Scarlet Blade

Walking Shadow: Book Two

By Jack Fields

Table of Contents

Dedication

For my father, who is a lion like his father before him.

Acknowledgements

Huge thanks to The Legion Publishers for their unwavering support, as well as editors Judy Roth and Michelle Dunbar for their perspective and corrections.
This book was a treat to write. But as with a certain October holiday it had tricks in store for me; challenging sections, difficult themes to wrangle and make sense of. The team was essential in realizing this best version of the book you're about to read.

Also many thanks to Agatha Christie, Arthur Conan Doyle, Terry Pratchett, and Stephen King for writing the murder mysteries that inspired this novel.

Content Advisory

This novel contains instances of the following:

Bugs and insects

Suspense/Threat

Strong violence

References to drug and alcohol abuse

Trauma linked to supernatural violence and child loss

Prologue
Something Buzzing

Marberry Dennings was on his way home from a long and arduous day at work when he saw a man jumping rooftops. This was odd for a couple of reasons, all of which occurred to Marberry as, overhead, the man bunched his leg muscles under him, folded in on himself like he had just sneezed, and then bounded from the frosty roof of a laundromat to the equally ice-studded roof of a pub.

Those reasons occurred to Marberry in an alphabetically structured list, as most conundrums did.

    a)   It was odd that someone should be taking their exercise four stories over a perfectly good street.

    b)   The man's tweed jacket was half-on, half-off. The arm—along with one strawberry-red suspender—flapped and fluttered behind him as he dashed across the dark slate shingles of Leonidas District.

    c)   What was really very odd was that the man had elected to perform these feats of aerial acrobatics during the coldest November the city had seen in years.

    d)   Now Marberry was examining it, the distance between the laundromat roof and the pub roof was actually quite a long way...

This last and inarguably strangest of points tickled some memory at the back of Marberry's mind. He grasped for it. No joy though. The memory was so much paper in a paraffin lamp; here one moment, gone the next.

Well, perhaps he'd remember later.

It was a little after eight o'clock. A scant few folk were going about their evening errands; it was simply too brisk and biting out. Marberry Dennings had been walking along Calvo Senatrucio Street when a walnut-shellish crunch had jerked his head around and up in time for him to spot the man. It was only a bit of ice gathered in a groove of slate breaking, but the sound had alarmed him almost as much as its source.

Now he paused to watch the man leap another gap. The fellow really was terribly spry. Amazing balance too. Marberry switched the parcels under his left arm to his right and squinted. A surge of admiration rose in him because, unless he was mistaken (which he wasn't), he thought he could see tufts of white hair sticking out from under the man's bowler hat.

There were many choices available to Marberry, things he could say in that moment. For example, he might have said:

a) "Good evening to you Mr. Roofy!"

b) "How's the view?"

c) "Shouldn't you be, ahm, a bit more careful at your age?"

d) (*sotto voce*) "I'd better not shout or else my friend up there will lose his concentration, and then I'll have a great explanation for being late home to Sue. 'What delayed me? Why, nothing much, dear. There I was hurrying to you and the kids when, by jingo, I happened to look up and see a man who was either enthusiastic about verticality or was in the midst of a mental breakdown engaged in what I can only describe as rooftop hopping. I say *was* because, calling out to him, I distracted this mysterious figure mid-leap. Whereupon he slipped, ragdolled in a flailing tangle of tweed, and plummeted thirty feet to the blacktop. Splat! Anyway, what's for dinner?' Yes. That'll go down well."

Marberry chose instead to say, in a quiet, timid voice, "Gosh!"

The street replied in the way of late autumn places that have forgotten to put up a fight against winter's pale boxing gloves. Yesterday's sleet mortified the bricks around him, sealing them in shaggy caskets of glittering white. Nubs of ice clung to the gutters, shortening here into stumps, elongating there into syringes full of the coming season's cold poison and glinting in the moonglow. For the most part the night was chill and clear and calm, but from the pub sallied swells of rowdy music and bawdy laughter, tankard thumps, and through the windows opened just a crack, the smell of gin and barley beer and musty, fraying, birthmarked fabric stretched over the barstool seats. Vivid red light spilled through those windows, the luminous sodium encased behind layer upon layer of glass. A little warming. A little malevolent.

The old man crouched and leaped. Two stories disappeared under him in a breathless moment. He landed on a barber's that overhung a chip shop, greasy aromas wafting over the hum of its neon sign. Landed. And stopped.

And looked down into the widening eyes of Marberry Dennings.

Who realized that his wonderment had already been curdling inside him. The old man raised a hand and wiggled his fingers. *Hi.* Despite the freezing chill in the air and the bony knots of rheumatism in the man's digits, there was no tremor. No shake. More unnerving still were the old man's eyes.

They're not empty, thought Marberry. *The opposite.*

They're...

That is, they look...

The word came to him. No alphabetical list this time. It came to him sure and steady as the movement of those swollen fingers up there.

The old man's eyes were deep set and blue and far from empty.

In fact they were crowded.

With what?

Again, the word arrived without tremor or complication.

Flies.

His eyes are crowded with swarms of flies.

The old man lowered his hand. Then he simply stood there on the roof of the barber/chipper, the arm of his jacket stirring softly in the breeze like a centipede with its legs torn off. Marberry for his part stood completely still, transfixed. Lumps of sour-milk fear began to stew in the pit of his stomach.

Up the street the laughter issuing from the bar had taken on an eerie quality. It seemed to mingle with the neon of the chip shop sign. With the *buzz* it produced.

And yes, those blue irises were not blue at all, but blue*bottle flies,* and rising as the temperature gauge crept down indoors, a creeping counterpart to the November cold, a burgeoning black on grubbish wings, a rising cloud of buzz-buzz-buzzing fli—

"Excuse me?"

Marberry dropped his parcels.

The speaker was a young woman holding a cigarette. With the perfunctory air of someone who is used to cleaning up after other people's messes, she tucked the cigarette behind one ear, hunkered down, gathered the parcels, and dumped them in a stunned Marberry's outstretched arms.

"I was just wondering if you had a light?" she asked, retrieving the cigarette.

How can you be so calm? he thought and turned back nervously to the old man perched on the roof.

There was no one there. The roof was

(not so crowded)

empty.

"No," he said. "Sorry. I don't smoke."

She gave a stiff little shrug. "No big hitch. You okay? Your complexion's awful."

"I've just had a bit of a scare."

"Yeah." She looked back toward the center of the District, a curiously haunted look crimping her face. "I know that feeling." She returned to Marberry. "Someone's birthday?"

"Sorry?"

"The stuff."

She nodded at his parcels and crossed her arms with the cigarette poised between her fingers. From Marberry's perspective the white line of it seemed to vanish into the ghostly bauble of the moon.

"No. No one's birthday. These are Tinfrost gifts," he explained.

This earned him a raised eyebrow. "A little early, no?"

It *was* early, not even December.

Marberry nodded awkwardly. "My wife and I like to get a head start." His stomach was feeling much better now. Rationality was reasserting itself. Ordinary conversation helped. Already Marberry Dennings was beginning to dismiss the old man on the roof as something he hadn't had the full context for. Perhaps Scarlet Citadel business, or a bit of extremely disturbing performance art.

Realization struck him.

"Hold on a moment," he said. "Could you..."

He held out the parcels to her. The young woman took them, her face puzzled. Rummaging in his pocket, Marberry took out a packaged long-nosed lighter, the kind you might use to kindle the ring of blue flame on a gas hob. He opened the packaging and lit her cigarette for her.

"Thanks." She exhaled through her nostrils, two huge plumes. "Norma."

"Marberry. Nice to meet you, Norma."

"You too. Walking this way?"

"Yes, I live on Giacomo Lane."

"Blackchapel Road."

Which meant they lived within hollering distance of one another.

With unspoken camaraderie they fell into step together. Norma asked Marberry what he did for work. He told her and politely returned the question. He was not altogether surprised to find out that she was a nurse. Marberry had two cousins who were nurses. They had a certain way about them, a certain solidity that he admired very much.

But something was wrong.

Fully in control of himself once more, Marberry Dennings, an observant man by nature, noticed that as she smoked, Norma's hands were not as steady as the peculiar roofjumper's had been. She did not have arthritis, but those smooth, unswollen hands were shaking badly.

He thought of that look she'd shot the center of the District and wondered what lay in that direction for her, what trouble she was leaving behind for the peace of home.

"I hope you don't mind me saying so, but you look like you could use a glass of—" he began kindly and broke off as she flinched. No, "flinch" didn't describe the spasmodic sharpness of it. Better to say she *recoiled* from him.

"—hot mulled wine," he finished. "What's the matter?"

"It's nothing," she said. "Look, I'm going to head home alone."

"But..."

"Thanks for the light."

He stared with his wrapped parcels under his arm and his mouth slung open as she hurried off, her shoulders hunched, her posture warding and tight as a shield raised against all potential protest.

And just like that he was alone again.

"What on earth was that about?" Marberry Dennings wondered.

All he'd meant was she seemed like she needed something soothing. A little nightcap to comfort herself. He tried to think how he could have offended her.

Maybe she was an alcoholic? He wouldn't blame her given her career.

Or maybe she knew one. Was close with one.

That struck him as nearer to true. Hadn't he read an article about the rate of alcoholism in Corinth City going up in the past five years? A ten percent increase? Twenty? Something like that.

And no wonder. Times were hard. The world could look pretty nasty until you viewed it through the bottom of a bluebottle.

He frowned.

A *bottle*, he meant. Yes. And hadn't Marberry himself been partial to a pint of Stoving's? Or six? Hadn't he flirted with overindulgence until Sue set him straight? That was a year before Adam—their first—was born.

Case solved then. Norma either knew an addict intimately, or was averse to alcoholism on account of her work in medicine, or was herself a booze hound and a sensitive one at that when the subject of drink was raised.

He decided one of these must be the answer and shrugged. No use in fretting. A bit of a social blunder, but a forgivable one, and oh God was that the time? The watch on his wrist read twenty-five past eight!

Marberry Dennings broke into that sort of lumbering jog all husbands and fathers become fast friends with, like the smell of talcum powder or the chill of your wife's cold toes on your warm ones. The alcoholism deduction along with the roof man encounter faded effortlessly into the background of his thoughts. He did not connect the woman's reaction to its actual cause—the word he'd spoken during his attempt at compassion. It was an ordinary word for him. Mundane.

But to Nurse Norma on that particular night, it was the very worst word. A jagged shard of language. It cut her when it passed his lips, cut her to the bone.

Pronounce it aloud if you like.

It won't hurt.

Promise.

After all, it's only glass.

***

When he hurried in out of the cold into the cramped, comfortably toasty apartment, Marberry smelled something good. He stamped his feet, stored the parcels for the time being in a shoe cubby under the coat pegs, and went in search of whatever owned the smell. It was potatoes cooking in goose fat. Their neighbor, Mrs. Orbiset, had dropped the goose fat over as a thank you for Marberry helping her with some shelves the previous week.

In the living room (which was also the kitchen and the kids' playroom, the Dennings family were happy in spite of their finances, not because of them), Marberry gave his wife, Susabeth, and their children, Adam and Ellen, a kiss.

The potatoes, green beans, and turnips were an excellent dinner. No meat, of course, with Sue putting money aside for Tinfrost night. But the goose fat was a treat and Adam Dennings spoke more than usual, which made it extra special for Marberry, who worried about his quiet son and despaired of his daughter, Ellen, who was as verbal as the radio and an absolute tyrant of a girl to boot. He loved them both so much that sometimes he forgot he had once been a soldier who had fought at the battle of Origné against Champleurs. Horror shrinks under beauty like a night flower in the sunshine.

When the kids were tucked into bed, Sue and Marberry made cocoa, curled up on the sofa, and had their usual chat. How was work, fine, same old same old, I still love you, well that's good since I'm still fond of you, love. Comfortable and meaningless, and yet so very important.

Sue had plunked into Marberry's life at a mixer for singles who had been affected by what had come to be known as The Hairy Autumn, that nasty bit of business that shook the city ten years before. They'd bonded over the fact that both of them had been transmogrified into animals (Sue was changed into a blonde Pomeranian and Marberry, luckily in the bath at the time, had been turned into a salmon). Additionally, they bonded over their ridiculous names (Marberry was a portmanteau of Mark and Hawberry, both popular names that his parents hadn't been able to pick between).

She thought he was solid and homey. He thought she was prim and hilarious. They hadn't hit it off so much as blasted.

Concluding their chat, they secreted the presents where Adam and Ellen wouldn't find them, kissed one another goodnight, and put the hot water bottle between their tangled feet. Marberry reminded Sue that she had to telephone her mother about Tinfrost arrangements. Sue reminded Marberry that tomorrow he must pick up condensed milk.

Later that night, she killed their children.

She used a knife.

Then she took the same knife and cut her husband's throat.

She did this because...

***

Sue Dennings felt them crawling all over her.

Earwigs and weevils, gall wasps and green orchid bees, woodborer and blister beetles, milkweed butterflies, metalmarks with gossamer wings, silkworms, slugs, caterpillars, and spiders too, fat ones and spindly-legged ones, cockroaches and crickets, midges, mealybugs, ants with short wriggling feelers and centipedes with long hairy ones, and flies.

The flies were the droning majority.

The monarch insect.

They crept and scuttled and squirmed and slimed and trailed and clicked and clittered and oozed over her skin.

Just because she couldn't see them didn't mean they weren't there.

She left Marberry and the children to rest in their crimson blankets. She had things to do if she wanted the bugs to go away. And she *did* want them to go away.

Needed them to, actually.

Their ceaseless march across her body, her face (even her mouth) was the most repulsive, flesh-prickling thing she had ever experienced.

She couldn't wait to tell Marberry about it. It would be good to vent.

Cleansing.

Things to do, things to do.

There was the kids' bedroom window to fling wide so the smell would carry. What smell? What smell? Nevermind. Done.

There was the front door to open in case Mrs. Orbiset fancied popping by. What if burglars got in? So much the better. Done.

There was the message to leave. A pen? No. Adam's markers? Ellen's crayons? No, no. Why, her very own hair! That would do splendidly! She hacked out clumps with the butcher knife and wound it in strands and spelled out the message by the Tinfrost tree.

What else?

That was all. Right?

Of course not. There was the most important thing of all. She would have to do that or else she'd never rid herself of... them.

She felt something thin caress her upper lip. A spider leg.

She whimpered.

18 SCARLET CITADEL

Out then, out the door left open for Mrs. Orbiset or a burglar or anybody, out to the apartment block's fire escape.

Up and up and up some more.

Up to where the night's a door.

Up so they would know the score.

Up to spring her heels some more.

Sue Dennings hurried to the roof, the flies urging her with every step.

<u>Act One</u>

Something Hushed

<u>Chapter One</u>

The man sat in the waiting area thinking about things in great detail to distract himself. Among other things, he thought about glass.

The waiting area was in the eastern wing of the Saint Wilhelmina Maternity Hospital in Ptolema District. The room had nice calming lemon-colored walls, seats that you could sleep in if you had a mind to (he did not), and a clock that told you exactly how long you'd been waiting so you wouldn't get addled by the human brain's rather mischievous habit for modified timekeeping. There were six windows, and if you stood at them you would have seen that unlike Leonidas District, the cold fingers of night had no handholds here. Everything in Ptolema was smooth polished glass and steel beams and impregnable marble. Petulant creature that the weather was, the best it could do was breathe a glaze of frost across the panes and skulk off for more promising parts.

At seven-forty-three, while another man called Marberry Dennings was paying for the last of his parcels, the waiting man's father arrived with a thermos of tea and an offer to wait with him. The waiting man told him it was okay, that he didn't know how long it'd be, and that he'd telephone the moment there was news. His father embraced him and left. The waiting man sat back down and drank his tea (sweet plum and mild fennel, his current favorite) and went back to thinking.

He thought about the strange smell you get inside tattoo parlors, new machines and newer ideas waiting in the newest ink. Ink silos shaped like porcupines, and all the quills sprouting from it were tapered needles waiting to render art on a canvas of skin. The high-pitched insectile drone as the liners and shaders danced their vibrational, almost sensual dance. He thought about his lover in the chair, chatting away to the flesh decorator with total ease even though she must have been in considerable pain. He thought about sitting in chairs or lying on beds and being in pain.

Mostly, though, it was glass he pondered.

In the theater of his mind it was the main feature.

When they had been dating for two years and eleven months, his lover had treated him to a delicious steak dinner and a few rounds of beer. Later, they'd gone to her room in the tower where they lived, since she didn't much care for the rustling state of his blankets. In bed she'd snuggled him quietly for a long time.

Then she'd told him about her aunt.

Her aunt had these boots that let her move between reflective surfaces. Any old surface would do. Kitchen foil. Jewelry. Puddles of rain water. Mirrors. It was a revolution in her aunt's life because she was a fighting woman and this teleporting power would be a marvelous feather in her cap.

But there was a price.

The boots would allow the aunt to go reflection-diving any time she liked. When she brought someone with her into the reflection, they would... stop. Forever. And that was a very useful technique for a fighter, especially when an opponent was extra tricky. However, the act of killing would brand itself on the aunt's body. When she dragged someone into the reflection, a bit of her would become glass. Only a teensy bit. But it would never go away.

His lover had looked at him, and she must have seen his fright because she spoke quickly, as though putting a halt on things now might plug them up. Stopped forever.

She told him that her aunt had grown older and had given her the boots to wear if she wanted. And of course she had, because they were fabulous and freeing, and so what if they cost something, what didn't? She'd developed her own taste for fighting, a palette enriched by adrenaline and fear and courage, and oh to hell with it, the fun! And, yes, some of her opponents had vanished into the fractal world of endless reflections, and that was why she got tattoos, right? To hide the fact that under the ink she was growing a strange second flesh. She reached over him and turned on the reading light, and by its glow she showed him the newest patch. He traced it with his eyes. Hidden until now by the incarnadine tumbles of her hair, it gleamed next to the scarlet-red bells tattooed at her throat. A smear of magical glass.

He noticed she was crying. Only a teensy bit. Never one for a sob was Cate Jubilee. There was too much merriment in her. But sometimes the party got maudlin.

"Thank you for telling me," he said. Into the ensuing silence he asked the most pressing question of many.

"Does it hurt?"

"Does it... hurt?"

"Yeah. The changing part. The progress of the glass. Does it hurt?"

She blinked. Broke into a crooked grin. Kissed him deeply. "No," she said. "No, it doesn't hurt."

He nodded, then voiced the second most immediate concern. "What happens when it covers you completely?"

"I don't know."

He gave her a squeeze that was both loving and automatic. As he did, the ball of his thumb brushed that spot of impossible glass on her throat. It was very cold. For every tattoo she wore, there was another just like it.

Her head had been resting on his chest. Now it turned so he could see her face in its naked totality, and vice versa. What she saw in his must have pleased her. She sniffled, then smiled a hopeful and rather spectacular smile. "Still want to be mine?"

"Don't be ridiculous," he said and bent to kiss the patch of glass.

The gesture startled her, but evidently it had been the right thing to do, just as waiting two years and eleven months for her to reveal this crazy and important truth had been the right thing to do.

She giggled. "Hey. That was really cute."

He smacked his lips. "Tingly."

"I'm getting it covered tomorrow at the parlor. Want to come?"

"Do bears shit in the woods?"

"Yes."

"Yes on all counts."

She nuzzled his jaw with the tip of her nose. "Love you, Puppy."

"You too, Kitten."

That had all been a long time ago, but he found he could still conjure it as clearly as his own eyes in a vanity.

And he still was. Hers, that is. Even in this yellow room, which reminded him of nothing so much as the padded cell of some asylum, he was still hers.

The waiting man sat and thought.

Over him, one of the anbaric lamps flickered, casting him in momentary darkness. The years had filled him out, but in that moment, head bowed and with his moth-gnawed coat pooled around him, he was every inch the shadow boy of his youth.

His name was Hughes.

Chapter Two

It might surprise you to learn that some years before the events of this story, Hughes crossed paths with the Dennings family. It was in a supermarket. And it was in December at the height of Tinfrost. An odd parallel, but hey, life is full of them.

Little did Marberry and Susabeth Dennings know that this chance encounter would lodge an idea in Hughes' mind, an idea that would grow and grow until he voiced it to Cate one night while the two of them were under the blankets in bed.

People think the largest gestures go the longest way, but often it's the small and completely unintentional ones that have the biggest impact.

That day Cate was running errands and meeting with her cousins, and Hughes was having a cup of tea on a convenient bench. There was a skylight over him, and the blue afternoon shone down on him as if preserving him in the blue amber of happier times. The Tinfrost decorations were up and the shops were as sweet and as busy as industrious beehives aflow with yummy honey.

It was with mellow amusement that he noted the Dennings family's approach. The little girl of four or five was perched atop her brother's shoulders while Mum and Dad looked on. The boy was six at most, but a burly strong lad and quite capable of keeping his sister aloft. In terms of speech they were direct opposites: the boy seemed monosyllabic, the girl unable to stop talking as if she had words instead of traditional blood and bone. Their familial parade stopped at the supermarket's Tinfrost tree, which happened to be about five feet from Hughes.

"Old Father Tinfrost has to be at the very top of the tree," said the girl (who was called Ellen) with all the confidence that only a five-year-old girl can muster. "Mum, want to hear the story of Tinfrosttime?"

Hughes watched as Mummy gave Daddy a look that was half pride and half exasperation.

Daddy shrugged.

Mummy rolled her eyes before addressing their daughter. "Yes, sweetie. Tell me in your own time."

"Can Daddy listen too, Ellen?" said Daddy.

"Certainly, you may," said Ellen graciously. "Also I want a... bubble."

"Bauble, sweetie."

"Yyyyes. Higher, Adam!"

The boy (Adam) went on tiptoe. The girl stretched and spoke at the same time.

Hughes listened, marveling at the child's vocabulary. He had never heard a kid so young speak with such... he supposed the word was grace, but a closer approximation would be fluency. Reaching for the sparkly red bauble on the Tinfrost tree, the girl told this story:

"Well, the story starts hundreds and hundreds and hundreds of years ago in this little village in Daethumberland. There was this rotten mayor in charge of things. He made everyone sad with his iron rule all year round. One night in December, he drank pots and pots of wine and his cheeks went red and his temper turned reddest! He sent out a decree that everyone had to give him a present to make his anger go away. Only everyone was already poor as pigs, so they had no gifts for him. So there was going to be *big trouble*. Almost there, Adam!

"Anyway, no sooner had the mayor given his order when the candles went *snuff*. It got so cold. In the dark, the mayor heard tiny feet thumping. Too small to be people. Too big to be mice. Outside the window the snow turned black as soot, and behind his gold chair the picture frames and paintings went *crack* with frost. And before the mayor could call for help, the tiny feet scampered, and the baldiebeards came out of the dark with carving knives picked from the house pantry and cut out all the mayor's bits and stuffed him with tinsel."

"Ellen!" Uh oh. Mummy was horrified. Judging by his expression, Hughes guessed Daddy wasn't exactly thrilled himself. The story had taken a gruesome turn that neither of them could have predicted.

Their daughter paused in her efforts. "What?" she said, bewildered at the anger in her mother's tone.

"Where did you hear that?" Mummy demanded.

"Hear what?"

"Those awful things about the gnomes hurting the mayor."

Ellen shrugged, her queenly demeanor scuffed but still intact. "In school. I haven't gotten to the bit where Old Father Tinfrost appears and tells all the people about the mayor's death, and that his wealth is up for grabs, and how the best gift of all is hostile takeovers..."

"*Ellen Dennings!*"

"*What is it, Mum?*"

Daddy made to weigh in before things got out of hand. His teeth clacked together in his mouth, curtailing what he'd been about to say. Hughes felt his own attention sharpen. Because the boy, Adam, was talking.

"Actually," he said, "I think the mayor heard something else in the dark."

Silence, deep as a basin. *Not so monosyllabic*, Hughes reflected. *Interesting*. The boy poured the story into the silence.

"I think the mayor heard the *rap... rap... rap* of a holly branch being used as a walking stick. And out of the black came a man in a cloak with a long white beard. 'Who are you?' asked the mayor. 'A saint for the saintless,' replied the cloaked man. 'If you want me to go away, take my hand, and it will happen.' The mayor wanted that very much, so he took the cloaked man's hand. And when he did, he realized the hand, and its owner, were made of tin. The mayor felt himself whisked out into the black snow on a sleigh pulled by twelve enormous squirrels. And the cloaked man showed the mayor all the houses in the village, how poor and chilly the people were. The mayor huffed and said, 'Well, it's not my fault they can't take care of themselves.' And the cloaked man replied, 'Then whose is the fault?' When the mayor didn't say anything, the cloaked man said, 'Come.' And he snapped his reins and showed the mayor a scullery maid who worked at the mayor's house. She had a cough that wouldn't stop. And the mayor said, 'Am I to blame for sickness too?' And the cloaked man replied, 'She blames no one.' The woman coughed and there was blood in her handkerchief, and as the mayor pulled away, he saw that he was in his house in the dark room, and there was no tin hand holding his. He was alone.

"Later that night, he gathered his servants and had them make squirrel masks and gnomish masks because he'd seen the little folk tend the wishes of the cloaked man. Then the mayor dressed up in a cloak and donned a false white beard. He visited each house for miles and miles around, offering presents of hot food and hotter drinks, logs for the fire, and medicine for sick people like the scullery maid. She got much better and married the mayor in the spring. Now everyone gives gifts and makes merry for Tinfrost, not just in Daethumberland, but all over the world. And... and that's it, really."

No one knew what to say. On his bench Hughes sat very still. His tea was cold by then, as you might imagine. Yet if you'd told him that, he would have glanced blankly at you and then looked away as if he couldn't give a shit. Which meant a whole lot, given who he was, and what his relationship to tea was like.

Even the boy's sister was momentarily spellbound, though she recovered quickest.

From her brother's shoulders she leaned down so they could look one another in the eye. "If he was made of tin, how did he speak?"

Adam gave this due consideration. "Wisely," he said.

Ellen nodded, satisfied.

Adam went on tiptoe again, and Ellen reached out and closed her small hand around the sparkly red bauble.

"There," she said.

Time ticks by. We forget a great deal. Even with his superb memory, Hughes forgot their faces, their voices, and didn't make the connection between their names and the gruesome article that would follow their misfortune years later.

He remembered the sense of that encounter in the supermarket though.

Remembered how charmed he'd been by them.

By those children, one on the shoulders of the other, telling the same story two very different ways, and both true in the manner that every yarn spun from a child's mind is true because the world has not taught them how to lie.

***

Cate Jubilee taught Hughes about romance. There was passion too, at the beginning. Inevitably you got over passion (which generally involves lots of going to bed and sorting out whose legs belong to who afterward), and then the really interesting part began.

It was this rather more enduring period that was called romance.

Hughes learned fast. There really wasn't an alternative. Not, at least, when subjected to the gusts of Hurricane Jubilee, which took no prisoners, and which incidentally had very nice legs indeed.

Romance, he discovered, was like building a house out of jelly. It was unlikely, amazing, rife with structural difficulties, and because no one had ever tried it before (each romance being unique), no one could tell you where the deck chairs were supposed to go.

Part of the integrity of the jelly house was finding ways to entertain the other person. A stomach wobbling with laughter makes for stable romantic foundations. Try spending time with a couple who have not laughed together in a long time, and see how long you can last before wishing the universe will spontaneously pop.

To this end, it was around the eighteen month mark, about seventeen months before Cate confessed that every time she fought, more and more of her body turned to glass, that the pair invented a game. The game had its roots in something astonishing that had happened to Hughes when he and Cate and a sublime man named Frank Gallant had gone up against a band of witches called The Nightjar Coven. During an induced dream, the witches had tried to overpower Hughes' mind. At the crucial moment, he had been protected by two long feminine arms that had emerged from his chest. It was not the first time Hughes had encountered them, having seen those very same arms plunge out of the chest of a monster, their huge, delicate hands offering Hughes the monster's still-beating heart.

From this clay was their game sculpted:

Cate would guess who the owner of the arms was, and Hughes would have to improvise a reason they might have protected him.

As you can imagine, the game grew silly very quickly.

See them in a café with glorious sunshine streaming through stained glass windows, tracing the rims of their cups in a thread of burgundy and turquoise: Cate throwing up her arms and shimmying to let him know she had a good one. "What if the Nightjar Coven had a secret maternal figure who disagreed with their plot, and the arms belonged to her?"

"Mm. Hoochie Mama Nightshade," Hughes offered. "She protects me because I've got a fungus growing in me I don't even know about, and when I turn thirty, it'll burst from my belly and become her mushroom-shaped familiar."

"*Verrrry creative*, Meester Hoos. End the name hoff thees fungal friend would be?"

Months spun into years, yet no matter how much time passed, her stereotypical vampire impression still got him.

"My fungal friend?" he said, gasping for air between giggles.

"Yezzzz. The mushroom mate! The spore specimen!"

Hughes threw back his head, his laughter utterly helpless now.

"I don't know," he managed. "Clarence."

"Clarence the mushroom familiar?"

Cate said it seriously, with just a little mysticism, as though Clarence the mushroom familiar were a hero to be reckoned with, but only at your own peril.

Then she doubled over, laughing until she howled like a giddy wolf at the roundest and goofiest of moons.

See them walking, hands laced together, under a wide-brimmed umbrella through a quiet rainy park in Nikandros District, hedgehogs and birds taking shelter under the nearby oaks:

"What if it's a fakir?" Cate presented. "From Horstesia where the bazaars are bizarre and the markets are markéd."

"Not just a fakir," said Hughes. "A genie *disguised* as a fakir."

"Yes!"

"The genie is protecting me because I am the fabled Lost Princess of Hortesia. Destined to shake up their socio-political climate, perform evocative and scandalous dances, cast down stuffy antiquity, and gyrate toward a better future."

"A flawless theory," said Cate Jubilee. "I tell a lie. There's one flaw. You're a man. You could be a prince, if you like, but not a princess."

Which Hughes took as a challenge. He dashed for an oak, clambered up it, and swung himself onto a branch. In one smooth motion he shrugged his coat to adjust its fit. In the diffuse gray rainlight of the afternoon it could have been an off-the-shoulder dress. A tumble of his dark hair fell over one eye. His face—which could balance all sorts of expressions with incredible flexibility—became that of a royal woman in hiding, proud yet furtive, staunch yet secretive.

Cate joined him on the branch.

"The genie is not the only one in disguise," said Hughes, Lost Princess of Hortesia.

Cate nodded, her face enraptured. "I'll help you regain your throne."

"Between your hobnail boots and my destiny, how can we fail?"

The abandoned umbrella rolled in lazy, thoughtless circles below them. Rain beaded their cheeks and chins.

"Can I've a kiss?" said Cate.

Hughes obliged. After, his dry smile caught in the kindling of her own. In intimate hours like these their love was a hearth. They burned logs of joy together.

"Plus we have Clarence," he said.

"HA!" she thundered, clapping a hand on her thigh. "I forgot Clarence!"

See them pick out an apartment in Cleomenes District. See them buying two-for-one mystery meat rotisserie sausages in the Leonidas bazaar. See them regret buying two-for-one mystery meat rotisserie sausages in the Leonidas bazaar.

See them fight in Iphigenia's toadish swamps, its faerie forest, its pale desert. See them carve a swathe through Eurydice, the dungeon dimension, vast and unknowable.

See autumn waltz into winter, winter foxtrot into spring, spring jive into summer, and summer tango into the great changing season of autumn once more.

Speaking of, see Corinth City change.

See it stay the same while you're at it.

And after a short time (or a quite significant time, depending on where you find your feet), the guessing game went the way of autumn and transformed.

"How about Evelyn?" said Hughes.

They were in bed. Through the window there were a few stars. Pink and purple light came up from the nightclubs, and in the walls the central heating pipes clunked and rattled.

Cate turned to frown at him. "Say again?"

"Evelyn."

"Who's Evelyn?"

"It's just a name."

"Lorna Blacktower's got a hamster called Evelyn."

"I'm not talking about Lorna Blacktower's hamster," said Hughes. "I'm talking about a baby."

"What baby?"

He smiled at her.

Understanding rode over Cate's face, tugging the frown into a wide-eyed look of amazement.

"Oh," she said.

"Well?"

"Oh Hughes, I don't know..."

"It's only if you'd like to."

"I'd like to. I would," she said. "I just don't know if I *can*."

"You think the boots have made it so you can't?"

"Yeah."

The subject of her hobnail boots had come up a few times over the years. There had never been an argument over Cate's changing body, but on those rare occasions Hughes had trod with the utmost care. Love someone deeply and receive their love back, and you get a feel for one another that is both panoptic and depthful. The jelly house of romance might have sterling foundations, but it's still gelatinous sugar. Sweet, sure. But delicate too.

Who knew what her body transforming to glass meant for her in the long run, anatomically speaking? Certainly Hughes had no idea. What he did know (but would never dream of articulating) was this: asking her to hang up her magic boots and quit the whole fighting monsters thing would destroy him in her eyes. It would be like asking a tiger to surrender her claws.

"Since when have you wanted to be a dad?" Cate wanted to know.

"I'm not sure," Hughes replied after a pause. "I think it's a survival mechanism."

She grinned, illuminating their private dark. "How so?"

He shrugged. "I love you, Cate. More and more every day. I think I need something to take the runoff from that love or else I'm likely to burst."

"Hughes..."

"So I thought, well, we're happy, and fun, and quite mad. Why not have a happy, fun, mad little boy or girl? That way I've got more space to accommodate it. To hold all this... fondness I've got for you."

She pulled him to her.

"And what if something happens to the baby?"

"We'll protect it."

"Because we love each other?"

He kissed her. A moment later she looked up at him with a devotion so strong it was almost fierce. Hughes gave it all back to her with his eyes, all that he had to give. Then he said, with complete sincerity:

"You're grand, I suppose."

Outside, a dog walker heard the squalls rolling through the apartment window, shook his head, and tutted to himself at the malarkey of young people nowadays.

Inside, Hughes begged for mercy. None came. Hurricane Jubilee blew like vengeance incarnate, and her tickles were lethal.

"I love you," he pleaded. "I love you I love you I love youuuuu!"

"*Too late Hoos!*" Cate roared, impish and wrathful. "*You arr done for!* And for your information, Evelyn," she added, "is a rubbish name!"

A year later she ran from the bathroom, wearing a t-shirt, socks, and no panties, and tackled him to the ground. In the mayhem he was able to see the object she was waving frantically in his face. Stubby and white, the pregnancy test had a little oval at its core. In that oval, Hughes made out two pink lines.

Pink for positive.

His happiness was so great, he felt as though he really might explode. *Surely*, he thought, *this bliss can't get any bigger.* Then, in September, it did.

A pleasant woman with spearmint breath and wearing blue scrubs smeared clear jelly (cold and not in the least romantic) over Cate's belly. She passed the transducer over Cate's skin, including the murder of inky crows flying from Cate's belly button, dark wings covering a patch of glass. Hughes held Cate's hand while, on the technician's monitor, their baby appeared.

"Everything seems good," said the technician. "Want to know the gender?"

"Please," said Cate.

"You're going to have a little girl."

I'm okay, Hughes thought valiantly. *So long as no one says anything else, I'm cool.*

The transducer slid over Cate's bump.

"See her pudgy hand?" cooed the technician.

Hughes burst into tears.

Up there on the monitor, that hand resembled nothing so much as a—

A noise in the corridor snapped his reverie in two.

Hughes got up. He left the supposedly calming yellow waiting room and looked down one corridor, then the other. Down the second, he could see the nurses' station, all transparent plastic walls, patient files, a fugue of gossip, and half-slurped coffees.

The head nurse was there, Sadie Somethingorother, the one who'd escorted Hughes to that unbearable waiting room. Someone else too. Another nurse. Hughes didn't recognize her, but it was clear she was upset. Actually "upset" didn't seem to cover it. He clutched for the word and found it. *Stricken.* This younger nurse looked stricken, and as he listened to what she had to say, a rusty razorblade of fear began to run up and down the column of his spine.

"... so awful," the young nurse blubbered. "You weren't there, Sadie. It's unnatural. I've never seen anything so unnatural in my life."

"Why did Doctor Lanmoor send you out?" the head nurse demanded.

"I told you, he *didn't* send me out. I left on my own. I had to, don't you understand?"

"Norma, for God's sake. You can't just scoot out in the middle of surgery. Go outside for a minute, clear your head, then get back where you're needed."

But the young nurse (*Norma*, Hughes thought. *Her name is Norma*) only shook her head.

"I'm going home," she said and set off to do just that. "It's too much. Too much to ask from me. I need a cigarette."

"That isn't how this works," insisted the head nurse, pursuing her with the air of a mother hen clucking at an errant chick. "Norma, now hold on a second. You'll be fired, Norma. I'm sure Doctor Lanmoor is spitting bolts right now, and... hey, *slow down, Norma...*"

As stealthily as he could, Hughes hurried to the nurses' station. He looked around for security personnel. Nobody. Only sterile overheads, glossy anti-slip floors, and the whiff of human beings striving through the strangeness of that night shift in early November.

He had no inkling where the right delivery room might be. Hughes had no intention of stumbling in on the wrong birth. The nurses' station had a cogwheel computer, and by a stroke of luck it was unlocked and awaiting inputs. He opened the Finder application and entered "Delivery" into the search bar. A list appeared, numbering them one through twenty-five.

His mouth pulled taut in an impatient grimace.

Nurse Norma's words stalked along the treadmill of his thoughts.

So awful, she'd said.

Unnatural, she'd said.

Cate. Honey. I'm on my way.

He began to click into the delivery room files, viewing their current assigned staff, scanning for any details that might indicate the rooms' occupants.

Delivery Room One:

Obstetrician in Attendance, F. Delaney.

Nurse Staff, A. Bracegirdle; N. Cross.

Patient, R. Fitchett.

No success there. Hughes' eyes darted over the lip of the computer. The coast remained clear for now.

Delivery Room Two:

Obstetrician in Attendance, Q. Rollinson.

Nurse Staff, E. Pardy; J. Stockton.

Patient, O. Poulter.

How long did he have? Hughes didn't think long.

Delivery Room Three:

Obstetrician in Attendance, K. Lutwidge.

Nurse Staff, H. Mallard. K. Ives.

Patient—

"Dumb little so-and-so," a voice opined. "She'll regret that, you mark my... Hey. Hey, what are you doing in there?"

Hughes didn't look up. Desperate, he read the patient for Delivery Room Three's name (I. Spindler, short for Irene Spindler, who would in eleven minutes give birth to a healthy baby boy).

Head Nurse Sadie materialized. "Mr. Hughes, I warned you once already when you arrived. I don't do second warnings."

"I was just checking in with work. I've got an email from Wendy Dragontail herself," Hughes improvised. "That's *the* Wendy Dragontail, of course. Leader of the Scarlet Citadel, wyrm who works atop the tower Redspire, and incinerator of those who oppose her will in any shape and or form." He stood. "I'm glad you've arrived. Wendy personally requests that I keep a close eye on my partner's condition. If you'll direct me to the correct delivery room..."

"Well, that's very interesting to hear," said the head nurse, each word adrip with caustic acid. "Considering our talk about colors and how they run. Of course her Ladyship is a law unto herself, it's well known, and I wouldn't want to put a spanner in her works. Why don't we have a look at that email so I can verify it, then we'll get you sorted at once, eh?"

Hughes stared at her, wishing his Performance could be tried twice in quick succession. This peevish old battleaxe had resisted it once, but if only he could...

"I'll go back to the waiting room," he muttered.

"That would be best."

There was a telephone in one of the corridors snaking off from the hub of the nurses' station. For the dozenth time that night Hughes tried the various numbers he knew of those in Redspire, including the ever-reliable Falstaff. No one answered. Probably busy. Out of seemingly nowhere, he remembered Miss Gleam saying something about how he'd troubled her ("too long have you been the ointment in my flies") and wondered if this weren't some cruel species of karmic retribution. He wondered if, wherever she was, his suffering brought a scalpel-smile to her lips.

That's just anxiety giving you dictation, he told himself. *Don't jot it down unedited. Anyway, it's possible the phones are out at Redspire. It's cold enough that the telecommunicog might have frozen to a stop in Ptolema.*

And he couldn't take a taxi back to the tower to fetch help in case there were developments here in the hospital.

Helpless but to wait, he slunk back to the waiting room.

He sat down.

What was it he'd been thinking about?

The ultrasound, right. That had been September, a hair shy of two months ago. The clear gel. Cate's stomach, formerly flat and hard as wood, now rounding with their daughter's slow growth. And the monitor. He could conjure the image of that screen so clearly. Grainy, kind of fuzzy, and shaped out of white wax in a blue drum was their baby manifested. Then, as if to say hello, the blobby almost-person had extended a hand. Through the blur of implacable tears, Hughes believed that hand resembled nothing so much as a seashell.

Delicate and brittle and beautiful.

Now it was November, autumn was taking her final bow before the cold curtainfall of winter, and the whole world seemed brittle with no beauty to compensate.

"Why couldn't you have worked?" he mumbled without knowing he spoke. "This one time. Just this once."

That was seven-fifteen.

Somewhere in the city, an old man was hooking fingers swollen with rheumatism into loose brickwork, his mind full of rooftops and sap-sucking aphids, his nostrils tickled with a coppery smell, and his eardrums beating with the buzz of sticky wings.

Marberry Dennings would spot this very same old man on his way home from work. He would meet a nurse named Norma, and he would go home to his wife Sue and his children Adam and Ellen, and then...

Well, you know the rest.

Chapter Three

arlier today, an unobtrusive afternoon cusping the outset of November, they had been enjoying some well-deserved rest when, quite suddenly, Cate gave a grunt of pain.

They were in the main square of Nikandros. Beneath the statue of The Tyrant a crowd had assembled to watch a band playing a new style of music, a sort of evolution of the blues blown in from southern Ikahagua. Hughes wasn't sure how much he cared for it. It had a certain irreverence that spoke more to his lover's sizzling blood than his own.

Loud as the tune had played, he nevertheless heard that grunt clear as you might hear your favorite person talking in the next room at a noisy party; an unconscious subaurale recognition.

He turned to Cate, whose palms were pressed to her stomach, her face a mask of bewilderment.

"Contraction?" he mouthed.

She shook her head. He watched her expression clear into a look of naked relief.

He thought, *Oh thank God.* Twenty-six weeks was early for a nativity, rather worryingly so in fact, but he was not about to lose his composure after all the preparations they'd made. It was only a spasm. A bout of natal martial arts, maybe. The thought wrung a smile from him.

A spasm. That was all.

Twenty feet away the band's singer swept into a baleful verse.

Righteous Momma, moo-hoo-hoove aside
Gonna court the devil, gon' be his bride
Black-haired Momma, better run your lip

Gonna summon evil, gon' sink this ship

The next few moments staggered into one another in a domino of horror.

First, the guitar sprang in with a chord that was low and reverberating and somehow savage. Next, Cate Jubilee's relief crumpled. Her eyes bulged. Her cheeks went chalk-white. She bent in a stoop, fingers curled into agonized claws over her abdomen. Air hissed through her clenched teeth.

"Fffffuckkk," she moaned. "Oh ffffuck me."

Hughes' Performance boomed across his brain, boiled his blood, broke along his windpipe in a chariot. He took hold of Cate, aimed them for that taxi rank over there on the other side of the square, and bellowed in a voice that overrode the music like a crashing cymbal, *"MOVE ASIDE! GET OUT OF THE WAY!"*

"Puppeeee..."

"MOVE, I SAID!"

"Hughes, it hurtsssss..."

"I know, Kitten. It's going to be okay, come here."

Muscle is denser than fat, or so goes the common maxim. It's right too. Babies are no lightweights either, especially snug in a pool of amniotic fluid. So Cate was damned heavy. But Hughes had been trained in the gymnasium by Cassandra of Troy, and he swept his lover into his arms and hurried for those glowing rectangles labeled TAXI, soothing her and ordering deaf assholes out of the goddamn way, and kicking the taxi's door to get the driver's attention, and asking the gawping moron if he hadn't seen a pregnant woman before, and sliding Cate into the back and thumping the doors shut, squeezing her hand as her white-knuckle fingers tightened on his, and using his Performance on the driver so he'd play the amber gamble at each shifting traffic light, then the superhighway threading the city like a thin gray vein, horns blaring, afternoon racing toward dusk, clear skies outpacing the slow indolent clouds, tick-tocking indicator sounds, the drive the drive the never-ending drive to the hospital, to the answers for whatever questions of pain sounded off in Cate's uterus, the drive to Saint Wilhemina's.

Their first suspicion that something was wrong came on the way to the emergency ultrasound. An orderly with hooded eyes that had seen just about everything pushed Cate in a wheelchair.

Ever by her side, Hughes had a front-row position to hear his woman, one of the most dangerous people in the city, someone who was reliably steady under pressure, murmur unbelievingly, "I'm weeing."

Hughes was no expert, but he didn't think she was. What's more, he was pretty sure Cate knew she wasn't. They had been told that her water breaking would certainly feel like she was urinating ("It's damp business, giving birth," a natal nurse and mother of four once advised them. "Every part of you wants in on the action. Your hooha will kick it off though, right as rain, excuse my pun."). But the color of the liquid was supposed to be clear, maybe a little yellow.

The orderly took a corner at speed, unsettling Cate in the chair. She didn't notice.

Spreading at her crotch and seeping through the fabric of her trousers was a stain. It was wine-dark and terrifying.

Cate looked up at him, her eyes wide and uncomprehending.

By simple chance their happy-clappy technician with her spearmint breath was on duty. "A little rupture would explain the blood," she reassured them. "I won't bullshit you, this is an early birth, Miss Jubilee. But you're in the best place for you. We'll keep you and the baby safe as houses."

"Thank you," said Cate, her voice thick with gratitude. "It hurts like hell."

"I bet. Let's see what the trouble is."

Much later, after things went from bad to worse, Hughes found himself remembering this random act of kindness.

The ultrasound process was bizarre for its familiarity. Up with the shirt. Smearing clear gel over the bare belly. The transducer doing its smooth powerslide.

"Okay," said the technician. There was a pause. Then she said, "I don't... ah..."

She beckoned the orderly who was standing by. When he was next to her she said, still chippy and confident, "This doodad's run out of juice. Let's get her to another machine."

"All okay?" Hughes asked.

The technician flashed him a placative smile. "All okay."

No smear needed this time. The gel glistened on Cate's skin. Mercifully, the contractions had abated. Even so, Cate wore a tiara of sweat.

There the transducer went, plowing a path through the jelly—*sliiiiiiide.*

The technician looked at her monitor, which neither Hughes nor Cate could see. She looked at Cate's belly, at the transducer making its arcs across it—*sliiiiiiiide.* Then she looked back at the monitor. "Okay," she said.

The no-problemo tone she'd used before was gone. The word came out of her like a lump of lead.

"I'll be right back," she told them.

On the way past she gripped the orderly's arm and dragged him into the hallway.

Hughes and Cate stared at one another. He held a finger to his lips. Quiet as he could, he went to the door—still open a crack—and listened.

Hospitals are loud places, organic and mechanical sounds cluttering the air prickly with the smell of anti-bacterial wipes. Through it all Hughes could pick out the technician's voice. He didn't catch it all, but one phrase stuck out and lodged in his brain like an icepick.

Foreign matter.

Hughes wasn't aware of it, but his lips moved, repeating them silently.

Foreign matter.

It was as though the words held a kind of profane current. After he heard them, things jumpstarted, a black engine carrying him and Cate somewhere they didn't want to go. The beleaguered orderly reappeared. No sign of the technician. In her place were a squadron of nurses, two young, one much older. This last was Head Nurse Sadie, or Sadie the Sadist as the other staff called her behind her back, although Hughes would never learn that for himself.

"Now, Cate, is it?" said the head nurse.

"Yes."

The orderly took the wheelchair's handles. Slowly, he began to wheel Cate along. The two young nurses followed at either side, a strange honor guard.

"Have you any personal items with you, Cate?" the head nurse clucked. "If so, leave them with your husband here."

"What did the ultrasound show?" said Cate.

"No personal items?"

"I'll be coming along," said Hughes.

The head nurse regarded him evenly. "I'm afraid not."

At a word from one of the young nurses, the orderly picked up speed. They were heading toward an elevator. It opened, a surgeon with a face mask and crinkly blue gloves exited, and one of the young nurses hurried to stop the doors from closing. Hughes went to sidestep the head nurse but she barred his way.

"Your wife is on her way to surgery," she explained. "The ultrasound showed a discrepancy that the doctor is going to investigate. Our delivery theaters are usually open to spouses, but this is an extraordinary case, and—"

In that moment Cate Jubilee vented a sound of unspeakable hurt. Whatever respite her insides had granted her was over.

All conscious thought ceased.

Hughes shouldered the head nurse, sent her stumbling, and ran for the elevator.

He was fast, but not fast enough. The doors sealed Cate from him a fraction of an instant before he could cram his arm through the gap.

"Sir! Sir, you can't just..." The head nurse was almost upon him, her face indignant, her neck darkening to raspberry. "You jostled me!" she cried.

Hughes spun. "Where have they taken her?"

"To be looked after by competent professionals."

He didn't have time for this.

Foreign matter. Two little words, yet they bothered him deeply. He was glad Cate hadn't heard them. For himself, Hughes could not unhear them. The idea that she might go through whatever was happening to her alone was impossible to reconcile with his love for her. The mystery of those two little words overhung them. They would learn their significance together.

Besides, that *sound* she'd made before the elevator closed...

God, even thinking about that sound rashed his skin out in gooseflesh.

"Take me to her," he snarled and pushed his Performance.

Hughes
Performance Level: 23
Influence the behavior of others using your physical and vocal performance, as well as your stage presence. **WARNING!** *Bad performances result in negative reception.*

Current Bonus: 49%	Next Level: +1% increase to Performance Level 25 Secret Ability: ???

The head nurse (Sadie, her name tag identified her) changed. Her features slackened. The berry-colored rage slamming up her neck began to drain.

Testing Performance...

A pigtailed nurse spied Sadie and approached.

Hughes held up a hand to her: *wait.* In the midst of his Performance, his movements held an irresistible gravity. Humdrum hospital sounds bled into insignificance; his clench-jawed silence reigned absolute. Dark-eyed, pale-handed, he seemed to emit, the way a bioluminescent flower emits a hypnotic glow through sheets of stagnant water. Pigtails halted, her mouth forming an 'o' of surprise.

Testing Performance...

Work.

He could feel the power suffusing the head nurse, probing and prodding her mind like a mouse investigating a ruined church.

Words and images flickered through him in a cinema reel.

(Cate's fiery hair strewn over their pillows like strands of fire)

(a smudge of glass under scarlet bells rendered in ink)

(*Ask not for whom they toll, they toll for thee*)

(grainy monitor screen)

(seashell hand)

(*Foreign matter*)

Hughes' power roved and rambled.

Work, you must work.

You've got to—

Registering Result...

—work because she's everything, everything to m...

That icepick of fear he'd felt lodge in him spread coldness. He felt it all over.

No, he thought. *Not now. My girlfriend needs me.*

Performance Failed
+ 1 Experience On A Failed Attempt
Congratulations!

To his mounting anger he watched the head nurse's features regain their focus. No outrage this time. Her lips pressed into a thin line of contempt.

"Mr. Hughes. I know who you are and who your..." Her eyes flitted to Hughes' nude ring finger. "... your friend is. Let me tell you something: sickness doesn't care what colors you wear. Blue, yellow... *scarlet.* When it comes to maladies of the body, you will find that all such colors lose their meaning. They run.

"In other words, *you have no authority here, you pompous little man.* Be glad that your... friend is in the best care the city has to offer. Be glad also that we live in immoral times that accommodate children born outside of wedlock. If I had my way your particular brand of fornication would be outright prohibited. And fie to sinners of your breed who cry wolf on the moral and the upstanding. Now unless you want me to call security and have you removed from this hospital, I suggest you tottle those revolting boots and swish that filthy rag of a coat down that hall to our waiting room. There are a great many phones around. You've my permission to use them. Call your Citadel riffraff to complain or rally the troops if it pleases you. But I warn you that they, like you, may have need of the staff here at Saint Wilhemina's before long. Despite our uncertain economy, we are experiencing a baby boom on a scale we haven't seen since the end of the war.

We who treat sickness wear its colors, Mr. Hughes. Those do not run. You'd do well to remember that."

Hughes said nothing. All of his attention was being brought to bear cooling the white-hot coal of his fury.

She gave him a stiff nod as if tying the cord on the matter and summoned Pigtails with her hand, taking the chart the younger nurse handed her.

"You'll be notified of any developments," she told Hughes without looking at him.

Hughes went to the waiting room.

Seven hours later he was still there, jaunting down Memory Lane, and sipping cold tea, and loving Cate harder than he'd ever loved anything in the world.

Somehow, he knew she needed that love.

And more.

He sat in the waiting area and thought about many things.

He thought about *Foreign matter*. The technician's chirpiness withering to puzzlement and... yes, doubt. Or maybe some shadow cousin that was worse than doubt. Fear. If she had turned the monitor, Hughes was sure that neither he nor Cate would have seen the blobby baby shape, or the extended seashell hand, but something else. Something other.

Foreign matter.

He thought of the stain at her crotch, wet and red and spreading.

He thought of that animal sound she'd made, a guttural moan evolving as dark mutations of pain grew inside her.

He thought about how she had always been there for him, even in the gloomiest extremity when the going got tough and Cate Jubilee got going, and how he was letting that flawed, flawless woman down.

He thought, *Cate, I love you so much.*

But mostly he thought about glass.

***

"Gormon Hughes?"

Hughes jumped. His trip down Memory Lane had put him in a kind of trance.

"Yes," he said, rising to his feet, his voice tight with real urgency. "I'm Hughes."

"Art Lanmoor. Come with me, Mr. Hughes."

Art Lanmoor was really Doctor Artemi Lanmoor. He was North Daethumbrish on his mother's side and Corinthian on his father's, and it showed in his complexion, which was pasty, and in his 'r's, which were strong and rolling as a hill of densely-packed snow.

His office was akin to those belonging to most modern physicians. There was a desk, a computer plugged into the hospital's database, cabinets, and some loose pages scattered hither and thither, probably for the look of the thing. A slightly musty, slightly tobaccoish smell pervaded the room. Next to a bottle of water on the desk was a stapler. It bore this simple tagline: *Try and hold it together.*

"Sit down, Mr. Hughes."

He did.

"Mr. Hughes, there's no easy way for me to go about this, so I'll just give it all to you and answer any questions you've got after. Your partner has just undergone surgery. I apologize for keeping you in the dark. I think when I'm done talking, you'll understand why I made that decision."

"Is Cate okay?"

"She's stable. Do you mind if I smoke?"

"No."

"She's stable," Lanmoor repeated, lighting up. Not a cigarette but a cigar, thick as two thumbs held together. "I won't bullshit you, friend. I'm too tired for that. It was a near thing.

She's made of stern stuff though, and I expect a full recovery. Hers was not what you might call a typical birth. The condition of the baby resulted in a cervical hemorrhage. Miss Jubilee required a blood transfusion." Through the pall of blue smoke, he saw Hughes open his mouth and held up a hand to stop him. "You've lost the baby. I'm sorry. Ought to have opened with that. Tell you the truth I'm a little off-center. One of my nurses ran out during the procedure. Ugly thing to do. It, ah, rattled me. But then my bedside manner's never been up to much.

"Miss Jubilee had an ultrasound in September, yes? Yes, that's what the file says. I've been made aware of her... what would you call them? Physical circumstances? Woman turning to glass. I suppose it's mundane to you, but to a man like me it's arcane. I'm not the only one. Dermatology is at a loss. Radiology wants to perform a whole anatomical survey on her. Magic boots." Lanmoor turned his cigar around so the burning end was pointing up at him, a smoking finger thrust as if in judgment. He looked at it while he spoke. "Sometime between September and tonight, Miss Jubilee's issue spread through her various systems. Digestive, respiratory, etcetera. No adverse effects for her, health-wise, but it did reach her uterine tissue. The fetus underwent a transformation. When Miss Jubilee's contractions began, it wasn't an early birth so much as her body trying to expel the glass inside it."

Hughes stared at him. "What are you telling me? That our baby was... made of glass?"

"That's what I'm telling you."

Understanding struck so hard it actually dizzied him. The ultrasound technician had looked at her monitor, and where two months before she had seen a healthy, normal baby, tonight she had seen nothing. Just an inexplicable lump in the fluid-drained cavity of the womb. *Foreign matter.*

The sound reoccurred to him, that bestial noise gushing up Cate's throat as the orderly wheeled her into the elevator. Hughes knew now that it was the sound of a woman being torn apart from the inside. Everything made sense. The dark wine-stain was blood pumped out of her body. The endless hours without updates were hours spent picking shards of shattered glass out of his girlfriend.

And those shards... Oh God, those shards of fractured glass were...

"I see I've upset you," Lanmoor said. "I'm sorry. All I can say in my defense is that in twenty-five years in and out of operating theaters, tonight's surgery was my strangest. And it has stiff competition." He puffed at his cigar, making it wink like a fiendish orange eye, and tamped it out on his desk without bothering to search for an ashtray. "Miss Jubilee is in Delivery Room 4. I'll have a foldout bed set up for you so you can spend the night with her."

Hughes nodded.

"We're going to keep her under observation," Lanmoor continued. "Anyone we can call for you?"

"Call?" The word pushed through his lips, slurred with shock. "Cll" instead of "call." Sitting across from the doctor, Hughes looked nothing like the man who had been hailed as one of the city's heroes during the mass hysteria known as The Hairy Autumn a decade ago. He had the look people get when they narrowly avoid fatal car crashes that claim the lives of everyone else involved. He looked stunned and bolted in place as if by invisible steel rods. He looked condemned.

"Cll?"

"Nevermind." Lanmoor stood. "My condolences. Truly."

Feeling as if he were walking in a dream for the first time since he really *had* walked through a dream years ago, Hughes made his way to Delivery Room 4.

It was a one-bedder, a rare thing even in privately owned hospitals. No window. No get-well-soon cards or flowers either, but why should there be? What would come as news to their friends and family would by then be olds here in Saint Wilhemina's. Of the surgery that had saved Cate's life, there was no hint. Not a single drop of red on the lime-green marmoleum. Only the smell of disinfectant lingered, a hygienic poltergeist haunting the space. There was a bed, elevated and railed to stop the patient from doing a roly-poly and breaking something important.

In the bed was Cate. She was asleep, and the dreams must have been pretty good because her lips were tugged in a faint but definite smile.

Wish I was there with you, Kitten.

The orderlies hadn't brought up his foldout, so Hughes stood by the bed for a while, holding Cate's hand in mimicry of a younger, blissfully ignorant version of himself. One who still believed he had a little girl to delight in, rather than a plastic bag that jangled when you shook it to mourn.

Now he thought of it, he wondered where they'd taken the remains.

Surely not to the recycle bin. The idea injected him with fresh misery.

He should have asked Lanmoor.

A few minutes passed. He hoped Cate would stir. A soft snore. A gentle noise. Some vocalization of life, that was what he craved. Some logogram, some sign that this numb ruin inside him would declutter and decobweb.

But Cate didn't stir. So he planted a kiss on her brow.

"Love you," he said and gave her hand a squeeze to show he meant it.

He did not weep. Weeping would come later, but for now there were no tears. That seemed right. Those ought to be saved for Cate. He owed her the full ambit of his grief, as she owed him hers.

For now, he confined himself wholly to his thoughts.

They plashed from subject to subject, not really finding firm earth in any of them.

He thought about his life, and what he was going to say to Cate when her dreams were cut like puppet wire (*snicker-snick*) and she woke up. And what he would do to comfort her when words fell short, as they inevitably would.

The only subject he did not dwell on, the one thing he shut out of his mind and his heart, was glass.

Act Two

Something Ripe

Chapter Four

It was December 17th, snowflakes fell like ash from the gray bier of the clouds, Corinth City rose with the morning as a great pale phoenix, and everything was different now.

Salted roads crisscrossed. Trucks, cars, carriages pulled by mechanical dray horses decked in tinsel and fake holly for the holidays, the metrotram, and what kind of cars? All kinds. All makes. Buffed or scuffed. They all rode the asphalt veins and tarmacked arteries, searching for something unnamable as the city beat its irregular cardiac rhythm.

Different.

Cars had chugged before. The first sixteen-wheeler truck had hit the roads in the glum healing period that followed the war.

Different.

Eight-hundred years of medieval drudgery, accidental industrialization, civil war, foreign invasion, territorial squabbles, not to mention shifts in sociological paradigms, cultural herky-jerks, psycho-sexual revolutions, and greed (always that) had carved the city up into its current fragmented gestalt. It was a rough-and-tumble place, a pearl that remembered it was once a brainless worm that found its way into an oyster.

But the fact that change can gather so quickly, the way frost accumulates on your car windshield overnight, that was the real shocker.

Take Ptolema District. Only a generation ago those glass spires pricking the coldly weeping sky were warehouses. Street upon street of storage facilities where boxed goods awaited delivery by sea to Daethumberland, Jaenqui-Across-The-River, or even distant Yi-Shi. There was the occasional industrial park, and God knew a few office blocks rubbing shoulders with Redspire, that neck-creakingly tall tower right *there* at the center of things. The tower cast its shadow a long way. Across the whole *city,* like the needle on a huge sundial. Only a few scant years in the past, the basins of the Ptolemaien public fountains wouldn't glimmer with the tarnished green of old pennies but with the quartzy-pink of credits. How flash. It was a ritzy overdog area lording it over the underdogs, but hey, the tail still wagged. Now, well. Now it was clear that time had taken all that smarmy, ambitious life and replaced them with the sort of architecture you could check your teeth in.

Venturing the eye a little eastward down the slope of the city's hill, down to Polydoros District all colorful stained glass windows, cosmetic factories, and shops with gooey cheese and hard crackers and succulent thin slices of meat that melt on the tongue. Shop awnings were so popular there, canvas of cobalt-blue and whiskey-orange. Where did they go?

Curling into artistic, musical Cleomenes, the three Districts almost melting together, lay Nikandros. Once it had been grim and gray as a thundercloud with frizzy buildings and lightning-purple rooftiles. Now, artificial hedgerows snaked everywhere, fake flowers bloomed in parks of real grass imported from the countryside, and the lamps all burned green, a warm spring green that defied the ice making the posts sticky black sugarsticks, mocking the snows that gilded each emerald edge.

Biggest of all, Leonidas District.

It looked...

It...

Oh, but perhaps not everything was different after all.

Take Ptolema. Maybe the people and the buildings were wealthier, but the quality of that wealth remained steady. It was still simply a case of *More.* And a dragon still roosted atop Redspire, Wendy daughter of Walsingham.

Down the hill, Cleomenes still boasted a healthy population of pigeons. They were roosting too (on the roofs, oh yes oh yeah, taller roofs, wider, sure, but still *roofs,* baby). Huge and dark, the anvil-shaped Foundry jutted its familiar jut.

Curling District into District, Nikandros remained after all these years a breeding ground for nightclubs. And... Why, there in the middle of the main square. If it wasn't the statue of The Tyrant! The last King of Corinth still looked as though he had a wad of sandpaper up his bottom.

Biggest of all, a fat pustule dangling off the city's icy skin: Leonidas District.

Le-oh-ni-dasssssss. Each syllable a curse on its tenemented residents, its ratty shingles, its bad hospitals and worse schools, overcrowded and overburdened and yet...

And yet so deliciously *hopeful*. So sumptuously fucking plump with the yearning for tomorrow to be a little better than today. It radiated from unheated apartments, tattoo parlors, boarded-up pubs, dingy pawn shops, and the tea houses: a rich perfume of HOPE.

From a perfectly unremarkable rooftop on a perfectly unremarkable street, the shadow felt a giddy rush she did not at first recognize.

When she did, she smiled, a huge and charming smile. Homecoming. That was what she felt. How nice!

As she smiled, a fly crawled out of her ear canal and up one nostril.

It was December 17th, snowflakes dandruffed down from the slate-gray sky, and she was back, and everything was exactly the same.

***

Whiskers Number 319 observed from his hiding spot under the crockery cupboard. Just what he was observing was not entirely clear, since it was Big Folk Business, and he was himself Small Pickings, i.e. a rat.

He had been pawing his usual beat in the meadow (rats consider every environment a meadow. Even a city is a meadow, only much more fun) when he'd come to the good-smelling place. He'd been led to believe that this was called a 'pantry.' Food and drink lived here in quiet abundance, although Whiskers Number 319 hadn't needed to be told that. The smell of herbs alone was enough to bombard his senses, and what a gorgeous nasal siege it was.

This particular pantry was in what was apparently called The Mysicordelian Embassy, whatever that meant. Whiskers Number 319 didn't have much truck with details, although his employer certainly did, and far be it for this rat to turn his twitching pink nose up at the whims of his betters.

He'd scampered in as quiet as... well, maybe not as quiet as a Mr. Squeaky, but pretty close, and he'd made an effort to ignore the amazing delights of the pantry to do his job. In the middle of the room were two Bigs. One Big was making noises at another, who didn't make any noise at all, only drooped his head so his chin touched his throat now and again. The talkative Big looked around, as if afraid someone might come in without warning. No one did. Wringing his hands, the talkative Big approached the silent Big and opened his mouth, looking scared. The silent Big put his thumb inside his own mouth, as an infant Big might, and then withdrew it covered in red. Then he put his thumb inside the talkative Big's mouth, who sucked it.

Whiskers Number 319 was not sure what was going on here, but he knew one thing with grave certainty: he did not like the smell of this silent Big.

It was the smell that only vermin recognize. It hangs around cooks with rolling pins, or Bigs that wear foot-clothes with toes that are harder than normal, so that whatever they kicked would remember. Or, in some cases, so that whatever they kicked would not remember anything ever again.

That sort of smell could mean trouble.

Taking extra care, Whiskers Number 319 exited the pantry by a hole no bigger than your thumb and forefinger pressed together might make. It was a tight squeeze, but he just about managed it. Here were hard lumpy things that groaned and rumbled like the bellies of predators, and which on rare occasions belched scorching air or squirted water so hot it could kill you.

Luckily no such incident transpired, and after fifteen minutes of retracing his way to the Embassy toilets and the wide wall crack covered by a discarded porcelain sink, Whiskers Number 319 fled into a dawn so bitingly cold it made him shiver all over.

He paused and gazed up in amazement. Whiskers Number 319 was eight months old (approaching middle-age) and had never seen snow before. Of course he didn't think of it as 'snow.' To him, it seemed the monster that lived in the sky who made him dry when it was happy and who drenched his fur when it was irritable, was in very bad form. So bad, in fact, that the monster had decided to fill the day with horrible white teeth. Bitingly cold was right!

There was nothing to be done though. His employer would be expecting him any moment. Paws going painfully numb as he negotiated the stiff-frozen cobbles and slurry where dirty bath and shower water had guzzled out of gutters to mix with the snow, Whiskers Number 319 hurried for The Mound.

The Mound was not at the heart of the pipe-tangled jungle of the city's sewers, or even in its kidney. It was, in fact, not in the sewers at all but could be found within the sarcophagus of a thing that had once been a sewer. It had been constructed before the most recent technological boom, only to be bricked up after its engineers discovered a spongy brown mold living there, which was quite harmless for many species of sewer-dwelling animal, though nevertheless in humans would cause the development of lip-sores, lymphatic swelling, and other unfortunate symptoms. Like death.

So it was a quiet, abandoned-feeling place where forgotten pipes trickled and mismanaged chutes coughed out the occasional treasure from the upworld. It was to this lightless subterranean damp that Whiskers Number 319 arrived.

He took his spot in line behind a Bruce, who was deep in conversation with a Mr. Squeaky and another Whiskers.

A voice rolled out of the gloom. It did not belong to a Small Pickings but to a Big. A special Big, in fact, one that made the entire line perk up with excitement because it was the voice of the one who gave them work.

"Is that so? No. Really? Well, well, wellingtons. That *is* interesting."

Rats cannot sigh happily, but Whiskers Number 319 gave it a fair go. Life was so much better with that voice dictating its shape. Before the voice, things had been helter-skelter and no mistake. A rat without a guiding voice spent his days paw-to-mouth. Then someone—maybe it was Whiskers Number 256 or one of the other old-timers—had told him that things didn't have to be that way. He'd had his doubts. The sewage was always drier on the other side, and so on. But in the end he had elected to come here, down into the fetid dark. Down to The Mound.

And he had never cast a beady-eyed glance back. No indeed.

The line moved forward, and as Whiskers Number 319 got closer to the heap of soggy lavatory paper, ironically discarded wastebins, beakless rubber ducks, rusted needles, and inexplicable shopping trolleys that The Mound was named for, his adjusting eyes fixed on his employer.

The figure was a Big, otherwise known as a human being, although he stretched that definition a tad. This was what he looked like: take some playdough and make a man, then leave the playdough man in the middle of a highway that is frequented by lots of motorcycles. One side of his head was larger than the other. Count his toes and fingers and be presented with an odd number. His resting expression would not be out of place in a painting made by someone on cocaine cut with washing-up liquid.

Because of the "Occasional" part in a phenomenon called Occasional Morphology, it was extremely uncommon for a magic item to warp the appearance of its bearer. Unfortunately Knickerbocker was one such case. His item, which was a little gray sock, allowed him to communicate and exert power over rodents of every stripe and sort. He had built a respectable spy network out of these odd instruments, which included old church mice, city squirrels, chinchillas, rogue hamsters, rats, and bats (which are not really rodents, unless you have one in your living room. Biological classification is all well and good, but if it makes you wish you were holding a broom or possibly a portable trebuchet, it's a rodent).

The sock had also transformed him into the squashed gargoyle that Whiskers Number 319 was currently looking at. The change was irreversible and tended to elicit screams from people who weren't expecting to see him. Actually, it aroused screams from most people. Nevertheless Knickerbocker was a kindly soul, and even though he was their squalid sovereign, he spoke to his rodents as equals.

The line shuffled, and before long...

"Hullo Whiskers," said Knickerbocker. "What have you got for me?"

The voice called to a part of his brain that most rats never used, a recess in which memories were stored. He recalled the pantry. The talking Big, and the silent Big with the frightful smell. He recalled the talk, every lipsmack and tonguewag. Whiskers Number 319 squeaked his way around the unfamiliar syllables. Knickerbocker nodded, taking notes on a fresh page with a greasy stub of pencil.

"The silent man," he said. "Was his tongue pierced?"

Whiskers Number 319 considered, then agreed that it was.

"Was the piercing glittery and red?"

It was indeed.

"Well, well, wellingtons," cooed Knickerbocker. "Taniko has sent an Incarnadine to Corinth City. Seems he's worried about the life of his consul, who just happens to be the emperor's second cousin. I do believe that is the most tasty crumb of gossip. Well done, Whiskers."

Knickerbocker slipped the paper into a file and stroked Whiskers Number 319 with a finger like a melted crayon. Then he stood up, tucked the file into a pack he kept lashed across his lumpy chest, and said, "That's enough for today. I've left a lovely meal for each of you in the usual spot. Wossat?"

A bat was flapping about his head, screeching frantically.

"Yes, all right, all *right*," said Knickerbocker. "Stop that racket you daft git. What have you to tell me that's so urgent, Bruce?"

The bat landed on his head and told him. The crowd strained to hear.

"Yeah. Yeah, I know all about that," grumbled Knickerbocker after a while. "I'm sure it's nothing to crimp your wings about. Hear that, all of you? I know about... the *sound*, okay? Close your ears to it for the time being and open them to really important stuff, like what Whiskers over there told me just now. It's Big Folk Business, and that's how it'll stay. Happy?"

A chorus of chitters that would have stopped the heart of a restaurant manager answered him. Knickerbocker grinned. "Toodle pip."

Whiskers Number 319 watched him go.

Then he went with the others and ate breakfast. It was good but nowhere near as magnificent as the best meal of the year. That was coming soon.

Any day now.

Lots of things were coming soon.

***

In the great chemical broth of the universe, there often arises certain chunks of formula that play themselves out.

One of these can be summarized like this: whenever a butler attempts to quietly insinuate themself into the room their master or mistress is occupying, some little sound will give them away. The groan of a floorboard. The creak of the unoiled doorframe. The rattle of keys or dinner bells or other miscellaneous items hanging from the butler's belt. Then the Lord or Lady will, without breaking concentration on whatever it is they are doing, say something along the lines of, "Ah, Jeeves. Do come in."

It's just one of those things.

That morning, the butler, Falstaff, slipped quietly into the office of his mistress. The formula attempted to follow its familiar course and found it couldn't. The floorboards were too well-mended to groan. The door jamb was too well-oiled to creak. Nothing jangled on his belt. The entrance was as smooth as it was noiseless.

This was because this particular butler was simply too neat for messy, ridiculous natural conventions to have any power over him. He was immaculately tailored, tucked, and tidied. His fingernails would have made many a manicurist hang up their files in shame. When he spoke, his sentences were cutlery drawers, his words polished silver. He made your standard Jeeves look like a baboon.

Nevertheless, before he could clear his throat to announce himself, Lady Wendy Dragontail covered her telephone's mouthpiece with her hand, and without looking up, said, "Ah, Falstaff. Do come in."

Falstaff offered a private smile and obeyed.

"Yes, I understand your grievance, Mr. Bileous," Wendy said, resuming her conversation as Falstaff refluffled the couch cushions, emptied the ash from the fireplace, and engaged in what you might call general primping. "Nevertheless, I must remind you that it is Tinfrosttime. The so-called Holiday Season. Those who are still working wish they weren't, and those who aren't wish that they never will again. It is a time of fantasies, Mr. Bileous. Small fantasies, I grant you, yet they do go a long way, don't they?

"Your network fills the home screens of the working woman and the toiling man with a convincing imitation of cinema. And home video, like cinema, has a kind of wizardry to it. A beautiful hypnotism. It makes fantasies feel closer to hand. Even the small ones, Mr. Bileous. Here we come to the crux of the matter," Wendy continued, scanning her notes on a separate issue entirely. "Take away those fantasies, and you force people to contend with difficult realities. Realities they would rather forget and certainly do not wish bandied about in the restless silence of a house where the screens receive nothing but static. Those kinds of hard truths might just aggravate otherwise ordinary people to the point where things that ought to remain fantasies become realities.

"I draw your attention to the crime rates before and after the introduction of home video. I think the results speak for themselves." Her eyes went to the window, its frosty pane dimpled with snow. "I know you and your fellow board members are aware of this. And yet we are in the third week of December, and you still have a labor strike in your laps. I would like to see an end to reruns, and if I may be so blunt, an end to excuses as well, and furthermore a return to scheduled programming by tomorrow afternoon."

She listened.

"Did I say anything of the sort, Mr. Bileous? I rather think I'd remember."

A brief pause.

"Yes. But while I of course know you to be a man whose shrewdness does little to curtail his generosity, I alas am not on the other side of the negotiating table. That would be your *union*, Mr. Bileous. Your extremely peeved *union*. They are not going to be corralled, so corral yourself on their behalf and pay them what they want, there's a good man."

Another pause, longer this time.

When she spoke again, her voice was like a plume of oily black smoke curling out of a cave where dragons were rumored to lurk.

"You feel, perhaps, that I am being... overly demanding?"

She listened. Then her face softened.

"Yes, thank you, Mr. Bileous. I'm pleased to hear it. Happy Tinfrost to you as well."

She hung up.

"That captain fellow has requested an audience again, my Lady."

Wendy perused a notebook, muttered something inaudible, set it aside, and selected another. Her desk was in a bit of a tiff with itself at present, each section vying for control over the others. "Captain?" she said absently.

"Hokum something," replied Falstaff. "He has a second name like the sound of being clubbed."

"Hoshrum Thud."

"Yes, that was it. He's very eager. Something about a spate of troubling murders."

"Murders are not troubling, Falstaff. In a city of a million people, in which tempers stack and teeter like plates in a kitchen sink, there are bound to be a few regrettable crashes." Wendy tossed the useless notebook aside, abandoned the desktop, and began to search its drawers. "In my experience, real trouble presents itself in subtler clothes than the blood-rags of common murder. Notify Captain Thud that despite his convictions to the contrary, this is not a Scarlet Citadel matter. I wish him luck in his investigations, my regards to his Commissioner, the usual drivel."

Falstaff made a mental note. "Yes, my Lady. Can I be of any help in locating–"

"No, I've got it." Wendy hefted the correct notebook triumphantly. She flipped it open, studying its contents. "What's the latest on the Dengue Virus?"

"Would her Ladyship care for the long or the short of it?"

"What did the great director say of edits? *Leave my bones on the cutting room floor, but for God's sake, leave my art unsnipped.*"

"Long it is." Falstaff whisked a clean white cloth from the cuff of his shirt and began buffing the stone dragons that framed the fireplace. "The Ereb mosquito doesn't die out in winter, but its population usually slackens dramatically. That might have meant a subsequent decline in infection rates. Unfortunately an unseasonably warm November across the southwest of Ikahagua has meant a slower decline than normal."

"I take it infection rates are still high?"

"Precariously so."

"Vaccine?"

"Still in preliminary trials, my Lady."

"What?" Wendy looked up. "That can't be. It's the Dengue Virus. As common as cows on a dairy farm."

"Evidently viral mutations are just as ubiquitous," said Falstaff. "I hope they discover a vaccine soon. The news says it's horrible in Ereb."

"What about John's team? Why haven't they sped things up there?"

Falstaff hesitated. "Doctor Isherwood has been... difficult to contact of late, your Ladyship."

A line formed in Wendy's brow. She opened her mouth just as the telephone rang.

"Yes?" A pause. "Who is this? How did..."

She held the receiver at arm's length, the way an arachnophobe might hold a spider at the end of some tweezers. Petulant chirps erupted from it, scrambled and keening. Slamming it down and ending the call, Wendy leaned over the desk.

"*I say, Montcrieff! Can you hear me?*"

"Urk."

Falstaff jumped, fumbling the buffing cloth. How had he not noticed the young man tapping away at his cogwheel computers in the room's corner?

There he slumped, pimply and slung haphazardly into a dun-brown cardigan.

The butler disliked Montcrieff. Not out of any personal qualm, of course. It would take a real nuisance to draw Falstaff's ire. It was more out of a sort of basic servile principle. Montcrieff was a dispatcher, a researcher, and a digital analyst. He was almost as good at his job at Falstaff was at his own, and that was, if not unacceptable, then at the very least a real pain in the bowtie.

Also, the man was too damn invisible by half. He simply melted into the background. And he never uttered a word, only faint sounds of inquiry or agreement. Not a single opinion except, *What is the job* and *I will get right to it.*

That was it. The man oozed conformity and submission. Many worked to live. Montcrieff lived to work.

Falstaff fairly smoldered with envy.

"Montcrieff, I've something for you," Wendy commanded. *"Trace that last call. Some vulture from the tabloids, I'll wager, pecking for a comment on that fiasco at The Hippodrome last week. I want their name, organization, and preferably one of their primal fears."*

"Urk?"

"Scratch that last. Can you do it?"

"Urk."

"Thank you."

That fiasco at The Hippodrome.

Retrieving the cloth, Falstaff grimaced. He'd heard about that. Tommy Fahrenheit really ought to be ashamed of himself. Nothing like that had ever happened before. And Tommy had always been so—

There was a knock at the window.

Wendy waved an order to open it, dialing a new number with her free hand.

Falstaff hurried dutifully to the window, swung it inward to admit the knocker, and did his best not to yelp.

"Guh-good morning, Knickerbocker," he managed.

The figure perched on the ledge gave a nod. "Falstaff. Got news hot off the street."

Falstaff glanced back at the desk where Wendy was pitched in a conversation with someone in portalology.

"Put me through to John Isherwood, please. John, capital. And here I expected to be told you were unavailable, what with your ongoing contributions toward a vaccination for Ereb..."

"Off the street, hm?" said Falstaff. "That's exciting. Erm. How are you, Knickerbocker?"

"Peachy keen, peachy keen. You?"

"Me?"

"Yeah."

"Splendid, thanks. Ahm. Her Ladyship is rather busy..."

Knickerbocker shook what Falstaff presumed was his head. "Can't wait."

"Right. I'll see if I can lure her from her desk."

"You do that."

Falstaff expected to find Wendy unloading a torrent of chastising poison down the phone line into John Isherwood's ear. Instead she seemed intent, almost fascinated.

"I was under the impression the project's findings weren't ready to be presented?" she said. And after a moment: "I see. Yes, of course. John, I want to hear these findings of yours. I want to hear them today." Wendy listened, her eyes twinkling. "Oh, I'm sure you'll bear through. And John? This is *excellent* news. Yes, Falstaff?" she added, hanging up. "What is it?"

"News, my Lady."

"Yes, it's marvelous, isn't it?"

"What?"

"Pardon?"

They looked at one another in shared puzzlement.

From the window came a sound like a watermelon being fed through a woodchipper. Knickerbocker had just cleared his throat.

Wendy said, "Good morning! I'll be over directly."

Her mood had certainly picked up.

"Right-o, Ladyship," said Knickerbocker. "Got a doozy for you."

"You tend to, my prime kobold. Falstaff, contact... No, I've reconsidered. *Montcrieff! Can you hear me?*"

"Urk."

"I'd be delighted..." Falstaff began, but Wendy overrode him.

"Contact the Ikahaguan Consulate. I'd like to affirm our commitment to assist in the production of a vaccine to the recently mutated Dengue Virus. Unforeseen delays have prevented

us from doing so already. Call them, oh, roadblocks on the highway of epistemology. More of a country path, really. Bumpy as anything..."

"Urk?"

"*Nevermind,*" called Wendy. "*In addition, to demonstrate our friendship with our southern cousins, we will be sending a member of the Scarlet Citadel to assist in the conservation and upkeep of their quarantine zones. It's imperative that this remain an epidemic and not escalate into a possible pandemic. Etcetera, etcetera. Read well to you?*"

"Urk."

"*Good.* Falstaff, be a lamb and draft me a list of candidates."

Candidates to send to distant Ikahagua. Not a position many here in the Citadel would relish, especially during the holiday season. Except...

"Might I suggest Tommy Fahrenheit?"

Falstaff felt a rush of pleasure at the approval he saw cross Wendy's face.

"A capital suggestion. See to it, Falstaff. Knickerbocker! You'll forgive the delay."

That was another thing.

Dress in sweaters and slippers though she might, wear tasteless earrings though she absolutely did, Wendy (short for Winnifred) Dragontail *was* the ruler of the city. Observe her for the length of a few minutes, and that fact solidified in your head. There were other giveaways, of course. Easy breezy phrases like "you'll forgive the delay" rather than "please forgive," or "won't you forgive." Or more sinister ones like "You feel, perhaps, that I am being... overly demanding?" that chilled the marrow of otherwise fierce television executives. Wendy's mind was wide enough to envelop every District, every street, every apartment block, and narrow enough so that the city didn't have much wiggle room, and so that it wouldn't question who exactly was in charge. Oh, there was a government who voted on things, true. And a judiciary system, yes. But they were rather useless and everyone knew it.

No, thought Falstaff. *It's the Last Dragon who presides over us. And thank goodness for that.*

He crept out as quietly as he'd come. Scurrying through the Lunarlight Wing, he reviewed the morning's affairs. The television worker union strike. The pleas of a streetbeater captain. The Dengue Virus in Ereb. Predacious journalists. Knickerbocker's pressing news.

Falstaff summoned the elevator, smiled to himself, and spoke aloud the words of an old Tinfrost carol. "*Good tidings we bring to you and your kin.*"

In his pocket, another list sent up hungry tendrils into the part of his brain dedicated to organization. It was stuffed to the brim with chores, problems, and little fiddly tasks. Thinking of that list, his smile didn't fade. Quite the contrary. It grew much, much wider.

It was almost Tinfrost, and there was so much to do!

The elevator chimed. The doors opened.

Falstaff's expression changed.

"Oh!" he said. "I wasn't expecting to see either of you!"

***

Knickerbocker climbed down the tower.

It was a little after seven o'clock in the morning when he broke through the heavy curtain of clouds and the city, well-salted with snow, appeared below and around him, little sullen buildings and high proud spires.

Although the bumpy things that could debatably be called his hands and feet moved expertly from nook to cranny, and his squashed nose began to run in the high cold air, Knickerbocker's mind was fixed firmly on the conversation he'd just had with her Ladyship.

She had noted the arrival of an Incarnadine in the city with interest, as he knew she would. When a member of a group known for their bodyguarding, anti-terrorist efforts, political assassinations, as well as their cavalier attitude to violence turned up, only a fool would ignore it, and Wendy Dragontail was no fool.

"I commend your informant, Knickerbocker."

"Whiskers, ma'am. He's a rat," said Knickerbocker helpfully.

"Do convey my compliments. And some cheese perhaps."

On the ledge, Knickerbocker's face twisted into a secretive leer. "I heard they call themselves 'Incarnadine' coz it means 'red.'"

"Pinkish red," Wendy amended.

"And *that's* coz they've got this ritual, see? After they trains them up in Mysicordelia, from kiddies to killers, they've got to knife their best friend in the world and take their heart's blood and put it in a magic jewel. That jewel of dead friend's red heart's blood gives them *power*, like what our Jolene forging does here in Corinth."

"Fascinating," said Wendy flatly.

He shivered. "Fairly prickles my nadgers and no mistake, your Ladyship."

"Really? I'm sure an ointment of some kind will help."

"Incarnadines," growled Knickerbocker. "Why do you think the emperor's sent a nasty customer like that here?"

"Perhaps Emperor Tanika is merely getting into the festive spirit." Wendy was looking at the fireplace where Falstaff had set a few logs burning against the pre-afternoon chill. "Perhaps it's a gift."

Knickerbocker was tempted to say that Whiskers hadn't reported any sign of a card or mentioned any ribbon attached to the Incarnadine but thought better of it. Wendy Dragontail was not a humorless woman by any means, and that was a blessing provided you weren't a joke, or God help you, a punchline in her estimation.

He watched her. She watched the flames.

Then Knickerbocker chanced his arm and broached a topic he really would rather not have.

"Eh, there was something else, your Ladyship."

"Do tell."

"You're not, er, too busy?"

"Always. Tell anyway."

Knickerbocker hesitated. "Lately a few of my more, um, lofty snitches—that is those who are more inclined toward chimneys, attics, and roof tiles rather than the lowly cobbles and tarmacs and so on—have told me about this sound they've heard."

"A sound?"

"Made them nervous, so it did." Knickerbocker had filched the truth, there. According to the various Mr. Squeakies, Bruces, Bushtails, and the rest, the sound pushed through them in sickening waves. Their teeth ached with it. It made their tiny fibrous ear hairs stand on end. So when they came, they did not appeal to Knickerbocker nervous. They appealed to him scared.

"Can you describe the sound?" said Wendy.

"A buzzing, your Ladyship."

"Could be a radio frequency. Subaurale sounds that don't bother the human ear have been known to disturb animals. Dog whistles and pest alarms, for example."

"Could be," Knickerbocker allowed, although he was ninety percent sure it wasn't, and he told her so.

"What then?"

"I don't know, ma'am," he said. "But I thought I should mention it to you. Far as I can tell the only alarm going off is the one in my head."

She looked at him for the first time in a while. "I shall put in a call with someone in the zoology department at the university. We'll silence that alarm in no time." She'd drawn closer to the fire, and her teeth gleamed orange when she grinned. It comforted him at once.

"Thank you very much, m'Lady."

"Your help is valuable to me, Knickerbocker. Where would a dragon be without her kobolds?"

"I expect we tip the scales in your favor all right." He'd seen the opportunity and gone for it.

To his immense relief her grin had broadened. "Scales. Very good. Will that be all, Knickerbocker?"

It had been. Now he was halfway down Redspire tower. His fingers and toes gripped each jut and ridge with the automaticity of a wizened rat avoiding a suspicious slice of blue-veined gorgonzola. He peered down and saw cars with defrosted windshields and raised fog lights. Cones of wispy gold in the strange streets. Knickerbocker increased his speed. He had no phobia of heights, but ever since his transformation he found he had a fondness for, if not solid ground, then whatever damp recess lay under it.

Highness is finest, but lowly is homey.

Ooh, he liked that. The warped canvas of his face painted itself a grin to match his mistress'. Down, he was bound. Down and down, and downer still below the roads worn smooth by rubber wheels and clopping shoes and atrophied bubblegum.

The Mound was calling him home.

Chapter Five

In the first year of meeting one another, Wendy Dragontail had tricked Hughes twice. The first time she tested his instincts. The second she tested his resolve.

With the medium of theatrical performance dead and all the old showbiz haunts demolished, renovated, or left to crumble, the only acting you saw was in the movies or on the vids. At least that was the prevailing belief.

In truth, acting was alive and well. It always had been.

Certain people like to front the idea that everyone is acting all the time. Tailoring who they are to suit a particular audience. Some argue that we even perform ourselves to ourselves. The ultimate solo act. Solitary dramas staged without applause in an even lonelier dark. *All the world's a stage*, there's a notion. *All of the true things I'm about to tell you are shameless lies*, there's another.

Maybe so, but in a much more immediate sense, acting and performance were still vital and flourishing in Gormon Hughes. He understood the craft, sure, but there was magic inherent to him that would dim the brightest stage light, hush the loudest clarions from the bandstand, evoke emotion and kill it in the same breath. He didn't understand it and had given up trying to years ago. If men like Doctor John Isherwood couldn't, what chance did he have? None, that was what.

Still, he'd nurtured it readily enough.

As a boy who'd slept under old play manuscripts stitched together for want of a blanket, and who still snuck out of bed sometimes when he couldn't sleep, careful not to rouse Cate, who took to the spare room, and snuggled up under a rustling story, the idea of Performance enacting real change sort of thrilled him.

Moreover, it had given him an eye for bullshit and the coy, nearly-invisible forms bullshit assumed in everyday life. With amazing regularity he saw masks put on and taken off, and here's the thing: There might be other masks under *those*. People were funny like that.

When they entered Wendy's office—often referred to as The Dragon's Lair—Hughes saw Wendy don such a mask. She donned it over her real expression, which was one of both astonishment and concern. Her new face was a portrait of composure.

It happened fast, but he caught it. Caught it and was wary of it.

This dragon might have white scales, but they had been bleached a long time, and her fire was still as scorching as that of the one chewing the logs in the hearth.

More so.

"Cate. Hughes. I wasn't expecting to see you so soon."

A vague greeting, but a pointed one. The implicit meaning was clear: *I wasn't expecting to see you so soon after that night in Saint Wilhemina's.* In other words, *What are you doing here when you should be in recovery?*

The image of Cate unconscious in the steel-framed hospital bed crossed six weeks and landed in Hughes' head. Her cheeks sunken. Her complexion yogurt-plain despite the blood transfusion. Her belly still big. It hadn't forgotten what had been inside it, the person who had become a thing that had become a shattering. Hughes dismissed this image. Doing so was hard.

Cate said, "My Lady. Hughes and I are hoping to speak to you."

"Have a seat."

They did. Over in the hearth a knot of wood exploded, showering the grate in glowing sparks. December poured wan light through the office window, and there were no lamps lit. So the fire sketched them all. It mingled with Cate's red mane, turned Wendy's hair into a burning nimbus, and even seemed to smear Hughes' dark locks with a molten varnish. The three settled themselves, Gormon Hughes and Cate Jubilee on one couch, Wendy Dragontail on the other.

A subtle tension moved unseen between them, like disturbing significance in a tableau.

"How are you feeling?" Wendy asked Cate.

"Fine. Look, Wendy, we've been—"

"And you, Hughes? You were both still indisposed when I called on you."

Indisposed was one way of putting it. Delicate and sharp as a thorn, that was their fearless leader's method of communication. Wendy had indeed visited Cate during her recovery though. She'd brought flowers, disarming sympathy, and a host of friends and colleagues from the Citadel. For the length of this visit, Cate and Hughes had been shocked out of their numb fugue of grief, an unthinkable result.

He remembered this gesture now, sitting across from the woman who had orchestrated it.

That was then, however, and this was n—

"Hughes?" said Wendy. "I asked you how you're holding up, my lad."

He didn't answer, simply turned to Cate and waited for her to continue what she'd been trying to say. She shot him a grateful look and plowed on.

"Hughes and I have thought long and hard about this. Deliberated, I suppose you could say. We've decided that we're coming back to work. Today, actually. Please," she said as Wendy drew a breath to reply. "Let me finish."

Wendy's shoulders relaxed a little. She waved an inviting hand as if to say, *Do go on.* Hughes, ever watchful, saw the stiffness in those fingers and realized this was going to be as difficult and unpleasant as he and Cate had predicted. Possibly worse.

"I'll speak about my own plans first," said Cate. "I'd like to get in on whatever it is you're planning with John Isherwood. Three clues have led me to believe something *is* being planned. First, the rumors. Even from home, it's been impossible to escape the avalanche of speculation about Doctor Isherwood's work. Members of his team are going on extended leave, maternity, burnout repose. Some are outright quitting, dissolved back into academia, presumably sworn to secrecy with their names scrawled on the bottom line of a nondisclosure agreement. There's a rumor about one portal technician experiencing a complete breakdown. Apparently he rushed screaming into Eurydice, never to be seen again."

"Baseless jabs," said Wendy, unimpressed.

Cate nodded. "I agree. It's my flimsiest evidence. Much more concrete is my second clue: you've mandated larger teams. Ever since I joined the Citadel under your tenure, we've been able to select who we venture through the portals with. Before I became Hughes' patron, I was able to lone-wolf it entirely. Yet in the past six months you've adjusted the system. In August the minimum became five members to a unit. As of October that number has risen to seven. Isaac Lawless and the other cartographers have been parceled out to join these units. You're sealing up ranks, my Lady. Something has changed."

To this, Wendy Dragontail made no reply.

"Third," said Cate after a tense moment. "I've been paying close attention to the situation in Ereb. Greasy though some of their printing presses might be, the papers are well-informed. There hasn't been a single headline about a delegation being sent from Redspire. Not one." She crossed her legs and leaned forward, her fingers laced. "Forgive my bluntness, Your Grace, but there's not a monkey's fart of a hope that this isn't intentional. John Isherwood has extensive experience with virology. He's written nine bloody papers on the subject, four of which tackle the vaccine skepticism that, you'll excuse my glibness here, plagued the former half of the current century. John would have been perfect as the top brass in a team sent to help stymy this mutation of the Dengue Virus. But he's not there. He's here. His continued work under your stewardship means that whatever *has* changed is so big that it eclipses a potentially global pandemic.

"I want in."

Cate finished with these three words, one for each bit of evidence. Her voice was steady and strong as a hammer.

Clever carpentry altogether, Hughes thought, admiring his lover. *She nailed it.*

He had no need to smother a smile. The moment was simply too intense for humor. But the pun knocked around his head for a moment, as though testing the integrity of his seriousness. Suddenly he missed his father.

Wendy Dragontail got up. Without a word she went to her desk and picked up the telephone. "Good morning. Two teas and a coffee to my office, if you'd be so kind."

Cate touched Hughes' hand, encouraged. With this small display, Wendy had established that she was willing to entertain the possibility of them returning to work, but that in this tower it was she and she alone who called the shots. Before vanishing into history, dragons had dominated with fireworks summoned from their guts. Now the Last Dragon dominated with heated beverages. The irony was not lost on Hughes, who felt a flicker of deep respect in the presence of this dangerous woman.

Drinks arrived while Cate talked Wendy through Hughes' reasons for getting back to work. For his part, Hughes listened and observed and drank his tea.

Onto the table that lay between them, the wood grain awash in fireglow, Cate laid a cutout from yesterday's copy of the *Corinthian Times*. The cutout was made up of a headline, three chunky paragraphs, and a picture. The writer of this article, a journalist called Tracer Gogen, informed the reader of the brutal slaying of Jodi Whitlaw (48), Penny Moore (32), Harris Stokely (46) and Marge Tinetts (22) in the Gallfer Canning Factory off Blackchapel Road. The chief suspect in the murder was a man named Nigel Ulmersten (55). The article related the day's events and the ugliness of the murders in exquisite detail (Hughes suspected Tracer Gogen had good contacts in the forensic and police departments, not to mention the chief coroner's office).

Then the article executed a radical but elegant pivot.

It turned the reader's attention to a recent but undeniable spike in gruesome slaughters. These incidents bore a striking resemblance to the Ulmersten case.

Take the murder of Marberry Dennings (41), Adam Dennings (10), and Ellen Dennings (9) in their apartment on Giacomo Lane. They had been killed in early November. The culprit was, according to the streetbeaters who had picked up and subsequently jailed her, the wife and mother of the deceased, Susabeth Dennings (40).

This, the article reiterated to the reader, was only one of many similar cases.

There was no evidence to suggest that any of the culprits were familiar with, or had even met one another.

Almost as bizarre as the murders themselves was the manner in which the suspects were apprehended. Susabeth, like Nigel after her, had been caught after being spotted leaping from roof to roof by multiple witnesses. This trend repeated itself across every single one of the seemingly unrelated cases.

The photo next to the article was a side-by-side comparison of two photos. Both were snapped at crime scenes (further cementing Hughes' suspicions about the journalist's contacts). In the first, there was a room at the Gallfer Canning Factory. Buckets of tuna stood by each workstation. A conveyor belt unwound from one wall. It was bereft of aluminum cans. What it was not bereft of was blood. A large splash of it ran over the immobile rubber of the belt and onto the nearby wall where a message had been written in gore. In the second photo, a little of the Dennings' apartment was visible. By a wall stood a Tinfrost tree complete with decorations. No blood here. Instead, the message on the wall was written using human hair.

Despite the difference in materials from photo one and photo two, the message was identical.

THEY ARE IN ME

Lastly, the headline read: *Jack's Back! Police Left Reeling By Rooftop Ravagers.* The alliteration was a cunning touch of journalism, a wicked flourish to snatch at the reader's imagination.

"Jack refers to the legend of Spring-Heeled Jack," said Cate. "Apparently a string of similar murders took place years ago. There were lots of convictions, but it was a more sensationalist time in those days. The public believed there was one killer behind it all, and that those arrested were being framed so Jack could escape scot-free."

Wendy said, "What has this got to do with you, Hughes?"

"The killings seem isolated to Leonidas District," he replied. "With your permission, my Lady, I'm going to defend my home."

She peered at him over the cutout, then lowered it so he could see the steel of her expression. "You wish to play policeman?"

Hughes nodded, not embarrassed by the comparison in the least.

Wendy exchanged the cutout for her cup and saucer, sipped tea, seemed to be mulling over everything that had been said.

Cate and Hughes kept their silence. Both sensed what was coming.

"Of course it's wonderful to see you both out and about," said Wendy with a fond smile. "And no one could call the pair of you unpersuasive. I note with approval that during your no doubt complicated preparation for this conversation, you elected to have Cate do most of the talking. Hughes, with his propensity toward swaying the minds of those he wishes to sway, might have risked offense should he have taken the reins. Or put me, as they say, on edge. That was sly of you." Another sip of tea. "Yes, very persuasive."

Here we go.

"However, it would be remiss of me not to prioritize the wellbeing of two of my finest agents. I have been called many things over the years. Negligent is not amongst them. Cate, I assume you've spoken to your physician."

"I have."

"And?"

Cate shrugged. "Says I'm fit as a fiddle."

"And I'm to take your word for it that this is so?"

It was a smart avenue to pursue, but they'd been ready for it. From the depths of his moth-gnawed coat Hughes produced a letter. He handed it to Wendy.

"My word wouldn't do," said Cate. "Take his."

In admirably lay terms from someone in the medical field, the letter summarized the three weeks of rest and treatment, as well as the subsequent three weeks of physiotherapy, undertaken by one Cate Jubilee. It laid out the facts. Sometime in the second trimester the baby gestating inside her had turned to glass. Cate's body, its cells alerted to growing danger suspended in her amniotic fluid, had tried to expel it. The damage to her womb and cervix were cataclysmic.

Here Cate's luck turned. Surgery was successful. Bolstering that success was a crack treatment scheme involving blood transfusions and an additional surgery performed by an international leader in gynecological reconstructive surgery who happened to be visiting his brother-in-law here in the city.

The letter went on to recount in frankly awed tones Cate's progress, discharge from intensive care, and ongoing evaluation. There had been minimal muscle wasting. Her vitals were good. She had weaned herself off pain medication twenty-five days after surgery. It asserted that such a rapid recovery owed itself to several factors, not least of which included the young Miss Jubilee's fitness and what the letter's writer delicately described as her "unique circumstances."

Meaning Cate's glassification.

The letter concluded with a recommendation that Miss Jubilee return to work when she should feel ready and furthermore expressed its apologies:

"I'm sorry. I wish there was more I could have done."

It was signed by Artemi Lanmoor, M.D. Saint Wilhelmina's Obstetrics Dep.

Hughes watched Wendy's face as she read. No movement. Not a single twitch.

She folded the letter and handed it back to Hughes.

"You will not be assuming the role of detective," she told him. "Reprise the part of the hero instead. You play it better."

The letter had surprised her. You didn't need Hughes' ear for intonation to recognize that. Right now you could extinguish forest fires with Wendy Dragontail's voice, it was that chilly.

"I'm sending you to Eurydice, Hughes. There's a matter there that requires your attention."

"Has it anything to do with John Isherwood's current project?"

"Yes."

"In that case Cate should go," said Hughes. "She's got the experience. Eurydice's her home away from home. I'd be surprised if the monsters there haven't set up a support group: We Survived Cate Jubilee And Her Hobnail Boots, Somehow. We Can't Remember The Details, It's All A Bit Of A Blur, Now You Mention."

He felt something stroke the knuckles on his right hand. Cate's little finger.

"Perhaps I did not make myself entirely clear," said Wendy, the dragon's irritation burning cold enough that it beaded the air between them with invisible ice crystals. "This is not a debate. This is not charming Sunday morning gossip over freshly baked buns. The nature of the problem in Eurydice is undergoing evaluation. I'm speaking with John later this afternoon and intend to be fully informed by tonight. My instincts, however, tell me that you are the man for the job, Hughes. They're rather superbly honed, though I don't need to remind you of that. You remember the events preceding The Hairy Autumn?"

He remembered all right. And Hughes wasn't touching that one. Ten years ago she'd brought him into the Citadel on the basis of those instincts of hers, that was a fair point. On the whole it had worked out well, especially for Hughes. And you didn't become the leader of a city like Corinth by being stupid. You did it by being Wendy Dragontail, or to put it another way, by being less stupid than everyone else.

There was also the nickname.

Where it had started, Hughes would never know. It had come to his ears out of the blue one day and it had jarred him to his bones.

Wendy's Bloodhound.

That was what they called him, in certain circles anyway, and out of his hearing if they could help it. Gormon Hughes, Wendy's Bloodhound. *Her Ladyship has a problem, she'll invariably send Hughes to sniff it out.*

The worst thing, the absolute cruelest thing about it, was that some tiny part of him perked up at the idea of being her favorite. It wagged its tail.

Well, he was damned if he was going to roll over obediently this morning.

"Maybe we're arguing a moot point," he said. "Might I make a suggestion, Your Worship?"

"I don't think anything short of an earthquake could stop you, Hughes."

"It's a good thing your authority is longer than that, your Ladyship."

He caught a miniscule twinkle in her hard hazel eyes.

"This job sounds important. Send Cate initially, and then once this murder business is wrapped up, I'll join her."

"And should your... investigations seem interminable?" Wendy demanded. "What then?"

"It's unlikely," said Cate. "My partner is, as you yourself admit, very persuasive."

"And pressing as this Eurydice venture is, the Spring-Heeled Jack issue needs resolving." Hughes tapped the cutout on the table with a finger. "If we don't, there's going to be a lot more headlines like this."

"You're insinuating that the streetbeaters are not up to the task?"

Hughes tried to keep his expression neutral. "I'm sure they're doing their best."

"You think the commissioner, a veteran of forty years of police work, will fail to find the source of these murders?"

"With all due respect, my Lady. Commissioner Vincent Winkles couldn't find his own bottom with both hands."

"That is extremely rude of you, Hughes."

"I did say *with all due respect*, Your Grace." He shrugged. "In my view Old Vinny Winky could use all the help he can get. Plus I've got Chimera, the backing of the Citadel, and my other little talent."

"You are referring to your Performance."

"Could be useful for interviewing the culprits, my Lady. Maybe I'll uncover something the streetbeaters haven't. Or couldn't, if you take my meaning."

She drummed her fingers on her lap, her gaze boring into him.

Then she sighed.

"You don't feel this is all a tad... premature?"

Cate shook her head.

"May I ask what *has* gripped you then?" Wendy pressed sharply. "Moral obligation? An evolved sense of duty to your fellow man? Simple restlessness?"

Both of her guests were studying the carpet, the table, the fire devouring the last of the logs. They looked at everything except Wendy. Or one another.

"Well? You must be feeling something, the pair of you."

It was Hughes who replied.

"Broken," he said.

Outside the wind hadn't worked up the courage to blow. Snow filled in the footprints Knickerbocker had left on the window ledge. Soon it would be as though he was never there. Morning ripened. Lumbering densities waked in the baleful white. Where it had cozened itself shelter the night's former frost endured, except where it had gathered near the tower's central heating systems which were protuberant and large as buffalo. There the frost melted and dripped, a clear sweet cordial for passing robins. Inside within the hearth vigiled by stony ghosts the embering flames spoke a language as old as the earth and cried out with tiger-colored tongues, cried of the babes who had been born, who had lived that evening chiseled out of autumn dark and who were yet living, and who had not tokened sympathetic letters from men who did not and could not understand.

Eventually Wendy said, "Thud."

Hughes and Cate blinked. The moment had passed and everything was going again. "Beg your pardon," they said in perfect unison.

"Thud." Wendy was on her slipper-clad feet and behind her desk before the word could register once more with either of them. "Captain Hoshrum Thud. You'll find him in the Leonidas Precinct Station, Hughes. Unless I'm mistaken, he'll assume the role of Ye Olde Grizzled Copper in this murder mystery of yours. As for you, Cate, report to Eilandri Titansgrave."

Cate was standing now. Hughes joined her. "The Pale Giant?" she said.

"I caution you not to use that particular title around Miss Titansgrave. I understand the last person to do so is still looking for employment, preferably in a career that involves a great deal of lying down."

"I heard Eilandri was comfortably retired," said Hughes.

"Indeed. And now she is comfortably... What's that winsome little phrase? Ah yes, *back in the saddle.*"

Cate said, "Is she leading this Eurydice assignment?"

"What gave you that impression? No, Miss Titansgrave and her unit are bound for Iphigenia. A crop of spritely new recruits aims to join the Citadel in the new year. In The Foundry, the Jolenes have begun stoking up their furnaces. Naturally they'll need the raw materials in order to forge the necessary magic items."

Cate was with her now. "Hence Eilandri's journey into Iphigenia. It's a stab-and-grab."

"Quite so. Assist them, Cate, and when you return I'll have a greater sense of John Isherwood's project. Next steps will doubtless materialize. You and I shall speak candidly, that I promise you. And Hughes, do try and avoid picking up bad habits where possible. Smoking. Drinking. Covering cork boards in photographs connected by red thread. Detective work has that effect on some.

"How nice of you both to drop by."

She sat behind her desk, chose a pen and a notebook, and began to scribble.

Dumbstruck, Cate and Hughes stood.

After a moment Wendy Dragontail glanced up at them, as though surprised to see them still here.

"Don't let me detain you," she said mildly.

***

After kissing Cate goodbye, Hughes headed toward the Leonidas Precinct Station.

He made a brief stop along the way. Wendy's mention of The Foundry had jumpstarted an idea, one he put to his friend Jo.

Jo heard him out, her mismatched eyes green and milky and intent.

When he was done she let him down gently.

"Sorry lovely," she said. "We've been working on that magic for ages and ages with no luck."

"It's impossible?"

"Didn't say that now, did I? I just said we've been going for yonks." She leaned on her workbench and settled into a ponderous slouch, her shelf of brow wrinkling. "Tell you what though. I got this thing I've been working on. I'd be well keen on you trying it out."

"Like a prototype?"

"Yeah, exactly."

He enjoyed the way her mouth formed that second word: sacked-lee.

"I'm game," he said. "What's this undertaking of yours?"

She told him.

You shall find out for yourself what it was soon, but not quite yet.

By ten o'clock Hughes was on the metrotram, and by a quarter to eleven he strode into the foyer of the Leonidas District Precinct, snowflakes glittering on his collar.

There was no secretary. The plastic-paneled box where one might be was empty. Hughes waited for them to appear. Instead a streetbeater who wasn't obeying his own NO SMOKING sign came and asked what Hughes wanted.

"Captain's on duty," he said after Hughes explained things. "Not sure why. Only get one day off a week, no point wasting it, that's what I say."

"Where can I find him?"

"Search me, mate."

"Who's this then?" said a new voice. There were two corridors that led deeper into the station proper and one door. Coming through that door was a jowly, grim-faced streetbeater with a mug in his hand.

"Just some bloke from up Citadel," said the smoker. "Looking for Captain Thud on account of the Jack story in *The Times*."

"Here, I know you," said the drinker. He approached, stopping close enough that the paunch of his stomach actually brushed the edge of Hughes' open coat. "You're on the telly."

"Maybe you caught me in the background of a shot," said Hughes easily. "I'm just a promo guy for the Citadel. Do you know where I can find the captain?"

The man was silent, slurping from his mug. When he lowered it, the bottom resting nicely on his belly, he was grinning.

"No, I recognize you. You've a beard now, that's what threw me. This," he told the smoker, pointing to Hughes, "is Wendy's Bloodhound."

"No shit."

"I shit you not, mate."

Hughes could smell creamy liqueur on the man's breath.

Smoke and booze, he thought. *All we need is a cork board with red thread and we're three for three. Maybe this is why Wendy discouraged me; these men are traffic wardens who scratch their balls while reading the speedometer. Here's hoping Captain Thud is made of sterner stuff.*

"You wouldn't happen to be bezzy mates with Tommy Fahrenheit, would you?" asked the mug drinker casually.

Oh no.

"I know Tommy," Hughes agreed, half-dodging the question.

"Only my wife's niece was in The Hippodrome when Tommy Fahrenheit flubbed his match." Still casual. All pals here. But the man's nose was spidered in the purplish-red veins of a seasoned alcoholic, and his eyes were narrow. "She was four-and-one-quarter. Poor thing flew like a doll when the monster got into the crowd."

"I'm sorry about that," said Hughes and pushed his Performance.

A minute later he thanked both men for their help and left.

The smoker fetched an ashtray from a counter with forms for police statements on it and stubbed out his smoke. He looked quite puzzled.

"You did a turnaround there," he told his drinker colleague. "Got very chummy."

"Did I?" The drinker shrugged. He felt oddly fuzzy, pleasantly mellow, a feeling as though he had lost some time. Even more so than usual after his third shot of the day. "Maybe I was. Nice young bloke, is all. Takes a lot to apologize for a mistake, especially if it wasn't yours in the first place. Bloody noble, when you think about it."

"Right," said the smoker doubtfully. "You feeling okay?"

"Hm? Fine. Some pelt this." He raised his mug to the snowfall visible through the foyer glass, went to drink, found the mug empty. He frowned. It had been half full only a moment ago, hadn't it? That strange feeling of having lost time niggled him again. Also he felt the apology Wendy's Bloodhound had given him like a rod of sincerity anchored in his chest, sending out vibrations that were... yes, that were fuzzy and mellow.

It occurred to him that he'd really liked his niece, and that some fantastically huge part of him had been seething after her unjust death. The apology, for whatever reason, was calming the storm. Poor girl though. Tommy Fahrenheit just let it happen to her and all those others. Poor wee thing.

"Thinking I should telephone Winky about our visitor," said the smoker. "Let him know thems up in the Citadel are peeking into our business. What do you reckon?"

He waited for the drinker to speak, but all the big man said was, "Like a doll. Just like a doll..."

***

No motorways or dual carriageways snaked out of Corinth City toward the eastern farmlands. If you wanted to get there, you'd have to take the metrotram or your chances with the sheepdogs and switchbacks, not to mention the woods of which there were many spanning from the miniature townships all the way south to the country's immediate neighbor, Champleurs, where fat grapes grew, champagne fermented, and old resentments lay shaken, bottled up to be sipped when needed.

Within living memory that country had thrust a finger into the chests of every other nation in the world and said: *You. I want to go to war with you.*

The conflict had swelled bitterly for years and had involved numerous declarations of alliance as well as too much death, eventually coming to a close at the battle of Origné.

Marberry Dennings had fought in that war, as had Cate Jubilee's father, people who were either dead or resurrected as ghosts (namely the children of one Priam King), hell, they'd all fought. Those that lived came home afterward, their hearts crinkled up and sapped of vitality like leaves come the patterns of October.

One man was Mr. Jurdels. He and his wife had both been in the war, he in the trenches and she in the communications depo. Desiring a quiet life, the pair combined funds and bought a plot of land in those previously referenced farmlands outside the bedlam of the city. There they raised their daughter to love animals and green things. Children will respond in all sorts of ways to being ushered toward something. In the Jurdels' case, their daughter rebelled. She went to Corinth City penniless, but was a fabulous girl, and by the time she was a young woman she had joined that most prosperous and awesome of organizations: the Scarlet Citadel.

Four years later she was dead.

Some folks brought her home, told the Jurdels they were sorry.

Why were her hands like that? The folks explained that their little girl had become a talented warrior, that her fingers had been infused with magic, that she could turn them into swords to defend her friends from bad trouble.

The Jurdels had not known what to say.

They buried her under a blackberry thicket.

Her name was Laurana.

That had been ten years ago, or thereabouts. Mr. and Mrs. Jurdels occupied themselves. They kept busy with the ins and outs of running a farm with lots of moving parts and were quiet but good company to one another.

That day in mid December, they had been summoned out of their routine by word of a Punch and Judy show rolling into town. Laurana had always been fond of puppets, and though Mrs. Jurdels had her misgivings, the pair decided it might further tighten old wounds rather than open them up again.

They expected to be mildly entertained and were ready for sorrow should it come.

What they did not expect was for things to turn odd.

But they did.

Things began normally. It was a healthy crowd for a winter performance. Like the Jurdels, the whole community had set out to see the show. Cunningly manipulated by their invisible puppeteer, Mr. Punch got up to all sorts under the glowering contempt of his wife, Judy. There was a baby, a hangman, a courtier, a clown, even a crocodile whose belly of emerald sequins caught what little light there was that morning. The crowd was pleased to note that the puppets were not the usual hideous batch but prettily painted and suspended on strings no less! No cheap glove puppets here, folks! Mr. Punch's nincompoopish voice caused ripples of giddiness among the assembled children.

Next to her husband, Mrs. Jurdels felt a tug at the stitching over the cut Laurana's death had left in her. She couldn't help it. Their daughter had been one of nature's gigglers.

The oddness happened right as Mr. Punch was about to take up his famous bat.

Above cruel Punch and cowering Judy, the strings snapped. Just like that. It was as though some secret scissors clipped them. The strings fell uselessly. Yet the puppets stayed aloft. The whole puppet cast rose into view together, including the crocodile.

With widening eyes, adults and children alike watched as the box in which the show took place fell apart. It was effortless. All four walls simply... toppled to the ground.

There before them stood the puppeteer, surrounded by his stringless creations.

The crowd watched him.

He looked as baffled as they felt.

Then, without warning, the puppets fell on him. They tickled him. They spanked his bottom lightly and without malice. They danced him around, a crocodile tango, a clownish foxtrot, a marriage waltz.

No one knew where the laughter began.

Except Mrs. Jurdels. And she only knew because it started right next to her.

It began with Mr. Jurdels, who had once taken up a shovel as he had taken up arms for his country and buried his only child.

He took one look at Judy patting the puppeteer's tushie like an old woman might pat her favorite moggy and burst out laughing. He brayed as the dancing struck up. He fairly *howled* when Mr. Punch put his bat between his teeth like a rose and pirouetted.

By then everyone was in on it. Even the puppeteer had gotten over his scare and was leaning into this peculiar development. Soon the fresh snow crunched underfoot as people danced and stamped a rhythm and hopped with the sheer joy of this very unexpected show.

Mr. Jurdels laughed and laughed. Tears rolled down his cheeks. He had not seen anything so hilarious in an age.

From the benevolent hysteria of the crowd, two figures detached themselves.

"I'm hungry," said one. "You hungry?"

"I am always hungry," replied the other.

"And here's me always forgetting. Burgers?"

"Yeah, all right. How raw?"

"Long as it doesn't moo when you pick it up, I think you're okay."

"Blue and bloody, please."

"Shit, how else?"

They went to find burgers, wild laughter lapping at their heels.

Chapter Six

While Mr. Jurdels laughed himself silly in the countryside, Gormon Hughes was turning the corner of Bromley where the sign for The King's Flagon tavern showed a beer crowned in froth. Snow transformed it into a woodcut with a white frame.

It did that for everything, and more. Without a gust to swirl it into a crazy gnashing cold-toothed creature, the unhurried clouds and the heavy flakes turned the world into a cake with thick icing to be cut by lovers. A line of poetry shook itself from the rafters of his mind.

Snow is the wedding of the world.

He waited with a hundred other people for a pedestrian light to turn green. One of them had a lead round a dog that looked eerily similar to one Hughes had met a long time ago under the Polydoros Overpass. A truck stuffed with bags of flour and baking soda clogged the cross section. Horns honked. Hughes and the crowd filtered by, some hands vanished into pockets, some throats scarfed, most taking the time to look up at the woman balanced precariously on a ladder and stringing Tinfrost lights over an off-license.

Here a row of parked cars on Diogenes Street lay enshrined in snow, their wheels glazed, their wipers laden down like swords embedded in ice awaiting the right knight to pull them free. The romance of that thought warmed him a little. No matter how many years passed, he still had a banner to carry for stories about gallant goofballs riding geriatric steeds into trouble that was both daunting and melodramatic. His favorite play was still *A Summer Knight's Stroll*.

He walked on through the pale.

Diogenes Street was unusually long for the District. Its red sodium lamps lay dark and would remain so until six that evening. By night the houses and shop fronts would be rosy. Ten minutes rolled by. *Very long*, Hughes thought again, glancing ahead only to see that the street had no intention of stopping. Most roads in Leonidas were stubby things, compressed like accordions and just as noisy. Diogenes was no exception there. Cold, bored cats mewled for lazy owners who snicked open doors and muttered them inside tenement apartments and shabby houses where arguments blended into harmless bickering, all underscored by the radio cycling through the suite of classic Tinfrost hits. Kids cackled as they sculpted snowmen with obscene alien genitalia, starfish cocks and squidlike vulvas. A strange woman with no teeth and a bell that tinkled silvery notes touched Hughes gently on the arm and told him to watch the roofs in case he saw an angel.

He thanked her, watched her shuffle toward a bus stop where no buses would come until January, and walked on.

Mercifully Diogenes finally ended in a messy tangle of lanes, most of which converged in the nearby Leonidas bazaar (like the sodium lamps, the bazaar would only gear up and go after sunset). One of these lanes took Hughes up the rise of a natural incline paved over a long time ago by site jockeys in hardhats, their nostrils singed with the smoke baking off the hot tarmac. At the summit he could see Taggart House.

Taggart House Penitentiary For The Criminally Insane was built as a corollary to the common wisdom that you cannot jail all convicted people, or people awaiting trial for that matter, together. This is because a small but definite minority will torture the larger majority, either with endless gibbering or the repossession of fingernails from those that are still using them. Also neurodivergence can affect vulnerability in plenty of criminals. Their exploitation would hang over the justice system like a bad smell. Hence the purchase of a rotting manor house occupying three acres in the boonies of Leonidas, its gutting, and its subsequent refurbishment.

Kindness abounds, but so does cruelty.

After opening without ceremony, locals had taken one leery look at the place and dubbed it the Toadhouse.

Hopping mad.

As Miss Gleam had once told Hughes, *If I wore a corset, my very sides would now be splitting.*

A fence enclosed the place. The paint job was terrible, globby and uninvitingly green. Each pole was tipped with an arrowhead-shaped spike. On the other side of the fence Hughes saw a sparsely populated carpark, and beyond that the asylum with its slanted roof and its barred and blacked-out windows.

He buzzed in at the gate. The nurse womanning the front desk sounded positively jolly.

"Come on in!" she bugled.

On his approach, he noted that some remarkable wit had graffitied one of the threshold pillars with lily pads.

It turned out the nurse was in such flying form because December 17th was her first day.

"Congratulations," said Hughes.

"Thanks. They're understaffed here and I need the money." Apple-cheeked, bubbly, and with a severely untucked shirt, she couldn't have been much older than twenty. Her peppy voice bounced around the admissions room as though seeking escape. "My friend Urujayne's a psychologist up on the third floor. You know psychology?"

"Not intimately," said Hughes.

"It's important in these walls. Everyone's got a big old dose of psychology. Anyway Urujayne got it all organized so here I am. You're from the Citadel, you said?"

"Yes, looking for Captain Hoshrum Thud."

"I haven't a betty-blue who that could be. I just got on duty thirty seconds before you buzzed. Ah hell." The untucked shirt had been spotted. She futzed with it, rolling her eyes with no small amount of charm. "Captain Thud, hm? Funny kind of name. Maybe he's around. I'll check. Get you a cup of coffee?"

"No, thank you." Hughes had managed to hold out against the coffee blight that laid waste to so many. Tea had its hooks in him, of course, but if there was a cup going he was sure Nurse Perky would already have the kettle on for him.

Instead she smiled. "Suit yourself. Take a seat, I'll be right back."

Hughes scanned about, wondering if he'd misheard her. He hadn't noticed a...

Oh. There it was.

The seat was nestled in a walled-off alcove that was only visible from where he stood by the front desk. There were, in actuality, two seats set tightly together.

One of them was occupied by a squat man with a receding hairline and the most spectacular mustache Hughes had ever seen. The man had a copy of the newspaper and was quite immersed in today's crossword.

Too awkward to stand and too polite to move the chairs apart a few inches, Hughes sat down. They were as cheek to cheek as a young couple at a cinema. The man didn't seem to mind, so Hughes tried not to either.

He was just beginning to think about the Spring-Heeled Jack article when a gruff voice beside him said, "Four letters; wears motley and bells."

Hughes glanced at the man, who had his pen poised over the empty white blocks of the crossword.

"King?"

"Good one." No smile to verify if the man meant this or not. "Think you've got the right setting though. A king's court. You're here for the copper?"

"You know him?"

"You've met one copper, you've met them all."

"Sure. How about 'jester'?"

"That's six letters."

"Right."

"Fat lot of good they do us."

Hughes blinked. "Erm. Jesters?"

"Coppers."

"Oh." His mouth quirked. "They can be a bit thick, I suppose."

"I want to write 'harlequin,'" said the man. "Only it doesn't fit. Coppers are always trying to make things fit. That's what I don't like. Nothing's ever neat."

"Have you had bad experiences?" said Hughes, warming to the conversation.

"With the streetbeaters?" The man snorted. "Plenty."

"Me too."

"Go on then."

Hughes considered. "I remember one who tried to give me a hidden camera so I could take photos of a friend of mine."

"What? Lewd ones?"

"Yes. I ended up with his umbrella. This was during that bad storm years ago."

"I dare say you rained on his parade," said the man dryly. "And a very nasty parade it was by the sound of things." He paused. "Got it." The pen scratched four letters; a perfect fit.

"Well done," said Hughes, eyeing reception and wondering if Nurse Perky would be back anytime soon. "To be honest, the streetbeaters have always been fairly rubbish. At least in Leonidas where no one can bribe them into decency."

"I heartily agree," said the man.

"Did you know the nickname 'copper' derives from the days before credits subsumed the market? The police used to jingle their change in their pockets as they patrolled. They were famous for it," Hughes said idly. "Of course, everyone else's pockets were conspicuously empty."

"Is that so?" said the man.

"Uh huh. Cut to the present day and nothing's really changed. Most coppers are still on the take. There's a few good apples, but the barrel's more or less spoiled, if you see what I mean."

"I believe so," said the man.

Hughes paused. An idea occurred to him. It was a horrible idea, one that couldn't possibly be true, because that would make mere horribleness look like a picnic. Slowly, very slowly, his bowels soured. They grew greasier and greasier. He looked at the man, praying he was wrong.

"You wouldn't be Captain Thud, would you?"

"Yup," said Captain Thud.

He showed Hughes the crossword answer.

Four letters; wears motley and bells.

Fool.

***

During one of their fun, useless, cozy conversations, Hughes had explained how height worked. The concept had never been a complicated one for Cate Jubilee. People were tall or... vertically hopeful.

No, her lover had said bemusedly. He was talking about dynamic theatrical height.

Ahhh, well, he ought to have said so.

She'd listened as he spoke about the way vid directors blocked out a scene using height to establish power between characters. Characters standing or in a lofty position were dominant. Sitters and lowlier characters were submissive.

Cate pointed out that sometimes stillness and motion could be used for that purpose. Say a character is pacing. That conveys unease, possibly even weakness. Another character sits nearby, perfectly motionless. That convinced you the sitter was strong, in control. In that situation, Hughes' idea sprung leaks.

He conceded she was right.

Then they had sex.

It was fantastic, really.

Anyway, all this (the height and motion stuff, not the sex) went a long way toward explaining why Eilandri Titansgrave commanded the space around her. Her magic item—a hammer that was as long as Cate was tall with a huge crushing head as large as a lampshade—performed the same transformative trick that Knickerbocker's gray sock had played on him. It had reached down into Eilandri, into the hot spitting plasma of her genetic code, and it had changed her.

A stately woman already, the hammer had stretched and widened her. With a straight spine she stood an inch shy of twelve feet tall. You could have held a banquet on the immaculate plane of her back and invited friends and family, first and second cousins included. Her biceps alone measured thirty inches at rest. Thick veins made a lattice across her forearms. She was utterly hairless. Strikingly, her skin was white as bleached bone. She might have presented a ghoulish skull-like figure had her features not filled her out.

Cate thought she got away with it.

In fact Eilandri Titansgrave had a certain otherworldly gravity to her, not pretty exactly, but captivating.

Maybe it was the eyes that sealed this quality. They were a deep lavender purple and gave you the impression they had glimpsed many things. Whether those things were dreamy or nightmarish was not immediately clear.

In the warehouse where the portal to Iphigenia caressed its own obsidian edges with slender fingers of fire, where technicians shouted over one another, knocked against potted plants and set them wobbling, and dashed helter-skelter to meet the drop's deadline, where engineers milled, lab-coated pencil pushers totted up the numbers, and a unit of no less than seven Scarlet Citadel members practically glowed with prowess and grandeur as they readied themselves, the Pale Giant sat without motion as though carved.

She took up more space than she should have (and that was plenty to begin with).

In summation, she was the only act Cate found herself able to focus on.

A member of the unit spotted her and grinned.

"Cate! You're joining us?"

It was Lorna Blacktower, whose magic item, a dark opal brooch, turned her body into a fortified tower (sort of. Lorna remained exactly the same in almost every way, except her skin became dark hornblende rock, tiny arrows fired from her pores, and sometimes she could decant burning hot oil from her ears).

"Hello, Lorna. Yes, I am. Hello all!"

A chorus of greetings, most of them enthusiastic. Cate was quite popular. She detected no furtive looks of sympathy or puzzlement. That was good, but some wise part of her cautioned they would turn up sooner rather than later. By now everyone in the Citadel knew about the baby. People hoarded gossip as eagerly as they hoarded bread in a storm. The rumor mill kept on turning. Believing otherwise wouldn't be merely naive, it'd be stupid too. "Eilandri Titansgrave," she said. "Her Ladyship has requested that I add my hobnail boots to your venture. The rest of me comes attached in the bargain. Pleasure to be working with you."

Mystifyingly there was no verbal response. Instead Eilandri reached into the satchel slung across her scarlet-red armor. She wrote something on a little yellow card and handed it to Cate.

"*Hello Cate Jubilee*," read the card. "*It's nice to meet you. I do not mean to dampen the merriment of our first interaction, but it is important that I disclose the fact that I have no voice box. Recently I was diagnosed with laryngeal cancer. They caught it early (yippee!), but in order to get the best result it was necessary to have my larynx surgically removed. I am quite well now. Please do not tell me that you are sorry. We will just take the boots, if that's all right with you.*"

Cate looked up.

Eilandri Titansgrave was not grinning. That last line was absolutely a good-natured goof and a rather delightful one at that. There could be no doubt that Eilandri had added it to garner some response, just as she'd taken the time to add Cate's name to the little yellow card. *Perhaps I'm reading into it.* No. No way. For goodness' sake, the word "yippee" had been deployed.

But there was not even a glint of amusement in the huge albino's face, and that meant Cate ought to keep a straight expression too.

"Who is your second-in-command?" she asked.

Eilandri took out a pen and a fresh yellow card, wrote, and showed it to Cate.

"*I am open to suggestions.*"

Cate put it to the unit. This was how command structures were handled in the Citadel. Wendy Dragontail was at the top. Everyone below her simply sorted themselves out. Generally proceedings were amicable, and blessedly that was the case today.

Cate was not entirely surprised when the group unanimously chose her.

Meanwhile Eilandri had been writing.

"*You will give orders,*" the card informed Cate. "*If I disagree, I will let you know.*"

"Sounds like a plan."

"Five minutes, folks!" a technician hollered in their direction.

The portal yawned invitingly. Another world awaited.

Cate Jubilee tied up her hair, which was just as bright as the liquid flame dancing in that jaw of dark stone, and as the prospect of a good old fashioned fight drew nearer she could almost have persuaded herself she was happy.

Maybe you could be, a coaxing voice inside her whispered. *Scuff those knuckles, pet. Get the good blood flowing. What do you say?*

"Whose turn?"

Cate jumped.

Lorna Blacktower was smiling curiously at her.

"Sorry?"

"You said, 'It's their turn.'"

"Did I?"

"Mm-hm," affirmed Lorna. "Who'd you mean? Their turn for what?"

Cate did her best to look clueless. "I'm not sure. Tell the truth, I didn't even know I was talking."

"Happens all the time," said Lorna cheerfully. "Sometimes I'm in the kitchen chattering away to myself. Only realize it when my dogs start whining. *Bow-wow, our mistress is crrrrrrazy. We'd leave, only she's got those sweet bags of doggie chow held hostage.* I think we've got the signal," she added, looking over Cate's shoulder at the bulwark of panels where the technicians were finalizing the drop. "Shall we go?"

"Ready Eilandri?" said Cate.

The Pale Giant lifted that diabolically large hammer of hers and slung it over one shoulder, a fireman's lift for seventy-one inches of arcane steel. The thing must have weighed as much as a sofa. She nodded, lavender eyes glued to the portal as if it were an old friend.

Whose turn? Lorna had asked her.

As their unit headed for the portal, Cate thought grimly, *Monsters, that's who. Ghoulies and creepies and long-leggedy beasties. I don't relish hurting things that have the brainpower to know when they're hurt. I think you've got to be ill to enjoy that part of combat. It's the adrenaline like boiling tar pitched and steaming through the capillaries that I like. Sometimes the fact that we're invading their home stings. Only I suspect lots of things on that side of the portal would happily come over here and kill me if they could, so that's all right then. Besides, lately my blood has flowed enough.*

Now it's their turn.

That's *what I say.*

The coaxing bit of her quailed. It had expected to nudge her toward the simple enjoyment of battle, not into this avalanche of cold and misting anger.

A rather bigger bit of her was mightily pleased. And eager.

This is because while grief is complex, rage is as simple as a dollop of butter on toast.

That's why you could digest it.

That's why you can spread it around.

Distantly, some engineer's radio was tuned to the Tinfrost megahits.

As Cate Jubilee stepped in a world full of strange creatures, some docile, some dangerous, and all with a great deal of warm blood pumping through them, that radio sent out a few trills of melody and then a lyric that was oddly prophetic.

The singer cautioned whomsoever might be listening:

"You better watch out..."

***

Hughes stared at those four letters as a condemned man might stare at the gallows.

Fool.

"You found him!"

Nurse Perky was back. She skipped over, her mouth beaming. "Thank goodness. I been asking all around. 'Where's this Captain Wham guy? Where could Captain Wham be?' Until somebody said, 'You mean Captain Thud?' and I said, 'That's him! Where's he at? I've got a guy from the Citadel who wants to speak to him.' And they said you were down in reception, Captain, and I thought, 'Oh my God, I'm such a goober. I've gone romping around this whole place when the man I've been looking for was right round the corner!'"

"That's all right," said Captain Thud, folding away his newspaper. "It gave this civic-minded young man and I a few minutes to get to know one another."

Hughes began to wonder if it was possible to actually die of acute embarrassment.

I told him coppers could be thick, he thought bleakly. *That they've always been rubbish. That they need to be bribed into decency!*

Again those four letters hemmed in by crossword boxes flashed across his mind.

Fool.

"Really, this is classic me." Nurse Perky giggled. "Momma used to say I was so dumb they could stick a handle in my ear, and Daddy would have a brand new hammer for his toolbox."

"I expect you've got something to tell me," said Thud.

"Huh? Oh yeah! That guest you were hoping to speak to woke up just a little bit ago. Isn't it kooky that we call them 'guests' as opposed to 'patients' like in a hospital?"

"Kooky is the word," agreed the captain. He was up now, tottling toward one of the corridors that curved and climbed deeper into the asylum. "Thank you very much, Nurse. Come along, lad," he called.

Feeling wretched, Hughes came along.

The walls of the corridor were made of screens. They played a looping vid of fish swimming through serene blue waters. Shoals of sturgeons, dottybacks, tangs and turbots, long-whiskered catfish and stubby-headed sharks finned and tailed their way over parti-colored coral beds and through the carcasses of ships, which were knobbed with white barnacles and glued with indigo starfish. Ceiling-mounted projectors ticked quietly overhead.

All this in an asylum hall that reeked of strawberry Jell-O and bleach.

Hughes might have puzzled over this frankly weird choice of interior decoration, but right now he had larger aquatic residents to fry.

Unless Thud fried him first, naturally.

"Look, Captain," Hughes stammered. "I know what you must think—"

"What do you know about Spring-Heeled Jack?" said Thud, very calmly, as though his voice might disturb the fish.

"He's an invention of the press. Or people who spoke to the press, I suppose."

"Tell me about him."

Hughes looked at Thud's profile. He seemed serious enough.

Not only that. He's got me on scales, Hughes realized. *Weighing me up. He knows Wendy Dragontail sent me, and now he wants to know if I'm a reluctant lackey, a starry-eyed idiot who's read too many toothless detective novels, or somebody who gives a damn about the actual case.*

I've got to convince him of my interest, or he'll dismiss me as a misery tourist. I'll have to work on my own without his expertise.

That couldn't happen.

After a moment Hughes said, "First and foremost Jack is a killer. He has no preference for tools or targets. He picks someone, or multiple someones, murders them in cold blood, finds the nearest rooftop, and goes for a jaunt. This last habit is what earned him the nickname 'Spring-Heeled.' Jack is strong, acrobatic, and utterly insane. He's also, as I said, an invention. Fictional." They crested a stair to the second floor. "Made up."

"Why fabricate such a man?" asked Thud.

In the buildup to the meeting with Wendy Dragontail that morning, Hughes had given this very question some thought. "Because it's better than the alternative."

They had passed lots of occupied rooms. Now they passed one with an open door. Inside was a bed dangling restraints like severed pig tails. A janitor mopped the floor.

"Go on," Thud said.

It was difficult to explain. Hughes tried nonetheless. "It's got something to do with the way people think. Imagine it. There's these horrible murders happening, right? The facts surrounding the case creep out into the public domain. They're disturbing facts, starting with this one: none of the culprits have anything much in common. Few have prior convictions, and none have any history of violence. That would be troubling, but it gets worse because while the blood is still slick and the bodies are still warm, the murderers go bounding over roofs. There's also no evidence to suggest they're copycat killings because according to the newspapers and the rumor mill, all of the culprits have gone mad. Which is the most terrible fact of all because in the hours leading up to the crime they were acting perfectly normally.

"Add that all together, and it's a touch too real, too close-to-home for the people of this city to cope with. So they cook Jack up. It's not lots of madfolk behind the killings but rather one extremely dangerous mad*man*. A freak with monstrous appetites and ankles built for lunging."

"Cooked up an entire person, did they?" said Thud, feigning astonishment. "Just like that?"

Hughes shrugged, playing along. "Happens all the time. Always has. Take the pagan beliefs that existed before the old church swept them away. People drew up huge lists of Gods to explain things. A God that makes the sun come up every morning. A God for wealth, giving it and taking it away. A God for the itch between your shoulder blades that you can't reach, so you're going to have to get a wooden spoon. When an idea is too wide to fit in the head, people squash it down into a shape that *will* fit. Usually it's a word," he said, "like how precipitation cycles become simple rain. But sometimes the idea becomes a person. Like Father Tinfrost."

"Or Jack," said Thud.

Hughes nodded. "Basic anthropomorphism, really. Anyway, the first murder associated with Spring-Heeled Jack happened before the war with Champleurs, about thirty years ago."

"Thirty-four," said Thud.

"It occurred during the holiday season. All of the murders followed suit. For two consecutive years, at Tinfrosttime, Jack cast his black shadow from the rooftops into the streets of Corinth. Entire businesses closed down; no one was going out to buy presents or binge drink at the pub, especially after sunset, when the moon and Jack were up to their pale work. There was a rise in spiritualism and the occult. The scare even ignited a short-lived but fiery resurrection of the old church. Then, as quickly as they'd begun, the murders stopped," Hughes concluded. "Now it seems they've struck up again. That was long-winded. Sorry. I'm new to the whole criminal deduction thing."

"Well you're better at it than you are at recognizing coppers," said Thud. "That much I'll grant you."

A harried-looking nurse was coming their way.

"You," she sneered when she saw the captain. "You here to tongue-wag at the loonies again?"

"I intend to interrogate the chief suspect in a murder investigation, yes," said Thud.

The nurse took this poorly. She fairly glowered at the captain.

"I wish you wouldn't grill them so. These are not gym rags for you to wring out, buddy. They are goo-gah crazy people. You give them the squeeze, they get jittery, and then it's up to us to get them under control again."

"I'm very sorry about that."

"Gee thanks," she said, storming by. "That's wonderful consolation."

She muttered round the corner toward the first floor stairs.

Thud seemed unbothered. Hughes thought about what Nurse Perky had said to the captain. *That guest you were hoping to speak to woke up just a little bit ago.*

Cables connected in his mind.

"You're going to speak to the one who killed those people in the canning factory the day before last," he said and looked at Thud. "Nigel Ulmerston."

The captain gave a curt nod.

The names of Ulmerston's victims came to Hughes from the article in *The Times.*

Jodi Whitlaw (48), Penny Moore (32), Harris Stokely (46) and Marge Tinetts (22).

According to that same article, Ulmerston was fifty-five.

"Even if he caught them by surprise, the victims were adults. How does a man approaching retirement age kill four people?"

"Economically," said Thud.

"I meant—"

"I know what you meant. Pay attention now because there'll be a quiz later if I feel like it. Questions from your throat are well and good, but it's the ones your other senses ask and answer that represent real policing. Your eyes. Your ears. Even your nose gets in on the action. *Observation*, my lad. That's rule number one of being a copper. That, and you can't underestimate the presence of a biscuit tin," Thud added with a gruff awe for nibbles in general and custard creams in specific. "As it happens I also wondered how the geezer managed four people in one go. I expect we'll find out once we meet Mr. Ulmerston."

The second floor of Taggart House was a very different ecosystem to the first. The fish were still there, exploring the walls like the glass fringes of an aquarium, but joining them was a nurses' station, a staff cafeteria, bustling people with clipboards, orderlies adjusting the contents of metal carts that walked by themselves, bandy tungsten legs twitching, set with trays of synthetic fruit, mealy custard, tasteless meatloaf and cheese sandwiches, tomato soup, wooden spoons, paper cups stuffed with pills, and the whole place honeycombed with rooms where the neurodivergent pottered about or read or slept the drooling sleep of the benumbed, and with sporadic offices sporting plaques telling you who worked within and what degree they'd wrangled from the university.

"There's one glaring inconsistency in your summary," Thud told Hughes. "You said the culprits don't have anything much in common."

"Right," said Hughes. "Of course. The timing and demographics align. The killings take place in-or-around the holiday season, there's the obvious pattern of execution, and there's the location. They exclusively happen in Leonidas District."

"You might think so, given how Tracer Gogen covers it in *The Times*," said Thud, his tone scathing. "In reality, the killings are widespread. The whole city has its fair share of rooftoppers, as I call them. Though it is true that Leonidas hosts the greatest majority of cases."

For the first time since they'd left reception, Thud looked at him.

"So what's going on here? Why are these people killing their coworkers? Their families? Total strangers? What is it about this time of year that sets them off? Why did the incidents stop during the war? Why'd they stay stopped? And why after so long an intervening period is it all starting up again?"

"I don't know," said Hughes honestly. "When you lay it out in plain terms it sounds like some sort of shared mania. Maybe a communal delirium, like the dancing plague in Champleurs or the spate of extraterrestrial sightings following that radio play scandal in my grandfather's time. Or perhaps there's magic involved. I bet you think it's exactly that, given how your eyes just lit up at the suggestion. I know you contacted the Citadel, Captain, so yes. Yes, you *must* believe that magic is at the root of these murders."

They stopped outside a room. Someone had written the name of the occupant on a whiteboard in blue marker: Nigel Ulmerston. Through the door's frosted glass, Hughes could see the bedbound shape of the man who had, less than forty-eight hours ago, slaughtered four of his coworkers before scrawling a cryptic message with their still-hot insides and finding the nearest fire escape, one that led down to the street, or up to the roof.

Thud regarded Hughes silently.

Somewhere, a telephone rang. Its forlorn burring went unanswered.

As though he were drawing a sword to match the one on Hughes' hip, Thud took a newspaper clipping from his coat pocket and gave it to his dark-haired, dark-eyed companion. Despite being laminated for preservation, age had yellowed the clipping. Its texture was delicate. Crumbly. The headline was dated thirty-four years ago.

It read: *Chimneystack Demon Strikes Again.*

There was an article. Hughes didn't read it. Not yet. His eyes were fixed on the clipping's photograph. It showed a grubby living room. Upholstery burst from the sofa cushions like wads of wet popcorn. At the edge of the image he could just about make out the blurry edges of a potted fern. No, not a fern. A small Tinfrost tree. On the wall overlooking the sofa, written in sawn-off lips, chopped earlobes, and scraps of fingernail, was this:

THEY ARE IN ME

"Holy shit," he said.

"What's your name?"

"Hughes."

"Wendy's Bloodhound. I might have known. Well look here, snifferdog, I'm not messing about with this. I'm the only streetbeater who grasps there's something binding these horror shows together, like an evil length of tinsel wrapped around one huge rotten trunk. You've got a personal stake in seeing justice done. I see that clear as day. You've got one of these legendary motivations. You want to solve the whole nasty business, to unwind the tangly mysteries and get at the rot they're concealing and purify it or burn it. I can tell, yes, I can. Now, I don't know why you're here, and I don't really give a damn. But what I *do* care about—and 'care' is too soft a word for it—is this city. It's mine and I'm its, okay? And someone," he said, jabbing a finger at the old newspaper clipping. "Some*thing* is hurting my city so deeply that when I'm walking the beat, I can hear its screams come up through my boots. That sound is the whole ruddy land crying out for help. If I'm going to heed its call, I need somebody like you. I need an agent of the Citadel. Because this thing that the dark street whispers have named Jack has been sleeping for three decades, and now it's awake again, and I suspect it's hungry. Thirsty too, for suffering. It'll slake itself and sate its belly until it's caught. Until we catch it and string it up by its shoelaces. Conventional coppering won't work. It didn't before; why should it now? I've got to get creative. I've got to go *off the book.*"

He stepped forward so they were almost nose-to-nose.

"So the root, Hughes? No," hissed Captain Hoshrum Thud. "Not the root. That is entirely understating it. I believe that when it comes to this case, magic is the whole bloody tree."

Act Three

Something Rotten

Chapter Seven

Facing her office window with the cold and brumal afternoon light accentuating the lines of her face, the Last Dragon stood with her arms clasped behind her like folded wings.

The wan glow spilled over her shoulder, brightening the carpeted floor and coming to gleaming rest on the shoes of Doctor John Isherwood. In the ten years since the Hairy Autumn, he had gained fifty pounds and lost a hundred and twenty more. His jowls had slimmed into full, healthy cheeks. His muttonchops remained, a little bushier, a little grayer. Though he was no longer a heavy man, John still moved like one. It was as if that catastrophe ten years ago with so much of the city becoming animals had evoked a congruent change in him. He stood in the middle of Wendy's office with the daylight not quite reaching him and the firelight soaking like liquid oil in his smart midnight-blue waistcoat, his spectacles perched on his nose, his shoulders almost imperceptibly stooped, and he looked like something his uncle Richard Isherwood would have shot down and scooped out and packed with sawdust.

There they were, a dragon and a bird.

No songs issued from the record player. Montcrieff had gone on some private errand. Down in the lower levels of the tower, Falstaff was overseeing that most complicated of afternoonly processes known as lunch. The dragon and bird were alone except for a silence as dense as treacle, only bitter instead of sweet.

"You're quite sure?" she said. "I don't mean to belittle your findings, John."

"No. I understand. When the scope of it hit me I fairly disintegrated. I got sick. Couldn't sleep for a week."

"I remember Falstaff saying something. I thought you had the flu."

"Virulent case of professional shock, more like." John smiled without humor, took off his glasses, and massaged one sore eyelid with the ball of his thumb. "The documents you and I have just gone through were presented to a panel of geologists, microbiologists, physicists, and a smattering of cultural savants. Anthropologists, philosophers, you know. They were sworn to secrecy and are currently under thorough surveillance. After the presentation each member of the panel was given copies of the documents and allowed to conduct their own series of experiments. Every resource they requested was given to them. No expense was spared." He replaced his spectacles and pushed them up the bridge of his nose. "During that time I worked with a team of neurologists to decipher just what those patterns were. There's no ambiguity, Wendy."

"Brainwaves," she said. "What does that mean?"

"How long do you have? The implications are staggering."

"And this panel of yours reconvened?"

"Yes. Total consensus."

"Even the philosophers?"

Now his smile was earnest, though not quite warm. "Almost total consensus, then. When you asked me if I was sure, you weren't belittling my findings. You see they can't be insulted, derogated, or undermined." Once more his lips were thin pink lines. "I've never been so sorry to contradict you."

"This is harrowing, John."

"Yes."

"I do not use that word lightly."

"No," he agreed. "Harrowing is right."

He opened his mouth, as if he might add that it was electrifying, goddamn terrifying, and... bewitching. Seductive in the simple way a bauble attracts magpies and in the complex way that ornithologists fawn over bills and beaks and wingspans and the rarer pigmentations of feathers. It lit up his head and shone out of the bores in his skull, a jack-o-lantern of sizzling newfangled thoughtbeams. It was a Discovery. *His* Discovery.

John Isherwood closed his mouth, and kept all this and more to himself.

Now was not the time.

"Brainwaves." Wendy Dragontail breathed the word like a furnace breathing smoke. "Impulses in the dark."

A pause. A subtle change in the room's atmosphere.

Then Wendy said, "What teams are out beyond the portals?"

"None in Eurydice. There's a unit in Iphigenia. Eilandri Titansgrave."

"And Cate Jubilee, yes I recall." Wendy pitched a sigh. "John, set up a drop, there's a good man."

"A drop?" He frowned, a proud owl with ruffled plumage. "For who?"

"Me," said Wendy, turning to face him. "Quick as you can. I do not wish to explain to Hughes that I sent his lady love to her death."

***

Maybe there was something to Thud's advice about the powers of human observation asking and answering its own questions.

Hughes took one look at Nigel Ulmerston and understood.

Under a face that was as vacant as a lot without cars, Ulmerston sported a bullish neck, broad shoulders, and a body that creaked the heavy-duty bed every time he moved during the interrogation that would follow. The man must have been an athlete of some sort who exchanged the weights for the expanding waistband sometime in his thirties. At fifty-five, Nigel Ulmerston was easily three-hundred pounds, fat slopped over embedded muscle. Encircling his wrists the restraints seemed inconsequential, almost toylike.

Hughes' senses asked: How did this man kill four people?

And they answered: loudly, with grunts hitching up the great pillar of him; aromatically, with a week's worth of sweat-stink coming pungent and sour from under the arms, the gut swells, the back flaps, the groin; and, yes, economically. From the moment the kill switch flipped behind those now empty eyes to the moment Jodi, Penny, Harris, and Marge lay crumpled in death poses, the whole thing had probably taken less than sixty seconds.

Observation. Go figure.

Hughes still wasn't sure what Thud had meant about the biscuit tins though.

"Nigel Ulmerston?" said Thud. "I'm a policeman. Can you hear me?"

No response.

"Mr. Ulmerston?"

Nothing.

Hughes read only the tiniest hint of disappointment in Thud's expression. He hadn't expected his suspect to talk to him. Now the captain gestured from Hughes to the insensate Ulmerston. "Watch this."

Hughes watched in growing bemusement as Thud sat down on the floor beside the bed. From where Hughes stood, the top of the captain's head was visible for a moment then that too was gone.

A noise emerged from the place where the hidden policeman sat, one so ridiculous Hughes wasn't initially sure what he was hearing.

"Bzzz. Bzz bzzzzzz."

Hughes drew a breath to say, "Excuse me. Can I ask why you are down there doing your best impression of an electric razor with one dead battery?"

He got as far as, "Exc—" when Nigel Ulmerston whimpered.

Hughes gave a start.

He stared at Ulmerston, whose eyes had unglazed and were now scanning the room frantically. His mouth must have been half full of spit because each breath passing his cracked lips was accompanied by a kind of labored slurping sound. The whimpers were consistent and horrifying; a kid's hopeless respiration when Mum and Dad are out of earshot and something hungry has just gone *bump* under the bed. At the same time the man was *cringing*. Doughy flesh amassed as his chin slid into his neck. At his sides both meaty hands were clammy, flushed with blood, and clamped tight on the mattress. They looked like a fixture from Taggart House's ambient wall aquarium, like starfish, only unnatural and seized on a muscular level with fright.

"Bzzz," went Thud. "Bzz bzz..."

The noise died away.

The effect was instantaneous. Ulmerston seemed to fill with liquid relief. His throat closed on another bout of whimpering. His fingers relaxed. He looked directly into Hughes' eyes, smiled a wide, beatific smile as if the two of them had been the subjects of a danger that had now passed, and lapsed into the same waking sleep they had found him in.

Much like the murder in the Gallfer Canning Factory, the entire event played itself out faster than the mind could be expected to digest.

On the other side of the bed, Thud rose.

"I thought so," he said. "Exactly the same as the others."

"What others?" Hoarse and rattled, Hughes hardly recognized his own voice.

If Thud noticed, he gave no sign.

"You read the Tracer Gogen article in *The Times*? Remember how he drew a parallel between the Ulmerston killings and the ones perpetrated by Susabeth Dennings? That's because she was one of the first instances of the Spring-Heeled Jack revival, and it remains the nastiest."

Hughes remembered. Sue Dennings had killed her husband Marberry and her two children. What had their names been? His excellent memory offered them with no small reluctance. Adam and Ellen. By the time she was done with them, their mother's arms had been sleeved in their blood.

"Well, I interviewed Mrs. Dennings," continued Thud. "Wasn't getting anywhere. She was about as lucid as a chicken sandwich. The room was stuffy. In my frustration I opened the window a crack. A fly got in. As soon as the sound of its wings reached her ears, Dennings reacted much the same as Ulmerston here. Sudden alertness. Clenching of the muscles. Vocalization of extreme distress. Dennings actually let out a single high-pitched shriek before I swatted the buzzing bugger with my newspaper."

"Are they all like that?" Hughes said, easing back into things now normality had resumed. At a nod from Thud, he mused on the idea. Giving up, he said, "What does that tell us?"

"Nothing much, nothing much," Thud conceded. "But it's a corroboration of what we strongly suspect. These people have been touched by the same... What's the word I'm looking for..."

"Vileness?"

"Yeah," said the captain. "Probably more apt to say, 'bitten by the same bug,' but yeah. Touched by vileness. Speaking of, you look a bit touched yourself. Sorry. I should have given you a proper warning."

"It's okay," said Hughes. "A few years ago my partner and I fought a huge, bloated monster that gurgled and cooed like a toddler when it was happy."

"How'd you know it was happy?"

"It almost got us."

"Ah."

"The gurgling was so... I don't know... incongruous. So jarring. Just now when he made that scared sound," Hughes said, indicating Ulmerston, "it made me think of that."

When he turned, Thud was giving him a hard gimlet glare.

"You're sure you're up for this, lad? I guarantee you it doesn't get any better."

Hughes' face clouded. He met the captain's glare with one of his own. "Were you a streetbeater during The Hairy Autumn, Thud?"

"Just a lowly lance-corporal then, but yes, I was."

"And would you call that a *bad situation*?"

"What, people turning into animals? I call that downright awful. Why?"

"No reason," Hughes said breezily. "Only I wasn't always called Wendy's Bloodhound. In those days it was just plain old Gormon Hughes, that scruffy kid whose father owns a teashop. But in five months I'd gone from the streets of Leonidas to the Scarlet Citadel, and my troubles didn't let up, Captain. No, they formed an orderly line to take turns. And then came The Hairy Autumn, only the real animals weren't people at all but witches who had the whole city under their spell. To slay the hags they sent a few capable people and also me. And we won. I don't claim to understand the magic behind these killings, but as far as I'm concerned it's just another case of the real beasts—whoever they are—showing their claws and baring their teeth. I'm up for this. More than up for it. Think of me, Captain, as the man with the net."

Their joint glares gained an extra level of depth.

Thud looked away first. "Fair enough."

Hughes felt a small surge of victory. "What happens now?"

"Not much else to do here," said Thud, scowling at Ulmerston. "I always hope the next one will be the one who talks. The only beans this fellow will be spilling will be the ones covered in brown sauce. Canned, of course. I can see the headline now. *Killer Canner Gets Thrown In Can.*"

"He won't go into general population though, will he?"

"Course not. He'll stay here, hopping about in the Toadhouse. Maybe he and Sue Dennings can compare notes in their spare time. She's on the third floor."

There it is, thought Hughes.

Brash, naked disappointment tightened the captain's face.

"Why don't you talk to us, Ulmerston? We know it wasn't you. Sure, all the evidence says we're wrong. Forensics are taking samples, bloody useful Bunsen burner-sniffing bastards. They'll say it was you too. But we know better, me and this articulate git here."

"Can I try something?" said Hughes.

Thud's eyes flicked up to him. Suspicion flared in them, but he gave a stiff nod and stood back.

Hughes studied their surroundings. Setting: unadorned. Lighting: drab. Audience: one very prickly copper indeed.

Oh well. It would have to do.

He drew himself up to his full height, and then seemed to summon a few extra inches of sheer charisma.

"Nigel Ulmerston," he intoned, and his voice was both the stormy sea and the calm black sand shore. "A vile touch has used you and set you loose into a world without sense. You wander there now, far away from the comfort of reason, the blissful cradle of the rational. Hear me and know that you have not strayed into a wilderness from which there can be no salvation. Hear me and know that you have been found." Hughes hesitated. What was the proper policeman's thing to say at a time like this? He struck blindly and scored a decent attempt. "Come back and answer our questions, you horrible man."

***

Out of the fug of bubbling marsh juice, wispy mist droning with the wingbeats of suckling things too big and bloodthirsty to be mosquitos, fat fungal pods and giant spotted mushrooms packed together like wrinkled housing estates, hot gassy smells, the carcasses of poor old bovines creatures picked clean and with bones yielding to spongy kingdoms of sphagnum moss, and all the other interesting attractions of the swamp region of Iphigenia; out of all that strode seven figures dressed in scarlet.

They were a bit rumpled but none the worse for wear.

Behind them came what was known colloquially in the Citadel as a pack mule. It was, when you got right down to it, a walking refrigerator. There was a metal chassis, a biomechanical engine to keep the exoskeleton moving plus a coolant tank for the organs packaged inside it. But indeed. Locomotive fridge pretty much summed it up.

The organs in question came from all sorts of unpleasant things. Ghoulies, creepies, and long-leggedy beasties, as Cate Jubilee might have dubbed them. Once slain these monsters underwent rapid decomposition, leaving only a single trace behind; an organ that glowed with a spring-green light.

These simple luminous lumps were base ingredients awaiting the Jolenes of Corinth City's Foundry, who would melt them down and shape them into magic items.

The seven figures weren't too concerned about all that though. They had magic items of their own; some sharp, some blunt, some weirder and more wonderful than others, and all unique and magnificent as snowflakes knitted by the arthritic hands of winter. Those instruments of war had seen plenty of use these past few hours and grim use at that.

But now the vapors were clearing and the unit had left the most loathsome part of the swamp behind. Morale was good, and they were discussing nightclubs.

"Say what you like, Cate. *Rhinestone Rhino* is the best place for a dance."

This from Robbie Slim, a shaggy-haired young man with great legs and a greater willingness to show them off, be it in battle or the boogie zone.

"The *Rhinestone Rhino*," Cate replied, "has got toilets I would not condemn my worst enemy to clean. The music is stale radio bubblegum. The drinks would not feel out of place if they were poured into these bog puddles. In fact they would feel as though they had returned home."

"And it's *horny*," said Lorna Blacktower. "A very *horny* establishment, I've always said."

"I was at one of their singles nights before I met Hughes," continued Cate. "You're more likely to meet an eligible bachelor in a dustbin than the *Rhinestone Rhino*."

"It's a lie!" Robbie Slim laughed. "I've made many a conquest at the singles night."

"My point exactly," said Cate.

Someone snickered.

"Get it? *Horny?* Because you see, your standard rhinoceroseros has got—"

"Yes, thank you Lorna," snapped Cate good-naturedly. "And you've got to stop pronouncing rhinoceros with an extra 'eros.' It's silly, and this is a serious mission. Right, Eilandri? Oh."

Eilandri had been writing something on one of her yellow cards. Now she handed it to Cate Jubilee, who read it promptly.

"*Ask Lorna if she's ever met an elephelephelant.*"

"What?" Lorna avoided a particular squelchy puddle and frowned over at them. "What's funny, Cate?"

"Nothing. Nothing."

"I think it rather must be. Your tummy and shoulders are shaking."

"It's the fetid reek."

"But your nose isn't wrinkling."

"The fetid reek of this extremely fetid swamp, Lorna Blacktower."

Lorna huffed.

Cate snuck a glance at Eilandri Titansgrave. In that smooth white face she could not detect even a teensy glint of mischief. Not a speck of amusement.

I swear, sooner or later I will have a smile from you.

"Well, I certainly hope none of you are convinced by the trash Miss Jubilee's peddling," said Robbie Slim. "She hangs out at *The Pear and Princess*, and that place is a dive."

"I like it," someone cut in. "Do a lovely pint of Scratch, so they do."

"It's a lie!"

"And to be fair, Cate took me to Boomsugar last year." This comment from one among their company began an avalanche that overrode Robbie's protests.

"Yeah, and she took a big group of us to *The Coconut.*"

"What about *Knuckledragger's?* She's famous there."

"*The Sloe Ginger.*"

"*The Judge's Wig.*"

"*Crunchie Kev's.*"

"*The Dumb Waitress.*"

"*Between A Rock & A Boat Race.*"

"*O-kay,*" surrendered Robbie Slim, throwing his hands up. "Cate Jubilee, I think you've taken everyone in the Citadel out for a good time except me."

Cate grinned. "It's a lie!"

Laughter rang out over the stagnant of the swamp, an antidote to its harmless, irredeemable poisons. Robbie's was loudest of all.

He had less than eleven minutes to live.

***

Performance Success
Level Up! *23 → 24* Congratulations!
New Perk Gained: Master of Disguise Assume the physical appearance of another person for one hour. This Perk can only be used **once**.

Current Bonus: 50%	Next Level: +1% increase to Performance Level 25 Secret Ability: ???

Hughes registered his increasing strength in as long as it might take you to stir honey into a cup of tea. Double quick! And here rose Ulmerston, tugged out of his fugue by the irresistible crank of the Performance!

Formerly slack, his expression firmed up. His eyes gained clarity. He blinked.

"Where am I?"

Nearby, Captain Hoshrum Thud had gone absolutely still, with only his mustache quivering to show the man had not departed his body altogether.

There was no time to explain.

Bleary and confused as he was, Ulmerston made to rub the crust of sleep from his eyes. The restraints held his wrists tight. Hughes watched bewilderment curdle into panic. "Whuh..." the newly returned man began.

Hughes' skill at improvisation took over. He smiled a wide, ingratiating smile, the sort of smile that says I Am Here To Help. "Hello, Nigel."

Ulmerston's gaze swiveled to him. His tongue roamed over his dry upper lip. "Who are you?"

"We represent the Gallfer Canning Factory. My name is Mr. Hughes. This is Mr. Thud. Mr. Thud, Nigel here is uncomfortable. I think the restraints can come off."

That broke Thud's trance. "They can?"

Hughes gave him a look: *play along.*

Thud nodded and bent to loosen the restraints.

His movements were quick and professional. It was a complete recovery from the shock of seeing the radical effects of the Performance, and Hughes felt his admiration for the captain ratchet up a notch.

Meanwhile Nigel Ulmerston was looking at Hughes the way a mouse looks at a cat who's just nudged a rind of cheese its way. A very large mouse accused of murder, to be sure, but a skittish creature just the same.

Looking into the man's eyes, Hughes decided something.

Nigel here doesn't remember what he did. If he did, then he'd be either a smiling lunatic or a screaming man wracked by guilt, but he's neither.

The fact that he could not recount the details of the crime didn't matter though. Thud had his first real chance at an interrogation, and it was up to Hughes to get the ball rolling.

Fortunately, Nigel Ulmerston got it rolling for him.

"You're from the company?" he said doubtfully.

"That's right. There's been an accident, and we're questioning everyone who might be able to help us get to the bottom of it." Hughes allowed pity to cover his face. "But you must be very disoriented. Let me tell you what's going on. Then we can take it from there. Okay?"

"Okay..."

"You're in a medical facility. We believe you might have hit your head during the accident."

By now Thud was done with the restraints.

Ulmerston squeezed his eyelids.

"I do feel fuzzy," he admitted. "What happened?"

"An equipment malfunction," said Hughes with suitable vagueness.

"What does that mean?"

"What it sounds like, Nigel. I'm not an engineer so that's all I've got."

Ulmerston grunted. "Anybody hurt?"

"Hurt? No. Not seriously," said Hughes without missing a beat. "We were worried about you, of course. But you seem all right. Would you be willing to answer some questions?"

"Sure."

Hughes raised both brows at Thud.

With no script to follow but the one his experience will type out as he goes, the grizzled copper enters stage left.

Thud went through the rigmarole of asking Ulmerston about his background. As the man in the bed wrapped up the major events of his life in neat parcels, two things became abundantly clear. The first of these had nothing to do with Ulmerston himself but rather the man interviewing him.

Hoshrum Thud was interesting.

According to Thud he'd been a lance-corporal five years ago. *Let's see, after that comes sergeant, then second-lieutenant, then lieutenant, and finally captain.* That meant that in five years Thud had received almost as many promotions. Hughes was not, as has been noted, overly fond of Corinth City's constabulary, but even so that seemed an astonishingly fast trajectory. Either Thud was bribing his way to the top, or he was almost supernaturally good at his job.

As to the bribing, a man who wore discount tweed trousers and whose coat had mended elbows was not a likely candidate for corruption. The only ostentatious thing about Hoshrum Thud was his mustache. By the looks of it he manicured those whiskers regularly and kept it shiny with just the right amount of pomade.

Evidence backing up the idea that Thud was simply really, really good at being a copper, on the other hand, *that* was swiftly stacking up. His gentle but firm method of questioning won them Nigel Ulmerston's whole story and had the additional effect of setting the poor man at ease. As the questioning evolved, Thud demonstrated an intensity of concentration and insight that impressed Gormon Hughes. He wondered how deep and varied that intensity ran and remembered the way the captain had spoken about the city.

It's mine and I'm its, he'd said.

Hughes had believed that to be a little exaggeration meant to gall the puffed-up Citadel kid, but now he wasn't so sure...

The second thing that became clear during the preliminary questioning was this: Nigel Ulmerston saw something on the ceiling that Hughes could not identify. He would be speaking quite casually and then without explanation his eyes would drift up and regard the ceiling for a while. He'd go on talking, and the eyes would eventually lower, only to be snagged by the impulse once more and drift upward. When this happened, Hughes observed that Ulmerston's rate of swallowing increased, as though something up above them, real or imagined, was drying his throat for him.

It made Hughes think of Thud sitting out of Ulmerston's direct line of sight and making that insectile sound. *Bzzz.* The translated Horstesian nursery rhyme reoccurred from childhood. *There once was an old lady who swallowed a fly, perhaps she'll die.*

For reasons he could not have explained if he'd wanted to, Hughes felt a chill coil up the bone pole of his spine.

"I understand you're a bit muddled, Nigel, but I'd like to go over the day of the accident," Thud asked Ulmerston. "This would be Thursday the 15th. What do you remember?"

"Not much. Clocked in a little before seven like usual. Harry and the others showed up right on time..."

"That's Harris Stokely?" Thud cut in.

"Yeah. Harry's my best friend. We catch a flick together every Friday."

"What cinema?"

"The Morvodolce." Ulmerston pronounced it "morv-oh-doll-see."

Thud jotted in a brown leather notebook he'd produced. "Right. So you clock in."

"Then we... worked." Ulmerston flexed his wrists and blew through his lips, flummoxed. "Belt starts up. Cans come out. Put fish in. Shoot the shit or listen to some music. I don't remember any accident. Hell, I can't even tell you where the memories stop. There's no clean break or anything."

"Relax, Nigel. You're doing fine." Thud put the full stop on whatever thought he'd been penning then turned a page and looked at the man in the bed. "If you'll do something for me,

I'd like you to shut your eyes and have a good hard think. Does anything strike you about that day? Something that was different from the usual routine. Even the smallest detail might be useful in our, uh..." Thud darted a glance at Hughes. "In the *company's* inquiries."

Nigel Ulmerston shut his eyes. He didn't look thrilled about it. A few moments passed. His forehead developed a few creases to join the age lines already living there.

"Oh," he murmured. His eyes flew open. "Oh! Margie's birthday!"

"This would be Marge Tinetts?"

"How could I forget about Margie! She was grinning like the moon turned sideways when she came in. Her man, Derek or David or something, he picked up tickets for them both to go across the river on one of those luxury barges. Margie blurted it out and clapped her hands together like a schoolgirl. Jodi and Penny were all over her after that. One thing led to another, and we decided we'd put the Tinfrost crap up early. Margie's wild about the holidays. Seemed a nice way to ahm..."

"Commemorate the day," offered Thud.

"Right! Yeah, that's it."

"And can I ask, Nigel. By 'Tinfrost crap' you mean...?"

"Oh the tree and shit."

"The decorations."

"Uh huh. Every depo gets their own. Gets delivered at the start of the month, but we get to pop it up ourselves. Part of the whole team building gunk upper management shovel. Oh..." Color rose in Ulmerston's bull-thick neck. "I mean... shit, I didn't mean to say..."

"Don't you worry," said Thud. "Mum's the word."

Ulmerston was pleased to hear that. "Thanks. I don't want to lose my job. And I'm not going to lawyer up or sue or anything, even if I did hit my head. I feel fine. Just a little cottonswabbed is all." His eyes began that peculiar, steady drift toward the ceiling again. Thud was writing quickly.

Faint voices outside. Hughes had a keen ear, and he thought they were coming from farther down the corridor.

With a click in his throat Ulmerston swallowed. He let his gaze come down and rest on the captain. "I don't know how I forgot about Margie," he repeated, grinning sheepishly.

"Anything else?" said Thud.

"Everyone needed a lie down."

Hughes' head snapped round. Out of the corner of his eye he saw Thud freeze at exactly the same instant. Ulmerston's voice had sounded suddenly abstract. Dreamy. A cursory examination of the man told Hughes that the Performance was wearing off. The length of the effects was varied, but it had never faded so rapidly before. Jack—or whatever vileness had touched Nigel Ulmerston—had left its mark in obvious ways and subtle ones too. Those eyes, alert only a moment ago, were slowly beginning to glaze.

Hughes could hear the voices growing louder.

"Who needed a lie down?" said Thud.

"Had to lay Harry and the rest down or they would have stayed."

"Who would have stayed? Where?"

Louder. Someone was shouting just outside the door.

"Stayed where, Nigel?"

The handle was turning.

"They were..." Ulmerston's face pulled itself into a rictus, a death mask of horror. "Oh dear God, they were laying eggs inside me. I could *feel it...*"

The door opened.

Chapter Eight

Lorna was squinting at something.

She had been the first to trudge to the top of a muddy hill that marked the frontier of the swamp. From there the group would thread the low sloping pasture at the center of Iphigenia, and onward to the portal.

Cate came to stand beside her, the rest of the unit close behind. Down the hill and spread out as far as the eye could see was a fog bank. It curled and fused and broke apart like milk poured into a glass of water.

"Must have rolled in from the forest," said Cate.

"What must have?" said Robbie Slim.

"The fog," said Cate.

Lorna mumbled something.

"Reckon it'll be damp?" Robbie asked the company.

"I'd say so," Cate replied.

"I have a spare cloak."

"What, another?"

"Swamps are rude places, Cate."

"How so?"

"Polite places have the compassion to stay dry."

"What's that?" said Lorna.

They looked at her outstretched finger pointing down the hill.

The unit strained to see. A smatter of murmuring broke out. Cate's search was as fruitless as theirs.

Then she saw it.

"There," she said. "Three hundred yards from us."

"Where? Oh," piped Robbie. "There, I have it."

He might indeed, but next to him Cate Jubilee was having trouble keeping her eye on it. Down there in that cauldron of fog the shadows were misbehaving.

"What on earth could it be?" said Lorna Blacktower.

Cate had no idea. "Looks like a machine."

If so, it was a fluid one. Unnervingly long, it rode through the fog with slow sinuous movements. From her vantage point, it looked like nothing so much as an immense snake. But if the mist ran as deep as she believed, then it couldn't be a snake because it wasn't soughing through the long grass. The shape was at least twenty feet off the ground.

Reluctantly, Cate tore her gaze from this unexpected development.

"Eilandri?"

The Pale Giant was watching the shape.

It paused, gyrating strangely, then went still.

Eilandri Titansgrave reached up and clicked the scabbard button on her back.

Then she wrapped her fingers around her hammer.

Out in the fog the shape erupted into motion.

"*To arms!*" Cate roared. Around her the unit scrambled to action. She wrenched the zip of her satchel open, filled her fingers with instant mirrors. She hopped to get the blood flowing in her cold, stiff legs. The enchanted hobnails in her boots sensed encroaching battle. Magic swept over her feet, tingling her toes.

The shape charged the hill, closing the distance with an asp's mercurial speed. Distance proved itself the great diminisher.

"Fuck me, it's big," someone muttered.

"She's bigger," said Robbie Slim, winking at Eilandri.

It's a lie, thought Cate, gallows humor diluting her shock. The elongated thing Lorna had spotted in the haze was not the shape's entirety.

It was the creature's neck.

The Iphigenian sunshine baked cold distortions in the fog, which, although no wind blew, seemed to be advancing up the hill, a silk carpet rolling out to welcome the creature to the killing spot. It crept over their feet, too quickly for Cate's liking.

"The fog is with our enemy," she growled.

No one questioned the truth of this. They were warriors of the Scarlet Citadel. A little naughty weather was standard fare.

When the fog lapped at their thighs with cool white tongues the creature reached the hill, and they saw it.

The hideously long neck ended in a bulbous lump that must have been its head, for the face was obscured by a veil of moldering cloth and fastened with a tiara of bones glowing blackly. Its shoulders, chest, and belly were that of a human woman's, draped in that same reeking cloth like the mummified queens of old Ikahagua. Sprouting from the torso were limbs of such grotesque spindling length they brought to mind those horrible torture racks where cranks are turned and the body is prized apart. But the effect was not spiderlike. Rather, here was a gargantuan feminine shape, her movements languid and balletic, evoking both the snake and the charmer.

From veil to foot, she must have measured eighty feet.

No standoff took place.

No battle cries rippled the alien air.

The red unit waded in.

Unstoppering a vial and stepping into a mirror, Cate caught a glimpse of Eilandri Titansgrave's hammerhead swooping, heard the *whoooo—*

(around her ten billion facets in a glass tumbler)

And she was through, under the oncoming creature.

Momentum lending her a modicum of extra force, she placed her palms flat on that glass, bunched the muscles in her legs, and sent both booted feet spearing upward.

The creature's left arm was ungodly heavy, but Cate was devilishly strong, and instead of warding the blow with its forearm, its elbow rose right into the path of Eilandri's hammer.

—*ooosssshhhhhh; CRRRRACKKKK!*

Some clever Jolene had honed the hammer's head into a thousand tiny cuspated points. It bit and crashed with the weight of Eilandri's shoulders behind it.

The effect was quite spectacular.

The monster's elbow joint bowed in at the impact side and exploded out the other. Cartilage, synovial fluid, and a thick mucusy blood sprayed in a ghoulish confetti. While it certainly relied on its legs for balance, the creature was top-heavy thanks to an abundance of throat.

It stumbled, its veil and spine going back and forth in a clockish pendulum.

Efficient and deadly the unit swarmed it, hacking and bruising and blasting with their wealth of Foundry-forged magic. But Cate's statement proved truer than even she could have anticipated. The fog whelmed up, coalescing, and in a trice the monster's elbow was set back in its crook and restored to full vigor.

"Over the hill!" Cate commanded. *"Drive it into the swamp!"*

Wise though she was to the fact that they would stand no chance against an adversary who could recuperate so quickly in its favored terrain, the notion was easier spoken than delivered on. Their foe was now wary of the mirrors Cate leaped through, and where it could it avoided Eilandri, who was the only one mighty enough to push it over the hill into the clear where it might be slain for good.

It was then that the creature scooped up a fist of curling white and fashioned the mist into a hooded lantern that poked forth a finger of lonely purple light. As though it were a mother showing her son a dark secret, it showed the beam to Robbie, who dropped the flail he was wielding and clutched his face.

"I can't see!" he cried, purple light washing over him. "Oh God no, not blind, don't let me be blind, nono*no*."

With its free hand the monster drew a sickle from the fog. Sunlight traced the blade in wicked gold.

Robbie!

Cate dived for him just as the sickle came down.

***

There are only so many ways to be thin, but there are an exceeding number of possibilities involved in being fat.

There are the pompous champagne sippers, the surprisingly graceful, the jolly, the fastidiously clean and pleasant, the determinedly smelly who are distinctly less so, the wrestlers, the shrewd foxy types, the chest puffers, the army colonels, and of course those who are addicted to cakes with pictures of pixies on them.

The list goes on.

It's no small business, being fat.

Commissioner Vincent Winkles of the Leonidas District Police was the sort of fat man who is constantly huffing at a cigar. The only reason he refused to have two in his mouth at the same time was that one would keep falling out. His red sideburns were streaked with gray and ended abruptly three inches over his ears, giving way to a bald and sweating dome he occasionally mopped with a handkerchief. No wedding ring adorned his pork sausage fingers, and you got the sense that if he did meet a woman he found attractive, some acidic part of him would assert itself, and he'd grumble the name of a lemon-flavored dessert before showing her the door.

He was, in round, the kind of person who gives the horizontally gifted a bad name.

"As I live and breathe," he said, issuing through the door in a cloud of smoke and grinning at Hughes and Thud. "If it isn't Wendy's Bloodhound and the Leonidas Labrador, thick as thieves and making trouble."

Hughes bristled. "Vincent," he said.

Prick, he thought.

Thud said nothing. He was speaking in hushed tones to a now unresponsive Nigel Ulmerston.

"Sir, you really ought to come out of there," whined Nurse Perky from the corridor. "These guys are questioning a guest."

"I can see that," said Winkles. "You know why I'm here, Thud?"

The captain didn't look around. "Commissioner, I–"

"I'm here because there's been another complaint about you disturbing the peace in the Toadh... erm. In this esteemed house of convalescence," Winkles amended quickly. "Which makes four complaints in total. Three strikes and you're out, as they say, to which I add: four strikes and you're buggered."

"Complaint?" Nurse Perky frowned. She had clearly been led to believe Thud's interrogation was legitimate. "Who complained?"

"I did."

Hughes turned and saw the harried-looking nurse they'd had the misfortune of meeting earlier. She stood in the corridor with her arms folded, her whey-face all pinched and smug. "Now you come away from here and let the commissioner handle things."

"Commissioner? Gee, I'm sorry sir."

"Quite all right," Winkles told the suddenly nervous Nurse Perky with a friendly smile. "Now piss off, there's a good girl."

Her face fell. She hurried off after her superior.

"How was the stroll, Vincent?"

The commissioner gave Hughes a suspicious look. "What stroll?"

"The stroll you were on," said Hughes innocently. "Only the precinct is a twenty-minute walk from here." *Closer to thirty for you, you worthless prick.* "Driving's right out; the streets are pedestrianized for the holidays. Even if the nurse telephoned you the moment after myself and the captain ran into her, you'd still be making your way here."

Out of the corner of his eye, Hughes saw Thud's mustache twitch.

Approval or irritation?

Hughes supposed he'd find out later.

Winkles closed the door, his cigar end smoldering like the last living coal in a furnace. "All right. Well spotted. The complaint was a bit of good luck. The nurse was shocked when I came in a minute after she'd hung up the phone. Said I was a *model of haste*, the silly cow." He pushed past Hughes, making sure to jostle him with a heavy shoulder on the way, and leaned over the recumbent Nigel Ulmerston. "One of my lads told me you'd come asking after our tenacious Captain Thud, Hughes. Got me very curious, that did. 'Thud's on his day off,' I tell my lad. 'No, sir,' he says. 'Thud's gone up to the Toadhouse to pick at some mad geezer's brains again. Even though you told him that was all finished with, sir.' Well," finished Winkles, exhaling plumes of smoke through his nostrils into poor Nigel's face before standing straight and glowering at Thud, "you can imagine my total surprise to hear it, Thud me old chum."

Hughes did not believe the commissioner was surprised in the least.

And the man wasn't done. "I wonder what part of 'leave it alone' wasn't clear," he asked Thud. "Seems a fairly simple concept to me."

"Commissioner. Hughes and I just spoke to this man. He gave us details surrounding the murder in the canning factory."

"Did he?" Winkles eyed the drooling figure in the bed. "Looks like he couldn't tell you the price of butter."

"Hughes was able to ah... break his stupor, sir."

"Mm. And what did he have to say for himself?"

Thud related Ulmerston's testimony.

Hughes watched Vincent Winkles closely. Thud's words skimmed off the commissioner like pebbles on a frozen lake. Only one thing cracked that facade.

"Eggs?" he said. "What's he talking about eggs for?"

"We're as intrigued as you, sir."

Winkles waved a hand impatiently. "I'm not intrigued, Thud. I am, in fact, completely disinterested in the lame poetry of killers. This case is cut and dry. Forensics will back that up, I'll tell you that for nothing. What we've got here is a plain old instance of bottled-up nastiness spewing over. Happens all the time."

"And the messages?" pressed Thud. "The rooftop running?"

"You're behind the times, mate. This whole Spring-Heeled Jack malarky is a classic bit of wonky-headedness on the part of the public. Call it mass hysteria or a media frenzy if you like. As far as I'm concerned," said Winkles, "it's all The Hairy Autumn's fault. It put the frights up everyone, made them think magic is lurking around every corner, when really it's on Hughes' hip, or in The Hippodrome for a few shards of credit. Sport and steel.

"Now, Thud, if you're going to work on your day off, I've got plenty of tricky cases that require a look. I promise they'll actually wind up with results. Remember those? You and results used to be on famous terms. Bosom buddies, you and results, I've always said. I suggest you take me up on it."

"No sir," said Thud stiffly. "Think I'll stick with simple, if it's all the same to you."

"Careful, Captain," said Vincent Winkles. "That badge of yours isn't stuck on with tape. It only takes a word, and it'll be plucked right off your chest."

"And just who exactly is going to pluck it, sir?"

"Me." The handkerchief mopped sweat. The cigar streamed smoke. "That's who."

Anger crackled between the two men.

Hughes could think of nothing that would cool their tempers. Fortunately, he didn't have to.

Thud wilted. "Apologies, sir. I'd be delighted to look at these richer, more complicated cases of yours."

Winkles grinned. "See? Was that so hard?"

"No sir. Not sure what came over me, sir."

"No harm done, no harm done. Come on with me, Thud me old biscuit." The grin faltered. "What are you writing there?"

"I've bothered her Ladyship Winnifred Dragontail for weeks over this lost cause," said Thud, finishing his scribble, tearing out a page from his notebook, and handing it to Hughes. "I owe her an apology too. Could you give this to her, Mr. Hughes?"

"Of course."

"We were barking up the wrong tree," Thud told him.

This elicited booming laughter from the commissioner. "The Labrador and the Bloodhound. Still thick, only not together, eh Thud?"

"That's right, sir."

They headed out into the corridor, leaving Hughes alone with Ulmerston.

Voices fading. Silence.

He unfolded the note.

Half-seven tonight. 13 Lombardel Road. This isn't over.

***

Robbie's death was only the beginning.

Like ants avoiding sunlight lasered through a magnifying glass, the unit from the Scarlet Citadel were forced on the backfoot by the monster's lantern. Insidious and purple, its blinding beam hunted them through the mist, which crept ever higher and higher until it kissed the napes of their necks with cool lips before engulfing them completely. And, of course, there was the monster's sickle, which cleaved flesh as easily as fog.

With her mirror-bound teleportation, Cate Jubilee had a better time of it than others. *Especially you,* she thought, spotting a pair of legs in time to step over them. Those legs had caused quite a stir across the city nightclubs, mostly the *Rhinestone Rhino.* Amputated, they'd become clutter. Watch your feet on the feet, honey. We've shuffled our last and that's no lie. *Sorry Robbie.*

Even for Cate there were a few close shaves. The lantern and the sickle came swooping and shining out of the gloom, and it was only her quick reflexes that pulled her low or tugged her tall in the nick of time.

Of their goal to drive the monster out of its protective mist, there was little hope. The simple act of orienting herself, her unit, and the monster, took every helping of Cate's concentration that she could serve. It was a bitter fight, the sort that injects your hip joints full of ache and dips your arms and shoulders in lead.

Yet in spite of all these things that would plant doubt and sorrow in the mind of pretty much anyone, Cate was having fun. At any moment she might have a limb, her sight, her whole *life* stolen from her, and she simply could not stop smiling.

A hand closed on her shoulder. She spun and found herself looking at a red breastplate. Only one person in their company was that large.

"Eilandri. Take a risk with me," she said and explained the plan she had not even known she was concocting at the back of her head.

When she was done, there was movement in the fog. It was Eilandri's nod: *Yes.* The albino swept off into the murk.

Careful of the lantern and the sickle, Cate tracked down the others and got them on board. Then she peered into the fog, found the purple beam, and sprinted for it. Her heart drummed her blood with heavy thumps, snares, and cymbal crashes of ecstasy. Strands of her fiery hair had worked loose from her ponytail. Sweat and fog damp plastered them to her scalp and brow—her brow!

For weeks it had been knotted with lines. Now it was clear and she was happy and—

Oh this was it.

Those fights she'd undertaken in the swamp, filling the pack mule, those no longer counted.

This

(sensing her approach and with a barely audible sighing sound that wafted its veil of mildewed cloth, the monster made to douse the little flame that was Cate, and instead experienced a crunch that flared up the left side of its body, followed by the most sumptuous agony)

was

(a loud metallic *thump* came to the little flame's ears, and her smile toothed itself into a grin; her unit came up behind her, working the creature's neck, cutting deep like some feverish decapitation squad, guillotine goons, and Lorna Blacktower foaming the monster's veil and the face under it with boiling oil, and in response to this onslaught the monster lashed with its sickle, too slow, too slow to match the speed of Hurricane Jubilee, a little flame waxing bright in this crucial moment, and she was on the beast's neck stamping with a hobnail boot, keeping its head low to the ground where it must remain if this madcap plan of hers was going to work)

IT

(where was its lantern? Where oh where?).

Try as it might to raise itself, the monster's curdy head squashed into Iphigenian grass. Cate ground her heel into the biggest spinal node she could see for good measure. Then she threw herself forward, gripped the monster's veil, and yanked it up, exposing the face beneath.

"Now!" she called. She screwed her eyes shut.

On cue, Eilandri Titansgrave emerged from the haze like a zeppelin from cotton wool clouds. Her eyes too, were shut, just in case. In her arms Eilandri carried the purple lantern.

Not one of them saw the monster's true face under the veil. That was a blessing. Partially melted by Lorna's oil, stitching itself together with needles of fog, it was the sort of face that might carve your mind into cutlets and fry them all mad. Chiefly, however, the monster did have eyes. They gazed directly into the spot below the lantern's hood. All five of them.

The purple light from its own lantern blazed. It leeched those eyes of color, transforming them into blind white billiard balls. The monster didn't sigh then. It *hissed*.

Now was the moment for the Scarlet Citadel, and they were fast in seizing it.

Filing out and getting a hold of the monster as it writhed and churned up tufts of turfy grass, the unit recognized their lost numbers. Eight had set out beyond the portal. Now they were five.

Three dead, thought Cate. *Then I must have courage for four.*

"Push," she urged them, and push they did.

Grunts rushed through gritted teeth. Tendrils of mist poured over straining muscle. As their struggles advanced and regressed, a vessel popped in Cate's eye. It gave the effect of her inherent redness spreading; red hair, red clothes, red rage, let's go. Blood flowed through the pale jelly of her eye as dye might soak a white shirt. She hardly noticed.

The unit heaved their enemy toward the top of the hill. Overhead the grotesque length of its neck wriggled. In one hand, its weapon changed in a melding of fog. A sickle. A sword. A cudgel. A knife. A slender whip that came within inches of snaring Cate and grinding her rib bones to a mealy paste. The monster's other hand was temporarily useless. Eilandri's hammerblow had mangled it so badly that the healing was slow. Repairing tissue *whumped* like muffled fireworks.

Again the unit heaved but the monster, suspicious at the antics of these little nuisances overcoming its panic, began to heave back.

"Heavy," groaned Lorna. "Too heavy by half. We ought to run for the portal."

"You three go. Eilandri and I will keep it here."

"Yes, Cate."

"Rally the troops, okay?"

No words, only a few desultory grumbles from the survivors. Orders were orders. She felt approval mixed into the bubbling gumbo that was her emotional state.

"Oh." Cate chided herself. In all the excitement she'd nearly forgotten. "Tell my Hughes that I—"

"I wonder," someone said, "if I might be of assistance?"

I know that voice.

Cate turned and saw the calm, unassuming figure standing to the side, admiring their battlefield. She couldn't help it. She gasped.

"*Wendy?*"

The Last Dragon had arrived.

With its sight returning in a pale gray blur, the monster was aware only that there was another tiny threat to bisect. It brought the sickle around in a fatal slash.

Wendy Dragontail batted it away. She was assessing.

"Miss Jubilee?"

"Yes my Lady?"

"Where does the fog end?"

Cate stood agog. "Um. We *think* on the other side."

"Capital."

The creature lunged for the elderly woman, hoping to squish her like a bag of blood, to chew her head like an apple, and munch the brain like cored pips, yummy-scrummy with harmless cyanide.

Wendy Dragontail grabbed it by both rows of teeth, and in one smooth motion, she dislocated its jaw. Then she crumpled its huge windpipe into a thin tube so she could close her fist around it.

"Come with me, please."

Thrashing feebly, the monster found itself dragged up the hillside, away from its soothing mists, into the swamp with its sickly brown smell and cancerous toadstools. The surviving members of the Scarlet Citadel unit watched its gargantuan mass pulled over the crest and out of sight. Its sighs and slobberings quieted. Then they swelled, growing much louder, rising to a high and keening scream. It went on and on. It was utterly inhuman.

Then there was nothing to hear.

The fog dissipated.

Looking out over the pasture, sunglossed and vibrant green, they could all see mounds of shaggy hair lying stickily in pools of gore. Before it had taken on their unit, the monster had evidently slaughtered whole herds of the cowlike things that grazed here in the rural soul of Iphigenia. Distantly, the great portal beckoned them home.

It had all happened so quickly.

Cate Jubilee's stunned face contorted.

It softened.

It broke apart.

"Cate?" Turning from stone to skin once more, Lorna Blacktower bit her lip and sidled up to her friend. "Cate dearie. What's got into you?"

"Her sweater."

Lorna frowned. "Sorry?"

Cate touched the other woman's shoulder, her own shaking uncontrollably.

"She came to save us in a wooly sweater."

Unable to stifle it any longer, she threw back her head and laughed long and loud enough to wake the sleeping dead.

Well, almost.

Chapter Nine

That afternoon, Hughes made two assumptions about 13 Lombardel Road. One was right. The other was dead wrong.

He assumed that the address was a house, and that he would find it in a rugged, homely corner of Leonidas District. In fact, growing frustrated and consulting a Corinth City street map, he discovered that while Lombardel Road was a residential area, it was actually in Cleomenes.

Cleomenes was a District of extravagant street art, bakeries whose ovens were equipped with little handles you could turn to rotate trays stacked in a grid, the world-class Wailing Lady Opera House, dance halls lit with rubicund chandeliers, restaurants boasting cuisines of every taste and presentation, and now that it was Tinfrosttime, skating. Premium boutique ice skating. Complete with flailing your arms about in an effort not to collapse, jeers from your friends holding hot wine on the other side of the skating rink's partition, and an experience generally replete with guarantees of merriment and the chance to make a total tit of oneself.

Cleomenes was prosperous, frivolous, and not the sort of place Hughes could picture Captain Hoshrum Thud living in *at all*.

Nevertheless, he had run a few errands, squeezed in a quick but much needed visit with his father, and now it was closing in on half past seven and here was Lombardel Road with its hedges clipped to look like ostriches, and the ostriches wrapped in Tinfrost lights of red and blue and orange.

Number 13 was the largest and prettiest house in an estate of large and pretty houses. On the threshold, the welcome mat told Hughes to tread softly, for he trod on its dreams. This made him vaguely uncomfortable. Welcome mats do not traditionally have dreams, unless they are in children's cartoons dreaming about becoming fine Hortesian rugs. Thinking about children's cartoons made him think about...

But no. No, he mustn't think about her.

Not her pudgy, seashell hand.

Not her nursing at her mum's breast, milk and glass and tattoos.

Not her learning to walk, or to spell her name, or to use the toilet.

Certainly not her getting big and curling up on the sofa to watch cartoons with her dad.

He mustn't think about any of th—

"You must be Mr. Hughes."

He looked up. The door to 13 Lombardel Road was open. In the frame stood a woman who had either run out of a painting or into one. Paint of every hue blotched her apron-clad body; rust red, burnt umber, azure and olive, and a whole host of other shades. Her hair might have been mousy brown, or it might have been ash blonde. Stiff as wheat with dried paint in cornucopious rainbows, it was difficult to tell. That small fleck of brown on her chin might be a dollop of brown paint or a beauty spot. Under it all she was an amiable-looking woman of, Hughes surmised, about thirty-five.

"Hughes," he said, flustered. "I am he."

"He you are," agreed the woman. "She am me."

"And you is?"

"Mrs. Thud is I."

He regarded her and her fabulous house. The pair seemed to summarize Cleomenes District.

Hughes could only smile. "If you say so."

"Would you like to come in?"

Past the front door was a wide corridor decorated with gilt-framed paintings. A central stair climbed to the second floor. A cabinet door lay ajar under the stairs, showing a broom handle, cleaning wipes, and a dustpan and brush. They must have been used often. Spotless wooden floors roamed elsewhere, through open doors leading hither and thither, though not yon because it was not a gigantic house, merely a very big one.

The paintings encompassed lots of styles but only one theme.

"You're pagan," said Hughes without pausing to think.

Thankfully, Mrs. Thud looked pleased rather than offended. "You recognize the characters in my paintings!"

He gestured from one image to another. "Isofer, God of Banquets and Honorable Combat. In this painting he devours his grandniece Loithohedra, Goddess of Winter, only to have her burst from his throat reborn, devoured, and reborn, in an endless cycle. Over there is Hereticia, Goddess of Spring and Betrayal. She sleeps nine months of the year thanks to a curse bestowed on her by those she, um, well, betrayed." Hughes turned to his host. "This is a hallway of seasons."

"That's right. They went out of fashion once the old church started burning pagans at the stake. It's wonderful that you recognized it. Let me introduce myself properly, Mr. Hughes. I'm Heavy."

Hughes' mouth fell open. "Your name is Heavy Thud?"

"*Hettie*," she said reproachfully.

"Oh God. Sorry. I misheard you."

"That's never happened before," Hettie said crossly. "I mean really." She maintained this for perhaps three seconds before bursting. "You ought to see your face." She giggled. "And they say art is priceless."

"Here he is. The very man."

Hughes turned in time to see Hoshrum Thud appearing through one of the doors. He had discarded his coat and was wearing a shirt with, unless Hughes was very much mistaken, one of his wife's paintings on it. Button-nosed, apple-cheeked cherubs flapped across Thud's midsection on wings of silver.

"Find the place okay?" Thud asked. Before Hughes could formulate an answer, he addressed his wife. "Supper's on the table."

"You're a dote," Hettie said, leaning to kiss his brow. "You know when you don't realize you're hungry until someone mentions it, then you're instantly ravenous? I've been pacing the whole house trying to sort this piece out in my head. I found Mr. Hughes on our doorstep. He looked glum. I hope you aren't grinding this young man down, Hoshrum."

"Wouldn't consider it, dear," said Thud. "Any more grinding and Hughes here will be sharp enough to shave with. Have you eaten, lad?"

"No."

"Should be enough for three. You and I can eat in the parlor. Hettie likes to eat alone. I hope you like duck with almonds, orange-peel, and stuffing in a nutmeg gravy."

Hughes did like it. He liked it so much he had seconds and sucked the last of the duck meat off the bones.

"You're from Leonidas, all right." Thud grinned. "Usually I'm the only person in the whole bloody District who licks the grease off his fingers."

The parlor was low-ceilinged and cozy, with nut-brown cushioned seats and a fireplace sporting two stockings stitched with the names Hettie and Hoshrum. A sculpture of a goatman fingering a flute hunched over the hearth.

Hughes and Thud sat together in a silence that was half prudence, half grudging respect, and all surreality. Two boys from the gutter. One a man of the Citadel. The other a man of the Law.

As the silence lengthened, it changed, becoming a kind of game. Whoever broke it first would lose. The stakes were nonexistent. Both men understood this, and yet for some reason winning was important.

After a while, it became clear that whoever spoke first would be the deputy in the case of Spring-Heeled Jack. The other would take the lead.

So the stakes were real after all.

As he smiled politely and admired the room's fixtures, Hughes' mind was cast back years to a conversation he'd had with Cate about dynamic theatrical height. Cate, ever brilliant, pointed out that different kinds of movement as well as height could explain the power in any given scene. Now he mentally added speech and silence to that list.

Stare into the fire and tug your whiskers all you like, Thud. I may be new to this, but when it comes to magic you're the novice. Your beat is the pavement and the city that formed around it. But my beat is this entire world and its two strange neighbors. That's the difference between copper and scarlet. You tread softly while me and mine tread dreams.

Silence.

Enveloping and fraught and flushed with meaning.

Silence.

With a tug of his whiskers, and not looking away from the skirts of fire whirling behind the mesh of the grate, Captain Hoshrum Thud said, "Right. I've got witness reports and contacts who can get you into a room with every single murderer; suspected, accused, convicted, the whole shebang. That's enough to put together a portfolio of interviews. From there we can get out the old corkboard and red thread because I like clichés and because Hettie used up all the other colors in a tapestry of the God of Sneezing Into Thy Enemy's Chowder When He Isn't Looking, or something of that kidney. It's hanging up in one of the bathrooms, and I see it every time I widdle, that's all I know. I've got coroner statements, access to autopsies, crime scene photographs, plus I know every officer who's worked on the case, including a few retired coppers who tried to bust Jack before the war. I'm not on hugging terms with the journalist Tracer Gogen, who between you and I is a bit of a weasel, but I know where he works, and I think I might persuade him into running whatever stories we like in *The Times*, should that be a strategy we'd like to pursue." His gaze bored into Hughes. "Your turn. How about you start by telling me what you did to Nigel Ulmerston."

His words had drawn Hughes forward in his chair, fingers laced together. "I'll tell you, Thud. But if it goes beyond us, I'll know."

"Intimidation, is it?"

"No. None required. Come on, Captain. You know as well as I do that the Citadel is secretive."

"Mum's the word."

Hughes held the man's stare for another few moments. Stony and quiet, Thud gave away nothing.

Here I tread.

"It's called Performance. It gives me a certain amount of influence over people."

"What sort of influence?"

"I can convince policemen to give me their umbrella during a storm. It can be more subtle than that. More drastic too."

"Like pulling Nigel Ulmerston out of his, whatchacallit... sounds like mayonnaise."

"Malaise?"

"That's it."

"Yeah, like that."

"Right. Okay. We're warming up the barbecue, you and I. So this Performance of yours, it comes from your sword?" Thud's eyes gleamed. "Or that slip of a knife you think you're hiding in your boot?"

Hughes let that go. His Krys knife was not important, and neither was Chimera. "Usually magic items are the source of each Citadel member's power."

"Only not yours?"

"No."

"Why?"

To that Hughes had no answer. He told Thud as much.

The captain mulled it over. Absently he opened a nearby drawer, took out a damp honey-scented cloth, cleaned the rest of the grease off his hands, and toyed with his mustache. "How does it work?"

"The best way I've found to describe it is that it's like dredging up a feeling from the loam of who you are. Then it's a matter of sending it into the target, fastening the Performance in them like a machine laden with seeds, hoping they take root and germinate into a success. Failure happens. There's a percentile chance involved."

"What dictates the chance?"

Hoochie Mama Nightshade and her mushroom familiar Clarence.

"I don't know," said Hughes honestly. "One thing I do know; I've gotten better at it over time."

He chose not to tell the captain about his secret ability, Chimera, which allowed Hughes to dramatically alter someone fundamentally, not planting seeds so much as sewing salt into the fertile soil of their personality. Regular Performance merely affected the target. Chimera changed them forever. He had only ever used it once, on a woman with a smile like a perverse surgery kit and whose skin sparkled even in dark places.

Two sharp tugs of the mustache. Thud's eyes narrowed.

"Don't take this the wrong way, Hughes. Planting seeds and other shiny metaphors aside, it sounds like mind control."

"Maybe. You use manacles. A truncheon."

"Lousy comparison. Yeah, okay, the cuffs chafe a bit. But at least they leave your brain where it is."

"And the stick?"

"It's only there in case the carrot doesn't work."

Hughes grinned a nasty grin. "If you asked them, I bet most people would take a few moments of cognitive influence over a flattened nose or mashed gums."

Thud scowled, rapping a knuckle on the arm of his chair.

"It seems like an easy thing to abuse. That's all I'm saying."

Hughes let his grin dissolve into a gentler smile, one he actually felt. He despised bandying about the morality of his power. It goaded something ugly in him he didn't much care for.

"Years ago when Cate and I were starting out, she told me that using a power like Performance on someone who means you harm is one thing. Using it on someone just because you can is another."

"Cate's your partner?"

"I'm lucky to say she is."

"Two Leonidas scrappers, punching above their weight."

Hughes laughed. "Don't forget both sporting canine nicknames."

Thud rolled his eyes. "At least yours has a certain, you know, *je ne sais quack* about it. Wendy's Bloodhound. There's a moniker to get the hairs on your kneecaps prickling. The Leonidas Labrador makes me sound like a soft touch."

"Wouldn't be too sure." Hughes chuckled. "There may be something in it."

"Oh?"

"You're working a murder case you don't have to for the sake of people you don't know."

"Ah, well, yes. Yes. Fair. But... that's the job, isn't it?"

"And you make your wife supper."

"True, eh... true. But Hettie's up to her eyes with this museum piece at the moment, I mean... she can't be expected to..."

"And I heard what you said to Ulmerston."

Thud's teeth came together with a distinct *click*.

Hughes savored the moment. "When the commissioner waddled in, I heard you tell Ulmerston that it was going to be all right. That you were set on seeing justice done for his friends and for him. And soon, so he wouldn't have to wait long. You said the city looks after her own."

There was a tactful pause. In the hearth, a log gave up the fight against thermodynamics and fell in on itself, tossing up sparks like delicate smoldering moths.

Thud shifted awkwardly in his seat. "What um... what else are you bringing to the case?"

Hughes let the man stew for a moment. Thud was a rottweiler with the heart of a labrador, and Hughes knew it. Eventually he relented. "I've got the support of the Scarlet Citadel. I can go where I like, speak to the people your commissioner forbids you from speaking to. Thanks to my Performance, doors that would be closed even to the Citadel might just open for me. There's Knickerbocker too. You've heard of him."

"I've seen him," said Thud. "Smelled him too. He talks to bats."

"Among other creatures. Knickerbocker owes me a favor. Last summer one of his voles was feeling low, and I got it back on its feet." Hughes chewed the inside of his cheek. "I suppose I could speak to Krys and The Mum."

"Who?"

"An old woman who gets lost in the past and a young girl who can see the future."

Thud was silent a long time. Then he said, "So what you can bring to the case, aside from your amazing gifts of persuasion, are some weird oracles and the master of a few depressed rodents."

"*Lots* of rodents. And most of them are quite content." Hughes gave the captain a winning smile. "Look, it's not as expansive as your list, but I'm sure—*stars shining bright above you*—that I'll think of other advantages we might call on."

"What?" said Thud.

"Sorry?"

"What was that about stars?"

Hughes frowned. "I didn't mention stars."

"Yeah, you did. Your voice got sort of sing-songy and you said something about stars."

"Captain, I know it's been a long day—*night breezes seem to whisper 'I love you'*—for both of us, so maybe I should..."

"There it was again!" Thud had perked right up in his chair. "You just sang 'night breezes something something I love you'!"

"What are you talking about?"

"You must hear yourself. Is it magic?" Thud's mustache quivered. "I knew I shouldn't have asked what you did to Ulmerston. Now your Performance knows I'm on to it and it's going clockwise cuckoo!"

"You're being ridiculous. Listen to me, don't you think I'd recognize it—*birds singing in the sycamore tree*—if I were singing? Thud, where are you going?"

"To open the parlor door and escort you out of my house. You and the bloody birds are in it together. Bloody choir invisible. You can stuff the stars and sycamore tree too. *And* the night breeze. We'll talk tomorrow when you're back to normal."

"If you insist—*dream a little dream of me*—then of course I'll go."

"I do—*dream a little dream of me*—insist."

Thud froze with his fingers on the doorknob.

"Did I say something just now?"

But his guest wasn't listening. Hughes was standing up. He was looking at the fireplace. No traceable emotion moved across his face. His hand, however, was on the move. It was curling around the hilt of his sword.

"Heard something..." he said.

As Thud was drawing a breath to reply, there came a rat-tat-tat knocking at the front door of 13 Lombardel Road.

It was answered. "Hello," said Mrs. Thud. "Oh it's you. I... I don't think we've met but I... Well it's the funniest thing, but I feel like we've been expecting you."

Thud paled. "Hettie."

"Come in, please," said Mrs. Thud. "They're just in the parlor."

Something was wrong. It thawed the captain's paralysis. He reefed open the door and readied himself to tackle the intruder.

And the intruder said, "Got yourself a lovely home, miss."

Hughes thought, *I know that voice.* "Hoshrum, wait."

"Bugger that. There's a stranger in my home. The moment he comes round the corner with Hettie, I'll..."

"Just wait. Please. I... think it's a friend of mine."

"A friend?" Thud was being knocked for a loop. "Of yours?"

"Here they are." Hettie arrived, smiling the smile of a woman who does not know exactly why she is smiling, but who is pleased to ride the wave so long as it is willing to carry her. There was a man with her. "Hoshrum, Mr. Hughes. This is... I'm sorry, I never got your name."

The man's skin was dark, and his suit was darker still, a piece of velvet-black night slit from the sky and sprinkled with crushed diamonds, or perhaps the residue of stars that had died a long time ago, when night breezes whispered and birds sang in sycamore trees now vanished.

His hair might have been as white as the snow nestling under the hedges outside, but it was lit up with the light of aurora borealis, the kind you might spot from the prow of a ship sailing the black and gelid waters of cold Daethumberland.

His eyes were the most striking feature of all.

They were yellow, and very beautiful.

"His name is Frank Gallant," said Hughes. "And those words that rose in us were from him, Thud. Frank is the master of the grand entrance."

"Hughes, my man." Frank opened his arms. "Gimme some candy sublime and a damn good time."

Hughes obliged, squeezing his old friend in the tightest of hugs.

"It's so good to see you."

"You too. Hey, let me look at you. How long's it been?"

"Nine years, give or take."

"That sweet clock time sure is in a hurry, huh? Hi," Frank said to a thoroughly disgruntled Captain Thud. "I'm Frank Gallant."

"The Dream Warrior." Thud's expression clouded. "How did I know that?"

Frank grinned and tapped the side of his nose with a finger.

Hughes was grinning too. He didn't seem to be able to stop.

"I'm just so happy you're here," he admitted. "Cate's going to pitch a fit."

"May I ask *why* you are here, Mr. Gallant?" said Hettie.

"Madam," said Frank. "Under your roof, the conversation flows as directed by the river of your whim."

"Oh!" She clutched her husband's hands. "Hoshrum, isn't that nice?"

"Nice as ice-cream dear. Though I'm not sure about the dairy farm, in this case, i.e. *the source*. Well, Mr. Gallant? Why are you here?"

"This case," Frank repeated.

"Pardon?"

Frank reached into his amazing suit, and with a rustle of fabric he produced a news clipping. It was from a paper called *The Klepu Inquirer.* Hughes knew that Klepu was the capital of Ikahagua. Thanks to that ravenous beast called colonization, the headline was in Champleurs and read: *Étain givré pour Jacques.*

"Anyone's Champleurs up to snuff?" said Thud.

"It means *Tinfrost for Jack,*" said Hughes. "Frank? You're not here to help us solve this thing, are you?"

"As it so happens, I am." The aurora in Frank's hair lightened from emerald green to mint, then sea foam, then chalky blue. He gestured toward the back of the parlor. "And I did not come alone."

It was at that moment that their ears registered something coming down the chimney flue.

They all turned, very slowly.

Out of the dark chute emerged a long-fingered hand. It gripped the mantelpiece and pulled. The fireplace seemed to give birth to a tall, thin figure. He wore a suit the smog and dust had barely touched, as though it had been designed for someone who enjoyed a messy lifestyle. The figure patted his bald head, reached back into the flue, and retrieved a coal-colored hat.

He parted the Thuds' hung stockings and stepped forward like Father Tinfrost's ignoble cousin who has spent time in jail and who brings the sort of gifts no one wants to receive.

If he says ho-ho-ho I'm going to snap, Hughes thought. *I'm going to snap in two and bad jokes and paper crowns are going to fall out.*

The figure seemed to feel the stares in the room.

He turned his gaunt face with its sunken eyes upon them all.

"There was a bird's nest in your chimney," said Mr. Glint. Reaching up one of his terrible hands, he wiped feathers and runny egg yolk from his lips. "It's gone now."

***

In Redspire, where the members of the Scarlet Citadel made their home, there were eighty-eight floors that everyone knew about, and two they did not.

Those two were almost as secret as Hughes' Performance. If you knew about them, you either worked or lived there.

One was below the ground floor of the tower. It was a cavernously large place full of scientifically minded men and women who spent most of their time reading graph paper and admitting how little they understood their field of study, and that the prospect of ignorance was, on the whole, rather exciting.

This floor also contained a door to another world. That world was called Eurydice, which some people referred to as the dungeon dimension, and which other people called "paydirt" because if you went there and killed a few monsters, you inevitably returned home with heavy pockets. Credits make the world go round, true, but they also make other worlds worth exploring.

The other secret floor could be found at the very top of Redspire. For security purposes it was impossible to reach unless you knew the passcode. Even then, you'd need to know that there *was* a passcode in the first place. Which goes a long way toward saying that it was isolated, the secretest of secret places.

Lonely too, if you cared about that sort of thing.

It was night, and at the summit of Redspire the tower walls were shaggy with ice, the lupine wind roved around howling, and moonlight blew moon-colored hoops in the snow clouds.

Somewhere far away there was a city. The people there did city things.

Up here, a jailer without any prisoners looked up from her book as the tock-tocking sound of shoes on the pinewood stair signaled someone approaching.

The jailer was the daughter of a self-important man and a prostitute who was important to other people.

Ten years ago when she'd met a young man named Gormon Hughes, she'd had an appetite for horrors that only a thirteen-year-old girl could conjure. Should a genuine horror have materialized before her, she probably would have done what any precocious and confident girl would have, and poked it in case it jiggled interestingly. In those days, she looked eagerly out at the world through eyes with deep purple pouches under them, as though she hadn't had a proper sleep in her whole life.

At twenty-three she still looked exhausted, only she no longer held that aura of girlish enthusiasm that said: *my favorite word is 'decapitate' because you can really hear the gristle in it. What's yours, and why are you backing away slowly?*

Now her aura was nervous, and she looked ill. Not ill as in feverish or jaundiced. Just starved or parched of something vital.

She looked sick.

The footsteps were getting closer.

Reluctantly, the jailer closed her book, which was called *The Little Book of Palindromes*, and sat on the edge of her bed. Her lips thinned into a hyphen. At the last moment, she tugged them up in a smile that didn't quite reach her eyes.

Lady Wendy Dragontail stepped into the comfortable reading light cast by the jailer's anbaric lamp. Here stood the most powerful woman in the city. Her hair, which had gone prematurely white in her girlhood, was pulled back sensibly with an ordinary pink scrunchy. Her face was lined: jolly lines crinkling her hazel eyes and severe lines framing the strong mouth. She wore sweatpants, hard-soled slippers, and two ill-fitting sweaters. The slippers were embroidered with little cloaked men bearing holly branches meant to signify Father Tinfrost.

In her hands was a tray.

"Good evening, Estelle."

"Good evening, Lady."

"I'm given to understand that tonight's dish is *le petit agneau avec jus de viande, légumes, et la purée de pomme de terre.* Our new chef is from Champleurs and delights in his mother tongue," said Wendy, setting the tray down on the bedside table. "I confess, to my uncouth imagination, it seems to be a... What would you call it? A splat perhaps. A splat of cottage pie."

"Yummy."

"To be sure. Also there is a bottle of red wine and... yes, I do believe these are mints covered in dark chocolate."

This last bit struck a puzzling chord in Estelle. "Is it Saturday?"

"It is."

"Oh." Well it must be. Mints covered in dark chocolate were the proof. Their presence on her tray meant it was indeed the third Saturday of the month, just as cream-filled eclairs meant the fourth Friday or gingernut biscuits meant the first Tuesday. The beginnings of a frown furrowed her brow. Hadn't she thought... Yes, she had been *sure* it was...

But oh. Oh no, but if it *was* Saturday, that meant it was the 17th of December, which meant Wendy would...

The thought was too awful to finish.

"And let us not forget the most filling meal of all," said Wendy Dragontail, oblivious to Estelle's fledgling despair.

From the droopy pocket in the back of her sweatpants she withdrew a book. The cover showed a woman who was without doubt some evolved species of princess. The good looks were one thing, but the crown was a dead giveaway. The princess was curled up in deep slumber in the depths of a dark wood. Standing vigil over her was a dragon, its wings folded against its lean reptilian body, its bullet head in profile, its scales like hammered pearls in the moonlight.

Estelle took the gift solemnly. "Thank you very much."

"Think nothing of it. What did you make of the last one?"

"It was good. Lots of twists and turns. An important character died at the end."

"Oh yes?"

"He was blood eagled by the villains. Blood eagling is quite interesting, actually. It's not at all what people seem to think it is. What you do is, you get this really fantastically big eagle, and you—"

"I dare say the subject would be a very suitable one," said Wendy, "after supper."

"Hm. Yes." Estelle deflated a bit. "Yes, it would be."

She picked up her fork and played about with her cottage pie.

It looked tasty, but she found she had no appetite.

December 17th, oh hell.

Her Ladyship approached Estelle's bookshelves, which had over time developed their own geography; separate countries of romance, cities of poetry, suburbs dedicated to particular authors of fantasy and science fiction, as well as chaotic apartment blocks merging all of these categories together. "You've amassed quite the collection."

"I haven't read them all from cover to cover," said Estelle modestly. "Only most."

"Fiction never loses its luster for you? You wouldn't like, say, a computer? Break up the monotony?"

"No, your Ladyship." The screens hurt her eyes. They hadn't used to when she was a girl. Over the years that particular ache had wormed its way into her. Books, on the other hand, they never bit. Lovingly she broke their spines. Lovingly they threw her parties where paper throbbed with second, third, and fourth lives, lives beyond counting, and the ink barrels never ran dry.

Without taking her eyes off the bookshelves, Wendy said, "Estelle. It is that time of year again."

Estelle squirmed internally.

"Your Ladyship..."

"Tinfrost Eve being a week away, I would like to extend you an invitation to the feast. I can guarantee you that there will be a private booth. No one will talk to you or eat with you unless you say so. Many people have asked for you."

"That's... lovely of them, but..."

What Wendy said next made Estelle flinch. It had made her flinch the year before, and the year before that, and holy God it did so now.

"I think it prudent to mention that Hughes is especially hopeful you'll make an appearance this year."

"Your Ladyship is so kind to offer," Estelle managed, wishing this wasn't happening. Images of such amazing dread were thunderclapping inside her, she could hardly bear it. Fingernails, fingers, hands, all capable of being held out to her, expectant: *shake me shake me shake me!* Endless featureless faces like sanded mannequins. And the noises! Repulsive garbled pots of words stirred up and spilled out without a moment's consideration for those who would rather staple their ears closed than listen to another second of it.

Wendy continued blithely. "At a moment's notice, I could have word sent to your mother, Gwendolyn. I'm sure she would be delighted to see you."

Her mother?

The very idea of seeing her mother—*of Mum seeing ME*—made her lightheaded, dizzy, instantly nauseous.

"No," she murmured, hanging her head to hide the tears that stung her eyes, and which she was not sure she could contain much longer. "Thank you very much but no. Your Ladyship won't think less of me, I hope. I... I just couldn't."

There was a pause. Then a pressure, another body joining her on the edge of the bed. A weathered, blue-veined hand gave her smooth, shaking ones a pat. And another. Two pats. *There, there.*

"No, my dear," said Wendy, her voice gentle. "I do not think less of you."

Estelle Corlum looked into the face of the woman who was ruler of a city in all but name. The jolly lines crinkling her eyes. The severe ones framing her mouth.

Despite all that this amazing woman dealt with on a daily basis, she still made time to come up here to the eighty-ninth floor. She brought food, and drink, and wonderful things like mints covered with dark chocolate. More nourishing than any of those she brought company, the only one Estelle could stomach.

"You're too good to me," she said, tears spilling down her cheeks.

The weathered hands did their thing. Two pats. *There, there.*

And without another word, The Last Dragon left the top of the tower, not to its princess, but to its jailer who kept no prisoners.

After a while Estelle felt better. She ate her cottage pie, chased it with water she cooled with ice from icicles that hung outside her bedroom window. She felt better still. Then came her reading, which involved chocolates and rich, mellow wine that held notes of oak and amber and juniper. On its nightly travel, the moon began to peep and then to peer into her room with silver binoculars. She shut the curtains. She was happy.

Before bed, she explored the eighty-ninth floor, as was her custom. The word "expansive" came to mind, but in reality it was much bigger than that. There was always something new to find.

That evening she discovered a series of pipes that started somewhere she couldn't determine, and which went through a locked door. When she was fourteen, Wendy had told Estelle that her father, Walsingham Dragontail, had stashed many of the spoils of his career on the eighty-ninth floor. In his dotage he had lost the keys and had forgotten what doors they opened in the first place.

Listening at the keyhole, Estelle heard clunking thunking sounds and decided through this door lay the heating system. She'd always wondered where that was.

Past the enormous, suspended skeleton of a dragon (which Wendy assured her was only a replica, though Estelle had her suspicions) was a ramble of rooms, one of which contained the bathroom where she cleaned her teeth and washed herself.

It was during this part of her evening routine that she sucked in a lungful of air.

She had forgotten to ask Wendy if she would tell Hughes that she, Estelle, thanked him for his hopes that she attend the banquet this year, that she gratefully declined, and that she hoped he was well. The message would have been stiff, and it didn't even scratch at how fiercely she missed her old friend, but hey, it was *something*.

Now he would have to settle for a curt refusal from Wendy.

You stupid bitch, she scolded herself. *Stupid selfish freak hermitted up here, think you're too good for politeness, self-centered bitch.*

Upset, she hurried back to bed, where her *Little Book of Palindromes* soothed her. It was toward the beginning of her stay on the eighty-ninth floor when she had discovered her love of palindromes. There was a comforting endlessness to them, not to mention how clever they were when teased out. Live Evil was one. Do Geese See God was another. Nurses Run usually made her giggle—Where to? Where to? Most splendid of all was this: Was it a cat I saw?

Back to front. Front to back.

Pure delight bounded by the first capital letter and the full stop.

"Gormon Hughes doesn't work," she said as drowsiness began to tug her toward sleep. "Sehguh Nomrog. How horrible."

Silence.

Somewhere far away there was a city. People there did city things.

Below her there was a whole tower's worth of commotion.

Here, there was silence, rimed in frost and sealed in stories behind a thousand book spines and lingering over her supper and the empty wine bottle.

There was a silence here that told you that you were not a girl anymore. That you had grown up, only instead of coming out of yourself as everyone had led you to believe you would, you came a little more inward every day until everything outside you seemed strange and somehow foreboding.

In the silence you could hear the palindromes going endlessly.

Back to front. Front to back.

"I really do miss you, Hughes," whispered Estelle.

She slept.

Act Four

Something Sharp

Chapter Ten

Sunday arrived.

It became clear to anyone who was paying attention that no one had killed anyone else on Saturday. There were no sinister messages written on any walls. Squirrels had been seen on rooftops, and pigeons, lice-covered possums, and the occasional cat, but no people.

In conversation with his editor, the journalist Tracer Gogen was faced with the choice of running a foreign interest piece about the Dengue Plague or reusing some pared-away material he had for the Jack story. Either way, he wasn't going to headline.

He went with the plague.

Lots of journalists from other papers joined him.

The absence of Jack's name from the broadsheet stands and tabloid stalls seemed to oxygenate Leonidas District. People breathed easier than they had in weeks. Further adding to their comfort were rumors that a member of the Scarlet Citadel had become involved in the case.

Who? said some.

Don't quote me on it, said others. But I heard it was Wendy's Bloodhound himself.

Well, said some, with the air of proud roosters, it must be over and done with then. He's a fine chap that Hughes. Comes from around here. Nice to know he's not forgotten his roots.

And so on.

In her flat above the liquor store and below the studio of an amateur saxophonist, the schoolteacher Rummy Lou sipped from a mug of piping-hot instant coffee. She had the slightly hunted look common to both academics and veterans of jungle warfare. Sunday classes, designed for those students who were desperate or delinquent enough to need them, were always a bummer. But three more shifts and she and the rest of the faculty would be free. Twenty days (almost three weeks!) of not correcting sloppy homework, of no breaking up fights, of no trigonometry or Corinthian history or supervising study hall. She and her girlfriend Brenda (also a schoolteacher, smart, ambitious, fluent in Champleurs, and *trés, trés* fetching) had no plans. Likely they would share a kiss, fall onto a convenient sofa, and slowly congeal into the springs. Vegetation of the soul. Bliss.

Finishing her coffee, Rummy Lou slipped on her shoes and headed out into the snow.

She would be the first.

In Taggart House, the custodian, Paulie Manzarek, listened to the bluesy music coming through his headphones, his head bobbing up and down rhythmically, his hands around the mop he'd dubbed Mae because that seemed like a good name for a mop. Right about then Mae was busy taking care of something one of the guests had upchucked, and Paulie was busy taking care of Mae, keeping her clean with his bucket (as yet unnamed) souped full of kettle-heated water and WAX-O surface disinfectant. The guest who had vomited was none other than Susabeth Dennings, who was lying half-in and half-out of her bed. Paulie did not know why Susabeth was in Taggart House, and that suited him just fine. Far as he was concerned, guests like Susabeth kept him in a job. Their histories were their own, just as his was his. Let the music play. Hurrah for the blues and neurodivergent folks. He set Mae aside and gently propped Sue Dennings back in her bed, though not before thanking her for getting her sick on the floor instead of on her bedclothes. Floors were a cake walk compared to bed clothes.

From his portable device the music underwent a change; one album blending into another. Paulie bobbed his head along, retrieving Mae and the bucket. *No rest for the wicked*, he thought. *And none for me either.*

He would be the second.

Preparing for morning mass in his sacristy, the reverend Taylet Gordon couldn't stop tonguing the bump on the inside of his right cheek. Goddamn bastard was sore, probably an ulcer. Well, no wonder he had a fucking ulcer. His congregation was shrinking every year. It's not safe, their carefully diplomatic, simpering shitheel letters confided. Our neighbors might catch on. My husband might find out. Parents, coworkers, the streetbeaters. Hell, fellow churchgoers. Rats in the walls, the usual paranoid crap. The message wasn't even a veiled one. The old church had been rendered illegal a long time ago. You, the reverend Taylet Gordon, may risk your neck at your leisure, but you will not risk ours.

Sinner was too good a word for them. Reprobate shits. The risk was theirs to bear, the highest risk of all, the one that fringed the sacred ectoplasm of the soul. Couldn't they see that? Was he so impotent a preacher that this fundamental thing had fucking failed to sink the fuck in?

Taylet Gordon paged the gospel, selecting a sermon. Something hot-blooded to warm them up in the cold pews he'd built with his brother Sam (another dirty shit) all those years ago when things were better, when Leonidas had the faith. He tongued his ulcer. It hurt.

He would be the third.

Laura Clemp, who was a popular young entrepreneur in the brothel *Pamplona*, plucked her eyebrows. Barclay Waters, fifth child in a family of ten and determined to drag himself from poverty, ignored his sister's pleas for him to unjam the stick from his ass and play with her instead of studying for the bar exam, which would plot the course for the rest of his life (or so he thought). Alma Coalman, who worked for the Sequins Messenger Club to pay the electricity bills and keep food on the table, headed toward the apartment of Cate Jubilee and Gormon Hughes. Karoliina Vaaca, recently emigrated from a small ice-fishing village in Daethumberland and now happily employed as a cocktail bartender in the *Rhinestone Rhino*, turned over under her warm blankets, gladly snoozing the morning away.

Fourth, fifth, sixth, seventh.

Saturday was over. Sunday had begun.

Buzzing and acrawl with bugs, the shadow moved on.

***

On his side of the kitchen, a pan of garnished sausages and bacon and black pudding sizzled. On hers, tomatoes were chopped, yogurt was stirred with honey from the Citadel's apiary, and butter spread gold-yellow over toast.

Hughes plated it all up. Cate cutleried and napkined.

"When's your meeting with Wendy?" he asked across the breakfast table.

"After the funeral. Two being cremated, one interred in the botanic garden."

"Who?"

"Robbie."

Hughes nodded, conscious of how juicy and sweet the tomato was in his mouth. Measured against the grave, breakfast was suddenly beautiful. "I'll go if you like. Can always meet Thud later."

"Hold up a murder investigation on account of the dead? The living won't thank you."

"Good point. Pomegranate juice?"

"Orange, please."

He poured. "Frank hasn't aged a day."

"I'd say his eyes are older."

"You'd say correctly."

"How does he intend to help you and Thud? I never asked you."

"Remember how we defeated the Nightjar Coven? After I get a few interrogations under my belt, Frank's proposing to take me into Nigel Ulmerston—or one of the culprit's—dreams."

"The Coven lived inside a dream realm," said Cate. "I doubt whatever is infesting people can be found through Frank's power."

"I agree. But delving into dreams will yield results, I think. Something Ulmerston said: *Everyone needed a lie down.* He said it right as my Performance was wearing off. What does that suggest to you?"

"That it was an idea kicked up from his subconscious mind. A thought slipping through the net, so to speak."

"Exactly. *Lie down* implies rest. It also implies death. I think the force that Thud calls Jack is puppeting these innocent people and then wiping... no... paving over their memories so they can't remember what they've done."

Cate nodded, swallowing a rind of bacon. "Ulmerston believes he's laid his coworkers down for a nap."

"When in reality he's killed them, yeah. I think using Frank's dreamstriding abilities, we can access the memory. It might give us a clue as to what we're dealing with."

"Clever."

From where Hughes sat, Cate's face was posed sidelong. His eyes traced the line of her jaw, the small shell of her ear peeping through her hair, the look of meditative distance in her eye. She looked reposeful. Thoughtful. And silhouetted by the dining room window, her brushed hair was a cloud full of a sunset's reddest promises.

"You look amazing today, Cate."

She turned to him, surprised. "Thank you, Hughes. You too."

"I need a shave."

"Don't slander your bristles."

"Okay. I won't. I'll shave them though."

"You wouldn't!"

"Do not tempt me, Mees Joobillee. Eet ees my raze-horr."

They shared a grin. It was the first goofy moment they'd had since the baby died. The fact registered with them both at the same time. Both looked away. Both experienced their own brand of shame, questioning why they should be ashamed, then feeling it anyway.

Their telephone rang.

"Yes?" said Hughes.

"Sequins messenger down here for ya, Mr. Hughes. Will I buzz em up?"

"Thanks."

The messenger told Hughes that a Jolene requested his presence at The Foundry at his earliest convenience. Hughes tipped generously and shut the door.

"Would you have time to come with me?" he asked Cate.

She checked her watch. "Should do. Everything okay?"

"I've a present for you."

"I'll get my boots on."

Which gave Hughes ample time to wash the dishes. Cate's hobnail boots had more laces than a queen's doily set. Glancing out the window it looked like Sunday had the makings of frostbite. Begloved, bebooted, and bejacketed, they set out.

"I forgot to tell you," said Cate. "Something interesting has happened to my hobnail boots."

"Something interesting like you've unlocked new power? Or something interesting like they've been knocking heels without telling you."

"Naughty. New power, of course. I felt it tingle all the way up to my head. Get this, darling: I can pull enemies into reflections *and keep them alive*."

"Really? Going through won't kill them anymore?"

"If I want them to die, I suspect they will. And if I don't, they won't."

"Only enemies, not friends?"

"I'm not sure. You know magic is terribly nebulous. Like concrete that refuses to set into an easy shape. With a friend I'd be scared to try."

Hughes considered the implications. "Interesting."

"Right?"

"Well, I'm sure you'll put it to good use, Cate."

He was wrong about that. Hughes was a man of many talents but foresight was not one of them. No, Cate would not put her new skill to good use.

She would put it to splendid, madcap, utterly and completely bananas use.

But that would not be for a while yet.

Their brisk jaunt through white snowy streets splashed with color gave Hughes the impression he was one of very few people in a tiger cage who knew the tiger, though presently absent, would not remain absent for very long.

Children tossed fistfuls of wadded ice. Retail workers on their smoke breaks leaned in their doorways, gossiping and adding their own tarry plumes to the cleaner ones everyone else was breathing. Cackles came through the open window of a hair salon. Whistling, a cheesemonger with no arms slid her stumps into a stationary set of mechanized limbs to cut slices of sharp smelling comté for a couple visiting from Jaenqui-Across-The-River. Radios played. Jived-up melodies hitched rides on the breeze.

"You'd think there hadn't been a murder in years," muttered Hughes.

"A cynic would say it's the modern news cycle making the span of our memories shorter." Moving with effortless grace, Cate reached down and plucked a little boy out of the path of a cyclist. She set the plump, giggling, ruddy-cheeked kid down and walked on. "I think people just have a larger capacity for happiness nowadays."

"You think so?"

She looked bemused. "You're seeing the same street I am, right?"

Hughes could only agree. And narrowly dodge snowballs.

They arrived at The Foundry. It was ten past eight in the morning, and everywhere they looked the Jolenes, who evidently kept the same schedule as farmers, were already tucking into the longest part of the day and looking forward to lunch.

"Cate Jubilee, as I stoke and smith!"

"Jo!"

The two embraced.

"It's wild. I met a woman who's even brawnier than you," Cate said. "Her name is Eilandri Titansgrave."

"Well, with a name like that, you've got to be a biggun or a littlun. Like when you meet a fellow called Big Dave and he's either so huge you could pop a sail up his bum and call him a boat, or a complete titch with barely a bum to speak of. But enough about tushes. Come inside." Jo guided them into the large inlet where she had her workbench. As ever tools of every size and shape were pegged and hanging from the walls: tongs, assorted bellows of fragrant brown leather, bags of coke and other grainy catalysts, prizers, hammers wide and narrow, and of course there in the midst of it all was the workbench itself, accompanied by an anvil of chipped iron.

Hughes shivered happily, unbuttoning his coat. "It's so toasty in here."

"Ah. That would be my cunning heating system," Jo explained. "What I do is, I take my furnace, see, and I put lots and lots of coal in it. Then I light the burny bit on fire. In a jiffy the place is tingly warm."

"I never know when you're joking," said Cate.

"That's because I'm so cunning. Got something for you."

With much ceremony and ahem-hem-hemming, Jo handed Hughes and Cate two identical sheets of thick paper. One side was blue. The other was red.

"Well?" Jo said expectantly.

There was a pause.

"What's happening?" said Cate.

"Oh right, right. So Hughes asked me if I could make him a telephone that works even if one person is in Iphigenia or Eurydice and the other person is here in Corinth. Told him there wasn't a pickled penny's chance. But I've been working on this prolapse..."

"Prototype," said Hughes while Cate got a hold of herself.

"Prototype, exactly. What you do is, you write a letter on one side, and the other person can write back on the other. Message ought to fade in a day or so." Jo planted both hairy hands on her hips. "Means you two can keep in touch while one of you is off roving in other peculiar places."

A moment ago Hughes had frowned at the paper handed to him. Now he was practically radiant; he was that pleased. "Red's for Cate. Blue's for Hughes."

Jo gave an endearing little chuckle. "Caught that, did you? Yeah, well. I do love a rhyme, me."

"Little gestures from a big heart."

"Ah, lay off it you soppy old thing. My ears are pink enough as is."

The letters were a marvelous innovation, less than Hughes had desired but much more than he'd hoped for. Now and then Jolenes going about their business would peek into the inlet to see what all the fuss was about. The three friends spoke and traded stories. It was a good visit. Its mood was as cozy as the temperature, yet as Cate lavished praise and delight on Jo, an odd disquiet began to grow in Hughes. Try as he might, he simply couldn't put his finger on it. It would niggle at him until they left The Foundry, and after a fond farewell with Jo, he set it aside, knowing the idea would present itself when it was good and ready.

The snowfall was heavier. Bursts of choppy gust swirled the flakes, sticking them like postcard stamps to Hughes' coat collar.

"Quarter to nine," said Cate. "I'd best hurry."

Hughes, who was fifteen minutes late to his rendezvous with Captain Thud, concurred wholeheartedly.

"Almost forgot," he said, leaning in to peck his lover on her cheek. "Thank you for the tomatoes, toast, and honey yogurt."

"Thank you for the sausages, bacon, and black pudding."

"I thought the pudding was overdone."

Cate kissed him, once quick and playful, once long and slow and sensuous.

She pulled away, gave him a wink.

"It was perfect," she said. "Later, handsome."

***

The feeling that he was a knight being outfitted for war was inescapable.

Over the course of their morning chat in a grotty Leonidas café, Thud armed Hughes with knowledge, armored him with strategy, and saddled him with the responsibility to use it correctly.

Having spent half the night on the telephone with retired coppers, Thud had gleaned valuable information. Thirty years ago those who had carried out their version of the They Are In Me murders, and who had later been committed to various countryside sanitariums and the city-based Taggart House, had over time made something tantamount to a full recovery. Pockets of amnesia forbade access to the memory of the actual killing, but the point was this: the killers' broken minds had repaired themselves. They had improved.

More interesting still: they had relapsed.

"When?" asked Hughes, intrigued.

Thud looked triumphant. "This year. The coppers I talked to last night are grouchy, grudge-bearing types. They never let the fact that the Jack case went unsolved go. So they kept tabs on the culprits, even after they got better. And now those same recovered people are back jabbering nonsense and staring at nothing."

Hughes thought of the headline. *Jack's Back*, it declared.

Jack's Back and the flies are buzzing again.

Thud took him through each incident.

Names, implements of murder, terms of sentence, and autopsy report details slotted neatly into files in Hughes' head. The vernacular of investigation. There was a craft to all this, and if Thud was not a master of it, he was damn close.

Explored one by one the differences between each murder in the Jack case were negligible, the commonalities staggering and irrefutable. The idea that Commissioner Vincent Winkles would turn his face from the situation appalled Hughes. Indeed, it seemed that while Thud had many a sympathetic ear bent his way at the station, his gruff persuasion had failed to galvanize the debatable might of the Leonidas police force into action. What help Thud could scrounge up amounted to insights pancaked one over the other, trickled in a syrup of bewildering apathy: maybe it is supernatural, maybe it isn't. Shrug it off and pass the donuts. This, the prevalent attitude of the streetbeaters.

The precinct cried out for reform, that was clear to Hughes.

"Reform takes time," said Thud. "It's revolution you want. That's quick."

"Don't you want it?"

"Sure. But when you've got a revolution on your hands, you're bound to get blood under your fingernails. And that's just for the crowd sifting about in the aftermath. In the middle of it all, right in the thick part where the future is uncertain and the past is unacceptable, so we're all making do with right here right now... During all of that there is a gibbet, and there are the people who've got to climb it, and there's the bloke at the top waiting for them."

"The axeman."

"Axeperson," said Thud. "Might be a lady. Probably do a better job of it than a man, if you ask me. Fewer cuts necessary, more results, that sort of thing."

"I suppose rapid change is too much to ask for," said Hughes, a twinkle in his eye. "Poor Vinny might lose his Winky."

Thud sputtered. "There's no cause for innuendo. Right when I was drinking my tea too."

"So sorry, Captain."

Thud grumbled to himself.

As the morning crept toward afternoon, it was mutually decided that Frank be kept in reserve for today. The list of interrogations was daunting.

Hughes rose, eyeing the street outside the café, feeling a surge of displeasure at the tempo of the wind. It was picking up. "I'm going to get started before the blizzard breaks."

"Blizzard?"

"Just a hunch."

"You might call on your friend first," Thud suggested. "The one who can see into the future. Might save some hassle. Divide the wheat from the chaff, if you take my meaning."

"I do. It's a good idea. Where are you off to?"

"*The Times* headquarters on Farrier's Row. I think Tracer Gogen and I need to have a little chat. Oh, don't give me that look. I'll ruffle his feathers a bit, that's all. Make sure he's on our side and not Jack's."

"I guess so. Luck, Thud."

"Same to you, lad."

Hughes was not two steps out of the café when he was intercepted by a ghost.

"Hector!"

Hector made a contented noise as Hughes threw his arms around him. "Such enthusiasm."

Hughes held his mentor at arm's length, grinning. "I missed you. I don't care who knows it. You there!" he said, accosting a ratty-looking man in a skewed bowler hat.

The man looked around, pointing at himself. "Me?"

"I missed my friend."

"That's nice. May I go now please?"

"By all means!"

The man hurried away, shooting mildly worried glances back at Hughes in case the young man did something odd, such as spontaneous combustion.

The whole display had succeeded in wringing a grin from Hector, something Hughes was not sure he'd ever seen since meeting his mentor, his confidant, his friend. "You're preposterous. And sentimental." He gestured to the scarf wrapped around Hughes' throat. Embroidered peonies bloomed across its hand-knitted softness. "And I have missed you too. Walk with me?"

"Course."

They fell into step together, the wind tickling Hughes' face with chilly rushes while having absolutely no effect on Hector, who was dead and therefore quite immune to the wind's ragamuffin mischief.

How long has it been since Hector and I saw one another?

Certainly not before November. Sometime in mid-autumn, then, he supposed.

That was around when...

Hughes' good mood evaporated as he remembered the rumors surrounding Hector and his siblings' reclusion. "How's Priam?"

"Poorly, I confess. My father is dying."

Then the rumors were true. The Old Trojan, dying. Hughes had never had much cause to speak with Priam King, though he was close with the man's children.

The dead ones, at any rate.

"I'm sorry to hear it, Hector." He hesitated. "Can I ask... what does that mean for you? For Cassandra and Paris?"

"Nothing unexpected. This second life we live is thanks to his magic item, the Crown of Troy. Once Priam dies, the item will cease to function. Cassandra, Paris, and I will follow our father into the grave."

"That's... God, that's terrible."

Hector shrugged languidly. "What is the poet's line? *Do not go gentle into that good night... Rage, rage against the dying of the light.* Tempting a dancer as anger is while the light called 'Hector' dims, I find my current blissful acceptance the more attractive partner by far. I'll go gentle enough."

"But what about Kim... I mean Creusa."

"What about her?"

"She's your sister. And more importantly, Priam's daughter. Most pressing of all, she's *alive*, Hector. Magic items can be passed on, right? They're hereditary. So... if your father dies, then Creusa could take up his crystal crown. You'd be saved."

"No, Hughes." Hector's tone was stern. "I confess you are of a mind with her in that she would do it willingly, but no. What you both suggest puts Creusa in danger, and the living must not pay the toll given to the dead. Cassandra, Paris, and I are in agreement."

"I don't understand."

"Of course you do. Have one of your Hard Thinks, my bright fellow."

Hughes gave him a despairing look. A Hard Think usually worked a treat, but right now he didn't need one. He knew why his ex-girlfriend couldn't be expected to put on her father's crown. It was an ugly truth, but yeah, he knew it.

"Occasional Morphology," he said. "The moment Priam donned the crown its magic wasted the tissue in his muscle. Made him feeble. I'd heard about that. Thought it was only a rumor, but I can tell from your expression it's true. What happened to your dad might not happen to your sister. But it might. You and Paris and Cassandra... you just want her to be okay."

Hector reached up, adjusting the scarf he'd gifted his pupil a long time ago.

"Death has waited patiently for Troy's firstborn son. So yes," he told Hughes and the snowy December afternoon at large, "yes, a gentle end for me."

Hughes didn't know what to say. So he said, rather meekly, and feeling more than a little trite and useless, "Is there anything I can do?"

Hector surprised him by replying, "Oh yes. If you're willing."

"You must be joking. Hector, of course. Anything."

"Anything?"

Tension now, no soft back-and-forth between friends. Theatrically minded as he was, Hughes was not one to miss a cue. In a voice as serious as drawn steel, he said, "I swear it on my tongue, my wit, my strong sword arm. Anything you ask."

"Noble of you."

"Not me," said Hughes. "Only loyal."

"What have I done to earn such fealty?"

Hughes gave him a look that summed up a decade of lessons, insights, supportive moments, favors, and a great deal more besides, expressing the idea that what Hector had done to earn such fealty was, in fact, lots.

This had the intended effect. In a moment the tension was whisked away along with a column of snow crystals in a cold gust.

Hector stopped. "We're here."

Hughes looked up. The pub was called *The Maedar.* Beneath peeling paint its sign showed a man with long green hair that was supposed to seem snakelike but which in reality looked as though the man had headbutted a mound of seaweed.

"Are we getting a pint?" said Hughes.

Hector sighed and went inside.

Oathbound, Hughes followed. "Anything" apparently included accompanying his friend into dingy Leonidas pubs at one o'clock in the afternoon.

Inside it was dark and ill-favored, with the air tasting of imitation mint leaves tossed from a grubby jar into mojitos you could clean toilets with. Two anbaric lamps flickered feebly over the bar. There were bottles and taps, and even a barkeep, although he was not fat or merry as in many of the stories Hughes had grown up reading, but thin and jaundiced yellow with liver disease, and poisonous-looking as a snake's tooth.

A neon anaconda ran the length of the pub's floor, winding between tables, its light dead in the daylight and unlikely to fizzle come the evening.

Surly and cleaning their pipes with apocalyptic cocktails, *The Maedar*'s patrons ignored them. All but one.

At a table by the bar, waving at them, sat none other than...

"Tommy?"

"*Bonjour*, Monsieur Hughes. *Asseyez-vous.*"

Hughes felt as though he'd been blasted by an autumnal leaf blower on max setting.

When he'd first met Tommy Fahrenheit, the man had certainly made an impression. Tommy defined himself by a creed that Hughes still did not completely understand, but which nevertheless was called ethnographic somatism. Cate had described it in simple terms: Tommy was serious about his body. Beneath a tumble of auburn curls and prominent features that harkened back to his homeland of Champleurs, Tommy's muscular form rippled like a lake being attacked by pebbles.

At least it had. Things had changed.

Redspire was a big tower. You lost touch with certain people. After a few pageant fights by Tommy's side, Hughes had quickly decided that The Hippodrome was not his scene. Crowds and applause were well and good, but something about killing monsters while the popcorn munching or TV-glued audience gawked made him oddly uncomfortable. After that he had seen Tommy in passing over the years, attended a few events together, that kind of thing, but Hughes would not have been able to tell you the last time he'd actually spoken to the man for all the credits in Eurydice.

Sitting on a wonky-legged stool by a tall table in a pub called *The Maedar*, Tommy looked terrible. His usually clean-shaven face was tarred in patchy stubble. Veins marbled his eyeballs. Lank, greasy-hair framed a face gripped by such misery, Hughes could hardly believe it. He reeked of sweat and wine. Dear God, but unless he was very much mistaken, Hughes could see the beginnings of a *gut* puffing out Tommy's midsection.

As they sat down with him, Tommy gestured to their surroundings.

"Is this not the bleakest hovel in hell? *Je suis désolé.* Nowhere else will serve me booze."

"Why not?" asked Hughes, although in his heart he knew.

"The girl was from here."

Hughes felt a gray bleakness settle on him as the meaning of that statement sank in. Less than a fortnight ago, Tommy had failed to put a monster down at The Hippodrome. It had gotten into the crowd. Eleven people died, one of them a little girl. Hughes suddenly thought of the copper at the Leonidas Precinct. He'd mentioned the girl because he was related to her. *She was four-and-one-quarter,* the streetbeater had said. *Poor thing flew like a doll.*

"Hughes is going to help you," said Hector.

It was so blunt it caught Hughes off-guard.

"What with?" he said.

Tommy grinned wretchedly. "I would like you to use your power on me."

Hughes stared at him, stunned.

"Nearby, a truck's gears linger in neutral. It carries tinned food, powdered milk for babies, morphine, penicillin, dissolvable steroid solutions. When I leave this shithole, it will also carry me. The truck's destination is Ereb, where the people are being mauled by the newest evolution of the Dengue Virus." Tommy's fingers prized a splinter from the tabletop. "I am being sent to the quarantine zone."

"By Wendy?"

"*Oui.* Who else?"

Who else indeed. Hughes mulled it over. A tactical banishment, all things considered. Remove Tommy from the city to let the crisis cool off. Meanwhile cultivate relations with the Ikahaguan Government. Two birds, one drunk Champleurs bastard. Classic Wendy Dragontail.

He couldn't help but notice the smudged glass topped up with wine in front of Tommy. It looked untouched, but not too far from the man's hand. Like a provocation. Or proof. But proof of what?

Hughes sat forward. "Tommy, what exactly are we talking about here? Whatever about your ex—exit." Fuck, he'd almost said *exile*. "I don't see how my power factors in. I can't turn public opinion in your favor, if that's what you're asking..."

"No. Not public opinion. Me. I would like you to change me. I have become disillusioned and have strayed from the path that ends in *splendif*. Alcohol and I have begun a romance." Tommy's voice was flat, strangely toneless. "*Malheureusement*, booze is a serial abuser. It destroys me, and I roll over to make space for it in bed. *Oui*, I tell it. Yes. Always yes." Bloodshot eyes flicked up from the splinter swiveling between clammy fingers, affixing Hughes' gaze. "I know of your ability to reach down into a man and transform who he is. Help me to say no, Monsieur Hughes. *S'il te plaît.*"

"Please," echoed Hector. "Hughes, before you protest that you cannot do it for moral reasons, because changing a person is wrong and you are a right-minded man, listen to me."

"Both ears," Hughes affirmed. "Double the dubiety, I'm afraid. But I'm listening, Hector."

"Tommy was recruited as a boy soldier during the war. He murdered many for his country, including me. I don't begrudge him this. Neither should you. He was eleven, palming blood instead of butterflies. And though I find his current beliefs about ethnographic somatism repugnant, I think here there is a decent jewel to be unearthed from the mud. He's willing to change but lacks the willpower to do so. Come Hughes," said Hector, gripping his student's shoulder. "You did say anything."

Hughes was studying the untouched wine in Tommy's glass. He felt hackled, backed into a nasty corner disguised as a five star hotel room. "I want to help you," he told Tommy. "It's complicated. And it might not work. That's important. *It might not work.*"

"*Je viex améliorer,*" said Tommy, and to Hughes' astonishment he heard a desperation in the man's voice that was whiny, almost childlike. He looked at Tommy, and Tommy said, "I want to get better."

Hughes looked into his face for a long time. He could feel Hector's eyes, condemned and glimmering with hope.

I want to get better. The phrase clanged with impossible force around Hughes' head, transmuting into something fuller and more arresting yet. *Je viex améliorer. My whole life is fucked up. Help me. Please. I want to get better.*

"Pick up the glass," he murmured.

They sat motionless, watching him.

"Pick up the glass, Tommy."

Tommy discarded the splinter he'd been toying with and obeyed.

"Touch it to your mouth."

"Hughes?" Hector looked uncertain.

Hughes ignored him. "Do it."

Not without reluctance, Tommy Fahrenheit lifted the glass. He pressed the smudged rim to his mouth.

"Part your lips."

"Hughes. Is this necessary?"

"Part your goddamn lips."

Tommy did it. He was calm, collected. But Hughes was observant. He saw the desire move like some black leviathan in Tommy's pupils.

"You want me to say glug it," said Hughes. "You want to say yes. Don't you?"

Tommy did. He wanted it so badly. His composure was cracking. *It's the smell*, thought Hughes. *The whiff of grape orchards in bloom. In this pub, this hovel from hell, it must smell like heaven.*

"It's asking you to move over in bed," he told Tommy, his voice coaxing. It was the voice of addiction. "It won't hurt you. It'll be sweet, Tommy. Sweeter than anything. Just move over. Take a sip. A slurp. Your throat's dry. Your lips are so parched. A gulp isn't so bad. It's asking you, Tommy. Asking you the most important question of all. If you will move over and let it into bed. Come on, now. Don't you want to?"

And when it seemed that Tommy must drink, drink or smash the glass and gouge out Hughes' coaxing throat or explode into guilty shreds of sanity (a doll, the dead girl flew like a doll), Hughes *pushed.*

His Performance rushed over the drunkard in a wave.

Tommy's face went slack.

Chimera, thought Hughes, and the Performance expanded and contracted, pulsing with newness and a power both terrific and consuming.

In the seconds that followed, Hector watched in silence so taut you could string bows with it. Heedless of the enormity of what was happening in his pub, *The Maedar's* barkeep and owner peered maliciously at his door, wishing more alcoholics would shuffle in, shamefaced and thirsty.

Eventually Hughes sat back. He didn't relax, so Hector couldn't either.

They both eyed Tommy Fahrenheit.

Who let the glass fall from his fingers.

It hit the table awkwardly, rolled, toppled, and shattered into shards the moment it hit the floor by the inert neon anaconda. Wine *glup-glupped*, spreading like a slow parasol across the floor.

"No," said Tommy wonderingly. "No, I do not think I will."

Feeling the (SUCCESS) gush through him, Hughes felt a hand close over his. He looked into Hector's face, which held such gratitude it nearly broke his heart.

Over the snarls of the barkeep and Tommy Fahrenheit's rising, delighted laughter, the ghost whispered six words that did break Hughes' heart. Then they put it back together, only wiser, enriched with ache. He grasped it then. Really fully got a hold of it. Hector would go gently into that good night. He might live to see another summer, or he might not make it to Tinfrost. This thing with Tommy was something he'd wanted to do before he died.

"My apt pupil," Hector said, his cinnamon carrot cake voice warm and happy. "My wonderful friend."

Chapter Eleven

Going to see Krys and The Mum no longer seemed a mere good idea. Rather it was absolutely necessary.

He'd thought he'd had it bad last night with the whole cartoon business, but his encounter with Tommy and Hector had left him feeling more vulnerable than he had since November punched out and December took over management. Shock is a tranquilizer; its numbing effects cannot be overstated. It was at times like this, when every conceivable emotion welled up and closed your throat for you, that Hughes wished for that, craved absence.

It didn't come.

Once Cate woke up in Saint Wilhemina's, absence, it seemed, was done with him. Who could afford it at a time like that? Not he. All of his investments were in love, and he'd spent it all on Cate and she on him.

Overhead the sky seemed immobile, the clouds sealing the afternoon in concrete. It was bitterly cold. Negotiating a parking lot forested in frost and overgrown with snow, and with a flock of abandoned shopping carts grazing in the crunchy white, he found himself lost in the word, vulnerability, what it meant for him, what it might mean for somebody else.

Estelle, for example. Poor Estelle. Agoraphobia had its talons in her, closing her off from everything instead of opening her up to the best years of her life. Just because she was isolated at the top of a bloody great big tower didn't mean she was out of harm's way. It just changed the shape harm took. Harm was slippery that way. Put up tough hard safeguards to protect your body and your mind, and nine times out of ten it would bypass them all and get you where you were soft. One time out of ten it would get you where you weren't just soft but vulnerable. That was what had happened to Estelle. Word had reached him that she wouldn't be coming to the Tinfrost Eve feast. Again. It got you down, it really did.

Then there was Thud. A more robust figure you couldn't hope to meet, yet put him in front of his direct superior and he was just another copper with his tail between his legs. Now he was slinking under the radar with Hughes.

That got him on to the victims in the Jack murders. Now *there* was vulnerability. The things he was feeling at the moment—sad, bitter, angry things—those didn't count. In fact most people in Leonidas (shit, the whole city) were unfortified and pregnable in ways that he had once been and now was not.

Out of the complicated bath of thought a simple bubble arose. A question. Before it popped he decided he would pose it to Wendy Dragontail when the time was right. *I wonder what she'll say.*

Wind fluttering his coat behind him, he trudged past the derelict datalog library and came to the garden that surrounded the cottage. Flowers were fabulously rare in the city, with many of the upmarket florists keeping pace with the profits of jewelers and bankers. The garden Hughes stepped into was walled-off from the rest of the District and heated with cylinders that beamed out absorbed sunlight, and in that lukewarm calm bloomed the most amazing range of flowers you could imagine. Being no student of botany, Hughes was content to let the formations and colors take the place of their proper names. There was fat-petaled purple, thin stalky blue, wide fan of yellow, feather of orange, white eye with a pink iris, tube of rusty red, hand of green with fingernails of black.

As for the cottage itself, it was made out of the bones of a carousel, such as you might find in a carnival. And a carnival is exactly where this exhibit had come from, The Rotbloom Carnival of Bright Oddments and Dark Delights. It had trundled into Corinth City many years ago and caused quite the stir. But now the cottage was all that remained of it, and of course its occupants, the carnival's former owners.

One of them was waiting for Hughes, as he knew she would be.

"Hello, Krys."

"Season's most convivial greetings to you, Hughes. You look very handsome if a bit rough around the edges today. I knew you'd come."

"Yes. I expect you did."

"The Mum is upstairs having a rest, but I'm bright-eyed and bushy-bottomed. Oh but you're cold! Come in at once. Don't stab him."

Hughes went stock-still, one foot over the threshold. "What?"

"Hm? Oh, I was telling my myrmidons not to stab you."

"Myrmidons?"

Krys gestured with both hands. Hughes squinted into the far corners of the room. Yes, there were two men in here, sitting in black chairs. With the fire unlit it was difficult to distinguish them. They had been in the process of getting up, but at Krys' word they sat down without a sound. Into their shadowy clothes he saw sharp things vanish. Hughes felt a shiver run up his back.

"Usually they keep out in their cars, watching the cottage, you know. But with the arrival of an Incarnadine in the city, Kim wants to be extra careful." Krys leaned close to him, her voice hushed and conspiratorial. "Kim never told us their real names, so I call them my myrmidons because it's a dreadfully fun word to say." Her brow clouded. "The Mum says I mustn't name them because they are dangerous men who lead horrible lives, and if they died I would be more upset since I went to the trouble of naming them. And anyway what was wrong with a solid name like Archimedes or Bernard, why did I have to make everything so silly?" Krys was cheerful again. "Then she grumbled away and made tea, so it all worked out in the end. How are you?"

"I'm fine, Krys." He followed her as she cartwheeled into the kitchen and put on the kettle. "Your dress is almost as lovely as you are."

She pirouetted so he might see that his compliment was well founded. The dress was daffodil-yellow with stylish straps girding the waist and shoulders. Every movement she made fanned the hem out like a flower opening its petalled face to the sun. "Splendid of you to say so. I get a new one every week."

In return for services rendered, Hughes thought. *Giving prophecies to my crime lord of an ex-girlfriend. Oh well, it really is a great dress.*

"And how are you, Krys? You seem in flying form."

"Soaring!" Her laughter filled the narrow kitchen. "Tie a basket to my toes and I should float away, hot-weather-balloon style!"

Hughes couldn't have resisted grinning if he tried. Still, those men that Krys had dubbed her myrmidons had given him a scare. They looked the sort to peel your eyelids off first and ask questions later. "And you're happy with your... current circumstances, then? You seem to be under close watch at the moment. One person's protection is another person's surveillance state, and all that."

She cocked her head, puzzled. "Kim wants to keep us safe."

"Yes," said Hughes, a bit stiffly. "I'm sure she does." He sighed. "As long as you're happy, I suppose. What was that about an Incarnadine? Aren't they those..." He debated several options, settling on, "Those really unpleasant men who work for the Emperor of Mysicordelia?"

Griffons and imps rose and fell as Krys shrugged her shoulders. When she had co-run the carnival, she had been called the Painted Girl, sporting enough tattoos to rival Cate Jubilee's growing collection. Unlike Cate, who covered spots of magical glass on her body with ink, Krys seemed to be tattooed for the sheer pleasure of it. Funny, looking at her now he was struck, not for the first time, that she never seemed to get any older. Ditto for the old woman who called herself The Mum slumbering upstairs.

He remembered asking her about it once.

"Krys?"

"Yes Hughes?"

"One of these days you're going to grow up, aren't you?"

"And become The Painted Woman? Never!"

"But it's not something you've got control over," he'd said, younger then, and more prone to argument. "I insist you tell me about it. Why don't you grow older?"

"Why do you?" was all she'd replied. "It seems terribly inconvenient."

The memory raised his flagging spirits. Not quite hot-air-balloon style, but hey, a little more fondness and he might get off the ground. He was glad he'd come.

Krys was rocking back and forth on her heels, her face expectant.

Hughes filed the knowledge of an Incarnadine in Corinth away for later perusal and turned to the reason he'd come.

"Krys, could you look into the future for me? I'm sorry to ask, but..."

He shut up as she took his face in her tattooed hands. Her palms were cool and soft.

"Never," she said and repeated firmly, "*Never* give an unwarranted apology. It thins out real sorrow. A sparing 'sorry' is one that lands true unless you're a walking disaster prone to mistakes. And you, Hughes, are no disaster. You are my shining star and darkest delight." She let her hands fall to her sides and inclined her head. "I shall look into the future for you."

"Thank you," he said quietly. "Thanks Krys."

"Just now I am too close to The Mum and can only see the present. Let's... Let... Oh." Her pupils shuttled rapidly, then her whole face lit up. "Two shadows, one pursuing the other. You're *after her*, aren't you, Hughes?"

"Her?" He took an unconscious step forward. Festooned in flowers, the kitchen window teemed with cold gray light. That same coldness seemed to sweep through him, electrifying him with icebolts of excitement. "Can you see the killer?"

"She doesn't know, Hughes. She knows the Cut-String King, but not you. She thinks she's the only shade in town."

"Where is she? Is she using magic?"

He watched in dismay as her forehead creased. "Is who using magic?"

"Nevermind," he said, bottling his frustration. Better to rage against the wind than Krys and The Mum's bright oddments. He forced a smile at her confused expression. "It's okay. You were going to show me the future. Someone is hurting our home, Krys. I've got to stop them."

"Hurting home? The scallywag! Come with me to the far corner of the kitchen. There we are. Hand me the biscuit tin."

"Here you go. Is that important?"

"Very."

Weird. She'd never needed a biscuit tin before.

"Is it like a talisman of some kind?" Hughes hazarded. "Like an object putting you in touch with the eerie mysteries of the universe?"

"Could be," said Krys, opening the tin. "Also I'm peckish. Ooh shortbread."

"Never underestimate the presence of a biscuit tin," Hughes muttered.

"Hm?"

"Don't mind me. How's that oracle vision thing going?"

"Any moment now, I'm sure. Bikky?"

"No, thanks."

"This one's got jelly crocodiles on it."

"Oh?"

"Look at the detail on the scales. They will meet you at the feast."

"Amazing," he said, admiring the jelly work of the biscuit makers. He looked up sharply. "What did you say? Who'll meet me at the feast?"

"They will." Krys smiled. "She and she and she."

"Try to be more specific. Who will meet me? What feast?" Cables connected in his mind. "The feast on Tinfrost Day?"

"Two will have your eyes, shadow man. The third will have your heart."

He was kneeling down in front of her, his hands clasped about her shoulders. When had that happened? It didn't matter.

"Please," he begged her. "Tell me what you see."

Her gaze clarified a bit. She was looking at him and *everything else.*

"I see a girl, brittle all the way through."

She might as well have dropped the cottage ceiling on him. Hughes' lips slid back over his teeth in an expression of incredible hurt. Spasm trembled his fingers. He was up and away from her in an instant.

"Hughes?" Krys was cogent, yanked back into the present again. She was looking at him with heartfelt concern. "What's wrong?"

"You don't remember what you said?"

"When? Oh Hughes, don't avoid my eyes. You look like I just walked over your grave."

No, he thought. *But you just rustled over my daughter's. Dead leaf words over a dead glass child.* "I um... Th-thank you again, Krys. I've got to go."

She stepped between him and the door to the main room.

"Stay. You're all crumbly. You need porridge and a hug to set you firm again."

"I can't," he said. "There isn't time."

"There's always time for porridge."

He hesitated. He wasn't hungry, not after that little brush with bad memories

(brittle girl)

(pudgy hand)

, but...

"Blackberry jam mixed in?"

Krys looked affronted. "Is this a house of jackanapes and jesters?"

"Doesn't look like it."

"How about misery thump-a-lumps?"

"None are forthcoming."

"No. That is because you are in a house of good things. A cottage of comfort and warmth. Here, in this happy hall," she said primly, "porridge and blackberry jam are the finest friends, and together, they are enemies of the *bad mood* and the *unwelcome frown.*"

This time he actively fought the grin. It happened anyway. "Damn your inky krakens, Krys. You've convinced me."

"Naturally," she said. And smiled. "Would you like your hug now, or afterward?"

What could he do? Not leave in a huff. It was impossible. She was the Painted Girl, her tattoos cyclopean and kaleidoscopic. She was Krys, and that look on her face would not take no for an answer.

"Well?" she said.

Hughes opened his arms wide. "Now sounds good."

***

Hughes spent the rest of the afternoon conducting interviews. With the help of Nurse Perky (her name was Ida Surries) he narrowly avoided those members of Taggart House staff itching to report the presence of Captain Thud or his accomplice to the commissioner.

Once Hughes was in the room with the sightlessly staring culprits, it was up to his Performance to yield results. That first day it didn't go well. In spite of the odds veering in his favor he got through to around one in every five people he spoke to. He could always allow some time to pass and retry the failed attempts, he supposed, but better to reconcile himself to the obvious now rather than later. *Some of these sad, dribbling shells of humanity will never speak to me.*

Thud hadn't needed to tell Hughes the goal of an interview portfolio is to establish patterns and uncover anomalies. Each testimony was compared against the others, superimposed like photographic images using computer software. It didn't take long for interesting things to emerge.

Only Hughes wasn't sure what to make of it.

It was just so damn *weird*.

He gave in to mental fatigue at a quarter of ten that evening. Ida distracted a group of other nurses while he snuck out the front door. Once this was over he owed her a deluxe package at the *Scriptorium and Flavored Tea Emporium*. All she could drink.

Outside under the vast black night the lane sloped down ahead of him. Distantly he could hear engines and raised voices, and he could smell the grease dripping off rotisserie pigeon and the chalky chocolate smell of cakes and nighttime pastries; the respiration of the Leonidas bazaar. Streetlamps glowed red, making the sidewalk drifts and the snowfall just as red. It was odd and very beautiful.

Heading back toward Diogenes Street, the cold did the work of five cups of coffee. His mind poured over the interviews, seizing large details and teasing them into small wafer-thin strands in case a pattern felt like offering itself up for study.

Broadly speaking, each of the murderers had led happy normal lives. Some had families, some didn't. Some were responsible for the fact that they no longer had families. None of them remembered the hours surrounding their crime or the act itself. It seemed a ridiculous thing to say, but abandoning the non-pedestrianized zone in search of a taxi, Hughes said it anyway. "They were all so *ordinary*."

Everyone he'd spoken to was just your basic humdrum, run-of-the-mill, good-natured person. One or two had revealed ugly sides of their character, sure, and one had seemed a bit of a git actually. That was Limley Olson, a mean-mouthed welfare officer who seemed to like movies about the poor rather than the poor themselves.

But yeah. By and large these murderers sure were nice people.

Significantly less so were Krys' visions of the future. He...

Hm.

Where am I?

Time apart and the weather had made his home District unfamiliar. Frost crept like blue-fingered ivy. Ice-packed and frozen these buildings looked strange to his eye, and many landmarks were swallowed in snow. He scanned about, retraced his steps, spun, executed a brisk advance along the road, and was at last rewarded. This street's plaque had eroded over time, but the abundance of chippers including *Jandy Mack's Jumbo Fried Shrimp Shop* meant that it was Pyrren Road, and he was on the right track.

Where had he been...?

Oh yes. Right.

Eyes scrunched, lashes flecked with snow, huddling into himself against the driving chill blowing over his neck and throat and filling his cheeks with warm compensatory blood, Hughes drew up a mental list.

1.   Krys identified the one behind all this as a "her." Jack was feminine, not masculine.

2.   Leading on from this, there was one evil intelligence behind the Spring-Heeled Jack crimes. One malefactor. One guilty bastard. Or, um... possibly a bitch, now, actually.

3.   Hughes would meet three people at a feast. She and she and she.

This last item flicked a switch inside him, and Hughes heard Krys' words as clearly as if she were beside him now.

Two will have your eyes, shadow man. The third will have your heart.

He shuddered, not entirely from the cold, and added one final item to the list.

4.   Whoever or whatever Jack was, she did not know Hughes. She did, however, know someone called the "Cut-String King."

Who could be none other than Frank Gallant.

Frank had freed himself from his mothers' control ten years ago, a puppet no more. The fact that Jack knew him suggested their investigation might not be dealing with a person wielding the supernatural.

We might be facing off against the supernatural wielding people.

Could such a thing happen? *Of course,* he reasoned. *The Nightjar Coven did it.* Those baleful hags—Frank's three mothers—had invaded ordinary peoples' dreams and transformed them into animals. The resulting violence resonated even now. In one case close to Hughes' heart, a husband had crushed two beetles only to discover his wife and daughter mangled in the trash can. There were lots of other horrors like that. And of course people felt they were responsible. But in truth it was the Coven who were solely responsible for those who died during The Hairy Autumn. The architects of that nightmare.

Why not Jack, then? The supernatural wielding people. For some reason it rang true for him.

Something with designs upon the city.

Something magic.

Something vile.

Something sharp.

At the end of Pyrren Road cars and motorcycles trundled and zipped by, wheels crunching in sand crystals laid to prevent slippery black ice forming. A taxi was coming. Hughes held up his hand but it drove by. He walked farther up toward a traffic light, fingers stinging with cold and stuffed into his coat pockets. He ought to invest in gloves. Earmuffs too. And the equivalent of mittens, only for your nose. His kept snuffling and dripping, insubordinate nose that it was.

His coat rumpled and snapped around him, the wind gnawing his skin with freezing gums. If the blizzard hadn't arrived in Corinth yet, it was close.

Looking at the row of apartments opposite him, Hughes found his eyes drifting up. And up. All the way to the rooftops.

No one there. Hard to tell with no moon and no stars, but yeah.

No one there.

He grunted disconsolately and went back to thumbing for taxis.

The pattern. That was what would solve it. He was sure of that at least.

Only the thing that the patterns offered was really, unbelievably peculiar.

He put his hand out, expecting this oncoming cab to pass by too, but it didn't.

"Where you going, mate?"

"Cleomenes."

"Hop in."

Peculiar, thought Hughes in the back seat, the city lights washing over his face like shadows glimpsed through stained glass. *Extremely fucking weird, more like.*

Here it was, then, the only pattern of substance that felt like it might lead to something, something concrete and powerful:

Before they were taken over by Jack, before they were touched by vileness, every single one of his interviewees had that very same day put up their Tinfrost decorations.

Back home in his and Cate's place, he telephoned first the Thud residence, then the hotel where Frank Gallant and Mr. Glint were staying. Lastly, he dialed the Citadel.

Before punching "call," he hesitated.

He toed his coat—which had fallen from the back of a chair onto the floor—and lifted it within grabbing distance with his socked foot. In one of its many, many inside pockets, he found the letter.

The red side was blank. Cate wasn't in the apartment and she hadn't written. He smiled a private smile. She was keeping busy. Good.

Two industrious bees, only together we're a whole hive, he thought. *Cate, I love you, honey.*

Replacing the letter he went back to his phone call.

"Hello? Yes, Falstaff please." A pause. "Gormon Hughes."

A moment later a neat, clipped voice said, "Good evening, sir. What can I do for you?"

"A few things, Falstaff. It's a stupid question since you're never not up to your ears, but do you have time for me?"

"For you, sir? Invariably, sir."

Hughes felt a soft twinge of love for the fussy little fellow. "Could you have Knickerbocker speak to me, soon as he can? I need to requisition some of his operatives."

"The Mr. Squeakers or the Bruces?"

"I'll know once I speak to him."

"Fabulous." Hughes couldn't hear a pen scratch. Falstaff never took notes. He didn't need them. "Do go on, sir."

"How's Priam King? I'm not asking for a medical opinion here, but ahm... Well, how does he seem?"

"Frail. He has a host of lesser illnesses nittering at him, but the man is old."

"I'd like to be notified if he looks like he's about to pass on. I want to say goodbye to Hector and the others." *But mostly Hector.*

My apt pupil. My wonderful friend.

Falstaff cleared his throat. "I'll see to it. Hector escorted Tommy Fahrenheit out of Corinth today. He left somber, yet returned animated. I think it would be fair to say he was happier than I have seen him in a long time. Am I right in assuming you had a part to play in his improvement?"

"Some part."

"Yes, I suspected so. I'll notify you, Hughes. Personally."

"Thanks, Falstaff." Pure curiosity caught him. "One more thing. Is Cate there in the Citadel?"

There was silence.

Then, "You hadn't heard, sir?"

"Heard what?"

"Miss Jubilee said she'd reach out to you."

"Heard *what?*"

"She's gone. She and the others."

"What others, Falstaff?"

"It's the largest unit in Citadel history," said Falstaff, his tone full of zest and vigor. "Bigger than Walsingham's Merry Miner's. Which is spectacular, when you take a moment to think about it, and in our lifetime! And as for..."

By chance Hughes' eye fell on the letter poking out of his coat pocket.

The red side faced him. Before it had been blank.

Now it was filled.

Falstaff was talking to him. Hughes didn't hear a word.

The phone slid into the crook of his shoulder, forgotten. By the time he was finished reading the letter, Falstaff had hung up and tried to telephone him back twice.

When the butler called a third time, Hughes answered.

"Is Wendy in her office?" he said.

"Her Ladyship? Not at present. I doubt she'll be long. What's the matter, Hughes?"

But Hughes was gone, slinging his feet into his shoes, and his arms into his coat, and barreling out the apartment door into the biting white storm and the howling night.

Chapter Twelve

Earlier that day...

"Quarter to nine," said Cate. "I'd best hurry."

She watched her lover's face change.

"Almost forgot," he said, pecking her on the cheek. "Thank you for the tomatoes, toast, and honey yogurt."

Charmer, she thought. *Two can play this game.*

"Thank you for the sausages, bacon, and black pudding," she said sweetly.

"I thought the pudding was overdone."

Cate kissed him, once quick and playful, once long and slow and sensuous.

She pulled away, gave him a wink.

"It was perfect," she said. "Later, handsome."

She set out, melting from romance into risky business, in which all can be lost and perhaps gained back and ameliorated, so long as you were willing to get your hands mucky and your mind grimed, here's to that then, here's to being a Woman With Important Shit To Do. Her cheek tingled where Hughes' lips had lingered. In fact she was tingly all over. Snow accounted for that, melting in its own right on the quiet furnace of her bare skin, and the bells inked at her throat, and her crooked lips. But there was excitement too. Movement. Life! A yesterday to solve. A today to mystify. And from the bottoms of her hobnail boots to the top of her molten-red head, Cate Jubilee felt ready.

She spied a faraway spire of glass, faceless and reflective in Ptolema District.

It would do.

She stepped onto a parked car, cleared the snow from the back window with her boot, and vanished through it.

Several onlookers gawped. Most, however, took no heed of the disappearing woman.

In Corinth City, things like that happened all the time.

***

After the funeral she took an elevator to The Lunarlight Wing.

It was a good service, Cate surmised. Good speeches.

There'd be celebrations later that night to honor the lives of the dead, and that was good.

Just overall goodness, really.

She hadn't known two-thirds of the deceased well, but she'd known Robbie, and he wasn't good.

Robbie was excellent.

No lie.

She smiled, and it was like a toast to her friend who'd died. Which was all for the best because though she did not know it yet, Cate Jubilee would not make that evening's festivities. She would be far away by then. A whole world away.

The elevator clicked and whirred deep in its mechanisms.

Listening to it, the sound reminded her of something.

A (sighhhh) as of monstrous breath wafting from behind a veil of rotted cloth.

Cate drew a deep breath of her own and let it go.

The moment passed.

Had it been a moment of significance? Yeah. It had. For an instant or two she'd been back on the hill in Iphigenia. Back in the unknown, where monsters she had never seen before could rise up out of the fog like a nightmare from a gauze of dream. Scary? Sure. Regret-tinged? Definitely. (Poor Robbie.)

But also... just a tiny bit fun?

Yes.

Maybe a big bit.

Yes.

In fact, fucking *deliciously* invigorating?

Oh yeah.

It had been a moment all right. So had breakfast that morning with Hughes. A gorgeous moment. Miserable. Cozy. Glum. Who had grinned last? Who had looked away first? A moment of togethermore. A moment of daughterless.

Over now though.

The elevator stopped. The doors slid open.

All good.

Cate strode under the lunar chandeliers and the crescent-curved lamps, her bootheels thumping softly on the cream-white carpet.

Past the antechamber with its tick-tocking grandfather clock, Wendy was waiting for her in the heart of the Wing, in an office that had very appropriately garnered the name The Dragon's Lair.

"Do come in, Cate. Falstaff has made you a coffee. You realize that 'latte' simply means 'milk' in Calcifern? It is an obscenely diluted drink. You may as well order it straight from the cow's udder and have done."

"Her Ladyship sounds envious." She took a whack from the dainty cup. Not one for sipping was Cate Jubilee. "How long has it been since you've had coffee, Wendy?"

The leader of the Scarlet Citadel raised an eyebrow. "That was a low blow. My dietitian makes the old church's inquisition torturers look like nursemaids."

"I'm sure he's not that bad."

"Watery vegetable soups, fruit and nut fiber bowls, and cakes so stiff you could build a roof from them and never again fear the rain. And they call me a dictator." Wendy stirred her tea (black and unsweetened) with the sullen grace of a wyrm who has been denied her dinner of thieving dwarven princes and is forced to make do with halfling fare. "Speaking of roofs, how is Hughes finding the life of a Spring-Heeled Jack investigator?"

"You know Hughes," said Cate distractedly. "Assumes a role and sinks deep enough that the role gives up being its own thing and sinks into him, breath to bones. I haven't seen this in a while," she added, coming round the huge board stationed opposite the fireplace. "When was the last time you wheeled this out for me?"

"Castle Aldersglen," Wendy reminded her.

Wow. Her first mission alongside her lover. Hughes had been mostly puppy in those days. Still, against Marrow King Maelen and the Bonemeal Boys, he'd demonstrated that while a puppy can be shy, naive, and impulsive, it is also capable of locking its teeth around something vital and hanging on for dear life.

In this way, small nuisances can become big problems.

Hughes made for a tremendously large problem to his enemies.

He only presented a problem for Cate Jubilee when he was hard on himself, or when he wore clothes for too long.

Anyway, here was the old board rolled out again.

She wondered what it was here to demonstrate.

Cate folded her arms, one hand tucked to her side and the other cupping the curve of her bicep, and gave the intricate work on the board a cursory examination. "Nope," she said eventually. "Can't make heads or tails of this. What are these squiggly things?"

"I believe it is the symbol for biomes."

Cate frowned. "I didn't know you were into that sort of film, Wendy. Little fantasy creatures going around and hooking up with one another willy-nilly..."

Wendy sighed. "Not bi-gnomes. *Biomes*, Miss Jubilee. As in geographical regions and their concomitant climates."

"Ah. Okay, I'm with you now."

Movement in the corner of Cate's eye. Wendy was next to her, looking up at the board, her sweaters smelling like fresh laundry and woodsmoke.

She had been behind her desk a moment ago. Now she was here.

Sometimes I forget how fast the old gal can be.

"I wonder, Cate, do you know how Iphigenia and Eurydice got their names?"

"I think I do. It was Lutz, right? Diedrich Lutz. The fellow who made the portals in the first place. He named them." Her aunty Trisha had divulged that to her in the days before handing the hobnail boots over. "I seem to remember Lutz was a few spoons short of a cutlery box too."

"Have you any idea where he got the names from?"

Cate shrugged. "Out of a paper hat for all I know."

"He says that they *came to him*, Cate. That he happened to be daydreaming while sketching a blueprint, and when he looked down, his pencil had scribbled both names, underlined them, and surrounded them with little notches and crosses for good measure. What do you make of that?"

"Not much *to* make of it, your Ladyship. Lorna Blacktower's got a hamster named Evelyn. She doesn't know anyone with that name. It came to her, you could say. Probably Lutz just heard someone use the names Iphigenia and Eurydice in passing and stowed them away in his head for later use."

"Reasonable. Reasonable." Wendy was looking at her out of the side of her face. "What would be your reaction, Miss Jubilee, if I were to tell you that the veiled figure, the Bride of the Fog in Iphigenia was, in fact, from Eurydice?"

There was a pause.

"You mean before or after I told you that would be impossible, your Ladyship?"

"Mmm. After, I should think."

"That's easy. I'd say, 'Just let me relace my boots and I'll be off.'"

"Off?" Wendy regarded her. "Where to?"

"To Eurydice. If there's monsters slipping from one world into another, what's to stop them learning they can slip into ours?" Cate turned toward the ashy hearth. "Getting cold up here. Mind if I restock your fire?"

"By all means."

As she tamped down the ash in the grate and fetched fresh logs, Cate said, "*Are* you telling me that it was from Eurydice, your Ladyship?"

"Indeed I am, Cate. John Isherwood was here yesterday. For the past several years he's been striving to advance the field of portalology. I shall forego decanting the details into your ear. In summary, we believe that Eurydice is invading Iphigenia."

Cate was trying to get Wendy's firelighter going. It clicked without spark. Maybe there was no fluid in it. Then her head caught up with her ears. She froze.

"Invading? How can a place invade another place?"

"I expect the same way people do it," said Wendy Dragontail. "With the deployment of ground troops."

In her mind's eye Cate watched that stretched leviathan of mummy cloth and clinging mist come toward her. Could the creature, the Bride of the Fog as Wendy called it, be Eurydice's perverse version of a soldier?

She guessed it could, although the implications were startling to say the least. For example, soldiers did not marshal themselves. It took a commander to send them out. A general. A queen or a king, maybe.

Hadn't Hughes once brought up something that touched on all this?

Hughes...

An idea wheeled across her brain.

"The two-headed wolf," she blurted. "The one Hughes killed all those years ago. Could that have been from Eurydice as well?"

"Yes," Wendy replied. "Yes, we believe it was. Moreover, we believe that worse is on the way." The Last Dragon's eyes twinkled darkly. "John and his people have detected electrical impulses deep under the tectonic plates of both Eurydice and Iphigenia. Strange charges moving faster than continental drift and slower than the systolic heartbeat of trees. These impulses have been examined. Findings suggest they're brainwaves. My God, it's gradually more surreal every time I say it. But it's true, Cate. Brainwaves. At Doctor Isherwood's discretion a team of neurologists have confirmed that these signals map quite tidily onto projections of human brain activity. See those ripples on the board? The real scans are much more complex, I assure you, but the conclusion is clear. The worlds are thinking about things."

Cate was dumbstruck. It was as though the fog from yesterday had crept into her and was pumping her mind full of pale white juice (latte in Calcifern). So she continued about the fire, getting it going and stepping back once it was and sitting on the nearby sofa and listening to Wendy talk about vast, incomprehensible matters that made no sense, no sense at all...

Wendy went on. "This opens up several uncomfortable but nonetheless intriguing possibilities. When Diedrich Lutz was relaxing that day with his pencil poised over his blueprint of the first portal, isn't it possible that another, much less tangible portal was opening in his head? A thought-vortex, if you like. Isn't it possible that he was thinking, 'What shall I name these big doors anyway?' And through that psychic link, the big doors told him? Introduced themselves, for lack of a better term."

She sat down on a chair by the sofa, tucking her feet under her, and opened a drawer with a false bottom. Inside was a single cookie. It was studded with chocolate. "The flesh, alas, is weak. I trust you to keep my secret. Falstaff is scrupulous with my diet, the loyal fiend. Where was I? Ah yes. When the two-headed wolf arrived in Iphigenia, it tore apart a group of dramen and pygmies. When the Bride of the Fog swept in, it cut down whole herds of cattle. The truth is plain. Eurydice is thinking red thoughts. Its agents are doing red work. Who can guess what motivates that? Not us. But we are the Scarlet Citadel, and we recognize the red.

"Not only that. I intend to outmatch it."

She dunked her cookie in the lukewarm dregs of her tea, raised it like something sacred, and popped it into her mouth. Wendy closed her eyes, smiling the happy smile of a wyrm who gets to enjoy sizzling strips of thieving dwarf prince after all. Storybook joy deepened the lines of her face.

"Does our world think?" Cate heard herself say. Her voice seemed to be coming from a long way off.

"Lowly," said Wendy through a mouthful of cookie. She swallowed. "Amazing. I find the forbidden quality only improves the flavor of treats. 'Slowly,' I meant. Our world thinks slowly. Much more so than its neighbors."

Frantic images of contamination, bombs blasting, pollution, acid rain, rainbows of oil shimmering on the surface of lakes, fish corpses baking on sunny beaches, deforestation, tar-black smoke boiling into the clear noon sky, tank nozzles thumping out cartridges; all of this and more occurred to Cate, who was no fool, and who knew that something capable of thought was probably capable of emotion.

"Doesn't it hate us?" she wondered. "Doesn't it feel betrayed?"

"Do weeds feel betrayed when yellow garden gloves yank them out? Certainly not. Weeds are weeds. Don't get lost in them, that's my advice. Mapping tidily to human thought doesn't mean a world thinks like a person. How could it? Imagine a human being whose mind stretched from one horizon to the other. The electrical energy generated by such a brain could power the galaxy for an hour, the whole expanding universe for a fraction of an instant. Would such a being think of injustice and retribution as we do? Of course not. Too alien. Too different."

Cate glanced up from her boots into Wendy's hard hazel eyes and smiled. It was a colorless curling of the lips, almost plastic.

"And you say you intend to outmatch that?" she said. "How?"

This time the twinkle in Wendy's irises was not just dark but dangerous. "With ground troops," she said. "How did you put it, Cate? Relace your boots and you'll be off."

Understanding dawned. "An invasion of our own?" Cate sprang to her feet. "Like Walsingham's Merry Miners?"

"My father was on an expedition. This is war." With a jerk of her wrinkled thumb Wendy indicated the lower area of the board.

Cate looked at the things drawn there. With new context they began to order themselves into units. No, larger than units. Contingents.

"A Scarlet army," said Wendy as if reading her mind. "Take.... mmm... half the Citadel with you. Eliminate these world-crossing monsters. Find out how Eurydice is empowering them and put a stop to it." She finished her tea, set it aside. "You will, naturally, require a second in command."

Cate Jubilee grinned. It had color in it now. A surplus of sweet and scarlet red. "I have just the woman in mind."

***

Eilandri Titansgrave was the first to appear that afternoon.

The subterranean floor that held the clerical and chemical machinery necessary to power the Eurydice portal was vast, though not so vast as to diminish The Pale Giant. Eilandri's bald head and piercing purple eyes were visible over work stations, insulated partitions, coffee dispensers, and the crush of people working here in the shadow of the door to the dungeon dimension.

Also the hammer was hard to ignore. Even sheathed it seemed to whisper menacing oaths, such as, *If I'm drawn because of you, you are going to wish I hadn't been.*

Next came Rosemund Valkyrie, broad of shoulder, fair-haired and wearing a cloak upon which a bloody battle raged eternally. With her was Steffan Cerulean, blue-bearded and blue-of-hair, his shirt rattling with beads dyed white and jade, so that when he walked he seemed a moving wave.

After them came Varjo Cutthroat, a man who reminded all who looked at him of a knife, gray and slender and sharp.

At his heels strode ugly Marcus Angel and beautiful Xacorca Demon, bright Rebecca Lupine and a darkly clad pair in tow, Igor Wight and Jennifer Goblingrin.

They came in groups and they came alone.

They came laughing. They came somber.

They came with misgivings. They came ready.

A hush had fallen over the engineers and scientists and interns recently graduated from university. They watched with a quiet that was partly reverence, partly unease, as the Scarlet men and women gathered before the otherworldly door.

No one had seen anything like this before.

Not even John Isherwood, who approached the leader of the outfit. Cate was holding a letter with red on one side, blue on the other.

"What's that you've got there?" John said, glancing up half-interestedly from the jumble of notes threatening to slip through his fingers.

"A magical letter that will allow me to talk to my boyfriend from another world."

"Uh huh. Uh huh. Great." John found the page he was looking for. With some effort he slid it to the front, his eyes scanning with a surgeon's speed and discipline. "Okay, all asses farting equally, these coordinates ought to get you to Eurydice with minimal tread. Take a look at this line. It spikes the graph here, here, and here. We think these spikes document moments of physical reality at its most strained. In other words, it's these monsters attempting to breach the boundary between worlds. Get into Iphigenia. Cause a little bedlam. You know."

"Can you drop us nearby?" said Cate. "Close to one or all of these creatures?"

"One yes. All? No, they're too spread out. It's a whole hell on the other side of that door."

"I can move quickly if I have to," Cate pointed out. "So can Rosemund and some of the others in a pinch. But not all. How do you propose we travel?"

"Wendy not tell you?"

"What about?"

The good doctor nodded over her shoulder.

Cate turned. Her stomach rolled like a cat in fresh and pooling cream.

Something began to march out of the shadows toward her. Stupendously huge, its footfalls shook the whole sub-Citadel underground. Perhaps they could feel it in the city like the memory of some ancient earthquake under their feet.

"Oh." She took a shaky breath. "Oh my."

"We've been working on it a long time. Traditional machinery doesn't work in Eurydice, after all. Bioengineering's come a long way since I picked up my first microscope. I've outfitted a camera to it, as well as an audio recorder. There's a few vacuum-sealed pods too, if you wouldn't mind collecting samples. I intend to do a little backstage observation on this show of yours." He paused. "You okay?"

"Cool," she said, "as a refrigerated parsnip, John. Nippy as a nip, if you like. That's me. Girlish glee? Never heard of it. Whimsical delight at unexpected awesomeness? Total stranger."

He nodded, some bookish cousin of bemusement twisting his lips, and stuck the wad of papers under his arm. "I'm no physician. Still, as your dimensional sawbones, I prescribe a course of good fortune. Take one a day. Come back safe."

She was genuinely touched. "Thanks John."

They shook hands.

Then the moment arrived. Ever since her meeting with Wendy, Cate had felt it closing in, and now it fizzled in her gut and vaulted up her throat. She pictured Walsingham Dragontail, felt her hobnail boots filling his shoes. The Old Dragon had stood right here before the portal, had set his gleaming gaze upon a force of very, very dangerous people, his Merry Miners, and he had said the words.

She called those same words aloud now.

"Scarlet brother be my shield."

And her siblings in scarlet replied, "Be the weapon that I wield."

"I will be your courage true."

"I will burn like fire for you."

"If I'm laid eternal low."

"We pray that it shall not be so."

"*Yes,*" she roared. "*But if it comes to be?*"

"*WE WILL CARRY ON FOR THEE.*"

Satisfied, Cate Jubilee jutted her chin toward their ride.

They mounted up, dozens upon dozens of really quite dangerous people indeed, and she joined them.

At his console, John Isherwood guided his technicians. "Drop's almost ready!"

Cate eyed the portal before them. It blazed, its liquid flame seeming to lend credence to the good doctor's words. *It's a whole hell on the other side of that door.*

So be it, thought Cate. *Abandon all hope, ye who make me come in there.*

John's voice. "It's open!"

Cate felt her ride surge under her. The Scarlet Army came forth.

And the portal swallowed them whole.

***

The monster Cate Jubilee would come to think of as Skuggs watched their arrival with interest.

From one of the caves in one of many mountains in these parts, there galloped a vehicle so odd that, in Eurydice, it practically seemed normal. It was immensely large with sloping legs as wide as tree trunks. In fact its legs *were* tree trunks, complete with bark and gnarly nodes of sap and growths of furry green moss and damp green lichen. The tops of the leg-trees came together to form a platform of hardened organic matter. On this platform was a fortress of steel and concrete. In the wicked tango-pink light of the moon (Eurydice had moons that misbehaved, wait and see) the vehicle seemed to offer a challenge to any who might take it.

Skuggs wiggled a finger in his ear, checked the fingertip in case he'd found anything exciting, and watched the fortress stop, orient itself, then trot off along the crags in the direction of the mountain pass.

Oh, but that was guzzlible luck. Going that way would take these newcomers directly to the Troll. And just when the Troll was about to make his—ahehn-hen-hen—*big breakthrough.*

Skuggs tittered. It sounded like ahehn-hen-hen.

Perhaps he ought to let old Trolly know he was in for visitors, eh? That way, the great big thrumpkin could cobble together a tarsty welcome. Skuggs should like to see that. He should like to see it very, very much.

And so what if it took him a littlest behind schedule?

He had been a head-and-throat-and-shoulder blades ahead only recently.

Surely the others would understand. Wouldn't they?

"Fat chance," said Skuggs, his two-throated voice sounding both cheerful and rueful. And without another moment's delay, he let the sparkling quartz of his home cover his whole body like an envelope covering a letter. Rock and soil opened under him, sucking and slurping the crystalline shape out of the moonlight. He sent himself west.

Postal service at its peak, thought Skuggs. *Ahehn-hen-hen.*

Chapter Thirteen

:01pm.

3   Rummy Lou was proud as any schoolteacher could hope to be. Honest-to-God, for a while there she hadn't been sure she could take another two days of this before the semester ended. Then something had changed, and for the better. For whatever reason the kids were chomping through her lesson plan. You got these days (regrettably infrequent) where they had the hunger, where due to inexplicable factors the lesson appeared to the children as a scrumptious banquet. Tuck your bibs in, gang. The calculus is *fine*.

Even rarer were days when no whispers or smothered giggles issued out of the cramped seats, sparking savagely against her nerves. Gum popping. Nervously joggling legs. The impudent (Rummy Lou hated that word, but here it was warranted) sighs that seemed to express that while school truly blew, she, the avatar of education in sensible shoes, blew goats.

Yet here such a day was, and boy was she glad to see it. Despite the classroom clock ticking toward afternoon's end, she felt full of energy. Vim and vigor, by God! Another easy hour and she'd be home to easy, love-drunk living with Brenda. One last course of the knowledge banquet. Just then, looking out at their eager faces, Rummy Lou experienced a mild shock. Why, Daniel Slone, the class thug, was actually smiling at her. She got a discussion on geography going, tossed Daniel a question, and holy shit he answered it! Correctly too! Wonders never cease, huh? And...

And she really ought to do something about the poor kid's hair.

Daniel came from a bad household. His mother and father could clean out a bottle with great diligence. Less so when it came to cleaning their boy. Didn't Rummy Lou have something in her desk drawer that might help?

What that something was, she was not altogether sure.

An odd buzzing was gradually beginning to fill her ears. Odd, but it didn't bother her. What bothered her—had in fact been bothering her for a minute or so now—was the sense of being... words failed her for an instant, then she had it!

The sense of fullness. Something was... filling her up, and she... had to get it out.

Yes, that was clear now.

How? How to rid herself of the

(buzzbuzzbuzzbuzzbuzzbuzzbuzzbuzzbuzz)

the stifling full-up feeling?

As Daniel Slone's smile fell away, replaced by a frown of puzzlement (most of the kids were exchanging looks now, whispering, buzzing), Rummy Lou understood.

Helping him with his hair... Helping them all with their hair...

That would do the trick. She'd be emptied out. Herself again.

It was important to be yourself.

Good lesson.

Yum yum.

Ms. Lou's class watched perplexed as she reached down into one of her desk's drawers. In there among the glue sticks, pens, and notepads, was a wad of steel wire Ms. Lou sometimes used to clean out the classroom sink on arts and crafts days.

Later, it would be bagged as evidence by the Leonidas District police, clotted with blood and skin and human hair.

Rummy's hand closed around it.

"Danny," she called to the Slone boy, her voice silken and inviting. "Come here a sec, would you?"

3:39pm.

Setting the mop he called Mae to one side, Paulie Manzarek switched off his music and removed his headphones. He was aware that some part of him, distinct but shrinking, questioned why he should do that.

Because, he thought. *I wanna hear the buzzing.*

The buzzing was important.

Why? said that shrinking part. It's only stupid flies.

Shut up.

And maybe there was rest for the wicked, and rest for Paulie too, because the nagging voice *did* shut up. He listened to the buzzing for a while, and then...

And then...

Paulie groaned.

He clutched at his belly, but the sensation overwhelming him was not isolated there. It was all over. Inside and all over and he had to *get it out.*

Before he could articulate his helplessness, Paulie Manzarek helped himself.

From where he stood in one of Taggart House's serpentine corridors, he looked through an open door and to the guest (some people called them patients, others said loonies, but not Paulie, no way) who was snoring softly in bed.

Cool relief gushed over hot, urgent dread, quenching it.

He got it now. It was the pillows. They were... wrong somehow.

It was, he decided, the position. The poor guest could really use his help. He was only a mop-slopper, sure, but he had always tried to make the poor guys and gals resting up here in Taggart feel... well, if not better, then at least a little more comfortable. Looked-after. Yeah, that was the phrase. Heck, if their places were reversed, Paulie was damn sure *he'd* want to be looked-after.

He went inside (shutting the door behind him for reasons he could not have explained under duress) and helped out. He thought, *There. That pillow looks good there.*

Only the daggum thing kept moving.

Paulie held it in place, first with one hand, then two. Eventually the pillow took the hint.

Paulie smiled.

He felt better already.

He had visited eight rooms before a nurse on her rounds poked her head in and saw the extent of Paulie Manzarek's help.

Her screams went on and on.

4:50pm.

The reverend Taylet Gordon perceived the buzzing and felt that stuffed-to-bursting sensation at the tail end of his afternoon service. Leading up to it he had been high-fired and swinging for the back aisle.

It was because of Miss Audripepper. She was one of those scuttling little old ladies who smelled of pocket lint, chewy toffee, and bedraggled linen, and whose general civility is only matched by her cunning. She had approached him before noon while Taylet was wrathfully tonguing his ulcer. With her she had brought a suggestion: why not, dear reverend, put up the Tinfrost tree a little early this year?

Taylet had snapped that putting it up late was the whole damn point. By erecting the filthy fucking pagan effigy in January, it gave the middle finger to the reprobate shit pagans who worshipped the parcel and the gravy-glazed ham more than their Lord and Master.

Miss Audripepper had nodded sympathetically, and then she'd said, in calm and reasonable tones that made him want to throttle the shrewd wrinkle-fisted nosy besom, that it was such a shame to see the church's numbers dwindling recently. Perhaps if the tree went up, people might be more inclined to think the church was moving with the times. Also, it might deter any people who thought the reverend himself was purposefully driving away the congregation with sermons dripping fire and sinful blood.

The reverend Taylet Gordon had drawn a breath to chastise her, really give her the flat of his tongue... Yet what emerged surprised him. Put up the tree early? Fine. He'd help. He might as well have told her he was part-timing as the messiah.

The bitch was delighted.

Oh Reverend, you won't regret it.

Oh, I'm sure. *But you will,* he'd thought privately. *When the cambions of hell are peeling flesh off your bones in big sticky flaps, Miss Audripepper. You'll regret it then.*

Surprises come in packs, he supposed. Slinging up the tree had been a pain in the ass and a worse one in the ulcer, but evidently the old lady had spread the good news. They turned up in droves for his afternoon service. There was none of the furtiveness he'd come to expect. People seemed glad and proud to be there. Many admired the tree, how sweet it looked there by the makeshift altar, how festive and nice.

Maybe it was the ambience, but Taylet found himself delivering a mass with none of his usual steel. He was softer than normal, even deigning to make a joke during the sermon.

And they laughed. Earnest mirth to warm the heart on such a chilly day.

His congregation, his flock. They stoked up a soul cry in him: Reprobates beware! The armies of the faithful can only grow from here!

As the buzzing ramped up, he excused himself for a moment, claiming he'd forgotten the sacramental wine in the sacristy. In fact the blood of the lamb was the farthest thing from his mind. Moving quietly, he crept up the side stairs, avoiding the creakiest boards.

God, was he *full.*

Even the sodomizing fuck-ache ulcer was full. Though not... particularly painful... now he thought about it...

He came to the balcony overlooking the haberdash church he and his brother had built so many years ago before the holy waters between their family had soured and thickened to pus. The balcony was dusty, and there were dusty rafters crisscrossing the air up here, and dustiest of all the chandelier holding the blessed candles and the winch roped to the chandelier keeping it poised over the pews.

Taylet hadn't reeled the thing down to ground level to refresh the candles in, hoh nelly, must be two or three years by now.

The winch felt sturdy under his hand. He looked up and saw that he'd been wrong. The candles were lit. Tiny glowbugs of light. Orange and red and gold as a sunrise in heaven.

His eyes widened at this subtle miracle, and then the truth opened in his head like a page of gospel.

What his flock really needed was a shepherd in such savage times.

And what better shepherd than the light?

His smile incandescent, the reverend Taylet Gordon reached into his vestments, produced the bottle opener for the sacramental wine, and bent to the rope...

6:22pm.

In the brothel *Pamplona*, Laura Clemp stared at the bare ass of her patron, who was undressing by the open window, which, while curtained, was flung wide, so wide...

6:28pm.

While his family spooned up supper, Barclay Waters locked all the doors in his house, one hand gripping his father's spare oil drum, the other a box of matches...

7:00pm.

Alma Coalman, arriving just in time for her Sunday evening dance class, could not help but think the instructor's refusal to face the mirror could be solved if he and the glass were on better terms...

9:47pm.

In the cubby below the bar where she and the rest of the staff changed the kegs and kept spare bottles of liquor and mixer, Karoliina Vaaca glanced over one shoulder, then the other, and then eased open the cabinet containing cleaning wipes, bleach, and cumbersome plastic bottles of the most efficient rat poison...

... and in the streets of Corinth City, people who happened to glance up at exactly the right moment, at exactly the right time, might have seen figures jumping from rooftop to rooftop.

The shadow took no heed of onlookers.

It had taken her all of Saturday to build up her strength. In the bleak planning hours she had begun to fret that her best days were behind her, back in the past where things were so very different and yet so utterly identical to the here and the now.

She needn't have worried. Exuberant and happy, she loomed high and high and higher still over Sunday, December 18th.

She did this, and she thought, *'Twas the week before Tinfrost, and all through the dark, the flies were a' buzzing, in search of a lark.*

And all of the girlies and all of the boys,

Dreaming of presents under the tree,

None, not a one, shall smile at their toys.

They'll open the wrapping, and what will there be?

A knife, a fly, a roof tile,

And me.

Act Five

Something Blunt

Chapter Fourteen

D^{ear} *Cate,*

Thanks for writing. It's funny; you write pretty much exactly as you speak, so I read the whole letter in your voice. It greatly improved the experience.

Sorry we'll be apart for a while. Will <u>miss</u> you.

But I want you to know that I support this adventure of yours wholeheartedly. I suppose it's more of a job, or at the very least a task. Knowing you though, <u>there will be something adventurous about it</u>.

I had a difficult evening. After I got your letter I went to the Citadel for a chat with Wendy. I wanted to get everything straight in my head. Worlds that think? Worlds that prey on other worlds? I mean it changes absolutely everything, doesn't it?

I've been wracking my brains, and it's only now that I've remembered. You and I spoke about the conjunction of the worlds years ago, around the time we beat the Nightjar Coven. This discovery of Doctor John's confirms my suspicion from back then: that the two-headed wolf was from Eurydice all along! Your Bride of the Fog sounds like an Echo of it. Or maybe a better way to put it is that the pair of them are Dark Cousins. That would imply a family tree of similar monsters (one whose branches you might have to prune on your current venture).

It also implies that what happened with the Coven might happen again.

Maybe that's what this whole Spring-Heeled Jack thing is.

A sort of follow-up of the Hairy Autumn, only in the winter, and with murder instead of transformation. An Echo.

A Dark Cousin.

Then again, I could be grasping at straws. But this whole thing is galling news, that's for sure. Worlds that think—holy shit.

Not that her Ladyship agrees. After I got to her office, and as I got myself more and more worked up, Wendy made out that it was all in hand, all being taken care of. I couldn't believe it. Oh, she gave some ground, admitting that the situation could "present issues" and that it certainly "required attention." It's all just water off a dragon's wing, as far as she's concerned.

I suppose sending you along with half the Citadel is a sign that at least it has *snagged her attention.*

But it ties into something that I thought about earlier today.

Cate, can you tell me why no one has any magic items? Except the Citadel, I mean. Why is it just us? Taking into account that there's people being killed by magic (vis-à-vis Jack), and that now there is a very real possibility *of our world being invaded by another, why should there be those who have magic, and those who don't?*

Wendy said it's because if ordinary people had access to magic, then it would be difficult to regulate. Arm the butcher who deals in offal, and you also arm the butcher who deals in awful. I said that when it comes to regulation, difficult *isn't the same as* impossible.

Ended up having what my dad calls an "argy-bargy," i.e. Wendy and I kept talking until we shouted, and then we shouted until we spoke in quiet, cold voices, and then one of us left, namely me.

I don't know. She's damn persuasive, but it just doesn't seem right.

And I object to her use of "ordinary."

The only difference between someone in the Scarlet Citadel and someone who isn't is that one of them has a questionable approach to safety while wearing red trousers. And the Jolene-forged objects in question, of course.

I could use your insight. (Thanks in advance.)

As I write this, I can look out our apartment window. Earlier there was a pillar of smoke and a winking orange light. Must have been a fire in Leonidas. Seems localized enough, and the firefighters and the blizzard took care of it quickly. Still, hope everyone's okay.

And I hope you're okay. <u>Better</u>, even.

Will write to you about the case tomorrow. Can't keep my eyes open. Look forward to hearing from you.

Love you, Kitten.

Hughes

***

What had he been about to call her?

She didn't know, that was the trouble.

It was a quarter to eight on Monday morning, her office window was firmly shut, the hearth with its six carved dragons was blazing merrily, and Wendy Dragontail was having breakfast with the cousin of an emperor.

The consul was a nervous little man tucked into a blazer that showed cream-white turtles swimming in a black cloth sea. He mewled over the pastries and fruit slices and bowls of probiotic yogurt. Hovering by the door was the Incarnadine, and in normal circumstances Wendy's scrutiny would have fallen directly on him. The killer was the consul's polar opposite, tall and broad and unwilling to part with his coat. He claimed the Corinthian weather did not agree with him. He had answered Wendy's question about never seeing snow with a curt shake of the head. Where the consul fidgeted constantly, the killer seldom moved at all. He wore sunglasses indoors. In her experience it was prudent to watch a man who hid his eyes. Chances were he was watching you.

And though she had invited the consul to breakfast at the Citadel knowing he would bring his bodyguard, and though she'd planned to lure or cajole or persuade the reason for said bodyguard's presence in the city from one or both of them, Wendy found herself distracted.

It was Hughes of course. This would not be happening if he'd simply finished what he was going to say.

An image of him came to mind effortlessly. Time wound back, white Monday morning becoming black Sunday night. He'd been standing over there by her office door, where the Incarnadine now lingered. Hughes' stance was unlike any she'd ever seen. It was difficult to describe, but if pressed she would have said their argument had somehow infused him, the way a teabag infuses boiling water in drifty clouds, only with anger instead of chamomile. His jaw had stuck out, his lower canines showing. The glare he'd fastened her with could have stripped paint off a wall.

You're a stubborn old...

And then he'd stopped, and turned his face so it was half hidden in shadow, and slipped out the door, and shut it quietly after him.

She wished he'd slammed it. That would have punctuated things, given them a crisp finality. But he'd closed the door softly, and that was how she knew he was not merely pissed but really and truly *aggrieved*.

"The headlines today are most interesting," observed the consul.

"Yes?"

"Poisonings at a nightclub. The sabotage of a chandelier at an illegal mass. The schoolteacher who attacked her students. The fire. I hear there was even an incident at the asylum people call 'The Toadhouse.' An orderly smothering patients in their beds." The consul smiled a fatuous little smile. "Evidently, your Ladyship, the city has gone, ahem, *hopping mad*."

"Extremely funny," said Wendy. "I can only imagine how hilarious your Excellence is when ingesting anything more exciting than fermented milk."

"I am told I am the life of any party."

"Know a lot of undertakers, do you?"

The consul frowned between yogurt slurps. "I'm sorry?"

"You were saying about the headlines, your Excellence?"

"Ah yes, there was another so intriguing that I read the entire article on my way here to your, ahem, *lovely* Citadel..."

He prattled on. Wendy nodded and pulled agreeable expressions.

A stubborn old... baggage?

Stubborn old... weapon?

They'd been arguing over what to do about Spring-Heeled Jack of all things. Of course it had been about more than that. It was always the way with passionate disputes. You skated over the ice waiting for it to crack, and then the cold fury of Opinion submerged you and any hope of reconciliation was drowned.

What it amounted to was this: Hughes wanted Wendy to give the order that the Jolenes were to expand The Foundry. Bigger building. More Jolenes. As a result of this expansion Wendy could commission an astounding haul of magic items, first by the hundreds, then the thousands. Hughes wanted these arcane tools (mass produced and perhaps less powerful than those wielded by the Citadel, but still leaps and bounds ahead of your standard kitchen knife) to be given to everyone. The police. The citizenry. Stewards to shopkeepers. Merchants to milkmen. He wanted to arm *everyone*.

Wendy, on the other hand, wanted Hughes to realize that what he was proposing was absurd.

"All this misfortune, and around Tinfrost," said the consul. "Here, my Lady. You keep eyeing these enchanting chocolate pastries. Have one."

"No, thank you, your Excellence."

"So it is true? In my home, there are those who whisper that the great, nay, the insurmountable Winnifred Dragontail eats only the still-warm ashes from briquette fires. Chews burning coals. That you... *dine* as the dragons of yore once dined, for want of a better phrase."

"Myth on both accounts, I'm afraid. Dragons have never eaten the residue of fire. They had quite enough combustion going on internally, I assure you."

"So, what did they, ahem ahem, eat?"

Why, men, your Excellence. Deep fried.

Wendy smiled her best ingratiating smile. "We continue to be diverted from the topic."

"Ah yes. Yes, you're right."

In her mind's ear she heard a door closing with a soft, goading *click*.

Stubborn old shrew? She sat opposite the peevish little gabbler of a diplomat, silently seething. *Cow? Witch? Grimalkin?*

What?

Stubborn old what?

The thing Hughes didn't understand was that the mass production of anything—absolutely anything—caused a corresponding dilution. Sometimes that was good. Take credits. One credit, faceted pink-quartz, otherworldly and dazzling, was a museum piece. A thousand was a rare black market thrill. A million was an economy.

But sometimes the results of mass production were nightmarish.

To explain it to him, she had used the example of the quickbolt. Crossbolts were a relatively contemporary invention compared to the long and shortbow. It took engineers longer to figure out the windy parts. Crossbows were also, until around a hundred years ago, utterly useless. You got one good shot off and then you were stuck winding the thing for forty seconds, which was plenty of time for your enemy to wander over and ask you if you'd like your bolt back, and if so, where?

The spring-loaded crossbow, otherwise known as the quickbolt, had changed all of that. It shot fast, reloaded fast, and basically made bows obsolete overnight. The aristocracy were delighted, and they thanked the clever people who had invented the quickbolts, and then they had those clever people cleverly done away with. This was because the inventors would never stop inventing, and you had to draw a line in the murderous sand somewhere. But it was too late, for the quickbolt was already being made quickly and cheaply, and because it was cheap to make, it wasn't too expensive to buy and sell, and one day you woke up and all your neighbors owned a quickbolt, and so did you, and, *well*, suddenly there were all these cases of people disemboweling one another and children accidentally shooting their parents and parents not-so-accidentally shooting children. Long story truncated, the quickbolt was recalled. The army got involved, and the police, and even the Scarlet Citadel. It was, in summation, a mess.

Wendy offered Hughes the idea that, should they give everyone a magic item, it might turn out very much like the quickbolt.

Only should things turn bad, and should bad turn to worse, magic items might not be so easy to recall.

"What I found, ahem ahem, *particularly* interesting," wheedled the consul, "was that despite all of this, ahem, disturbing and eye-catching material, your city's most popular paper, *The Times*, ran a headline... about the state of the... weather."

"It's the blizzard," said Wendy. "We don't often get extreme weather in Corinth."

"Nevertheless... isn't there a certain... journalistic responsibility to, ahem, inform the public?"

"In my experience the public informs itself. A sort of 'all you can eat buffet' with words instead of lukewarm curry." Wendy came back to herself. Something in the consul's tone had raised fluorescent warning signs in the busy highway of her head. "Have these other headlines given you pause, your Excellence?"

"Um." He glanced at the Incarnadine as an apprentice roofer might glance at a ladder to make sure it is still under him. "Rather more than pause, my Lady. It embarrasses me greatly, but the headlines have given me sleepless nights. While the Embassy is well protected, it seems that the recent incline in, ahem, gross barbarity does not discriminate between those with guards and without them. Also, the Embassy does possess a roof."

Wendy looked at him blankly.

Understanding opened her face like a surprised flower. "You're worried about Jack."

The consul wrung his hands. "Perhaps it is unwise to invoke his name, good Lady."

"You're worried about Spring-Heeled Jack so you had your cousin send him?" Wendy jabbed a finger at the Incarnadine.

The hand-wringing intensified. "His radiance the emperor and I are *second* cousins."

Yes, and a good thing too, thought Wendy. *If you were brothers he might have sent a war elephant.*

She sighed inwardly. Politics was a wily beast. Perforce one was charged to wrangle it to one's purpose. Often it bucked. On occasion it bit. And then there were mornings like this, when you got exactly what you wanted while you weren't even trying. Yogurt and silence; evidently a remedy for one's every diplomatic woe. She wondered if Hughes had meant to call her a stubborn old pot of gut-friendly gloop, then decided no, probably not.

"The Citadel has a roof," she commented, as one might comment on the weather (blizzardy as it may be). "Far more difficult to reach than the one at the Embassy. Also far more difficult to be reached *by*, I suppose."

The consul perked up. Fretful as he might be, the man was no fool.

"I would never dream of inconveniencing her Ladyship..."

"Inconvenience? For our friends from Mysicordelia, there is no such state of being. *I say, Montcrieff! Can you hear me?*"

"Urk."

"What?" The consul had jumped at her shout. Now he was looking around frantically, though Montcrieff was quite elusive to those who didn't know where to find him. "Mont—what? Can who hear you?"

"*Send a message to Falstaff,*" Wendy continued, ignoring him. "*Consul Isshin is to be escorted to the forty-fourth floor, where he shall enjoy the full suite of satisfactions available to our honored guests. Once settled, the consul shall provide a list of everything he requires from his former domicile; that would be the Embassy.*"

"Eurk?"

"*Em-ba-ssy, Montcrieff. It is a large building where foreign people do important work and also complain about what the locals have done to their food. Nevermind that now. Inform Falstaff that we are also hosting an Incarnadine. Word is to be spread that he is not to be interfered with or harangued in any way, should his conduct remain reasonable. Fair enough?*"

"Certainly. Absolutely." The consul bobbed his head, but Wendy wasn't looking at him.

It was barely perceptible, but she thought the tall man in sunglasses gave a nod.

"Excellent. *Have you got that, Montcrieff?*"

"Urk."

"*Thank you.*"

The consul had recovered. He got to his feet, clasping those nervous, powdered hands of his together. "One thousand blessings upon you, my Lady."

"Just one will do, your Excellence, so long as it's yours."

"I shall sleep easier than I have in weeks!"

"Wonderful." Her smile was one that monarchs everywhere deploy. Technically Wendy was not queen, but she had this smile in her back pocket for a snowy day. It said, *That will be all.*

Bowing and scraping, the consul made to leave, leaped three feet in the air as Falstaff appeared to escort him, then bowed and scraped and wrung his hands a bit for good measure.

Wendy went to her desk. She jotted a thought in one of her many notebooks...

... and was aware of the fine hairs on her arms raising like stiff white pins.

She looked up.

The Incarnadine was there.

He was in the doorway, unmoving, and suddenly Wendy felt the amulet at her throat respond. Faethe, it was called. Amulet of Dragons. It kept her safe, changing her body at a moment's notice; light and quick as silk in a strong wind one moment, hard and heavy as tungsten the next.

Out of the man's sight, she curled her fingers round the wooden lip of the desk.

She was not afraid exactly (not since her girlhood had Wendy Dragontail felt the cold clutch of fear), but rustling through her was an enriching breed of curiosity.

The Incarnadine watched her. She, in turn, watched him.

Then he did something that would influence the course of important things to come, not just for Wendy but for Hughes and poor tower-bound Estelle, and perhaps many more.

He opened his mouth and slowly, almost conspiratorially, slid out his tongue. Embedded in the fleshy wet pinkness was a stone—a piercing. It caught the firelight, especially the lapping warm redness. Faintly, Wendy remembered Knickerbocker's words. The giddy gargoyle had been talking about the Incarnadine, how they were rumored to have killed the person they were closest to in order to become what they were.

She stared at the piercing and thought, *That jewel of dead friend's red heart's blood gives them* power.

The Incarnadine retracted his tongue. Without having spoken a single word, he turned on his heel and left. The door closed softly. *Click.*

Wendy let go of the desk.

Indents shaped like her fingers remained in the wood.

Suddenly the room seemed stifling. Undoing the shutter and flinging wide the window, she was treated to a view that even a dragon of yore would have envied. Something about the currents in the air above the clouds. Poor scaly devils couldn't manage it. No matter. Their inheritors had defied gravity's curt refusals. Walsingham had often called Redspire the Tower of the Elegy. Her father was an introspective man, jolly in his youth yet prone to melancholy in his dotage, as though the things he'd seen inside grew more and more sombering with age.

He hadn't understood when she'd left for a year. See the woman (young, so young then!) with the white hair scamper down the tower without a speck of wealth or a scrap of knowledge about how far over her head she was. A year, a year, a brave and bold year! As she'd fled, she had believed she was leaving for far longer. Down there (from her vantage she could actually see the District between the pregnant bellies of cloud, swollen with hoarfrosted raindrops, birthing a million snowchildren into the natal glow of morning), down there in Leonidas she had believed she had not left anything but rather found something worth staying for. Delicious hot drinks. Stories without end. Responsibility of an earthier variety than any she had ever known and far more attractive for it. And love, naturally.

Yes. Love most of all kept her keen on Leonidas District.

Not love of the place (though that played a part) but love of the man she'd met there. Love that drank you up and infused you with, oh hell, all the gooey things that shabby poets scribbled about in the moonglow and candlekiss of romantic dusk.

Then Frank Gallant had come through the Eurydice portal, and Wendy's father had been driven into a dream from which he would never wake, and the prodigal daughter had returned to take up his suit of scales, his invisible crown, his scarlet tower. The elegy became hers to embody. Some welcome. Some home.

But it was her cherished year in Leonidas that had taught her valuable truths, and one truth above all. It was something she could not disclose to Hughes. The anger it would incite in him would make last night's tantrum seem a pale and bloodless thing. Here, now, with her shoulder pressed against the lining of the window and the cold breath of December blowing her cheeks full of plum-dark flush, and with the city huddled against the blizzard below her, she might as well disclose it to herself.

Quickbolts and regulation; it was all bunk. Pithy rationalizations meant to placate a young man with a kind heart and a head fizzing with tomorrow. What it might look like. How he might realize it. She grasped motivation that fierce, even sympathized with it. But it was doomed because of the fundamental truth underlying the matter.

The real reason she could not condone the arming of the populace was that Corinth City had no stomach for a militia. Here and there you got a civic minded lass or bloke who would stick their neck out to save their neighbor from the headsman, supernatural or mundane. But by and large people were happy to get on with their lives. Pass from point A to point C, willfully oblivious of the screams emanating from point B. People wanted to wake up and have a warm shower and work the job and kiss the lover and take turns cooking dinner and read to the kids and watch a vid and go to sleep. They did not want to be handed a magic item and told they were heroes now. Much more comfortable was the idea that their hero was out there, taking up ether and performing various feats of derring-do. Surely they would do the saving where required.

Hughes would never accept that.

How could he?

He was, after all, one of the civic minded ones. Given the rising severity of this Spring-Heeled malarky, his neck was seemingly poised in the vicinity of the chopping block. Once it was over (she was surprised that no conscious part of her entertained the idea of Hughes failing) she would endeavor to change his mind on the whole "magic item mass production" business. Make him see sense.

Hughes had Performance, but Wendy had a surplus of the next best thing—style.

He would come around. She was quite sure of it.

"My mistake was referring to them as *ordinary people*," she murmured tartly. "He looked as though I'd just called them serfs. Well, maybe it was tantamount to that. Even a dragon errs, on occasion."

Against all odds of gravity, a snowflake blew in. It landed in her hair, white-on-white.

Stubborn old me, mused Wendy, before shutting the window 'gainst the dawning of the day.

***

There was a doll in the road.

Hughes saw the little girl drop it, excited by what her mother was showing her in a large Tinfrost hamper: raisin and walnut cakes, lemon shortbread, chocolate-covered almonds and other things for Father Tinfrost (despite being made of tin, it was said he was as peckish as a man of flesh and blood), as well as carrots and parsnips for the gnomes (who are reputedly heavy smokers trying to quit, and thus appreciate thin food) and assorted munchable things for the twelve giant squirrels who pull the sleigh every December.

A few steps later the little girl noticed she was minus a doll, and with a lackadaisy Hughes could not understand because he had not grown up with money, she shrugged and cooed at her mother to give her another peek in the hamper and did not even go to the trouble of looking behind her.

If she had, she would have seen Hughes bending to pick up her doll—which was lacy and pink and wonderful—and opening his mouth to call out to her. She would have seen his lips freeze and the muscles in his throat contract and lock around the words he might have spoken. She would have seen him staring at the doll as though he were staring at a ghost.

But she did not turn around, and the busy street whelmed over the little girl with a jingle-tinkle-ring of festive bells.

Hughes mastered his nerve, which had been frayed for a second but was gradually mending. He ran a hand over the dark bristles of his beard.

Before him, among the footprint tracks and scraps of colorful bunting that had come loose and floated down from the streetlamps and signs, the doll seemed to speak to him in a voice that crossed a decade of his life.

It was not splayed out, as one might expect a fallen doll to be. On that note its skirts were neater and tidier than reason could account for. He looked at the stuffed limbs lying reposefully and at the one that defied the others. One stitched arm pointed down a side alley that abandoned the light and bustle of the main thoroughfare for stillness and the dark. It might have seemed random to most, but Hughes knew better.

It was not the first time he'd received guidance from a marionette, you see.

He set off down the alley, freezing hands plunged into the depths of his coat and eyelashes blinking away the morning's snow. The blizzard had broken for now, hence the flurry of shoppers behind him, but the wind still held bite. Through its cold teeth it seemed to whisper promises of the blizzard's return.

Sealed off by a brick wall at one end, the alley was sheltered from both daylight and the worst of the breeze. Warped and indistinct, his reflection regarded him from the red stainless steel of two huge bins. Downspouts dipped low from the buildings on either side of him like ladles in the slush. They rattled, and below that he could hear the *trickle-drip* of water sifting through the sewer grates rimmed in ice and gripped by tenacious winter slugs, small, shriveled things whose glossy slime seemed a parody of the morning light's gleam on the snow covering Corinth.

Something else too. He could hear voices.

Recognizing one and feeling a rush of vindicated pleasure, Hughes rounded the second bin and saw two figures sitting in the snow.

"Good morning, Frank. Who's this?"

Frank leaped to his feet, his face a portrait of joy. "Well I'll be a monkey's uncle and an auntie's cool vermouth cocktail on a sunny veranda—Hughes! Great to see you, man. I think you'll find it is a *great* morning, not just *good*. Smell that rare air in fair abundance? Smell it there, that rare fair air."

It smelled like bog-standard alleyway air to Hughes. Only...

Only quite suddenly, remarkably, Hughes felt his mind switch gears. It *was* pretty nice outdoors. "Nice" didn't cover it. Crisp and sharp, the perfume of the slush and the snow mingled with the richer, dark-sweet smell of hot chocolate brewed fresh in a nearby café. He oughtn't to have been surprised at this change. Frank Gallant was like wet paint on life's railings; lean for just a moment and you found yourself marked and grinning helplessly.

"This here's a friend of mine," said Frank of the other figure squatting in the gloom. "Tookus Argyle Vercingetorix of Demeter."

"Good day, young man," said Tookus.

He extended a hand gnarled in varicose veins. Hughes shook it and had the impression he was gripping a leathery glove. Mr. Vercingetorix was what a diplomatic person would have called "venerable," and what a significantly less diplomatic person would call "old as Grandad's hand-me-down trousers." Frail though he might be, Hughes liked the man's wide, avuncular smile, even if it was brown and several teeth short of the average set.

"Let me help you up, Tookus," said Frank.

"Much obliged, Mr. Gallant. Much obliged."

"My pleasure. Up you come. There, ain't verticality a treat after sitting in the street? Yes indeed. But introductions remain open when they ought to be shut tight by now. Gormon Hughes is only a name. This is *him*, Mr. Vercingetorix."

"Wassat?"

Frank canted his head to one side, the aurora in his hair a playful periwinkle blue. "You heard me."

The old man looked at Frank.

He looked at Hughes.

He looked at Frank again.

"*Him?*"

Frank nodded.

Tookus brushed the snow off his rear and regarded Hughes with a new respect. That avuncular smile appeared again, even wider this time. "I'll be an uncle's cookie jar and an auntie's cookies." He stepped forward, regrasping Hughes' hand in both of his own and pumping it with gusto and good cheer. "Oh merriness and mirth, young man. Let both eclipse your blackest suns and blot your sinistrest moons."

Hughes wasn't sure you could qualify "sinistrest" as a word. He wasn't sure what was happening either, except that he was on the receiving end of a truly vigorous hand-pump. Mr. Vercongetorix showed no sign of stopping. Standing there in the dimness of the alley, they looked like salesmen agreeing on the most splendid deal, or perhaps a malfunctioning winch—*pumppumppump*. Feeling thoroughly ridiculous and just as baffled by the situation, Hughes shot Frank a look that said, *I really am pleased you're back in my life after so long apart, but right now ours is a precarious arrangement. Help at once, or I'll... Well, I shall think of something very vengeful, Frank, just you bloody wait and see.*

His old friend took mercy on him. "Mr. Hughes and I had best be on our way."

"Hm? Oh yes. Yes, of course." Tookus Argyle Vercingetorix let go of Hughes' hand. There was a rumpled hat on his head. He snatched it off and gave Hughes a creaky-jointed bow. "Distinguished to have met you, young man. Dis-tinguished. May She Whose Favorite Gift Is Ambrosia Fudge walk by your side *and never behind you.*"

And with that, he set his hat back on his head, embraced Frank, and shuffled out of the alley and into the wintry morning.

"What was that about?" Hughes asked Frank. "How does he know me? And what did you mean, 'of Demeter.' Like Demeter Road?"

"He doesn't know you," said Frank, leading him out of the alley and east toward Leonidas District. "Heard of you? Sure. There's a lot of speculation about you amongst people like him. As to Demeter... One second. Anybody peeping?"

Hughes glanced about. "Plenty."

"Good. I do love an audience."

Frank was wearing a suit of gorgeous white cashmere, its three buttons silver squirrels, its cufflinks holly berries of green and red stone. He was wearing a tie too, green as a Tinfrost tree, but before Hughes' eyes (and a great many other people's, the street was busy), the tie split apart into a hundred strings of nylon, lengthening, reforming, and all at once Frank was not wearing a tie but a heavy green scarf that warmed his throat and drifted behind him.

A few people walked briskly by them, keen to put distance between themselves and anything so odd as this, but most ignored it, and some were even charmed, nudging their children or their friends and nodding at the striking figure Frank cut that day in middle-late December.

If only his mothers could see him, Hughes thought. *They would be completely and utterly livid.*

In the depths of his perplexity, the notion gave him a flash of pleasure because the Nightjar Coven would not see their son or anything ever again on account of being cadaverously inclined, i.e. dead.

Frank wrapped his new scarf a little tighter.

"Cold as a farmer's bed at lunchtime. Wind's working its way up to a big statement, see if I'm wrong. Where was I?"

"Demeter Road," said Hughes. "But hold on..."

"No, not Demeter Road. Tookus is from the *town*, man."

"Is there one?"

"There used to be. Corinth City ate it up a long time ago. Demeter's where the kings of this country used to rule."

"Ah. That one." Hughes was no scholar, but he knew his city. "So the old geezer thinks he's from a town that hasn't existed for ahm... about three hundred years, give or take?"

"You're from a teashop?"

"Yeah."

"I'm from a dream realm. Don't blight a man's origins as strange when ours are equally peculiar. Tookus was once a hedge knight summoned into service by the fourth King of Corinthia. Does that make said old man older than you initially believed? Yes, it does. So what? Tookus is what you might call one of the in-between people. People like your Painted Girl and her Ringmaster Woman."

Why don't you grow any older? Hughes had asked Krys.

Why do you? It seems terribly inconvenient.

Somewhere in a fictional universe, a version of him called Hughes 2 doubtless enjoyed a suite of the most ordinary friends and acquaintances.

Hughes 1, meanwhile, had the sort of friends and acquaintances who looked into the future because they were bored and who remodeled ties into scarves because they were chilly.

"But why me?" Hughes asked.

"If you existed on the periphery of the world, and you heard about a fellow who could do the things you do, wouldn't you be interested?"

"It would depend on the reasons behind that intrigue. Do they want something?" As they'd parted, the old man had invoked a blessing for Hughes, something about someone walking beside him rather than behind him? And what had he said about fudge? "Is it a religious thing? A cult?" Krys and The Mum had never struck him as cultish types. Deeply weird and amazing, naturally, but never that.

"No, Hughes. They're interested in you the way the moon is interested in this world we walk. The same forces that act upon you act upon them. Unseen gravities. You get me?"

"Not really."

Frank chuckled. "Give it time, and time'll give it back. Trust me?"

"You know I do."

"I've got something important to tell you. Would have told you before in the Thud household, but I figured you'd want it to just be me and you."

"Tell me."

"I believe I can take you to the place where your power comes from."

Hughes' heart skipped a beat. The phrase "get the shivers" doesn't even touch the intensity of the prickles that swept his body. Senses heightened with shock, he was aware of small things rendered somehow significant in the snowfall. On his left a metrotram was leaving the station. Shopping bags crinkled. Coats rustled in the breeze. Snuffs and whines rose as a newborn collie tried to make sense of a synthetic dalmatian, its spotted fur so convincing to the eye, so repelling to the nose. Above and to the right, on a balcony smelling of pork chops marinated in soy sauce, a waitress was taking her break, red-painted fingernails poised around the day's nineteenth cigarette, one for each day of December. Hughes was not sure why, but this last image filled him with what his childhood hero Gwendle Gardener would have called Fell and Fabulous Omenhood, a sense that behind the scenes hidden players rehearsed and set pieces changed, and without his knowledge lots of terribly crucial things had been building, and he mustn't flub his lines or miss a cue now that the moment was here!

His fingers closed round Frank's wrist.

"No mischief, Frank. I said I trust you and I do, so don't tease or say something glib or... or glamorous, or anything. I want to go," he said. "*Need* to. Take me there now, please."

Frank was looking at Hughes' hand. With an effort Hughes peeled his fingers away.

"We'll need a quiet place," said Frank. "Someplace we won't be disturbed for a long time."

"How long?"

"I don't know. Could be hours." The blue aurora deepened in his hair, an oddly foreboding violet. "Could be days."

"Days?" Hughes looked aggrieved. "I can't... Oh Frank, what have you done?"

Hughes covered his face with his hand.

The air might be rare indeed, but the sight of Frank Gallant taken aback was rarer still. Through the curled slats of his fingers Hughes was treated to that sight now, much good it did him.

"I don't understand," said Frank.

"It's okay," Hughes said. His voice was a nerve-gnawed whisper. "I can't go for days. Even hours might be disastrous. I don't suppose you've read the newspaper. Yesterday was filled with horror shows of the most despicable kind. People crushed under a chandelier, teachers attacking students, mass poisonings at a nightclub, a fire. Captain Thud's assured me Jack is behind them all, and I think he's right. We've got to focus on that now with all we've got, and you..."

"I've cast uncertainty into the mix," said Frank, comprehension dawning. Sorrow creased his face for him. "And that's not all there is. There's more. You're getting it from all sides. Can't believe I missed it till now. It's on your face like a cracked mask. Talk to me, brother of mine. I love you. I'll help you if it is within my power to do it, and if it is not then by the ceaseless tones of the clock that sends hour chasing hour, I will *try*."

"My friend Hector is going to die." He paused, thinking, *Don't talk about it*, and found himself doing it anyway. "I guess there is more. Cate and I... we were going to have a baby. A little girl. She um..." A sound of despair (controlled, but only just) escaped him. "Something awful happened to her, and Cate almost died, and I... Oh God. Oh I can't do this right now."

He wiped his face and put out his hands and caught some snow and wiped his face some more. The feel of the flakes melting against his cheeks soothed a little. A little, but not enough. In his mind's eye he could not escape visions of recycle bins and plastic bags jangling with shards of bloodied glass lobbed into them. He saw Cate in a hospital bed, blissfully asleep, smiling faintly. Foreign matter. Pudgy seashell hand. The message on the stapler in Doctor Lanmoor's office: *Try and hold it together.*

He felt something warm pushed against his palm.

Frank was there, offering takeaway tea, and with a look of beatific sympathy etching his face like a carving of an angel who deals in sins more often than miracles, but who is no less lovely for that.

Hughes sipped his tea.

"Cardamom and fennel," he said wonderingly.

"It's your favorite."

"It was. Sweet plum and fennel now."

"Things change," said Frank Gallant. Gently, he brought Hughes' fingers closed so he was holding the cup with both hands. "Things stay the same."

"I'm still an open book with mussed-up, inky-splotched, dog-eared pages."

"I'm still a puppet who has been handed his own strings, lost trying to figure them out. Tangled and cryptic. I'll make a concerted effort to be clear now as things look dire and in need of clarity. Sound good?"

"Sounds great."

"Great as the day with its whole self set on becoming evening. Walk and talk?"

"Walk and talk."

They walked and talked.

Mostly Frank.

He told Hughes about his adventures across the world. They were not altogether dangerous pursuits (it is hard to be in danger when your companion is Mr. Glint), but obstacles arose as Frank sought the answer to a question that could not be articulated, yet which played the strings of his soul with a melody that was both bewitching and urgent.

"I found many answers," Frank confided. "None of them *right* though, and I'm sorry that that's as exact as I can be. Could be I got the same wanderlust that pulls kids from the shelter of Mom and Dad's roof, sends them off across the world in search of something vital, something without letters or pictograms, which nevertheless spells 'Growing Up' when arranged in the rebus of the heart."

"My dad calls that The Autumn Waltz," Hughes put in. "Makes sense. Autumn is the season where change shows itself most vividly."

"The Autumn Waltz." Frank regarded the slate-dark chimneys poking up from shingles encased in ice and sealed tight in a fusion of snow. His smile was faint but definite. "Not bad."

One by one Frank accumulated knowledge of a group he deemed the in-between people, or the midwayers. Those who had fallen through a crack. Which one—who could say? To what end? Frank did not know. He knew only that of the many he and Mr. Glint encountered, these in-between folk were the most memorable. Frank liked them. And, intriguingly, to a one they had all heard of Gormon Hughes, or at the very least someone fitting his description and accreditation.

"Talking to them, I started to assemble a sense—or the *hint* of a sense—for a place where Dreams and Death meet."

"Why are you saying it like that?"

"Like what?"

"Dreams and Death," said Hughes. "See? Like they've got Capital Letters."

"Was I doing that?"

"You were."

Frank frowned. "Huh." He shrugged. "Well, they're big ideas. Only natural to treat them with respect."

"And what is this place, where Dreams and Death coincide?"

"We'll find out when we get there. All I'm certain of is the name. Dreaming Jija."

Dreaming Jija.

The name held an odd malevolence. He told Frank as much.

"More mystical than malevolent for me. But I get you. Tookus and the others didn't want to go into it. Had to coax it out of them. They said I must make sure you don't go there. That it might incur the ire of She Whose Favorite Gift Is Ambrosia Fudge." Frank smiled. "Goes without saying, I'm taking you there as soon as you say so. Years ago I was your guide through dreams. I intend to do it again. What's the theatrical term? *Once more, with feeling!*"

"And this Dreaming Jija. You think it's where my powers come from?"

"I know it's on the way. As to what comes after, you and I will find that out too."

Hughes pondered a moment. "Whose favorite gift is ambrosia fudge?"

"Lots of people. Fudge is a glorious invention designed to keep the masses happy. Propaganda of the bowel."

"Frank..."

"Yeah, yeah. Look, this is going to sound... It might rub up against your understanding of the world." A woman carrying a bouquet of flowers, fat and lush and burgundy, paused to offer one to Frank. Why she did this, Hughes was not exactly sure, though he guessed it was another symptom of his old friend's charm. Frank took the bloom, blew the woman a kiss, and walked on, inhaling its fragrance. "She Whose Favorite Gift Is Ambrosia Fudge is what Tookus and the rest of the midwayers call Death. And that's not a capital 'D' based in respect, although there's good reason to respect her. It's because it's her *name*."

"Death?"

"You know it, man."

"Like... with the black hood and stuff?"

"That *stuff* is called a *scythe*. And yeah. Far as I know, that's her."

"That's patently ridiculous."

Frank shrugged one of his eloquent shrugs. "In that case we ought to have no trouble getting to Dreaming Jija."

"Right."

"We needn't worry about the whole *walking alongside her* shtick."

"Right."

"About her *getting behind us* with that scythe of hers."

"R—right."

Hughes felt a needle of unease trace the flesh between his shoulder blades. He wondered how much of that creeping dread he'd felt at the mention of the place between death and dreams was the name it held, and how much was owed to the one who might stop him from reaching it. She Whose Favorite Gift Is Ambrosia Fudge. It was an absurd moniker. Almost clownish. So why did he have the distinct impression something was tickling the fine hairs on the curve of his back? Something lifelessly cold. And *sharp*.

Frank was holding the flower outstretched, expecting him to take a whiff.

"No thanks," Hughes said. "Peony."

"Now who's being cryptic?"

"Never you mind. We'll talk about dream journeys later. For now, we've got a..."

Hughes petered off into grumbles. His ears began to redden.

Frank grinned. "A dream journey to make?"

"Shut up," said Hughes.

"Susabeth Dennings." Frank tried her name on for size. "Su-za-*beth*. Funny kinda name."

"Less amusing circumstance."

"I heard that, brother. Why'd you pick her?"

"Her recollection of the murder is the best defined. She can recall minute details that seem to elude the other cases."

"Who'd she off?"

"Husband. Children."

"Damn."

"Yeah."

"How many?"

"Two," said Hughes. "Adam and Ellen."

Adam's teacher was Brenda Kofatch. The reason Hughes knew that was because Rummy Lou, the woman who had taken a steel wire brush to one of her students (a now hospitalized boy named Daniel Slone) had her next of kin listed as her girlfriend. This woman had been interviewed by Captain Hoshrum Thud at half past six that morning. Thud had sent the notes to Hughes, and though it was unlikelier than unlikely, the world had sent forth a connection. Brenda's mother was the late Sheila Kofatch, a woman who before she had gotten married and moved out of Leonidas, had let Hughes use her bath once a month. Blush had crept up her neck as she'd handed him the towel, her face turned aside for modesty's sake. Sheila had been killed during The Hairy Autumn. Ten years later, her daughter's partner and one of her students had been touched by the vileness that was Spring-Heeled Jack.

Funny old world. No, what was the other one? Dreadful.

Dreadful old world.

Well, he wasn't going to stand by and let it go on. Today they would venture into Susabeth Dennings' head, and they would unearth some essential clue that would lead them to Jack. Or the feminine idea that was Jack, he amended mentally, thinking on his chat with Krys the Painted Girl.

Jack infested innocent people, and afterward he wiped their memories. There had to be a reason for that. Something awaiting discovery behind the magically-stunned skulls of the victims. *Something there*, he mused. *And I want it.*

I want you, Jack.

Unconsciously he brushed the ball of his thumb over Chimera's lion-headed pommel.

I want your thumping-pumping heart skewered and leaking your life on my sword, my knife, my rage.

His mind moved freely over the conversation with Krys then, and with the wind stating itself in freezing lashes and whip-strikes of bluster as Frank had predicted, Hughes recalled the predictions of the carousel-cottage oracle.

Two shadows, one pursuing the other. You're after her, aren't you, Hughes?

That thumb-brush over the pommel again. Snow glistened in Chimera's ramhorn cross guard and in the grooves of the sculpted dragon head breathing its finger of steel, its killing edge.

Next to him, the Dream Warrior plucked a petal. "She loves me," he said. Another. "She loves me not."

"Ever find her, Frank?"

"Huh?"

"Your Lady of Evening."

He watched Frank's lips tug up at the corners. The smile was as enigmatic as any Hughes had ever seen, with extra helpings of mystery, inscrutability, and conundrum. His fingers plucked another petal. The wind carried it away.

"She loves me..."

Chapter Fifteen

The ex-criminal and the policeman sat next to one another outside Susabeth Dennings' room. One of them was there under the pretext of investigating the crime that had taken place in this building the day prior, and the other was there simply because he wanted to be, and because no one dared to ask him why.

"Thanks for clearing out the bird nest," said Hoshrum Thud.

"Don't mention it, gov," replied Mr. Glint in his voice like two gravestones grinding to horrible sour silt.

In its ceiling fixture the corridor projector whirred. The walls swam with oceanic blue. Animated catfish whiskered and whelmed over them.

"Traveled a lot, have you?" said Thud.

"Been about."

"Far afield?"

"What?"

"Travel far afield?"

"Some," said Mr. Glint. "They had donkeys."

"Right," said Thud. "Rrright." He opened his mouth... and closed it.

A nurse hurried by, her nose in a chart.

Taggart House as a whole was a profoundly anxious place that Monday morning. A custodian caught smothering patients has a tangible effect on morale. Ashtrays piled high. Doctors were jumpy. Nurses had steelier nerves, though they were not faring much better. Administration chewed pens. Cooks nicked their fingers, burnt breakfast, accidentally elbowed cutlery pots that toppled to the floor in a clatter and clash that raised eyebrows and sent hands fluttering over bunned hair and chests and mouths whose lips made perfect "o"s of discontent. Two additional guards had been hired overnight, big no-nonsense men with backgrounds in law enforcement. Custodians mopped with heads bent, watching the wet acrid-smelling trails gliiiiiide back and forth across the linoleum. Orderlies spent as little time around the fruitcakes... around the *guests* as possible. Drool went unwiped. Bedpans and clothes changed with less frequency, ditto showers doled out. Some of the sweeter nurses had taken time to read to their favorite guests. This practice did not see the light of the new week and might never again. There had been a mistake. A man had snapped on duty. More importantly he'd been *allowed* to snap, had been permitted to vent each burst of insanity room after room without intervention. As a result scrutiny was ratcheting up to match the sheer enormity of this fuck-up, and it was in unspoken agreement that the trivial kindnesses of normal day-to-day operations were ousted for the foreseeable future.

All this goes to say that there was a hard, inflexible tension in the air, and maybe that was why Hoshrum Thud said, "If memory serves, there was a Mr. Glint who occupied a somewhat... How would you put it? A *prominent* position in the city underworld."

"That so?"

"We were up to our ears in cases pertinent to Mr. Glint."

"Yeah?"

"Mutilations. Brutalizations. Assault and battery, like. Arson. Destruction of property. Violation of city ordinance on every possible indictment from murder to loitering with intent to murder. Even had a pest control service call in, said Mr. Glint was putting them out of business. It got to the point where we had our own classification for him. A normal person dumps an overdose victim on a sidewalk, that's a major incident. But Mr. Glint dumps a body, well, that's littering, isn't it?"

"Sounds like a nuisance."

"You could say that. You could, in fact, say that." Thud fingered his immaculate mustache. "On the other hand, you could say he was a one-man-case for bringing back public hangings."

"Wouldn't have worked."

"No?"

Mr. Glint shook his head. "No."

"No. I suppose not."

Thud took a tiny box of pomade from his jacket, daubed his fingers, and smoothed the syrupy stuff over his whiskers (which made the catfish look like amateurs).

"Always wondered what I would do if I met the infamous Mr. Glint."

"Sort of..." Glint's brow wrinkled with the effort of conjuring the word. "Idle speculation, yeah?"

"That's right."

They sat there, Thud stony faced, Glint sour-mouthed.

Then Mr. Glint stood up, and he wrenched the projector off the ceiling. With a sickening *crrrrack* he opened his mouth wider than a man should be able to widen his mouth. The projector and all its blue currents and its jolly swimming fishes disappeared down his throat.

Mr. Glint sat back down.

The corridor was gray, and unmoving, and silent.

Thud's face was still completely impassive. Not one single muscle had changed, not even a twitch. In a flat, matter-of-fact tone, he said, "Come to think of it, we caught him in the end."

"Yeah?"

"Nabbed him good, we did. Locked him up to rot in a cell. Justice served. Threw the book at him. The whole library, in his case. We rested a damn sight easier after that, I don't mind telling you."

"I bet you did."

"You'd win that bet. Yeah, we said. There he is behind bars at last. Mr. Glint in that cell."

"Which one?"

"Which one? Ahhh. Thir... teen."

"Thirteen?"

"Thirteen. Lucky thirteen, we said. That's where our man is."

"Give you much trouble, did he?"

"No," said Thud quickly. "Model inmate, I always said."

"Well done."

"Gentlemen," came a new voice.

Both looked up and saw Hughes and Frank appear, Hughes in his ultralight scarlet armor and his tattered coat, Frank fixing his tie where only a moment ago there had been a scarf.

"I've got to check in with the commissioner in half an hour. How long will this take?" asked Thud.

"Not long," said Frank.

They filed inside.

None of them had known Susabeth Dennings before she'd taken a knife to her family and lapsed into her current lethargy. Still, it did not take a genius to see that her body had undergone changes that were both recent and drastic. She had that slightly sagging look of someone who has lost a lot of weight too fast. Where it wasn't loose, her skin was riddled with the blue and purple passage of veins. She had carved out her hair in clumps to write her message at the crime scene. Damage to the scalp was minimal, yet what had grown back was not the healthy dun-colored hair that had been with her since girlhood, but thin strands of iron-gray. Her bed was tilted at a forty-degree angle. She lay there with her eyeballs wide open, seeing nothing, her slow blinks like habits hard to break.

Without exchanging a word the four men took various positions in the room, as though obeying instructions in a script. Frank and Mr. Glint removed the spare plastic-sheeted mattress from where it had been stuffed in a storage unit. Hughes washed his hands at the room's hygiene station, took out some petroleum jelly, and applied it to Susabeth's dry, cracked mouth. Captain Hoshrum Thud went to the bedside table opposite Hughes. There was a heart-shaped biscuit tin there, newly bought. A little note next to it said, *Your safety is our heart's desire. From all your friends in the Taggart House staff.* He stared at this piece of mealy-mouthed tripe for a while, wondering who it was for. Not Susabeth Dennings, certainly. She wouldn't have known an elephant if it was placed on her bedside table, much less a biscuit tin.

Some thought moved behind his eyes, some flash of instinct. His wife had seen this expression across the dinner table more times than she could count, and far more often than she liked. She called it one of his namesakes. A moment in which he stopped thinking about clues and started cluing about think. In other words, a moment of irrational yet total focus upon an idea that, while not valued by the currency in the troubled market of policing, nevertheless held a formidable promise. A thud. Hettie always said that when her husband got that look, things were about to get very interesting indeed.

"I'm going to stay out of it," he said.

Hughes glanced at him. "Of what?"

"The dream."

"No need for caution. Frank can pull us out at any time."

"Guarantee that, can you?"

"Jack is long gone." Hughes replaced the petroleum jelly, his brow creasing. "What's got you nettled?"

"Instinct, lad. Primary tool of police work."

"I thought observation was the primary tool of police work."

"Yeah. Course. Only instinct is the other one."

Hughes opened his mouth to defend the sanctity of the word "primary," then thought better of it. "We might need you in there. Details that would strike you as obvious might sail by us unnoticed."

"I don't think so. This whole dream business is a bit big for my boots. Give me honest cobbles and I'm flying, or patrolling at the very least. But dreams..." Thud pursed his lips, made a thoughtful smacking sound. "I'll have a devil of a time finding my feet in dreams. I'll stay here. Consider me Plan B, as in Plan Bloody A didn't work so let's rely on the other one."

To that Hughes had no reply. He looked expectantly at Frank who was lying down on the spare mattress. Frank shrugged.

So it was decided.

"Don't touch the strings," Hughes warned Thud.

Thud nodded absently. He turned the biscuit tin over in his hands, his gaze distant.

A look of mild irritation crossed Hughes' face.

Meanwhile Mr. Glint turned to Frank. "Aren't we going to Creamy Ginger?"

"*Dreaming Jija*, Mr. Glint. Sure we are. Not today though. Today we're going to help Hughes with the Spring-Heeled Jack murders."

"What, like disposing of the bodies and suchlike?"

"What? No." Frank's eyes had been closed. Now he opened them and sat up slightly. "Hughes is not Spring-Heeled Jack. He wants to *stop* Spring-Heeled Jack."

"Gotchya." Mr. Glint nodded. "That way he can do the scragging himself. Free up the playing field."

"Aren't you going to ask?" Hughes prompted Thud.

"Sorry?" said Thud.

"Mr. Glint," said Frank. "I feel like we have got our wires somewhat tangled. Hughes is not going to scrag anybody."

"Only Spring-Heeled Jack."

"'What strings?' I thought you'd ask me what strings," said Hughes.

"Why should I do that?" said Thud.

"Well, we'll see what we can do," said Frank. "Hughes says that Jack knows me. Calls me the Cut-String King. Could be one malicious momma-jamma."

"Why?" said Hughes. "Well, I don't know. It was vague, the statement I made. Don't touch the strings. Sort of an evocative... thing. Like when someone looks outside and goes, 'Oh bugger,' it's very... evocative."

"Oh yes?"

"Someone looks outside and goes, 'Oh bugger.' And someone else says, 'Nasty out, eh?' You know."

Thud opened the biscuit tin, examining the treats cozy in their aluminum casing. "I expect you'd tell me if I needed to know."

"If Jack... knows you, Mr. Gallant," said Mr. Glint, slowly, as though pulling each word up his throat like a husk of mummified bone from a tomb. "Then... maybe Jack knew your mums... before I ate them."

"The thought has crossed my mind," said Frank.

"If Jack knew your mums... Jack might make mischief... that's just right... or just wrong... for you. Because your mums knew you, and how to hurt you. And if Jack tries to hurt you, then I'll hurt Jack," affirmed Glint in a growl that would make the flesh of the long-dead crawl. "Not a little, either. I will hurt him lots."

Frank smiled. "We'll be careful."

"Careful as lambs, Mr. Gallant."

"Big man," said Frank, lying down and closing his eyes once more. "For the wolf who mistakes you and I for lambs, I have nothing but the deepest and sincerest pity."

Hughes leaned against the wall, one leg tucked pensively behind the other, his arms knotted over his chest. "These strings," he muttered.

Frank's body transformed. Tendrils of nylon swept over the left hand-side of the room. Place a camera in front of an abandoned space, preferably a warm and sheltered and slightly damp space where spiders of robust size may roam and plot and plan thin spindly plans. After a month has passed, edit the recorded vid so that it plays at a dizzyingly fast speed and watch as the spiders unfurl their pale sticky schematic in quicktime, constructing a palace of cobweb, stringing the whole place full as if in celebration. That was what it looked like when Frank sent forth his puppet strings. They covered every surface from the wall, the sink, the storage cupboard, the bed with Susabeth Dennings, Frank and Mr. Glint and Hughes, all becoming immersed and vanishing into strings, stopping just shy of Hoshrum Thud and the bedside table.

"Those strings," he echoed pleasantly.

He closed the biscuit tin, slipped it under his arm, and went to see if he could find a nurse.

***

He opened his eyes and for a moment was overwhelmed by the feeling that he was inside a photograph. Lightheadedness spilled over his brain, a cerebral paint striped in vertigo and nausea. Hughes closed his eyes and silently mouthed the flavors of his favorite teas, starting with the very best, which was sweet plum and fennel, and going down all the way until he reached the more uncommon teas he was only in the mood for on rare occasion, such as liquorice and infusion of dogwood.

It settled him, and with a deep steadying breath, he opened his eyes once more.

He was in an apartment. Tinsel hung from green cabinets and drawers, and everywhere he looked there were candleholders with frames sliced into different shapes. Red and green flames shone from these, not wholesome comforting shades but festersome ones; the red of an infected wound, the green of fresh-squeezed pus. In these colors the candleholders stenciled shadows on the walls, the sofa cushions, the decorated Tinfrost tree. That sense of stepping into a photograph had not been altogether wrong. The apartment had been home to Marberry, Susabeth, Adam, and Ellen Dennings. He had seen it in November on the front page of *The Times*.

There were two differences. First, those heinous candles casting the room and his face and body in eerie light. Second, the message on the wall by the tree.

It was no longer written in human hair as in the photograph, but rather in nylon strings. Moreover the words were different. Gone was the freakish confession THEY ARE IN ME. As he read what the strings had to tell him, Hughes felt the disorientation he'd conquered make its return. It spoiled into an unease that tasted like rotten cabbage soup. It slinked from his head, into the canal of his dry throat, and down into his guts.

HUGHES I WAS WRONG JACK IS STILL HERE.

DON'T KNOW HOW BUT I'M SURE OF IT.

MR. G AND I ARE HIDDEN.

GET HER TALKING. GET HER INTERESTED.

WHEN SHE COMES WE'LL TAKE HER TOGETHER.

F

If Hughes had been of different stock, he might have wet his lips, or let his lower one creep beneath his teeth for a nervous nibble, or he might have clenched his fingers or let the sudden judder of his heartbeat wheel him into the spokes of panic.

But he was a man prepared in the stock of the worst trouble you can imagine, and so when the message sank in he let his weight shift ever so slightly, creating a solid foundation on the apartment's hardwood floor, and on that bulwark he began to stack the blocks of a Performance. It used the surreal cottony silence. It used the malignant lights flickering green and red. Tilting his head and letting the room's shadow taste his jaw with probing tongues of dark, and smiling faintly, he seemed for all intents and purposes to be a personality corrupted, as sinister as this dead home dream in Susabeth Denning's head.

The voice emerging through his lips was quite unlike his usual one. It was the sort of voice that would make even the frightful Mr. Glint turn around and take notice. He really was quite the performer.

"Good morning," he said.

"Good morning yourself," replied Jack.

***

"Telephone for you, Captain," said the nurse.

"Me?" Thud was fiddling with the ice dispenser on the staff fridge.

He came out to the front desk, picked up the phone, and put it to his ear.

"This is Thud," he said at exactly the same time he realized he was holding the dispenser, and the ice, recently topped-up, was about to tip over.

"Was he a gospel monkey?" said Commissioner Vincent Winkles.

"Sir?"

"Well, was he?"

"To whom are you referring, sir?"

Thud slid the handset and receiver under his chin and caught a pair of ice cubes before they could slide from the dispenser onto a computer keyboard.

"Who do you think, Thud? The nutcase who smothered all those hoppers in the Toadhouse." There was a pause, during which Thud was sure the commissioner puffed at a cigar as tobacco-packed and ugly as he was, and during which Thud tried to signal the nurse clicking away at her portable screen for help. She smiled a blissful smile and took no notice. "How are the interviews going up there?"

"Fine, sir. *Pssst.*"

"They're about to undergo a significant improvement, Thud me old ham sandwich. I've got a theory. It's one I am particularly proud of."

"I'm all ears, sir. *Pssst. Nurse.*"

She glanced up, smiled at him vaguely, then walked away, mumbling to herself about the guests on the second floor needing a look in.

"Thud?" The commissioner sounded irritated. "What's that sound?"

"One of the patients here, sir. He's impersonating a man in distress." A battalion of freezing cubes toppled. Somehow he caught all of them. His fingers had gone tingling numb ten seconds ago. Now they were starting to throb. "There he goes. Carry on, sir. Your theory?"

"You're going to interview the rest of the staff there," the commissioner told him. "If you've got their statements already, just say you've got one or two more questions, the usual. Then, right... sort of sneakily, mind... ask them whether or not Mr. ah..." a pause as notes were scrutinized and a cigar was suckled, "Mr. Paulie Manzarek ever tried to recruit them to attend mass."

Thud made like the cubes of gelid water. He froze solid.

"Sir?" he said.

"Maybe go about it even more stealthy-like. Ask them if he ever wore a crucifix under his uniform, or if they ever saw him check nobody was around and cross himself. You know the whole sacred bless-yourself thing."

"I'm afraid I don't understand, sir. What exactly is this theory?"

A grunt of exasperation came from the other end of the line. "For one of our brightest, Thud, you really are dim as a broken bulb sometimes. The church! I'm talking about the old church!"

"What about it, sir?"

"This fellow we've got, Taylet Gordon. According to the survivors of that stunt he pulled with the chandelier, Gordon was performing illegal services at the scene of the crime. Mass! In this day and age! Can you imagine? I heard that, and Thud me lad, it was like all the circuits in my head came on at once."

"Been off for a long time, had they, sir?"

"What's that?"

"Nothing, sir." Thud was no longer aware of the frigid pain threading his hands. His face was very still. Terribly, fervently still. "You're not suggesting that the link between the cases that have been attributed to Spring-Heeled Jack... You're not implying that those cases are joined up by a thread of..."

"Religion, Thud." The commissioner's tone was grand as a grand piano with ambitions of becoming an orchestra. "That's the motive. Your standard plague of religious mania, like what our grandfather's fathers saw in the days of the old church. Don't you see? It explains all the culprits being zonked out of it. Probably driven mad by *zeal*, so they are. Used to be zeal coming out the wazoo in those batty old days of the batty old church. Now, don't waste time speaking to me. Get back into those interviews and get me a corroboration, there's a good copper!"

Thud thought of Hettie. She would not approve of him losing the rag with his superior. She was a stout-hearted woman, a patient woman, and to her conversation was an art as much as the sort that went on one of her canvases.

Hoshrum Thud gave it his best attempt.

"Commissioner Winkles," he said stiffly. "The Spring-Heeled Jack murders are not the work of sectarian vigilantes smiting the unbelievers. It is not a crusade against the heresies of the contemporary epoch of Corinth City. It is *not* a religious crime spree. To be honest, sir, I wish it was. Could solve it overnight. Spread the word that there's going to be a holy summit. Stoke the fires of theistic reverie. Nab them there, call it a day. But, and I really do want you to hear me closely on this, sir, your theory holds as much water as my hand. Which, and I can tell you this from recent experience, *is not very much water at all*."

Through his fingers, icy rills dripped and trickled.

There was silence on the other end of the line.

Thud's moustaches twitched.

Oh well. He'd tried. Hettie wouldn't approve, but then again she might.

There was an art to pissing off your superior. In that field, Hoshrum Thud was a full-blown prodigy.

"Incidentally, are you thinking of going on any impromptu strolls today, sir? Only I ought to prepare the staff here for that possibility. They've only just had the place fumigated to clean out the smell of death, and your perfume of *eau du swaggering twerp* might offend. You understand, sir."

There was a click. The dead line *burr-burred* at him, taunting. Thud glowered at the receiver, replaced it in its cradle, and hefted the ice dispenser. Nearby, the biscuit tin sat open, and Thud set about filling it up, grumbling all the while.

***

When he was four, two years before the arrival of Krys and The Mum's Rotbloom Carnival and twenty-five years before he ventured into the dreaming mind of Susabeth Dennings, Hughes spent an hour with a bee in his head. It was a large springtime bumblebee. Slow and striped and bobbing in lazy, pollen-drunk bobs, the bee had meandered from a florist's over the District border into Leonidas. Finding no flowers to sample (weeds and bad habits and hope grow in Leonidas, but not much else), the discerning bee had become first disgruntled, then really unbelievably angry, and in its anger it had steered itself headfirst into Hughes' ear canal.

Neither participant had been happy with the arrangement. Little Hughes had howled himself raw, and the bee buzzed itself into a frenzy that Hughes could feel shivering down his cheek and filling his face with warm hysterical blood and his skull with the sawing-sizzling-humming-drumming-buzz of electric razors dialed all the way to maximum. A pair of calipers his father sourced from their neighbor Ernie Wilks had set things right, but two-and-a-half decades later Hughes had cause to remember the bee.

The voice of Spring-Heeled Jack was that cause.

It buzzed through the dream apartment walls and up from the floorboards and down from the watermarked plaster of the ceiling. It was insectile, a droning swarming susurrus, but it was also distinctly human. A woman's voice, charming and rich and relaxed, a radio DJ's timbre in the bug-stuffed stereo system of some sultry hell. "Good morning yourself," she said. "Where's Frank?"

"Somewhere decadent, I'm sure. He told me the way here. I've come to meet you, Jack."

"Jack?" The presence he felt all around him chuckled, a little sensual, a little mocking. "My name isn't Jack."

"Who are you?"

"You first, stranger." Was that a smile he heard in the fuzzy core of her tone? His curiosity deepened.

"I'm Gormon Hughes."

From the red and green candleflames crawled a legion of flies. Before his carefully calm gaze they spelled a name out of their twitch-wing bodies.

GORMAN HUGHES.

"Two O's in Gormon."

"Oops. Like this?"

The flies corrected their mistake.

"Like that," he affirmed. While the flies vanished behind picture frames and under lamps and tinsel fronds, Frank's instruction recurred to Hughes. *Get her talking. Get her interested.* Succeeding in that would give Frank and Mr. Glint time to assess and execute their ambush. Also, there was a chance this vile presence would reveal itself to Hughes. If the presence did that, his Performance would wash over it in waves, oh yes, he would *ensure* it. Still so cool and calm, he took a seat on the Dennings' family sofa between two cushions and said, "May I guess your name?"

"May I guess why you've come to meet me?"

"Yes."

"Then yes."

"Your name is Arachne," said Hughes. "Weaver of bedlam and chaos and woe, queen of things that scuttle in the dark."

"Not I," buzzed his company. "You're here because… you're a scholar. A mystic with a house full of books, eager for profane knowledge on subjects that defy the prosaic. A real leather-bound-hound."

"Wrong," said Hughes, not liking how close "house full of books" had been to the truth, for he had spent much of his life in his father's teashop, which was for the most part fashioned out of manuscripts. He sat forward. "And I was wrong to think of spiders. Your chief agents are airborne, not scuttlers, and you speak as though your throat were coated in them. Your name is Beelzebub, Lady of the Flies."

"Not even close," hummed the presence like a bumblebee lodged in both ears. "My turn again. You're here because… you are an enemy of Frank Gallant. He's lured you here so I'll dispose of you for him."

"I'm no friend or enemy of Frank's," Hughes lied smoothly. "Will you?"

"Will I what?"

"Dispose of me?"

"No. I like you," she soothed him, and though his ear was a finely tuned machine when it came to telling truth from lies, Hughes detected not one hint of deceit. "As far as I'm concerned, the only way you could be nicer was if you enjoyed rhymes."

"As it happens I do."

"You do?" Genuine pleasure. Once more he had to resist the tempting questions. *What the hell are you? What do you want?* It was hard. If his curiosity got any deeper he'd have to start shoveling other emotions aside to make room.

"Tell me one," she bid him. "One you're really fond of."

His composure almost faltered, he was that off balance. Desperate, he spoke the first rhyme he could think of. "Mirror man, mirror man, fool me, trick me, if you can."

A sound like a busy apiary surrounded him. It was a moment before he understood what it was. She was laughing.

"Short and sweet. Want one of mine?"

She didn't wait, instead reciting for him eagerly.

"When we smooch farewell in the hall/I shall hug you as close as can be/And as you head home keep so warm/With thoughts of little old me."

"I like that one too," said Hughes. "I like the whole song. An oldie but a goodie."

"Mine comes crooning from Tinfrost jukeboxes. Where's yours from?"

"I don't remember."

"If you do, let me know. Mirror man, mirror man. Sort of... creepy, huh?"

"Most nursery rhymes are."

"That's true. Innocent witches in houses made of sweets," she prompted.

"Wicked orphans making use of convenient ovens," Hughes said, never one to miss a cue when it was offered to him. An impulse arrived in his head. He followed it. "There was an old lady who swallowed a fly, perhaps she'll die."

"It was the horse that did her in, of course."

"I don't know," he said. "Horses are pretty agreeable, even if they are huge kicking biting bastards on occasion. One fly, okay, probably no big deal. But a hundred? A thousand? Swallow enough flies and if you don't die you'll wish for it."

"Only there weren't a hundred or a thousand," she said. "Maybe it felt that way when it was wriggling down her throat. But there was only one. Just one fly, and nothing *perhaps* about her. She *will* die."

Hughes made no reply. His mind raced, sorting the useful details from distractingly alluring conjecture. It was a while before he spoke again. When he did, his voice held none of its former friendliness. "Why are you in this woman's head?"

"The previous tenant moved out and the rent's affordable."

He supposed he deserved that. Okay, a different vector of approach. She was talking but was she interested? "When I spoke to Frank, he told me you were behind all these incidents in the city."

"He did? That's funny."

"Funny?"

"I'm wondering how he knows it's me. Could be anybody," she pointed out. "Could be *him*. It would make sense, actually. Frank comes from a bad family. *Bad stock*, isn't that the Corinth City term?"

"He seemed sure it was you."

No response.

"Are you still there?"

Nothing.

Hughes opened his mouth... and felt something on his hand. Something small and hairy and quick.

He looked down. The fly wandered between two of his knuckles. It twiddled its front legs. It looked at him with eyes faceted like greenish black gemstones.

The electric razor buzz of her voice came from the fly and from all around him at the same time. "I have another guess."

"Go ahead," he murmured, thinking, *If I use my Performance now, would it work? Dare I risk it?*

"You're here because you want to help me. You like what I'm doing as much as you like anything; that scarf you wear with embroidered flowers, your coat with all its clever pockets (I counted them, hope you don't mind), rhymes and words and being alive. You adore what's going on. You see my feast being set, and you want a seat at the table. Don't you, Gormon Hughes? Well, don't you?"

Feast. The word rebounded in his mind—FEASTFEAstfeast—and he thought of Krys and her prediction. *They will meet you at the feast. She and she and she.*

The fly skittered up his middle finger, stopping at the nail, looking up into his face. A fly cannot show expectation, not with its alien features, yet somehow this fly did. "You see it, right? You do, I know it! You see it because something in your life has cleared you out. Bared you. Pared you down to the nub. Emptied. So won't you eat with me?" she asked him. "Eat and be made full?"

Two things happened at once.

Frank and Mr. Glint unfolded themselves from the sofa cushion disguises they'd been wearing, and as strings and long-fingered hands made to capture the fly, Hughes pushed his Performance.

***

While Hughes' imagination could be akin to a mean aunt who whispers nasty nothings and smiles like a cheese grater, his Performance was like an estranged yet doting uncle: reliable in a pinch and yet completely unreliable the rest of the time. Actually, even in a pinch things were touch and go.

At least you could always rely on it being unreliable, which was some comfort.

And there were rules, that he was sure of.

Performance had limitations, such as being limited to a single target, and an extremely inconvenient cooldown that prevented the same target being selected twice in quick succession. It also only worked when he could see his target in the flesh. This meant he couldn't compel people simply by aiming his intent at their photographs, or at their recorded image glimpsed in the cinema. Effigies were insufficient. Only the real thing would do.

He had learned a lot about the creature who didn't call herself Jack during their conversation, and at the moment he pushed his Performance to force her to relinquish her hold on Susabeth Dennings and reveal herself in the waking world, he learned something else. He felt his power roam out of him and find... nothing.

There was no consciousness to root itself in, grasp hold of, affect.

No target.

The significance of this did not immediately sink in because at that moment there were more pressing matters.

"Got her!" Frank reveled as strings enclosed the fly and Mr. Glint curled his hands around the ball of nylon. "I'm bringing us out of here. Be ready to gobble her up, Mr. Glint."

"Goodie goodie gumdrops," said Mr. Glint dourly.

"Here goe—" Frank gagged. His eyes widened, very white in the gloom of the now-hushed room. From that hush crept a voice, amused and velvety and buzzing.

"I'm a little Dream Kettle, short and stout."

Saliva beaded and began to run from Frank's mouth.

"Here is my handle."

Frank doubled over.

"Here is my spout."

Frank fell to his knees.

Veins stood out in his neck like cords of piano wire. The aurora in his hair swam in a crazed kaleidoscope; greenbluepurplepinkredredred, strobes of red, the red of autumn leaves before death's brown wilting strikes, the red of metal before it whitens and melts into molten slag, the red light of a borealis streak as though the sky was stuck like an animal with a knife and was now bleeding helplessly in the hospital ward of the cosmos. He retched and gagged and looked at Hughes, his gaze imploring.

"S-Stop," Hughes hissed. Then, louder. "Wait, please! You've got to stop!"

"When I get all steamed up, hear me shout," continued the buzzing voice blithely. "Tip me over..."

Mr. Glint unhanded the nylon ball, which unwound instantly. The fly crawled onto his hand.

"Please," Hughes said. "We'll go. Right now, I swear, and—"

"... and pour me..."

Mr. Glint raised his other hand and smashed the fly flat.

"... out."

Through the wall that had borne messages written in human hair and now puppet strings, there first pulsed and then emerged in a spray of plaster and woodwork a pair of huge multifaceted eyes, buggish and baleful and orange. The Tinfrost tree melted into a mound of goo-seeping slugs. The cabinets eroded into rivers and lakes and seas of ants. Cicadas and cockroaches and beetles scurried from the tinsel. Moths boiled from the candles in colorful clouds. The sofa exploded with spiders, fat hairy ones bloated with poison, thoraxes bobbing with tiny young begging to burst free, thin long-legged ones that moved with wild herky-jerky sprints of terrible scuttling speed. Mosquitos probed the air with their tapered noses. Worms and lice jiggled and threshed from under the dining table.

Frank's back arched at a grotesque angle. He screamed, and his scream foamed from his lips in a seethe of flies. Their drone slammed Hughes' eardrums. *The bee*, he thought. *Stuck in my head, Dad. Get it out! It's in me,*

(they are in me)

in me in me so get it OOOOOOOUT!

Frank was paralyzed, a man transformed into a scream. The flies fountained up into the air and splattered the ceiling in their carrion stink, a smell that made Hughes think of sour gone-off chicken and moldering fruit shriveling and caving in on itself and sickly sweet soup filmed in a layer of grease and bins, refuse dumps, the gorge-tickling high-fright smell of flies.

Words failed Hughes.

He yanked Chimera from its sheath and waded in.

***

A very different scene was playing out behind Sue Dennings' closed door in Taggart House. The strings Thud had watched appear from Frank's body now stiffened and convulsed. He recalled a fixture in one of Hettie's galleries, a replica cow's heart built from the parts of a decommissioned machine that processed giblets in a burger factory. Doubtless something very meaningful and amazing was at work in the piece, but Thud had found himself struck not by the heart's artistic merits, but by the odd spasms of its contractions. It got him thinking about cardiac arrest. A simple yet disturbing representation of a heart attack.

Hettie's father had died of a heart attack when she was seventeen. Strange how the context around a thing informed the perception of the thing itself. Observation and instinct. Marital awareness. Being a copper.

And...

And as he looked at the strings shiver and quake as though signaling for help, Thud saw the patch of skin. It was pale. Fine blonde hairs stood up on it. It was, without a doubt, the thigh of Susabeth Dennings. When he'd covered half the room in strings, Frank had left that patch exposed. Thud grinned without knowing it. He hadn't noticed her thigh earlier when he'd formulated his plan. But now it was here, it was damned useful.

His belly cramped as it digested the madness of the situation, own heart whamming in his chest, Hoshrum Thud prepared to do what Plan B does best.

That is to say, make like an apple once Plan A goes pear-shaped.

***

Hughes carved through droves of bugs feeling like a hunter in a jungle that was clotted and dense and utterly against him. Warmth and cold all over him. Inert things. Living things. Everywhere he looked, wriggle-flit-squirm. Skin wet. Lips pressed tight against intrusion. Earholes yawning invitations; things with too many legs were starting to crawl over his sensitive lobes and into the canal toward his brain. Severed wings spun to the floor like maple seeds.

No conscious thought in his mind now, only an inarticulate and ferocious need to find his friend in this black and heaving malaise. The hint of a name. Names. There had been something about names, forgotten, lost, the buzz. The buzz and the things that made it were finding ways inside.

Inside what?

(bzzzzzzzzz)

Inside what?

(zzzzzzzzzz)

Inside me.

He blanked his whole head, ridding himself of fear of revulsion of hate, because acknowledging them in the thick of this nightmare would unscrew the cap of his sanity and shake it and fizz

(zzzzzzzzz)

him until he was empty

(filling filling filling)

He passed Mr. Glint, an insane art exhibit of a man gulping live insects by the throatload. Voracious sounds emitted from him, the exhibit's audio featurette cranked up to match Radio Beelzebub.

That wasn't her name though.

Whose name?

(*No!*)

Hughes stopped himself just in time. He would not let himself think.

Instead he hewed, and he swung, and he unsheathed his Krys knife, and he let instincts (which are wonderful for police but for warriors they are *better*) engraved in his muscles like the aspects of gods upon the totems of the pre-church pagan world take over. He and Chimera became one. Steel edge. Steeled courage. Warm insides gobleted as he cut. A banquet of blood. The blade fairly feasted. His Krys knife bit and tasted and chewed, a counterpart to the mayhem he was meting out upon the chittering, chirping, slime-slick horde.

He bumped into something.

For a moment it seemed as though Hughes might saw it apart and move on.

Instinct (which is *best* for fellowship) stopped him short.

Frank was no longer screaming. He had vomited his last fly and broken free, the fabulous man! With his pale hair and his suit spindling into a vast array of nylon, his fly-ravaged lips peeled back in a snarl, Frank was throttling a shape that looked like a woman composed of insects. She batted her fists against his chest.

Frank Gallant took no notice.

"You like nursery rhymes, motherfucker?" he growled. Choking with his right hand, he raised his left and transformed it into a mass of writhing strings. "Here's the itsy bitsy spider. You're the water spout."

And with that, he crammed that mass of strings up through the woman's abdominal wall into the cavity of her chest. The strings went taut. They lanced out of her in a spray of gore.

The buggish woman *shrieked.*

***

At that crucial moment, Captain Hoshrum Thud of the Leonidas District streetbeaters took hold of the heart-shaped biscuit tin, the base of which had grown freezing-cold to the touch, thanks to its insides packed with ice, and with a look of regret should he cause this poor woman pain without knowing it, he pressed it to Sue Denning's bare thigh.

***

All over him the bugs atrophied with chill. Hughes could actually feel the centipedes struggle out of his head through his ears, dozens of legs clittering down his neck, only to freeze solid and fall away. Before him, he could see Frank's body enshrined in ice. Not a killing sheet. Protection, a barrier of solid sleet. The bug woman was gone, melted back into the endless flood of quivering, skittering, itching-alighting-biting bugs.

Her voice, however, had gone nowhere. It was still here and it was furious.

It roared over the trio of interlopers, particularly Hughes, who felt her anger keenest of all.

"Go ahead. Run away. Only stay away from me, or I will eat your friends and drink your families. Vanish home, icicles. Dream a little dream of spring. It'll come, and I'll be gone for another year. If you spot a figure on a roof, avert your eyes. If you read the paper and see something you don't like, just remember this. Remember the day you dipped your flaccidness in the wrong shadow and were revealed as impotent. I mean really fucking *powerless.*"

Hughes felt himself fragmenting into glassy shards, an ice statue breaking apart and leaving the dream behind. Before he awoke, she had something for him. He experienced her sense of grief at his betrayal of her trust as sharply as if it were her own. It was insane, and yet implacably strong. It was as though in that last moment of connection, he and the killer were the same.

One final time her voice buzzed, soft and glum, then hard and savage.

"And in the end, can you begrudge a starving woman her hunger? No more than I begrudge you your attempts at me, at my life. You can't have it. It's mine, and the feast is mine, and the City is mine all mine all mine, and my name... Mmm. Gormon Hughes, you want it you got it, babe."

As she disclosed herself in part, Hughes was confronted by her face. It was dark-haired and dark-eyed, which was stranger, and stranger still were her expressive features. But the strangest thing of all? It looked like his.

His face.

"Know me, and know that when you fuck with me, you're fucking with the best. 'Tis the season, and jolly-folly, roguery, and rascality are not advisable for those who want to watch the springtime bloom. Get gone and stay gone. The holly-branch bearer is eyeing chimney stacks, sleigh bells are ringing, parcels are being placed, the rooftops are singing, and while Jack might be back, the *name* is *Jane*."

Act Six

Something Frozen

Chapter Sixteen

The fortress was as tall and wide and complex as Cate's girlhood school, all inglenook rooms and rambling corridors and arched doorways and stairs that crept into the lower chambers or swirled up into the highest climbs. Unlike school, it was not a place of education, unless you wanted to learn about very dangerous people, how they prepared themselves for moments of deadly excitement, or how they passed the time between such invigorating bouts.

Some time has been devoted to descriptions of the fortress' exterior—its magnificent mossy tree trunk legs, its stabilizing platform, its walls and watchtowers and crenellations of steel and concrete that seemed to exude a direct challenge to any looking at it. *Come and try your luck, you small and nugatory agents of evil, if you think you are hard enough*—yet little must be devoted to its interior.

You might take a moment to admire the anbaric lamps that had been painstakingly molded into the shapes of hobnail boots to honor the commander of this mission. The pantry was a thing worth salivating over, with its silicate walls cooled by the respiration of the Daethumberland fjerta fish stationed in pools ice-fed like clockwork by timed chutes and its fragrant herbs and jars of multicolored delights from organic honey to juniper berry jam to crushed spices to clear-brown fish sauce, not to mention the slabs of pork and lamb and beef defrosting, soon to be lathered in all the juiciest and tastiest garnishes and marinating sauces and served at the dining table, which was long enough to sit thirty people quite comfortably. And, actually, it would be a grave injustice not to peer into the training room, which was exquisitely good for keeping fit, and the bedrooms, which while ensuring protection with their toughened-frame windows and flame resistant sheeting and suchlike, were also the very height of luxury, boasting curtains you could use as blankets and blankets you could roll up in and forget you were in a hostile world full of things that would be very pleased to eat you and only delighted to do worse.

Anyway, suffice it to say that the assembly of Scarlet Citadel warriors, who came to call themselves Cate's Company in the days that followed, had no complaints whatsoever about their lodgings during their short and eventful crusade in Eurydice. The fortress operated on the principle that if advanced technology ceased to function here in the dungeon dimension, science would start at square one on the organic scale and work upward from there.

The fortress was, in short, a miracle of Corinthian bioengineering.

Cate had named it Betty.

This had attracted disapproval from some of the stuffier personalities onboard and general hilarity from everyone else.

That Monday morning, while Hughes met the estimable vagabond named Tookus Argyle Vercingetorix of Demeter, Cate Jubilee was trying to be a Responsible Leader.

In her case the emphasis felt necessary though not altogether earned.

She was bent over her desk, her writing hand working feverishly, her face six inches from the page and screwed up in an expression of urgent determination.

The page in question was a mess of scribbles and scratched-out musings that would have made even the most illegible doctor's scrawl pack up its bags and retire. At the top the document was labeled *Useful Combinations.*

Examples of such combinations included:

The Rope Squad—Marcus Angel, Eugenie O'Nine Tails, Niccolo Bluescarf, and possibly Ulf Seamster paired with Rebecca Lupine.

Death From Above—Rosemund Valkyrie, Morvran Oats, Liddicoat Smite-The-Naughty-With-Large-Implements, and Xacorca Demon.

Murky Lurking Lads—Igor Wight, Varjo Cutthroat, Jennifer Goblingrin, and Brecht Bedlam.

There were several more of these, each promising since she'd thought about them in great detail, and each sporting the same crap quality of name. Cate was fast discovering she wasn't much up to naming. She wondered how much better she'd fare at commanding. Experience in the field told her to be confident. A career that started out as a lone wolf operation before graduating to half of a two-hander counseled that she was likely to make mistakes. How many? she wondered.

Not many, said her confidence.

Lots, warned her doubt.

It was a bugger. Nevermind. Movement. Progress. That was the ticket.

It was the way with her. Go forward as shrewdly and as stylishly as possible. Take nothing, except what mattered, an attitude to luggage that had served her well in the past and was serving her well since...

Well since November.

Her hand did not unconsciously reach down so her fingers could brush the network of still-lumpy, not-quite-silver scars, souvenirs of the operation. Those which could be conveniently reached, that is. They were numerous, if mercifully free from itch.

And if she did screw her features a little tighter, so what?

The prospect of a good fight. The fortress called Betty. Even the bloody Responsible bloody Leadership.

I'm enjoying this immensely, said her confidence.

I miss her even though she wasn't born, said her doubt.

There was a knock at the door.

"Come in."

Ducking so she didn't thump her brow on the door frame, Eilandri Titansgrave came in. The huge bald woman was in full armored regalia as per Cate's instruction. They had to be ready for anything at the drop of a hat. She was also, much to Cate's pleasure, carrying two bottles of Stoving's Apple Throatwinkler.

"What's this?"

Eilandri held one of her little yellow cards out. Cate took it and read.

"*Some of the others are comparing this mission of ours to Walsingham's Merry Miners. As one of the original members of that troupe, and as your second in command, I thought it best to make myself available to you in case you had questions.*"

"I do." Cate set her pen and page aside for now. Being too large for the chairs to accommodate, Eilandri sat on the edge of Cate's bed. They cracked the ciders. They sipped the ciders. Cate mulled some questions over. She knew some rudimentary details about the Merry Miners; how they had been the finest exemplars of the Citadel, hand selected by Walsingham Dragontail. The Old Dragon himself had led the sojourn into Eurydice with the express purpose of exploring the depths of its secrets, or failing that, gleaning a larger haul of credits than all previous expeditions combined. The secrets had eluded their grasp. The credits, and the monsters that fostered them within their bodies, had not.

Her first inquiry was one born of simple curiosity. "What was it like, working with the Old Dragon?"

Eilandri wrote, "*In those days he was young and fierce. White Flame Walt, we called him. Working under his command was like eating a street vendor sausage roll; you never knew what you were going to get.*"

"What qualities of leadership did he demonstrate that you liked?" said Cate. "Which could you have done without?"

"*Good: He led from the front. Bad: Sometimes it blinded him to what was going on behind him.*"

"What was he blind to?"

"*His losses. Fifteen set out on a rainy day in late summer. Seven returned. It was early autumn by then. Sunny. Somehow that seemed inappropriate. But I was happy to be home.*"

Eight claimed by Eurydice. When Cate considered that all eight of the deceased wielded unique magic items whose power would likely be lost along with them, those were hefty casualties indeed.

"Did you encounter anything like the Bride of the Fog?"

"*No. She was the largest and cruelest monster I have ever seen.*"

Cate looked into Eilandri's eyes. Their lavender hue spoke to an unwritten sentiment: *I wouldn't mind seeing another as large and cruel as that. In fact I crave it.*

To this Cate Jubilee could only smile, a small and conspiratorial smile that said, *Me too.*

They remembered their ciders. They gulped their ciders.

"Advise me about Eurydice. What trouble would a diligent woman be on the lookout for?"

"*Be wary of the terrain and the sky above it. Eurydice changes. For the most part those changes are slow enough that you might not notice it, but compared to our world's geography and astronomy, the shifts are astonishingly quick, as well as nonsensical. An example: the Merry Miners were here less than a month. On our way in we crossed a stream that was narrow enough to jump over. On our way back home we crossed a river with a strong current, which had developed an ecosystem of toads whose touch corroded our skin like battery acid.*"

Cate read this, nodded, hesitated.

"What do you mean, 'for the most part the changes are slow'?"

"*Once I witnessed the moon and the stars wink out. It was instantaneous. Like someone had turned out the lights and stuffed us in a dark room. There are lots of moons and suns that visit Eurydice. Constellations change night by night. Either this is a rest-stop for various cosmos, or the position of Eurydice in one unwavering galaxy alters without pause.*"

Cate studied her second. "You think it's the latter."

Eilandri nodded.

"It thinks, Eilandri. This world. So does ours. Measurable electrical impulses; thought voltage, I mean. Wendy Dragontail says there's proof of it. Something John Isherwood and his people have been pouring over for years. From possibility to actuality. And if a place thinks, it's got personality. It's uhm..." Her fingers rolled round the neck of the cider bottle. "It might explain the way Iphigenia is split into three stable regions, and why Eurydice is anything *but* stable." Her eyes roamed Eilandri's face, seeking any clue that the woman was shocked, confused, even suspicious. But there was none.

Sensing how flummoxed she was, Eilandri wrote, "*Makes sense.*"

Cate waited for more. None was forthcoming.

"Does it make sense?"

Eilandri nodded.

"Oh." Cate drew a breath, puffed out her cheeks, let it go. "Well... good. Glad to hear it. But don't you worry that ah... Doesn't it sort of raise questions about..."

She stared into those unblinking lavender eyes. They regarded her evenly.

"Nevermind."

They swilled their ciders. They finished their ciders.

"You know, you're remarkably solid, Eilandri. I expect it takes a lot to phase you."

The Pale Giant seemed to ponder this. Eventually she scribbled, "*Ovens.*"

"Baking or cooking?" asked Cate, bemused.

Eilandri held up two fingers. *Both.*

"*You know the scorch marks on the ceiling in the kitchens of Redspire?*"

"Oh. Yes, I think so."

Eilandri hooked a thumb at herself.

"You?"

A nod, this one less solemn and more playful.

Cate's eyes widened with a special kind of scandalized glee. "But those marks are enormous! Falstaff glares at them daily, swears the moment he gets a chance he'll devote an afternoon to them with a handful of sponges and scrubbing foam. What on earth were you making?"

"Breakfast."

When the fit of giggles had subsided, Cate stacked the yellow cards and handed them back to the fantastically huge, hairless, purple-eyed woman sitting on her bed. "You're easy to talk to."

Eilandri stowed the cards, pointed at her throat that was bereft of voice box, and tugged an ear that worked perfectly well.

"Yes, good listening makes for splendid chats." Cate paused. "Good reading, in my case."

Standing, or as close to standing as she could manage with the room's low roof, Eilandri circled the air with an index finger, as if to say, *Let's do it again.*

"I'd like that," said Cate.

They both turned as the second knock of the day arrived at her door.

Without waiting for a summons Lorna Blacktower bustled in. "Cate, I think this could be serious and there's no time for one of your jokes that whistle over my head like migrating starlings so I'm going to blurt it out here goes—"

Cate listened intently.

She made no jokes.

This is it, said her confidence as Lorna babbled on.

For once her doubt lay quiet.

***

All that morning Steffan Cerulean had plucked at his shirt of dyed beads, causing them to rattle. Gathering that something was the matter, his close confidante Rosemund Valkyrie approached him. "The air," he told her. "Cold."

"Is it? I shall fetch several nubile courtesans and a leopard to warm m'Lord," teased his friend good-naturedly. Rosemund was from Daethumberland. The recent snows in Corinth City had made her feel closer to home than she had felt in years.

"Colder than it ought to be," Steffan insisted. "See ahead of us?"

She did. They were in a pass that grooved like a wound through the craggy face of the mountain. To the left shaggy-haired trees made a beard on the rock, and to the right the mountain was gouged deep with caves, some small nooks, others vast caverns bored into the deep of the mountain. Low drifter clouds patrolled the slope. There was a subtle glittering blue-whiteness to the scene that prevailed on the eye. It could have been the sun, which shone with a strange blue light, but Rosemund knew ice when she spied it.

"See?" said Steffan. His fingers rolled a jade bead anxiously.

"I see. What's wrong, my friend?"

"Come with me, I'll show you."

They headed around the parapet, taking care where they stood. The fortress named Betty ambled forward at a smooth yet surprisingly fast clip, and the view through the slats reminded them it was a long way down. Initially they had been at the front of the fortress. When they reached the back, Rosemund felt a pang of disquiet, as though Steffan's might be catching.

Here before her was the pass they'd just come through. It was, all in all, fairly similar to the pass in front of them.

Except for the ice. There wasn't any. Nothing glimmered from the lines in the tree bark. Nothing gleamed from the mouths of the caves.

"Good morning," came the grumbling voice of Morvran Oats. "Not that I believe it. I'm only being polite."

"Morvran," said Steffan. "Could you fly down to the icy trees ahead of us and tell me about the roots?"

Morvran peered warily at him. "Why?"

"I'd like to know if they're dead."

"The roots?"

"The trees."

"Don't be stupid," said the grouchy fellow. "Trees can die and their roots can continue on without a by-your-leave. Seen that lots of times."

"Look, just do it, all right? I'd rather not get unpleasant with you, but—"

"I'll go," said Rosemund.

"Yeah," leered Morvran. "If I can go, Rosey here can go just as easily."

Steffan opened his mouth to protest, then subsided. His nervousness seemed worse. "Yes. Yes, all right. Only please be careful, and *make sure not to land.*"

"Give me five minutes."

Launching herself from the lip of the battlements, she snipped the clasp on her golden cloak. It flowed out around her, the magic firming up its soft material into a stiff bed of muscle sheeted in feathers the color of fresh marmalade. Her wings beating, Rosemund flapped high into the air. At once she felt warmer, warmer than the rising of hot air could account for. That dull disquiet sharpened a bit inside her.

She took a moment to scan for signs of monstrous activity. Seeing none, she instead found something that might have thrilled her, had her friend's observation not struck a chord with her. Ahead, the slope slouched precipitously, taking the path with it. Yet instead of descending into an area clear of the symptoms of the unusual cold she'd felt, the fortress was heading for a region encased in ice. The forest swelled into the path, choking it. The trees there were dead, sketching sinewy blue shadows on topsoil frozen solid.

Frowning deeply, Rosemund Valkyrie flew down for an inspection of one of the closer specimens. Not dead, but getting there, she supposed. The wooden flesh around the roots was brittle. Avoiding the ground, she tested leaves near the top of the tree, then the ones lower down. Those near the summit were normal. She held and put a little pressure on one of the lower ones. It broke with an audible crack. Cored with cold. Her breath clouded in front of her. It had not done that while she was near the top of the tree. She shuddered, once, and took wing.

These findings were related to Steffan, who vented them to Lorna Blacktower. She had heard the commotion and hurried to investigate. So it was that she related them to Cate Jubilee, who wasted no time in raising the alarm.

***

It was an hour later. The entire company were wearing sweaters over their armor, courtesy of Ulf Seamster who'd been hard at work with his enchanted knitting needles and about eighty yards of yarn. He was hard at work on a second set, and a good thing too.

It seemed that every step Betty took thrust the fortress and its Scarlet army deeper into the heart of something utterly invisible and unspeakably cold. To either side the slopes were littered with the carcasses of dead animals, none of them familiar to their eyes, and even if they had been, the frost would have rendered them unrecognizable. Bird and beast lay stiffened and sparkling like the victims of some diamond gorgon. Each tree on the mountainside was a province besieged by ice. In some cases the ice had actually split the tree apart, the frozen leafy crowns parted by glittering horns that rose up to gore the morning air.

"Set foot down there and die shivering," Marcus Angel had muttered grimly when he'd laid eyes on this bleak panorama. Cate was inclined to agree.

She had arrayed the greater part of the company around the battlements as best she could, hoping one among their number would spot the enemy. If they did not, surely those she had sent to loftier pursuits would spy something.

And there *was* an enemy, she was quite sure of that.

Cate almost wished she could be as severe as Marcus. A Responsible Leader ought to project a certain gravity. That would have been proper. Yet eyeing her forces clad in sweaters, she had been struck by the image of Wendy Dragontail slaying the Bride of the Fog while decked out in her own wooly clobber with fairy tale characters on them. Coupled with her customary giddiness before a fight, containing a grin was proving really very tricky indeed.

No wind or breath of breeze. The air hung on them like a sheet of hard-packed snow. They stamped their feet. Betty plodded onward. Cate felt a tap on her shoulder. She turned and saw Eilandri with her hammer lashed to her back, dormant and deadly. The mute nodded north-west.

Cate followed her gaze. At first she saw nothing, until...

Yes, she had it!

Movement among the raggedy limbs.

"Gone," she said after a while spent in watchful stillness. "Covert little bugger. Not nearly so big as I was expecting. I wonder what it is?"

Eilandri made no move to produce one of her yellow cards. Instead she strode back to her post, leaving Cate to rub warmth into her arms and resume her portion of the vigil alone.

Seconds quavered into minutes.

What had that shape out there been? It hadn't looked human.

Out here, what does?

Some things, she reminded herself. Years ago she and Hughes had taken on men-shaped foes called the Bonemeal Boys. Granted they were motorcycle riding skeletons, their skin hanging from their bones in gross greenish flaps. But when it comes to physiological symmetry it's the thought that counts.

She stuck out her jaw, parted her lips, and blew a fantastic cloud that dissipated over her head in a corona.

Ulf arrived, offering her a second sweater.

"Has everyone else got theirs?"

He shook his head.

"See that they do," Cate told him. "I'll take your last one, okay?"

From under a floppy-eared and cozy cap of plum-colored wool, Ulf gave her a once over. He took in her ruddy cheeks, chattering teeth, and her fiery hair pinned up in a bun, exposing ears turning puce with chill. "Aren't you nippy?"

"Are you mad? It's *freezing*, Ulf. Go on, now. Gloves and extra socks for all afterward. You're our only hope against frostbite."

"Yes, yes Cate."

His gaze was lowered. Sixty-one, bushy-eyebrowed, and gap-toothed, Ulf was a handsome silver stag of a man in a rustic way. She watched him peel the hat off his head and felt a rush of emotion when he held it out to her.

"Don't be ridiculous. You must... Oh come now, you old softie..."

But he wouldn't go until she took it.

Cate wore the hat, smiling a private smile at the togetherness of their little army. She felt the fortress' gait under her. When they'd arrived the tick-tock, back-and-forth quality of it had made her mildly seasick. She had acclimatized. Already it was relaxing, even encouraging. Rocked in a cradle of impregnable strength, of Corinthian ingenuity. It was enough to make a woman a patriot. Good grief.

Out in the crags, the ice seemed to be growing more compact. She wondered again what was out there. For a moment her thoughts rested with Hughes. She hoped her goofy, gorgeous love was doing well. His letter had touched her, and worried her.

The only difference between someone in the Scarlet Citadel and someone who isn't is that one of them has a questionable approach to safety while wearing red trousers. And the Jolene-forged objects in question, of course.

Should the public have access to magic items?

Her immediate reaction was no, they shouldn't. But how much of that was an automatic reaction grounded in her cultural predispositions, her heritage of blood and glass, her mistrust of that irredeemable creature that skulked about even in her world's most cordial societies; the mob?

She would approach the idea in a fairer state of mind later when she wrote her Puppy a reply. *Hughes*, she thought. *Sending you a warm toasty hug, you gormless Gormon. Lord knows I could use one.*

She hopped on her hobnail boots and tried to keep her teeth from doing the pink-gum-polka. Sweet holy shit, it was so, so cold.

Suddenly there was noise like blasting thunder from the front of Betty's battlements. That could only be Clothilda Toffington, whose magic item was a handkerchief that, when sneezed into, produced a concussive wave of force that could level a cottage. Clothilda, who could not sneeze on demand, always carried a jar of pepper grains from her partner's restaurant, which was labeled *For My Darling Clothy Wothy, The Ravaging Sniffler On The Go*. Cate joined the rush toward the sound. They converged and beheld what Clothilda had seen.

Directly ahead of the fortress, about the length of a football field away, was a large bridge. It connected one slope of the mountain pass to the other and was built out of ice as smooth and unblemished as glass. Standing next to the bridge, admiring it with its hands planted on its hips, was a monster of such incredible proportions Cate Jubilee's first thought was, *A statue in the road, must be, couldn't possibly be alive.*

But it was very much alive.

It turned and raised a hand in greeting. The monster stood as a man might stand if he were seventy feet tall and built like a piece of industrial equipment. Its face was long with, thankfully, the usual number of eyes and mouths and noses one might expect in a person's face. The features, however, were mashed and lumpy, coated with the chill. The effect was like being stared at by a garden of vegetables dusted in hoarfrost.

"What the devil is it?" said Clothilda Toffington, whose voice was so posh you could clean silver with it.

Studying that upraised hand, Cate said, "Polite."

"Politeness in this disaffected waste?" Clothilda sniffed. "Unlikely."

Absently giving Kelly Cinch (their company's improvised pilot) the signal to slow the fortress to a stop and the flying cadre of her forces a different signal that meant, "if anything weird occurs, unleash hell," Cate Jubilee took a calculated risk. She raised her hand right back.

The monster's face contorted. *Surely that's not a smile?*

It must very well have been because in a booming, cheerful voice that whelmed over Betty's crenellations in boreal-cold waves, he said, "Charmed. May I approach?"

Much to the alarm of those around her, Cate cupped her hands around her mouth. "Yes!" Their surprise was allayed when she issued instructions under her breath. What martial preparations that could be made without attracting undue attention were administered to. Above them, intermittently blotting out the light of the soulless blue sun and casting feathery shadows down among the dead trees, were Rosemund Valkyrie and Morvran Oats astride his magical owl. They ferried Liddicoat and Xacorca, each one of the four fostering their own thoughts about the creature now approaching the fortress in long, gentlemanly strides.

As the monster closed the gap between them, Cate could make out finer details. Its eyes were the turquoise of frozen Rhönland lakes. It sported a pair of ibex horns that curved from its scalp to the small of its back. Ice studded its chest, belly, and groin like a tunic of pale jewels. As it neared, it occurred to her the temperature was actually growing even chillier, a fact her sinuses would not have believed possible, yet it was true. The monster sat comfortably, its head still level with the platform the fortress was set upon. The very air around it crackled.

Unable to resist the temptation, and keen to meet this weird adversary on its terms, Cate climbed the battlements and sat with her legs dangling, both hands tucked into the sleeves of her sweaters. "I'm Cate Jubilee."

"An honor, I'm sure," he boomed. "I am a Troll."

"Have you no name other than that?"

"Troll is quite suitable, thank you."

"Welcome." She managed to suppress a shudder and tried to think of hot baths, saunas, and scalding coffee. It didn't help. "What do you want, Troll?"

"To work. I've been given a task, you see."

"What task?"

"To breach the barrier between Iphigenia and this world. I am to go there and kill as many things as I possibly can."

"A pitiless task."

The Troll shrugged in the manner of all those who do dirty jobs. The shrug conceded that, yes, it was a pitiless task, but as with cleaning toilets and the shooting of rabid animals, it is work that must be done. No point grousing or making a fuss of it.

"And who gave this task to you?" asked Cate.

"Eurydice, of course."

"The world?"

"The very same. The Lady and the World."

Cate didn't need to look. She could feel her company's unease. Not everyone had been as stoic about the whole "worlds that think" business as Eilandri had been.

"Why has Eurydice got you playing the murderer?"

"I don't know," said the Troll. "Truly, I would tell you if I did."

Cate could only smile at the absurdity of all this.

"You're very talkative."

Another shrug. "I believe in honesty. I have reason to believe you've come to kill me. If we are to fight, I think we ought to be up front with one another, so that when we enter the fray we might slaughter one another as equals." Eyebrows like huge white foxtails rose expectantly. "Have you come to kill me?"

"Yes, we have."

The Troll nodded as if this were par for the course. "My informant was correct then. I don't suppose I might dissuade you at all? I am a venerable Troll, and my kind do not grow weaker with age. On the contrary, we get stronger and stronger until at last we cannot control ourselves and fall into a sleep that is like the true death, which is so loathsome to necromancers."

"The wheel of life must spin."

The brows climbed further. "You know the motto of the necromancers?"

Cate's mind showed her an image of Marrow King Maelen. "I've had dealings with them. Their... what would you call it... their dark labors."

"That is very nicely put," complimented the Troll. "Speaking of labors, how did I do with the bridge?"

"What about it?"

"Is it good?"

"Very," said Cate, bewildered. "Starts there. Has the decency to finish on the other side. Lots of bridges give up halfway."

"Sounds like a jetty."

"Yyyyyes," said Cate, wondering if she had fallen asleep in an ice-water bath and was now dreaming. "Yes, it would do."

The Troll looked over his shoulders at his handiwork. "I'm given to understand your species has expectations about Trolls. I was able to get the bridge sorted." He sighed. "Alas, there is no toll booth."

"Fine. Um. No worries. Who is your informant?"

"Cate! CATE!"

She jerked about to see the source of the hullabaloo.

One of the people she'd asked to remain hidden in order to ambush the enemy, Jennifer Goblingrin, loped out of the shadows into the throng of the Scarlet Citadel. "We found a creature snooping around inside Betty. Tried to catch him and the little shit leaped out a window. When we looked out, he'd vanished."

"That would be my informant," said the Troll sagely. "Cunning fellow."

"Who is he?" asked Cate.

"He does not have a name, not caring for such, but in Eurydice there are many who call him Skuggs."

"Why Skuggs?"

"You know, I don't really know why." There was a thoughtful pause. "I suppose it is because he *looks* like a Skuggs. Now, I think that is enough gabbing for the moment, though you have a knack for it."

"You too."

"Have I dissuaded you, Cate Jubilee? I have no quarrel with you, and you may pass unbothered through this land I have made cold and beautiful with my company, should you wish to."

Cate smiled. "I'm afraid not."

"I see. One final question, then?"

"Okay."

"Who is Betty?"

Despite the fact there was about to be a battle (or perhaps because of it, anticipation casts odd spells on us all), there were groans and sniggers from behind her.

Cate felt her smile mature into a broad and lusty grin. "Our fortifications."

"Really?" The Troll pulled a face. "Well. You learn something new every day." Then he swung his body around, crouched, and sprang at Cate, who was ready for him.

Chapter Seventeen

This is the way a fly is born.

Its mother lays it along with dozens of brothers and sisters wherever she deems fit—preferably somewhere moist and decaying, such as inside the bellies, sores, and weeping lacerations of recently dead things—whereupon she flies off in the direction of her fancy. Mothers are not immune to the prospects that abandonment whispers into the ear of countless absent fathers. The children are on their own. But safe and nurtured in compost bins and loamy blood-soaked alleys and dog turds, the maggoty larva focuses its whole self on becoming. Metamorphosis works its warlock incantations on it. Now it is a pupa. Soon it will be born for the second time. Insane and yet entirely logical forces strand legs from the single tapered lobe. Veiny wings are woven. Bulbous opals protuberant and gazing at a beckoning world. Here it comes. There! See it fly? It's fully formed! Hear its buzz thickening the hours from noon to midnight?

That was how she took them for herself.

On Monday she found a woman who trained dogs, a man who laid brick, a girl who was just about tall enough to reach the kitchen butcher block with all its sharp residents, a boy who dreamed of being a man and who never would be. Not if she had anything to say about it.

Jane went from mind to mind, laying little eggs to hatch, and she did not think of dark-haired Hughes. She did not picture his dark eyes so much like her own.

She found a retired man who had loaded fish in Jaenqui-Across-The-River all his life, and who had two children he spoke to on the phone every day, and who was happy. Happier still was the young woman who worked in the cinema because her partner had just proposed to her, and for now it was a secret from her parents, but goodness weren't they going to be thrilled? Yes!

Only they never would find out.

The shadow moved on...

And then she just... drifted for a while.

Oh hell. Fine. She was thinking about him.

As she floated in hollows unglimpsed by mortal eyes, Jane crossed the idea of her arms over the idea of her chest.

But he was fascinating! She had every right to dwell on him a bit.

Of the three that had entered Sue Dennings' dream, Hughes had been by far the most... the most... *tantalizing.*

Why? she probed. *Why him?*

She sampled the mind of two siblings enjoying a coffee and watching the weather worsen through the stained glass of a café window. Both brothers hadn't seen one another in a long time. One hid his surliness behind a smile; she retracted from him, her taste buds cringing. The second brother was content all the way through, an unsuccessful man but one who found small pleasures like coffee with his sibling sufficient, particularly during the holiday season. He was delectable and perfect. She spilled her delayed poison inside him, her squadrons of buzzing guzzlers. But her heart wasn't in it and she moved on quickly.

Why Hughes?

Easy.

Invading Frank Gallant's mind would be risky, and she was not sure what to make of the sour-mouthed man who'd tried to vacuum up her bugs with his greedy tongue. Those two were simply abnormal. Abnormal she could deal with.

Hughes was something else altogether. His mind had been... had been... How she ached to find the words! Eventually she tried, *At first I thought he was ordinary. Then he changed, and he was anything but. It was as though I were staring into a mirror of myself.* That seemed grossly inadequate. The closest thing she could use for reference was the sea. You can pour a bucket of water, a stream, a river into the sea. But you cannot pour a sea into a sea. *He was she and she was me.* Which was impossible. Spring-Heeled Jane was one of a kind.

No, some wise side of her counseled. *You are many things, but you are not one of a kind. You are one among very few.*

And it was this, this realization that Hughes was like her, that edged her enticement in a feeling entirely unfamiliar to Jane. It was unpleasant, as though someone had filled her throat and mouth with sawdust and her stomach with a hairy layer of black mold topped up with a sloshing quart of bleachy black mold remover. He could not defeat her. No one could do that.

But he could badger and browbeat and discommode her.

She would have to keep an eye on Hughes. *An eye,* she thought, grinning, *or a million.* Bulbous opals all, sightseeing and keeping peeled for devilsome Gormon Hughes!

Reconciled to her feelings and on much firmer footing, so to speak, Jane turned from her elevenses plan in Cleomenes District to her luncheon plot in Leonidas. The smell of the fare huddled in their tenemented shambles was intoxicating, headier than any alcohol. It was Tinfrosttime, and they were so glad to be alive. She loved them for it. Loved them to death. Over the rooftops the shadow prowled. Inaudible for the moment at the back of many peoples' heads, pupas became larvae became flies, soon to gather and raise a droning, skull-filling symphony. But not yet. For now there was the laying, and patience. She would wait longer this time before submitting to her cravings. Hunger, after all, is the best seasoning. And more than that, thought Jane gleefully, there was this:

Candy is dandy but liquor is quicker.

Yet here in the houses and hovels flea-bitten,

Here lies a flavor that cannot be beaten.

This is the way a city is eaten.

***

Near the battlements where the fight was just beginning, darkness that should not have been present under the wide shining light of the blue sun crept closer. Igor Wight controlled that patch of mobile inky black, a skin-and-bones coatrack of a man. Guided by their grip on Igor's long coat of replica raven feathers were Varjo Cutthroat, Brecht Bedlam, and Jennifer Goblingrin, who had made a mad dash to assemble this band during the last moments of the Trollish conversation. They were mismatched in temperament, those four, but united in style. All of them would have been quite comfortable fitting in the sort of stories featuring misty moorlands, abandoned castles on the top of hills, and the occasional black-clad figure hoping to add more hemoglobin into their diet.

Cate stalled this furtive team she'd dubbed the Murky Lurking Lads with a gesture. She barked a few commands, stopping many advancing scarlet figures short.

Thwarting the Troll, she had teleported through a mirror she'd made in the nick of time. Now sitting on the ledge of a window thirty feet above her former position, she watched the Troll's eyes swivel in search of her. He had launched himself with spritely force, landing with his gnarled toes digging into the lip of the parapet and his hands with their fingernails like splintered white fence boards scrabbling. Not a moment later he'd found those hands lashed together with the glowing golden chains of Marcus Angel and his arms pinned to his sides by Niccolo's scarf of soft yet implacable blue stuff. Most insulting was the cat o'nine tails whip Eugenie used to muzzle him. He could not bite. Could not burst forth at a sprint. Could not roar or exhale a cloud of fatally frigid air.

But Cate had stopped Igor's group and the rest of the close combatants like Yussuf Copper and Margherita Stranger from moving in what the Champleurs would call a *coup de grâce.*

She looked at her left hand, her lips pulled back over her gums in a snarl. In the instant before teleportation as the monster bore down upon her, she must have raised it. The skin was cream-white, blanched with cold. It stung savagely, throbbed, then abruptly numbed, the horrible numbness that turns the fingers to clumsy broom handles and the wrists to curled lock-jointed shelves of ache.

"Don't get close," she told the company. "You'll freeze to death. Kpelle, I need heat."

Kpelle Cinder snapped to attention. She and Rebecca Lupine had been fueling Kevlin Paladin since the Troll had claimed his seat before the fortress. She saw Cate's plight and clicked her tongue. The stone embedded in the wet pink muscle flashed. A globule of fire appeared next to Cate. She held her hand to it, wishing the numbness would siphon away and the pain would saunter back. *Not nerve damage*, she prayed. Out loud she thundered, "Kevlin, spear him!"

With his spear topped with sunfire, amplified by Kpelle's flame and balanced by Rebecca's cosmic counterpoint, Kevlin Paladin charged, reared back, and let fly.

The spear sank into the Troll's cheek. Great as their enemy's chill was, the sheer heat was too much for it to bear. The cheekflesh blistered instantly, and as the superheated spearpoint dragged down, it unseamed the bone and sent the Troll's blood splashing in gallons.

Red like ours, thought Cate.

The Troll's gaze fixed on her. "There you are." He chuckled, voice muffled through Eugenie's cat o'nine tails. "And it seems I did not miss you entirely. Frostnip will become frostbite if I have a second chance. Ah, but you are fleet and fine. Speed trumps strength four times out of five, wouldn't you agree?"

"Clothilda," Cate said, simultaneously motioning to the Death From Above contingent soaring overhead. "Get him off my fortress."

The Troll's fearsome cold was disrupting its bonds, crumpling the chains and the scarf and brittling the whip. All at once the pressure released.

He made to stand... and found himself staring at a respectable distance into the small, imperious face of Clothilda Toffington, who inhaled sharply and sneezed like an elephant convention with hay fever.

A thousand tons of Troll catapulted backward. He hit the ice bridge at terrific speed. The resulting *CRRRRRUNCH* echoed through the mountain pass, the caves throwing the noise back and forth in glorious fanfare.

Before he had the wherewithal to speak, much less regain his footing, wings flapped over the Troll. As Rosemund and Morvran tore through the sky, Xacorca vented a foul-smelling gas up from her guts, and Liddicoat struck it. Dread combustion rolled through the gas, lighting it up in a blast that both singed and boiled the Troll's clavicle and shoulder in soft pustules and hard buboes.

Kelly Cinch poked her head out of the pilot room window and called to Cate, who gave the order to advance. In the brief time it had been stationary, Betty had acquired socks of twinkling frost as the power of the Troll seeped up from the ground. These socks *crickle-cracked* and billowed and sprinkled ice as the fortress got moving.

Kevlin Paladin retrieved his spear. He eyed it speculatively.

"My spearhead parted the beast's cold aura," he observed. "I think it could do more."

"Create a gap," growled Rebecca Lupine in agreement. "Let Cate's Murky Lurking Lads sneak in for the kill."

"Very good. We'll funnel you with flame and moonglow until you're about to burst," said Kpelle. "Aim for his jugular next time, Kev."

"Yes. Well. I shall do my utmost best."

While Cate disseminated the company's next move, those three took cover near the foot of the stair leading up to the parapet. Orange and white lights danced upon the stonework. Eventually one of them snickered.

"Murky Lurking Lads."

"Shut up."

Up amongst her vanguard Cate flexed her fingers. The skin looked crusty, almost flaked, and under the pallid cast it was taking on a bruised purplish color. The palm and knuckles were okay, but it felt as though someone had packed her fingers full of crushed charcoal and struck a match. She tried curling them into a fist and a little groan escaped her, but that was all. Her eyes crinkled at the corners. The numbness was tingling away and she could not remember ever feeling so grateful for hurt.

Ulf Seamster appeared beside her and began to busy himself popping warm gloves over her hands. When he got to the left Cate sucked in air. Son-of-a-bitch, it hurt. Ulf gave her an apologetic smile and hurried off to glove the rest.

"Yes, yes. Good, good," she heard him chirp. "Socks next."

"Cate," reported Steffan Cerulean. "That ah..." He waggled his fingers in a sort of body emanation gesture, searching for the right word. "Snowy billowing," he settled on, "is part of the Troll. Imagine the opposite of an oven; the cold is rolling off him in waves. No luck thawing it or drawing the water droplets into a prism we could pass through. I was able to help Eugenie and the others keep him in check by manipulating his blood, but the stuff is as thick as mucous before it touches nitrogen-rich air of the kind we're breathing."

"Try to slow him down, Steffan."

"At once."

"Inez?"

Inez Symphony stepped forward, a willowy woman of an age with Cate. Sandy blonde hair framed an avid, intelligent face, one that understood a great deal more than just the mastery of her magic item, a violin of polished rosewood Inez had dubbed Seismichelle.

"How can I help?"

"Head up to Kelly. Have her give us a burst of speed when we're within fifty feet of the Troll."

"Shall I play a ditty at the same moment?"

"Bring the house down, baby."

"Hurrah!"

She sped off.

Cate turned back to the Troll, eighty-odd feet away and struggling back toward a fighting stance. Eilandri shadowed her. Cate could feel the Pale Giant's presence the way you might appreciate a well-lit and populated street in an otherwise dark and still and above all unfamiliar town. They watched the Troll together. Despite their raised hackles, both acted too slowly to prevent the battle's next hideous development. Who could blame them? He was a wily old Troll, and he was not about to underestimate these little scarlet folk again.

In the time it would take you to fill a kettle and turn on the hob, he spread the rime ice studding his chest until it covered him in a coat of milk-white chainmail, and raising both hands he caught the thing that came crunch-snapping out of the largest tree and *whum-whumming* through the blue morning. "Well struck," they heard him holler. "But the riposte is mine. I will make that marching home of yours a tomb. Those of you of faith shall freeze unanointed." The hilt was one of those oblongs of ice that had unnerved Steffan Cerulean earlier that day. But the head was a polearm, one half hammer, the other an axe bearded in glittering frost that was, if not sharp, then at the very least like something dragged from a nightmare of winter turned bad.

Fifty feet, and the fortress increased speed. Notes sawed out through the pilot room window. Melancholy notes. Sorrowful notes. The earth responded to Inez's tune at the very instant the Troll came to meet them. It split with low tectonic groans. Fissures opened. He might have gone sprawling, but his chilly grip on the terrain saved him. Firmer footing arose as frost coagulated, cementing the ground under his feet.

Turning his shoulder to the fortress platform, he gave a triumphant caterwaul and smashed into Betty, shaking her to her foundations. Jarred, upset-balanced, Cate and the others grabbed hold of whatever they could. Some fell; others heaved them back into the thick of things.

Meanwhile the Troll scaled the walls, his polearm swooping and making deadly pendulums, his face plastered from cheek to chin in frozen gore.

"Your halls long coffins!" he bellowed. "Your beds sepulchers. A tomb, I say! A strolling tomb haunted by scarlet ghosts!"

***

Standing with a good view of the battle within their thicket of darkness, the four members of the Murky Lurking Lads went about their personal rituals.

Varjo Cutthroat checked his poisons and his knives, making double-sure each was paired correctly with each. Jennifer Goblingrin picked her teeth, which had been the delight of her schoolmates ever since she was a girl and a source of sleepless nights to those who saw what she could do with them. Brecht Bedlam tossed his doorknob from hand to hand. For his part, Igor Wight followed the doorknob's progress for a while. He did not play or fiddle or check up on his magic item, which though it summoned forth a deep, gloomy shadow, was not anything sinister or gaudy, but rather a simple hearing aid he had worn since his thirty-third birthday.

After a while he became bored with Brecht's doorknob juggling act and began to whistle. It was, "Deck The Halls," that old chestnut. An oldie, Gormon Hughes Senior would say, but a goodie.

Serendipity is quite a thing, and at that moment in Corinth City, a whole world away, a radio jockey pressed a button that started the next song. Tens of thousands of car radios and household portables sang out that familiar number; boughs of holly, season to be jolly, yadda yadda.

The poisons and knives were checked. The teeth were picked. The doorknob went from hand to hand. All inside Wight's whistling dark.

The four watched and they waited.

They lurked in the murk, as it were, and they were indeed lads.

And Jennifer.

***

From a perch atop one of the livelier trees where the creeping cold could not sap his toesie woesies of warmth and brittlest his feets till they turned black and fell off, the creature Skuggs was also watching.

His eyes followed the action unfolding in the fortress courtyard in the manner of an audience member at The Hippodrome or a game of football in which both teams' reputations were at stake and the outcome of which held great consequence.

Skuggs was feeling very low.

He was rattled because they had almost caught him while he was sneaking about in their fortress, and he was irritated that despite his cleverness and quietness, Skuggs' only takeaway was that there were more of the enemy than he'd at first presumed. Much more. Down in the pass by the ruin of the Troll's bridge, the fortress was chock-a-block and glutted up to its stony-home gizzard with the people who wore scarlet. The agents of the Red Death.

Skuggs wondered what the Troll had said to them. He'd heard the huge fellow's voice through the fortress walls but hadn't been able to discern what was said. Knowing the Troll, Skuggs bet it was pleasantries aplentiful. Maybe even something important to the war effort. Military intelligence.

Even the idea made Skuggs' throats dry into papery tubes. The agents of the Red Death furnished with scrumptious secrets of Eurydice.

That would be just his luck.

By the Lady, there were lots of them down there. Blood-colored ants wrestling an icy colossus... and winning!

Oh the Troll would do his best. That went without saying.

But would he win? Against such bleak odds, was that even possible?

Skuggs asked himself that question as his eyes affixed on one figure in particular. She was larger than the others, so large she and the Troll might have been very distant relations (in other circumstances this thought would have made Skuggs titter, *ahehn-hen-hen*), but to his puzzlement she wasn't getting involved. She stood quite apart from everything, and though Skuggs had really marvelous peepers for deducing all manner of tiny details, he found the expression on her face totally unreadable.

She had no hair, and her neck bore laparoscopic scars. A surgeon had fiddled there, but why? Skuggs decided that he did not like her. He did not like her eyes, and the less he thought about her hammer, the better.

Why wasn't she using it? The Troll's frostbite aura was a deterrent, true enough, but with all that muscle surely she could—

In a blur of movement, the pale purple-eyed woman threw her hammer.

Skuggs' felt horror plop into his belly in a sour-grape dollop.

He really did have the most guzzlible luck.

***

She'd been picking her moment.

Eilandri Titansgrave had a sharp eye for openings and an arm that you could hang small lorries from. The Troll had been trying to hew through the scarlet fighters like the universe's most homicidal lumberjack. At the same time, he'd been championing his foes, showering them with praise as they dealt him glancing blows, lauding them as formidable as they ducked and dodged the frost-serrated axe and the bashing hammer of the polearm. He moved with a grace that defied his enormity, and with a mind to defense, keeping his guard in a constant state of flux. So hitting him with a good strike was a tall order.

One Eilandri was happy to meet, giant to giant.

Crucially, Cate brought the majority of their combatants in for an encompassing offensive. It was no use employing close-up fighters; the Troll's cold was too stubborn a menace. But there were a plethora of long-rangers, including Marcus Angel, Niccolo Bluescarf, and Eugenie O'Nine Tails, who between them caused the Troll no end of grief. Chains and blue scarf fibers and the whip that had sprouted rosy thorns snared him and snicked him, and the Troll found himself buffeted by Clothilda's sneezes and the combustive clouds of pestilence from the team Cate had dubbed Death From Above. Also, Cate had chosen that moment to deploy Elowen Trammel. Elowen's cardigan buttons became massive tent peg-shaped nails, each one capable of piercing steel should the proper pressure be applied. That pressure came from Cate Jubilee, who risked another onset of frostbite to leap from the highest tower of the fortress named Betty, plunging down with the air scooping her hair out in a fluttering, blazing torch and slamming the trammel home with both hobnail boots.

It sank into the Troll's naked calf, squirting blood.

A spasm of pain pulled his features tight. Those graceful movements slowed.

For an instant, just the smallest sliver of a second, his guard became predictable.

Eilandri's hammer took him in the side of the head. It partially caved in, making a crater of his temple. The sheer strength behind the blow sent the impact up and down the arc of his skull. One turquoise eye popped out of its socket. The left portion of his jaw disintegrated. Tiny filaments of bone shredded his gum line. Blood jetted from his mouth and nostrils in bright freshets. Shock quivered his whole body. He fumbled the polearm.

Rolling across courtyard stone, hearing the *thunk* of Eilandri's hammer as it landed nearby, Cate Jubilee looked up in time to see the Troll bring his hands toward the sagging cataclysm of his face. Pity rose in her. As monsters went he was practically a gentleman. Almost noble. In tandem with that pity rose her fighting spirit. *Your halls long coffins*, he'd taunted them.

Yours will be this mountain pass, she thought. *Sending you there is an honor.*

Out of the corner of her eye, she spotted something gold-white and fizzling. It was Kevlin Paladin. Sunlight and moonlight shimmered off his spear in dazzling sheets.

Without a word he flung it headlong. Icy chainmail melted instantly. Through its running, steaming rings the spear delved, earthing itself in the Troll's throat, specifically its jugular vein, which popped and immediately cauterized with a smell like frying copper circuitry. Golden light propelled by lunar energy washed away the cold barrier surrounding the Troll.

"Igor!" Cate roared.

The whistling stopped.

Until now she hadn't been aware there *was* whistling. But there had been and now it was replaced by a silken silence. From the otherwise inconspicuous shadows pooled southwest of her boots crisped in the Troll's frost, the Murky Lurking Lads came. They spilled out of the dark, three of the four, for Igor's job was done and the others' was about to begin.

With daggers coated in the most caustic of poisons and teeth of the nastiest rending variety, Varjo and Jennifer peeled open the Troll's chest, exposing the heart nestled in its bed of cardiac muscle. Brecht Bedlam stepped forward, brandishing his doorknob.

"Wait," gurgled the Troll, and Cate almost bade them stop.

But she didn't. Pity and fighting spirit were joined by a firm iron-tough resolution: even for someone like the Troll, who was a HE and absolutely not an IT, closer to a person than any monster she had ever met... even for him there could be no mercy. Kindness at the extremities of reason, where worlds thought and marshaled troops to carry out their blitzkriegs, was a poisoned chalice. Drink and die. Such was Responsible Leadership.

She could have looked away when Brecht touched the doorknob to the Troll's heart, or when he turned it, opening a door-shaped hole, or when the chambers of the heart slopped out through that hole in a slippery chum. She really could have.

Instead she made herself watch it all, and when the rich dark heart's blood reached the soles of her boots she made herself step across it until she reached the place where the Troll lay. His good eye was at a level with her. It blinked at her slowly, indolently. Then it looked over her. Cate followed it, and felt her breath catch.

On the slope amongst the crooked-limbed trees, a shape was vanishing into a mound of pink-quartz crystal. It was exactly the same sort of crystal that credits were made of, the kind the Troll would become after he died. She had never, not in all her missions to Eurydice, ever seen the stuff form a mound all on its own without death being dealt out.

To her astonishment, the Troll spoke. "That will be Skuggs making his exit. He has harnessed the crystal in his body to cover him and ferry him in any direction he chooses. I'm afraid you stand no chance of catching him, Cate Jubilee."

Her mind blocked out the pain in her hand (which had graduated to a gasoline fire) and the shiver threading her poor frostnipped legs, and examined the situation.

(harnessed the crystal)

(covered in it)

(images of credits scattering and spilling from her fingers)

(each of them valuable, sure)

(sure and)

(and)

"Reflective," she mouthed.

The word filled her brain in phenomenal italics.

REFLECTIVE!!!

Moving fast, she dove into her satchel with questing fingers—suddenly atremble with urgency, for if she fucked this up *oh God God GOD*—snatched hold of a mirror-making vial, *whumped* it out, fell to her knees not caring if the stone skinned them, and rammed a hand through.

It closed on something that had not expected a hand to appear and close upon it, and which was willing to express that surprise violently.

Cate screamed.

In her haste, she had used the hand purpled and swollen with bruise and stuffed with throbbing, ugly agony. Her friends and allies rushed to help her. She stopped them. "I've guh-got it." That last word perforated into another scream.

The thing at the other end of the reflection was stabbing her wrist with something sharp. Stabbing and *twisting*. Vision blurring with tears, her lips unseamed in howls of mingled pain and fury, Cate hauled it through.

A wicked little horror wriggled at the end of her arm. It was small as a boy of six or seven. Its face was a mass of furrows and pockmarks, the skin ribbed and faintly glossy like pumpkin flesh in an autumnal market. Four ears stuck out pointed as knives from that head, and its nose and chin were just as sharp. Two Adam's apples bobbed crazily in its neck, which was strangely thick and veiny. A single eye rested in the middle of the creature's brow. It was black, with a ring of crystal-pink for the iris. It wore tight-fitting clothes, boots, and gloves, so black and wet-looking that you might have believed they were painted on. Its weapon was a dagger of that same pink-quartz Cate had seen passed from hand to hand in transaction ten-thousand times.

The creature called Skuggs slid the blade from her wrist and lunged for Cate's throat. She cocked her head, felt the point open her neck, not grievously but quite painfully, in a hot red line, and punched Skuggs, once in the head, whereupon it went limp in her grip. She held it aloft. Everyone stared at her, amazed, or agog, or both.

There was a rumble of amusement.

"Impressive," said the Troll. A moment later he was dead.

The mountain began to thaw.

Chapter Eighteen

*D*eck *The Halls* diminished on the radio. Another caroling classic struck up, only to be switched off by the barman of The King's Flagon. He opened his mouth to comment that if he heard one more Tinfrost song today, he was going to give up the genial innkeep demeanor and burn the place down. Just in time he remembered hearing one of his patrons tell him about the Waters household a couple streets down, how it had gone up in flames last night with everyone inside it. Cooked alive. Why hadn't they run outside to safety? The patron didn't know, but he heard from his brother-in-law who was a firefighter that there was no way it was a faulty socket or pot roast neglected in the oven. The odor from the blaze had been redolent of the smell you get from gas stations—unleaded petroleum. Air drenched in it, he said. It had to be arson. In fact, the brother-in-law had reason to believe that not only were the doors of the house shored up with fire, but they had been *locked*. Freaky stuff.

In his tenure at the Flagon, the barman had often served a young man who he'd gotten friendly with named Barclay Waters. Kid was studying to be a lawyer. What a dreamer. Leonidas District to the law department at the university. Not likely, but the kid seemed awfully sure of himself. Nice kid too. Very polite, very mannerly.

With his trap shut against crude comments that might upset his customers, the barman set to aimlessly cleaning glasses while the radio cranked out the moody tunes of the blues, some part of him wondering if it was the same Waters family, and if he'd ever see that Barclay kid again, and what sort of lawyer he'd make, or would have made...

Meanwhile at a table across from the bar, the Citadel man, the Cut-String King, the copper, and the ex-criminal sat and discussed previous steps. They would get to next steps, but it was easier to gather where they were going when they had a firm knowledge of where they'd been.

It was late afternoon. Only a moment ago it had seemed like early afternoon, but December fancies its days short. Already dusk was dimming, and the red sodium lights of Leonidas were beginning to flicker on. Outside the blizzard had returned with a vengeance. It rattled the sign, hooted down the chimney, roared over the cobbles, soughed in the chimneystacks, and howled wolfishly, and it stalked the streets with paws that snapped washing lines, toppled the streetlamps, and slapped the snow into a white flaky frenzy.

"Let's go over the facts," said Thud, flipping his notebook to the pertinent page. "We have our primary suspect." He circled the name *Jane.* "We have a method." He circled the verbs *Infest* and *Abandon.* "We have a motive." He circled and recircled the phrase, *She does it because the crime is a feast. She feasts because she is hungry.* "Enough to make an arrest by any court's standards. Now we've just got to arrest her. I will admit I'm something of a novice when it comes to women with appetites and abilities like this. My wife Hettie is an artist, and she's signed her name on many a transgressive latrine over the years, I don't mind telling you, but even she's got limits. Plus Spring-Heeled Jane is magic, and I'm about as arcane as a jelly doughnut. Anyone have any ideas?"

"We've got to get her in the act," said Hughes tonelessly. Their table was stationed by a window, and he was looking out its grimy snow-laced panels, not seeing anything, his dark eyes roving in that skidding way that indicates deep consideration, what his father always referred to as A Hard Think. "We've got to get her while she's still inside."

Thud frowned. "I thought she was in the Dennings' woman's head?"

It was Frank Gallant who replied. "Nah, man. Just a piece of her. A memento of their time together. A keepsake of the time Jane was jerking her around on buzzing strings." His voice, lush and powerful, practically glowed with contempt. "We know because, on the face of it, it adds up. How could she reap all the havoc round town while stuck in poor, excavated Sue Dennings? She couldn't, that's how. That thing we faced off against was a part of her, both present and cast off, like a molted insect skin the bug remembers wearing and can slip into at any time."

"A shadow," said Mr. Glint.

Hughes started.

They turned to him. "You okay?" said Frank.

"Yeah." Hughes elaborated no further. He took a mouthful of warm, sweet cocoa with its splash of creamy liqueur. Then he said, "To Frank's point, we can confirm Jane wasn't in the dream since my Performance had no effect. That fly on my hand was like... how to put it... a kind of avatar for her. A receptacle she'd filtered her personality into. But it was only a bit of synecdoche."

"A bit of what?" said Mr. Glint, avid pupil of language.

"Synecdoche. When a part of something is substituted for the whole. Like 'I got some new wheels' means 'I got a new car.' That fly, in fact that teeming mass of bugs we encountered in Taggart House and Sue Dennings' dream, was not Jane herself but a piece of her that spoke for and gestured to the entirety of her."

Mr. Glint nodded. "Makes sense. When you scrag a fly, the hive is okay, and the spee, the specky..."

"Species," supplied Frank gently.

"Thanks, the species goes on like nothing happened. So when I squashed that Jane fly, she was still tickety-boo and raring to go."

"So we've got to use your Performance on the real her," Thud said glumly, for he saw the whole picture now and did not care for how it influenced his investigation. "The only way you can do that is by targeting Jane while she's infesting a victim, making them carry out one of her crimes."

"And we've got no way to find her while she's playing mind-snatcher, roof-jumper," said Frank. "In other words, we're up a certain creek without a certain paddle."

"Well bugger."

"No," said Mr. Glint. "Not bugger. Shit."

Thud stared at him.

"The creek," said Mr. Glint by way of explanation. "We are up shit creek without a paddle."

"Ah. Right. Thank you so very much for that contribution." Thud drained his pint. "That tastes like paint thinner. What the hell is it?"

"It's a brand of beer," said Hughes.

"What brand?"

"Paint Thinner."

"I'm getting another."

As Thud left beneath a cloud of displeasure, Frank leaned his elbows on the tabletop and canted his head toward the streetbeater. "He know about Eurydice?"

"No," said Hughes. "Citadel secret."

"Jane is from Eurydice."

"I suspected so. You're quite sure?"

"Positive. While the flies were foaming out of me I couldn't tell up from down. Everything went warped, sights and sounds hurtling harum-scarum past me. After a moment or two I recognized it. The carousel where we fought my moms."

Hughes pondered that. "None of the people she's infested had knowledge of that. They'd all probably heard of The Hairy Autumn but not the Nightjar Coven. Yeah, the only way Jane could know about that is if she's part of the ecosystem of Eurydice. What does that mean?"

"I don't know. But she was into you, Hughes. Not attracted but *enthralled*. You had her multifaceted eyes out on stalks, and no mistake. Maybe it's because you participated in the downfall of my moms."

"That doesn't make sense," said Hughes. "If that were the case, she'd have been focused on..."

Together their gazes found Mr. Glint, who took the hint. "On me. 'Cos I ate them. Well, not all of them," he amended regretfully. "One got squashed by Miss Jubilee's boot."

Frank patted him on the arm. "Hey. Two outta three ain't bad."

"You reckon?"

"Whose deceitful doyen mothers ended up in your guts? When it comes to the subject of Mr. Glint devouring people's murderous mommas, I am the world's most prodigious expert."

"Fair enough," said Mr. Glint, pleased.

Hughes was left to mull the connotations over for himself. Jane had indeed seemed riveted by him. How much of that was his natural skill in assuming roles, and how much of it was the innate power casting itself long like a second shadow over the suspicious sands and hopeful dunes of his heart? He did not know. Resolve erected sand castles inside him. He would find out.

Thud returned with a fresh round for everyone.

Hughes	Thud	Frank	Mr. Glint
One cocoa with creamy liqueur	One pint of Paint Thinner	One Summer Fling (which is like a banana daiquiri mixed with the idea of sleek hotel room sex)	One whiskey glass containing three shots of whatever cleaning fluids the barman had under the sink

"There's something else," Hughes told them. "I think she's lonely."

"So not all bad news, then," said Thud.

"Don't be droll," Hughes snapped. "People are dead."

There was a crowded silence.

Hughes pushed his drink away, rubbed his eyes, and gave Thud a mournful look. "I'm sorry."

"Sticks and stones, lad. What were you saying?"

"Really, I—"

"Hughes. We're listening."

Hughes ran his lower incisors over his upper lip. He had a hold of himself once more. When had he grown so exhausted? Night hadn't fallen, and he felt washclothed, that phrase his neighbor of yesteryear Sheila Kofatch had trotted out on occasion. It meant wrung out. Gray and useless. Tired.

"During her speech about us leaving her to her business, Jane admitted that we'd only need to hold off until the season was over. She'd be gone come spring."

"The month or the idea?" said Thud.

"How do you mean?"

"Some people believe spring starts on February 1st, the Feast of Saint Brigitte. Others believe it comes in March. And then there's the other sort who are a bit more airy fairy about it; those people believe that spring starts with the blooming of the first daffodils."

I forgot his wife Hettie is pagan, Hughes thought. "It's a good distinction to make," he said. "But one I can't shed light on. Based on our clues connecting the victims, I think it might be sooner than all of those."

Thud's mustache twitched. "The decorations. You think she'll stop around Tinfrost."

Hughes nodded. "That would align with the Spring-Heeled murders thirty-four years ago. She'll stop after Tinfrost, I'm sure of it."

"What's the lonely angle?" asked Frank.

"I think her life cycle depresses her. The solitary nature of it. Imagine someone being born once a year and only getting to live for a few paltry weeks. That's a miniscule period of time for something as advanced as Jane clearly is. We spoke about the nursery rhyme about the old woman and the fly."

"Perhaps she'll die," intoned Mr. Glint like the wind through autumn leaves in a graveyard, scattered and dry-stemmed and dead.

"Exactly. It's a rhyme about increasingly dramatic measures being taken to solve a simple situation, and to disastrous effect. The old woman swallows a fly, then a spider to catch the fly, then a bird, a cat, and so on, until she swallows a horse and dies. But that's the human interpretation. Take the rhyme from the point of view of the fly. It doesn't care about the escalating nutritional developments in the life of some doddery windbag. It cares about the spider coming to eat it or the old lady's stomach acid dissolving it. It cares about death. It cares that it was going about its life and now it's going to die alone."

"After someone interfered," said Frank. "Clearly the irony is lost on our Spring-Heeled friend."

"The point is the isolation," insisted Hughes. "It could explain what Jane is getting out of this. She's hungry, right? What if she's eating her way into people's heads, chewing up their sense of selves because she's starved for company?"

"Then she is not the merry genius of her own household," said Mr. Glint.

The group blinked at him as one.

"Apologies, Mr. Glint. I didn't catch that," said Hughes cautiously.

"It's from a poem about loneliness. This poet, yeah? He's lying in bed and thinking about what would happen if, while his missus and his moppets stay asleep, he gets up and takes off his clothes and has a bit of a wiggler and a gabbler in front of the mirror. It ends with the lines, 'Who will guess I am not/the merry genius of my household?' Course no one will say that," finished Mr. Glint, raising his glass and inhaling the nostril-hair crinkling musk of his... well, his what might hesitantly be called a drink. "Being lonely is the time when you get to think about all sorts. Entertainment in your noodle, like. And then you can sing or dance or whatever, and no one will care. Company is dandy but lonesome is winsome, as the other poet wrote, and what a toff he was. Cheers." He knocked back his drink in one heinous throat-bulging swallow and declared his satisfaction. "Ahhhh."

"Strange as it might sound, that rings truer to me than your theory, Hughes," said Thud after an extremely necessary lull in the conversation. "I've seen lots of violent people over the years, and the reasons behind that violence always show. Domestics, robbers, well-meaning blowhards, and mean-minded clobberers. Motive is like cream, Hughes. Or scum, I suppose. It rises to the top. Spring-Heeled Jane is more sadism than sorrow. I'd stake my badge on it."

Frank had been quiet as all this played itself out.

Suddenly he spoke and with such intensity they all caught it and gave it back to him in spades. "What was that you said before? About the Tinfrost decorations?"

"It's the one factor connecting the victims," said Hughes. "Age, gender, social demographic, economic background. There are some similarities and conventions, but the one uniting element is that the victims recalled with vivid clarity the putting up of the Tinfrost decorations."

Frank turned to Mr. Glint. "My shiny-suited friend. You are a master of elliptic deduction."

Mr. Glint nodded. "I'm a regular bloody sleuth, me."

"What's it like putting up the decorations?" Frank asked Hughes and Thud, who were looking at him with naked bewilderment. "Come on, man. It's Tinfrost time. What's it like?"

"Can be a bit of a lark," said Hughes.

"Generally it's a pain in the arse," said Thud.

"Right. Okay. Now tell me, what is it like after you're done? When you're standing back, your knuckles kneading ache from the small of your back, and the tree baubles up like a pretty lady showing her gorgeous self to the room, and splendid as that same pretty lady having a good time doing so, and all the trouble of getting your tree organized behind you?"

"I... guess it feels nice?"

"How nice?"

"Nice, you know. Really, um, nice. Lovely." Hughes and Thud seemed to be having a contest to see who could frown deeper. "Where are you going with this, Frank?" Hughes asked.

Frank plucked the umbrella from his Summer Fling and skewered the syrup-covered cherry bobbing amid the ice cubes. "Our Spring-Heeled virago and vexatious vixen is not a voracious eater of company. Look around you. What is there in abundance at this time of year? What is the thing Mr. Glint so smartly pointed out that you can slurp up when you are lonesome and left to your own devices? More importantly, if I've got the timeline right, what was there *before* the war with Champleurs, what went *away* during those turbulent times, and what has taken a long-ass-span coming back *after* all the bullshit going on in this city during the intervening years? Think about it. What are there *tidings* of during the holiday season?"

Hughes concentrated. Thud was less patient and made to demand an answer, but before he could, Hughes' brow cleared and his face lit up with a mixture of inspiration and utter dread. "Tidings of comfort and joy," he said softly. "Jane eats happiness."

"Bingo," said Frank Gallant, and he ate the cherry in one sumptuous bite.

***

The investigation team agreed among themselves to go home and rest and think about ways they might capture Spring-Heeled Jane while she was still, as it were, in the driver's seat. It had been a long day. They had done much. There was much more to do.

As with the team, the blizzard was made up of four parts, and it seemed to reflect and parrot them. For the ex-criminal, the blizzard was sour-souled and strong, and it picked at your clothes and your exposed skin with too-long fingers. For the copper, the blizzard was hard and scrappy and intelligent; it moved through Leonidas District like an old friend, uncovering every secret it could. For the Citadel man who thought of himself as the teamaster's son and the lover of a woman of glass and fire, and who others thought of as the Bloodhound or the shadow man or the mirror man, for him the blizzard was a tempest of memory, a storm belabored by the past, driven by cold gusts and frozen flakes and hard lumps of icy necessity into the future. And for the Cut-String King, the Dream Warrior, the blizzard held a dreamy, somnolent quality, at least for those indoors. The next time there is a storm near you, and you are lucky enough to be tucked beyond its grasp and all its component parts, listen. You might just hear them. You might recognize something of yourself in it too.

The ex-criminal and the Cut-String King took their leave, heading about the business that only strange folk such as themselves could attract and dabble in.

The copper and the Citadel man fell into step.

They would part company in three stops. Their first stop, or shelter if you prefer, was in the lee of a big blue lorry parked on Bromley.

"Sorry again," said Hughes.

"What for?"

"For calling you droll. That wasn't you being droll, it was me being a dick."

"Oh, I don't know," said Thud, redoing the buttons on his coat so they aligned properly. "A bit curt, I suppose. You're under the kosh."

"The what?"

"The truncheon. Under pressure, like."

"We all are."

Thud grunted eloquently.

Their second spot was farther along. Some weirdly prescient street artist had made a sculpture out of brass umbrellas. Hughes wasn't sure of their aesthetic merit, but for their shield he was immensely grateful. Around them the blizzard wailed and whistled shrilly. Their facial hair was clumped in sticking snow.

"You seem stiff-shouldered," Hughes told Thud in a loud voice so he would be heard. "What's up?"

"Nothing. I said something I shouldn't have to someone on the telephone, that's all."

Hughes considered pushing the streetbeater on it. He let it go.

"Come on. We'll turn up Callimachus. After that we're both home free."

"I could use a drink."

"We've just come from the pub."

"I know. Fancy turning back?"

"Come on."

For a few appalling moments it seemed there would be no third stop. Callimachus was a north-facing street. The blizzard was using it as a funnel to get to south-easterly Leonidas. Gusts lengthened into knives that cut the remaining warmth from Hughes in an instant. The snow was no longer satisfied with clumping. It swirled and stuck and glued wherever it could find and finagle room. Where it gathered too-thick on roofs and gutters, it crashed and avalanched and brought tiles and piping down with it. A lumpen white shape nosing up a glowing red point in the middle of the street was all that remained of a fallen streetlamp. All in all, the weather on Callimachus was as cheery as Mr. Glint's countenance.

Thud spotted a wee titch of an alley. They dove for it.

Hughes blew his runny nose into a handkerchief. "I've never told you this," he began.

"Save your breath, son. You'd never make it as a full-time copper. There's jib in your cut, don't get me wrong. Fierceness in your fettle. You've a scrappy side, I grant you. But you need real hoodlum spirit to make it in the streetbeaters, and you left your rowdy roughneck delinquent days the moment you took the red."

"I was going to say you've an incredible mustache."

Thud looked taken aback. "Sorry?"

"Your mustache. It's the best mustache I've ever seen."

"I see."

"No, I see. I see your mustache, Thud."

There was a mildly embarrassed pause.

"Thank you," said Thud.

Hughes relaxed. "Bet it takes a lot of effort to maintain."

"Course it does," said Thud with a hint of pride.

"Why do you? Maintain it so well, that is?"

"A man has his reasons like a copper has his truncheon, lad. Sometimes it's best to keep such things in the pockets they belong in."

"It's because Hettie likes it, isn't it?"

"Certainly not."

"It is."

"Hughes, I do not purchase pomade that costs a whole month's salary a tin, keep a pair of trimming clippers in my coat, or pluck the scraggly grays and oranges... I do not do any of these things because my wife likes my mustache."

"Sorry."

"Just so that's all clear and firmly stated."

"Sorry."

"Good. Glad we've got that sorted." Thud peeked out of the alley. "I do it because she *loves* my mustache."

There was a break in between gusts.

They ran for it, Thud hunched low, Hughes even lower because he was laughing.

There was something tickling the outermost peripheries of his head. Something important about the investigation. Maybe it was a solution to finding Jane. Maybe it was something insignificant, half-forgotten and better off without being recalled. He didn't know. He'd sleep on it. On a lot of things.

First bed. Mmmmmbed. And a letter to Cate. And a telephone call to his dad to make sure he was all right. Also he should probably eat. He was getting bad at remembering to do that. Oh, and obviously his mind ought to slink over the details of the case, and hopefully, cough up some way to catch Jane before she could—

The blizzard roared in his ears, blotting out all conscious thought. He ran like a man possessed through that twinkling white savannah, leopard-spotted in red where the sodium lamps sparked up with the drawing in of night, fragrant with the cheap warthoggish smells of difficult times trying to mask themselves as better ones, and musical with radios and chatter from narrow tenement balconies where smokers shivered and talked about anything, and beautiful because Leonidas was his home before he'd found the home of Cate's heart and the Citadel, and terrible because of what would happen to it if he didn't get his act together and solve this thing.

Second, he needed to recharge. Get back to one hundred percent.

First, he ran, bidding Thud farewell as their routes diverged and carrying on alone. Alone as a fly. Perhaps he'll die.

***

In Nikandros District, in The Foundry where the Jolenes of Corinth City worked with greasy brows and sooty aprons, fussing over the creation of bright, exquisite things, in her private alcove wherein lay her workbench and her tools and her whole life, really, Jo was trying to be convincing.

More specifically, she was trying to convince plate steel that it wasn't plate steel. Or, even more specifically, that it wasn't *quite* plate steel. If things turned out well in the end, the material would believe it was what you might call metallurgically adjacent, i.e. plate steel*ish*.

The process was not without its difficulties. Metal knows exactly what it is. Put metal alongside wood, animal skin, or synthetic ceramic alloys, and see who gets picked first in the annual material contest. Metal is the prize show dog of modern armor. Steel is particularly popular since it's the child of two hard working and successful parents, iron and carbon, and it's never had to work a day in its life to be as good as it is. And popular things are confident. This is why CEOs and recently elected civil servants are so difficult to have 'round for tea. Questions and responses slide off them. They hear what they want to hear. They talk to themselves. Steel talks to itself, and even if it *was* willing to chat, it certainly wouldn't be interested in someone telling it that it isn't what it thinks it is. The word steel*ish* makes steel nervous.

Jo finished setting the breastplate up on its rack. She walked over to where she had constructed a large ballista. "Alley-oop," she said and thumped the release.

There was a noise like a sharpened rolling pin skewering a hundred layers of tinfoil. Jo ambled back over to the breastplate. As part of her efforts in persuading it, she'd tried alloying several complimentary metals along different sections of the steel, infusing one or two of them with the weird alchemy bubbling and broiling in her head, as well as in the various vials, jars, and grainy sandy kettles she kept in her alcove cabinets. This trial, alas, was a failure. The trebuchet arrow had slid off the attenuated ridge at the front of the breastplate, but that was normal, and the puncture was otherwise clean. She shook her head dolefully. "No promise at all. I'm not even one step closer to adaptive metallurgic folding." Then she smiled, a crooked-toothed smile "Not true. I know more ways it *won't* work. And that means I've narrowed the playing field. Back to the old drawing board, as they say. Though who 'they' are exactly, I've never been really sure of," she added in a musing voice, heading back to the schematics on the workbench. "Whoever 'they' are,' they must be clever, coming up with all these little sayings. Clever as my friend, Hughes, even." She scrunched up her most recent blueprint and binned it carefully, her mismatched eyes lined with laughter, her belly all a-rumble, her mouth full of giggles. "Not likely! He's as sharp as a tack, and tacks are sharp as... um. As Hughes!"

It was for the benefit of Hughes the Clever, Hughes the Kind, Hughes the Splendiferous, that she had chosen to re-embark on this attempt to tell metal that it was something else. If she could make him something even better than Jolene steel, but Jo's Special Steelish Stuff, then he would be pleased as punch, and she wouldn't get a punch for her trouble, no not ever, but a hug! Her high humor climbed up even higher.

As did her eyes. She wasn't aware of it, but there they went. They drifted up... and up... and up toward the ceiling, a faraway look in them, as though the ceiling was of little interest compared to what could be found above. The next floor, say. Or the roof.

Then the spell broke and Jo was sketching a new design. This one would hold promise, she would bet her last lank hairs on it! It would hold promises and oaths and swears and vows, that was how good it would be. She would show that stubborn metal what it could become. Show, don't tell. That was another of "their" sayings, those people not-quite-as clever as Hughes.

A kind word. A hug. She wiggled her hips and bottom. A hug!

And if she could hear—on some subsonic level—the buzz of a fly, what of it?

She was a woman about her work, and a bug would not deter her.

Skulking around in the interesting mind, Spring-Heeled Jane paused just long enough to try Jolene and pronounced Jolene delicious.

Act Seven

Something Charred

Chapter Nineteen

*D*ear Hughes,

I shall have to write as small as a cat trying to blend in at a mouse-only festival to get everything down on the page; there's so much to tell you!

Before I forget, I both prize and lionize your insistence on underlining for emphasis. It is utterly adorable and you are a dote.

Will start with your updates, since you sent me two letters before I've taken the time to send you one. (Thank you for your patience!)

I'm sorry you had an argy-bargy with her Ladyship about magic items. My initial reaction was that she has the right of it. But the more I mull the idea over, the more I dismiss my qualms as prejudice, a kind of paranoid reflex. Maybe a public militia is a wonderful idea. Inspired, even. On the other hand, Wendy has ruled over Corinth City for almost thirty years. The government is a figurehead; they're good for ordering curry take-away and keeping the roads supplied with the acceptable amount of litter and traffic and not much else. Whereas Wendy has juggled international relations and domestic policy so complicated, it makes my head spin. I'd be interested to hear her justifications for keeping magic item ownership localized to the Citadel, but what I am sure of is that there are justifications to be presented, if you see what I mean.

(Now I've begun underlining things; you're a contagion with a pretty jawline, Gormon Hughes.)

I'm still reeling over what you've told me about Spring-Heeled Jane. She sounds like something from an old horror flick, one of those ones where the girl clutches the guy, howling her lungs out while the monster slithers toward its next victims. The main difference being that Jane is genuinely terrifying. So take the utmost care. I'm pleased that Frank, Glint, and Thud have your back. They are grossly inadequate substitutes for me, but you shall just have to get on with things as best you can, and try not to be too devastated, or make a spectacle of yourself, you swarthy, swashbuckling, sparklingly dramatic circus of a human being.

If it isn't clear, I miss you too.

One last note on your business with Jane; I have a suggestion. Desdemona Cauldronpot (I think she's had the name legally changed from Denise Caldwell as of recently) has grown in experience and power. She used to be relegated to guiding people into deep, dream-rich sleep. To my understanding that has changed. Now while she herself sleeps, she can induce powerful visions. These visions are anchored in her past. Years ago she put you into a dream that carried your mind to the Nightjar Coven's realm in Eurydice. That means Eurydice is in Desdemona's past. In theory, does that not also mean she could go to sleep and latch onto a presence in the city that doesn't belong there, which does in fact belong in Eurydice? Namely Spring-Heeled Jane.

It's a stretch, but a bit of occult yoga never hurt anyone, eh?

Yesterday we fought a bizarrely amiable Troll and captured a much more predictably devious shitstain named Skuggs. According to the Troll, Skuggs has mastered the pink-quartz rock inside himself in order to travel great distances. It's the equivalent of a person from our world using their hemoglobin to fuel their car. Amazing, undoubtedly, but we've discovered the ability's constraints. Skuggs must be in contact with the ground in Eurydice in order for it to work. Shackled in our fortress, he's completely trapped.

He eats happily enough, but spared his venomous little tongue, other than to call me some colorful names, some of which I even understood, I think I'm the first instance of someone thwarting his escape method. Reflections in the crystal. Go figure.

As we searched Skuggs, we found a device. It's on my desk now as I write to you. It's a disc compact enough to close your fingers around. It reminds me of an old-fashioned clock face, rimmed in that pink-quartz we use for credits. It has lots of clock hands, some thick and heavy, some so faint as to be almost invisible. Instead of numbers running round the edge, the device has symbols. One of them looks a bit like the Troll from yesterday. So the symbols might represent creatures of his and the Bride of the Fog's caliber. Jolly good if so; a compass that points toward our monstrous targets is a welcome boon indeed.

Some of the others wanted me to draw information from Skuggs, sharply. Of course I told them where they could put that idea. Pain is a useless motivator; I, for one, would say anything if it would only stop. What unfeeling sod could claim differently? Cajoling was out too, since Skuggs is, as mentioned, a rude and odious pile of compost. Much as it's proximal to physical malevolence, and is pretty damn odious in and of itself, I ultimately decided to opt for dosing him with fright.

To this end I had Margherita Stranger prick his finger with that sword of hers. At a party once when we were younger, I had her prick my finger for a lark. And let me tell you, lover, when I heard the whimpering start from Skuggs I felt sympathy. That sword can show you horrors that are very tailor-fitted for you. I don't know what Skuggs saw, but when the clouds of terror vaporized behind his black eye, he was bathed in sweat. Only it didn't work, my darling. He grinned like a slashed Halloween pumpkin and asked me, if I wouldn't mind, to prick him again. Preferably his thumb this time, and deeper, so he could avoid my company a few moments longer. A cheeky grotesque, but a brave one.

Trusting that my conclusions about the device are solid, I've directed Betty (it's a good name for a fortress, shut up) toward the heaviest of the clock hands. When last I looked out from the parapet, I saw that we've entered a topsy-turvy country. Below us and as far as the eye can squint, the ground is a starry expanse with twelve moons suspended in the velvet black like Yi-Shi lanterns sunk beneath a pond. Above us stretch endless checkerboard fields, their grass and hedges dark with nightfall. Here and there the grass rises in chunky rectangles, becoming stairs that climb down toward us. Walking these steps are pale figures with robes that remind me of Hector and the other living ghosts' clothes, all translucent and flowing and spectral. The figures are singing. Everyone is reacting differently to the songs. I think they sound like lullabies. Lorna Blacktower says they sound like sea shanties. Rebecca Lupine hears the mournful howls of wolves. Igor Wight insists they're screams, but I think he's bored and winding people up. Hard to tell though.

Searching the Citadel notes, I've found coverage of this place by none other than Burnished Isaac Lawless, your biggest fan. Now there's someone who would find camaraderie with Skuggs. Isaac writes that this region of Eurydice is home to a group of ghostly types led by someone called William o' The Wisps. Apparently William has unique travel arrangements of his own; a giant flying manta ray. There's going to be a fight, a tricky one if Isaac's information is good.

I am as excited as a cat that the festival mice have accepted as one of their own, and now that the coast is clear the budgerigars are on their way, and bowls of unsuspecting cream. But you know that because you know me. And you know how I feel about you.

Something else before I sign off. If she ever tires of the fighting life, Eilandri should think about a career in therapy. The woman is much too easy to talk to. She visited me yesterday, and again today. Things were okay, and then out of seemingly nowhere I got it into my mind to tell her all about our bad November. The shock of the initial bleed. The hospital. Our baby. Everything. I could actually feel the words struggling to get out of me, as if they'd been as trapped as Skuggs and were desperate as hell to break free. I stopped them before they blurted out, but only just. It scared me. Vulnerability comes easier to you; you've a heart like a gift, made to be opened up for people (including a lucky girl like me) and delighted in. Sometimes I wonder if the glass hasn't reached mine. I put my hand on my chest and it beats fine. Regular healthy heart here, ma'am. Nothing to worry about.

But our baby was regular too. Ordinary and sublime. I think about the ultrasound, the subsequent change our little girl underwent, and some part of me whispers: for that baby's mum, the change isn't going to happen in the future. It already has happened. Am I different now than I was in November? Last Tinfrosttime? Different in a way that time can't account for, and which would only show up in the right kind of mirror, one embedded in my skin?

I don't know. No clues in this case. Investigators baffled. Head scratches all round.

I think I shall tell you how I feel about you, Puppy.

Just in case.

I love and admire you with all my heart. Flesh or glass, it's yours.

Now go catch a killer.

C. Jubilee

***

When Denise opened the door, she found herself staring into the faces of four strange men. One of the men was familiar. Three were not. But they were all of them, without exclusion or gripe or possible argument, strange.

This, some tidied-away part of her advised, boded poorly.

She smothered that part with authoritative mental hands.

"Good morning, Desdemona," said the familiar one. Humbert Something. He seemed to reconsider his greeting. He spread his arms wide. "Um. Blessings of the incipient umbra be upon this..." He looked at her apartment desperately. "Ummm... Be upon this very blessed domicile."

"Why's he blessed it twice?" asked one of them, tall and grim-faced, with a voice like gravel from the driveway to hell, a truly repulsive example of humanity.

"I don't know," replied the admittedly fetching one with... yes, what looked to be moving aurora borealis in his hair. Some technical wizardry involving LEDs perhaps. "Why'd you bless it if it was already blessed, Hughes?"

Hughes, that was it. Not Humbert.

"Look," said Hughes. "Can we come in?"

"Certainly not," she said huffily. "I'm very busy. Who do you think you are?"

"Sorry. Gormon Hughes. We've met several times."

"Yes, I remember you. I meant who—"

"Oh I see. This is Mr. Glint."

The awful-looking man nodded. "You got any sisters?" he asked. "Only I've eaten several people what look just like you."

"Anyway," said Hughes, sweating.

"If you have lost relatives to my belly, madam, I should like to apologize. I am, you see, a rough diamond what requires much polishing—"

"*Anyway!* This is Captain Hoshrum Thud, a commendable policeman of singular reputation and investigative skill."

"Ma'am," said Thud, giving a little bow.

"And this," continued Hughes, "is—"

"Mr. Hughes," she snapped, interrupting his torrent of introductions. "I mean who do you think you are barging in upon my day like a hedgehog prickling all over a perfectly good picnic?"

"Lot of Ps," said Glint.

"A preponderance," said the man with the aurora in his hair.

"Miss Cauldronpot, I..." Hughes broke off. He looked at the aurora man. "What did you say?"

"A preponderance."

"Did Cate tell you about that?"

"Tell me about what?"

"Nothing. You... But she... Nothing." Hughes shook his head as though clearing it of distractions. "Miss Cauldronpot. We've come to... That is we are hoping to invoke your considerable talents in the field of occultism and oneiromancy, and—"

"Caldwell."

"—furthermore we're under a lot of time pressure... Pardon?"

"My name," she said primly, drawing herself up like a hen. "Is Denise Caldwell."

Hughes gave her a look so blank you could use it as an art canvas.

"But you had it legally changed."

"*Back*," she said. "Legally changed *back*. To Denise Caldwell. My name."

Hughes looked at her arms, her clothes, and seemed to search for something else about her person.

"You will cease ogling me this instant," she berated him, drawing her bathrobe up tightly as if warding away the most lecherous of degenerates. "For shame, young man!"

"Where are your bangles?" he murmured. "Your ceremonial robes and the baubles and enormous great big jewelry. Where's your circlet with the magic tourmaline you drew a dot on to make it look like a third eye in your forehead?"

"Oh them. Dumped them in the rubbish. Good riddance, I say."

"Rubbish?" His mouth fell open. "You binned your *magic item*?"

"Don't be ridiculous. It's in the loft, I think. But I'm quite finished with all that. It's drivel. Avery has shown me that. Good day, young man."

"Wait, waitwaitwait." Hughes came forward as she shut the door. The outrageous man had the gall to stick his foot in the door. "Who is Avery? Quite finished with all *what*?"

"My boyfriend. Thanks to him I'm finished with the cryptic. The recondite. The esoteric. The supernatural and the hermetic. All in the rubbish. Tom-foolery." She tried to kick his obstructing foot out of the doorway. "Go away, good morning."

"But we need your help. There's—"

"None of my business, I'm sure. Quite positive. Good day to you!"

"Lady Caldwell," said the aurora man. He gently pulled Hughes back. Denise made to slam the door... and instead found herself keeping it open. She retreated farther into the safety of the apartment, but... she supposed she might keep the door open. Just a little bit longer. The aurora man smiled, and she opened the door a smidge wider.

"Lady?" she said. "I'm not some pompous little grand vizier."

"A deplorable loss to those courts that make use of the position. There are many," he said. "I have laid my eyes on them, just as I lay them upon you now. And yeah. For sure. Their loss."

She swallowed into a throat that was suddenly dry.

"That is very gracious of you," she allowed. Then proprietary reasserted itself. "Now I'll thank you to make yourselves scarce. Avery and I are watching a program about people being mean to one another in a village."

"I'm sure he won't mind us coming in and having a chin wag," said the aurora-haired man. He was still smiling. Denise had never been to a cabaret, had never danced at a nightclub or gotten drunk and climbed atop a table with her friends, shook her hair out and thrown her arms up and roared the words to a song about love and danger and passionate breakups and even more passionate reunions, but something about that smile made her want to try all those things, and more. Much more.

"Avery's not really up to talking in the morning time," she said doubtfully, even as she opened the door another smidge.

"Even when it concerns his stupendous and tremendous girl doing her thing?" said the man. "Even when it means helping him out?"

"Helping Avery out?"

"Avery lives in the city, right?"

He did. And... yes, it made a sort of sense, didn't it? Help the city (did these men intend to do that? They must, she decided, they absolutely must), and thus help Avery, who lived inside it.

Denise Caldwell hesitated... then stepped aside. "Do come in..."

"Mr. Gallant," said the man. "But you can call me Frank, if you like. Whoa, hey, take it easy—"

She fell. He caught her.

"Did you say Frank Gallant?" she said breezily.

"Sure did."

"But you can't be. That's the Dream Warrior's name."

***

In his living room with its silk curtains, wall-covering television, and valuable whiskey and rum cabinet, Avery Mullinger fumed. He was the manager of one of the three major national banks in Corinth City, a short, neat man with white fluffy popcorn hair curling over his ears and a tendency to wear waistcoats. He was the sort of person who will retire at sixty-five and take up several undemanding hobbies, most of them punctuated by conversations about how the city has gone to the dogs, the scourge of young people nowadays, and the absolute shambles of modern taxation, which should be high and punitive for other people and virtually nonexistent for men like Avery Mullinger. He was a gentleman of hard work and orthodox leisure. When people referred to him as an Old Soul, he nodded modest thanks, and inwardly swelled with pride. In his spare time he perused catalogs about horses. He was extremely used to having his way.

He was not used to the women in his life fluttering... no... *fawning* over other gentlemen in his presence. Particularly ones that looked so (Avery eyed the group with particular focus on Frank Gallant)... well, so bohemian.

"Let me get this straight," he rumbled irritably. "You want Denise to go gallivanting about the streets of the city in search of Spring-Heeled Jack—"

"Jane," interrupted Hughes.

"I have thoughts on that, young fellow. A masculine serial killer is an unfortunate reality. But a woman? That reeks of fiction. Women are givers of life, not takers of it. I should know," said Avery Mullinger, self-appointed expert on social dynamics. "I was in the war with Champleurs."

"Does the name Miss Gleam ring a bell?" said Mr. Glint.

"Gleam? Certainly not. Sounds like your sort of rabble."

"I figured you hadn't heard of her," continued the insolent man.

"That so? I suppose she would label me old fashioned for my beliefs on the subject of men and women, eh? Crusty and outmoded? Make me eat my words, eh? Eh?"

Mr. Glint seemed to weigh this idea. "No," he said. "Probably just your kidneys."

Avery Mullinger blotted Mr. Glint out of his personal world. He turned to the other trespassers in his luxurious apartment. "Regardless of your good intentions, those are your aims, yes? To lure Denise out of her comfortable Tuesday morning into the clutches of her potential murderer?"

"She'll be safe with us," said Thud.

"Forgive me, Captain, but I've a mind to report you to your superiors for flagrant violation of our rights."

"Really? And what rights would these be, Mr. Mullinger?"

"Well most importantly our right to... to..." Avery was not about to admit his shortcomings in the knowledge of privacy laws. "Our right to go about our lives without being conscripted into dangerous ordeals, by jingo!"

"She'll be asleep for pretty much the entire time she's in danger," said Hughes. "If that helps."

"Dreaming sweet dreams," said Frank, grinning at Denise.

Avery felt a rush of indignance at the way Denise clasped her hands together and returned that grin. There was something silly and girlish about it, and there would be none of that under his roof.

"Now look here," he began.

"Another slice of fruit cake, Mr. Gallant?" said Denise.

"That'd be real nice."

"You're fond of it?"

"Tasty dried fruits, candied nuts, just the right amount of brown sugar, and unless I'm mistaken the whole affair soaked in a delicious liquor. Yeah, Denise," said Frank. "I'm fond of it."

"Now look *here*," steamrolled Avery, who had not even been *offered* fruit cake. "While I can respect that this is Citadel business and am myself a great admirer of Winnifred Dragontail and so on and so forth, I will not assent to my beloved being hoodwinked out of her self-imposed retirement and thrust into the lion's jaws. She is not a part of your red world. That is all behind her. Binned. Rubbished. Finished." He thumped his fist on the little coffee table he was sitting at. "That's my final word."

Thud looked to be on the brink of losing his temper, but it was Frank Gallant who spoke next. "And what about yours, Denise?"

"My what?"

"Your final word."

"Oh. It's 'yes,' of course."

Avery's face fell. "But but but *Denise*," he stammered. "You can't be serious."

"Serious as a ouija board that stops being moved and starts moving you," said Denise happily. "Mr. Gallant has explained everything to my satisfaction. I'm quite moved myself, actually. Supernatural murder. How frightful! But welcome journeys can have unwelcome beginnings. I've been considering a return to the enigmatic arts for quite some time now."

"But you never said anything!"

"I couldn't have voiced the desire if I'd tried. My role as a medium never left entirely. It merely percolated inside me for a time like thaumaturgic coffee. Mysticism *is* mysterious, Avery my dear. They don't sound so alike out of convenience. Tiny dollop of cream, Mr. Gallant?"

"Please."

"Sugar in your tea? Honey?"

"Present company is sweet enough, thanks."

"Oh Mr. Gallant."

"But my dearest darling heart," said Avery, feeling his iron grip on matters begin to slip. "You could be hurt. Killed!"

"Don't be absurd. Mr. Gallant is the Dream Warrior. I have been aware of his existence ever since I was a skirt-twirling child running a palm-reading service in the girl's lavatories during school lunchtime. He is a puppet who defied his dark puppeteers and stole his strings. It was only after The Hairy Autumn when I realized that the rumored prisoner in Idris Corlum's Perfect Prison was that same figure I'd glimpsed in my most nascent visions. He had unwelcome beginnings of his own and is all the better for having embraced them and soldiered on. I trust him with my life."

"But I—"

"And of course I know my wonderful boyfriend will support me in my decision."

"Well, naturally, naturally. But—"

"Good. Now be a swain and fetch me my circlet from the loft. As for me, I shall get the scissors."

"Scissors?" Avery frowned. "What the devil do you need scissors for?"

"My guess is for the curtains," said Frank. "A medium must have her raiment. Am I right Miss Caldwell?"

"Right as rain, Mr. Gallant. And to you it is Miss Cauldronpot," she said, her eyes shining with cosmic energies and her voice like the rustle of beaded curtains being drawn. "Then again, dash the honorifics. Call me Desdemona."

Chapter Twenty

In the courtyard of the fortress named Betty, Cate Jubilee was up to her elbows in trouble, and sinking.

She was fighting William o' The Wisps, her hobnail boots against his sword, and she was losing. There were many reasons for this unfortunate state of affairs. One reason could possibly have been balance. It's best to have both arms at your disposal when you fight using your legs. The limbs accommodate one another. And thanks to Skuggs and the Troll, Cate had her left arm splinted and lashed to her chest. But really, she probably could have bested William in double-quick time if not for the fact that she could not find his reliquary.

You see, in his logbook, the cartographer Burnished Isaac Lawless had noted that William and his fellow wisps could not be hurt by any means whatsoever until their reliquaries were destroyed. Any attempt to do so would result in your weapon sailing harmlessly through William and his wispy chums, whereupon they'd cut off your arms and your legs, and then, if they were feeling conclusive, your head. For the benefit of Scarlet Citadel agents like herself, Isaac had taken the trouble to describe these reliquaries as "distinctive figurines worn about the neck on a bit of string, each one like a sort of wonky badger, only really wee and teeny." It was a very Isaac way to put it.

So the task was set forth: Break the reliquaries, make William and his wisps vulnerable to harm, then harm them with gusto.

Simplicity itself.

Only Isaac's insistence that the wisps kept the reliquaries fastened around their throats like necklaces was wrong. William and his posse wore no jewelry at all. Of wonky badger figurines, there was no sign.

Which struck Cate as rather odd since Isaac was usually so reliable. He'd stated that it was absolutely necessary for these aggravating wisps to remain within ten feet of their reliquaries or risk dissipation on the slightest puff of breeze.

So where were they?

William o' The Wisps swept his sword. It trailed milky-pale globs and tendrils of light as though haunting the air it passed through. Cate compressed her stomach muscles and rocked back on her heels. The sword point missed her armored belly, which it would have opened like a sack of warm butter by a third of an inch.

She forfeited ground. He advanced, eager to kill her.

Around them the scene was a crazed and savage riot: it was morning, yet no sun had risen below their feet to replace the twelve moons. Instead the moons had formed a diamond made up of lunar lanterns, each flashing brightly one after the other, painting the whole topsy-turvy land above indigo, peach, taxi-sign blue, and on and on in a polychrome shuffle that flooded the blood with a sick decoction of wooziness and glee. It was disco ambience. Deathhouse rumba light. Puce-red, jade, snowdrop white! Change, change, change! Up in their grassland steps, the pale things she'd written to Hughes about wandered and sang endlessly. Closer to the sky-floor but still overhead, splashing its pectoral fins through the air as if it were thick as saltwater, was a manta ray the size of a small forest. Each movement of those fins simulated gales of a tornado, blasting the fortress walls and filling Cate's eardrums with WHHHHOOOOOOOOSHHHH– WHHHHOOOOOOOOSHHHHes that shook the skeleton and joggled her brain full of ache. Purposeful and slow as continental drift it circled high above them all, its rough midnight-colored skin catching all light and damping it, its toothless mouth wide and displaying a highway of cartilage. From the ray's back not three minutes ago, William and his other wisps had descended, floating down to the parapet and the inner courtyard, snatching their swords from their scabbards, and charging the scarlet invader. Since then both forces had entered an uneasy stalemate. The wisps were not skilled enough to slay the scarlet army outright, and for their part the scarlet army was equipped with bad information. Neither foe could fell the other. They tried anyway.

Of course, the wisps, unlike her company, would never tire.

They would fight on and on above the waxing waning lights of schizophrenic moons, below dark melodies and the swimming bulk of the manta ray until scarlet armor sundered and red blood trickled into the cracks of the courtyard stone.

So Cate Jubilee, hobnailed hero, set her body to fighting William and her mind to unknotting the mystery of the missing wonky badgers.

Say Isaac was right about all of it except the distance. Say the wisps could be a hundred feet from their reliquaries instead of ten.

Another swipe of the ghost sword, too close for comfort. The face of her attacker was inhumanly round and poked full of holes instead of normal features. William o' The Wisps was not a gloater, or much of a talker in general. On occasion his smooth doll-like mouth hole would part a trifle wider and a snatch of eerie song would come out, a chant with words she did not recognize but which nevertheless made her think of haunted houses strewn in cobwebs and pruny, creeping myth. Ghosts held no fears for Cate Jubilee. Not merely because she knew a few who counted as undead (Hector being a fully fledged friend), but because ordinary life was plenty spooky. Specters needn't bother. People frightened themselves. How did that one poem begin? *One need not be a chamber—to be haunted.*

The problem spun in her head. She attacked it eagerly. A hundred feet, thirty-million leagues, distance made no matter! The reliquaries, those were the key! Yet here was the question: if she were an evil-minded bastard, where would she put the one thing that could make her vulnerable? *Where's the last place my enemies would think to look?*

Oh.

Oh surely they wouldn't...

William aimed an overhead chop meant to split her shoulder. Cate flipped, her boots settling firmly on the sword blade and pinning it for a moment in place. Her gaze snapped to the leviathan above them. William o' The Wisps must have seen the glow of realization in her eyes. A reed-pipe whistle of anger escaped him. Over his shoulder Cate spied Kevlin Paladin rushing toward them. His timing was fabulous.

"I've got to find Clothilda," said Cate. "Or one of the ropers."

"Eugenie has taken a wound and retreated for now. Marcus and Niccolo are due north-east where yesterday the crenellations took the brunt of the Troll's onslaught." Kevlin's sunlight spear joined her hobnail boots. It was all William could do to keep up with both of them. "I've not seen, or more importantly *heard* Clothilda since her last sneeze. That was about eighty seconds past. I fear she got a chill yesterday, which plays havoc with her power."

"Oh dear," said Cate.

"We're in straits ourselves," said Kevlin. "Not dire yet, but getting there."

"I'm sorting it."

"We're with you, Cate."

"Can you take him?"

"Take him?" said Kevlin, chuckling at William's expense. "I could buy him and sell him. This one fights cheap."

She grinned at that and took off. A mirror's length later—*whump!*—she was on the battlements. Here the atmosphere was a sizzling, smoky thing. Her nostrils filled with a sulfurous eggy smell. Beneath her the wedge-shaped stones snaked in a curve that encompassed Betty's perimeter. Between the gaps that were called embrasures, the crenellations jutted up in toothy merlons biting at the song-strewn morning. On Cate's left, Rebecca Lupine was lending her boon-based power to Igor Wight. His darkness swallowed the immediate area, a massive moon of swirling black. *That was mischievous*, she thought approvingly. *If we can't beat this enemy, then at least we can blind him. Make it a hunt we can hide from until the moment to strike comes.* To her right, a group of scarlet defenders kept a squadron of their foes at bay. All were splendid, but that day Nyoni Snickerdrake distinguished herself. The wild-haired girl, only newly recruited to the Citadel, had the power to pull an unlimited and highly volatile supply of fireworks from a box she kept on her back. She hopped and hollered, her big lighter *clickety-clicking* as she lit the fuses, and the fusillade of explosive pops and fizzles resulted in a smash and smatter of dazzlesome light that only augmented the disorientation of the strobing moons. *Hughes would gawp like a boy*, Cate could not resist musing. *Gawp and glory at this extravaganza of light.*

But there was no time to yearn for shining Gormon Hughes!

Across her satchel, Cate affixed Nyoni's most promising firework—a gnarly looking fox-faced rocket of crinkled paper—and hurried on.

Amongst the glut of defenders, she found the angel she'd been looking for.

"Marcus," she said. "I've a use for your chains."

"Anything. What do you need?"

Cate jabbed a finger at the manta ray. "Get me inside that."

He didn't even blink. Tinkling and jangling as they moved with sinuous animation, Marcus' chains curled around Cate's ankles. Their links had always looked gaudy to Cate, shimmering with their golden light, but in that moment she found their hue encouraging. Gold light, golden opportunity—and BANG-FLASH went Nyoni's fireworks in glitzy green—and PEARLESCENT swam the whole madcap scene. With a bright happy howl Cate dived over the fortress wall. The spangled sky opened below her. She fell into the network of stars, saw Betty's legs like mossy pillars, then fell onward, down and down into the twinkling moon-clogged fathoms, the pale harmonies of that grassy aboveness softening, the *whoooosh* of the leviathan's pectoral fins barely tousling her hair now, and her cheeks unseamed in a smile miles across and spanning the whole beautiful breadth of war.

Then the chains snapped up and she was flying. Hurtling up out of the void, she had the appearance of a rogue red comet.

Cosmic dust kiss my bootheels, she thought. *Death withhold your lips from mine.*

The manta ray was there. Spreading to fill her whole field of vision. There were the slit sofa cushion flaps of its gills. Here came its dark mouth, scaffolded in white.

But then momentum played a damnable trick on her. She slowed. She wouldn't make it! She would land on the lower plateau of its crescent head. There would be an instant of excruciating pain, then nothing. Lights out.

From somewhere below her there came a booming trumpeting sound that could only be Clothilda Toffington's thunderous snoot. That sneeze, as it turned out, was not intended for the enemy. It was intended for Cate.

Shooting up and overtaking her with tremendous speed was a full-length gilt-framed mirror. In her muddlement, she vaguely recognized it as the mirror from the fortress entry hall. It lodged in the roof of the manta ray's mouth, one end of the frame splitting and one quarter of the glass spilling away in shards. But the majority of the mirror was intact! Quick as a lynx, Cate had her satchel open and a vial squeezed. *Whump!* She vanished into hardening glass and reappeared in warm, wet, and cavernous quiet.

Beneath her feet the floor of the mouth was uneven, and thank goodness for the thick soles of her boots because that irregular quality came from the teeth. They rutted the road of the manta ray's gullet, row upon row of pointed white. Over one shoulder Cate could gaze out of the ray at the vista sprawling all about them. Her eyes fixed on a point in the distance. Yes, those were the peaks of the mountains the company had traveled from. No dusting of snow with the Troll vanquished. If she could spy a reflection there and step through it, some part of her knew she would emerge into a place bathed in solid blue sunshine, and the lightshow of the luminous moons would be a memory. Eurydice was a jumble-up tumble-down world indeed, and without being able to stop itself her mind conjured the Troll's words. It was Eurydice that had tasked him with breaking into another world and sewing chaos and ruin there. *The Lady and the World.* Cate had her share of troubles, but the idea that the landscape was a mess of inconsistencies because of its owner's psychology made those dooming doubts in her brain feel oddly comforted. Plus she was jipped full of yummy adrenaline, and that was a very good balm for conflicting emotions too. As her favorite tit-for-tat mantra went; you try to kill me. I try to kill you.

Fighting was a telescope. Life was simpler when viewed through its hazy maroon lens. Fewer bad Novembers. More eventful Decembers. Change! went the moonlight outside the ray's mouth. Move! sang the macabre choirs scoring the battlefield. Red comets burn out fast! All things do! Impact and smolder in the crater, only not yet! Never yet! Move! And her heart responded.

She studied the long tube of the ray. Questions swarmed her mind about Clothilda and the mirror, but she brushed them aside for the moment. There would be time enough to ponder catapulting furniture later. Darkness ahead; the yawning chasm of the ray's mouth only did so much to dispel the damp shadows. Breath wafted over her, drawn up from the gills, fainter here, heavier farther into the tube no doubt. She inhaled the odor of the bacterial slime coating the teeth. The recycled gill-brushed air. The putrescence of many things, slender and small, caught in the bony matrix of the mouth. Skyfish, flyfish, do you wanna diefish. Dead black eyes stared at her from the decaying aquarium as though the manta ray were collecting and displaying its diet for visitors like her. An abyss of cool organic smells and suppers long forgotten. Somewhere in here she would find the reliquaries for William o' The Wisps and his gang.

By now the moist grotto around her was a blur.

She was running. When had she started?

Who cared?

Cate knew one thing though. She was in the belly of the beast, and the thing she wanted to do, more than anything, was laugh.

So she did.

One need not be a chamber to be haunted.

One need not be the girl she'd once been to be young and to be happy.

***

They went out into the blizzard, mostly for ambience.

A ceremonial candle was lit. Mr. Glint held it, cupping the rim of the candle as well as the wick and flame so the orange light scampered over his fingers. He seemed to take special pride in being such an excellent windbreaker. Frank held two spangled dream catchers they'd salvaged from the apartment loft. Thud held a piece of resin. It was black. A raven's head had been sketched on the resin in chalk. Everyone agreed this was very occult. They stood in the street. The wind bugled. Snow sheeted around them. Hughes' innate theatricality stirred. As backgrounds went, this was a dramatic one. The players and the symbols were set.

"We shall begin the ritual," said Desdemona Cauldronpot. Garbed in luscious red silk cinched about her ample waist with an improvised girdle of rhinestones glued to a belt normally reserved for Avery's trousers, bangled and braceleted from wrist to bicep and bejeweled so she sparkled from kneecap to earlobe, she seemed restored to her former majesty. And if not majesty, then at the very least maje.

Glint turned to Frank. "Is this the bit where she goes, 'Ommm'?" he asked.

Ignoring him, Desdemona pinched her fingers together and made them bloom out from her forehead where her circlet was affixed. The sunset-colored tourmaline sat at the circlet's core. There was a dot in it.

"Spirits," she said. "Hearken to me."

Make my third eye open, Hughes thought, amused. *And my fifth ear close. It rings sometimes. Tinnitus or something. And actually, if you wouldn't mind, unclog my forty-eighth nostril. This cold plays merry havoc with my sinuses. Praise be.*

"Is something risible, Mr. Huckles?"

His reverie broke. Desdemona was staring at him.

"No."

"Only you're grinning, Mr. Huckles."

"It's Hughes. Am I? Grinning?"

"Yes."

"I'll stop."

"That would be best. Sanguine humors have no place in our..." She scanned their number, ran through various arcane shapes, and gave up. "In our sacred square."

"How about choleric humor?" said Frank.

She favored him with a milksop smile. "Indeed, Mr. Gallant. That is exactly what is required. Let our fervor enrich the magic. Our ambition shall shudder the attic of consciousness."

"Get the cosmic apparatus going."

"And the power out of the loft," finished Desdemona cheerfully. "Twice in one day, no less." And without further ado she fell asleep. Just like that. One moment she was alert and awake, and the next she was falling with what Hughes suspected was more than a little calculation into the arms of Frank Gallant.

There was silence.

Apart from the purr of traffic from the nearby main road, the crocodile-snap of the tarpaulin from the construction site opposite the apartments, the radio from one of those apartment windows, its music not Tinfrost tunes but that new sound graduating from small time undertow to the real mainstream roster, a fuzzy almost leering sound like the blues with its sleeves rolled up and its collar popped, rock and roll the kids had dubbed it, who could think why, and the throaty bark of a dog, replica or genuine it didn't seem to matter, all compressed and siphoned off in every snow-seized direction by the voice of the blizzard, whose shrillness took no prisoners.

But in a very personal and confined way, there was silence.

"What now?" said Hughes.

"Bet she'll get up with her eyes rolled back in her head and say 'ommm,'" said Mr. Glint.

Frank was peering down at the slumbering woman with interest.

"Anybody want coffee?" said Thud, tossing the dream catchers into a random snowdrift and removing a thermos and some disposable cups from his jacket. "Only Hettie made me a hazelnut coffee."

"What happened when she used her power with you, Hughes?" asked Frank.

"I can't really remember. I think it just sort of... happened."

"It's very hot, mind you. I'm not sure you can burn coffee when it comes out of a sachet, but she seems to give it a go."

"You sure this'll work, my man?"

"Frank, we're not in different mazes. I'm as oriented as you are."

"Did I mention it was hazelnut?"

"Besides," grumbled Hughes, "it's not as if we're bursting with other solutions."

Frank winked at him. "It's all gonna work out. We're on to a good thing here."

"Looks like a good thing is on to you."

"What can I say? You get raised by three women—even the nasty villainous kind—you learn a few things."

"Suit yourselves, suit yourselves."

Thud began to pour. He regretted this a moment later when Desdemona Cauldronpot shot up from Frank's arms, her eyes rolled back in her head, exposing the vein-marbled whites. Her voice was a husky monotone that cut the wind. On her brow the tourmaline glowed with a caramel-colored light.

"The shadow squirms. She looms. Two arms and two legs, she has, and two-million of each. She has lain many an egg since yesterday, a fresh batch today, and shall lay many more tomorrow if she is given the opportunity."

"Jane looms?" said Hughes, bolting over and grasping Desdemona by the shoulders. "Where? Where is she?"

"Bugger, bugger, bugger," Thud muttered, sucking coffee drops off his scalded fingers. Mr. Glint scooped up some snow, which Thud accepted gratefully.

Meanwhile a vision-possessed Desdemona went on. "She doesn't want to eat yet, wants to save them all for the last big feast, but with this one she cannot help herself. This morsel is so plump and juicy with the stuff she hungers for most. She will taste of tenderest veal. We have a train to catch."

With a vacant expression yet a firm-handed grip, she extricated herself from Hughes and set off into the blizzard.

"What train?" Hughes demanded. "Destined for where?"

"She can't hear you," said Frank. "Dreaming deep dreams and not sweet but sour as mulched grapes from a rotten vine by the sounds of them. Come on." He slipped his hands in his suit pants pockets and started after her, his shoulders hunched against the cold and his lambent yellow eyes like torches beaming through the haze. "All we can do is follow."

So they did. Frank and Mr. Glint assumed their customary pace alongside one another. Hughes and Thud strode a tad farther ahead, keeping close to Desdemona as she brought them through cul-de-sacs with wreaths on every door, past busy roads and traffic lights ticking through their tri-colored pixel sculptures, by hopeful shops with holiday special sale stickers blasting window to window, and other sundries of the frost-whittled city.

What few people they did pass were full of festive friendliness. They smiled at Hughes and company, tired but earnest smiles that said, "Some bluster, huh? Hope you've got somewhere warm waiting for you," and other pleasant messages of mutual wellbeing and shared plight and stubborn kindness in the face of callous gray-cheeked winter.

As he kept an eye on their spiritual guide, Hughes was aware of that niggling worry popping up again. It was the feeling he had missed something quite obvious, and that if only he could unscrew his tightly turned nerves, he might inspire a revelation. It was a conundrum. The more he sought to relax his mind, the closer it came, though never close enough, which tightened him up all over again.

Something about eyes. Desdemona's rolling to the whites, Frank's blazing out like foglamps. Pupils, sclera, those little pink bits that got crusty with sleep the names of which he could never remember. Eyes. Something about eyes, yes, but what?

"Is that woman high?" a passerby asked, pointing at Desdemona.

"Close," said Thud. "She's a medium."

"Oh."

"Police business."

"Oh I see! Good luck to you, officer."

"Thank you. Be safe. It's not exactly strolling weather."

"Too true! But it's the last day of sales at Maple's the clothing shop." The passerby brandished their bags. "Couldn't be helped. Goodbye."

"Everyone's in such good form," said Hughes wonderingly as they headed on.

"Must be the excellent savings."

Even troubled and distracted Hughes had to huff a little bemused huff at that. "No. I don't think so. I think people would be much more reticent about being friendly in the street if they'd read about the awful events from Sunday. How the hell did you convince Tracer Gogen and his editor not to run a Spring-Heel story?"

"I appealed to their sense of public duty," said Thud. "And instructed them as to the manner of the law."

"It's not illegal to print articles though. Even if they are inflammatory."

"Yup."

"So what do you mean, 'instructed them as to the manner of the law'?"

"Fairly simple," said Thud, sipping his hazelnut coffee and dabbing at his immaculate mustache. "I showed them what it's like when the law doesn't have manners. They put it out eventually."

"Put what out?"

"The fire. Ah. One of these trains."

They were approaching the Polydoros District station. Thud and Hughes scanned the train schedule with its neon red numerals on a black field, the former hazarding private guesses to himself about which train they were bound for, the latter thinking that the bespectacled logo on the advertisement flanking the entrance to the station resembled nothing so much as a pair of—

Eyes, thought Hughes. *Something about eyes. What could it be? What have I forgotten that's so damn important?*

Behind them a little ways came Frank and Mr. Glint.

Frank felt his companion was overdue a compliment. "That was a cool poem you rattled off in the pub."

"You think so?"

"Yeah man, it was cool. Know any about blizzards?"

"Wrote one."

Frank was flabbergasted. "No shit. A Glint original?"

Glint grunted, indicating that it was so.

"Written down, like?"

"No. I don't write poems down because if I did I wouldn't have to remember the words. Then if someone stole them they'd be gone, and I'd never be able to read them again."

"Sage of you."

"Thyme is good. Parsley's better. Marigold is best."

"*Sage* as in *wise*, Mr. Glint. Well, now I've got to hear this thing."

In his tombstone tones, Mr. Glint rumbled, "It's called After The Blizzard, The."

"The what?"

"Hold on a tick and you shall know." And he told Frank his poem:

"What happens when the blizzard is over?"

Said the boy to his mother while the kettle filled up.

"Will there be fields all covered in clover?

And long sunny stretches to run our good rover?

Oh what oh what comes when the blizzard is over?"

"What happens when the blizzard is over?"

Said the mother to her son while the kettle boiled hot.

"Sad to say there are no fields covered in clover.

No long sunny stretches to run our good rover.

When the blizzard is over, we pour tea with codliver rum,

And we stay nice and precise with our letters and sums.

We listen for goose-gusts and thumps of snow-drums,

And we wait with hearts braced should another pale come."

Silence for a time. Into that whistling windy quiet, Frank said, "After The Blizzard, The After The Blizzard, The, and so on."

Mr. Glint looked at him.

Frank's brows knit together. One side of his face hooshed up at the cheek and the corner of his mouth. "Suddenly I feel late to something. My bones all marrowed up with urgency."

"Him too," said Glint, nodding toward Hughes. "He's trotting faster and faster, Mr. Gallant."

"So he is, Mr. Glint. So he is. And us with him."

They saw Hughes veer close to Desdemona. He nodded, turned, and projected his voice with astonishing volume, so loud Frank and Mr. Glint could hear it even over the din of the white storm. Evidently they were aiming for a westbound train that would take them past the minor stations of Illmet and Porringebee toward the major hub in Nikandros.

At the station till Hughes bought them all tickets. Hurrying through the corridors of glossy, wedge-shaped yellow brick, they found the right set of steps and took them quick as they could. Luckily a westbounder was pulling into the station when they arrived on the platform. The station was open air, and as the first carriages flashed by in a flurry of snow, the group got a brief glimpse of themselves, and Hughes in particular was struck by the oddness of their company, by his own place in it, and more troubling than either of those, the look he'd seen skulking like some nocturnal animal behind his dark eyes. *Go ahead. Run away. Only stay away from me,* the insectile woman had warned them. *Stay away from me or I will eat your friends and drink your families.*

That look in his eye, the one he'd seen skimming by in the frost-framed glass, seemed to fashion this reply:

You know I can't, Jane. Both our bellies have made implacable demands, only while your appetite is satiated by comfort and joy, mine has designs on you. Here I am closing the distance between us with my Performance ready to snatch you out of whoever you've infested and make you tangible. Touchable. God, but I feel half-cut-drunk with nerves and exhilaration. I can hear my heart jam-juddering, drowning out the blizzard. And I'm angry, no, furious, as though I've taken huge gulping swallows from a tankard called Rage. The train is slowing now. More reflections. More mirror men. Thud looks staunch. Frank looks focused. Mr. Glint looks... well, he looks as horrible as ever, but he looks especially nasty today. The upcoming event has us by the lapels. No dinner jackets required, Jane. Just you, you buzzing menu listing all your evils from starter, to main course, to dark desserts. You who are hungry for them and the four of us for you. The table is laid. You bring the napkins. His fingers closed round Chimera's hilt. *I'll bring the cutlery.*

The train crawled a little farther, then stopped. The carriage doors hissed open. They filed on.

A very unexpected thing happened then, something that did not bely Hughes' fury and determination but rather turned it over inside him and gave it a different shape. How strange such a thing was as to be on a train enclosed in the frigid fist of December.

But then, the state of the railway can do a great many things. Importantly, aside from sincerely affecting a man on a mission, as Hughes was, it can tell you lots about a city. Hear the information tubes amble and rattle and rush! Not simply the cleanliness or the engineering, you understand, but the frequency of the transport and the substance of the people going on long-legged journeys or short-legged journeys without needing to use their actual legs at all, except for standing smartly straight if the seats are all claimed. Thirty-odd years ago during the conflict with Champleurs, the trains were all commandeered for the war effort. Ownership was forcefully changed, private to public. Routes were reconfigured; all tracks eventually veered south toward the front. Many carriages were gutted and converted into silos for every manner of supply, from tinned rations to packaged weaponry. And if you were lucky enough to find a spot for a civilian journey, you were likely to be crammed chin-to-elbow with soldiers. Board a train like that, or watch it pass with its deadly, solemn-faced cargo, and you'll have the city totted up in your mind in a trice. Bleak locomotions *chugging* and *chuffing* like wheeled summaries of a bleaker time.

That wintry day, led by Desdemona Cauldronpot, Hughes found himself boarding a train carriage stuffed to the upholstery with revelers. The revelers were engaged in what seemed to be, for all intents and purposes, a truly marvelous holiday party. Crushes of people shuffled and danced everywhere, whether through the aisles of cramped two-by-two seats or the clumped betabled four-seater spots. The overhead baggage compartments and their laminated advertisements were awash in popper confetti stuck to the plastic with winedrops and the fantastic damp heat of the carriage. Lovely jazz music permeated the air, along with a warm fruity-cinnamony smell. Women had shaken off their coats, men had loosened their ties, and kids had kicked off their wellington boots to waggle along with their biggers.

Hughes wasn't aware of it, but his eyebrows were dancing too, a slow rising motion called the Forehead Shuttle.

"Come inside!" cried a man with a merry complexion and gray hair. "Come inside at once out of that horror and into the wholesome! Have we mulled wine for these pilgrims all shaggy-bearded with snow?"

"We couldn't possibly—" Hughes began.

"Nonsense, nonsense. There you are." The man handed Hughes and Thud each a Styrofoam cup full of delicious-smelling mulled wine. He turned to the man operating the dispenser. "Two more, squire, even hotter than those! Say. Can any of-of-of you *sterling* gentlemen play an instrument?"

"If it has strings, I can play it," said Frank.

"Any good?"

Frank smiled modestly. "Oh, I've got a few ditties in me."

"Splendid! Come with me, our band is down a man. Concussed, poor chap. Hit by an aerodynamic daughter, but that's Tinfrost for you. Flying families with no thought to the timbre of a quintet. Come along, come-come-come."

Frank gave Hughes a shrug, his face blooming into something gorgeous, a flower that showed itself only for the sake of a really excellent party in the making, and with a rich rising laugh he turned and went off into the excitement. Lots of excitable young men and women followed after him. On such occasions Frank had the gravity of a small planet, people were drawn to him like giddy asteroids, circling in the belt of his charm.

With nothing to do but sip his mulled wine and wait for Desdemona to rise from her seat and announce they'd arrived, Hughes did just that. Next to him was Hoshrum Thud, who was reorganizing his whiskers after the trouncing the blizzard had given them.

His gaze came to rest on one of the few un-confettied advertisements. It showed a cartoon hand pulling a pocket from a trousers leg. The pocket was empty.

Times are hard, the advertisement told him. *But harder times could be just around the corner. It's never a bad time to get yourself insured. Call Bivvywaker's Insurance NOW for a quote on a comprehensive policy!*

Despite the churning sizzling thing at his core, Hughes' lips curled up at the corners.

Times are hard. Sure they were. He glanced around him at the horde of unlikely partygoers.

"What's that?" said Thud.

"Hm?"

Hughes turned to the grizzled copper.

"You said, 'but we are harder still,'" said Thud.

Hughes gave him a puzzled look. Puzzlement evaporated. He made a small sound of amusement. "I was just reminded of something my girlfriend told me. She said that people have a larger capacity for happiness nowadays."

Thud seemed to ponder the idea for a while. The train was headed up an incline. The rattle of the tracks was not something they could hear (not with the palaver of the party and the band, which was sounding even better with Frank Gallant on the guitar), but rather something that rose up through the seats and into their hips and spines, train talk, the language of the journey from uncertainty into danger. Through the foggy carriage windows, they could see nothing but the blizzard having its chilly way with the city. It felt far away, for the moment.

"Bit of an optimist, this girlfriend of yours?" said Thud.

"I think she just observes," said Hughes. "Sound instincts too. You'd like her."

"I expect I would."

There was a pause.

"Think we've got her?" said Hughes.

"Your girlfriend?"

"Jane."

Hughes watched Thud's face sober to match his own. The policeman's eyes drifted to a spot in the midst of the party, an alcove in the action where two hard-working, hard-bitten, hard-shouldered Leonidas women were giggling with two other ladies, soft, rich women from a whole other zone of life. The subject of their delight was none other than their group's fifth member, Mr. Glint. In violation of every reasonable code of human survivability they had shuffled their bums and made space for him. In violation of rationality they also found his curt, sour-mouthed answers to their questions uproariously funny. As Hughes and Thud watched, a little girl tugged Mr. Glint's sleeve. A few seconds later she was drawing on his long-fingered hand in crayon. This served merely to increase the nearby women's gaiety. Over the laughter and shouts and round guzzling gulps from Styrofoam cups, the band spooled the air with luxurious crooning tunes. Tempos switched. The drum beat its irresistible tattoo. Out in the throng the dance changed to meet the music. More and more wine was ladled by the moment. Pink and yellow streamers flew and tasseled overhead. And the westbound train trundled on.

Part of it all yet somehow separate, Hughes mentally replayed his question, totally unsure as to how he'd answer it if asked to do so.

Think we've got her?

Your girlfriend?

Jane.

He studied Thud, who was seemingly transfixed by the crazy carriage scene surrounding them. Hughes imagined the streetbeater would choose this particular moment to mutter something gruff yet kind like, "I hope so, lad." Or possibly, "We shall just have to wait and find out." It seemed the appropriate time for that sort of thing.

But Thud surprised him. He jutted his chin toward the revelers and said, "This lot reminds me of those people who were poisoned in that nightclub. A nice night touched by vileness. And that makes me think about the Dennings children, Adam and Ellen, murdered in their beds. And that little boy—the one who got his scalp peeled in school—he's never going to be able to look another teacher in the eye. I know I don't look it, Hughes, but I'm as riled up as I've ever been. Getting on this train has only made it worse."

"I'm there with you."

"With me?" Coarse and craggy, and with an edge in his voice and demeanor that was sharper than a knife, Thud took the measure of him. "Yes, well I suppose you are at that. Wendy's Bloodhound and the Leonidas Labrador. Anyone's judge whether or not we're good or bad dogs. Well, the jury remains undecided on you. Me, I'm on temporary leave. Suspension from duty. Should have told you. Doing it now since waiting in silence feels like being a teapot with no spout, left to steam and explode."

"Suspended?"

"The commissioner doesn't appreciate my devil-may-care attitude. Shocking, I know. *A propensity toward aggression and a distinct lack of respect for authority.* I believe that was the main feature in his report."

Understanding shone in Hughes. "That thing you mentioned yesterday," he said. "Something about a telephone. This is what you meant? You were insubordinate on a call with the commissioner?"

"I'm not sure it's possible to be subordinate to Old Vinny Winky," Thud mused. "He's a naturally inferior sort. Bog toadstools are superior to Old Vinny Winky. Oh don't trouble yourself. I know what you mean. Rank, and all that. Well, as of this morning I'm a copper without rank and without a badge for that matter. But I've still got what counts. Any ideas, Mr. Bloodhound? Come on. Show me you're not completely outclassed by this partner of yours I keep hearing about."

His stare bored into Hughes. Another bulb of understanding flickered on.

"You've still got your other badge," Hughes said quietly. "The one that can't be taken away."

Thud grinned. "Correct. Our Spring-Heeled Jane has broken the laws of the city: the lofty magic ones guarded by you and the ordinary ones you can find down in the street with me. Have we got her, lad?" He poured the rest of his mulled wine into Hughes' cup, produced his thermos, and took a huge mouthful of Hettie's hazelnut coffee. His whiskered face seemed to glow like a watchman's lamp against lengthening shadows. "You bet your arse we do."

Chapter Twenty-One

In Eurydice, in the topsy-turvy region beyond the mountain pass, a manta ray flew high above the fortress called Betty. Inside the manta ray was a house. Its welcome mat was stitched with five words:

Will's Will Wills The Wisps.

Cate Jubilee stood over the mat, looking down at it with an expression of deepest puzzlement. Her mouth moved silently. She raised both brows. "William's willpower wills the actions of the will o' the wisps. Good grief."

She peered up at the house, an air of mistrust permeating her, as a general might peer at an enemy's newest siege weapon. She counted its five stories, watched its wide milky windows, and noted its bricks sifting and curling like clouds, yet somehow remaining solid and neatly fit together. The house was set into the slick, ridged wall of the manta ray's insides, the way an architect might set a house into a cliff by the seaside.

If the reliquaries were anywhere to be found, then it seemed quite likely that they were here.

Cate made to open the front door, hesitated.

It's a trap, she thought. *There'll be blades, or hatchets, or spikes tipped in something noxious that will turn my veins into deadly conductors.*

No, surely not. She was being paranoid. But then again... then again, this was Eurydice, a world whose very moons got up to mischief in their spare time. It was a world partially plumbed by Walsingham's Merry Miners, who had numbered fifteen strong when they had come in and seven when they had come out. Maybe in Eurydice a tiny dose of paranoia, even when it seemed the least suitable medicine for your present woes, cured you of fatal mistakes.

Standing back, Cate unlaced a boot, slid it off her double-socked foot, and feeling more than a little bit ridiculous she flung it hard at one of the downstairs windows.

To her astonishment the milky glass did not shatter. Rather it *spludged*. Drop a lead ball into warm custard, and that will give you a fair approximation. The moment the boot passed into the house and out of sight, something happened, something that startled even Cate, who had been expecting trickery. The front door melted inward, leaving its frame empty. From its edges to its knob the door gooped up into itself, forming a long, bulging slug-shape of gelatinous ooze. The ooze was white, and end to end it was about the length of a car. Tutting and burbling to itself like a fussy housekeeper roused from a nap, it went into the house in search of whatever had so rudely disturbed it.

Cate stared after it, wide eyed. At length her shock abated, replaced by a feeling of vindication and pleasure.

I think that's zero to Eurydice and three to me, said her confidence in a tone of voice that was very smug indeed. The Troll, Skuggs, and now this. Her doubt, which of late could be quite the chatterbox when her confidence preened, voiced no objection.

So Cate grinned and felt all the happier with her cleverness.

Taking special care to make a hushed and stealthy showing of herself (Cate rightly suspected that the ooze was, while extremely sensitive to sound, completely blind), she went inside. Gazing about her, she thought the interior of the house bore a striking resemblance to William o' The Wisps' head; everything smooth and white and driven deep with holes. Treating these holes like corridors to explore, and avoiding the tuts and burbles of other guardian oozes patrolling the place, Cate found herself slipping out of her role as a Responsible Leader and into that of a hunter. *Wonky badgers*, she thought wryly. *We'll see.*

Ahead, between two strange lamps that looked like those slightly goofy, oddly mesmerizing lava-lamps that were the height of avant-garde fashion in Corinthian decor nowadays, all globulous and suspended and bright, she spied a funnel that curved upward toward a higher floor. There were grooves in the funnel. *Steps.*

Cate took them as fast as she dared, her eyes and ears alert to the telltale shuffling-quiver of an ooze. On the pearly surface her boot *tepped,* her sock whispered. The stairway emerged into a circular chamber. Eight funnels led out of it, presumably into the wisps' equivalent of living rooms, dining areas, and lavatories. Cate tried one of these, discovered a dead end printed in ghoulish images of figures bent around musical notes like melodious torture racks, and retraced her steps. Urgency made her swift. With her companions in trouble, there was no time to inspect each path. She decided to trust a candle of Cate-ish instinct flickering in her chest. She would go as far up into the house's reaches as she could. Satisfying herself that the cast keeping her injured arm tight to her body was secure, she set out to do just that.

Up Cate climbed, and up, and when she could crest no higher she prowled searchingly with her hair fastened back from her face and the alien glossy whiteness of her environment egging her on and goading her; a red hunter in a pale game ground.

Tep, tep went her boot.

Whisperrrr, went her sock.

Where oh where could the reliquaries be? Not in here, in a rhombus-sharp room. Not in there among big columns like punctured reed pipes, either. Perhaps an ooze could offer her direction. Her investigation made her think of Hughes. After all, wasn't a detective simply a hunter armed with the law instead of a spear? The *law and other bad habits,* she mused, recalling Wendy's dry little warning. *Smoking. Drinking. Covering cork boards in photographs connected by red thread. Hughes, we're in different domains but against all rules of spacetime I feel you here with me. Dear one, I'll take you and one boot over a matching pair anytime.*

Suddenly, Cate heard a wet, gummy sound that froze her stiff.

Burble-sclup.

She pressed herself flat against the cool, smooth cusp of a new chamber, holding her breath as an ooze slithered by. It took its time doing so, and it was close, so terribly close that the rubbery pulp of its body revealed its little wrinkles to her eye. She could have reached out and crammed her thumb into its maggot-pale softness. What would happen then? Would the skin slough off her fingerbones? Maybe her thumb would disappear, and the ooze would suck the rest of her hand, her wrist, her whole arm inside it. Tut-tut. Yum yum. Trespassers like her were fucking tasty. *You just hold now, breath of mine*, she commanded. It held, good old lung gust that it was. Hemmed in by the odd surroundings, stock-still, tight-lipped, and wearing half of her usual footwear, Cate realized she must look like nothing so much as a bizarre slapstick heroine in a surrealist comedy. Thankfully, her potential audience took no notice of her. There went its tapered end. The ooze trickled on by, turning a corner. *Tut-tut-burble-sclup.*

It was odd, but in that perilous moment an association made her smile. Once in their cuddlesome quietude, her Puppy had described their romance as a jelly house, sweet yet delicate in some vital way. "Delicate?" she'd asked crossly. "Not strong? Robust? Solid?"

"Those too," Hughes agreed.

"Then how precisely is our relationship delicate, Hughes? What vital way do you mean?"

"All great love is delicate, Cate. One harsh mistake is enough to bring the whole thing wobbling over as a jelly house wobbles off its plate in extreme circumstances. A love that endures in spite of everything, good or ill, would be tedious, utterly without risk. Every day I risk losing you. Every day I want to be my best so it does not happen. That is the jelly house. Delicate, yes. But sweet also."

Charming bastard. These wisp house walls were not near so smooth as him. How weird and how weirdly nice, remembering that in this oozy-riddled warren.

Speaking of, the creature she'd narrowly avoided was gone. Its burbles were distant now, almost imperceptible. Exhaling softly, Cate peeped round the edge of the chamber entrance, saw the coast was clear, and slinked in.

Okay, she thought. *Same shiny white textures. Same funnels tubing off in every direction. But ahhh. What are you?*

One of the funnels, taller and wider than any she'd seen in the wisp house, led toward a pale glow. More of those prints of people bent crooked over music notes lined the funnel. The glow was like a lonely sodium lamp on a street of starless dark. Cate followed it. She came to a room.

In the topsy-turvy place, in the manta ray, in the house of William and his fellow wisps, that room was a sacred, special place.

When she saw what was in there, Cate's once brave breath turned cowardly. It escaped her in a helpless rush. The residue of good Hughes memories were bleached of all meaning, sucked away like a dumb thumb into colorless Jell-O. Her whole brain was blasted blank. Seized with a spasm she could not have controlled if she'd wanted to, her good hand bunched in a fist, rose, and half-covered her mouth.

"Oh my God," she said.

***

A long time ago (she was not altogether sure when), the eldest of the Jolenes had overheard one of her girls talking about her. The girl—another Jolene, blonde, chippy, smart—told her little group that she always knew when their elder was on her rounds, checking up on each workstation, the usual shtick.

"How could you know?" another Jolene asked.

"Well," said the blonde, "isn't it obvious? She *sprauchles.*"

Eavesdropping and befuddled, the elderly Jolene turned the word over in her head. *Sprauchles.* She had never heard the term before. Later, looking it up in her little pocket dictionary, she'd discovered just how accurate and ugly a word it was. Sprauchle: to move clumsily or with great effort.

Do I?

Of course not. But just to be safe she'd tested it out, pacing her own workstation. Once, okay. Twice, real nice. Thrice, hey, no big deal. Were her steps a little measured? Yeah. Were her ankles pounding like old church bells? Sure! But damn, it felt good to one-up the younger generations. She drew a breath to give a contented "hmmf" that would draw the whole business to a close... and the noise stopped.

What noise? she thought numbly. Some part of her, a crusted old scab of rational thinking, replied, *The wheeze.*

Before she could question that, the air she'd drawn in let itself go. It passed her chapped lips in a dry, papery sigh. A *wheeze.*

Her hand fluttered out, clutching the edge of her workbench as if for support. A kind of palsy overwhelmed her, a soul-deep paralysis.

She moves with great effort.

Her windpipe clenched and unclenched, the loose skin at her throat shivering.

She sprauchles.

The sound that swept out of her then was part wheeze, yes, and part moan. *Is that how they see me now? A... a windbag to hang jokes on like plastic jewels on a Tinfrost tree? A creak in the corridor? A nuisance?*

She thought she'd raised them better.

It took a while to break the palsy's grip on her nerve. Longer still to get to work. But she *had* gotten to work, and that was what mattered.

And so it was that on that particular Tuesday, around the time Cate Jubilee pulled off her boot and Gormon Hughes remembered what he had forgotten, the eldest Jolene made her rounds, checking up on the younger ladies who filled the Foundry with ting-rings, hisses, heave-ho bellows rushes, and furnace growls of industry. Between visits in which she ran her discerning eye over work, pronouncing it shoddy or middling or (and this was a rare and splendid compliment) very fine, she hid herself in the Foundry's inglenooks and alcoves, listened, and when she was sure she was in a private way, she took great big sucks from her inhaler. It was not like the inhalers handed out by physicians and pharmacies across Corinth City. It was quite unique. It was tinkered-with and matte-black and full of clever innovations to the mainstream model. It was Heavy Fucking Duty. And if the elderly Jolene did sprauchle, just a little, then she did it with dignity. Of late there were no rolled eyes. No snide comments. Nothing to overhear. It did an old gal good, right enough. Even longer than long ago, she had borne witness to Hughes' bonding with his sword, Chimera. On that occasion, she had given the young buck a useful piece of advice. *When in doubt, hold your tongue and perk your ears and hope the world doesn't whack you so hard your brain falls out your arsehole.* In her present wintry days, she added this follow-up: *If it does whack you, make sure you thump the world back, and twice as hard!*

She had just visited the young lady who had the temerity to mock her, the one who'd said she sprauchled. "This is very fine," she told the girl, admiring a shoulder pauldron enchanted with magic.

"Thank you, Jolene," the girl replied. "Coming from you, that means a great deal."

Ah yes. It did, didn't it?

She walked down the gentle decline of the Foundry. At ninety-one years, she was by leaps and bounds the oldest of her kindred. Despite the change in perspective her inhaler provided, she took no special pride in that. As far as she was concerned, age was no guarantee of anything, except that you became a complaints department. Muscle grumbles. Joint grievances. Sciatic quibbles up the backside, often literally. The old fielded all of these. Every day.

Still...

Coming from you, that means a great deal.

She took a deep breath, let it go.

No wheeze.

Jolene grinned.

It was Tinfrosttime, the stocking of her heart was chock-full of respect like wrapped and ribboned gifts, and all was right in the world.

She arrived at a Jolene's workstation. This one was a friend of that nice boy, Hughes, and his busy-body of a lover, Cate Jubilee. This one had been named Last Resort by those with sense in their heads, and Ogre Jo by crueler minds than even those who had cooked up 'sprauchle.'

The workstation was impressive, not tidy, but organized as the irreverent minds of genius are organized. Spindles of warm orange light spilled through the teeth of the furnace grate. Swollen and knotted with benign cysts, Jo's back was hunched. The elderly Jolene couldn't see her face.

She cleared her throat to announce herself. "Happy Tuesday, Jo. Hard at work, I see."

No reply.

The elderly Jolene sniffed, an extra pair of icy-blue lenses clicking into place over her spectacles. "Everything all right?" Usually Jolenes spoke purely in direct statements. Questions were a sign of great intimacy between Jolenes and those they trusted, as you have probably gathered. So when the eldest Jolene voiced a question she damn well expected an answer.

None came.

To hell with dignity. She hurried forward. "Jo? Can you hear me?"

"I hear them."

Jo turned. Sweat plastered the few strands of hair she had to her brow. Her eyes were... crowded somehow. In her hands, a pair of tongs and a hammer. The furnace glow gave them the look of a cambion's weapons, devil tools handled in a heathen dark.

"I hear them because they're inside me," said Jo.

A sensation pumped up the elderly Jolene's legs, buttocks, and back. It was not the paroxysm of her nerves, or cramp. It was worse. She felt it pool and cloud through her pubic bone like nitroglycerin. When she looked into Jo's eyes, she didn't wheeze. She made a little sound, fright making a child of her.

Jo advanced, her hands with their gleaming implements rising up like carrion promises over a gibbet.

She backed up, her own wrinkled hands shaking violently.

"You've got all the wrong gasses in you," Jo told her. "I've seen that thing you use. The inhaler. We all have. The relief it gives you is only temporary. If I help you... it'll make us better. Make it go away. The *buzzing*. It'll shine us both free and bright. You'll see."

"What's the matter, girl? What's gotten into you?"

"Nothing really," said Jo. Tugging up her victim's lips, Jane smiled. "Only flies."

***

Thud was running.

Not the bushtail softneck gumsweet run you get along suburban sidewalks, hello neighbor bullshit barely overshooting jumble-footed jogs, no, by God, he was hell-for-thunder *running*.

They were in Nikandros. Train station a blur of images and sounds now left behind. Frank Gallant and Mr. Glint outpacing him, and Hughes a shape half-glimpsed with each burst of speed. Wendy's Bloodhound hell. The kid was a Greyhound, faster than fast. Lost for a moment. He called out, heard Frank Gallant's voice shout something (what? Shout what for God's sake?), and took off in that direction. The blizzard was a roaring wall. He traversed it, demolition with a snow-shod mustache parting bricks of solid white, his pupils dilated, chest heaving, arms going herky-jerk to spur his legs to stir his circulation to go-go-GO!

Something—a telephone pole, maybe—smashed his shoulder on the bypass. Thud grunted and dashed on, pinheads pricking his whole arm numb. Hazelnut coffee sloshed in his gut. He blinked. Acidic smog mixed with the snow. His eyes stinging, hot-cold flakes clotting his lashes like dust kitties on broom bristles. There! A tall shape leaping a stalled car. Mr. Glint!

Thud ran.

Hughes' words echoed through the black imperatives driving him. The lad had uttered them just as the train doors parted. His eyes had fixed on a bit of Citadel propaganda adorning a station wall—just a simple rendering of the anvil-shaped Foundry where the Jolenes kindled and caroused and made magic—and the words had boiled out of him. Thud was not sure what to make of them then, and he was no closer now. "The ceiling. She kept looking up, past it. To the roof."

The roof was a Spring-Heeled Jane reference that chimed alarms in Thud. But who was "she"? Jane herself? There'd been no time to ask. No sooner were the words clear off his mouth than Hughes took off, leaving Desdemona Cauldronpot and the rest of them behind, hopping the ticket booth in one easy gliding motion, speeding off into the thick of Nikandros District as if the hounds of hell were after him. Or as if he *were* the hound and the chase was on. That clove closer to the truth for Thud.

There'd been nothing for it. Frank Gallant had broken Desdemona's trance in an instant and then the three of them were Hughes hunting, squinting and sprinting and closing in on who? What? Jane, please God. Thud wanted her as badly as Hughes did. The Leonidas boys, two good hounds, bark-bark, good dogs, and when they found the bitch they'd bite her throat out if they could. *She kept looking up, past it. To the roof.* What had the lad recalled? What desperate knowing was playing compass in his head, leading the way where their dream dial could not?

A horn blasted. Ghastly yellow lamps beaming out of the haze. Growing larger, larger than life, and the truck coning them from its glass fixtures coming to wrench Thud's life away. It was on him. Its breaking wheels (too slow, breaking too slow, oh holy shit) foaming up huge brown-white waves of road slush. His instincts were sharp, but he was not a young man and the truck was on him.

He had time to think

(Hettie, I'm sorry)

before long-fingered hands seized him. A change in pressure. Flying, he was flying. He hit a car bonnet, rolled, fell face-first into hard-packed ice. Cold crystals filled his mouth, his nose, one of his eyes was burning with the chill. He wiped his face with a gloved hand, stood, his breath like a bull's. The truck had slowed down but not quite stopped, skidding on a slick patch up the street, its axles oscillating. Thud barely noticed. Mr. Glint was there. The truck's enormous tires had rolled over his legs. They were squashed boneless things. Mr. Glint regarded them as Thud might regard a mild spate of spring rain.

"Saved me," said Thud, still not quite believing what he was seeing.

"Can't have," said Mr. Glint. "I'm locked in lucky cell 13."

"I'll phone an ambulance."

"Nah. Be mended in a jiff. Go on with Mr. Hughes and Mr. Gallant."

Thud opened his mouth. *Earlier this week you saw this man swallow a projector.* He shut his mouth, nodded, and was running once more, head down against the savage gale. Turned around again, he spied a flare of shifting colors, recognized Frank's aurora borealis hair, dug deep in his reserves, lungs afire, mind still twitched and twisted around the truck's headlights, and there before him rose the Foundry.

"Where's Glint?" shouted Frank, materializing beside him.

"Truck hit him. Says he'll be okay. Hughes?"

"Ahead. Come on."

On they went, the Foundry looming high, its oblong immensity evoking something monstrous and otherworldly, something pressing itself up from the city as if in answer to the frozen questions of the blizzard.

And Hoshrum Thud, suspended captain of the streetbeaters, let his observation answer its own questions. *Hughes saw a poster of the Foundry and remembered someone, someone whose eyes drifted up to the roof. Roof-obsession is one of the symptoms we've ascribed to the Jane possessions. And who works at the Foundry?*

"Oh no," he said. "Not one of them."

The blizzard howled, and for a moment he was sure he could hear an insectile triumph on the wind.

He ran, a Labrador pushed too far, the ancient wolf inside every dog growling.

***

At the Foundry entrance Hughes went down on one knee. He wrenched his Krys knife from his boot. His eyes roved up the Foundry's vast hollow. The anbarics were dim. From down here with its busy workstations pouring out their lights in blues and greens and yellows (when the Jolenes dealt in fire, it did not always have to be red), the structure gave the impression of... Hughes' lip curled savagely. *Of a beehive*, he thought. *Hold on Jo. You just hold on because you've got a friend coming, and his love for you is thicker than clotted cream.*

Moving again. The mechanized stairwell folded into place underfoot. At this hour the Jolenes' work was in full fling. The sheer heat of the place rolled over him in waves. He lost his bearing, regained it, ran on with curious eyes on him, he could feel them.

Someone called his name. Just who it was he could not be sure.

Instead he heard with astounding clarity the *flap* of his coat behind him, the boat-rudder-*shudder* of his heartbeat. *Chunk* went the furnace grates. Their glow bathed him as he hurtled by, dyeing the melting snow in his beard all sorts of vivid colors. It looked like a bristly nest of gemstones. And on some subaurale level where dread played its little symphonies, Hughes could hear flies.

Jo, you told me once I would be beautiful no matter how I looked. Now we're in Jane's domain, her hive, and no matter how fierce the infestation you've got to fight like a cornered animal in the poacher pens. You've got to be beautiful here at the extremity or you're done for.

Close now. A few more flights and he would be there.

(too late)

(no, can't be, can*not* be)

His lungs hummed. His stomach lurched and swam with sickening greasy fright and lurched some more. He thought of her lank hair brushed by long, whispery cockroach feelers and his heart gave an almighty squeeze.

Desdemona's words occurred to him, the ones she'd uttered in tones that had seemed to carve the blizzard like some great frozen bird: *This morsel is so plump and juicy with the stuff she hungers for most. She will taste of tenderest veal.*

Of course it was Jo the Spring-Heeled killer found so irresistible. Hughes knew of few people who could match Jo's enthusiasm for the sweeter things in life. She saw a good world and met it on even terms. A woman with physical deformities who had always made Hughes feel perfect because if he was high in her estimation, then hey, he must be doing something right. That was Jo.

To Jane, she would be a feast.

He tore Chimera from its scabbard. A few more steps, and he was...

He...

What Hughes saw there in Jo's workstation defied everything he knew about his friend. Everything kind and mild and thoughtful about her sketched itself over the scene in his mind, a sort of volitional graffiti. Later, he would struggle to remember, even though such a thing had every right to be remembered. That was a mercy. For both of them. It wasn't Jo. She was not in the driver's seat.

When he stumbled to a heel-rocked, sweat-drenched stop, and looked into that room, and saw the bloody tongs and claw-headed hammer and the eldest of the Jolenes lying there, her clothes stripped and her chest cavity parted like the doors of a weathered wardrobe; when he saw Jo lifting up the old woman's spongy, glistening lungs as though offering them to him...

When he saw her wide, beatific smile, Hughes knew who was moving the muscles in her cheeks. The flies were not in his imagination now. They *buzzed*, loud, a sickening static gathering on the death stink in the air.

Jo hoisted the lungs a trifle higher. They did not look deflated at all. Full of the old gal's last breath, some part of Hughes hazarded. *Her breath or her scream.*

"Gas these," Jo bid him, shaking the lungs. "Mustard gas to muster her spirits."

"Come out, Jane."

"Dijon, dijon, mustard gas. Vapor. Squirt it up her ass."

"Come out of there so I can kill you," Hughes said and pushed his Performance.

***

Caviar, Jane thought, sucking drops of Jo's happiness off her fingers. *Truffles. Crab meat. Veal. Warm chocolate pudding you probe with a spoon, only to have the rich dark stuff inside come spilling out—it's so hot it* steeeeeeams.

She dove in for another mouthful, her whole body jerking and joggling, giddiness-gripped. She had a very wide mouth, like a praying mantis wife biting off her husband's head, and yet at the same time, paradoxically, she had a very thin one, like the proboscis sucker you might find on a household mosquito. She gnawed and slurped and suckled and swallowed and oh, oh, oh, it was so yummy and tasty and *good*. The disfigured woman's joy was pillow-soft and yielding. For the lovely, lucky life of her, Jane could not recall the last time she had eaten so well.

And the thing that made her meal all the better? All the more savory?

The secrets.

She was learning so much about Jo. An uncommonly ugly lady, it was amazing that she hadn't killed herself when she was a little girl, when the teasing had reached a crescendo. A miracle. And here, sliding over her gums, another miracle, this one even more scrumptious. Jo had been close once, right on the cusp of despair, when falling on one side meant recovery and falling on the other meant suicide. Someone had tipped the balance. Hughes. Jane could taste the woman's love for Hughes—the friendship and trust—like the most elegant seasoning in the restaurant of the soul.

And now I get to eat her, Jane thrilled, her pleasure very great.

I get to munch your friend, Hughes. The next time you see her, she'll be a vegetable. Drooling like a head trauma case. Blank-eyed and unresponsive like a stoned crow. That was funny. She had to stop herself from laughing. Her mouth, after all, was terribly busy, and she was hungry.

She craned down, spit running in anticipation, and stopped.

Something changed in the unseeable dark of her feeding spot. Something *adjusted.* Something *let itself in.*

Before Jane could react or formulate a thought more complicated than

(*What?*)

that same something collared her. Collared her like a naughty bitch pup. Long feminine hands. Red nail polish. The fingers smelled like ashtrays.

Jane's eyes narrowed instinctually as her cozy dark filled with a light that was painfully bright. The light was green. *Green as springtime,* she thought.

And just like that, she knew who had barged in on her.

Suddenly she was excited all over again. Let the rude interruption become a meeting between like-minded peers. And they *were* like-minded, she and Hughes.

She had known it ever since he'd come to her in the Dennings' woman's dream. Maybe they weren't family, and the possibility of being friends was virtually nonexistent. But looking up at him, a woman who was a fly and a man who was a mirror for her, she had understood with *absolute certainty* that they were meant for one another. *Something in your life has cleared you out,* she'd told him. *Bared you. Pared you down to the nub. Emptied.*

And now, thanks to her most recent chow, Jane knew what that something was.

See? I'm a better detective than you are, Hughes.

The arms pulled her out of the dark.

Jane went willingly, laughing a high, lunatic laugh.

Chapter Twenty-Two

When the cloud of insects boiled out of Jo, Hughes spared no time for pleasantries. He waded in, first with Chimera, then with the Krys knife. The swarm rippled with the first strike, then parried the second in a clash of steel. His eyes widened.

She formed up so they could see one another. She stood of a height with him. Her hair was dark, and her eyes were darker still. He had expected them to be faceted and alien, like a bug's eyes, but they weren't. He took in her long, intelligent face, which was very animated when any emotion touched it. Her coat was made of moths. Holding his Krys knife at bay was a sword that was, for all intents and purposes, a hideous reflection of his own. Where Hughes' Chimera was a blade of dragon, ram, and lion, Jane's weapon was a blade of weevil, spider, and clusters of fly eggs at the pommel.

As Hoshrum Thud and Frank Gallant crested the mechanical stair, both men believed they were seeing double.

Then Jane grinned and the illusion broke. A brown-and-orange spotted millipede scurried out of the corner of her mouth and into the pink corner of her eye. Behind her, Jo slumped, her eyes rolled back to the whites. She fell flat on her face, her nose squashed, lips mashed, and the lungs *splatting* wetly on the stone floor.

Things seldom play out in sequence. When it comes to moments like that, everything tends to happen all at once, and those involved form their own scattershot picture of it afterward, the photographs they mentally snapped either blurred to obscurity or sharply focused depending on the mind rendering development. Hughes was aware of bugs issuing out of Jane from her pant legs, like blackly buzzing urine, or fumy kerosene leaking from a faulty tanker. Sounds behind him would later reveal themselves to be Thud and Frank fending off a legion of creepy crawlies and zipping, flying things that would sting and bite and bury under the skin if they could. Mostly though, he was aware of Jane's eyes, which were so much like his own it gave him chills.

Two will have your eyes, shadow man. The third will have your heart.

Was Jane one of the women Krys had told him of?

"So you're Iphigenia's shadow," Jane said. "That's fun."

Hughes had no idea what the fuck she was talking about. Just then he didn't much care either. Signals too rapid for his conscious mind to register were shooting through him, making electrical runways of his system. He whirled, Chimera skimming shy of Jane's throat. The bug bitch went on talking.

"I was worried it was the Pale world or one of the really nasty ones. Love the sword by the way. The knife too. See mine?"

Hughes feinted, thrust, and found himself locking blades with her, sword against sword, knife against... yes, against a knife of her own, short-handled and wicked.

"My Chrysalis knife," she whispered conspiratorially. "I always keep it handy."

A memory exploded in the maroon-tinted murk of his rage. The Painted Girl. Rain. A thunderstorm. She was pressing a knife into his hand. His knife. "You keep your Krys knife handy, Hughes," she'd said. "You hear me?"

He met Jane's gaze. Reason sent up a flare, another burst temporarily dispersing his anger. "Are you me?" he asked.

"Uh huh. Of the same stuff, the way human beings and stars share a suite of gasses. You and me, honey," she said, her smile beetled and teeming with lice. "We're the big time. Walking shadows. You, Iphigenia's. Me, Eurydice's."

(walking shadows)

(*two will have your eyes, shadow man*)

"I don't understand," said Hughes.

"Be with me, then. Give ignorance a funeral. I'll show you how to really be, babe."

"Don't talk to me—"

"But—"

"Like that, don't you *talk to me like that!*"

They came apart. The room was stifling hot. Hughes could feel the tip of a dehydration migraine testing and making wand-brushes across his brain.

Frank and Thud were in trouble. The impulse to help them motivated what he said next, but that was only part of it. The rest was selfishness. "Let them go," he said. "I want to speak to you, Jane. Only let them go and leave Jo be, and it'll... it..."

"It'll just be you and me?"

His face had been lowered, flushed, and pinched. Now it came up, and he looked at her, and her expression was so eager it galled him and cored him out like fruit, and sweet as fruit were the answers hidden behind her rhyme-loving lips.

"Yeah," he said softly. "Okay."

Words could not describe the surprise, then the outrage, then the blood-sizzling fury that rose in him when Jane's eagerness melted away, replaced with peels of laughter.

"You're so quick!" Huge death's-head hawkmoths fluttered from her giggling mouth, evaporating into the lengthening shadows as the furnace fire dimmed low. "So quick to snuggle up to me. I've got half your friend's cheer stewing in my guts. Do you give a flying fuck? Nope! Oh Jane, Janey, Janey girl! Tell me more, I need it, I want it, I gots to have dat good, good knowing or else my poor sad noodle gonna pop."

Hughes tried to stick her with Chimera. Jane turned the strike, nicked his chin with her Chrysalis knife, then slipped beyond his reach.

"It's a relief, it really is," she said. "I was scared you had some mischief up your sleeve. I do, so I thought: he must too. But I was wrong. The best you've got is a tongue that's graduated from silver to the gold podium. Gift of the gab. Numb slum-house magic. Rudimentary." Another bout of steel, another stalemate. Jane was quick as a hornet, deadly as an Ikahaguan brown widow, and her words just as venomous. "I'm so happy we found each other, Gormon. We're meant to play, I think. Gifts passed from world to world. You for me and me for you. Real seasonal. It would have been different if you were a daddy."

The blood drained from Hughes' countenance. His cheeks were waxy. The cut on his chin wept a mixture of blood and sweat. A vein throbbed caterpillar-thick at his temple. In a voice that was horribly quiet, he asked, "What did you say?"

"You would have been happier, just another basket of goodies to taste. Whereas miserable, we can fill one another up. You trying to guard the banquet table and me slipping through your grasp. Did they really put her in the bin?" said Jane sweetly. "Just more glass for recycling? That's brutal, even for a connoisseur like me. I bet she *made a tinkling sound*, Hughes. I bet your baby girl *tinkled like fucking sleigh bells.*"

A vital wire snipped inside him, and what came for Jane in that instant was not a man, only man-shaped.

Crushing aphids as big as rats underfoot, swatting and ducking and spitting, Thud and Frank could only struggle on while there in the dusky purple light of Jo's fire the shadows crossed swords.

Nearby, under a few discarded blueprints and a bit of old ham sandwich, someone small and entirely unnoticed, and who had been watching events unfold with interest, issued a squeak and scampered away.

***

Burnished Isaac Lawless had nailed one aspect of the reliquaries. They were pretty silly looking. It was hard to appreciate it though, to be amused. Hard to think at all.

The reliquaries were arranged in a prism that floated forty inches above the floor. They were black and white and strangely badgerish, like a kid's trial attempts at carving a totem. According to Isaac, each reliquary corresponded with a wisp of William's retinue. Destroy one, and the wisp died. But Isaac must have only observed their culture for a short period of time, or perhaps William and his kin had evolved because the reliquaries weren't just objects made to seal the life force of the wisps away and keep them safe. They were sources of new life too.

The reliquaries had these little strands coming out of them, and the strands went up and came together over the prism, and amassed like that they made a womb. Inside it floated a little thing.

A baby.

Cate approached. She reached out. The baby held out a hand.

A short, sharp sound escaped her. She recoiled. The hand stayed out, as if to say, *hold me.*

Cate stood, looking at her boot. She brushed a few threads of hair from her eyes, tucked a few more behind one ear, pressed her lips until they made a hyphen of her mouth. She thought about her life. She thought about the view from the manta ray's mouth, the landscape that was a thinking world that was a woman. *The World and the Lady.* She thought about glass.

Her gaze darted about the chamber. Smooth and white and part of an ooze house inside a sky leviathan, it was a place totally removed from the bounds of her conception. She returned to the boot, possibly hoping for solidarity.

In her mind's ear she could hear beeps and clicks of hospital equipment. Bustling nurses. Ropes of pain in her groin and lower abdomen, dulling to an ache, then a throb as the intravenous drips did their version of Hughes' Performance; the drugs say out and out the hurt goes. Abracadabra. *My boots and I do magic too.* See that monitor? See that ooze? See it firm up into a little thing? Watch the baby. Watch closely. Poof. Alakazam. Look again. Empty screen. Magician bows. Rustle of curtain. Waking up to Hughes' face wearing all the cosmetics of grief. How softly they talked as if talking too loud might wake the baby that wasn't there. His eyes like lakes of Novocain. He told her she'd smiled while she slept. "I dreamed of you," she said. *And the baby*, she didn't say. *We were in the park and you and our little girl fed ducks. She picked one up, and it didn't seem to mind at all, not at all...*

Glass. What a pretty curse for Cate. Gorgeous. Merciless.

What had the ultrasound technician called the ornament inside her?

Hughes had told her afterward. Right, right.

Foreign matter.

Had she spoken?

Cate didn't know. There was a crinkle-thump as something fell to the floor. She looked down. The firework Nyoni Snickerdrake had given her was there. Loose from where she'd affixed it against her satchel. Fox-faced, it made a weird symmetry with the badger-faced reliquaries. She'd planned to blow the latter up with the former. Or just William's. Will's will willed the wisps, after all. A little lightshow inside the Manta Ray stadium. A jubilee. Eurydice, zero. Cate, four. *This world, zero*, she thought with a bitterness that scared her. *Foreign matter, four. Make it five for November.*

She glanced up. The wisp baby didn't have a face, merely a smooth white sphere with holes. Not even a head, really, just a... just a seashell...

"Oh."

After what seemed like a long time, she slid a finger through the ghostly light from the reliquaries, which was cold, and let the little hand touch her and close into a fist, which was warm.

A tear rolled down her cheek. Only that and nothing more.

Not one for sobbing was Cate Jubilee.

No sir.

***

"It's times like this," muttered Frank Gallant, his clothes and fingers spindling out into ten-thousand filaments of nylon string, putting bugs by the score to sleep and melting them away into dreamstuff, but never enough for there were always more scuttling and bumbling and susurrating over him. "Times like this Mr. Glint comes in *really* handy."

Thud grunted. "And wives."

"Say again?"

"Hettie didn't just pack me a thermos."

The superbly-mustached man dropped his sticky, dripping truncheon and produced a can, the contents of which rattled when he shook it. Frank read the label: *Hothouse & Byrne's Jumbo-Size Insecticide.* Also there was a splat of graphic design on the can, red and stark, and the text there told the reader: *Bug Be-Gone and Nests De-stroyed or Your Money Back!*

"An artist with common sense," Frank said. "Well I'll be."

"Don't be daft. This is just a bit of cleverness. Hettie has no common sense whatsoever."

"How can you tell?"

"Would *you* marry a policeman?"

Frank grinned. "Spray these suckers, man."

Thud did.

His world became the *hisssss* of the can, the puffy, rippling chemical mist, the nostril-hair shriveling smell, the satisfying picture of hundreds of winged shapes falling limply mid-swoop and the thin-and-thick crawlers and creepers curling in on themselves.

Vaguely his ear registered a dry *thwapping* sound.

What could that be? Thud thought and promptly turned his attention to more pressing concerns, namely the long-legged things climbing his leg.

The source of the sound was a very large lappet of cow-leather, cured and ready to be worked, and hanging from a hook suspended from a steel railing. Hughes had, only a moment ago, sent it careening toward Jane. They stalked one another among the animal hides. With an instinctive cunning that made use of the familiar environment, Hughes guided the fight toward the storage compartment in the western wall, his knife-clutching fist thumping the button that hitched the conveyor belt system into action. A mechanized arm with a cogwheel core swung round. Hughes, ready for it, vaulted over its titanium strut. Jane, not ready, was knocked off her feet.

Reeling, she made an ugly glottal noise as Hughes stuck her legs with both blades—Chimera lodged in her left calf, the Krys knife sank to the hilt and twisted in her right thigh. Blood pumped over his fingers. No, not blood. Jane's gunk was gooey, a pale amber plasma. "Here's your pollen," he mumbled thickly, not conscious he was even speaking. "Here's your honeycomb." He dug about, the steel grinding her bones and nuzzling her nerve endings. Jane screamed. Overhead the metal arm sorted in the compartment, found a supply box packed with crude ores, and emerged ferrying it. If Hughes had kept Jane there she would have been squashed flat

(good enough for a fly)

(too good for her)

but she was crafty. She could not bring her elbows back for a decent strike. So tossing her blades aside with a clatter, she grabbed two fistfuls of his hair and brought his face to hers, noses mashed together, two sets of dark eyes glowering, pupils contracted, and with a roar Jane vomited a clot of locusts down Hughes' throat. Windpipe locking round the quivering creatures inside it, Hughes gagged, color slamming up his neck. His complexion went puce. He was forced to jerk aside, retching. The supply box came down heavily, wafting Jane's hair but nothing more.

Messily, a real caterpillar throbbing at her temple like an exerted vein, she pulled Chimera and the Krys knife out of her legs. Just in time too, for Hughes was on her, slashing wide, cutting narrow. They fought with one another's weapons, he a dog and she a swarm of fleas. Hughes' offense was not wild, far from it. It was terribly controlled. Hector's teachings were embedded marrow-deep. His body went through the motions, even if his mind was a nest of cobras, coiled anger and molting calm and carefulness like skin. Ideas accumulated and dripped through him in cloudy venomous jewels.

(kill you)

(I'll kill)

(you you)

(bloated leech)

(dark mantis)

(I'll bite)

(your head)

(off and)

(shit down)

(your neck)

Spring-Heeled Jane was laughing. Limping, bleeding, laughing. The reverberations of it shook something from the damp cave walls of him. The man-shape with propane for blood that was Hughes heard her say, *I bet your baby girl tinkled like fucking sleigh bells.* Totally without plan or mischief, just an animal doing nature's fierce labor for it, he drove her toward the furnace. Kicking the lever, he triggered the metal grille. It shucked high so the coals and the bright lavender flames showed. Jane tried a counteroffensive, was thwarted, gave more ground. No laughter now. She had joined her noise to Hughes', a sonic consummation. Together they breathed, almost perfectly synchronized. As they neared the furnace Hughes' body snapped in a pirouette. The movement allowed him to slide the tip of Jane's sword (which felt like a second Chimera in his hand) under the coals. With a flick he sent hot sparks into Jane's eyes. She sucked in air, her lids shut, squeezing out tears like larval jelly.

"Jolene," said Hughes. His throat was raw, swollen-feeling. His voice was a vagabond's rugged rasp. Pressing his advantage, he made quick work of her guard and drove both steel points home.

"Rummy Lou. Paulie Manzarek. Adam and Ellen Dennings." He yanked the Chrysalis knife, opening Jane's side like an envelope. "My daughter had no name to invoke, but I'll have theirs from you, Jane. Adam and Ellen Dennings. Say their names."

"Gladly," she said. "Adam and Ellen Dennings. At my behest their momma did unspeakable things to them. How is Susy-Q? That night when I ate her, she tasted like lamb casserole."

She snapped forward at the neck, her mouth stretching grotesquely. Hughes sensed more than felt her teeth about to close on his lower lip. His reflexes saved him. The lurch started in his core and radiated out, drawing him away from her in the nick of time. Instead of mutilating him, Jane succeeded only in ripping a string of soft skin free. He watched her tongue it, that little strip of lip. Then she sucked it into her mouth, closed her eyes for a moment, and wiggled all over so Hughes could see how *good* he tasted. She tugged her Chrysalis knife and her sword out of her torso, then bowed a deep and mocking bow. That gooey plasma seeped down her side and chest, sticking her clothes to her skin like the most malignant glue in hell.

Backing up, Hughes' ankle nudged something. He slid his foot under it and gave a fleet, flicking kick. Something sharp rose. He caught it. As Jane charged, he met her with Chimera. The clang of their clash jarred the first really clear thought he'd had since Jane had mentioned his daughter. *I'm baking alive.* Warm drops of sweat rolled down his own sides and between his shoulder blades. His eyes stung. Sour perfumes filled the room, sweat and some chemical agent Hughes could not identify. His chin was hot and wet and purple-red in the firelight, a pageant half-mask of blood.

As he recouped his stamina, Hector's composite subrules of defense asserted themselves in Hughes: assessment; parrying; riposting. His footwork was immaculate, though doubtless his friend and teacher would have found his parries profoundly sluggish and his poise wanting. Hughes could not help it. He was used to battle in demanding circumstances, but his unmeasured onslaught at the outset of this melee had robbed him of that which separates the good from the merely competent. Besides the blanketing heat was murder. How Jane was still going high-octane with so many wounds—not superficial scrapes but normally crippling injuries—was beyond him. On the other hand, it made a perverse kind of sense. When you kill a fly, or even a hundred flies, does the swarm die? Does it even falter? Hughes supposed it did. The bug bitch was limping, after all, and she kept her knife-wielding arm tucked close to her goop-weeping side.

Still, the fact of her endurance rang clear with each steely impact. And through her smiling mouth, her cruelty spilled out, so as to drown him in despair.

"Rummy Lou, steel wire for a hair sponge, scrubba-dub-dub," Jane taunted. "Taylet Gordon dropped a chandelier. Barclay Waters. Alma Coalman. Karoliina Vaaca. Laura Clemp, that slut was succulent. Paulie Manzarek smothered lots of people, some of them my former hosts. Neat, huh? You already brought up Susy-Q Dennings, but listen to this Hughes, get a load of this. There was another one that night in November. A man. An old man who spent his whole life trying—I mean *striving*— to make something of himself. And you know what? He did! He made himself a palate cleanser. Sorbet, so I could really savor Susabeth. Isn't that a knee-slapper?"

Somewhere distant, a forlorn rattling.

It was Thud's can. Empty.

He tossed it aside, scrambled for his truncheon, hissed through clenched teeth as a hairy spider nipped his knuckles. Before his eyes the flesh began to swell. He cast about, seeing his insecticide had done a fair job, dead bugs dissolving into shadow.

"Still too many," he said. Looking past the chirping, flit-wing tide, he could see the shadows. "Hughes is on the backfoot."

"I'd ask you to cover me while I help him," said Frank. "But you'll die."

"So I'll die."

"Heroic." Frank's aurora hair shone turquoise. It was breathtaking. "Hettie a widow though? You want it?"

Thud made a small, savage sound, but said nothing. The spider bite on his hand itched monstrously. From the corner of his eye he saw Frank's smile. It was vexing, enigmatic, the sort of smile that makes the cowardly bold and the weak gain bursts of unlikely strength. "Swing that stick, policeman. In a sec we're going to make a break for Hughes. Jane's a demon one-on-one. Let's see how she likes one-on-three."

"There's too bloody many," Thud protested, gesturing to the insects. "We'll be eaten alive."

"Yeah."

"You don't give a damn, do you?"

Nylon strings captured the spider that had nipped Thud. Hairy legs waggled in the air. The strings tore it apart. Meanwhile Frank's smile had eased into something approximating... what? Thud had no idea. Whatever it was, the emotion was directed at Hughes, who Frank was staring at with great intensity. "I give a damn," he said. "A drat, a blast, a cataclysmic fuck. I give the whole kit-and-kaboodle." He looked at Thud sidelong. "Ready?"

Thud wasn't. "Course I am. Asking me am I ready. The cheek. Are *you*?"

But Frank wasn't looking at him anymore. He was looking at something behind Thud.

Thud turned. And yelped.

"Well, well, wellingtons," said Knickerbocker. "Whiskers 319 sold it poorly. This is worse than a right mess. It's downright wrong, and no mistake. But don't worry," he said, patting a petrified Thud on the shoulder with a hand like a chewed mitten. "The cavalry has arrived."

Out of the holes in the walls, the tiny inglenooks that no Big Folk see because their eyes skim right past the domains of Small Pickings—out of these scampered the Whiskers and the Mr. Squeakies.

***

The impasse between the wisps and the Scarlet Citadel ended even more strangely than it had begun.

Two buoyant little *whumps* signaled the arrival of two new mirrors on the battlefield, one directly below the manta ray, which Cate Jubilee plunged into boots-first, and another in the courtyard, which Cate appeared through a moment later.

She strode up to William o' The Wisps. William, who was trying with all his might to cut down Kevlin Paladin, paid her no great mind. Then he noticed what she was carrying. To Kevlin's astonishment, William's sword-arm froze... and slowly lowered.

All over the fortress called Betty, the wisps stopped attacking and retreated a few steps. *Will's will wills the wisps*, Cate thought. "Wait," she commanded as Kevlin prepared to thrust his spear. He flinched, held back. At her nod, he bellowed, "*Company! Hold fast, Cate's orders!*"

Murmurs. Uneasy glances. Scowls from Xacorca Demon and other foul-tempered fighters, but even she held fast and made no move toward hostility.

Stillness then. Restless peace made almost unbearably tense by the *WHOOOOOSH* of the manta ray's fins scooping the wind. Those who could not see the courtyard chewed their cheeks and whispered to one another and began to carefully make their way there. Those who could see waited on tenterhooks—what was going to happen? What was in Cate's arms?

She drew up before William. His hole-riddled head seemed to regard her evenly. Or perhaps that was only her imagination. He could have been anything: aggrieved; truculent; afraid. That last one would not do.

Cate smiled a warm and friendly smile. "Here."

And she handed William the wisp baby. He sheathed his sword and cradled the child automatically. Threads of light still enfolded its form. The threads stretched back through Cate's courtyard mirror, out the other one, and sailed up into the air, all the way into the manta ray. The reliquaries didn't fancy relinquishing their hold on their creation, and Cate had made no attempt to sever that bond. Giving him the once-over, it was impossible to parse William's reaction to being handed the baby, but Cate would have bet all the credits in Eurydice that he was staring at it in disbelief.

As if on cue, the child gave an odd, high-pitched fluting toot. It sounded happy. *Hey Dad! That red lady brought me down from the ray, and boy, was it a trip.*

Cate pushed the firework nestled on her satchel aside, rooted in it, and produced the disc she'd taken from Skuggs. Its pink-quartz rim glittered. "This compass led us to you," she said. "Has Eurydice tasked you with invading Iphigenia, William? Has she asked you to kill as many living things as you can?"

He nodded twice.

"Can you tell me why?"

Nothing. *Like the Troll,* Cate conceded glumly. *He doesn't know.*

Resolution overwhelmed disappointment. When she spoke, she did so with a strange blend of confidence and reluctance. Her tone was Cate-ish though, infused with the flicker-flame of honesty burning through the center of her, and that could not be feigned or faulted as it sent the words luminous from the wick of her spirit.

"William, I cannot know what sort of man you are. I've never met a wisp before. There are writings on you, but my doubts about their accuracy began earlier today and have only deepened since then. My name is Cate Jubilee. I know you here in Eurydice call us Agents of the Red Death. We have names for the creatures and people here. Perhaps... perhaps we could set those names aside, the way useless old furniture is set aside, maybe to be refurbished, or taken to the dump. Why not you be a wisp and me a woman. Those are better terms than the ones we met on. I'd shake your hand only yours are occupied." The baby was fluting, plaintive now, reaching for her. Cate let it hold her finger, which seemed very much to the child's satisfaction, as though it had discovered in her finger a whole carnival of wonders. Cate cleared her throat and addressed the leader of the wisps. "As a wisp I know you've an obligation to your world. The Lady and the World, both being the same. And as a woman who takes her work seriously, I respect that obligation very much. Still, I'm asking you to stay here. Don't go to Iphigenia. I..." She wet her lips, her gaze fixed upon him and so intent it might have bored a fresh hole in his head. "I cannot know what sort of man you are," she repeated. "Whether you are the sort who will obey an irrefutable command from your liege or heed the impassioned plea of an enemy. A woman who has..." She bit the coming words back. That Cate-ish candle in her had guttered a warning; whatever words she'd been about to speak were for her to contend with and not for anyone else's ears. Not yet. "Of an enemy," she amended. William stood before her, holding the baby who was, in turn, holding her finger firmly. His expression was unreadable, mostly on account of there not being any expression to read. Desperation seizing her, her composure grappling it, she smothered anything more complicated than her plea. Three words would suffice, a "full stop" to mark the moment for good or ill. "Please. Stay here."

William's head canted and tilted. Cate believed—or maybe just hoped—that she could glean a little something from those cants and tilts, namely William's eyeline, his focus. Later, she thought this was how it shook out:

The wisp man looked at the baby in his arms. He followed the threads of reliquary light leading from the child to the manta ray. He looked at Cate, at the firework—the fox-faced, undetonated firework. He looked at the child's fingers like tiny round piano keys, all smooth and white and pure, locked in that vice-grip babies have around Cate's finger. Then his gaze did a circuit. The firework. The baby. Cate. Then he just stopped. His focus settled on her and he *stopped*.

Slow and rattly her breath came.

Colors painted the landscape above, fluctuations of moonlight as the twelve moons jived, their radiant dance ratcheting up the tension Cate felt like a live animal inside her. The ray's circles above them sent waves of wind ruffling her scarlet shirt, planting strange cool kisses on her sweat-dappled brow. The fine hairs on the back of her neck whispered up and stiffened.

When the sound arrived, it seemed to begin in her head, only reaching her ears as a matter of courtesy. When she was in her early twenties she'd seen a film called *The Forest God Pan*, and the score for that movie had been crazy, a discordant maelstrom of piccolos, pan pipes, baroque, bansuri, dizis, and fues. All that musical wind had whisked her right into the weird woods of the fair folk, and she'd felt stirred and sublime and very much enchanted. The sound of William and his wisps saying farewell was like that. It flowed over the battlements and filled the courtyard, and as the wisps performed this eerily beautiful song they began to raise themselves up into the air as though lifted on cinematic stunt wire. Cate inhaled softly as the baby let her finger go. William carried it up, and up, and here came the manta ray with its tail swerving in the sonorous dark. The reliquaries gave up their links, safe in the knowledge that their little one was on its way home.

A minute later the ray was going off, seeming to take on the look of a huge scaly cloud that had solidified for a time and was now content to vanish once more, and the scarlet men and women hurried to pose every question bubbling on their lips. Cate answered them as best she could until Eilandri Titansgrave, mute yet ever wise, managed to convey that now was not a good time for an interrogation, and everyone had best bugger off and get some much-needed rest.

There was some grumbling, but it was perfunctory. In truth everyone looked wrung-out and haggard with exhaustion; it had been a long and grueling morning.

"Cate," said Jennifer Goblingrin, taking her aside. "Went to check on the prisoner—that horrid little crookshank, Skuggs—in case he decided to pull a bit of mischief during the battle. No problems, he's chained up good. He says he must eat some of his supplies we confiscated or he'll starve."

"He'll last till morning." *And maybe a flirtation with hunger will do what Margherita Stranger's visions failed to and get him talking.* "How's morale, Jen?"

Jennifer Goblingrin smiled, an expression that reminded Cate of a cluttered toolshed. "A few close shaves tonight, but the Company is solid, ma'am."

A kind lie, but a lie nonetheless. The chalky complexion. Difficulty maintaining balance. Sluggishness and slowness of reaction times indicating lightheadedness. These were signs Cate recognized all too well. She had been a long hauler in her day. Beneath the cheerful exterior, Jennifer was dog-tired. Worse, she was shaken. Most of her Company were, if not all. The wisps had left peacefully enough, but Cate had only to look at the faces of her friends as they quit the courtyard to see the afterimage of William's menace.

"Did we win, Cate?" said Jennifer.

Cate returned the young lady's hopeful smile, as sweet and soothing as she could manage. "Probably," she said.

Eilandri was nowhere to be seen. Maybe that was for the best. Maybe, but Cate could have used the giant's presence, even for a minute.

She went to her quarters, all her kindled and bright qualities extinguished for the time being. The room was very comfortable, but she felt absent from it somehow. Where the wisp baby had held it, her finger gave a tingle. At the same time, she felt a deep, sinister ache. It started in her lower abdomen and reached out, krakenlike, with slow, groping tentacles that wrapped around some vulnerable crow's nest in her lower back. For an instant she thought, *Oh fuck, my period.* It had been so long, she'd actually forgotten that spotted-tampon specter that roosts nastily over half the population. Sitting on her bed, she curled up a little. It helped. But that was impossible. She couldn't *get* a period. That bleak cycle had relinquished her with a reluctance that mirrored the reliquaries and their baby in a way that was too close for comfort. For God's sake, she didn't have a scrap of lining to shed. She didn't have a *womb.* Not since the bad November.

This is phantom pain, she decided. *Phantom pain and stress, and those words I was about to speak to William sneaking up on me. It's crimson magic, thought-alchemy, and I'm going to get better. A little rest is all I need.*

She lay down, breathing in through her nose and out through her mouth, her whole self curled around that awful ache.

Oddly... but no, there was nothing odd about it.

Not so oddly, then, her thoughts scrawled across the red paper of her mind like one of her letters home.

Hughes. Your Kitten is in _real trouble_ here.
Be safe for both of us, okay?

***

The rats and the mice struck the insect horde in a phalanx of pink tails, twitchy noses, and chisel-shaped teeth. Mandibles were trod on. Stingers nimbly dodged. Wings nibbled.

His ears full of squeaks, Hughes saw a gap begin to form in the wretched ranks. The bugs' line broke. Frank Gallant strode through it, his face an education in the loveliness of dreams and the wickedness of nightmares.

"Jane, Jane, Jane," he sang, encasing her wrist in a manacle of strings. "*Had this girl on my brain, brain, brain.*"

Hughes lunged. Jane's sword skittered, spidery-quick. But Thud was coming, truncheon adrip with unthinkable fluids, mustache quivering, and Frank's strings were giving the queen of the flies no end of distress.

"*Got to scoot on a train, train, train.*"

"Let me go," she spat. Her dagger hand sawed at him with a sound like a night-chirping cicada. The Dream Warrior caught the hand, tightened and twisted it, pushed it till it snapped. At that exact moment Hughes drove Chimera into her armpit. Jane's whole body went taut. Her eyes were out on stalks. Her jaw unhinged. Flies began to stream from her nose and throat, their senseless buzz a corollary of their mistress' pain.

Hughes felt a thrill of absurd pride. Suddenly the flies changed course. They converged on Frank. There was a rush of sound, then a fantastic *crunch* as Thud's streetbeater kosh stove Jane's cheekbone in, caved it *right the fuck in.* On the upswing he shut her mouth, closing off the parade of flies and bringing her teeth together with a distinct *click.*

"*She's no fan of sunshine,*" Frank sang on lustily. "*Jane cloaks the sky in a gray mantle, uncorks the sour champagne, and makes it rain, rain, rain.*"

"Sing on, Frank," Jane slurred. Thud had broken her jaw. Her grin was crooked. "Your mothers loved a song. Lullabies like dream nectar in the naked yesterday. I'll kill you. I'll fucking kill youuuuuuuuuUUUUUUUUUUUUOOOOOOOOOO–"

Hughes' hackles were raised, his temper irrevocably lost, his teeth bared. Not Winnifred Dragontail's Bloodhound but the city's dark watchdog. With her threats washing over him he'd turned his blade, got the angle good and true, and punctured Chimera through Jane's heart.

From his perspective, slightly crouched, stare zeroed-in on the line of that broken jaw, Hughes saw a frantic, erratic spasm worming around the scourge of Corinth City. Her fingers fluttered as if playing invisible accordion keys. Somewhere close by there were disappointed squeaks as insects melted away from the hungry mouths of Knickerbocker's informants. For her part, Jane was also going to pieces. It started at her core and worked its way out, her body peeling away like pencil lead, and then even that dissolving into nothing. Only a suggestion of a woman. A shadow. Thud stood riveted, Frank mesmerized.

Jane sighed, or seemed to sigh. Another convulsion moved through her.

Through the lattice of her ribs, which Hughes could see very clearly as her skin and muscle wilted, he watched her heart beat once-twice.

Impaled as it was by Chimera, it called to memory another heart. That one he'd pierced too, only it was his Krys knife that time. It was the heart of a two-headed wolf, the one who had killed a unit of the Scarlet Citadel, including a much beloved young woman named Laurana. Weird, but

Hughes had thought of mustard gas that day, that gruesome chemical deployed in the trench war against Champleurs. Jolene had mentioned it just a few minutes ago, glistening lungs weeping blood through her fingers. Amazing how parallels presented themselves over the course of a life. *Amazing*, he thought, looking at his parallel, his fellow shadow (whatever that meant), his Dark Cousin. *And spooky. Downright terrifying.*

Hughes watched Jane's heart, her face a window to his own.

He counted the beats.

Once-twice.

Once-twice.

Once—

Still.

One second fused into the next, a hair's breadth of accountable time, that was all, and abruptly Jane was gone, taking a good bit of Hughes' consternation with her.

The dancing plum-purple glow of the furnace fire showed the three men to one another. Purple is a color that means different things to different people, yet almost always evokes strong emotions. Twilit skies spur romance. Grapes sate. Lavender calms. Hughes had even heard that purple posters sold more suspense movies, as purple covers had sold more horror paperbacks in the bygone days of Corinth City literature. With Frank Gallant's aurora burning a cautiously optimistic yellow that made the purple light very vivid, and the paler bristles in Hoshrum Thud's mustache going purplish-pink as the glow soaked in, Hughes felt a strong emotion. Actually it was two strong emotions, and he let them both out, a big burst of laughter that said, *I am relieved and I am holy-smoke delighted!* Frank's brows went up. He laughed his big, tremendous laugh. Even stoic Thud could not resist a gruff huff of amusement. Why, had Mr. Glint been there, he himself may have broken his surly custom and cracked a smile.

Don't push it, Hughes thought to himself and laughed all the harder.

It died in his throat as the voice whispered in his ear.

No. As it *buzzed* in his ear.

"I have another rhyme for you, shadow of Iphigenia, ditch dog of a dead-end cause. Listen close:

The whole high hill stank
Dog soldiers in the sun
They say that flowers will grow there
But spring will never come

And lo, I met her majesty
There on the charnel rise
She said that she will never die
That empress of the flies."

"Hughes?" Frank, approaching him, face pinched with concern. "You okay?"

"I have a long list of your friends, Hughes," the voice told him. "I got their names from that mutant Jo's head. I know their names and I know their faces, just like I know about your baby. Enlighten me to something. Does the idea of glass not freak you out? The fact that you might not be drinking from a regular coke bottle, or mixing your bakery ingredients in a regular bowl, or rolling up a regular car window? So much glass is recycled in this city. If I were you, I'd think, golly! This ordinary glass object might not be so ordinary after all. It might be made from the remains of my infant daughter. Does it scare you? Give you the heebie-jeebies? If it were me, I'd go nuts. Carted up to live with the loonies, hopping mad in the Toadhouse."

Frank and Thud were talking, their cadence urgent.

Hughes couldn't hear them.

His attention was completely fixed on the buzz, small but definite, in his ear.

"You keep curious company. A Ringmaster Woman and a Painted Girl."

Krys, he thought, numb with horror. *Krys and her myrmidons.*

"That human pustule I chewed on, Jo, she's taken care of. Who else? Who else? There's Daddy Gormon, yeah. The butler, Falstaff. Rosemund Valkyrie. Penelope Auspice. Isaac Lawless. Lots of Scarlet Citadel, my my. Oh and there's your hobnail whore, Catherine Jubilee. So many juicy names."

"This is between you and me," said Hughes.

Confusion on Thud and Frank's faces. Knickerbocker was there, and his Whiskers and Mr. Squeakers gazing up at him pinkly, perplexed.

"Sorry. It's too late. I told you, Hughes. What did I tell you? When you fuck with me..."

"You're fucking with the best."

A wheedling, keening drone filled his senses. His burst of humor was a distant memory, something that had happened to another man. He was a statue carved of cold fear and the flies were laughing at him.

"Now you're getting it," said Jane. "Father Tinfrost has his list and I have mine. I guess that's all, dear friend. Track me down and kill me again. Do it a hundred times. I'll keep coming back. How do you propose to slay a shadow when that which casts it remains alive and well? Solve that one, hotshot. And Hughes?" He heard the grin in her tone, slimy as a batch of slugs. "Do something for me, okay? Watch out for glass. I'd hate for you to get swallowed up by grief and forget about the good times, the pregnant pause before the... what would you call it? The shattered silence? Oh mm-mmmmm. You really are the tastiest bon-bon in the box. And one more thing: *Fuck you.* Your father takes it up the ass, your mother pimps her pussy out for bus fare, and I've beaten you without trying YOU LIMP DICKED LOSER! Go lick scraps from a garbage bag like the castrated mutt you are. There's my pollen." The buzz faded and faded. Around him the room seemed darker, the purple light transformed. To Gormon Hughes, it was the cover of a horror novel blown up into reality.

"There's my honeycomb," Jane whispered.

Then she was gone. Hughes felt hollow all the way through.

"What's the matter with him?" Thud's voice, suddenly clear.

Frank's eyes searched Hughes' face. There was so much concern in them that when they turned grim, their headlight-beam brightness seemed to darken with an absolute totality. "She isn't dead. Jane got away."

Thud's face fell. "How?" The man sounded devastated.

"We're gonna find out. Hughes, look at me. *Look at me.* We *will* get her."

"No Frank," he said gently. "We won't." And he covered his eyes with his hand.

Act Eight
Something Bloodless

Chapter Twenty-Three

It was Tuesday evening in Corinth City, and the blizzard was trying its hand at both architecture and amateur construction. Snowflake laborers built up the cottages, the schools, the apartments, the hospitals doctored and patiented with frost, churches steepled in crunchy ivory, powdery neighborhood parks, gymnasiums of graupel, songhalls of sleet, and when the blizzard was finished with all of that, it took up rustic pursuits and transmogrified the streetlamps into a glimmering forest whose leaves you'd best not hold your hand to for any length of time, lest you have the devil of a time getting it back. From clinical, officious Ptolema District to pretty Cleomenes to the unpolished... well, not a diamond... the unpolished amblygonite called Leonidas, the city was turned into ice.

Unfortunately, it was not a case of architecture and construction all around. Quite the contrary. That evening, at about six o'clock or thereabouts, there was actually a kind of quiet demolition happening in select places. It was not a concerted effort. No one site of bulldozing or clearance happened in communication with the others. In some cases, you would be hard pressed to see the demolition at work—you and the perpetrators, both! But it was at work. Yes, indeed.

In her tall tower home, happily apart from the comings and goings of the city, in quite the same way a hedgehog who has been convinced that it is a bird is happy to stay up in the nest while the rest of the hedgehogs shuffle about their business and worry about their zoologically discommoded friend overhead, Estelle Corlum finished her book. With the last sentence held firmly in her mind, she turned the book and set it on the bed where it resembled a very badly pitched tent, and she looked out the window behind the headboard of the bed, not really seeing what was going on out there (chilly things), instead seeing the world she'd only now finished visiting. It was an odd book. There'd been a chase scene at the beginning and some dastardly villains, one of whom died at the end while the other turned over to the good side. Lots of mysteries were presented, though only a few satisfactory answers. She hoped the sequel cleared those up. Bloody authors. Teases, the lot of them.

There had been a few words that had given her pause though, haunting or suggestive or grotesque words that had wakened the mannerly yet monstrous imagination of her girlhood from the deep sleep of Getting Older. She'd particularly enjoyed, "carbuncular." That sort of word got you thinking about inflamed flesh, sloughing skin, necrosis—gosh, but that was the stuff!

She seemed to grow a little taller, broader, *bolder* somehow... then she shrank. A sigh puffed out of her. "Goodbye then," she said. Then image by image, line of dialogue by line of dialogue, word by sound by smell by word, she made her way back to her towertop home, breaking the fantasy apart as she went.

A single floor below (really it could have been miles and miles below, for all it mattered to Estelle), Wendy Dragontail and Falstaff were breaking down a problem that was mountainous in size down to small, much more manageable chunks.

"Where to begin, Falstaff?"

"The roads, my Lady."

"Yes, the roads. Drivers have twice the vitriol of public transport users, and ten times the destructive power, since they are the ones behind the wheel."

"Quite so, my Lady."

Wendy closed the notebook she'd been working in, opened a desk drawer absently, removed a thin envelope marked *E*, and set it next to a Happy Tinfrost card she'd received from the High King of Daethumberland, who had probably gotten someone to write it for him, the evidence being that all the words were spelled correctly.

Not missing a beat (possibly a teensy one, she had a lot on her mind), she said, "Right. If we cannot close the roads without causing a holiday-season riot, which is quite impossible, then we must attend to their upkeep. The major points of ingress and egress to and from the city are... have you a map?"

Any other butler might have rushed to find an atlas, but not Falstaff. "Here is one I prepared earlier."

"You'd have to get up very early to get the better of you, Falstaff."

The butler smiled a neat and tidy smile. "You would need to never go to sleep, my Lady."

Wendy spread the map. "The largest minority group in the city is Hortesian, followed by Mysicordelian, then Champleurs. Some thirty-seven thousand, twenty-two thousand, and eighteen thousand respectively."

"Seventy-seven in total."

"Rather unluckily these are also fellow citizens on the continental highway, that great gray artery, let me see, let me..." Before Falstaff's admiring eye, Wendy circled the key routes with a scarlet pen. She hesitated over one, put a square around it, and capped the pen. "Have the dig crews focus their efforts on these," she indicated the circles. "Rouse the road engineers, putting them on triple pay. Call it The Blizzard Blitz Rate. Incentivize professional traffic wardens with a similar scheme. Get them out to these cleared areas, have them lash up some of those signs. The twinkly ones. Our chief concern after that is potential flurries, patchy ice, and the coordinated flow of vehicles. Designate one lane per route for emergencies. There'll be crashes, and ambulances still need to get to and from hospitals. The flu and its kindred are as determined to enjoy themselves at Tinfrost as those they afflict."

"What is this, my Lady?" Falstaff tapped a flawlessly manicured finger on the squared zone. "No regional markings, as far as I can see."

"That, dear man, is where the motorway runs alongside the Ferryman's Hat."

"Ah." The Ferryman's Hat was a large slopey landmass, popular for climbing, and possibly skiing, at this time of year. "I understand. It's an avalanche hazard."

"And it's the only way for those who want to go home to Champleurs for Tinfrost to get there. Likewise for our people returning to Corinthia."

"We can have some sort of emergency scaffolding built."

"Difficult in the blizzard." Wendy drew a breath, let it go, her frown not peevish but actually an indication she was, if not enjoying herself, then at the very least in her element. Blizzards were bastards, but you knew where you stood with them, i.e. up to your navel in snow. "Steffan Cerulean would have been ideal."

"Or Kpelle Cinder."

"Mm." *Or Hughes*, she thought. If anyone could convince a landslide to reconsider its direction in life, it was him. "Elena Longfellow might do. *Montcrieff! Can you hear me?*"

Nothing.

Wendy's frown changed. "Where's Montcrieff?"

"Oh, he left earlier today."

"Left? Left where?"

"Family, I think, Your grace. Tinfrost obligations and so forth."

"Montcrieff has family? Why has he never visited them before?"

"Apparently some broken bridges have been, ahm, mended, my Lady."

"Irritating, but not disastrous. Thankfully you are ever dependable, Falstaff."

Falstaff managed to suppress a smug smile. He opted for a polite bow to further disguise it. Meanwhile Wendy was back amidst the issue. "Contact Elena. Nevermind, I'll meet with her. I'll have to speak with our publicity department about an emergency communication campaign anyway."

"On to trains, then?" said Falstaff, falling into step behind Wendy as she marshaled out of her office.

"Trains," Wendy agreed. "Then electricity pylon repairs. We are done with roads?"

The butler nodded. "The roads are covered, my Lady."

"Not if I have anything to say about it, Falstaff."

And far away from the tower called Redspire, in his house at 13 Lombardel Road, Hoshrum Thud was on the jar. Now, when people say "on the jar" they can mean "having a few harmless pints" or they can mean "getting absolutely gazzoongad on peach schnapps and embalming fluid." It's a very expansive phrase, is "on the jar." Thud was actually occupied by the third, least known interpretation, which involves sitting alone with a beer that has gone too warm too quickly, staring off into the middle distance, and occasionally muttering, "To hell with it anyway," and other disconsolate grumblings of that sort.

Hettie poked her head in. "Are you still in a mood, Hoshrum?"

Thud grunted something vaguely hostile.

"I shall take that as a yes."

She walked over to the chair he was fermenting in.

"Have I given you sufficient time to recognize that even though you are currently suspended, you are an excellent policeman, and that the affairs of the Scarlet Citadel were always going to frustrate you on some level, minimal or drastic, because their bread and butter is the magical and yours is not?"

A petulant grunt hinted at the fact that while this particular point had indeed had sufficient time to sink in, its recipient was not entirely pleased about it.

"Hughes will think of something. Or that nice Mr. Gallant."

A harsh grunt pointed out that leaving aside his professional pride, handing over the reins of an ongoing investigation had never been Thud's style. He liked to see things through. The fact that Jane had thwarted them, and that there seemed no recourse, no handhold to grip now that the team had slipped, was throwing up useless sparks from the stony grindstone of his soul.

"I see."

A glum grunt said that he saw too. He saw only too well.

"And isn't that beer a bit warm by now?"

A reluctant grunt admitted it was pretty warm, yeah.

Hettie stood there, her hands caked in clay, knuckles planted on her hips, her hair standing out in paint-stiff multicolored stalks. She reached a decision.

Thud looked up sharply as she enfolded his hand in hers. Grudgingly he allowed himself to be drawn out of the chair (where the beer sat wedged by the cushion and abandoned), up a few flights of stairs, and into Hettie's art studio.

Thud's mouth grew thin under his whiskers. Generally speaking he was not encouraged to hang around up here. His wife always made him welcome, but there was an edge to that warmth that he only felt blunt and diminish once his boots plodded down the steps, as if the space were exhaling. *Now that he's gone,* the studio seemed to preen, *Hettie is free to create.* So he was even more hesitant than before... until he realized that the edgy sensation wasn't there to usher him out. There was only the atmosphere of welcome. Soft and warm. He glanced at his wife. She was mostly turned away from him, her fingers laced in his own, her stride strong and determined. What was she planning? Thud had no clue whatsoever.

Hettie led him through sculptures, frescoes, tapestries, paintings, experimental engines that curled sweetly and swelled disturbingly—all of these things ongoing, incomplete, unsealed by his wife's approval. He spied a mock-up of some street art commissioned by anti-monarchy anarchists. They wanted the statue of Corinthia's last king, The Tyrant, toppled from its plinth. How these geometric graphics designed by his wife would achieve this aim of public fixture destruction was not entirely clear. Not that Thud disagreed with the anarchists in principle. He thought the statue was bloody ridiculous. The problem with anti-monarchy anarchists was that they didn't enact much social change, although they did smoke lots of cigarettes (so that was okay).

His reverie broke as Hettie stopped. She turned and smiled at him expectantly. Thud peered at the piece. Several figures were there, posed in a tableau.

"Clay," he said. "I take it this is your current fascination."

"It is."

"Where'd you get the clay?"

"Pottery shop."

He gave her his best Nettled Husband expression. "Where did you bake it, love?"

"In the clay oven." She hooked a thumb back toward the main thoroughfare of the studio. "Back there."

"I didn't know we had one."

"And right under his nose too, your honor. Honestly, and they say he's the finest copper in Corinth."

Thud offered the grunt this sly comment deserved. But it was not nearly as gruff as the ones he'd huffed out in the chair with the warm beer in his hand, and as he eyed the clay figures narrowly, Hettie smiled a secret smile.

"This one," he said, standing in front of one. "Looks familiar."

"I should hope so. You've been so closely involved."

It was Frank Gallant.

"You've really captured him."

"You know, I rather think I haven't actually." Hettie went on tiptoe next to him. She made clawing gestures, not vicious but thoughtful, round Frank's face. "Something in the nose, maybe. Or the eyes, those outrageous and inexplicable yellow eyes. What makes them like that? What makes him, him? Elusive. You know all art is the same, Hoshrum. All fiction, and that means lies. Only good fiction is the truth contained within the lie. Anyway, yes. I don't think I've captured him in the slightest. They have."

Thud stood back. Now Hettie put it like that, it did seem as though the other figures were... What?

He wasn't sure. Like they were... holding him from a distance. Not an embrace. *Holding him in a cell.* He blinked twice, in rapid succession. Where had that come from? The thought had arrived in his head with the bizarre clarity of a lightbulb switching on. Thud examined the tableau with his streetbeater eye. Almost instantly he was uncomfortable. There was something off about the figures around Frank. About their shapes. On one hand they looked like innocent partygoers, yet on the other there was a definite sinister quality. Their faces were too long, he supposed. And while Frank's eyes were glad and charming, even rendered in clay, theirs were simply empty. And there was that feeling. He couldn't shake it. That feeling like they were holding him in a cell. Hettie hadn't noticed his discomfort.

"Hettie?"

"Yes Hoshrum?"

"This um... arrangement. Where did you get the idea for it?"

"You know, it's the funniest thing. I dreamed it."

"Did you now?" Thud stroked his mustaches. "Did you indeed?"

"Anyway." Hettie clapped her hands, startling her husband. "Shall we?"

"Shall we what, dear?"

"Oh don't be silly. You know why we're here." She was rolling up her sleeves. "You want first go, or will I?"

"Hettie, I have no idea what you're talking about."

"Corinth's finest. Well, you've had three-quarters of a lager, so I'll forgive you."

"Hettie."

"It's clay, Hoshrum!" She waggled her eyebrows. "Clay!"

And suddenly he had it.

A slow, unwilling grin spread across his face.

"Clay!" He slapped his brow. "God, how could I be so dense?"

"The penny drops for the copper. Good man. After you?"

Thud lumbered behind one of the figures, jostling it hard with his shoulder. It fell. The shatter of the clay was *immensely* satisfying. Hettie's turn. She used her hip. Elbows flew. Smash-clatter-crash! It felt good, Thud knew, seeing this weird tableau decimated. What felt better was that his wife remembered their wedding night with such intensity that she could recreate it. They had gotten married very young, much to both of their families' collective chagrin. That night on the jar, they'd gotten gazoongad on peach schnapps (there was no embalming fluid to hand) and headed for an exhibition hosted by a rival of Hettie's. The rival was incredibly vicious and had pull with the critics, so much so that he'd tried to ruin Hettie's career as an artist before it began. He was also partial to clay sculpture. The exhibition was of course closed. The Thuds went in anyway, giddy and itching for trouble. The policeman who arrived later might have heard the racket the drunken newlyweds were causing on his patrol route, or maybe someone called him. Either way, they were booked by the streetbeaters on their wedding night. Instead of getting pissy, the grizzled old copper had let them off with a warning. He'd been so nice about it, Hoshrum Thud elected to make a career change. He'd quit his job stacking storage crates and applied for his badge the next day. Plus the old copper had boasted a very respectable set of whiskers...

He pushed over the statue of Frank, hoping the scene was just moon whispers Hettie had rustled up during dreams. He felt light. That special lightness that comes after being so heavy you don't even realize.

"Thank you, Hettie."

She pressed close to him, went up on tiptoe, and kissed him. "Welcome."

And far away in the abandoned leisure center, unaware that a sculpture made in his likeness was being smashed to pieces, Frank Gallant walked with his hands in his pockets. He was walking through the bowling alley, his gaze falling onto things and off of them with the same level of interest. The narrow lanes, the return system, the digital scoreboards, the pins, the balls with their two finger holes and one for the thumb, and the serried rows of extra-grip shoes behind the counter. Dust had laid claim to all of it. Idly he wondered if any of it still worked. Shafts of diffuse light came down into the alley from the high windows. Dust had even conquered these, dancing a microbe dance that would probably go on forever, unless someone ordered a wrecking crew for this husk of a building. That was another thing, why hadn't they? Who owned the remains of the leisure center? Why after ten years of total abandonment had nothing been done?

Responsibility seemed the word of the day. Loops of it (strings upon strings) connecting people and perhaps not connecting those it ought to have.

Frank looked up at the sign of movement. From the lightless black hollows of the pin-replacement system came Mr. Glint. He was chewing. The reason behind his chewing was this: when this was his lair, Mr. Glint had become something of a plague for the creatures who inhabited the leisure center, fat, bloated, damp things that matched their environment and who skittered and crept about it willy-nilly before Mr. Glint arrived with his sunken eyes, his mouth like a box of cemetery stones, and his appetite, which was ravenous. Now, a decade had passed without disturbance, and the creatures had flourished, repopulating the drippy warrens and moldy nooks and crannies. They had gotten comfortable. A fatal error. Out of the blizzard Mr. Glint had arrived. He was displeased he had been injured. It meant he couldn't eat Spring-Heeled Jane, and given her treatment of his friend Frank and her general insectile nature, he would very much like to have done just that, chomping and gargling her and washing bits of her down with her own blood. So the comfortable creatures of the leisure center had not been prepared when long fingered hands had emerged into their nooks and crannies, in other words when the plague had come back for seconds.

"How's the legs, Mr. Glint?" said Frank.

Glint swallowed the unspeakable thing he was munching. "Very tasty, Mr. Gallant."

"I meant yours."

Mr. Glint gave his regenerated legs some consideration. "Peaches and cream."

"Cool."

The tall, gaunt man stalked away, no doubt hungry for thirds. Frank walked on. On an impulse he checked behind the clerk counter. The remains of a smashed phone were there, draped in cobweb. Something tiny-footed went over his foot. Frank sat on the counter, his face unbothered and unaware that he was cribbing the stance of Mr. Glint's former partner. The bowling alley was on full display. Utter desolation. A threadbare stocking stuffed for Tinfrost with soft mushy fungus and squishy brown mold.

He had meant the things he'd told Hughes earlier that week. He loved his freedom, a puppet with no strings except his own. But the freedom to do what you wanted meant the unraveling of different choices, any of which a guy might take, and that meant delighting in the good times and feeling culpable and miserable in the bad.

During his eventful travels with Glint, there had been times he'd forgotten Corinth City, his first taste of life (no, LIFE with all the gorgeous trimmings), but if he tried with all his concentration and devotion he could not forget Gormon Hughes and Catherine Jubilee. His desire to help them—the flat, uncomplicated sense of responsibility—was not going anywhere. Shit, if those two lived any closer to his heart, he'd have to start charging them rent.

A hairy, many-eyed thing flopped down in front of him. Mr. Glint descended after it, climbing through a crumbly bit of ceiling and dropping down, unearthly quiet but for the muffled *thump* of his shoes on the floor.

"Tell me something," said Frank as Glint scooped up the twitching abomination, *crrrracked* wide his jaw, and slid the thing inside. "How does it feel, being back here after so long?"

"Peaches and cream, Mr. Gallant."

"Not a little sad?"

Glint shrugged. "In a slanting wise, maybe she and I will meet again."

By "she" he meant Miss Gleam. Frank had never met a more evil woman, and he'd met his mothers. But Glint had held her in the same regard Frank held Hughes and Cate in, plus that line "in a slanting wise" was a callout to some advice he himself had given Mr. Glint at the outset of their partnership. Frank could only crack a little himself—mind you it was only a small smile rather than his whole jaw as Mr. Glint so often did.

"You've got peaches and cream on the brain," he commented.

"Had peaches and cream pie with Miss Gleam. The seller didn't have ankle."

"Apple?"

"Ankle."

"Gotchya. How inconsiderate of him."

"That's what I thought." Mr. Glint adjusted his hat. It was a hat from the Jaenqui-Across-The-River marketplace in Derbisdale, popularly known as a Derby Hat, and it suited him the way a dark raven suits a mantelpiece skull. "You all right, Mr. Gallant?"

As a matter of fact I am not. I am flummoxed and bamboozled. I am at a loss that makes my former state of orientation look positively geographic. I am, not to put too fine a point on it, old buddy, feeling culpable and miserable. Ever since Jane escaped I've been untangling my strings, trying to think of a way to beat her. No dice. She's beyond me. That cuts me deep. And you want the worst of it? I promised Hughes I'd try. I said I'd try and I'm bum-fresh out of ideas and that Spring-Heeled creep is going to go on yanking people around by their wiring.

But what good did spouting such bile do? No good, that's what.

So Frank smiled, not without melancholy, and he said, "Screeches and screams, Mr. Glint. Let's go check in on Desdemona, make sure that boyfriend of hers is minding his Ps and Qs."

Desdemona Cauldronpot was going to contact him the moment she sensed Jane's presence manifesting in the city. There was no way to isolate her before that, but if she took over another person, the team would know. A decent alarm system, as these things went, but still Frank was dispirited.

Even if we find her, it won't amount to shit.

He followed Mr. Glint out of the leisure center, his fabulous posture stooped, his aurora hair seeming to blend in with the blizzard, cold and gray and bloodless and hopeless.

And back in Redspire, in the gardens where wintry pansies and cyclamen and Tinfrost roses bloomed, the leaves of the bushes and trees were a whitish blue in the nighttime garden ambience, and those flowers, pink and red, stood out very nicely. Hughes was there and he certainly thought as much.

He looked somewhat the worse for wear, standing there under a large rose hedge (the garden tenders could afford to plant real trees in Redspire, which was quite rare, although not unheard of in Corinth City). His eyes were pouched in crow's feet, his teeth unbrushed, his breath smelly, his hair mussed. His beard, unchopped since Cate's departure to Eurydice, was growing scraggly. The moth-gnawed coat he wore seemed to have absorbed into his being—he was moth-gnawed all over.

Hector, son of Priam, took all of this in within a moment.

His voice, unchanged from his life as a man to his life as a ghost, and very resemblant of a slice of cinnamon-seasoned carrot cake enjoyed on a drizzly autumn day, in other words a spectacular register on the ear, surprised Hughes.

"Pariahs have lonely refuge in times of strife. The popular have friends they can call on. Why act like the former when it is not the case?"

"Company is dandy but lonesome is winsome."

A line formed in Hector's brow.

"Something Mr. Glint said," Hughes told the swordmaster. "Apparently a famous poet said it first."

"Is the expression not, 'candy is dandy but liquor is quicker'?"

Such a goofy phrase coming from severe Hector. It almost wrung a grin from Hughes. Almost, but not quite. "How's your father?"

"In and out. That vulture, dementia, has its talons in him. It has pecked his mind to ribbons. I've heard about it. Thought I understood it. But when your own father looks into your eyes without recognition, it pulls a cord inside you that brings on total despair." As he spoke Hector drew his sword and snipped a Tinfrost rose, its petals lush and carmine. "Father woke three hours ago. He gawped around, vague but reasonably in control, until he saw Cassandra. He recoiled from her at once. Pleaded with her not to kill his children."

"Who did he think she was?"

"General Ulyssé. Paris and Creusa and I stood like waxworks. We couldn't believe it. It fell to Cassandra to do what we could not. She smiled at our father, and she told him that her forces had surrendered and all his children were alive, and his wife was asking for him with a wreath of victory in one hand and the other meant for his cheek, the back of his neck, his own hand. Mother has been dead for years. Father calls for her often, just the same. His children were alive and close by, Cassandra assured him. He would hear their laughter in a minute. Father looked mistrustful, but as Cassandra persisted we could see him begin to believe it might be true. By the time he lapsed back into sleep he wore the same smile she did. A good smile, warm and happy. He murmured something the others did not catch, but I did." As Hector handed Hughes the rose, a thorn sliced his finger. Ectoplasm welled up from the wound, a milky bead. Hector brought it to his mouth, paused, and before sucking the cut clean he relayed the words Priam had spoken before he slept. "Bring me my children. Bring them to me so I might hold them."

Silence in the garden.

Hughes said, "I'm so sorry. Are you okay?"

"Better now." Hector eyed the cut, saw it was fine, and folded his arms pensively across his spectral chest. "Cassandra held her grief inside until we left Father's room. Then she fell to pieces. I have never seen her so distraught."

Hughes didn't know what to say. The image of Cassandra weeping didn't simply stun him. It thunderstruck him. Made him mute. For something to do he rooted in his pockets, found a pin, and pinned the Tinfrost rose to his coat. Coupled with his peony scarf he was beginning to look like an extremely morose bouquet.

"Why linger here?"

"Here?"

"This spot," said Hector. "There's handsomer places in the gardens. Here there's only this scrub of hedge. Seems an odd place to be dour and alone. Not winsome in the least."

For a moment Hughes debated keeping the truth from Hector. Only for a moment though. "This is where they spread Walter's remains. Walter Pillion. Do you remember him?"

"Vividly."

"Yeah, colorful bloke."

"Colorful, yes. You could say that."

A delicate pause.

"You could also say he was a complete and utter penis," said Hector.

Laughter erupted from Hughes before his sadness could think to lower the portcullis. It slammed down, too late. "Hector!"

The ghost held up his hands in a way that said, *The thrust was there, I took it. What else can a swordmaster do?*

They sobered. Hughes could feel the stormy atmosphere permeating him mellow out. Only a little, but still, right now a little felt like a lot. With some preamble he began to tell Hector about the Spring-Heeled Jane case, some background details, most of the developments. He told him how the day had started so promising, and how catastrophically it had panned out in the end. Lastly, he told Hector his suspicions and the things he was increasingly sure of. Convictions sealed up as the blizzard encased the city. The buzz of Jane's voice was like a counterpart to Hector's lovely one. *I'll kill you*, she'd chuckled in spite of her pain. *I'll fucking kill you.* Hughes had expressed the same sentiment, hell, used those exact same words cupped in the same poetic precursor. The knife, the sword, her very appearance—they were clues that pointed to a single conclusion. He and Jane were the same. That was one of the definites, irrefutable. *Of the same stuff.* He could see her despicable maggoty smile in his head. A white smile under black eyes. *You and me, honey. We're the big time. Walking shadows. You, Iphigenia's. Me, Eurydice's.*

Hector mulled these over with care.

While he did, Hughes bustled on. "And here's the thing: I don't think it's gobbledygook. I think Jane knew that, for whatever reason, talking about shadows would ring true for me. A lie I could brush off. But by giving me the smallest sliver of a large important truth, she's torturing me psychologically."

"I agree," said Hector. "Repeat those words she spoke when you slew her physical form. That question about shadow."

"*How do you propose to slay a shadow when that which casts it remains alive and well?*"

"Your memory is exceptional. Yes. Yes, to me that suggests Jane is connected in a powerful way to Eurydice. Eclipses happen when the moon blots out the sun, casting its lunar shadow across the face of our planet. Perhaps Jane is like that," mused Hector, and his gaze met his pupils. "Perhaps you are."

"What's the source of light, then?"

"Who knows. And what does it mean for you, Hughes, if you and Jane really are shadows cast by strange worlds?"

"Who knows," Hughes echoed. He thought it best to confide a touch more on the subject. "Frank Gallant has promised to take me to a place where I can find out where my power comes from. The only problem is that it'll take hours, maybe days. Jane isn't going anywhere—how can I?"

"You can't."

"Exactly. You asked me why I've lingered here. I told you this was Walter's gravesite, the place his mulchy remains were buried to feed the roses. But that's no answer." He plucked a petal from the rose pinned to his coat. It was silky soft between his fingers. "After Jane lauded her invulnerability over us, I became a kind of automaton. We have an alarm system in the form of Desdemona Cauldronpot, thank God, but we're no good to Jane's victims if she inhabits them and causes more carnage before we arrive. Her threats against those close to me constitutes an emergency. I made telephone calls on the way to my dad's place, the *Scriptorium and Flavored Tea Emporium*. He's under guard now, three of them in case Jane infests one. Warnings have been sent out, protection hired. It's mad," he said, his mouth lopsided in an expression too bitter to be purely nostalgic. "Ten years ago I'd have been concocting a hair-brained scheme to keep everyone safe. Now I throw money and resources around and the emergency contracts. A Man of the Citadel, indeed, and speaking of shadows, Redspire is one influential tower. Its shadow is long." He plucked the petal. "You have to understand I was like a machine, a machine running on dread instead of electrical energy. After the immediate safeguards were in place and no alarm had been sounded, that ebbed away. I felt defeated and used up somehow. Drained. Jane is queen of flies, but she's a mosquito too. Dealing with her has left me feeling as empty as a well with no bottom. I tried to make myself better, and for whatever reason I thought of you and Tommy Fahrenheit. His joy when the alcoholism snapped like a rotten branch inside him, and the way you called me friend. I've always wanted that. To be your friend." His fingers let the petal go. It seesawed back and forth, yet inevitably downward, a tiny red thing submitting to a force it could not hope to overcome. Hughes' brow clouded. "Then I thought of Walter Pillion. Mean, brooding Walter, who was never anything but a dick to me. I found my way here, and you know what I've been thinking about, Hector? Not Iphigenia. Not Eurydice. Not Jane or the case or anything to do with it. I've been thinking about bloody Walter bloody Pillion. Whether or not I could have saved him."

"If you'd done for him what you did for Tommy, you mean." Hector shook his head. "You mustn't think that way."

"Why not? It bears up to scrutiny. Cate has always encouraged me to be cautious with my Performance. And she's right. I can change people. In subtle ways, sure, but drastically as well. I can provoke sobriety. Instill madness. Boost confidence. Traumatize. A power like that... It shouldn't be anything other than a last resort. If I thought about it differently, Jane and I wouldn't just be *of the same stuff*. We'd be identical. Vile." He scrunched his nose a little on that last word, a small spasm that spoke to the dread still lurking inside him.

"And yet you can't help but fixate on that tantalizing question that occurs to all who wield a bit of power," said Hector sagely. "*What if...*"

Hughes nodded. "I could staunch the invisible wounds people carry inside themselves. I could heal, bring succor, soothe, and satiate. The personality is a stage in uproar. Sometimes it could use a bit of management. A flair for direction... Ahh." He made a choleric sound and scratched an itch at the nape of his neck, his face crimping in an expression of such damp anger it might soon attract mildew. "I've just been in my head, is all. I had an argument with Lady Dragontail about why people outside the Citadel don't have magic items."

"I think they should, given the influx of magical dangers."

"Right? And would she hear about it?" Hughes' anger grew even wetter, bogged down in that particular memory. "Evidently the 'ordinary' aren't of reliable enough stock. The dragon ought to watch in case she blows up, she's so full of her own hot air."

Hector reached over and gave his shoulder a squeeze. "You've suffered a setback. You've come here to punish yourself."

"No..."

"Yes, you've come here to punish yourself. Don't look so agape. It's quite understandable. All this navel gazing is needling you, and the more you agonize over duty and morality, right and wrong, and the endless mysteries, the deeper the needles dig. One problem at a time. Think of your troubles like swordplay. Big overarching issues—"

"And composite sub-issues."

Hector smiled and Hughes' mood improved at once. "That's right. Leave all these feelings aside. Channel the role you've taken up with seriousness. Be a conduit for the spirit of the perfect investigator."

"Well, there's our stumbling block." Hughes chuckled without mirth. "Jane is immortal. She survived an onslaught that would have taken down a God, if such a person were flesh and blood, and which Jane is certainly not."

"Which leaves..."

"What do you mean, *which leaves?* It doesn't leave anything. I could attempt a Performance, use Chimera on her, but there's only a half-and-half chance that it might anchor in her personality. Besides, if she's able to withstand death, then I'm sure she can withstand change. What do you suggest? That we destroy Eurydice? If Eurydice casts Jane as a shadow, then we've got to kill a world in order to beat her?" Dripping with fresh fuel, his anger splashed and sizzled. "What are you looking at me like that for? Honestly, you expect too much of me, Hector. You really... Will you stop staring at me with that stern, heroic, 'I know you can do this, so shut up and think your way toward a solution' frown—it's not going to work. We can't win with arms, and she can slip right through armor. There's no magical barrier we can employ or bug repellent, not unless the elderly Jolene had a moment of inspiration and left a plan for it before Jane did her in. And we absolutely can't imprison..."

He stopped.

Hector was not usually one to raise an eyebrow. That sort of roguish gesture was more at home with his younger brother, Paris. Sometimes, however, these things cannot be avoided in good conscience. He raised an eyebrow. "Yes?" he prompted.

"The Perfect Prison! It builds a cage especially fitted for its captive!"

"Even Jane?"

"Even her!" Hughes' excitement fizzled into his limbs. When the idea had come to him he'd begun pacing, his fingers clutching into exhilarated fists, his spine bowing as if the (EUREKA!) moment had made him smaller of body and wider of mind. Suddenly all of this goodness crumbled. "Oh, but Wendy will never go for it."

"Why not?" said Hector. "Have you spoken to her?"

Hughes would rather have spoken to one of the dragons of old about the benefits of treasure hoard taxation, but his mentor's voice carried an excellent point. What would be the harm? All other options were exhausted. It was Perfect Prison or bust, and Jane would win.

"I will," he said. "Speak to her, that is."

"Good. I'll walk you to the lift." They left the spot where a bastard of a man had grown into a rather beautiful hedge, their gaits brisk and very similar, as if they were brothers. Hughes would have liked that. He was an only child, and though he loved his dad dearly his memories of his mother were scattered, unreliable, and as misty as the breath of this blizzard they were enduring. He could have done with a brother to share things with, secrets, grievances, stories. The only brothers he'd had were Gwendle Gardener and other fictional heroes from plays. That didn't count because it was one-sided, and you needed dimension for fraternity and friendship. Hector though. Hector would have been a great brother. On the way to the elevator, he told Hughes something that he would never forget. "You know, the other day when I left that bar the Maedar, and Tommy was going to the truck that would take him to Ikahagua and you were going off to work on your case, I sort of got into it like you have now. My head felt like a silverware drawer with too many forks. Clatter and no sense. I walked down the street, and with all the snow everywhere and good things happening here and bad things there, and me in the middle, I thought, 'This isn't just a street, it's my life. It's too short and hectic and it ends in a cold, narrow point. My life,' that's what I thought. Then, an odd thing happened. A band was on the street, and they played some of that new music that's getting very popular these days, and as the lyrics started, mingling with the tune, I still felt cold and I still felt like things were unfair, but I felt good too. That made it bearable."

"What were the lyrics?"

"What do you do?/When you get so deeply moved?/Do you stall up on the wall? Or do you move on through?"

They came to the lift. Hector pushed the button to summon it. They could hear the wind howling outside the tower walls, and behind them the garden was still and dreamlike and winsome and lonely.

"I wish you wouldn't die, Hector."

"I've done it once before. The second time ought to be easier, if God is good. Right now, it's not the dying that matters to me." Hector's face broke into the biggest grin Hughes had ever seen on him. "What matters is that I got to meet you while I lived."

Chapter Twenty-Four

Hughes stepped into Wendy's office in the Lunarlight Wing at a quarter past six. The door was open, so he expected to find the Last Dragon poring over her notebooks, but she wasn't. The office was deserted. Presuming she'd be back in a moment, he moseyed about the place, his hands slipping naturally into his coat pockets. In the hearth with its six stone dragons snapping and snarling, the fire was lit. But then it was always lit. Wendy was a dragon in more than name, and though she lacked for scales and fire, she craved heat, electing to wear sweaters and wooly slippers even during the hottest Corinthian summers. There was a large supply of briquettes. They smelled earthy and wholesome, stacked so neat and high next to the fire. *Winters must be hard for her.* The window through which Wendy admitted Knickerbocker for his daily reports was shut.

Hughes' eye skimmed her desk, taking in the customary notebook pile, the potted eucalyptus (the gift of some delegation from Jaenqui-Across-The-River, probably), the envelope marked with an *E*, not paying any special notice to any of it. His demeanor was relaxed, his conversation with Hector having attuned him to his investigative role more effectively than a bucket of ice water, smelling salts, or the mumbling of an audience behind a curtain. And while Hector had taught him discipline, his sister Cassandra had taught Hughes patience. *Her and the peony.* Some bruised part of him still flinched every time he caught sight of his own scarf and the flowers embroidered there. Compared to his vendetta with peonies, his opposition to Jane was practically normal.

"*Bonsoir*, Your Worship. Oh! Monsieur Hughes."

Hughes turned to see the source of that pristine little voice. Its owner was a man in his late fifties, not as prim and precise as Falstaff (who was like a spotless resumé with ears), but very respectable. With his clean, folded sleeves, a white shirt, apron, and tight-fitting white pants, the man seemed to be doing his best impersonation of a handkerchief.

"*Bonsoir,*" said Hughes, bidding the man a good evening in Champleurs. "*Désolé. Madame est absente pour le moment.*" *I'm sorry. Her Ladyship is out at the moment.*

"*Pas de problème, pas de problème.* You speak Champleurs with a nice accent." The man came forward with a tray. There was a silver dish on the tray, a bottle of wine, a napkin, knife, and fork. "My name is Pierre Barrault. I am the new chef."

"I've heard your dinners are superb. Pleased to meet you, I'm—"

"Oh, there is no need to introduce yourself!" Barrault set the tray down on a side table next to Wendy's sofa, rushed toward Hughes, and shook his hand with a rigor that would have embarrassed even the great wrist-pumper Tookus Argyle Vercingetorix of Demeter. "I am familiar with your work, Monsieur Hughes. Very familiar. You do good work."

"You're very kind."

"*Non!* There is no kindness involved. Only," the man spread his hands, which were nicked with many cuts from years of chopping, "the obvious facts. The Citadel has much wealth, lots and lots of it thanks to you and Cate Jubilee, and that is why I came to the Citadel. Such pretty money this country has! And some of it mine, thanks to my ability to keep the staff full and fat and happy. You are coming to the feast, yes? You must, you absolutely must, for I have so many things for you to enjoy. Perhaps that flat, hard belly of yours will not get fat overnight, but we can see about happiness, eh? Such pretty money, and me, so grateful to have so much of it now. Ah, but Eurydice and its plunder is a very great secret, one I was vouchsafed with under strictest confidence, and I must not discuss the wealth of the Citadel so... *comment tu dis...* flippantly!"

"*Pas de problème,*" said Hughes, bemused. "What's her Ladyship enjoying tonight?"

"Her Ladyship?" The chef followed Hughes' gesture toward the tray. "Ahhh, *non.* You are mistaken, Monsieur. That is for the girl at the top of the tower."

"Estelle?"

"*Oui*, Estelle, that is her name. Comes from Champleurs. The name, *si tu comprends*, not the girl."

Hughes nodded that he understood fine. But he was frowning. "Why have you brought it here instead of up to the tower?" *And why not give it to her guards?* he thought, for like Krys and her myrmidons, Estelle Corlum was—as well as being a pitiable creature—a terribly valuable asset to the Citadel and worthy of a little extra stewardship and protection.

"Oh but it is a heartwarming thing, is it not? That her Ladyship would take the time each night to bring the girl her meal?"

"Every night?"

"*Absolument*! I was informed about it by the last head chef when I came here. Every night I must personally deliver Estelle's meal to the office of her Ladyship. I must be punctual, and well dressed, since Winnifred Dragontail is a fastidious woman, much as though she were a chef and this fine city her kitchen, yes?"

"Yes indeed."

"Should Lady Dragontail be off doing something important, I must leave the tray here on this side table. *Alors*! And it is done. Now, Monsieur, I do not like to be rude, but I must hurry back to my incompetent staff. If I leave them alone, they become arsonists, charring everything until it is black and despicable. Goodbye! You will come to the feast?"

"*Certainement, Monsieur. Avec plaisir. Bonne nuit, et merci pour votre introduction polie.*"

"Nice, very nice! And you as well, Monsieur Hughes! Goodnight!"

The man hurried off, a handkerchief whisked away by the fingers of obligation.

Hughes stood looking after him for a while, only really he was looking at the conversation. He had an appreciable talent for this, recalling the back-and-forths of casual speech between two people, or even small groups, and seeing it like a script in his head. He stood quite still for about ten seconds, then he moved to the desk and picked up the envelope he'd seen when he'd come in. At once something shifted inside with a *sift-sift* noise, the soft sound sand or powder of some kind might make. Hughes held the envelope in front of himself with the fire backlighting it. No good. The paper was thick. He couldn't see inside. With no other avenue to take he pinched the top of the envelope and tore it the smallest bit open. He decanted a few tiny granules of the contents onto the side desk. They were not sand but rather similar to crushed spice, although there was no smell. Hughes brushed the granules off the desk, careful to use his sleeve and not his naked skin. Then he went to the side table and lifted the silver covering. The food looked exquisite. Hughes studied it for a moment, paying special attention to the consistency of the sauce the prawns and lentils were swimming in.

He replaced the dish, his frown now extremely deep as though carved with a hammer and chisel into his brow.

He consulted the improvised script he and Barrault had spoken aloud just now.

Estelle, that is her name.

Oh but it is a heartwarming thing, is it not? That her Ladyship would take the time each night to bring the girl her meal?

Every night?

Absolument!

Hughes checked the envelope once more, moving it a little. *Sift-sift.* A spice without a smell.

Every night?

Absolument!

Estelle, that is her name.

Sift-sift.

His gaze drifted back to the letter printed on the envelope.

E.

***

The eighty-ninth floor of Redspire was like a celibate person's undergarments: only accessible under very specific circumstances.

Firstly, there was the fact that the eighty-ninth could only be reached if you summoned the elevator on the eighty-eighth floor. Then there was the passcode—a recorded failsafe featuring the voice of the Old Dragon, Walsingham Dragontail. Not to mention the guards, who were stationed outside the lift doors in the Lunarlight Wing and who were the sort of silent, unblinking people who make those thick-necked, veiny-forearmed bouncers outside nightclubs look like wimps. And of course, there was the key.

While Wendy Dragontail did not keep that key on her person, it would take a really keen nose to sniff out its location in her office—a doggish nose. A Bloodhound's, maybe.

But at twenty-five-past six, it was not a dog that came ambling toward the guards. Curiously, it was not Gormon Hughes either, who only ten minutes ago had nodded at both of them as he headed for the office that was known locally as The Dragon's Lair.

Considering the identity of this person, their approach might have been a cause for some unrest between the two guards because they had seen her take the elevator down only twenty minutes ago in the company of Falstaff the butler. But nothing could be further from the truth. This person, the approacher, was known to appear in improbable ways all the time, as if she could teleport like Cate Jubilee or become a cloud of ether like the Citadel hero Quorlo Paradise. It was remarked upon by people more intellectually disposed than the guards (who had the general dispositions of sedimentary deposits), that she probably used secret passages to go hither and thither about the tower with impunity and speed, passages designed by her own hand after the extensive renovations to the tower twenty-eight years ago. So the guards were not at all surprised when she approached them carrying the crazy girl's dinner tray.

"Good evening, Cornwell," Wendy Dragontail greeted the first guard. "And to you, Palcibayne. I'm going up."

Palcibayne, the friendlier of the two guards by far, gave what might, conceivably, have been the slightest of nods. He had pushed the elevator button as soon as he'd glimpsed the glint of silver from the tray's dish. Now it opened and Wendy went inside. Stony and bored, the guards heard the doors judder closed behind them. Neither had noticed the rill of sweat trickling down Wendy's cheek. They could not have spelled the word "perceptive" if you promised them pots of money for doing so. Muffled through the doors there was the minutest *click* as a certain unique key was turned in a unique lock. Then came the hollow clunks and mechanical whirrings like a bucket-shaped machine being dropped down a foxhole. Only the lift didn't descend. It rose.

Several floors below, at that precise instant, Lady Winnifred was deep in discussion with the Scarlet Citadel's publicity team.

In the rising dark of the lift, on her way to the eighty-ninth floor, someone who was the spitting image of her Ladyship, and who had also sounded exactly like her to Cornwell and Palcibayne, wiped away that traitorous bead of nervous sweat and gave a broad, manic grin that stretched from ear to ear. The effect of the Perk began to dissolve. Wendy's hair unwrapped itself from its tight packed-snowman-looking bun, shortening and darkening, an infusion of black. Her clothes lost all their snugness, sweater and slippers becoming outdoor shoes and a long, moth-gnawed coat. Her wrinkles smoothed out.

The grin though, and the eyes twinkling with merriment above it, did not change.

They stayed almost exactly as they were, as if a building were being renovated with only a piece of splendid graffiti left untouched.

Master of Disguise

Assume the physical appearance of another person for one minute.

This Perk can only be used **once**.

Hughes let the pleasure of success go and braced himself. A moment later the elevator lurched to a halt, his stomach somersaulting, the knife and fork rattle-tattling on the tray.

The silence that followed was taut. Expectant.

Words were required here, words rooted in the history of the Citadel. *Drearier days,* Wendy had once dubbed that span of time in Hughes' hearing. Here in the dreariest December where tempers and fear made a kiln and burned all good sense and hope and wrathful blizzards scattered the ashes far and wide, the battle chant of his forebears held a quality both uncanny and oddly relevant. He felt dipped in the dark, in the immensity of what he'd done, what he was doing. In his pocket the envelope marked *E* seemed suddenly heavier. Elevator engines filled his nostrils with a smell like car exhaust. So dark, so pitched and tarred with anticipation.

Words were required here.

Steeling his resolve, Hughes let his vocal impression of her Ladyship melt down into the recesses of his throat, and in his own voice, sharp and clear and strong, he felt the words' weight and spoke them aloud.

"Scarlet brother be my shield."

"Be the weapon that I wield," replied the recorded voice of the late Walsingham Dragontail, Wendy's father.

"I will be your courage true."

"I will burn like fire for you."

"If I'm laid eternal low."

"We pray that it shall not be so."

"Yes, but if it comes to be?"

"We will carry on for thee."

Heavy noises emerged from the blanketing blackness in the lift.

The doors opened. Hughes stepped out into the Wing of the Dragonlords. His shoes whispered over the carpet in the hallway and the grand foyer. Ahead, wending up to the balustrade above, was a stairwell. He took it, bootheels clocking on the pine. Like the hearth in Wendy's office the stair was embossed with dragons. Three of them were there rather than a clutch of six, yet instead of fireplace fieldstone these drakes were carved from precious stones. In a bright light they would glimmer, the glow passing through their scales and shining them full of life. But that evening the foyer was dark, the anbaric lamps unlit, the windows admitting only a paltry scrap of cloud-soaked moonlight. To Hughes' eye each dragon he passed was more drab than the last.

In the hub area at the top of the stairs, Hughes made for the ninth of the nine available corridors without hesitation. It had been a long time since his last visit to his towertop friend—longer than he cared to admit—but he remembered the way to her lodgings. The eighty-ninth floor occupied the summit of Redspire. Owing to the attenuated architecture, the floor was, by necessity, much smaller than the others. Still, this was like saying that a knife is the least deadly of an assassin's tools, and yet those small blades were employed constantly by professionals. In other words, despite its comparable smallness, the Wing of the Dragonlords was still the size of a modest housing estate. It was Hughes' understanding that Estelle explored its secrets to this day. A galling prospect, if true, given her self-imposed confinement began almost ten full years ago.

He passed doors and rooms half-remembered. Adrenaline—coursing strongly through him even as far as the stairs—had ebbed to a trickle. Even so, he walked briskly. He didn't know how much time he had.

Less and less, his caution warned.

Okay, said his legs. *So what?*

Should Wendy return to her office and see no tray, then she'll telephone the kitchen. Barrault will tell her there must be some mistake—he dropped the tray up. Where was it then? Je ne sais pas, maybe the last person who saw it may know. Who might that be?

Hughes broke into a jog.

At least both ends of his body were in agreement.

Not that he was in mortal peril, or anything so dramatic. There was nothing criminal afoot. Unless...

Now he mulled it over, there probably didn't have to be a law against assuming the likeness of the most powerful figure in the city. There are no laws against immersing your head into a psychedelic jellyfish tank, either. It's just not advisable, especially if you value your frontal lobe and would rather it not leak out your eyeballs.

It had been a razor-thin thing, getting past the guards before Master of Disguise wore off. Replicating Wendy's voice had been simplicity itself (Cate often good-naturedly got him to roll out his vocal prowess party trick. Hughes would trot out some impressions of figures from popular culture, which impressed and delighted. Then he ratcheted things to the next level by selecting someone in the crowd he'd never spoken to, asking them to say one, maybe two lines of dialogue, and then shocking and amazing everyone by speaking flawlessly in that person's voice. No one was more pleased by this than Cate, who knew Hughes selected those lines of dialogue from a play he'd read as a boy. His theatrical mind had identified the words as being wonderful testament to rhythm and intonation—catalysts for mimicry. To put it curtly, Hughes' brain was more than a match for his cunning tongue and shrewd ear. Only his impulses invite speculation). The appearance shift, however, had given him the jitters. A minute can flow like treacle or sugar, and those sweet seconds between rounding the corner during which the guards could see him and the lift doors closing had filtered by with a pace that terrified him.

And lest he forget there was the envelope in his pocket. He'd pinched that from Wendy's desk, mysterious odorless powder included.

Hughes ran.

***

Estelle Corlum was expecting her usual visitor, so imagine her astonishment and happiness at seeing not Wendy, but Hughes.

Her eyes flew wide open, showing hope (could it be true? Really true?) like window shutters flung wide to admit streaming June sunshine. One hand trembled and covered her mouth, as if not trusting what it might say. The other hand went out, reaching.

Setting the tray aside, Hughes rushed forward and took it. He saw her fingernails had been bitten to the quick. Another of his famous impulses seized him. He planted a kiss on them—those raggedy, gnawed fingernails—and lifted his face so she could see his smile. Hughes' face was wonderfully malleable. His smiles could say a lot when he wished them to. This one said, *Hey you. I don't see your reservation. I don't see your sickly, cottage-cheese complexion. I don't see those gray hairs like streaks of fear made physical on your head. Instead, I see a girl who, when I met her, wore a backless dress, winged eyeliner, and laddered stockings. I see the woman that girl has become. I see my friend, Estelle, and nothing is going to change that.*

Her eyes misted with tears. "Hughes. Oh *Hughes.*"

They hugged tightly.

He held her at arm's length. They looked at one another for a long, fantastic moment, letting their friendship refit and stretch, like old boots, or new toffee.

"Can I sit?" he asked.

"Down here next to me."

He did.

"You look washclothed, Hughes," she told him brusquely.

Washclothed. It was Sheila Kofatch, his old neighbor's phrase. Hughes and his father used it from time to time. It was nice hearing it from Estelle, really nice.

"I'm tired," he admitted. "But listen, I've got to talk to you about something."

"Anything."

"Okay, but... first I want to ask you... Estelle, do you take supplements with your dinner?"

Relief wrapped him in warm vines as she nodded. "I've got iron and calcium deficiencies. Vitamin D too. I can sunbathe just fine up here, but sometimes I forget. Why?"

"Nothing. I was worried."

She gestured to the table he'd set her tray on. "They're in there. I'll take them when you go."

Short lived, relief withered and died. "They're not mixed in?"

Her features pinched, bewildered.

"Your supplements. They're not mixed in with the sauce?"

"No. They're pills. I take them with water after dinner."

What the fuck, he thought sharply. *What in God's name am I doing? So the powder raises a few red flags. They look more like yellow flags now with the benefit of hindsight. Possibly bad. But then, just as likely, nothing to worry about. And another thing: E is a common letter. It's a vowel, you paranoid fuck. E does not have to mean—*

"Hughes," said Estelle. Her tone was all concern. "You're frightening me."

He gave her another charming smile. "Sorry. Away with the birds there. I lied before. I wasn't worried. I've been at my wit's end. And I'm sorry I haven't come sooner. My friend Frank says that sweet clock time sure goes by in a hurry."

"Frank Gallant?"

"You remember him?"

"Ps and Qs," she said, and for a second he thought he saw amusement sparkle in the cold dark of her pupils. "He said I was his warden now, rather than my daddy. I'm glad I'm not. Yes, I remember."

The change in topic had relaxed her. He watched some fresh emotion fill her up. She looked at her library, the door, her feet. These last she twiddled, a gesture that took him right back to their first meeting. "I missed you," she said.

"I missed you too," said Hughes.

In his coat pocket, the envelope was heavier than ever. To cope with new demands, he found that his mind became a volunteer postal worker. It took the envelope and filed its mystery away in a section called LATER. It did not throw the envelope into the rubbish bin. Hughes would not put it back in Wendy's office where he'd found it. This was a friend's situation he was thinking about. Paranoid, okay. Fine. But he would take no chances.

"What was it you wanted to talk about?" Estelle asked him. Her stomach rumbled, startling them both.

Hughes grinned heartily. "Maybe you should eat while I jaw."

"Maybe I should. Join me? We can share the cutlery."

"No thanks."

There was a beat as he thought, *How do I handle this?*

Estelle ate her prawns.

"Estelle, for the past few days, there's been—" He broke off. "No. I'll—I'll go further back. Um. Estelle, for a very long time now—years and years—there have been very big conflicts in this country. There was the Hairy Autumn, which you had an important role in, but before that there was the war with Champleurs, and before that there was local strife as the suffragette movement lost and gained traction, labor strikes, quibbles of industrialization. You get the picture. Now if these conflicts involve periods of pain and suffering on a large scale, then it makes sense that the periods that break from that mold must be, however ephemeral, times of trust and happiness. What if I told you there was a creature—similar in some ways to the Nightjar Coven, those witches who invaded dreams and turned people into animals—yet almost wholly unique?"

Almost, he thought.

(*You and me, honey. We're the big time.*)

"What if I told you this creature was a serial killer? One that feeds on the happiness of these periods between the conflict? A bug that drinks joy and eats hope."

Estelle had put down her fork. He was not sure when exactly, so fierce was his concentration on the subject at hand. He went on.

"Of course I'm not speaking in hypotheticals. This killer looks like a human being, every inch of her infested with insects. Only she's the one who does the infesting. She gets into people and makes them do unspeakable things to their friends, their coworkers. Their families. Jane—the killer's name—doesn't just do it either. This is not an automaton going through the motions. She likes it, Estelle. She gets off on it in a way that... No, it's not a sexual crime. Forgive me, I haven't been sleeping."

Another beat. Estelle's stare seemed to gain dimension, deepening and deepening.

He met her gaze, felt oddly encouraged by what he saw there, and once more continued.

"It's a crime of craving. My dad used to gamble. He's kept me away from it as well as any parent can. His carpings and mutterings on betting culture lend context to Jane. What is it inside a rational thinking mind that can drive it to wager the college fund, the car, the house? What emptiness? Or maybe another rather radical way to think about it is this: Desperation doesn't arise from a lack but rather a surplus. In the gambler's case and Jane's too, it's a craving for some other state of being. Craving exchanged for craving. Fullness for fullness of another kind. But of course she'll never be replete. That's what I'm getting at, Estelle. This killer will never hang up her knife. The bug house will never go out of business. She'll go and come back. A cycle of vileness.

"I've tried to stop her. Frank Gallant and Mr. Glint and a policeman—a dutiful one, imagine that. We've tried with everything we've got and been thwarted. Jane claims to be a shadow of Eurydice, and while that world endures she can't be put down. A lunatic's claim. Maybe I'm crazy too, but I believe her. A discounted immortality, but as far as we're concerned she's quite invulnerable. Which leads me to you... and the Perfect Prison."

Until that moment Estelle Corlum had been so on board with Hughes' topic of choice, she could hoist rigging and call herself a boat. You must remember that when she was a girl she had been fascinated with evisceration and beheadings and other things young women consider to be absolutely brilliant. Now in her early twenties Estelle was an altogether different person. But some things, no matter how compelling the changes around them, stay the same. At the mention of a serial killer who ate joy from the brains of her victims—and who left a trail of corpses in her wake—years of bloodlust unscolded by maturity had fizzled and brightened like a magnesium flare in Estelle's chest. She was waiting for Hughes to tell her the entire story, and most excitingly how he'd bested this apparition named Jane. With any luck there'd been iron maidens in the story, which weren't at all what people thought when they pictured iron maidens (the real version involving iron-clad and profoundly aggressive virgins), ooh and maybe even a defenestration (which is the throwing of your foe out of a convenient window). There was no doubt in her mind that her friend Hughes was excellent at defenestrations.

But then he'd started talking about how Jane wasn't defeated—could not in fact be killed by traditional means—and a quiet dread had put out its hand and smothered the fizzling flare inside her.

He won't, she thought. *He won't say it.*

But he did.

"Which leads me to you... and the Perfect Prison. If Jane can't be killed, let's stop her the way Frank Gallant was stopped by your father. Let's jail her forever."

He must have seen the sheer panic in her face.

"You wouldn't have to be outside for long," he soothed. "Only a few hours."

"Hughes, I couldn't."

"I'll be with you every moment. There won't be an instant where you look for me, afraid I've left you. Not a single second. That's how close and careful I'll be."

"You don't understand."

"Estelle—"

"You should go." She got up, putting her back to him, her arms couching her elbows, hands hugging herself or warding Hughes away, he could not tell which. "I want you to stay and you can. You can *if* you let this drop. Don't ask me to imprison your killer. You know I can't do it, so why ask me? Why ask me?"

"Hold on a minute now," he said, staying seated, his voice calm and coaxing. "Just hold on. There are ways we could keep you completely divorced from the company of other people. We could organize specially outfitted taxis to collect you, partitions keeping you from the driver's prying, blacked-out windows so no one could see into the back seat."

One set of fingers kneaded her bicep, the other set massaging her side. "Thanks for staying relaxed with me. I wish I wasn't so fidgety. I can't help it. But you must understand, there's no precautions you could take that would make me okay with leaving the tower. Maybe..." She took a breath and let it go. Shaky. Scared stiff. "I adore you, Hughes. You and Wendy are so good to me. Let me prove that to you. If you bring Jane here, I'll do it. We'll put her in the Perfect Prison, and I won't have to leave the top floor." She still wasn't looking at him, but he could hear the strained smile in her tone. "Everybody wins."

"Bring her here?" Hughes was not strained. He was appalled. "You're mixed up, and I've contributed to that. When I said Jane infests people, I mean she moves in a kind of psychic leap from mind to mind. She's unpredictable. Maybe if we baited her... No, how could we? Estelle, stop for a minute."

She was moving again, agitation oozing from her every pore, her hands restless, bitten fingernails dancing as her fingers kneaded her skin through her clothes.

"Stop. Stop and listen to me. There's this alarm system. Desdemona Cauldronpot's at the heart of it, and—"

"You'd better go."

"—at her go-ahead, we launch an ambush."

"It can't happen."

Damn it, why wouldn't she look at him? If only she'd do that he was sure his eyes—the hurt combined with the boldness in them—would give him purchase here on the futile slopes of Mount Estelle. "Look at me."

She didn't.

"There's a plan. A good one, guaranteed to work, I'd bet my life on it." *Gambling is a mug's game.* His dad's warnings, no use now, why should they occur to him now? "Please, Estelle. Just hear me out."

"No. Get out."

"Haven't you heard me? Haven't you heard a word I've spoken?"

"All I hear is a man acting like a stupid boy. What you want I can't give."

"Dying." His tone delivered that word like a blade wrapped in velvet. "Adults. Children. Innocent people, *real* people. She's slaughtering them. Here, I'll make it concrete, cold hard facts so you know."

"Hughes—"

"This year's crop started in November. The Dennings' lived on Giacomo Lane. Susabeth and Marberry were the mother and father. The kids—"

"*Don't,*" she cried, turning so he could see the passion glowing pinkly at her cheekbones. "Oh Hughes, *don't—*"

"Okay." He held up both hands, mollifying. "I won't. I can see the idea of getting details scares you, but I won't lie; that in and of itself frightens me. A few short years ago such details— no matter how grisly—would have electrified you, spurred you to action. You're a good person. Kooky and strange and incredible. That's why we're friends. And I'm terrified for you, Estelle. What's happened to my friend? What's that head of yours so stricken by that you—"

"Chemicals," she snapped, and he had to hide his shock at the anger in her voice. "They're imbalanced. Enlargement of the whatchamacallit and a reduction of the rest. What are you, a psychiatrist? Are you here to visit me or diagnose me?"

Hughes' brow creased. "That's too far. Upsetting you is the last thing I want, but we've got to be realisti—"

She surged toward him. Her table and the dinner tray tipped over, the silver dish circling itself, making round silvery sounds on the flagstone. Stunned into reacting, Hughes made to rise but her hands clamped on his shoulders and forced him back down. She wasn't particularly strong, but the storm of her rage lent her a lightning flash quickness and a timbre like thunder. "I knew a girl once who was afraid of spiders. With the best of intentions, her mother took her to Mysicordelia where jungle tarantulas grow as big as kittens. On the advice of specialists in trauma therapy, the mother had the girl covered in spiders. They didn't strip her or have her suffer any indignity. It was all very above-board and ethical. They just put her in a room, alone, after covering her in the things she was frightened of most. That was all. And, you know, the most wonderful thing happened. She was cured! She was so cured that she screamed and screamed until a tarantula put its fat hairy leg on the tip of her tongue, and then she screamed until her throat fled in hysterics. Then it was just the girl and her weepy, red-raw-throated silence and the spiders crawling all over her, and the trauma therapists jotting down notes and nodding to themselves, and one of them patting the girl's mother on the arm. 'It's for her own good.'

"When I first got sick I made myself go outside, Hughes. I was the girl and the mother and the trauma therapists. Only the outside and the company of other people, as you put it, *wrongly by the way*, isn't like spiders. You can brush spiders off if you're frightened, provided no one has tied your hands. You seem mixed up so I'll educate you. Agoraphobia is a fear of the feeling of being encased in a very personal hell. Open spaces are bad, but closed ones, like a cinema or the line at the post office, are actually worse. You can leave at any time, only that's not the opinion of the chemicals. Stay, they say. Be paralyzed and acrawl with invisible spiders. It's for your own good. Agoraphobia also poisons social settings. A smile, kindly offered, cords your whole body in coarse, itchy ropes. Handshakes send senseless messages to your bladder, making it weak and quaky. Friendly conversation cramps your bowel and floods your head with helium and damp, moldy dough. Your brain is soggy bread and your muscles are squirming and your bones are calling out for comfort, and you think, 'I'm a child, oh God help me, my illness has put me back in *Pamplona.*' Only it would be better there. That girl was happy. So you see, as hells go, it's rather adaptable. Inescapable too *because the snare is inside your head.* Do you have the slightest idea what that's... But no, that's a dumb provocation. You wouldn't ask me. Wouldn't *think* to ask me.

"Go," she muttered, releasing her grip and stepping back. "I could say more, but I'll spare you that. Our friendship's on thin ice as it is. Leave me alone. It's—"

"For my own good," said Hughes.

Estelle froze.

And no wonder.

Hughes' voice had been a thing worth freezing over.

A word crept inaudibly through Estelle's trembling lips. She walked over to him, slowly at first, one-step, two-swift-steps, then sprung full of hurry. She went down on her knees, that too-quiet word pulsing up from a band of muscular survival expanding and contracting inside her. In caricature of his former fondness, she took his hand with its unbitten fingernails. She took it and kissed it.

He gawked down at her, confused beyond belief.

More kisses peppering his fingers. More murmurs of the word, barely perceptible.

If he concentrated, he could just barely make it out.

Please, he thought. *She's saying please over and over. Please what? Please what?*

With an acuity that was almost supernatural, she tilted her face up, sniffled, and said, "Please don't use your power on me."

She may as well have punched him in the gut. He had no air. No breath to chase a reply back into his lungs and up to his mouth. He simply stood with the cold moonlight coming through the window and tracing his silhouette, a woodcut of a man too jolted to think.

"I heard a little about it before locking myself up here. After the Hairy Autumn everyone was speculating. Who did what against the witches. And over time, I heard it more and more: Hughes has got the power to change people. He can get in your head and when he's there he can do two things. Make or break. The Nightjar Coven fought Cate and Frank Gallant and Mr. Glint, but they couldn't fight Hughes. Not with this thing he had. Has." She bit her lip. "One time when her Ladyship and I were talking, I sort of... broached the subject. I thought she'd laugh me off, make a joke of it or something. But she didn't. She said it was true, but that I shouldn't be freaked out. You were still you, and you exercised your best judgment. Hughes, please don't use it on me. I'm begging you."

Not getting a reply of any kind, she bent to his fingers again. Hughes didn't know much of anything after the mental wallop he'd just received, but he knew he would rather she chopped off his hand than kiss it again. He pulled back.

Another wave of shock crashed through him as she cringed away, the color draining out of her cheeks.

What happened to "I adore you, Hughes. You and Wendy are so good to me"? What happened to proving it to me?

He answered himself. *I did. I happened. Me and this rotten, shitty thing I call Performance, but which Thud described a hundred times better: mind control.*

"I won't," he said. "I would never."

Estelle smiled through her fear. "You won't?" She sounded surprised. *And happy. I guess the woman can be as happy as the girl she once was, if the circumstances are right.*

"Can I ask you something?" he said.

Now that she was in no danger of being afflicted by his magic, she seemed glad to talk, almost eager. "Of course you can."

"What did I do?"

"Pardon?"

He looked at her. "What did I do to make you think I could do that to you?"

To that, Estelle Corlum had nothing to say.

He left her alone.

Alone, that is, except for the crawlers.

Not spiders. Worse.

Regrets.

Chapter Twenty-Five

What are you?

The question had been nettling her since she had captured Skuggs. Lots of things about Skuggs nettled. He was squat, rude, ugly, contumacious, contemptible, generally repulsive, and about as friendly and charming as a genital rash. A more generous disposition than hers would have called him interesting to look at, but Cate was pretty satisfied with "ugly."

One pink eye ogling at her through the bars of his cell in Betty's dungeon, Skuggs sat and exuded malignance. Top-heavy with his glossy orange wrinkle-sponge of a head, and with his thick, veiny neck craning that head in front of his child-sized body, he resembled nothing so much as a rancid pumpkin. He was not speaking now, but he had before, and Cate was struck by the queer quality of his voice. It seemed that Skuggs had two of them, two voices arising from two throats and merging in his mouth, dual resonances of every word mingling together in a loathsome little harmony. She had not heard him laugh. Cate hoped she never would. It would sound terrible.

It was the evening of Tuesday the 20th of December, Hughes was disguising himself to look like Wendy Dragontail, and through the door of fire in Eurydice a whole world away, Cate was sitting in her fortress' dungeon, her huge hobnail boots resting atop a stool, the anbaric lamp in the dungeon burning red and accentuating the natural fire of her hair, and there, through the bars, only ten paces away, was Skuggs.

"I've never met another teleporter before," she told him. "A man I knew back home had a localized variety, but that's an entirely different pot of coffee. Interesting how our limitations reveal themselves. I've got to be in contact with a reflective surface in order to pass from here to there. You've got to be in contact with the ground of your world. Why has no one come for you?"

The quickness of the pivot did nothing to phase Skuggs. He closed one nostril with his thumb and fired a gobbet of snot from the other. It hit the floor, jiggling and greenish-white. His pink eye narrowed, hinting that he'd have preferred to aim for her face, had it been but a little closer.

He was a tough customer. But then he'd proved that by keeping his nerve after Cate's fellow Citadel agent, Margherita Stranger, nicked him with that ghoulish sword of hers.

She rummaged in her satchel and pulled out the crystal compass. "I've been thinking about this. At first I surmised it pointed to places where the boundary between Eurydice and Iphigenia is weak. Nice and thin, so Eurydice can send her best killers through. Now I think not."

Skuggs said nothing. His dimpled, pocked, pumpkin-skin visage gave nothing away.

"I've deduced that this—" she hefted the compass, "—points not to places but people. Powerful people like the Troll and William o' The Wisps, and who knows who else. They're to be given Eurydice's commands, the order to invade Iphigenia. For people like the Troll and William, the partition between worlds isn't weak in certain places and strong in others. It's thin all over. They are the deciding factors."

She made the compass vanish into her satchel, and she crossed her arms over her chest. She wore a scarlet t-shirt, and her forearms were marbled in veins, masoned in muscle. "Shall I tell you something else? Something tantalizing in its repercussions?"

Skuggs offered no opinion. His expression said she could tell him the secret mathematics of universal dark matter, and he would not give the smallest iota of a shit.

"Someone entrusted with both the task of relating those commands and the navigational means to do so would be an important fellow. That's you, Skuggs. And no wonder. Teleportation is an elegant talent in a messenger. No, you're more than that. You're a diplomat. An emissary of Eurydice, from her to her people. A mouthpiece, your two throats a substitute for your Lady's. So I ask again, why has no one come for you?"

Nothing.

She shrugged. It was no skin off her elbows. A tiny flicker of amusement at that. The phrase belonged to Hughes. Thinking in his vernacular could mean only one thing. She missed the handsome rascal. *And I've had enough of this caged one*, she thought, giving Skuggs a parting grin as she got up to go. He wasn't even handsome, the inconsiderate prick.

But when she set her boot to the lowest step leading out of the dungeon, a double-throated voice said, "Why haven't you pokeled and prodded me?"

She turned, pleased to finally get him talking, but not quite sure what she'd heard.

"Sorry? Why haven't I what?"

"Pokeled. Prodded. Pinched." While her back was turned Skuggs had retrieved the Tupperware box they gave him his meals in. His rations were a gruel the color of red wine vomit, and about the consistency. Dreadful, but it was all the bastard would eat. "Teased. Tickled. Torn. Trounced-on. Trampled."

"Tortured?"

"Good one, good one."

"Why haven't I had you tortured?"

"That display with the nicking-sharpest swordle, that wavy-haired tart with the name like a cocktail."

"Margherita Stranger. She cut you with her sword, what about it?"

"That was pitsiful."

"The reviews are in. I'm coming to sit back in my chair by the spell. If you throw your food at me I'll do something disturbing to you. Fair enough?"

He nodded, his mouth full.

She wasn't sure she bought it. She chanced it, anyway.

This time there was no propping her boots on the stool. She sat with their soles firmly planted on the floor, her forearms resting on her thighs, her back bowed, her curiosity firm and straight and flowing from her through the bars of the cell to where Skuggs sat munching.

He swallowed. "Spooks don't loosen tongues. Scares in moving picture format are only threats without words. Torture, on the other mitt. *That* would make me squeal. Take that cocktail sow's sword, take it to me *properly*," Skuggs said, his ears wiggling as he smiled a wide and wicked smile. "Then I'd sing for you. I'd sing till all the cows come home."

"You clearly haven't heard of Infiltrator David Hogmanay."

That wiped the smile off his leering face. "Whossat?"

"In my world there was a war between a country called Champleurs and a lot of other countries who weren't thrilled about its approach to foreign policy. Infiltrator David Hogmanay was a spy sent by the allied forces into Champleurs. There he had a false identity, and he lived what spies call a 'double life.'"

Skuggs grunted deep in his double-throat.

"He was caught—not his fault, spying is a tenuous, delicate game with many moving pieces and constant flux—and in a cell much like yours, Skuggs, he was interrogated. They tortured Hogmanay, sure they would get information. And they did."

Skuggs chewed the last of his gruel. He looked smug.

Cate lulled him into remaining so. "Hogmanay gave his tormentors the names of several dissidents who were planning a toothless assassination attempt against the King of Champleurs. His info was good. The torturers congratulated themselves on a job well done. Then they wondered if Hogmanay knew some things he'd kept secret from them. So they tortured him again, and he gave them the name of an officer in the Champleurs army who was feeding military intelligence to the allied forces. Again his info was spot on. The torturers were delighted with themselves, and moreover they were securing awards and promotions and letters of thanks signed by the king himself."

"I bet they paid the gabber another visit," said Skuggs cheerfully. "Made him sing to their tune."

"They did pay Hogmanay another visit. This time, while they were smashing the bones in his legs with hammers, he gave them the names of key members of the king's war cabinet. This was a shocking revelation, and the torturers were reluctant to pass on what they had learned. But the info that Hogmanay had given them before was rock solid, and so they went for it."

"More fuel for the screamy fires," chortled Skuggs. "Ahehn-hen-hen."

Cate had been right. It was a mean, conniving laugh. She envied the Cate she'd been a few moments ago, who hadn't heard it. Then again she relished being the Cate of the present moment because the ruse was over, and Skuggs was in for a nasty surprise.

"You might think so," said Cate. "Only the members of the war cabinet were innocent."

Skuggs stopped giggling. His lumpy face took on a suspicious cast. "But you said the information was tarsty and true."

"It had been. But David Hogmanay knew he was going to die in his cell, and that his enemies would make it painful. He decided to dish out some of what they were serving him with their pincers and hot irons and hammers. So when the cabinet members protested, they had a hard time convincing the Champleurs interrogators, who were sure they were on to a good thing. Meanwhile the allied forces took swift advantage of the unexpected sag in Champleurs' formerly tight onslaught. Hogmanay actually survived, and though he was crippled forever, he was given the pleasure of seeing his persecutors hanged by the neck until they were dead. Oh, and we won the fucking war, in no small part thanks to his cleverness and courage.

"Why haven't I tortured you, Skuggs? Because torture is an abandoned refrigerator. You can approach it with high hopes, but its contents will be spoiled. I won't torture you because I'm smarter than you are. I know you'll give me spoiled goods. So I'm taking you to Corinth City. There are people there who can plunge into a head—even a squashed fruity mess like yours—and root around in your dreams for the truths you would never, not in a million years, divulge. In other words *vee hev vays hov makink you talk, Skoogs*. I look forward to the melodies that day promises. I'm sure you'll sing beautifully."

She would savor the look on his face for a long, long time.

As she left the dungeon she hesitated a moment on the top step. She leaned over the banister so he could see her. "Ahehn-hen-hen," she said.

***

Somewhere lovely, a telephone rang.

A hand picked it up.

"Thud residence," said Thud. "Thud speaking."

"Thud, it's Hughes."

Thud's heart trilled a trumpet's tune. There was a tenacious tempo, a thunder thumping in the lad's tone.

"I need you to look into something for me."

"Okay. Tell me."

Hughes told him.

Ninety seconds later a call was placed to the streetbeater forensics facility in Nikandros District. The groggy night watchman (who was only starting his shift) was told to admit a young man matching Gormon Hughes' description, who should be arriving at the facility in twenty minutes. The young man was to be escorted to the laboratory, where undoubtedly Doctor Tyrae Leborski would be at her various vials and test tubes. There Leborski would test and identify a substance in the young man's safekeeping. She was to do this promptly, at the pleasure of the Scarlet Citadel, for the young man was a respected member of that organization. Once Leborski had results, she was to relate them to the young man, again with the greatest haste possible. In return Captain Thud would buy her a mojito.

***

John Isherwood went to bed expecting no sleep—he was too clipped full of excitement.

But he would. He would sleep, and without dreams. That would be swell.

Maybe when your life was flying high you had no need to dream. Sleep was merely rest. Recovery. A silky black injection, and—

It was cold under the covers. Outside the blizzard roared a challenge, one he was not inclined to take up. He turned on his electric blanket, setting the timer for half an hour (you can never be too careful), then just...bathing. In the heat seeping through the blanket, driving out the chill. And bathing in the memories. Another amazing day!

If he wanted to, he could fixate on a point in the dark of his room and picture the faces of his team. Diligent, hard-working expressions. Serious mouths. Happy eyes. They were as addicted to it as he was—to discovery. On a lunch break (most of the team worked at their desk so as to minimize downtime, himself included), he heard one of his favorite technicians remark that what they did was a kind of teleological poetry: making sense out of nonsense. A little fustian, okay. A little chi-chi. But when he heard it, it gave him one of those tingles, the sort that reminds you of childhood praise. Good job! Ridiculous. But then, that was what made a comment like the technician's all right. Appropriate. They *were* doing a good job. A *spectacular* job.

He lay there, luxuriating in the idea.

Teleological poetry. Pretentious, stuck-up crap. But true all the same.

He wondered if the geniuses who had solved the Champleurs communications code during the war felt the same way he did. If they got the tingle. Good job! You helped win the war. Or, in his case, Good job! You led the discovery of *a whole new form of life*. What was the code's name again?

Tigresse, that was it. Tigress.

So much for the survival of the fittest. Give a bunch of pencil pushers a few prehistoric computers and a soda machine and presto—they'll down a tigress.

He supposed there was some poetry there, if you cared to look for it.

The electric blanket, not one to be outdone, was doing its job admirably. He felt cradled in snugness and warmth. Hoh man. Soon sleep would come. But not yet. First the restlessness. The tossing and turning. The small, indulgent smile as he remembered yet another great part of his day.

This had become his routine. Work like a woodpecker nosing its way through the thickest redwood, not because of obligation or pay, but because it felt so damn rewarding. Then the rigmarole of exhaustion, denying it and fighting it with caffeine and yet another late supper, then giving up the goose and driving home, grinning like an asshole with his foot on the gas. Then to bed, thinking over problems and potential solutions until his head switched off and the twiggy nest of his labors became first bright, then grainy, then a fading sepia snapshot, and—

John Isherwood woke up.

He thought, *It's dark.* It was a stupid thought, languid, a get-me-back-to-sleep thought. Well, maybe not so stupid. He inhaled unhappily. For the life of him, he could not remember the last time he'd woken up in the middle of the night. No pressure in his bladder—the wizz fairy had not chosen tonight to make a house call.

Fine but... but if not that, then what had roused him?

It was the sound, Johnny.

His mother's voice.

It had been a long time since he'd heard her. When was it...

The bird, he remembered, and in response the moisture in his mouth evaporated instantly. *The bird outside my window. The one that killed the starling. Tore its throat out.* That was ten years ago, when the Nightjar Coven had raked their claws over Corinth's exposed belly. Weird dreams. Morphic fields changing. People becoming animals. And that bird. That immense bird on his balcony had been a herald for it all. *Its beak. I remember...*

(the drip, Johnny)

... yeah. The drip.

A pause. A skip in his chest as his heart fluttered.

What sound, Mom?

And thinking that, he shifted under the covers...

... and realized that something heavy was pushing down on his legs.

Without a single coherent thought and tucking his chin into his neck, he looked down at the end of his bed, a motion that didn't involve his shoulders or upper back. So he was flat as a board except for his head when he saw the shape squatting monstrously on top of him.

"Whadda fuck?" He meant to shout but the words came in a stridulant whisper. His dry throat gave it another shot, this time a little louder, though the words "fuck is that" stuck together in a mushy wad. "What the fucksat?"

"That" was a shape almost totally indistinct in the room's deep gloom. It was the size of a steering wheel, two rounded bulges looming over his crotch, curved things sticking from its sides, and six thin stalks propping it up like some perverse old-fashioned camera.

Bizarre, but his first thought was, *It's going to spear its beak into my groin, pierce two layers of cloth, and puncture my balls.* Fright was contracting his testicles up against his body—he could feel a prickling tightness radiating up from their base and into his penis. *Maybe it'll peck that after. Then I'll be the starling. I'll be the one who drips.*

Mercifully what little scraps of judicious thinking he had in that moment drew his gaze to the anatomy of his nighttime guest. No feathers. Those curves might be wings. He wasn't sure. But there was no beak. And no beak, no bother.

A lot of bother, he corrected savagely, staring at the shape, trying to make out more details. *More than a lot, unless I'm having a hallucinatory experience.* Possible, he supposed. He was not an insomniac—as the most common sufferers of sleep paralysis were—but he was working in a high stress environment. High yield, yes, yet right on the cusp of that graph was a spike of massive responsibility, and its hooded, evil partner, stress. John Isherwood was no shrink, but he knew plenty, and those guys were always good for a story about the things some of their clients saw in the dark.

Convinced themselves they saw, that is.

The stare he'd fastened on his guest was beginning to mutiny against him. Tension leaked into the muscles around his eyes, much as the heat from his electric blanket had comforted him earlier. That reversal—relaxation to dread—was creepy. The shape was worse. It stayed right there, as though his unblinking eyes were pinning it somehow. Perfectly still. Perfectly alien. How long had he been looking at it?

Sixty seconds?

It felt like more.

That was when the shape flickered its wings, and John heard the sound they made. Not for the first time, either. It was the sound that had stirred him to begin with, pulling him out of the blank sightless pit of sleep.

A *buzz*.

Oh God. God, was that it?

His eyes were adjusting, or was it his mind sculpting the shape out of the shadows? The bulging round things on its head, the six legs (not stalks), the curves of wing, translucent now with the faint moonlight slipping in through a sliver in the curtain.

A fly. A giant fly.

(just like the nursery rhyme, Johnny, my sweet boy)

(there was a fly who swallowed an old lady)

(he ate her head, her smock, her frock)

(imagine, he ate her up, how crazy)

(AND YOU'RE NEXT DOC)

His body was bathed—not in electric blanket heat or memories, but in sweat. Dirty stinking gunk griming up his flesh, making him slick and icy-hot. His hands were useless stiff meat under the bedsheet, palms and fingers gloved in that filthy sweat, sweat dripping off the hairs on his knuckles, running in beads down his back.

Bzzzzz.

The wings flickered again.

Bzzzz. Bzzzzzzz.

This was no illusion, no symptoms of moon whispers or phantasmal fugue, nurse. The diagnosis is REAL *and this time there's no glass partition between me and the danger.*

His vision was very shivery now. A point behind each eyeball was throbbing. The eyeballs themselves were like parched garden roots, wrinklesome and bone-dry, screaming for rain, flowing faucets, puddle flecks, tears. He had to blink—knew he could not, could absolutely not.

"Hey Johnny."

That rumbling, husky, sensual drone of a voice was not in his head. Thank God it wasn't his mother. If he'd heard Ella Isherwood speak aloud, her voice emanating from that bloated bug on top of his legs, he would surely have lost it.

If I haven't already, he thought. *Sane men do not see flies the size of Huskies in the full bloom of evening. Come to think of it, how often do their dead mothers speak to them? Even twice over a decade seems twice too often. But then I am overworked. Deliriously happy, decadently overworked...*

(And crazy)

"I am not crazy."

Bzzzz.

"I never said you were."

"Who are you?"

"Only a shadow."

He ran his tongue over his lower lip. Both were unutterably dry.

"Are you with the bird?" he asked the fly.

"What bird?"

"The nightjar?"

"No, Johnny. I'm with you."

"Okay," he said, trying to stop the shakes rocking through him, unable to do so. He felt queasy. The taut skin on his balls was crawling. "Okay. That's good. With me. Good."

Babbling. He couldn't stop that either.

The fly did.

"You can blink," she said. "I won't hurt you."

On the word "blink" he did. Three times, very rapidly. The relief was palpable. True to her word she didn't hurt him. She did raise her front legs.

Don't come any closer. He wished he could say it, but his throat locked at the very thought of it.

She didn't. She brushed them together, hairy fly-flesh rasping.

"Have you ever heard of the idea that when you look into the abyss, the abyss looks back into you?"

"Yeah." He nodded, as much as he could nod. It made him aware of a bitch of a cramp seizing and clenching in his neck. "Yes," he said. "I've heard of that."

"Do you believe it?"

"Sure. Sure I believe it."

Anything you say.

"You've looked at her for a long time."

Puzzlement mixed with the sour sick feeling in his gut. "Who?" said John.

"Eurydice. You've courted her with your sly glances, Doctor. You've looked for her through the door of fire. I'm here to tell you she has looked back." *Bzzzz.* "It gives me great pleasure to tell you that your affections are reciprocated. Both parties like what they see."

Again the tongue swept over his lower lip. There was moisture to go around now. Confusion had beaten fear, for a little while.

"Are you... some kind of envoy?"

"Sit up, Johnny."

When he tugged, the fly raised itself, ever so slightly. He whipped both legs free fast. He drew them to him protectively as he sat up. The fly seemed smaller from this angle but still grotesquely large.

He could make out the patterns and clusters on its eyes now. *Watching me.*

The wings flickered, droning their drone and snapping his attention to them.

Maybe when your life is flying high you have no need to dream, he thought. Maybe that success and happiness attracts nightmares instead, like a daub of honey

(or a cadaver)

(a dead woman)

(Momma's insides are full of them, grave grubs galore)

like a daub of honey attracts swarms of—

"I can go," said the fly, making him jump. "I've disturbed you. In more ways than one I guess."

Was that... humor glazing her voice? John thought it was.

"So sorry to wake you, Johnny."

"No," he said. "No, there's... Don't go."

"You sure?"

John Isherwood thought about what she'd said.

His affections were reciprocated. He'd searched for Eurydice through the doors of fire. Thinking Eurydice. The thoughtful world. *Both parties like what they see.* Could such a thing happen? Could a planet, a changing, endlessly complex thing have a gender? Emotions that a person could feel out, understand... reciprocate?

"I'm sure," he told the thing in the darkness. "I'm listening."

Later, after the fly and the good doctor had parted company, Jane allowed herself a brief moment of gratification. It was the first she'd enjoyed since Hughes had rammed a sword through her heart earlier that day.

Usually when she laid her eggs inside someone, they burst and birthed her into the midst of their joy, otherwise known as the buffet table. The eggs she'd lain in John Isherwood were completely different, with the small exception that they would hatch as normal. The man had been eager enough. And smart. The plasma pool of his intellect was very fertile.

Yes, the eggs would hatch.

In due time.

Chapter Twenty-Six

Emboldened by her chat with Skuggs, Cate fetched a couple beers from the pantry and set out for Eilandri Titansgrave's quarters. The two of them were due a chat of their own.

The fortress halls were quiet, almost serenely lifeless. A few galactic-level snores from Morvran Oats' room. Some cigarette smoke filtering through Igor Wight's door. That was all. The wisp battle was taxing. Everybody was bushed. Cate understood. In fact she preferred it this way. She wanted them ready, after all, for whatever came next.

Still... try as she might, she could not resist the teeniest pang of jealousy.

Sleep and Cate Jubilee were in a feud at the moment. There were the phantom cramps earlier, and now she was busy. She was a woman with appointments. Pain, then Skuggs, then Eilandri. Sour, sharp, then sweet. Though all three were strange in their way, she supposed.

Morvran's snores dimmed as she trotted up a set of stairs and hung a left into another hallway, this one equally deserted. Exhaustion made itself known—a little lightheadedness, a touch of befuddled fog and emotional vulnerability every few minutes—but in majority she felt great. Limber. Part of Cate wished her body and its rest could reconcile. It was a slumped, drowsy part that bitched and moaned and rubbed its bleary face. Fortunately the driven, energetic parts of her were much more experienced at getting her attention. *For now the feud must go on.*

Cate walked and Betty walked with her—the fortress matching its commander's pace across foreign terrain. Cate barely noticed that rocking seesaw motion under her feet, the way fresh sailors grow accustomed to the push and pull of the sea. Around her the wall-mounted lamps burned green, a nice organic shade like a woodland in early August. Appropriate, Cate conceded, given that the path to the next target had taken them into a forest. What little she'd seen of it through the fortress windows gave her the sense of an ordinary countryside forest, only stuffed with the tallest, widest trees she'd ever seen. Nocturnal animals hung upside down from the branches like bats. They blended in well with the cloudy night, when the moon peeped out only occasionally, green like the lamps in the fortress, only paler and eerier among the twinkling stars. Of the upside-down creatures, Cate could tell only that they were larger than a bat had any right to be and that their hooded eyes seemed to blink at her, red and narrow and cunning.

Looking at them, Cate had thought of Hughes' journey through dreams. In a candlewax swamp her lover had met Badger, a warden of that dreamy in-between. Badger's swamp was filled with trees, and there were baubles on the branches, red and green apples made of tin. She found the idea sort of enchanting. Her own journey through dreams had not been so folkloric.

For a moment her addled brain filled her senses with the ugly, mephitic smell of cigars, orange juice, and that cloying sour reek of sweat.

Cathy. Come here and give us a kiss.

Turning from the view of the woods, she'd dismissed her father's harsh, pettish voice. It was easy to do thanks to softer, kinder memories of her mother. *You look just like that actress Ginger Dujour*, admirers used to tell Cate's mum. Now, Cate Jubilee had fancied her mother was a deal prettier than Ginger, who was a starlet, and from the screen achieved a kind of plastic loveliness. But the way Mum brushed off such compliments without giving offense was both instructive and dazzling—there was a beauty to humbleness, as well as a species of pride that made her even more beautiful in her admirer's opinion. Yes, her mother's life was better luggage. A woman on the move had to be careful what she brought with her. Cate stored memories like that up in case of rain or snow, or baleful visitation from her father and other unwelcome visitations from her past. *What would the screen make of me?* Haunted Daughter. Responsible Leader. Troll conqueror. Forger of Peace, no matter how wispy. Sufferer of unaccountable twinges, isolated in a womb she did not have. A golem of fire and glass.

Aren't I a catch? Hughes ought to count his lucky constellations. I'm who he's chosen to share his heart with, and God help him.

She passed the fortress gymnasium. There was an honest, clean sweat smell. You could be hard on yourself at the gym and be rewarded with uplifting feelings, and that smell of course.

What about being hard on yourself as you passed the gym?

Cate was not aware of it, but in her eyes a few twigs of cheerful kindling caught fire, and her stride grew less stiff and much more smooth, and her chin moved up as though a secret hand were giving it the old "chin up, kid, it ain't so bad" routine.

Aren't I a catch?

Well, she had a great laugh.

And her nose too, that was cute. It was her mother's before her. Thank you genetics. Oh, and she was a fun date. A stellar lay. Respected, passionate, sharp as a tack, strong as an ox on whatever oxen took to overachieve in competitions, probably steroids with little horns on them. And she loved Hughes, that gormless gorgeous man. Worshiped him. Took care of him just as he looked after her.

Hell, maybe he was lucky. He seemed to think so.

So why don't you believe it? her confidence wondered.

Because of what you are, her doubt replied.

What am I? I thought I was a catch. What else could I be?

Don't you know. You're a falling chandelier, babe. Glass all the way down.

She walked on, closing herself off from that line of thinking entirely. But it was too late, and the fire in her eyes had snuffed out, and there was a subtle stiffness in her stride, and her chin moved back down to where it had been before.

Moved to distraction, her ear registered the enormous crunch as Betty's pillar of a leg drove itself through an impeding tree. Her imagination conjured the splinters as they flew and flew. That recentered the mission in her mind. Somewhere in these woods there was another

(person?)

another *entity*, to use a piece of clinical verbiage. This entity called Eurydice "mistress," and on her orders it would break into Iphigenia and cause some mayhem if given the chance. Unless it was put down or negotiated with (if such a thing were possible twice in a row, William may have been a fluke).

Kelly Cinch, the woman Cate had appointed as the fortress pilot thanks to the additional arms and mobility her corset granted her, was at that very moment consulting the crystal compass, which Cate had dropped up after her trip to the dungeon. Whether the company's next target was a monstrous gentleman like the Troll or an unconventional patriarch like William o' The Wisps remained to be seen. Regardless, it was a long way off yet, if Cate's reading of the compass could be relied upon, and there was a rotating shift of watchers on the battlements. Safety and slumber for the scarlet tribe, that was the meal on the menu for tonight.

Cate being one of the exceptions, naturally, as she so often was. Her appetites lay with a Pale Giant and a wonderfully cold bottle of Stoving's Dandified Eyewaterer (with mint). She could not be sure why, but something told her Eilandri would be awake and doing something interesting. She was right too. Hunches, like hobnail boots, are weird phenomena.

She reached the end of the hall and was about to turn the corner when hushed voices gave her pause.

"—what she's doing. She's embarked on diverse journeys here, and for longer stretches than any of us." The speaker was Marcus Angel. "Not to mention she worked entirely alone for years. You cannot doubt her experience."

"I think that... that *lone wolfism* has instilled the wrong instincts." This second voice belonged to Xacorca Demon. She and Marcus had been romantic for ages, as long as Cate could remember. Uncomfortable with eavesdropping, yet flexing instincts that had served her well on numerous occasions, she decided not to announce herself to them, instead flattening herself against the wall, keeping her mind and her ears wide open.

"I think it's fostered an attitude that cozens itself to the idea of success," said Xacorca. "While at the same time increasing risk."

"Well, she's a risk-taker. There's no denying that."

Who? Cate thought.

"What I still don't see is your evidence," continued Marcus. "Something you can point to and say: here, here's proof she's not a competent leader."

"You're absurd."

"Certainly. But the point stands."

"On wobbly legs, Marcus. A newborn giraffe has firmer footing. Have you forgotten that our fearless leader spoke to that icy colossus, letting it get close enough to spring an ambush? That against the wisps she left the battlefield to go searching for a solution in a giant manta ray?"

Fearless leader, eh? Cate felt even less comfortable eavesdropping on a conversation about herself. Still, maybe there was something useful here, a slice of wisdom to be cut from the cake of uninhibited discussion.

"I haven't forgotten anything, my love," said Marcus gently. "I recall that no ambush materialized. We beat the Troll handily, thanks in large part to Cate's natural authority on the battlefield. And she proved selfless as well as tough. The only case of frostbite was her. So much for *lone wolfism*, as you call it. She's a pack animal and no mistake. As to—"

"But a commander endangering themselves actually illustrates—"

"My darling demoness, please."

Grumbles as Xacorca assented to him finishing his point.

"As to the manta ray," Marcus went on, "there was a solution to be found. What choice did Cate have?"

"Retreat," pressed Xacorca. "Say she hadn't found anything up there. Too much time had passed for us to make a vigorous comeback, allowing the creation of space for a good, calculated retreat."

"That's... not a bad point," mused Marcus. "I suppose it was touch-and-go for a while there. Sometimes a tactical retreat is what's called for."

"And this time Cate wasn't the one who got hurt. Her harum-scarum approach to fighting meant the rest of us were left to hold the fortress while she investigated a fish. Eugenie was slashed across the face. She might lose an eye."

"I didn't know it was that bad."

I did. And it would have been much worse if I hadn't found the reliquaries. Besides, the ray was huge. There was no outrunning it.

Bitter thoughts, but not without merit. Xacorca hadn't a clue. For God's sake, when Cate had visited her after the battle, Eugenie had *thanked* her, had gone so far as to praise her ingenuity. "Without you I might be wearing a bandage over both eyes instead of the one," she'd said, and Cate could only hug her and tell her that her depth perception would be restored in no time.

"It's late," observed Marcus. "Too late for lovers' quarrels. Betty has a soporific gait, doesn't she?"

"That's another thing. Why are we still moving?" Xacorca's nattering grew distant as the pair strode away toward their room. "We ought to find somewhere to rest for a few days." Her gusto was undercut by an enormous jaw-crackling yawn. "Get our bearings."

"A few days, a few hours," said Marcus breezily. "We are men and women of the Citadel, we have obligations to her Ladyship, and moreover I would like to be home in time for Tinfrost." Now he was yawning. "The hastier our progress the better, I say. We've lots of credits for the coffers and samples for Doctor Isherwood to fawn over. Anything else is a bonus, but remember that those stack, and Cate was right when she said that these incursions into Iphigenia mean trouble." Another yawn. "Goodness gracious. Well, for the moment all this angel cares about are his pillows. And the demon who hogs them and slobbers them in drool, of course. Mustn't forget her."

"And, lest it slip your mind, she can strangle you with your own magic chains."

"Yes," said Marcus happily. "But only if I'm very good."

Cate listened to them banter and bicker. Then they were gone.

All in all not the most pleasant listening for eight o'clock in the evening.

But there was no time to dwell on it. The beers were warming every moment.

When she arrived at Eilandri's quarters she was surprised to see they were pretty much on par with her own. Apparently while there had been time to mold the fortress lamps to look like hobnail boots, there had not been enough left over to build Eilandri a higher ceiling. Cate wondered how the woman got by. Stooping, probably.

Cate's prospective drinking partner was sitting in a chair by her window. Like Cate she was in a t-shirt, although instead of jogging pants Eilandri wore shorts that made the impeccably toned muscle in her upper thighs stand out starkly. That eerie pale moonlight passed through the windowpane and mixed with the greenish woodland lamplight. It shone over Eilandri's bald pate, her bare shoulders, and—Cate could not help but notice—a nasty gash on her knee. This last she was stitching up, needle-and-gut style, old fashioned. Those knowing purple eyes rose to meet Cate's as she came dawdling in, knocking on the door afterward with a sheepish grin on her face.

"One of the wisps nick you?" she asked.

Eilandri nodded.

"I brought beer."

Nod.

"Am I imposing?"

Headshake.

Cate shut the door and sat on the edge of the bed. In contrast to the rest of the room its proportions were actually suitable for its designated occupant. Set Eilandri in normal sleeping arrangements—even super deluxe king-size—and her arms and legs would stick out like laces from a shoebox.

Cate cracked the beers with her thumbs (a trick she'd learned from a bartender in *The Coconut* club), hooshed off her butt, set one of the bottles next to Eilandri on the windowsill, and sat herself back down again.

She watched the giant suture for a while. The needle slipped through; the thread of catgut flowed; every movement graceful and slow and measured.

Slip. Flowwww.

Slip. Flowwww.

"Would I be right in guessing it was your idea to grab the mirror from the foyer and have Clothilda sneeze it up to me?"

Nod. Slip. Flowwww.

"I bet you even hauled the mirror yourself. Faster that way."

Nod.

"Thanks for saving my life."

A glance from those lavender eyes. A wink. Nothing else changed on that long hairless face. Just a quick flash of the eyelid. Then Eilandri returned to her suturing.

It happened so fast Cate wasn't sure she'd seen it at all.

She smiled in case she had, embarrassed and pleased, her face listing away from the window so she seemed half-damasked in shadow.

An odd thing happened then.

All at once the happy-go-lucky vibe faded and the smile broke apart and dissolved on her lips. She sipped her beer without tasting it. A lock of hair stuck to the wet rim of the bottle. She teased it away between two fingers.

"Do you think it's wrong to love fighting?"

Headshake.

"Even... even if it costs more than you originally bargained for?"

Quizzical glance.

"Never mind."

Hesitant nod. Slip. Flowwww.

"Xacorca thinks I've acted recklessly. Marcus disagrees. I'm not sure who's right."

Without skipping a beat or peeling her attention from her wounded knee, Eilandri tapped her chest with the tip of the needle.

"You do?"

Nod.

"Marcus?" Cate said with faint hope.

Nod. Slip. Flowwww.

Obstinate, Cate's spirits refused to be raised. "But maybe Xacorca has a point. I went straight for the manta ray as soon as I guessed the reliquaries were there. Inspiration struck and I just went with it. I didn't question my instincts for a second. Is that responsible? The ray was terrifyingly large, sure, but maybe there *was* a way we could have escaped, something I haven't considered, or which only a truly brilliant mind could plan and execute. Besides, isn't a tactical retreat sometimes what's called for?"

Nod. Shrug. A few thoughtful nods. Eilandri lifted the thread to her mouth. Biting it in two, she made sure the knot was good and tight on the suture, reached for a first aid kit, and began to pack away her supplies. When she was done she picked up her beer by the neck, walked to the wall (with only a minor stoop so as not to whack her head on the ceiling) opposite the spot where Cate was sitting, and held the bottle out.

Cate leaned forward.

Clink.

"I wonder why they call it Eyewaterer," she said.

They sipped the beers. They grimaced at the beers.

"God. Well, mystery solved. That's horrendous."

They studied the beers. They took another gulp of the beers.

"Actually, the mint does leave a distinctive aftertaste."

Nod.

"Will I grab your cards so we can chat?"

Shrug. Headshake. In other words, *this works fine.*

"Okay. How are you?"

A turning corkscrew motion of the hand. The gesture meant *comme ci, comme ça,* very common in Champleurs. Given she was from Daethumberland, the Pale Giant curled her fingers a trifle more than a Champleurs person would, and her thumb hooked onto her index finger as the hand swerved back and forth. Translated to Corinthian, Eilandri was saying, *Not bad. I've been better.*

"You think I made a bugger of things with the wisps?"

Emphatic headshake.

That flickered her flame a little brighter. Cate got the impression Eilandri's praise was not a thing lightly given. Any more of it and her spirits would rise in clouds of billowing orange smoke, suffusing her full. *Maybe I'll be myself if that happens.* Fully yourself, said her confidence.

Never again, said her doubt. Drink your beer, you delusional piece of shit.

She physically flinched.

Eilandri shot her another quizzical look.

Cate shrugged it off, drank her beer, and felt like a delusional piece of shit.

Aloud she wondered, "*Comme ci, comme ça.* Okay, the wisp thing doesn't bother you. I admit, that's a relief. I worried the company wouldn't understand. But if not that, then what's the matter, Eilandri? Worried about Eugenie?"

Headshake. The pale woman closed one lid and tapped the skin with the rim of her bottle.

Not worried, but she'll lose the eye.

There was a coldness to that assessment. Then again the last time Eilandri came to Eurydice her troupe had returned home with less than half their number. Necessary cold, then. Cate could respect that.

Out of reasonable choices she took a wild stab at the reason behind the giant's mixed mood. "You're tired?"

Nod.

"No way."

Nod. *Way it is.*

"That's loopy. Come on. Really?"

Nod.

Cate was grinning stupidly, unable to stop. When Eilandri didn't crack a smile (big shocker there) or give any other sign she was kidding, the grin pursed into a bemused little curl of the mouth. Cate snorted, giving a little "hokay, laydee, whateva choo say" jerk of the head. "Well ah. If you're tired, I must be... I must be a zombie. And I don't know how I look. It's possible I look dead on my feet, but I feel fine."

Eilandri took a swig of her beer.

"I don't know."

A swig for Cate too. "Nice," she said. Her mouth scrunched. "Interesting," she amended. "You think we're out here too long? It's only been a few days."

Shrug.

"I've been on month-long journeys in Eurydice." What was it Xacorca had called it? *My lone wolfism.* She wouldn't dare relate that to Eilandri, but it did spur her to say, "Our supplies are plentiful. Moods are testy but morale's solid. There's been one serious injury, but no..."

She stopped.

No what? her doubt asked.

No casualties, said her confidence. Nobody dead.

Oh you arrogant fuck.

Cate felt as though her stomach had crashed into her lower abdomen, tangling in a mesh of intestine. A bitter bile taste washed up over her mint-tingled tongue. Seizing and holding her own, Eilandri's gaze pierced deep.

"Hey..." Cate said. She made to rest her beer on the reading-light table by the bed. Paying more attention to her blunder, she misjudged the angle. Instead of staying put, the moment she released her grip the bottle tumbled. Cate winced the instant before she heard the *crunch*.

"Shit." Cate took a knee. The bottle had broken in two jagged but otherwise cleanly severed pieces. Still a tad humiliating but not a disaster. All she had to do was pluck the shards up, fetch a cloth from the pantry for the spill, plus another beer (a palatable one this time) while she was at it, and they were good to go. "Sorry. Butter fingers. No, don't move, I've got it. Let me... let... Oh."

Blood welled up from where the glass had broken skin. Cate stared at her hand. Somewhere in the hard, framed, reflective center of her, a few hairline cracks developed...

What else could I be?

(a falling chandelier, babe)

(glass all the way down)

And the cracks grew...

What else could I be?

(Unique circumstances, signed Artemi Lanmoor, M.D. Saint Wilhelmina's Obstetrics Dep.)

(foreign matter)

And grew...

(seashell hand)

(Hughes saw that hand on the monitor and cried like a)

And grew...

(Cried like a)

What else could I be?

Blood dribbled down her finger. It dropped. She watched it go. Red stuff red woman red choices red outcomes. She watched as a drop of her blood fell on the bottle. On the glass.

She thought, very clearly, *Hughes saw that seashell hand on the monitor, and he cried like a baby.*

And then it was over.

All the defenses she'd put up, like a fortress against a fierce enemy, came down. All the humor, the Cateish candle flickering, the charm, the goofiness, the memories of her mother who people compared to the film star Ginger Dujour, the letters she and Hughes had scribbled to one another to bridge the distance between worlds... everything vanished. All it took was a drop of blood on broken glass. All it took was an instant in which movement, that cornerstone of her soul, was impossible.

Her face crumpled.

She put her hands over it, covering her stupid face as fucking stupid heat rushed into it, and tears too, oh God, God, her baby, her baby girl...

Cate Jubilee, never one for a bad cry, always stoic, always fiery and respectable, began to sob. She sobbed hard. She dredged them up as soupy mud and snarls of weeds and trash are dredged out of a dockland from which all ships have sailed, and over which a red sun now sets, a bloody bit of glassware suspended, a harbinger of bleakest, vaporous doom, or night, or some apocalyptic combination of the two. Even when her father beat her mother to death, when the grief had been unbearable, she had not wept like this.

This was beyond unbearable.

On some level reality was going on, and someone very large and very strong was holding her. But here inside her nothing made sense.

There had been a baby, and a womb, and something indefinable and really quite beautiful for that lack of definition—tomorrow, there should have been a tomorrow and a seashell hand to squeeze it and suckle it like a soother and wear nappies on its head and drink down sweet milk and upchuck it and smile toothlessly while Mum cleaned up the yuck, and saying "Mum" and Mum's face lighting up—A WORD A WORD A SPLENDID WORD—and the smelly sick forgotten and Mum lifting up the magnificent new talker, the best orator of this and any age, and blowing on the soft belly making raspberries, gigglesgigglessqueaks and pumping chubby legs and laughter, *and gone all of it gone November took it from me...*

Not November. Enough was enough. She was the locus of hurt, not a month. A month couldn't be bad, she was, *I am.*

(glass all the way down)

(cold jelly smeared over her bump)

(gliiiiide went the transducer)

(you're going to have a little girl)

She moaned and sobbed and felt as if she were a monstrous piece of shit.

I am, I am a monstrous piece of shit.

Tongueless confidence.

Doubt braying triumph.

I could have saved her. If I'd stopped using my boots she wouldn't have died. Aunt Trisha had babies and they were healthy. You would have been too, she told her daughter who never was. *You would have been okay too...*

It was too much, too much for her. She felt it anyway. All of it.

She screamed and begged and sobbed uncontrollably.

As tears convulsed her frame, she told God to take His own medicine. She prayed whatever divine womb He had would dry up and kill him. She asked for forgiveness. She hoped for hell.

A big hand, firm and implacable, held her own as she tried to claw her cheeks.

Another slipped its fingers through her hair and flowed comblike through it.

Slip. Flowwwww.

Cate whimpered.

Slip. Flowwww.

Outside the window, the moon succumbed to the clouds, and the forest was so dark, so very dark...

Act Nine

Something Scarlet

Chapter Twenty-Seven

Wednesday, and the blizzard was a murderer in white.

There was a cold gray dawn. It smothered that, as Jane—wearing Paulie Manzarek like a skin suit—had smothered those poor helpless people in Taggart House.

There was a pre-Tinfrost sale. The blizzard starved those. No one could get to work, much less go shopping.

There were points of brightness in the pale day that carried the essence of dark with it. Streetlamps refusing to blow over. Board games and books with something warm sizzling on the stove. Kind souls inviting shivering homeless people inside—Tracer Gogen, who along with his fellow columnists tended to sleep in his office in *The Times* building, led a sortie of journalists with the aim of getting as many people in out of the chill as they could. His selflessness saved thirty-five people, got them a hot shower (thank God for back-up generator power), a toasted cheese sandwich, and a carton of apple juice each. Against the urgings of his colleagues to call it there, he went out to see if could help just one more person. As he braved the blind, bellowing streets, streets made unrecognizable they were so overcome with ice, he thought about Hoshrum Thud warning him off the Spring-Heeled story. Normally Tracer would have nodded along, making placative noises, and later discarding the strong-arming censorship crap in the garbage where it belonged. But Thud had been weirdly persuasive, arguing that sometimes on the scales of judgment, public safety was heavier than the truth. Tracer wasn't sure about that. *Then why am I out here, when I could be at my computer typing up a digital article?* Why indeed.

In the crook of a side-street alcove, he came upon the body of an old woman. Frozen solid. The breeze moved in her eyelashes, making Tracer think of a black butterfly he'd netted one summer. It was hot then. Funny how distant you felt from the sun when weather like this bashed its solar brains out, spilling slush and dandruff crisp as death. *I'd better get back to the office, or else I'm gonna lie down and never get back up.*

A block from *The Times'* front door, he slipped on a patch of ice hidden under a scrap of canvas awning. He went down with a yelp, the impact singing up his tailbone and spidering his back and underthighs with ache. "Shit." He got himself halfway to his feet, lowered his face to blink his stinging eyes, groaned, shook his head, and looked up.

Brightness. Two points of light busting out of the murk, swallowing his field of vision. The blare of a horn.

What's tha—

And that was the end of Tracer Gogen. There was a crunch of a windshield partially caving in, a series of rolling judders, and a final boneless noise as the body landed in the street. The car slowed down for a moment, brake lights like baleful red imp eyes peering out, assessing the damage. Then, without coming to a full stop, the car's gears were changed. It sped off rapidly.

Almost priestlike, the snow anointed the body. The body, in turn, anointed the street, only its sacrament was a wine-dark and seeping scarlet.

Wednesday, and the blizzard was a murderer in white.

It was not alone.

A killer skulked and capered through Corinth City. She would wear white before today was over. And in Eurydice, a white killer waited for his moment.

Hughes and Cate knew none of this.

But they would.

Very soon.

***

Estelle thought, *Maybe I could have a little water now. Water. Yeah.*

Weakly, slowly, she lifted her head off the pillow and squinted at the water jug. It was there on the bedside table, just out of reach, cool and oh-so clear in the morning light that slipped like a white-gray intruder through the curtain. She could get it if she sat up. Even the thought of that seemed to seal her in concrete. Never in her life had she felt so listless. *So washclothed,* she thought and smiled.

Smiling took a lot out of her, so she lowered her head back to the safe territory of the pillow, and for a little while, she forgot about the water and remembered. Those memories were not pleasant, but rather insistent. And refreshing, in unexpected ways. *I'll just rest a moment to make myself better. Then I'll try attempt number two for that jug handle.* She lay still and remembered.

Yesterday there had been two visits; first Hughes then Wendy Dragontail. After Wendy was gone—after Estelle had drifted off to sleep, actually—she'd awoken to a horrible certainty that she was going to throw up. The bathroom was a ten second sprint away. Too far, in other words. And Estelle Corlum would not have trusted her legs to run, anyway.

She'd grabbed her wastebin, leaned over it, and yarked up watery stomach acid and half-digested prawns. Lumpy and chunky-wet it splattered against the bin's bottom. No relief came, just that hot-cold prickly sensation on her skin and the knowledge that her gut had more to give. The hair on her brow was stuck to her skin, sweat wringing itself from her pores like warm poisonous glue. She pushed a few damp strands back and inhaled through her nose; a mistake. The smell was not foul. It was rancid. Her gorge rose...

... and at the same time, a peculiar little palindrome bloomed in shades of violet through her head. It was a good one.

Rise to vote, sir.

Back to front. Front to back. Same as same. Delight contained between the capital letter and the full stop.

Predictably, her gorge was not politically motivated.

She retched and retched, and as her throat hitched effortlessly and spit flooded her mouth and ran in drips down the inside of the bin, she thought, *I don't get it. The food here is superb. The best in the whole city!*

A possible explanation struck her.

The new cook. Wendy had talked about him last week. He was from Champleurs. *Not a cook,* she amended, gathering saliva and gobbing into her own vomit. *A chef. He mustn't be as...* What was the word? *As* scrupulous *as the previous guy.*

Okay, so the new king of Redspire's kitchen had underdone the prawns. Now she had food poisoning. Despite the chills and rumbling abdomen, Estelle felt a trifle comforted by this snatch of logical reasoning. It would be a rough night, but then it'd be okay. What was that line from one of her favorite novels?

This too shall pass.

Not a palindrome, but nice. Soothing.

Only the night had not been rough.

Her grab bag of words—passed into her mind by years bent over books—offered her a more appropriate description. The initial nausea was a picnic, and the night that followed was long, virtually sleepless, and excruciating.

On the plus side, she made it to the bathroom after all.

She had shit herself until she cried, her bottom sore and too hot. And then, utterly bizarrely, she'd kept crying, even when the diarrhea pangs played themselves out and she was dry gagging, when all but nasty yellowy bile was cleared out of her belly. Crawling back to bed she had simply felt terrible. Low. Lonely. God, how could anybody be so alone and survive? How did the lack of others, the sheer staggering scraped-outness of loneliness, the fear and self-loathing and shame not gang up and decide, as a collective, to put their host out of her misery? She wished they would. She had not looked at her window longingly; a flight down the tower's frosted edifice was not an invitation Estelle's mind would ever have considered. But she did wish for oblivion of some kind, a gushing pale nothing that the blizzard taunted her with. *Howl*, it whistled and shrieked and whispered. *Howl as I do, and lose consciousness, and be free.*

But she didn't scream and she could not sleep and the depression only deepened with no sign of abating.

There was not a single one of her beloved palindromes—not even Drab As A Fool, As Aloof As A Bard—could allay her sorrow. Rattling around in her head with that sadness, they worsened it. *Naomi, Did I Moan?* Back to front. Front to back. Not comforting. Confining. Enclosing. Claustrophobic. Oh, she had not screamed, but the moans were another matter. Her voice had reverted to girlhood, high-pitched, cracking now and then and upsetting her even more.

Remembering it all from her current vantage point—i.e. the morning after— as she peered at that damnably distant jug, well, it actually made her smile. She had braved the worst, out of the woods now, thank heavens. Delicate, but much improved. Estelle was pleased with herself—an unfamiliar (though not unwelcome) shift from her usual attitude. A truly awful evening, yet now the sun was up and her health with it. She *was* better. Better every moment.

Better enough to give this another go.

She made a feeble grab for the jug handle. The tip of her middle finger actually nudged it a centimeter across the table. A whole centimeter.

Astounding.

Really a sterling effort from the keeper of the Perfect Prison.

She laced her fingers over her chest and turned a bit in bed so she was looking at her whole room. She stared at the view this position offered for some time. A line furrowed itself on her forehead. The corners of her mouth drew down. As sour expressions went, it would have given even Mr. Glint a run for his money.

There it was. Her room. Same as always. Only...

Only had the place always been so absurdly *cramped?*

Surely not.

The vast majority of her teens she'd spent here, and her early twenties. True, there'd been expeditions, truant escapades where she'd hunted around the eighty-ninth floor in search of secrets. But, for the most part, she and this room had been in it together. Boon companions. Friends.

She had always considered it perfectly spacious. Roomy, even.

But her "library" was just a titchy bunch of shelves; flimsy wooden things holding little stories aloft. And the distance between those rows of books and her bed was intolerable! Tinned peaches would lodge a complaint.

She closed her eyes and held the image of the room, expecting it to change back to the way it had always been when she opened them. She closed her eyes, and remembered.

Before the sickness, there had been Wendy.

The Last Dragon's visit had started out so strangely too.

She'd come in wearing her usual comfy combination of sweater and sweatpants and slippers, but there was nothing at ease about her expression when she asked:

"Forgive me, Estelle, but is this the first time we've spoken this evening?"

What a funny sort of question! Estelle hadn't known what to make of it then, and she still had no inkling now.

"Of course, my Lady. Are you feeling all right?"

"I am given to understand that you had another visitor this evening."

"I did," Estelle said, and though she wanted very badly to distance herself from that agonizing conversation with Hughes, she found herself recounting it to Wendy. Her Ladyship was so kind to her, so patient, so accommodating of all Estelle's idiosyncrasies. Withholding things from her was... well, it was unthinkable.

"Thank you, Estelle," Wendy said when the young woman had finished her tale. "I can see that the encounter has taken a toll on you."

"I feel completely dreadful. Hughes would never have used his power on me. Only after I lost my temper, he spoke with such a... I can't describe the tone of voice. It frightened me."

"You were quite right to be. Hughes' skills are exceptional, his capacity for action swift."

Estelle heard something in Wendy's voice that made her look up sharply. She wasn't sure, but under the admiration, she was sure that Wendy Dragontail sounded bitter. What should the most brilliant woman in the city have to feel bitter about? Hadn't she fostered Hughes' development, had him trained and given him purpose? Estelle's confusion melted into insignificance as her Ladyship met her gaze intently and said, "You were doubly right to refuse his request. The Perfect Prison is one of the City's greatest resources. Its use is not to be condoned unless absolutely necessary."

"Oh but this Spring-Heeled Jane character—Hughes painted her like the worst villain, my Lady. And he said she can't be killed by conventional means."

"Immortality is for children."

"Children?"

"Kites in the wind seldom trouble themselves with thoughts of the ground."

"Surely they must have started there?"

"Ah, but they don't remember." With her white hair loose for a change, and Estelle's many room candles like ghosts of dragonflame scoring the lines of her face, her Ladyship looked like an abode haunted in some truly odd and beautiful way. "Children are only concerned when the wind behind them slackens; the death of a parent, for example. The constancy is interrupted. Other than that though, they are content to fly."

"Until the ground calls them."

"Ah, growing old. And more things, besides. Some descents are sharper and messier than others. I'm sure this Spring-Heeled Jane will fall, in time. She must do, given her scattered appearances throughout our history. No, the Perfect Prison must address threats of a more abiding or world-threatening quality. Don't you think?"

"I think that you are very wise, my Lady."

Wendy's face changed. Her eyes twinkled. "Thank you," she said with a genuine warmth that thrilled Estelle. "You're a charming young woman, I ought to tell you more. But forgetful me. I have three new novels for you."

"Oh!"

"I note your shelves are otherwise occupied. You might consider pruning them? Some of the stories you have no intention of rereading, perhaps?"

"Of course!"

Exuding that tired excitement that was as close as she got to happiness these days, Estelle went to her library and began the difficult task of choosing books for the chopping block.

(And behind her, moving with a speed that defied her age, Wendy Dragontail snatched up Estelle's open wine bottle. Now Estelle hadn't taken a sip of that wine, only opened it to let it breathe for a while. From her pocket, Wendy took out an envelope. With a flick of her fingernail it was open, and into the wine she poured a colorless, odorless powder down the bottle neck. She swirled it, the mixture clouding and then settling, and by the time Estelle turned around with a stack of books in her arms for Wendy to take away, her Ladyship was sitting on her chair as she had been before, admiring the icicles dangling outside from the top of the window ledge.)

"Ah, capital." Wendy took the books. Estelle had struggled with their weight. Wendy held the stack aloft with one hand quite effortlessly. "I'll take these down. Have them donated somewhere. Here, three new stories, as promised. I do hope you'll find them diverting."

Estelle clutched them close, eyes roving greedily over the covers, not knowing that first illness, then new unexpected fancies would prevent her from reading them. Wendy bid her goodnight, but not before pouring Estelle a big glass of wine. Gratitude had welled up in her, so much, she'd only been able to mumble a reedy excuse of a thank you. Wendy told her to think nothing of it, and to drink deep and well. The wine was from a vineyard in Champleurs, a rare and delicious vintage.

She really was the kindest woman in the world.

Estelle enjoyed the rosy memory a moment longer.

Then she opened her eyes.

And frowned.

She looked at the paltry shelves, the low ceiling, the stuffy little nook for her bed, the tiny, almost surreptitious furniture (the side table in particular rankled because the wine glass on it seemed to dwarf it in size—incidentally the wine glass was full, despite Wendy's generosity Estelle hadn't much been in the mood for boozing). In short, she'd opened her eyes and her room was not restored to its former spacious quality. If anything, it felt *smaller.* What did that mean?

What's happening to me?

I want to see the sky, she thought suddenly.

She made to gently turn her body over so she faced the window, and without warning every ounce of desire in her cried: *NO!*

Estelle froze. *No, I'm not freezing, not at all, but here's a wild bit of trivia. I want to be. I want to run to the lift and ride that elevator down and run out of this tower directly into the blizzard. I want to feel the snow on my face, a thousand tingling mouths. December smooches. Then I want to go and find Hughes and leap into his arms and hug him while he carries me laughing, his best and brightest laugh, my wonderful friend escorting me somewhere cozy*

(and wide)

yes WIDE and open-ended and rambling, no corridors just colosseums, and heat from good fires and coats and rugs to romance away December's icy kisses, yesyesyes, I want to I want to...

"I want to see the sky. Even if this is just a passing thing. I *want* it."

Her voice emerged, not weak or raspy, but with a strength Estelle would have associated with Cate Jubilee. *Or Hughes.*

She had to find him.

Find him and apologize for how she'd spoken to him.

Forcefully, fighting fatigue with nails and teeth and an untapped vein of secret steel inside her, she sat up. She reached out. Her fingers curled around the jug handle.

Estelle grinned. She could have giggled, and ho-lee-shit, she was going to.

The daughter of Idris Corlum and Gwendolyn Gardener let loose a high, bright giggle and poured herself a glass of water.

For the first time in her entire life, she did not look in the least bit tired.

***

It was three-and-a-quarter hours past dawn, and as Cate made a difficult decision in Eurydice, as Gormon Hughes dreamed of Jane and his own features blending into one singular face, Estelle was on her way to the elevator.

Princesses dress to reign, warriors for combat, and Sequins Messenger Club members for maximum dazzle. There was no uniform for a bookish, whey-faced jailer preparing to reenter the world after her own self-imposed custody, but in her sturdiest shoes, a simple brown-wool sweater, a white skirt, three pairs of tights (badly laddered, some things change but some things stay exactly the same), and a white woolen hat to keep her ears warm, Estelle gave the whole uniform thing a fair shot. Plus if agoraphobia wasn't going to knock her down, she wasn't about to give the blizzard a chance to do so. She had what Hughes would call the "stage-fright jitters." Currents of nervous energy crackled up her legs and down her arms, making her fidgety and futzy. Her fingertips and toes were tingling so intensely, she actually entertained the idea that the first person she touched would get a shock of static. No pep talks were needed though. She was in control.

Finally.

She reached the elevator and thumbed the summon button without a shred of hesitation. Rocking back and forth on her heels, she totted up the things she wanted to do after her reconciliation with Hughes. The list was long, and though she was more than a little scared while making it, it wasn't fear of doing all of the cool things she could think of but rather a fear of herself. How easy it was, picturing herself visiting her mother in *Pamplona.* Going to a restaurant and ordering the most decadent thing. Five courses! Ten! Walking through a park in the rain, trying to tell the cheaper fake trees from the more expensive real ones. Throwing snowballs. Learning to drive. Twenty-four hours ago this last one would have plugged her up with cotton buds of dread. Now it was enticing. And that was pretty scary when you got right down to it. Again she asked the pertinent question, *What is happening to me?*

And on the heels of that: *Is this how it felt before? Like I can do anything I want, like the world is a library full of blank pages, and I am the only person with a pen?*

The elevator was taking its sweet time.

She tried the button again. Wasn't it supposed to light up? Yeah. She was sure it was. She had a clear memory of a ring of orange light. It came on when you pushed the button. So why wasn't it coming on? She pushed it again, held the pressure, released. Nothing.

Bad electrics? The universe might reckon she was due some faulty wiring, given the bold, brave voltage coursing through her right now.

There was a telephone in one of the rooms. Up until now, Estelle had never used it. All her meals were brought to her. When she wanted something, she asked and sooner or later it arrived. She found it without too great a search. Next to the dusty phone was an equally dusty card. There was a number on it.

Estelle dialed and listened to the *burr-burr,* knowing in her heart who would answer.

"Speak," said Wendy Dragontail.

"Wendy!"

She hadn't meant to be so shrill, but Estelle couldn't help it.

"Something's happened, I don't know what exactly but—"

"Estelle?" Puzzlement. No wonder. Her Ladyship was probably expecting calls from a hundred different projects she had on the burner. The last person she'd anticipated was the girl from the floor above who not once in the past decade had ever picked up the phone.

"Estelle? Are you there?"

"I'm here." She smiled. "More than I've been in a long time."

She wasn't making sense and she knew it.

"Listen, I've got to go out this morning. Not out into the tower, I mean the city. I know there's a blizzard, but I'm wrapped up, and I won't stay outside for long. Could you turn on the elevator? I think it's broken."

Silence on the other end of the line.

"Wendy?"

"I think it's a splendid idea."

"You do?"

"Naturally. Wrapped up, you say? Full marks for cold avoidance, that woman."

Estelle giggled.

"And a spell of mirth too."

"I'm just excited. Can you—"

"The elevator has been defunct for some time. It needs special inputs to work properly. Here's a thought. How about I come up with some breakfast for the two of us, and then we'll head out together?"

"Oh I couldn't eat, I—"

"I insist, Estelle. Do the adventurers in your books ignore their rations before setting out on an eventful—and physically taxing— journey?"

"I guess not. Um. Well," she said, rallying and beaming a big grin. "Breakfast sounds great."

"Capital."

"Bye Wendy. See you soon. And thank you. Thank you so much. Wendy?"
But the line was dead.

***

The same dawn that broke in Corinth City arrived in Eurydice, only golden-green instead of white. The rustle of the forest leaves seemed to meld in some incongruous way into the sweetly rushing hiss of a shower. Cate stood under the showerhead, her palms flat against the cream-colored wall tile, arching her back and rolling the stiffness from her shoulders, and feeling altogether like she had been through war and the hot water was a letter calling her home. A relief rinse. A washdown of light after a burlesque of shadow.

Scrubbing her face as the shower trickled its last and then wringing out her hair, she stepped out and toweled her body and set the towel round her hair in that beehive some long-locked people do after a shower or a bath, and she looked at the bathroom mirror all fogged up and thought about her baby. An image came to her. A handprint, tiny and pudgy-fingered, right there on the glass. *Look Mum! Small.* Another handprint, the fingers spread out instead of clumped together. *Now look! Big.* It hurt more than she hoped for but a good deal less than she'd expected.

Cate thought that her grapple with grief the night before represented a large contributor to this level of emotional stability. She felt her surrender to it was even more vital. But the note was mixed in there somewhere, and Cate did not discount its value to this... What? *My recovery?* That didn't strike true.

My tomorrow, she thought, and that was better. A lot better.

When she'd woken up, tucked up with a blanket in Eilandri's vast bed, the pale woman was nowhere to be seen. Only a few buttered and jammed slices of toast, a cup of tea (almost as good as her Puppy could brew, though not quite), and the note, which was written on a familiar card of yellow paper.

Cate,

When I got my cancer diagnosis, the doctor wrote in my patient file that I was "calm and determined to recover." That was true—in his office. Later, alone, I was so scared, I thought I would go insane. My body, which had been my closest friend my entire life, was now a dirty, cruel, and ravenously hungry traitor against which my mind (as well as a fusillade of chemicals and surgery) would have to do battle.

Sometimes the world is unpredictable. That is a trite, lukewarm thing to say, but the only thing more real are the results of that randomness. I don't know what tomorrow has in store for anybody, myself least of all. But I know that the person I am then will be a reflection, no matter how warped or distorted, of the one I am now. I am not normally so wordy (haha), but getting to know you has inspired me. When we met that day at the portal to Iphigenia, you said that Her Ladyship requested that you add your hobnail boots to my venture. The rest of you came attached in the bargain. That is how I feel about the random cruelty and kindness of life. The only thing we can be sure of is our own shape in the shapelessness. That when we go into the unknown, the best parts of us that made it through yesterday will carry on. I'm scared the cancer will come back. I'm scared of hurting.

But that luggage, those best parts of who I used to be, and still am, help me to be brave.

You should not blame yourself for what happened to your baby. You could, but it would be a huge and tragic waste. There are other ways for you to start a family, just as there are many ways for a mute woman to speak. Trust me—I would know!

Your friend,

Eilandri Titansgrave

P.S. From now on, you can call me "Ella." Walsingham did, and even though he was a dragon at heart, I like your fire a lot more than I respected his.

P.P.S. "Betty" is the worst possible name for a fortress. I have been meaning to tell you this for some time. It is not intimidating. It is exceedingly silly. And I would not change it for the world.

So it was that with a belly full of tea and toast, and with a body showered and a mind feeling just as fresh, Cate reached out and put a handprint on the foggy bathroom mirror.

There it was.

Her face in the glass.

She was not completely surprised to see her nose scrunched up, her eyes crinkled, her lips curled, and the high row of her teeth showing in an imp-like and distinctly Cateish grin. It was short lived, fading fast and gone by the time she was out of the bathroom and dressed. But it had been there. No use denying it.

"Hurricane Jubilee," Hughes had dubbed her early on in their courtship.

He had a flair for that sort of thing, and in this case the naming was especially good. For when Lorna Blacktower knocked on the door and announced there was something Cate had to see, she blew out toward the battlements like a red wind, all hobnail boots, tattoos, glass, and flame.

Chapter Twenty-Eight

The dragon lay in a clearing in the forest, surrounded by bodies.

It was long and slender, serpentlike rather than the massive bulky brutes depicted in illustrated Corinthian histories. There was something of the wolf, or perhaps the wild boar about its snouted head, and something of the snow leopard in its fur, mottled red-and-white and wafting in the breeze. Its claws were each as long as a woman standing tall, and if they were unfurled its wings would have cast a shadow like an effigy of despair. The wings, however, were not unfurled but rather splayed at unsightly angles, as if the membrane of muscle connecting wing to back had been twisted cruelly until it snapped.

The dragon lay in the clearing, its eyes rolled to the whites and staring sightlessly up at the sky, its body tortured and ravaged, surrounded by its slain enemies.

The dragon was dead.

From the battlements of Betty, the scarlet force studied it, their leader closest of all. "Why've we stopped?" said Nyoni Snickerdrake. She turned toward Kelly Cinch's pilot nest, her hands cupped around her mouth. "Oi! What's the big idea?"

"Keep your voice down," snapped Steffan Cerulean.

"Why? They're all brown bread down there."

"Brown bread?" murmured Yussuf Copper, politely curious.

An avalanche of whispered slang piled atop him from the Corinthian members of the company.

"Kicked the bucket."

"Bought the farm."

"Six feet under."

"Pushing up the daisies."

"Popped the clogs."

"Taking the dirt nap."

"Joined the choir invisible."

"Dead," translated Rosemund Valkyrie, bringer of clarity and stauncher of linguistic flow states.

"Yeah, exactly," said Nyoni. "Brown bread."

"Oh." Yussuf peered at the dragon. "I quite like brown bread. I do not, however, like whatever that is." His face lit up. "In this case it is not 'dough,' but 'donut.' Like to bee or not to wasp, eh? Eh?"

Nyoni gave his shoulder a pat. "You're really grasping the lingo with both hands, Yussuf."

"More idiot than idiom," sneered Varjo Cutthroat.

"Eugh, it's *furry*," said Clothilda Toffington. "I'm with Yussuf. That abomination makes my skin crawl. Bravo to whoever killed it, that's what I say."

"Seems as though it killed them in return," said Lorna, looking at the tangle of corpses scattered about the dragon. "Cate?"

They all looked at Cate, but their leader kept her silence. She had procured the crystal compass. Now and then Cate would glance down at it, her expression tempered with a concentration so hard you could shod a horse with it.

Glances passed through the company, this time intrigued, almost excited. What could Cate be pondering so deeply?

"It cannot really be a dragon," said Kevlin Paladin, frowning at the distant clearing. "Can it?"

"With fur? Don't be absurd," dismissed Clothilda, amateur zoologist. "Dragons have scales, Kevlin darling. They're famous for it. And they are stouter stock than that beast. Besides, do you see scorch marks? Cinder? Is the forest ablaze?"

"No," said Kevlin. "No sign of fire at all. That's something."

"It doesn't look particularly reptilian either," put in Steffan Cerulean. "I'm not sure *what* it resembles."

A thoughtful pause fell as a breeze brushed over the fortress merlons and fluted through the embrasures. Elsewhere the undergrowth, the warm tree sap, the round leaves made coinish in the sunshine and the nobbled, dusty, cypress-like bark of trees mingled in a perfume redolent of August, or early September. But the wind struck the clearing before rising up to Betty's battlements, and the only perfume they could smell was one whose ingredients were putrefaction and rot. A death reek for a pretty morning.

Without exception their gaze was arrested by that confusing fusion of features. Its mottled red-and-white hair. Its large eyes tugged by rigor mortis or whatever pain it had endured in death so the whites showed. Its wings so cataclysmically ruined, and yet studying them it was impossible not to imagine them healed and spread wide like a pale shroud over the face of a child.

(Dead or sleeping?)

A few of them shivered. None of the others judged them for it.

"It looks," said Igor Wight, his sibilant voice slinking among them, "like the boogeyman of dragons."

More glances were exchanged at this, considerably grimmer than the last. Though everyone agreed that the beast (most still thought of it as "dragon," Clothilda be damned) did look pretty ghastly, trust it to Igor to put things in the most unnerving possible way. It was a talent of his, in the same way that headsmen are very good at chopping onions.

The reason Nyoni had said "down there" earlier in the conversation was because the dragon and its foes were arrayed below and at a sizable distance from the fortress. A few minutes ago Betty had scaled a natural incline, thousands of leaves gossiping as the moving stone passed by. The sun was climbing, a golden cup raised to pour itself down the blue throat of the day. From the top of the hill the company could see for miles and miles in every direction. It was a remarkable view, provided you liked trees. There, adhering to her inner tactician, Kelly Cinch braked, and with a grinding sound like mountains getting overly familiar, the fortress came to a halt. Fortunately for Kelly, part of the view included the very clearing with which the entirety of the company was now fascinated. With many of the enormous wrinkle-faced trees cracked in half or beheaded, their canopies like fallen crowns, it did not take a genius to figure out the story behind this scene. The dragon had been flying. Something—perhaps the human-shaped, human-sized things sprawled out in a death rug around it—had torn it from the sky. In its plunging descent it had broken and churned a swathe through the woods, and in return the woods had given as good as they got. It explained the sorry state of the creature's wings.

The air smelled very bad now, a rich feast of spoiled flesh for the nose.

"Ella," said Cate. At her side, Eilandri stirred, a pale continent of muscle and compassion undergoing continental drift. "Give Kelly the signal. About turn. Head for the portal."

"The portal?" That was Xacorca Demon. She sounded puzzled, hurt, petulant even, the way a child sounds when she finds out the park is closing for the night. To her credit, she was not the only one incensed by Cate's declaration. "You cannot mean to *retreat.*"

"That is exactly what I mean to do. Full speed, Ella."

Xacorca gawped as Eilandri clenched a fist and slid it along her palm. The fortress was turning, secret organic levers turning around fulcrums of cunningly-placed stone. With a lurch that sent most of the company reeling and staggering and snatching the crenellations for support, the fortress began to gallop.

In the hullabaloo that followed, voices lashed up around Cate, ranging from honest inquiries to thorny comments that veered awfully close to insults. Loudest amongst the indignant was Xacorca.

"If you don't mean to follow the compass toward our next target," she said, "then at the very least we must go to that clearing and harvest the dead with our magic items. The sheer amount of credits those corpses will yield might rival the amount we earned from the Troll."

"Hear hear," said Varjo. "As it stands our haul is merely impressive. It could be legendary—triple that of the Merry Miners and over a shorter span of time. Quadruple, even! Turn back, I say. Delve deeper."

"Have you given the order to retreat because we're all a bit bushwinkled?" said Lorna Blacktower.

"Tired," Rosemund translated for Yussuf.

"Ah, thank you."

"Have you, Cate?"

"Partly." Cate gave Lorna a stern look. "Partly I did."

"What was the other part?"

"I don't fancy dying today."

"Cowardice." Xacorca laughed. That earned her a few stern looks of her own from the company, and worse. Completely unabashed, the Demon plowed on. "You've decided that there was a third combatant, the one who brought the dragon down and slew the smaller creatures. The clearing was directly ahead of us, and that means whatever the crystal compass was pointing toward lies beyond it. The possibility of such an enemy has bleached your otherwise colorful courage, Cate. The fact that we are turning around now is ill-advised and spineless and supports my argument no end. I'm sorry but that's simply not good enough."

"As it so happens, I believe nothing of the sort. The compass... Oh hell. *Down!*"

They obeyed, diving to hunker and crouch behind the merlons or down the battlement steps.

A particularly gigantic tree had reared up before them. Betty's legs crunched its huge sun-dried roots like snail shells. There was a breath—then the front legs struck the trunk. The *crrrrunch* was confounding, a noise that knocked Cate's teeth together like jousters in one of Hughes' plays. Branches exploded, bark blasted, shredded leaves, sheets of heartwood, the whole tree undone in a shower of splintering brown-green like sparks off some crazed druidic anvil. Pattering all around as the detritus fell amongst the company, and still they stayed low as Betty surged on, a chainsaw surgeon in this vivid wilderland, the great arboreal groan behind them as the lumber came crashing down, hearts hammering, on and on until the bedlam blurred and the fortress was stampeding heedlessly through the crush of the woods once more.

"Perhaps Cate is demonstrating a modicum of caution," said Marcus Angel. "Could it be that she simply favors our wellbeing? Needless to say, she's well within her rights to do so."

"Bit of caution sounds wonderful," said Eugenie. The bandage over her injured eye had bled through. "I'm enjoying the sight of the sun, and I shall savor the snow we've likely got waiting for us back home just as deeply, thanks very much."

"And even if 'twas only 'partly,'" said Liddicoat Smite-The-Naughty-With-Large-Implements, "I'm glad you're factoring our exhaustion into things, Cate. I love a bash-up and snuffer—"

"A fight," translated Rosemund.

"Thank you," said Yussuf irritably. "I got that one."

"—and even a bit of tosh-down and tousle-tackle-squibbler once in a while."

"That means—"

"I do not wish to know!"

"But, tell you truly, I'm knackered. Never had a fight go on for as long as the wispy one did. Downright indomitable, they were, and it were your gumption what took us to victory, even if a strange victory 'twas."

There was a chorus of general approval. If Liddicoat (who had once headbutted a monstrous billy goat so hard, it had started to moo in taxonomical bafflement) was for a withdrawal, that spoke volumes. It spoke entire libraries.

Even Varjo and Jennifer looked mollified.

But Xacorca Demon was far from satisfied. "This whole thing lacks honor. We're representatives of her Ladyship here in this cretinous country. We must make our mark or face ridicule, shaming, perhaps even censure."

That did it. Cate stormed up to the woman, so that Xacorca's hawkish nose and Cate's buttonish one were almost mashed together. "Honor is it? Good grief. *There was something wrong.* Didn't you feel it? A sense comparable to being followed in the dark. I'm talking about a very strong hunch here, the sort a wise woman heeds if she knows what's good for her. Honor is brilliant when you've got both your kidneys and an uncut throat and every chance of keeping it so. Now look, we've achieved much in Eurydice and learned more. Yet most important is the prisoner in our dungeon who lives high within the enemy's estimation, who has been privy to Her counsel. We've nabbed him and now we're taking him back to Corinth."

"A Tinfrost gift for her Ladyship," squeaked Lorna Blacktower.

Cate nodded, not taking her eyes off Xacorca. "Something like that. That creature Skuggs is our ticket to beating Eurydice—the woman and the world. And he's below our feet, clapped in irons thanks to me. Course if I'd been honorable I'd have let him scarper. At the very least given him a head start. Maybe I'm not the honorable type. Too busy getting stabbed in the wrist and getting things done, possibly." There was a beat as the atmosphere of the situation changed, and a nasty little thought occurred to Cate. She seized it. "Honestly, Xacorca. We must not cozen ourselves to the idea of success," she said sweetly. "Especially if it increases risk."

A hit, she thought as Xacorca went first pink, then puce.

"Cate seems to have won the bash-up and snuffer," said Yussuf mildly.

There was general snickering.

Oh a palpable hit, Cate corrected. *The woman's gone lilac.*

Marcus Angel took mercy on his girlfriend, slipping his arm around her and leading her to another lookout station. *There will be words between those two in the coming days.* Xacorca shot a look over her shoulder, so filthy it would make even Knickerbocker suggest hiring a cleaner. Cate paid it no attention.

She found herself drawn to the opposite end of the battlements, staring back at the obliterated tree dwindling behind them and the hill beyond that. Her mind's eye drifted farther than that, back to the clearing and what she'd seen there.

The compass had indeed pointed that direction, Xacorca was right there. But had it been pointing past that stinking arena, past the men-shapes and the beast that Igor Wight had described as the boogeyman of dragons? Cate did not think so. No, she did not think that was the case at all. The gallop of the fortress was equine—it pitched every view and panorama helter-skelter. A flock of animals shrieked up, disturbed by Betty's frenzied passage. Their ribbon-thin bodies curled and spiraled in colorful patterns like those twizzling vaudeville things in circus vids. *Even at the height of horror's carnival, hope cannot help but show us its ribbons.* She thought that was hokey. Hughes would have loved it, the soppy git.

God, she missed him. Fecundity is an odd phenomenon—the brain unleashing new ideas like coy into an already busy river. Simply thinking the word "hope" was enough to give her powerful associations. For example, she hoped Hughes had an Eilandri of his own. Someone to guide him in his grief as a poet might guide the lost through the ragged rings of hell to some limbo perhaps, or paradise.

Oh piss. She scowled to herself. *Piss and bother.* She was being Poignant. It never amounted to anything worthwhile, being Poignant with a capital "P." Cleverer people than her had fallen for its trap. She would relegate the poetical thinking for when she was deeply wankered on her next jar of Stoving's Apricot Jawglobber.

Still, the hope clung willfully on.

Take care of yourself, Puppy. I'm on my way, she thought resolutely. *Won't be long.*

Movement in the corner of her eye. Cate glanced over.

Eilandri was there.

"Good morning. A friendlier face I couldn't imagine. On the other hand, a happier one I could picture quite easily. Go on then, for the morning that's in it. Give us a grin, Ella."

Scribbling sounds. Cate was handed a small yellow card.

She read it.

"Please?"

Scribble. Yellow card.

"Oh all right."

***

As the booming crashes of the stronghold faded to distant thunder, as the reverberations gradually lessened underfoot, silence seeped into the clearing.

A woodland toad hopped from its muggy, slushy-wet home beneath a rotten moss-devoured tree. It blinked about at the carnage with chrysoberyl eyes. It took in the garrison of dead men, all chip-toothed and grinning skulls, tufts of licey hair wafting, and scraps of torn skin clinging to yellowing bones. Any coroner worth her salt would have pronounced them "very dead." The toad was not up-to-date on the entropic arts, however, and so didn't pronounce them anything except perhaps slightly uncomfortable lily pads. It was also not a toad trained in the rigors of blacksmithing either, and so the fact that the armor was in gleaming, top-notch condition was completely lost on it.

Taking an interest in the largest lily pad available, the toad hippity-hopped and quarkity-croaked its way onto the furry shape, smeary-spotted red-on-white. Here was a thinner patch (the neck) and a blunter bit (the head), and here something moist to have a squat on. The toad did just that, contenting itself and croaking absentmindedly, enjoying the sun that was warming and gold on its back and unwebbed feet.

As well as being a stranger to coronary and metallurgic work, the toad was also not a perceptive creature, much like the toads in the woods and creeks in the southern reaches of Corinthia, a whole world away.

It barely noticed as beneath its toes the moist surface rolled, no longer a blank white billiard ball but an eye—ivory-pale and slitted with scarlet. It did not notice as, below its squatting position, the shape's mouth parted and began to inhale through teeth like a graveyard for old trowels and rusty shears.

It did, however, notice a feeling of becoming very lethargic and dehydrated, a desire to hop away back to its damp home but... not quite being able to find the will to do so. It made a single noise of pitiable amphibian distress.

Then...

Well—take a sponge and plop it in a basin full of red food coloring. Let it soak. Then pick up the sponge and squeeze it in your fingers as hard as you can.

That was what happened to the toad.

All of its blood, every single drop, was extracted in an instant. Its body shriveled, the flesh pouching and sagging hideously, yellow jewel eyes seeming to bulge, and then it was falling, a dry papery husk sliding uselessly through the fur down to the forest floor. The toad's blood didn't splash or spill. It filtered as though being passed through a straw, or intravenous equipment in a hospital. Through the jagged teeth the blood went, the breath sucking it inside a parched throat.

The dragon sighed. A beggarly breakfast.

Oh well. Lunch had all the prospects of being much better.

Around it the corpses were beginning to stand. Clumsily, the dragon raised itself, just enough to give itself room. With a series of pops and snicks it twisted its wings back into shape. The long wolfish jaw reset itself. Dislocated limbs clicked back into place. The dragon moved, clumsy no longer. Agile. Sinuous. Quick for a form so large, much in the fashion of black mamba snakes. Its wings were as furry as its body, soft white tiger-esque fluff raindropped and tattooed in patches as red as the toad's succulent insides.

One of the dead men adjusted his skewed helmet. He looked much the same as he had in life except for the fact that all the skin and muscle and hair on his head had been removed in a chemical bath accident. A bit of melted chin, that was all that remained of his face. Nothing more. He glared with empty sockets at the empty hill.

"They didn't go for it," he said. "The master's gonna be miffed."

"Not half so miffed as his mistress if we don't catch them," said the dragon. "Send a flitter to Burrows. Inform him that the Agents of the Red Death are headed back to the mountain pass under Golgosuet."

"Golgosuet," the dead man repeated, dipping his bony finger in an inkpot he kept in his pocket and writing the word on his ribs in case he forgot. He turned to the dragon, whose gaze unnerved him. He was not special. Those eyes unnerved everyone in Burrows' army. Everyone in Eurydice, probably. They might even give Burrows himself the craggles! But ah... then again probably not. Burrows was what you might call an exception that proves the rule on the old terror front. "Going after em on your own?"

"Yes," said the dragon.

Even its voice was awful, as though someone important to you had had their hand lopped off, and their fingernails were being stroked up your back. A silky, sibilant, fundamentally wrong voice.

"I will go after them and liberate my fellow counselor."

And because I am hungry, those red slits seemed to add pleasantly.

Dead men have a wider range of emotions than many people think. Even so, fright is not a feeling that comes easily to them. The worst has happened, after all. Once you lay down, all you had to do was get back up again. Basic principle of necromancy, that.

Still, the dead fellow felt like cringing under the dragon's stare. His marrow felt meager, his gusto and bravery suddenly frailer than frail. He'd been itching for a fight against the Agents of the Red Death. Now...

Now, he was pleased to be on messenger duty.

"Luck then," he mumbled.

The dragon peered down at him a moment longer, as though considering something amusing, or sad, or tasty.

Then it turned toward the hill, dipped, drove forward, and snapped its body into flight. Flaring wide, its wings were as scythes reaping the ripe morning air, its heart and its mind orchestral, synchronized, in flawless harmony. Lovely listening, those scarlet aubades. Preludes of a kind.

It (or rather, he) was a great admirer of music. He shared Skuggs' regard for the symphonies that can only be played on that unique instrument. What was the name? Not *vertical flute*. Not *violin*. *Victim*. Ah yes, that was it. Melody and counterpoint. Question, answer. Culprit and victim. Not for the likes of sadism, of course. Sadism was a trough for pigs to snoutfuck.

The dragon's predilections hinted at something far worse than the derivation of simple pleasure from pain.

What songs will you have for me, Cate Jubilee?

He flew on, laughing, the forest rustling beneath him, and both sounds indistinguishable in that pure, pretty, putrid morning.

***

Hughes surfaced from bad dreams into wakefulness. There was no jump, no dramatic blurt or blubbering.

Only a slow intake of breath chopped in half and the eyes sliding open like shutters in a fairground ghost mansion, dark and rumored to be really, truly haunted.

That was all.

Cobwebby and cotton-mouthed, he rolled his wrists and cracked his knuckles and toes, looking around. Bars of cold light punched through the windows. Daytime then—he'd slept at least three hours. That was exhaustion for you. What a guerilla warfare expert. You did your best to fight but it snuck up on you anyway. A noise registered with him, so constant he actually hadn't heard it till now. Wind. Gusting wind. It sounded as though the blizzard was having a ball out there. Further examination reminded him just where the hell he was. The forensic lab hallway was a good index for the rest of the building, dull and washed out, appropriately clinical. The one exception was a poster pinned directly across from where Hughes sat. The poster showed a bloody splatter on a gray background like a promotional piece for a b-movie horror flick. Written underneath the blood were the words, *It takes guts to be a forensic scientist.*

He remembered this particular bit of wit from last night. He hadn't laughed then, and he didn't now.

"Sleep well?"

Hughes turned. The owner of the question was from Yi-Shi—unruly-haired, very round, and mellow-looking in an open lab coat, blues concert fan t-shirt, trainers, and maximum-comfort pajama bottoms. Tyrae Leborski was her name

"Yeah, not bad."

"You looked like you could use it," Leborski said.

"What time is it?"

"Not quite eight."

Make that five hours. He hadn't fallen asleep so much as crashed.

And straight into bad dreams at that. Most of them had vanished on waking like magician cloth. But the image of Jane's face superimposed over his own, the work of some demented internal photographer, stayed.

He rubbed it away as best he could along with the gunk gathered in the pink of his eyes. "Thank you for putting in an entire night on this," he told Leborski.

"I'm here anyway. Insomnia, man. What a bitch."

"How is it?"

"Insomnia?"

"No, that's a bitch, you've made that one clear. The sample."

"Oh right, right." Leborski was rummaging in her lab coat. She found what she was looking for—ChapStick. In no great hurry she applied it, smacked her lips, put the stick back in her pocket. "Yeah, we should talk about that."

Hughes stood. "You've found out what it is?"

"Sure," said Leborski, ambling at a snail's pace down the hall toward the main testing lab. "Figured it out at six or so."

"Six?" Hughes frowned. "You said it was almost eight o'clock."

"It is."

"Pardon me, Doctor. I don't understand."

"Neither do I, man. What's the problem?"

"You figured out what the substance was at six and waited two hours to tell me?"

"You were sleeping."

Anger thrust the poker of his temper into a lit fire, heating it up.

"I don't understand. Captain Thud communicated that this was an urgent matter?" said Hughes.

"Yeah, the nightwatch guy said something about it being important. But a couple hours won't make a difference with this stuff. It isn't Blackbird being dealt to street kids wanting to get high."

The flames guttered in Hughes, the poker getting hotter and hotter in his belly.

"Plus you were out, man," Leborski disclosed. "Like... out, out." She heaved a big, lackadaisical sigh. "I envied you, you know. The whole insomnia thing. But hey, no biggie. You seemed like you were having good dreams too, big smile and shit." She pushed the partition door open, held it for Hughes. "After you."

Hughes went in, resisting the urge to snap something ill-advised at her. It took effort, but he slid the poker out. It was a damned stupid thing to have happened, but he let it go. His mood cooled almost immediately, the blunt anger set aside, curiosity rattling and steaming. There were, as his father was wont to say, bigger kettles to boil.

"What did you find out?" he asked as Leborski made her way down one of many aisles where microscopes and petri dishes and vials of every shape and size held court.

"Well at first I had no idea what I was looking at. Initial tests showed the composition of this stuff's similar to fluoxetine."

"Fluo—"

"Prozac. So I thought, okay, we've got an antidepressant here. No big mystery." Leborski spread out a number of pages, each one scrawled in such illegible chickenscratch, Hughes wondered if the doctor might have a promising career in anarchist graffiti. "But I'm a cautious lady. Second round of tests are more thorough. There was a fair amount of the powder to work with so I tried various combinatory methodologies. Little mix and match. Those tests show that there are trace amounts of colloxin and hydroneurcide. And here's the really freaky thing. You want to know?"

"Of course I do," he almost growled.

"Chill out, man. I'll tell you. The freaky thing is this: the compound intended to increase levels of serotonin in the brain—normally present in fluoxetine—are not."

"What does that mean?"

"It means that while Prozac bumps your nuts, this stuff crushes them."

"Look, I don't have time for—"

"Chill. Out. My guy. My lab. My pace."

Your ChapStick rammed up your nostril.

But Hughes let it go again. Second verse same as the first.

"Your lab," he said, injecting genuine-sounding remorse into his tone. "Your rules. Sorry. That sleep wasn't half as nice as it looked. Grogginess makes me a real P-O-S. If you um... dig my meaning."

Leborski smiled a smile that said, *You are so lucky you got me and not some impatient harpy. No matter, you numbskull oafish dingbat. All is forgiven.* "P-O-S. Piece o' shizz, I dig that. Have a look into the scope."

Hughes saw no choice but to do as he was told.

"What do you see?"

Blobs.

"I take it I'm looking at the stuff from the envelope," he said.

Leborski nodded as if Hughes were really turning over a new leaf. "The name of that 'stuff' is rhylocaine. In Hortesia, it's known as... well I can't pronounce it, but it translates to 'The Emperor's Final Chalice.' And the street name for this particular mix of substances is 'Primer.'"

Rhylocaine. The name meant nothing to Hughes. Ditto on the nicknames.

Flexing his natural talent for theatrical roles, he assumed a chastened demeanor, his head slightly lowered while keeping his gaze unwavering and his voice soft and inquiring, sprinkled with eagerness. "Emperor's Final Chalice, huh? That's quite the evocative phrase."

"It's quite a powerful narcotic," replied Leborski breezily, pleased to be prompted. "It got that name during the Yobura dynastic hubbub in the 14th century. Lots of inventive poisonings in that time."

Hughes' heart skipped a beat. "Poison?"

"Yyyyyup. In high enough doses this stuff will shut down the production of vital proteins that keep the machinery of the brain ticking over as intended. One emperor liked to drink out of these huge, huge chalices. His wife had designs on her brother in law, so she loaded one of those chalices full of this." Leborski tapped a finger on the envelope, which Hughes could see still had some of the powder in it. "Emperor drink-ah dah chalice. Emperor brain cells go blammo."

"It's deadly?"

"In massive doses."

"I've heard lots of medicines fall into that category," Hughes said, not admitting that he'd actually read this in whodunnit mystery plays and crime novels.

"Yeah, lots of people believe that. There's some truth to it. Take enough paracetamol and your kidneys and liver will go kaput. Anyway, in micro doses rhylocaine's serotonin inhibitors comingle strongly with dopalate—you'd know it as the narcotic white gull—to produce stronger, more vivid highs."

"Hence the nickname 'Primer,'" Hughes deduced. "Like a primer applied to a surface before a paint job."

"Exactly."

"Doctor, may I ask you something?"

"Yes, you may."

"What would happen if you took rhylocaine every day?"

It was Leborski's turn to frown. "Huh?"

"Say you ingested the amount that was present in that envelope, once a day, every day," said Hughes, his pulse quickening as his eyes cut to the letter on the envelope itself. *E. E for every possible connotation of that letter. Or was it E for Estelle?* "What would happen to you?"

"Every day?" Leborski seemed taken aback. She scratched an itch on her brow, her face molding itself around the idea. "It would be bad, a weird thing to do, unless you were an addict, of course. But 'Primer' is expensive, it'd be cheaper just to join the rookery and get it over with."

"Purely hypothetical," Hughes encouraged her.

"Well... I suppose you could develop an anxiety disorder. That would take months and months. Maybe years. Depression, for sure. Maybe some symptoms comparable with post traumatic stress disorder—dissociation, fibromyalgia. Shit. Do it for long enough, you might gain an honest-to-God complex."

"Such as?"

"Well, agoraphobia for one."

And there it was.

Hughes stood with his hand on the scope, the other in his coat, quite literally stunned into a trance. He felt as if the world had accidentally shifted under his shoes, and any moment it would realize its mistake and fall apart.

Agoraphobia. A word that, like all the other phobias, seemed to have a kind of magic to it. Thalassophobia. Hypochondria. Entomophobia—fear of insects.

(Jane don't you worry I'll get to you)

(You bug bitch)

(I'll get to you)

(But first Estelle)

(Oh God the poor thing)

(Letter E printed on the envelope)

(*E for emergency, entrapped, escape!*)

(*Estelle!!!*)

A few minutes later, reflecting on the way Hughes had muttered something inaudible before executing a fast getaway, Doctor Tyrae Leborski slipped three bars of Tart Heart gum (extra citrus flavor) from her pack, peeled off the aluminum wrappers, and chewed them into a lemon-sharp wad. Some people were in such a breakneck hurry. It boggled the mind. What was so damn important that you couldn't take your time, do it right? A little twinge of bitterness rankled her— ghosts of boyfriends past who told her that her laconic disposition made her distant somehow, superior, a real laid back too-cool-for-school P-O-S.

In order to nudge such unwelcome thoughts aside, she worked and dwelt for a while on what Hughes had said. *Say you ingested the amount that was present in that envelope, once a day, every day.* Leborski peered into her scope. Where Hughes had seen amorphous blobs, she saw elegant chemical compositions. *Every day.* She couldn't conceive of a person doing such a thing. If they did, she did not envy the withdrawal symptoms they would surely exhibit if they ever stopped. No, she did not...

Chapter Twenty-Nine

The elevator doors parted and Wendy Dragontail stepped out. She held a tray that sported two hearty breakfasts. "Hearty" was definitely the word—sausages, poached eggs, well-salted bacon, baked beans, puddings white and black, fresh baked multiseed bread all brown and warm and soft and delicious, as well as a veritable cornucopia of jams, butter, marmalade, and other enticing spreads. There were lots of things to choose from and all choices in great amplitude. Wendy's dietitian would have had a conniption.

But it was of the utmost importance that Estelle enjoy her breakfast. It was a good and hearty meal, as has been made clear. If Wendy had to indulge herself so that Estelle felt encouraged to eat up, then that was the price of admission. Estelle's appetite might be small at first, but doubtless when she saw how much Wendy was gorging herself (no acting required there, those sausages were practically calling her name), she would feel compelled to tuck in.

And what went superbly well with such a meal?

Why, a tall, ice-cold glass of orange juice. Nothing better.

Wendy was counting on it.

But the best laid plans of dragons such as she often go awry.

She took the stairwell, walking past the gemstone dragons curled protectively as they were about the banisters, and when she got to the central hub from which the nine passages trailed away, each in their own precious direction, she would have taken the ninth toward Estelle's room, when, terribly sudden, she heard the faint noises of someone being violently ill.

Naturally there was only one person to whom that miserable retching could be ascribed.

Sending a wave of psychic spite toward Hughes, wherever he was, Wendy bent, set the tray on the floor, and hurried toward the sounds.

First the desire to play storybook detective, next the argument about magic items being handed out to the general populace, and now this.

Stubborn, she thought. *Stubborn young him.*

She passed a door to a locked room that contained the diaries of her maternal grandmother, five pillars holding aloft five tributes paid to the Dragontail family by the five Overqueens of Rhönland, a woven tapestry of her great-grandfather Wynford Dragontail, a closed window with a hand groping to find purchase on the ledge, another door leading to... leading...

The Lady of Redspire halted. She darted back to the window, her eyes wide. But there was nothing to see, only the juggernauts of cloud hauling snow out of the atmosphere, intent on dumping them in cold fistfuls over the city.

I could have sworn that—

Piteous crying jerked her attention back to the present issue. A normal person would have rushed on, business as usual, eye on the prize and so forth. Well normal could go hang. Wendy had not remained in her position through indolence and the inherent dictums of hegemonic power. She was still in charge because she recognized that the life of a ruler bore certain similarities to a restaurant experience, in which boldness and decisiveness certainly paid, but a fat helping of caution ensured that you stayed alive to ask for the bill.

She slid the window open and peered into the snowy murk. No one there. She made a point of leaning out in case a sly someone had leapt to the upper ledge or to one of the buttresses connecting this floor to the much larger one below. Snow tickled the tip of her nose and pecked her cheeks and brow with freezing beaks. Speaking of, there were a few birds roosting in various weathered crannies in the stone, ruffling and puffing their feathers out to fend off the grim morning gusts. No hand. No owners of a hand either. With her hair whipping into her face, Wendy stayed very still, looking and listening. A doomed attempt, unfortunately, for it was ferociously loud and so milky-thick that lightning could have struck three dozen feet away, and she would not have seen it.

Resigning herself to the idea that her elevated senses had transformed the flight of a passing bird into a groping set of fingers, she leaned in out of the blizzard and closed the window tight, locking it for good measure. Then she followed the sounds of tears.

The bathroom door was shut.

"Estelle?"

She heard an unobtrusive little *plip*.

"I'm afraid I'm not feeling up to breakfast, my Lady."

"Are you very poorly?"

"I was better for a bit, but I got too big for my boots and drank a pint of water. Sipped it to be careful. Not careful enough, I suppose."

The *plip* came again.

"Why do our mouths water so much when we get sick?"

"Saliva is mildly alkali," said Wendy blithely. "It counteracts the acids brought up by vomiting. Fabulously adaptive thing, the human body."

"I hope mine liquifies soon. I feel dreadful."

I'll bet. I hope you're happy, Hughes.

"Your system may cope better with something that replaces natural sugars," she suggested gently. "I'll leave a glass of orange juice in your room. Try it, and if you feel better in an hour, nibble some of the bread. Who knows, breakfast may become appetizing faster than you think."

"Thank you, Your Worship."

"Shall I carry you?"

A pause.

"That would be very kind."

"Can you make it to the door?"

"In a moment. I'm a bit weak."

Wendy put her shoulder to the door, activated her amulet Faethe, and applied pressure. The frame protested, then the door was open, the only evidence of force being the bolt, which had encountered stone, been bent, and now stood out awkwardly like a smashed iron limb.

The young woman was dressed to go out. Her color was a dour sight to behold, pasty and slick with sweat, her hair mussed, her eyes as watery as her dry-lipped and sour-smelling mouth.

"Ah, the princess of this tower," said Wendy. "Might I escort you to your room?"

Estelle's lips twitched. "My dragon protector."

Wendy picked her up and carried her as easily as you might lift a bar of dry soap from the sink. She strode back down the hall, keeping half an eye on any windows they passed, noticing nothing out of the ordinary. Why should there be? The tower was not a mere eighty-nine stories tall, but far larger, with each floor boasting ceilings that could range from corporate building size to the height of a cathedral's belfry. *There was no hand. Fatigue, stress, and this damn blizzard are conspirators in trickery, playing my suspicions against one another.*

She passed the tapestry again. Her great-grandfather sported a cankerous face, she thought. A certain stubborn cast about the mouth and jaw. Perhaps the trait had been passed on, like metabolism or propensity to disease or eye color. *For want of dragons to gift their sons and daughters, my ancestors opted for flaws.* What sort of justice was that?

The same one as dominated the restaurant of rulership, the kitchen games of society, the banquets of decisions facing a person when they reached the top of the ladder and discovered there were no more rungs to climb. The same authority that brought Frank Gallant to Corinth and took her father as a consequence.

No justice, in other words. *Only me.*

"Your scales," she heard the young woman murmur. Estelle held a lock of Wendy's hair braided in snowflakes. "So white."

***

Not for all the tea in his father's *Scriptorium* would Hughes have dared to imagine he might be genuinely thrilled to see Tookus Argyle Vercingetorix of Demeter.

There was a boarded up coffee shop in Cleomenes District, near the psychedelic jellyfish museum. Dazed and stricken, Hughes had been wandering, trying to get his thoughts in order, when through those boards he'd spotted fire dancing. Moving on autopilot as much as his sense of civic decency, he opened the door and saw—not a site of spontaneous combustion—but a fire made out of smashed cabinets and furniture. The room was smoky and stripped as a priest's opinion of hell. Tears sprang to Hughes' eyes, a cough to his throat. It was all he could do not to turn around spluttering into the snowstorm.

"Hot damn! I'll be an uncle's cookie jar and an auntie's cookies—it's you!"

Hughes had an enviable ear for voices.

"Tookus?"

In the oppressive fug of smoke the old man's avuncular smile materialized.

He waddled up to Hughes and pumped his hand vigorously.

"How can you breathe in here?" Hughes asked, his senses pleading for water and fresh air, the column of his throat itching savagely.

"In the nose, out the mouth, just like my daddy did before me. Livia! Livia come here, lemme introduce you."

A woman so wizened and frail she made Tookus seem positively spritely by comparison came pottering over.

"Who's this young man?"

"Gormon Hughes."

"This is *him*," whispered Tookus. Clownishly, he waggled his eyebrows at the woman—Hughes presumed her name was Livia—and gripped his fingers in excited bunches. Grip, grip, a crab showing off some priceless treasure.

Livia pursed her mouth in a fishy pout. Her gaze was pure skepticism.

"He don't look like much. Frank say this was him?"

"You bet your bloomers."

Livia extended her hand, the way a novice marine biologist might extend their hand into an eel tank too gunked up and cloudy to peer into. "Livia Massicordesto of Middlewich."

"Pleasure. Tookus, I'm happy I ran into you. I need to find Frank."

He hadn't realized he had until the words were out of him, but now that it was out the idea shaded his entire body in truth. Need was the word. He needed his friend now, and badly. Doubts crept in, but they were dispersed almost as quickly as they appeared.

"I'll take you to him," said Tookus.

"Really?" Hughes blinked. "Just like that?"

"Yeah, come on."

There seemed to be no explanation forthcoming. Hughes reassured himself with the knowledge he would not have understood it. He tried anyway.

"I suppose it's a 'people betwixt' thing? You all know one another?"

Tookus was fetching his coat off the defunct coffee machine. He seemed more bothered by Hughes' question than the room's intolerable smokiness. "What are you talking about?"

"The manner by which you're tracking Frank?" said Hughes. "I assume it's a 'betwixt'... You know... A thing those of you who live 'in between' things understand. Right?"

"What's he talking about?" Tookus asked Livia. He turned back to Hughes. "What are you talking about? Frank told me the name of the hotel he's staying at."

"Oh."

Hughes was too addled by recent revelations to be crestfallen. Still, it seemed a bit unfair that the reason wasn't a bit more... razzle-dazzle. Oh well. He supposed even Frank Gallant put his feet up somewhere.

"Let's go," said Tookus. "Livia, my fever, my whole heart keeper."

Her face did not soften a jot. "Get your ass out of here, you dirty old dishrag. Close the door, heat's getting out."

"Isn't she beautiful?" Tookus asked Hughes as they crunched their shoes in the deep street snow.

"Your girlfriend?"

"Yeah."

Hughes struggled. "She seems very cultural."

"You know, funny you say that. She *is* very cultural."

Examining their retreating backs through a gap in the coffee shop boards, Livia Massicordesto of Middlewich thought maybe Hughes was him after all. Strangeness, you learned, was all in the face, and that boy had some face. Everything he felt was like a surging tsunami rising up and crashing down inside him. The tide of him would push and pull this world. Bet the horse and saddle on it. Bet the rider! And that face showed it all, a shore and sea and all the hazel-dark constellations above them you could chart the course by. He could hide it from most, she supposed, but not from her and not from Tookus, nor from anyone like them.

She shuddered. Mighty cold. She chose another bit of broken cabinet and flung it on the fire. The flames chewed hungrily, orange gums working hard.

Those who live "in between" things.

Livia snorted.

"How you gonna tell the gaps if you can't even spot the solid blocks that define them? Lord have mercy." She got as close to the fire as she dared, willing them to warm her throbbing joints.

That long, animated face stayed fixed in her mind. "Maybe when you're a man it'll be different. But for now, shadow boy, you don't look like much at all," she said.

***

True to its name the *Upright Domino* hotel was a thin, rectangular building, its facade decorated with five craters or "dots" separated by a thin line. High roller casino joint and guest suite bonanza, the *Domino* raked in obscene credits, the average opening gambit amounting to the cost of the Dennings' entire apartment complex in Leonidas. The hotel's light fixtures were not sodium or anbaric but a newfangled type of neon. Combined with the distinct pineapple hum of early bird special piña coladas, copious cigar and cigarette smoke, and the raucous, almost hyperreal laughter of loose-collar-and-tied tycoons, the blue and pink lights gave the effect of a sensorial pan-fry. Neurons cooked while the cards were dealt out.

It was an ominous place, slightly sacred, undeniably profane, and Frank Gallant was having a blast.

He had not been on a winning streak so much as a winning marathon. The dealer—a professional who did not cheat, but who had a foxy sense for it—had developed a tiara of sweat, not because the man with the weird hair that went pink when the lights were blue and blue when the lights were pink was enjoying such enviable success but because of the fact that he seemed to be doing so honestly. Stranger still, when the furious casino management had sent two orangutan-shaped men to escort Mr. Gallant away from his table (presumably to beat him up and toss him out into the blizzard), there had been a hushed conversation during which Mr. Gallant did a great deal of talking and the men did a great deal of nodding. Frank had handed them each what looked like a length of metallic string. Then they had simply left, though not before offering to shake Mr. Gallant's hand and buy him a drink.

The dealer could not help himself. "What's with the strings?"

"A guarantee."

"Of what?"

Mr. Gallant smiled an enigmatic smile. "Good dreams."

A consummate veteran of the dark green cloth tables, the dealer had seen it all; dreams fulfilled, lives destroyed. He had never seen anything like this.

Things reached their culmination when two other men, one scraggly and old the other clean and young, arrived. To the dealer's surprise, Mr. Gallant wanted to go with them. "Where do I cash this out?" he asked, gesturing to the insane sum he'd accumulated.

The dealer pointed to the conversion booth. Then he got the attention of a waiter and ordered himself a stiff drink. It was nine o'clock somewhere. It felt like midnight in this hotel, as a matter of fact, a witching hour in which things outside the ordinary could—and probably would—happen. But that was Frank for you.

In the lobby, Hughes thanked Tookus profusely.

"Don't mention it, please."

"Really, I—"

"No, I mean it." Tookus' forehead laddered in deep, serious lines. "Me and Livia could get in trouble. Not our place to get involved with the likes of you."

Most other people would have inquired after the meaning of this. Hughes was in the role of the detective, though, his case beyond urgent and outside of that role his friend was in terrible danger. So he gave an earnest nod and said, "It's our secret," which satisfied the old man.

"Okay," said Frank, carrying a comically large duffel bag full to bursting with credits. "Hughes, you say Estelle's being poisoned?"

"Yeah, I said that, but I'm riled up with panic. *I* would call it poisoning. Drugging, definitely."

"Why?"

"Frank, your guess is as good as mine. We've got to rescue her."

"We will. How much will a cab cost?"

"One with ultragrip ice-resistant tires and willing to go out in this?" Hughes calculated quickly. "Depending on the distance I'd say between two and six." A despicable amount of money—six credits was enough to purchase a new grand piano—but realistic. That blizzard had buffeted and bunched Hughes in a strong, white-fingered fist as he'd labored to keep up with Tookus. Every step was a gamble in a casino unlike the one in the *Upstanding Domino*—one in which slippery ice constantly upped the ante. Driving would be even more hazardous.

Frank fished six credits from the bag and handed them to Hughes. He gave the rest to Tookus. "About three-hundred left, give or take."

In other words, a substantial fortune. You could purchase a chunk of Ptolema District real estate with three-hundred credits.

"Much obliged, much obliged. Uh. Who should I give it to?" said Tookus.

Frank shrugged. "Use your imagination. Later."

"Sure thing, Mr. Gallant."

He waved farewell and trudged off, a wrinkly walnut of a figure carrying a truly nutty amount of dough into the snow.

"Who is he?" said Hughes. "Who is Livia?"

"A knight and a handmaid. Don't bend your mind, Hughes. Now's the time when we've got to be arrow-straight."

"One problem at a time, right?"

"Right as rain. You call a cab, okay?"

"Frank, what are we going to do?"

"Here's how it's shaking out. You can't go because you stole the envelope. I can't go because Wendy holds me in the most caustic contempt. So while you phone a cabbie, I'm going to find Mr. Glint."

"Talk sense for God's sake. Mr. Glint is even more conspicuous than you are! If you can't enter Redspire without drawing attention, how is he to manage?"

With his yellow eyes narrowing for the tiniest instant Frank looked as wily and devious as any person Hughes had ever seen. "Hughes, my mothball closet of an angel. Who the fuck said anything about him going *inside?*"

***

When he got a firm handhold on the ledge, hoisted himself up, and spied the white-haired woman with her back turned on the other side of the window, Mr. Glint moved fast.

From his hiding spot in a hollow inside one of the buttresses, amongst a group of fiery-breasted and disaffected northern cardinal birds, he heard the window come open. He waited till it shut. Then he waited some more.

One of the cardinals had a nervous moment on his suit.

Mr. Glint snared the bird in his long fingers, wiped its own gooey shit on its tropical sunset feathers, debated eating it, then decided against and set the bird back where he'd grabbed it. The bird cheeped bewilderedly. It was the first time in avian history that one of its kind had ever cleaned up after itself. Also, it was unsure as to whether or not it was now a napkin. Biology pointed to no. Recent escapades pointed to an enthusiastic yes.

Mr. Glint gathered up some snow and rubbed it into the remaining stain on his suit. His mouth, lugubrious though it was, quietly recited a few lines of poetry from memory. Always a bit of company in a pinch, your basic verse. Scattering the cardinals, he unfolded himself from the hidey-hole. He had waited long enough.

Climbing back to the window, he saw that while it was possible to lift the window up a few centimeters, the lock would prevent it from rising any higher than that. Of course that was no problem to resourceful Mr. Glint, who crushed the bones in his left hand with his right. He squashed his pulverized fingers and thumb, all fishlike and floppy, under the gap.

In about forty minutes they had healed adequately. Now his left hand was inside, and it was a simple matter of flicking the lock off the hook. The window opened with hardly a creak.

And that was how Mr. Glint broke into Redspire.

Soon thereafter he found Estelle curled up in bed. Her eyes gave a butterfly-wing shiver and opened. She looked at him with that expression people have when they've recently been terribly ill—glassy flat eyes unimpressed by anything, even the end of the world, or the arrival of a tall, gaunt man in a snow-encrusted and wind-slapped suit.

"Are you... a fever dream?" she asked so very softly.

He began gathering more layers of clothing from her drawers. Belts too and all the spare blankets he could uncover.

She reached forth an arm and pawed feebly at the glass of orange juice set very close to her on a table. Remembering a warning Mr. Hughes had given him about exactly this sort of thing, Mr. Glint dropped the things he was carrying and took the glass from her unresisting fingers.

The girl followed him with her gaze as he went about his business.

Down went her eyelids, and up—somnolent curtains. "Who are you?"

"Mr. Glint is my name."

"And have you... come to gobble me up... like a girl... in a fable?"

"No," he said, and against her groans of displeasure he sat her up and dragged the extra layers over her. When this was done he covered her in the blankets and strapped them tight with the belts.

"I shall melt," she muttered crossly.

"You do look a bit like an ice-cream cone in that get-up."

"Sweet and short-lived?"

"Just the sweet."

"You're very polite for a fever dream."

"Put your arms round my neck, little vanilla treat."

She did. He fastened them there with the last belt, then he fastened her shins to his waist so she would be comfortable upon his back. As comfortable as possible, anyway. It was a long climb down.

She yawned against his neck and said sleepily, "What now?"

Mr. Glint set off. "This is the part where the monster rescues you from the tower."

Chapter Thirty

Knickerbocker was being followed.

This was, on the whole, a first for him.

When you look like a banjaxed ogre that has been struck by several dining tables and then squashed by God's bottom, people tend to give you space.

Nevertheless as he limped through the neglected tunnel network that led to The Mound (limping because in his scramble to get out of the blizzard into the moldy, damp, and dark safety of the underground, he'd barked his ankle on a fallen motorcycle that had been entirely submerged in snow), Knickerbocker sensed he was not alone.

Ahead of him the tunnel was a cobbled mouth yawning very wide. Pipes that ended without ceremony were its teeth, dribbling and dripping onto carpets of thin bell-hatted things that looked like mushrooms, gray-spotted and spongy, but which were not fungi at all, though Knickerbocker often cooked them into a detestable stroganoff.

Using eyes well-accustomed to such a heady gloom as was present, he spotted a small white form sitting on a phosphorescent bulb of some kind—today's sentry. The rest of Knickerbocker's employees had fled into the deepest hollows beneath the city, as far from the cold onslaught as they could be.

The mouse called Whiskers 319 perked up at his arrival. Knickerbocker put a finger to his lips. Obediently, the mouse did not squeak. In fact it went very still all over. Even its fretful twitchsome nose went still.

Knickerbocker gestured, a furtive gesture that the mouse recognized at once. Together they hurried down the tunnel's gullet, their ears alert to the *trickle-plurp* of the visible pipes and the *gurgle* of the unseen ones, and the *titter-tatter* of Whiskers' tiny pink feet on the slimy stone and alert to anything else, anything at all.

"Hello, Knickerbocker."

Both man and mouse almost leaped out of their skins.

Above them, standing on a strut made out of hardened nylon strings were Wendy's Bloodhound, that young fellow Hughes, and another man with eyes that split the murk like foglamps and long pale braided locks that fluctuated with colors. Knickerbocker knew that second man. He had seen him only the day before in The Foundry—Frank Gallant, that was the name! He was responsible for Walsingham Dragontail taking a long sleep and dying in it.

Her Ladyship might not be pleased to see her Bloodhound in such company. Then again she gives him a long enough leash, and where do I get off judging the lad? I like him well enough. But what's this ambush about?

It was Hughes who had addressed him, so Knickerbocker gave a cordial, oblong sort of expression that could have been anything from a grin to a grimace, and said, "And a good morning to you, sirrahs. What can I do for you?"

"Something I'm not sure you'll be keen on, Knickerbocker." Hughes looked down reticently, then back up, and he was different.

A shift in the stance, could be. Or the face. Had he glowered before? Loured? Leered? Knickerbocker felt a fin of fear plashing through the pool of benevolent acids in his stomach. He had heard whispered nothings, nothing to give credence to

(*I am now, I am now*)

that Hughes was capable of something, some manner of 'fluence as some called it, that he could reach in and—

"Wait," he said.

Whiskers 319, sensing its master's mounting dread, gave a squeak, wrinkling its nose and baring its garbage-enameled teeth.

Knickerbocker made to turn away, to run...

... and then rethought the matter.

Why should he run? Why not listen to what Hughes had to tell him? *Not keen on it?* How could Hughes know a thing like that? Knickerbocker was a sport, ready and game for most adventures of every stripe and kidney, especially if the cause was just and not too bothersome.

He was not in the least aware of it, but Whiskers 319 was staring fixedly up at him, confused. Because Knickerbocker's face had gone slack, all emotion drained out of it like sewage slop from a gouged septic tank.

"Listen to me carefully," came a voice. Was it Hughes speaking? Well, well, wellingtons. Wowser. Talk about vocal resonance. There was something richly... richly uhm... *compelling*, yes, compelling, about that voice.

Knickerbocker resolved to listen carefully. It was a fine idea.

And it wasn't as if he didn't like the lad...

***

It is so often the case that those delivering bad news have no sense of its scope.

When Rosemund flew to Clothilda and urged her to sniff from her pepper jar and sneeze, Clothilda dabbed delicately at her nostrils with a handkerchief and said in a nasally tone, "Now tell me what is going on at once."

"A dragon pursues us."

"*Pardon?*"

But Rosemund was already soaring—marmalade-golden wings catching the sun—to spread the word where Clothilda's thunderous honk required confirmation, and that word was *blood.* As in *prepare for it.*

Gallop as Betty might, the dragon was closing the distance. It was the one from the clearing, there could be no doubt.

It looked stone dead, murmured Cate's doubt.

Shows what you know, sneered her confidence. *Shut up, naysayer. I'm all that's required here.*

She stood with one hobnail boot braced against the stone of the battlements. Eilandri was at her side and Steffan Cerulean. More would come. For now...

"Steffan."

"Cate." His fingers were plucking apprehensively at his beaded shirt.

"I want impaling spikes and I want them now."

His head snapped around so jarringly she heard a click in his neck. "Spikes?" he said. "What spikes?"

"You control water, yes? We're in a forest. Stick it to the bastard."

The rattle of the beads stopped.

"Oh," Steffan said, eyes like gleaming wet river stones, fingers coming up to toy with his dyed blue beard. "Oh, you are an adversary worth avoiding and an ally worth keeping happy, Cate Jubilee. Spikes it shall be."

He raised both hands, stumbled as the fortress' frantic speed jostled his balance, then gaped as he suddenly became steady as a rock. Strong hands gripped his sides. Steffan looked over one shoulder. His gaze drifted up. A bald face with purple twilit eyes was there.

"I–I–I say, ahm... Th-Thank you, Miss Titansgrave!"

She jived her jaw toward the dragon.

"Certainly. Umm. Here goes."

He swept his arms wide, tapping into the ample reservoirs of his shirt's magic, and in his expression Cate saw the complexity of the task. Every leaf out there murmuring to its neighbor, and all the while the transportive xylem working under the veiny green flesh, the vacuole a goblet basking its liquid in the lightfilling, chlorophyllic sunshine, all those emerald discussions whetted with saliva, the swollen secrets of the wood, and Steffan seeking it out desperately, muscles in his hands contracting, veins just like the leaves' thumping under his knuckles.

Cate didn't want to distract him. She held her tongue and wished him well.

Do it Steffan, do it now.

Closer the dragon came. Closer. Closer still—not as enormous as the Troll and yet somehow far more terrible!

Raised voices nearby. Their allies on the approach, too late to interfere.

Steffan, you don't dare quit. You've got it so do it, nownownow!

She watched in feverish dread as the dragon's mouth slung open. Fangs stuck out. Cate was reminded of her father's toolbox. Daddy always packed too much crap in it, an overflow of screwdrivers and pliers and claw hammers

(just like the kind he used on Mum)

and screws, endless screws.

That was what the dragon's mouth was like, and she wanted nothing to do with a thing so foul.

Do it, for God's sake, IT'S ON US IT'S RIGHT—

Her opening horror capped itself closed as, with an almost wrapping paperlike crinkling sound that filled the world, all the leaves for five hundred yards in every direction withered. It was as though October had come for this section of the forest while all the rest of it was left intact, luxuriating in June. Rising up from the flimsy brown husks of the leaves was a lance of water. It was not broad, but it was *sharp.* Before their eyes it hardened to ice and took the dragon in the chest.

An ugly thing happened then, something Cate would rather forget in a hurry. It seemed impossible given the relatively modest size of the dragon (about as long as a long-hauler truck from muzzle to tail tip), but blood exploded from the wound Steffan's frozen lance had left in it. The scarlet army were forming up now on Cate's position, and with the sun on their faces there was nowhere to hide their revulsion. The stuff would simply not stop gushing. A foaming waterfall cascading down and down, as though to meet their rising spirits, since it is pretty encouraging to see an enemy so badly afflicted by an attack. As the dragon flapped into the sky to escape any other pointed surprises, the blood did not sprinkle so much as drench the desiccated part of the woods.

Steffan went limp in Eilandri's arms.

"I have just the thing," declared Clothilda.

"Cattle prod?" said Jennifer Goblingrin.

"Don't be crass, Goblin. Here, Eilandri, tilt his head this way. Smelling salts from Hortesia. Gloriously strong stuff."

With a rattling breath Steffan was conscious again. His eyes bugged out then focused on their worried expressions. His hand groped out, found Rosemund Valkyrie's, and squeezed.

"What's that smell?" he asked vaguely.

"Blood," replied Rosemund.

"It's wretched."

Cate agreed wholeheartedly. The breeze conveyed the coppery tang of it to them, holding it under their nostrils as urgently as the smelling salts had been deployed.

Their eyes were drawn overhead, where the dragon was circling. The disgusting flow seemed to have slackened. Still dashes of it dripped here and there, hideous holy water anointing the crenelations.

"Is it dying?" said Steffan hopefully.

Cate spoke at once, leaving no room for speculation. "No. It didn't even cry out when the lance struck home."

"I didn't wound it?"

"The blood tells a different story. But what do you do if you get a papercut?"

"Suck in air through your teeth," said Liddicoat Smite-The-Naughty-With-Large-Implements. "*Whisssht*. Like that."

"When the ice pierced it, I heard something that's only now registered in my mind," said Cate. "It was much the same as the noise you just demonstrated, Liddicoat."

There was a pause as everyone put this information into context. Then the atmosphere thickened with a vein-cooling understanding.

"But there's so much gore!" protested Elowen Trammel. "You cannot mean that all this is equivalent to a small cut."

"Bogeyman of dragons, Igor said," said Cate. "An unlikely bit of prophecy but one that looks truer and truer every second." The dragon had amended its course, overtaking them. Cate gave Kelly Cinch the signal to turn the fortress then continue the race toward the portal. She felt the weight of the company's attention settle on her. As she spoke she undid her scrunchy, shook her furnace-colored mane out, pinched a few of her loose hairs from the scrunchy, and retied it. "This is no thick-headed lizard we're dealing with. He's a thinker. That first charge was a test. We passed. Stands to reason the second approach won't be as obvious."

"Shall we spread out and keep our eyes peeled?" asked Kevlin Paladin.

Cate shook her head. "I'm not a wise woman, but if I were him I'd hope we all spread out so he could sneak up and torch us one-by-one. Turn us into candles and Betty our stick to melt upon. We stick together as a group, except for the Murky Lurking Lads. Is there something funny, Rebecca?"

Rebecca Lupine clamped both hands over her mouth. "Sorry."

Cate allowed a little sunshine to pass through the clouds in her expression. "Don't be. I'm tense too, as well as being rubbish at names. Igor, Jennifer, Varjo, Brecht—you four take up position in the dungeon. Even though it's a bit too big to fit down our halls, something tells me that dragon has plans involving our prisoner. Thwart them."

Brecht Bedlam tossed his doorknob. Caught it. Glanced at his fellow Lurking Lads. "If a nick causes the dragon to bleed in gallons, our efforts will surely cause a flood." The doorknob rose into the air, dropped, and was caught again. "Luckily for you, I had the foresight to bring snorkels."

Contagious, her bit of bright humor had caught in them, enough so that a joke like that was met with grins. Cate felt a spark of pride. "Everyone else, with Ella. Erm. *Eilandri.* I've got some Jolene-forged paper in my room. Hughes and I can write to one another with it. I'll let him know we're coming home, but that we've got the bogeyman of dragons hunting us. He'll drum up help. In the meantime, patrol the major entrances to the keep. Steffan, Kpelle, I need the two of you to be ready. At the drop of a hat, you've got to be able to douse and divert the dragon's fire."

They nodded.

"I don't plan to burn today," said Steffan. His smile was forced, but Cate thought it all the braver for that.

Her hair was out of her face, her satchel was full of mirrors waiting to be made, her feet tingled as the magic in her hobnail boots rallied itself, and somewhere out there a dragon schemed and plotted her demise.

Rather a typical Wednesday for Cate Jubilee, all things considered.

***

Though he and Frank had mutually understood that it would take Mr. Glint far longer to climb down the tower than to scale it; that was poor consolation to Hughes. He was beside himself with nerves.

They were in the parlor of the Thud household, Hughes himself, Frank Gallant, the captain, his wife, Hettie, and Desdemona Cauldronpot, who had sallied in out of the snow with a sheen of cold murder in her eye, a displeasure that had only thawed when Frank offered to discuss the role of the haruspex in ancient Corinthian religious ceremonies. ("The thing you've got to understand, Dez, you mind if I call you Dez? Okay, Dez it is, and meantime you can stop all this Mr. Gallant cockamamie and call me Frank. The thing you've got to get ahold of is the fact that divining the future from entrails was never intended to become a religious practice. It started out as a shamanistic medical praxis—take a farmer's dog and cut it open to see how best the farmer's liver might be treated. Superstition, sure, but they don't call it mediocre-stition. That hokum and nonsense has *tremendous* power," and so on.)

Minutes ebbed into hours. Cups of tea and lunchly bites were set out and ignored or nibbled at. Frank took special notice of the fact that Hughes paced and paced and drank nothing. No appetite was fine, but Gormon Hughes turning a blind eye to a cup of tea was serious business. Whenever he could he caught his friend's eye and winked. Hughes would give a thin smile and go back to pacing. Midday came and went.

"Where are they?" muttered Hughes.

"Coming," soothed Frank. "Hold your stallions, ponies, and horses. They're coming. You'll see."

Another warmthless sugar-caned smile from Hughes, sweet without substance to lend it solace, and when Frank went back to Desdemona, the dark-haired, dark-bearded, dark-eyed man turned and gave the clock a dour look. His hunger for Jane was as contagious as Cate Jubilee's fighting tendency, only where Cate shone up a place Hughes had the effect of charcoaling this one, an Etch A Sketch hate shading off him, every grunt a pettish deepening, every footstep and glance at the clock another cooking of the mood in a bath of flint sparks and liquid lead.

By one o'clock you could have cut the tension with a pie slicer.

By half-past, a plastic fork would have achieved the same thing.

Thud huddled by the window overlooking his backyard, smoking a cigarette that he offered to Hughes each time the lad passed his chair on frustrated rounds. He always offered—Hughes always accepted. Both of the Leonidas hounds felt like growling. Between mouthfuls of ginseng tea and teak-black coffee, Frank was a curator in a museum of answers giving a tour to Desdemona's endless questions about the occult. Along with Hettie, who was doodling them all without their knowledge (artists are thieves of image, give them an inch and they'll take your smile), the two mystical talkers were the only points in the room not wholly affected by Hughes' ashen impatience, his simple black-and-white appetite for insect meringue carved right from Jane's heart.

There was a knock at the front door—a single, heavy knock like the toll of a funeral bell.

"Mr. Glint!" said Hughes and Frank together.

The commotion started there and didn't stop until Mr. Glint was inside the parlor and Estelle planted right next to the fireplace, which Thud stockpiled with peat briquettes to combat the girl's snufflesome shivers.

Desdemona took advantage of the hubbub to slip out and place a telephone call to her boyfriend, Avery, who begged her to stop this foolishness several times and griped when she showed no signs of doing so, much to Desdemona's joy.

Back in the parlor, procuring a brush from its nest in the parlor dustpan, Frank set about ridding Mr. Glint of the sleet encrusting his suit. "Show me your hands."

Glint obeyed.

Frank tutted. "Frostbite. These are going to blister and go black as night."

"Faster if I grow them back."

"Good idea. Mrs. Thud?"

"Just Hettie, Mr. Gallant. Everything all right?"

"I need to chop Mr. Glint's hand off."

"Goodness. Doesn't he need them?"

"They'll regenerate."

"How novel!"

"Sure is," said Frank. "Could I impose upon you for a cleaver?"

"I'll do you one better," said Hettie. "I've a buzzsaw I use for working with wood. Does that suit you, Mr. Glint?"

He nodded. "You're a proper toff, Miss."

"Come along."

At the same time as this scene played out, Thud was tamping down spare ash in the hearth grate and feeding bricks of organic fibers and beeswax to get the fire good and hot, and Hughes was tending to Estelle.

"These blankets are soaked through," he said as he got them off her. "How long ago did you start feeling wet and cold?"

"Don't know," she said, teeth chattering. "Sometime after we stopped climbing down."

Hughes worked faster, encouraged. Ten or twenty minutes of freezing damp wasn't ideal, especially for someone with Estelle's constitution, but he knew from his own cold winters as a boy that the body can endure much and more before it stages a revolt. Plus you needed to be immersed in an intolerable chill for half an hour before hypothermia sank its cold claws into you.

"Thud, a dressing gown. Warm socks."

"Earmuffs," Thud said, setting down his iron poker and giving Estelle's stiff pink ears a pitying look. "I'll get it all. Hold her feet against your stomach."

He hurried out of the room.

Hughes slid the last pair of stockings off Estelle, wrapped her quivering body in his moth-gnawed coat, and moved the chair she was curled in closer to the fire. Then he took a chair for himself, sat opposite her, lifted his shirt, and put her frozen toes and soles against his belly.

"Hot," she whispered.

No, he thought. *It only feels that way.* Perhaps it had been longer than twenty minutes, after all. He hoped not. God, if she... He couldn't live with himself if she...

"It's so good to see you," he told her, tearing himself from the implacable gravity of worry. "There's—"

"Hughes, I've been suh-suh-so sick."

Withdrawal. Oh Estelle. "Yes," he said softly. "I know you have, sweetheart. There's something I've got to tell you. It'll shed light on your illness. But for now I'll praise you, since praise is what you deserve. Well done, Estelle. Well done."

Her gray-cheeked face peered out at him from the depths of his coat. "What for?"

"For coming down."

"The muh-monster did all the work."

"Mr. Glint?"

Her eyes closed. A spasm rocked her whole frame. "Cuh-cold."

"*Thud.*"

"Here, lad, I'm here."

They got her bundled up toastily. For a while things seemed touch and go as to whether she'd improve or worsen. Such moments when a person's health lies in question stretch as long and unpleasant as tuneless piano wire. As Hughes fussed and rubbed at her ankles to get the circulation going, Thud observed him as was his custom (he could sooner turn off his eyesight than his ability to use it for police work). Hughes was utterly changed. Gone was the grayscale passion that had wound him in knots. Of the bug hunt singeing and galvanizing him, Thud saw no sign. Hughes had seen his friend come in out of harm's way, and now he wanted to look after her. The Jane case was off the table to make room for Estelle, the girl's warmth and wellbeing. And just like that, Hughes trimmed himself a little higher in the suspended captain's opinion. Maybe a lot higher.

As for the young lady, Thud had the sum of her in a trice. Here was a woman, a jailer of enormous importance if Hughes was to be believed, who wore the evidence of her own imprisonment as obvious as those warm new clothes he'd given her. Restless limbs that the shivers wouldn't account for. Furtive, slightly stunned expression. A subtle glee. An overt terror. Now and again she gave Hughes a little smile, loving, yes, but contoured in scandal, as if to say, *This is really happening, isn't it? I know it is, but somehow I just cannot for the life of me believe that it's true.*

Thud gave the pair some space. He hooshed up the window a few inches, admitting some tiny threads of snowy cold, but not so much as would affect Estelle's recovery. More importantly it let him dump his cigarette gunk outside. Damn ashtray was full.

He let the muffled blizzard and the feel of its blue-lunged respiration on the backs of his hands drone out Hughes and Estelle's conversation behind him.

Poisoning. Poisoning a girl until she was a grown up and then poisoning her some more. Why?

Unlike the world beyond this pane of glass I haven't the foggiest.

What did a woman like Winnifred Dragontail have to gain from inducing agoraphobia in a nice girl and keeping her in a tower? Was it a punishment? If so it was a despicable skewing of the Citadel's scarlet justice. And what crime would warrant the Dragon's wrath? What was behind it? You could dismiss madness and deranged fetishism right away. If the city's leader was involved, then there had to be a reason. Winnifred's reputation spoke for itself, but the city gave it a voice and those syllables were strong—many people owed the humdrum shape of their lives to her Ladyship. The trains, for example. They ran on time. Lots of other things worked as was intended also, but the main thing was that the trains ran on time. The person who could guarantee that had power. The city moved and grew and shrank in no small part thanks to her Ladyship's whims. Maybe that was right and maybe it was wrong, but it irrefutably *was*. No arguments there and all translated to the fact that there was a motive. But what?

It's like Hughes, he deduced, taking a long musty pull at his smoke. *Like his mind control. And the Jane case too. There's magic at the root of this, and the trunk, and the whole ruddy tree.*

A link formed in his brain—tenuous but right-feeling in the way crucial clues always signposted themselves.

The young lady's magic item created a so-called Perfect Prison. Was it irony or something more that she had been locked away in circumstances she herself had been tricked into realizing.

Hoshrum Thud gazed out at the fuzzy white afternoon, his cigarette and his numbing fingers and his impeccable mustache forgotten while he spun over the noisy gravel of motive in his head. In the mystery, one fact shone very clear: her Ladyship would answer for this. It might not be to the law, and it might not be to him, but when the time came she would answer. Distantly, he could hear Hettie's buzzsaw. Odd time to be making contributions to the art world. But that was prolific visionaries for you. Always turning their hand to the next project.

A while later, Frank arrived with hot soup in one of Hettie's thermoses, checkered red and green and echoing the holly that added flair to the Thud house's Tinfrost decorations. Estelle sipped timidly, then gradually she seemed to build up a queenly appetite. She slurped and asked for bread and dunked it and munched and asked for seconds and a glass of warm milk if her hosts would be so good. Hughes and Thud shot one another sly looks of approval. This was more like it. The parlor clock struck two. In keeping with his transformation from obsessive to caretaker, Hughes paid the hour no notice.

"How do you feel?" he asked Estelle.

"Much better," she said. "Mr. Thud. Could I borrow some more clothes?" She eyed her fluffy sleeves and socks critically. "Outdoor ones."

"Course you can. But maybe another hour or so of recovery—"

"Yup. Very kind. Let's go to the part where we agree that I'm ready and raring to head off. Don't look so chagrined, Hughes. You asked me for my help, and now I'm here to deliver."

Thud watched Hughes' face, could actually see the lad replace his eagerness with concern. "You shouldn't be so keen to head back into the storm."

"I can lean on you."

"Your color could be better."

"Pale as December, I'll bet. Well, myself and the month should get along then. Kindred spirits."

"Estelle—"

"Come on, silly. Help me up. Spring-Heeled Jane won't hang up her garrote, her noose, her nursery-rhyme-horror knives. So I can't afford to hang up this either."

And she raised her right arm and clenched her fist tight.

Emerging from her skin so it fitted snugly around her forearm and wrist was a vambrace of leather. Two straps adorned it, one for each remaining use of its power. Once, there had been three, Hughes knew. On Hallow's eve, almost thirty years ago, a man had come through the Eurydice portal, stirred up a dreamy/nightmarish havoc, and put Walsingham Dragontail in a coma that would last until his death, and that man was...

"Frank Gallant," said Estelle. "You can lead us to our killer?"

"Desdemona can," he replied.

"Have you been minding your Ps and Qs?"

"Tell you the truth, ma'am, I've never been much for either. I prefer Fs, as in Freedoms."

Estelle laughed, shocking the Dream Warrior and the rest of them besides.

"That makes two of us, Frank. Oh thank you, Mr. Thud." She accepted the clothes Thud handed her, gave them a once-over and pronounced them very fine. Then she turned to her friend. "Hughes, you said you had stuff to tell me. About my sickness. Is it urgent?"

"Yes."

"More urgent than Jane?"

He frowned. "No."

"Then it can wait. How would you rate our chances of nabbing her today?"

"Now?" His gaze traveled and came to light on the leather vambrace. For the third time that day, Thud saw the lad change. First it was haste and hatred, then loyalty and consternation. Now with flecks of snow dusting the floor under the window and the briquettes burning in the hearth, Thud could not really place the emotion Hughes exuded, only that it was damned infectious. His arms itched to slip inside his heaviest coat, his hands to ram a hat atop his head and to reef open the front door, his feet to get loose from here where it was safe and go out there where victory and defeat hung on the edge of a fly's wing. He buzzed for the buzz, the Jane anthem. This was it, then. This time they'd throw in the towel or catch her. There was nothing in between. They could all seven of them in the house sense the totality of that sizzling, humming, buzzing in the air. And what were their odds? That was what young Estelle had asked. Thud wondered himself. He joined the rest in ogling Hughes.

The lad tore his focus from the vambrace. He returned their gazes evenly with one of his own. One by one he looked them each in the eye. Then he grinned, a Bloodhound's fierce and toothsome grin.

"Our chances? They're not perfect. But they're ours, and they'll do." He seemed to search for what to say next. A bolt of universal inspiration struck. "Dead or alive, I'm getting too old for this shit."

They stared at him.

His grin curdled. Grouchy-faced, he swept his coat over his shoulders and stalked toward the door.

"Something something, dirty son of a bitch. Let's go."

Chapter Thirty-One

There was a *tip-tip-tap* at her office window.

On the phone at her desk, Wendy motioned for Knickerbocker to come inside.

He did so, shutting the window behind him, moving as surreptitiously as he could. You'd have to have marbles for brains not to recognize when her Ladyship was in a fouler. Times like this a spymaster watched his footing, lest he step on a dragon's tail and end up a pile of smoldering, sticky bones. He took up a position on the absorbent mat Wendy had laid out for him so he wouldn't drag the wet inside and endeavored to look as though he were not listening to her side of the call.

"Yes, they are well within their rights to protest," said Wendy, her voice several shades cooler than a frosted cucumber. "But if those pylons fail, then the city will go without power. Oh there are backup generators of course, but not enough to make up the difference. That means no lights, my dear fellow, and no heating systems. Listen to me. I have contacted the Jolenes of The Foundry. They have suffered a very recent tragedy among their ranks. Still, their civic duty perseveres. They have offered to help ensure the pylons remain functional. Your workers are in fear for their lives, sir, but with cooperation they will prevail. After all, the blizzard is only a natural force. I am sure I do not need to tell you about the last man who mistook me for anything less than an *un*natural force. My butler, Falstaff, still winces when I mention the words 'concrete' and 'shoes' in the same sentence. Am I understood? Good."

She hung up and fixed her spymaster with a look that could persuade a surfer to take up skiing; it was that frigid. "You're skulking, Knickerbocker. Bad news, I take it?"

"Woeful bad. Horrible."

"Out with it then. Wait." She pressed her eyelids, drew a deep breath, and let it go. No snowflakes, which only partly surprised Knickerbocker, who'd been wondering if dragons had ever been known to disgorge ice as well as flame. "Forgive me," she said. "I'm at my wit's end. No excuse to berate you. I haven't had time to contact the zoology department at the university."

Knickerbocker performed some mental gymnastics without success. "Zoology, Your Worship?"

"You told me about a noise your loftier spies had complained of. A buzzing. I haven't done a thing about it. Rude of me."

Awkward as two thumbs on one hand, Knickerbocker bowed his head, unable to meet her gaze. "Er. No trouble, m'Lady. Better things to do. Uh, that is, more important to the—errrrm—general thingness of the city. Thing. Eh. Begins with a double-yew."

"The *wellbeing* of the city?"

"Yeah, that."

There was a brief silence. "You know my father used to call Redspire the Tower of the Elegy?"

He couldn't resist—he glanced up. "Elegy?"

"A lament for the dead." She was leaning forward on her desk, one arm flat upon the polished wood, the other up with the hand flat and the fingers a platform for her chin. "I asked him what died to make him say so. He never explained. Do you know what died, Knickerbocker?"

"Couldn't say."

"Nor I. I must make it a point to find out." She straightened, selected a notebook from the stack she kept on her desk, and clicked her pen, ready for dictation. "What was your bad news?"

This was the moment he'd been dreading. "It's about the girl, Your Worship."

"A touch more specific, if you please."

"The ah... the one what lives on the eighty-ninth floor."

There was a blur, dizzyingly quick, and there she was looming over Knickerbocker.

Her eyes bored into him.

"What of her?" she said. "Tell me at once."

"She's gone. Hughes got her out of the tower."

"How?"

"Dunno, Your Worship. But they were seen. One of my—"

"Where?"

She seized him by the shoulders. Knickerbocker's eyes darted to the amulet she wore. Gold, it was, and ominous. *Times like this*, a part of him whispered, *a spymaster ought to watch his footing real careful-like.*

He told her all he knew, quick as his quavering throat permitted.

Hughes and a young woman matching Estelle's description had been spotted by a trio of squirrels who had been sheltering in the remains of a crumbled chimney. One of the squirrels hurried to notify Knickerbocker, who on Wendy's very orders was keeping a close eye on Hughes. The other two followed and later reported that both Hughes and the young woman had boarded a 1 o'clock train bound for the eastern reaches of the country, and beyond.

"Heading for Jaenqui-Across-The-River?" Wendy asked. "Or south-easterly, bound for Calcifern? Hortesia?"

"I don't know, Your Worship. I've got the train's information though," he said with the enthusiasm that grips all those who really, really do not want to hear the words "concrete" and "shoes" in the same sentence. "The squirrels can't read, but they can remember the shapes of letters and numbers."

"Give them to me."

"A91 Eastbound, 9C, 13-00."

Moving to the desk, she snapped a few commands. "Go to the grandfather clock outside my office. Call out the exact time."

"Right away, m'Lady!"

By the time he declared that it was almost three o'clock, she had the Corinth City stationmaster on the other line and was calling out the details to him.

Heeding his mistress' forthcoming fouler (even worse than the last, he predicted), and exercising his admirable self-preservation instincts, Knickerbocker shut the office door quietly and headed for the elevator. Sometimes you went out the window you came in and sometimes you found another. Life was often marzipan—nutty as can be. Speaking of, he silently wished Gormon Hughes and Estelle Corlum all the speed they could muster. They were going to need it.

***

The Mysicordelian consul was in bed with a migraine when Lady Winnifred Dragontail stopped by his quarters in the guest wing.

"Ahh," he whined. "Oh your Ladyship. Come in. And close the door, I beg you. The light is like hammered nails, my head the shelving unit."

She shut the door behind her, her attention drawn not to the exquisite furnishings, or the homey touches the consul had put up to make his stay in Redspire a cozy one, but to the man sitting on the first step of the stairway that led up to the suite's bathroom. Even in the near-total dark he wore sunglasses. Absurd... and yet if the Incarnadine radiated one thing, then it was not absurdity. It was threat.

"Please, accept my humblest apologies. I cannot bow. I am plagued with fortnightly sinus trouble, and this most recent bout has escalated. The migraine is bad," said the consul, mostly submerged in blankets, his face pinched with pain, a cold compress sweating against his brow. "Impoliteness to my munificent host is worse."

"Your unflappable courtesy does you much credit, your Excellence. I hope to take but a few moments of your time."

"Of course, Lady Dragontail. Sit anywhere you wish, won't you?"

"I won't, thank you. Consul, your stay with us has brought to mind a kernel of gossip I once heard. Will you indulge me?"

His lips peeled back, exposing teeth, an ugly sibling to a smile. "To be sure, my Lady. What gossip is this?"

Wendy's vision was excellent. Still, the painting of the consul's cousin, Emperor Tanaka, hanging over the consul's bed had an eerie, louring quality. It robbed the emperor of his famous handsomeness, made him look even more wretched than the stricken creature bedded down in darkness before her. "It's only a bit of idle talk," she said. "It pertains to your Incarnadine."

No reaction from the man seated on the stairs, not as far as she could tell. *But then, his eyes are covered.*

Quite the reverse, the consul was squinting at her through his one open eye, his curiosity plain despite the gloom.

Proceed delicately now. A harmless creature has flown in for a visit, not a dragon but a bumblebee. Let them feel the bee's soft striped sides before the stinger.

"I have heard that the Incarnadine are observant of certain rituals. Rumor lends these rituals an air of barbarism that crosses the line from insensitivity to sensationalism, I don't doubt, but nevertheless one cannot help it if one hears a tidbit that pricks one's interest. Grains of truth from deserts of uncertainty, and so forth."

"Indeed, my Lady. There is wisdom in your words."

"Glad to hear it. So, your Excellence, is that an admission?"

"An admission?"

"About the Incarnadine. Such as, for example, the man you have in your service," said Wendy smoothly. "You admit that he observes some sort of rituals as determined by his organization."

"I... Yes. Well, yes, that is true, I suppose. Everybody has their customs, big and small. I dare say.... Ahh..." Looking at her was too much for him. He closed his squinting eye, massaging his temple vigorously while beads of moisture ran down his cheeks. "What was I... Right, I dare say that your Citadel is like a great symposium of rituals, my Lady. It is famous far and wide for them."

"Indeed?"

"Yes, yes. Absolutely. A good fame, of course, not infamy as the Incarnadine have accrued. There are actually two rival factions within their group."

"Did they schism?"

"Schism! *Ahh.*" He sucked his teeth. "*Meishife*, that hurts. Indeed, Lady, indeed. A schism that separated the merely violent counter terrorists and the bodyguards from the political assassins and criminal syndicates. The Incarnadine can be viewed like a partially blighted fruit. Let me assure you that the one I have been sent by my cousin, the emperor, is not part of the rot. He is vicious, true. But I trust him with my life."

"You display oracular talent," Wendy complimented.

"My Lady?"

"I simply say because you have accurately foreshadowed the nature of that tidbit of gossip I alluded to earlier." *There goes the soft,* she thought. *And without a hitch. Now, the stinger.* "Your Excellence, is it true that when they take on new employment, the Incarnadine demonstrate fealty by binding their lives to that of their employer?"

It was only because she was on high alert for it that she caught the movement. A casual watcher, and even an acute perception in fact, would have missed it.

But she saw.

At the mention of binding one's life, the figure on the step went as rigid as a broom. *Not what you were expecting, eh? Stick your pierced tongue out at this, then.*

"Since you have entrusted your care to the Citadel during this," she smiled without humor, "rather tumultuous holiday season, I feel it's my duty to understand what might be dubbed the 'relevant factors.' That is, any and all information conditional to your health and comfort."

"Ahm." The consul ran his tongue over his cracked, dry lower lip. She could practically sense him curling his toes under the sheet, weighing his cultural obligations versus his perceived debt to her. Gratitude rushed through her for the room's endarkened state—if it had been bright, the Incarnadine might have given the consul some signal. As it was, his Excellence had to figure things out for himself, which was favorable for her. No more words were spoken for a tense while. Wendy let silence do the rest of the convincing. It lengthened, and eventually worked as she knew it would.

"Your, ahah-hum, *tidbit* is correct, my Lady. In some practical semblance, anyway."

"Such as your own situation?"

"Yes. When the Incarnadine arrived in Corinth, he and I exchanged blood. A simple transfusion."

And one that was observed by a tiny rat, thought Wendy. *How puzzle pieces love to arrange themselves when they are good and ready to do so.*

"Our lives are bound until the employment contract ends," said the consul. He stopped massaging his head long enough to gesture in the Incarnadine's direction. "If he dies, I die, and vice versa. About the breaking of the binding, I can't tell you anything because I don't know anything. I... Oh *Jifur,* my head. Deepest apologies, I'm half-blind and thick-tongued with the pain. Suffice it to say I am telling you all of this information because of our strong diplomatic relationship, my Lady."

You're telling me because it behooves you, you fawning little frog. You verify the truth of some gossip, I continue to keep you here in the tower until this serial killer pantomime has run its course.

Aloud she placated, "Strong diplomatic relations grow even stronger when tempered by such honesty. I commend you, sir, truly I do. On your honor, as well. I wish my own people had your capacity for it."

He took her danglingly obvious hint.

"Your own people? What's happened?"

"Well, you know, it's the most inconvenient thing." She spoke nonchalantly, injecting some worry and emphasis here and there, and all the while she watched that stiffened, motionless form on the stairs. "A young woman in my care named Estelle Corlum has been taken abroad by Gormon Hughes."

"Your Bloodhound." She noticed the consul's waxy complexion grow paler still. "Oh, I do apol–"

"No harm done. Yes, *that* Gormon Hughes. And let me tell you something, your Excellence: Estelle is incredibly important to the Citadel, and to me."

"And Hughes has taken her? Why?"

"He seems to think she'll help him achieve success in some dangerous venture. He's concocted some plan. Who can say why young, impulsive–"

(*cheeky, impudent, priggish, headstrong, fucking* stubborn)

"–men do what they do?"

"You must be so worried, my Lady."

"Why, I'm sure I am as worried for her health as you are about your own," said Wendy.

And there.

It.

Was.

The proverbial cat was out of the metaphorical bag.

The consul prattled on, but Wendy wasn't paying him the slightest attention.

Do you take my meaning, Incarnadine? I struggle to think how I might say it in a more digestible way. The man you've bonded yourself to will receive my best protection, my concentration, and my care. For the rest of his tenure in the Embassy, he will walk safe, and you along with him. In return, I want Estelle. I want Hughes. The dragon demands her due. Not a bee, alas. In the end that stinger was a claw.

What shall it be, then?

The protective heat or the scourging flame?

The dim shape slumped a bit. He gave one of those barely perceptible nods, stood, and went to the consul's side.

Protective heat it is. A sublime choice.

The Incarnadine spoke into the consul's ear. The consul did not look happy with what he was being told. To Wendy's mild approval, he managed another of those anemic smiles. "My Lady. I may have the solution to your woes."

"Oh?" she said, a picture of surprise. "Do tell, your Excellence."

A minute or two later, she and the Incarnadine were standing together in the corridor. There were pillars lining it and windows on the left ferned in frost. All the flowers and plants on the right side of the corridor were uncovered but rather shrined in snow (the filtration system in the guest wing led to the outside). Wendy knew how they felt. In her chest her heart felt gelid and artificial, and ice lolly stuck with plastic. Everywhere else she was inflamed and ferocious. But where it counted she was flash frozen, a spurned icicle woman, nasty and cold and sharp as can be.

"You know," she said. "I also heard a rumor that members of your organization have a unique ability to locate lost people." She went to one of the windowsills she'd visited earlier and came back with a book and a great many newspapers folded into a single thick square. "Estelle recently held this book. For years Hughes slept under these newspapers for a blanket."

The Incarnadine took them wordlessly.

"I want them both alive," said Wendy. "And unhurt, if you can manage. For the rest—the policeman, the puppet, the gaunt, grim man—exercise a gallow's judgment. It must be clean and quiet and done with caution."

If he heard her he gave no sign of it.

He opened his mouth. His tongue came out, a damp pink mole emerging from its hidey hole. That piercing, a glimmering red stone, began to darken. She watched, fascinated, as blood seemed to fill it. Then the stone dripped—once on the book, again on the newspaper blanket. Scarlet seeped into age-yellowed pages.

The Incarnadine straightened, retracting his tongue.

Then he turned on his heel and marched toward the elevator.

If I let him turn the corridor corner, I'll let him go. Hughes and Estelle will be at the mercy of that man. True, he has a vested interest in keeping them alive for me. But who can say what will happen?

She had heard as many exaggerated stories about the Incarnadine as Knickerbocker. But she was Wendy Dragontail, and she had access to more than the usual loaves churned out by the rumor mill. This was a killer she was dealing with. Not a serial-murdering lunatic but a man who killed people because it was his job. What did it do to someone, approaching life and death with a barman's attitude to bottles of beer? Stack em up, knock em down.

She supposed it made you wear sunglasses all the time so people never knew where you were looking. It made you stick out your tongue at the most powerful woman in Corinth City. It made you curious to see what she would do because when murder was your friend, other company became a bore. You did little things to keep yourself entertained.

He was almost at the corner, about to walk out of sight.

I could stop him. Handle things myself. I won't lie and say I hadn't considered it. I could stop him.

Wendy opened her mouth to do just that...

... and closed it shut.

She thought of Estelle. She thought about what she'd had to do, and the methods, and the concessions she'd made with what she believed. Right and wrong. Negotiations in the bedbound night.

She thought of Hughes

(what? stubborn old what?)

, and she pictured his face when he found out those things she'd had to do.

Would there be a negotiation in his heart? Would he exhibit the frostiness she was, on a heartbeat basis? Would he say, *Oh, well, look. You know best, Wendy. You always have done. Now is no different.*

She doubted it.

She really, truly did.

The Incarnadine turned the corner and was gone. A red man conducting red business.

And on my behalf.

She stood alone, half of her bathed in the gray-white light spooning in from the windows the other half dimmer but still quite luminous in the reflected pale of the snow alters, the ice tabernacles.

And that was it. When you got right down to it, anyway.

The heat flowing all around—her cheeks, her neck, her mind. It was anger. Simple outrage channeled into fury. But her heart was a cold abandoned house. Shame squatted there. Shame and guilt and a wretched, loathsome stubbornness.

The Last Dragon, guilty.

Like something in a tragedy, and a bad one at that.

She was only delaying the inevitable, of course. Sooner or later she would see Hughes and Estelle. They would say what they had to say to her. Why bother sending the Incarnadine at all? Why not do as the dragon was wont to do and resolve matters herself?

Rational idea, that. Robust. Sensible.

And yet she hadn't stopped him. She wasn't planning to either.

She could feel the shame crickling and crunching like fresh snowfall underfoot. Its glitter was evil, yet by the same token irresistible.

When had she last felt this way?

When I wasn't here for my father. When I ran away all those years ago to pursue who knows what. While I gallivanted he must have chewed his cheeks ragged, worrying. Then the news was out that he was hurt. We never spoke again. I shouldn't blame myself—how could I have foreseen Frank Gallant? But I do. Blame myself. Parents and children. What a joke. Why must family be the only place where reason and good sense hang up their hats?

"My Lady!"

She started.

"Falstaff," she said, regaining control. "How are you?"

"Splendid, now I've found you. First I lost track of tasks, then time, and finally you. It's a day of misplacing, I suppose."

You have no idea, she thought.

"Some urgent matters require your attention," the butler said. "Will you follow me?"

The Last Dragon quenched her anger as easily as you might use a candlesnuffer on fiery wick, and with a proud, matronly tone, she said, "Lead on, Falstaff. The city calls and the tower answers."

Yes, the anger went away without umbrage or fuss.

But the shame didn't budge.

Not one bit.

Act Ten
Something Very, Very Loud

Chapter Thirty-Two

Later, when Jane had been dealt with (although Thud was never convinced she *was* dealt with, not completely) and the case had been filed away into the drawer to gather infamy and dust kitties, Hoshrum Thud reflected on that final chase. How it had passed in the ugliest fashion possible from day to night through dusk's infected kidneys. How it contained all the bad things—the vileness—that daytime or night could accommodate. How violent things grew. How violent he himself had to become to survive it.

Yet at the same time, there was an undeniable rosiness to the memory. Danger is never so terrible when viewed through a lens of years. Often the opposite veers closer to truth. That brush with one's own doom paints itself in motley clown getup, capering around. Talk to someone saved from a car filling rapidly with seawater, and they will inevitably tell you some odd detail that sticks in their head, an anecdote about the song on the radio being Muddy Waters, or Credence Clearwater Revival, something to that effect. Off-putting, to be sure, but also sort of amusing.

As they set out from his house on Lombardel Road, the group hot on Desdemona's heels as she guided them, Thud was not aware that while they pursued Jane, they were themselves being hunted. He wasn't aware of Cate Jubilee's predicament in Eurydice either.

He learned about those off-putting and perhaps amusing coincidences in good time.

In the thick of it, when it was happening around him, to him, things were not so pink. So rosy. They were white and red, blood and snow. One mission. One case. Three deadly chases.

As far as Thud was concerned, you had to laugh.

It was that or go crazy.

***

They found both men dead on the floor. Throats cut wide, second mouths gaping. Still wet.

"Who are they?" asked Thud.

"Myrmidons," said Hughes. "Hurry."

The carousel cottage blurred as they ran for the stairs leading to the second floor. Dog legs. Hare ears pricked high. Hippopotamus jaws yawning, four teeth like doorstops in the noisome dark. *Howwwwwwwwl,* went the blizzard outside and a pack of wolves joining in silent communion from the banister. Wild boar tusks. Ostrich necks. Horse hoofs. Monkey hands, humanlike, seeming to clutch at their clothes. Leonine snarls. Tiger teeth. Leopard, locust, and lanternbug. All plastic. All melded together to form the cottage walls and doors. Blind yet eerily lifelike eyes stared at their party. Blood on the steps. Droplets, slippery. Hughes stumbled, regained his feet, ran on. There was the top of the stairs, then the sweeping curved hall leading to the bedrooms and the broom closet. Hughes' frantic gaze snapped to the only source of light. The Mum's bedroom door was opening, a wedge of orange glow growing and growing. Krys the Painted Girl was there, turning the handle. In her other hand, the kitchen knife.

"*Jane,*" Hughes cried, and pushed his Performance. "*Get OUT OF HER!*"

The magic encompassed her, a gloved fist wringing the hideous grin, and all other trace of emotion, from Krys' face. She went still and slack and flat-featured, as though she'd put on an unmarked theater mask.

With Frank, Mr. Glint, Thud, and eager Estelle at his side, Hughes charged, a bark of triumph tearing up his throat.

The unthinkable happened.

Performance Failed

+1 Experience on a Failed Attempt

Congratulations!

There was a blocked sinus snuffling, as of someone with a cold waking from sleep. "Wossat?" The Mum's voice came through the door. "Is that you, girl?"

Estelle was reaching for Krys, her vambraced arm shaking with anticipation.

"Estelle, stop!"

She froze. "What is it?"

"It failed," said Hughes. "My Performance. If you imprison Jane you'll take Krys with her. *No, no–down!*" he roared as Krys wheeled and bolted into The Mum's room, knife swishing and carving madly. "*Bring her down, bring her–*"

A velvety sound, and Krys' fist was netted in a mesh of nylon strings. She glowered at Frank, whose jacket sleeve was unraveled to the elbow, the fibers transmogrified to the very strings snaring her.

Voices mingled like this:

The Mum: "What do you think you're doing, girl? And what are you doing here, Gormon Hughes, you and this lot of larrikins and bruisers? Up to what? No good, I'm sure!"

Hughes: "The knife–get the knife away from her!"

Frank: "Watch the tattooed girl, Estelle. Jane might leap out anyway, you just watch her now."

Estelle: "Should I... Hughes, what should I...?"

And Mr. Glint advanced through the crush, nimbly avoiding Frank's strings as they wrestled to keep control of the girl's flailing knife-hand, sidestepping big-eyed Estelle who was clearly knocked for a loop by Jane's unexpected resistance to Hughes' power, and in one fluid motion he took the knife blade-first. It sank into his skin. Mr. Glint seemed pretty unbothered by this. He yanked it from Krys' grip, *crrrracked* wide his face, mouth stretching cavernously, and in his way, he tidied up the mess.

A protesting metallic sound gave them all the impression the blade was being bent into a weird crescent by his gravestone teeth (which indeed it was). Then it was over.

The glazed look faded from Krys' countenance. She blinked at the first person she happened to look at—Mr. Glint.

"Good evening," she said. "I don't think we've met."

"Only a glint, Painted Bird. You've got all your morning songs inked on you."

She smiled happily, as though Mr. Glint had just spoken in her native dialect.

"Twitter-tweep," she said.

Hughes felt The Mum's glare and in that moment knew what Thud's fireplace had felt like when the streetbeater had thrust a hot poker into it.

"I don't pretend to understand what's going on here. What time do you call this then? Honestly, we're not all young as new daisies, Gormon Hughes. What are you cutting that tea of yours with—Irene Partridge's Extra Go-Go Powder?"

"It's only five o'clock, Miss," Thud pointed out.

"It's dark out, isn't it?"

"Darkish, yeah..."

"And who are you calling *Miss*, boy?"

Hughes turned to Frank. "Desdemona's downstairs, I think."

"Way ahead of you." Frank's sleeve was reforming, strings thinning back to jacket fibers, his stride elegant as he made for the stairs, eyes headlight bright and avid. "I'll find out where Jane's headed next."

Hughes spared a fleeting moment to thank whatever divine fortune had sent him his friend, Frank. When he turned back, Mr. Glint was helping Krys up. Krys was frowning her puzzlement at the indentations crisscrossing her palm and fingers—relics of her recent run-in with a certain Mr. Gallant.

"What now?" said Thud.

"We make sure these two have someone guarding them," said Hughes. "Then... I don't know. My Performance failed. There's an interval before I can try her again."

"How long?"

Hughes steeled himself. "Varies. Could be hours."

Right on cue, Thud's mustache twitched. But that was the man's only concession to their plight. He was a hard man, was Hoshrum Thud, and the despair he'd shown in The Foundry would not make a second showing. "In that case we thwart her, just like we did here. Almost did," he amended. "Poor bastards downstairs. Everything we can do is what we will do. Woof, woof, eh?"

Hughes grinned despite himself. It felt good. "Be faster with the truncheon next time, Leonidas Labrador."

"File a complaint with my superior. He can't take my badge twice."

"True." Hughes went into the bedroom. "You okay, The Mum?"

Her grandmotherly face was more flushed than usual. The skin around her nose was an angry red and flaky. Tissues formed stiff little processions up and down the bed, pooling on the floor.

"Have you a cold?" he said and regretted it at once.

"What clued you in? You're wrong, anyway. I've got what you might call stoic leprosy. Any moment now my patience is going to turn black and fall off."

"Let me explain."

"*Miss* indeed," she grumbled, snatching a hankie from her quilted pajama cuff and honking her stuffy nose into it. "Haven't been called *Miss* since the old Ringmaster took me for a carnie strumpet. Had his job in two years. There's *Miss* for you. Bloody cheek. And a policeman too! I'll pluck his whiskers for him. See if I don't."

Hughes gave Thud a look that said, *Make yourself scarce, I'll take it from here.*

Thud nodded and left.

Mr. Glint, Krys, and Estelle were exchanging pleasant introductions.

Hughes turned back to The Mum, took a breath, and felt his attention pivot dramatically as, downstairs, the front door slammed open on its hinge.

There was a pronounced clicking sound that traveled up the stairs, then a rush, a heart-jarring *thump.* Then a voice began to shriek.

Desdemona. Hughes moved fast, but Glint was faster. The gaunt man vaulted the banister. One second he was there. The next gone. Hughes was right behind him, reflexes built by Cassandra and Hector of Troy taking over. Taking the impact in his knees rather than his back, he gave a grunt and surged into the sitting room.

Desdemona was there, no longer wailing her banshee lungs out. She was on her knees by Frank, who was crumpled against one of the plastic animal walls. Tears made wild track streaks in Desdemona's makeup—eyeliner splotching blackly. Frank was shot, a crossbow bolt propped out of his chest like a flagpole inviting salutes.

The shooter was a woman with the look of the two guys Krys had dubbed her "myrmidons." Like them she was dressed darkly for stealth. Expensive shoes. New manicure. In her hands was a lean implement of murder. A crossbow with a narrow stock and a mechanism that was already loading a fresh bolt into the triangular nook of the string, nocked back and ready to loose. A quickbolt. Hughes couldn't believe it. The very weapon Wendy Dragontail had used as her example during their argument about mass deployment of magic items. Apparently they were not all decommissioned.

The shooter's face held an abstract quality, a little glazed, a little happy. It was an expression Hughes was becoming more familiar with, much to his grief and fury.

He did not need to tell Mr. Glint it was Jane.

Maybe it wouldn't have mattered if he did.

As Mr. Glint came for her, the shooter unloaded. It was an admirable shot, taking the gaunt man directly in the breastbone. Not a winner though. When it came to Mr. Glint, there was no such thing. He crumpled the bones in her wrists, took hold of her head, and punched her. Just one punch. One was all it took.

She slumped, falling backward bonelessly into the soft garden snow. Thud jumped over her in a limber bound, his truncheon out, disappearing into the flurry of white.

"She shot him. Kicked open the door and shot him like he was a rabid animal," Desdemona babbled. "No bleeding. Shouldn't there be... Oh Mr. Gallant. You mustn't die."

"Just Frank, baby." He gave her hand a pat. "Didn't I tell you that?"

"How bad, Frank?" said Hughes, leaning down next to him.

"Hurts like a sumbitch." Frank's mouth went crooked, his hair waxing and waning, turquoise to coral blue and back again. "But it's all good like Gielgud. I won't unravel."

Smiling. How can a shot man smile as charmingly as that?

Easy, he answered himself. *He's got to be Frank Gallant.*

Estelle appeared. "What happened?"

"I got shot," said Frank. "We're not making a big deal out of it."

"Estelle," said Hughes. "Go and get Krys for me. Tell her Jane's possessed one of Kim... eh, one of Creusa's men."

She gave a dutiful nod and hurried back upstairs.

"Sorry I hurt you," said Mr. Glint, dragging the unconscious shooter inside by her ankle and depositing her by the unlit fireplace. "Oughtn't to have shot Mr. Gallant, but seeing as you were *non compost marble,* I suppose that's all right."

"There's another bloke in a car out there," said Thud, arriving back. "Dead. Crossbow bolt in him. Looks like this one," he said, nudging the unconscious shooter with the toe of his shoe, "did for him before taking her chances with us."

"Not her," said Hughes. "Jane."

"Go get her," said Frank.

"Yes, and best of luck," said Desdemona.

"Save some for yourself. You're going too."

She stared at Frank with open astonishment. "Do you mean to suggest I leave you here? Like this?"

"Sure do."

"But you're shot!"

"It's inconvenient, but—"

"It probably punctured something important. You're quite delirious! Humbert—"

"Hughes."

"—you must do something right this moment. Your betters are pincushioned."

"Desdemona," said Frank, and his tone was a testament to that moment of bliss when the first good dream scoops you up and promises you that more of its kind are on the way—mighty phantasms, candy imaginings, sexy, joyful, and oh so nice.

"Desdemona."

"Yes, Frank?"

"Go with Hughes. Do that voodoo that you do so well."

Her soggy demeanor dried into a tough, unyielding resolve. "Yes. If the spirits decree it, and with all my heart I know that you, Frank, are the vessel for every benevolent apparition, every ethereal, fluctuating, evanescing—"

"Yeah, that'll do, Denise," said Hughes. "Frank, I love you."

"Love you too."

Krys backflipped down the stairs, stopped, and cocked her head at the two dead men and the one unconscious woman. "Who hurt my myrmidons?" she wondered.

"Krys, I wish we had five minutes to explain, but we don't," said Hughes. "Have you a telephone here?"

"Yes. But—"

"Call Creusa. Tell her your myrmidons were magically possessed and you need three more, pronto." A somber possibility occurred to him. "Tell her that the possession is catching—she needs people around her who can keep watch, both on her and one another."

"A potential target?" said Thud.

"My ex-girlfriend," Hughes replied.

Thud grunted. "That'll do it. We better move."

Hughes turned back to Krys. "Have you got all that?"

"Have it, worn it, hung it on a hanger."

"You're remarkable."

With her tattooed hands she fanned out her dress in a curtsey. The dress was new, a brocade of silks shuttle-woven to look like leaves. And on the leaves, ladybugs.

Hughes didn't much believe in omens.

His heart took it as one all the same.

As the rest filed out of the cottage, Frank sent out a string to bracelet Hughes' wrist.

Hughes' brows went up, and as Frank spoke they sank down again, furrowing a bit and relaxing, as though what his friend said troubled him greatly, yet at the same time applied balm to an open sore he did not know he had.

"Something that needs saying, Hughes. Maybe you win, maybe you don't. I think you've got a good shot with Estelle in your corner, but you never know. If you do win, and Jane loses, keep your grace. Do the killing or the imprisoning because it's got to be done. Don't like it or take pleasure in it. I was muddled before, when she brought up my moms. Made me happy to hurt her for what she said. But that way is hers, and it'll eat you up just as greedy as a swarm of flies on old chicken if you aren't wise to it."

"I'll think about it."

"I know you will."

"Sorry you got hurt."

"Hey, in adversity or prosperity, this too shall pass."

The string slipped off his hand, and Hughes went out into the storm.

***

A hair shy of an hour later, Krys the Painted Girl saw the shape of a man coalesce out of the blizzard. She was in her bedroom upstairs, stretching and contorting her needle-inked body next to her window, which overlooked the front garden. She stopped her circus gymnastics as soon as she caught sight of the shape. It crossed her mind this was another myrmidon, the first of the three Creusa promised her on the phone. But there was no one else with him, and she felt an eerie disquiet come over her.

There was nothing to see in that garden, with the flowers covered in tarps, the sunlight cylinders stowed away from the gusts that might knock them over, and the heavy snow covering the passage of Hughes and his friends.

If Krys' eyes were to be believed the man didn't care a jot for any of that. He moved about down there, searching or something, and all the while that disquiet inflated in her head.

"Go away," she whispered, a touch shocked at how unkind her tone was. "Go away. You're not wanted here."

He stopped what he was doing. His head swayed a little, side-to-side.

Then he looked right at her, and she felt as though the winter had pushed right in through her window.

He did something strange, turned his back, and walked away. In a few seconds he was enveloped in the mist and the whirling white.

A star, she thought. *A red dwarf star sparking in his tongue.*

***

Say this for the dragon—he was a crafty bugger.

All through the dense forest and the daytime, he'd staved off attacking. It hadn't lulled Cate and the others into a false sense of security. This was not their first monstrous rodeo. But it did tickle their imagination some, and when the attack did come, it meant that those who had formulated plans in their heads executed them quickly, without the good sense to adapt to changes in circumstance. In other words, Kpelle and Steffan reacted to what they expected to happen rather than what did happen.

The company was in tightly-knit formation, favoring the battlements rather than the courtyard for the elevated view of their surroundings. It was a quarter-to-six in the evening and they were back in the topsy turvy country where they had battled William o' The Wisps and his manta ray crew. The sun was gone, replaced by the twelve moons that circled below them. As evening deepened each moon winked out until eventually only one remained, a fat gibbous moon taking up a huge swathe of the sky, yellow-and-white like a cat's shining eye glimpsed at night.

If you peered at the fortress' feet, you'd have seen them running on thin air with the consistency of firm earth. It was enough to give you a nasty case of vertigo, made worse by the fact that Inez Symphony was shaking the terrain by sawing at her violin. Inez's geographic mischief was part of Cate's defense plan. At her best guess a dragon had two ways of assaulting a fortress: from the air or from the ground. The ground was slow, but it was quiet and subtle. While the company patrolled, they might well miss the dragon skulking up one of Betty's legs and gaining the ramparts with its sinuous speed. With Inez playing, the ground near the fortress was unstable, too-tricky to navigate. Which meant the dragon could only come from the air. While they couldn't hear its wingbeats over the violin-scored rumbling and crashing, they would see those wings just fine, like leathery pirate sails skull-and-crossboned in veins.

"It comes," said Marcus Angel.

Cate looked along with all the rest. The dragon was indeed coming. It unfurled out of the black landscape like a swatch of poisoned silk. Its wings spread out, and it plunged directly toward them.

"Good," said Xacorca Demon. "I am sick to death of waiting."

Inez's violin scratch-scriddled out that old song—the one that sounds like a graveyard full of jaunty skeletons, ghouls, and ghosts hopping up out of their plots and dancing, arm in arm, or in the case of chopping block traitors, head in arm. The "Danse Macabre". Cate knew this song.

Oh yes.

She and it were bosom friends.

There was a collective bracing, a steeling of bravery, a shunning of fright. Steffan Cerulean drew the water from twelve big barrels the company had hauled up from the pantry for him. It swirled and flowed with the music. Kpelle Cinder rolled her wrists, her fingernails ten flickering candleflames. Those two were the breath battlers, extinguishers of the first dragonfire to be breathed upon human beings in a hundred years, and they were ready.

"Stay together," said Cate. "Claws, jaws, and searing fire. Watch for those at any cost. Strike hard, strike true, our lucks conspire. And gift ourselves long lives this Tinfrost."

Combat stances flourished. Gilbert Wildsmith summoned his pack of spectral dogs. Rosemund Valkyrie's cloak fanned wide in golden wings. Nyoni Snickerdrake's matches poised over her fireworks. Morvran Oats was astride his indestructible owl. Rebecca Lupine was transformed into an empowering moon, orbiting Eilandri Titansgrave and making the Pale Giant faster, more perceptive, stronger even than before if such a thing were possible. Niccolo Bluescarf, Eugenie O'Nine Tails, and Marcus were readying their lengths of fabric, leather, and chain to catch the creature's wings. Margherita Stranger stood with her nightmare blade across one shoulder; Kevlin Paladin with his sunspear gripped firm. More and more, a scarlet brigade. Cate's company.

"Did you do that on purpose?" said Lorna Blacktower.

"Do what on purpose?" Cate replied innocently.

"Make your pre-battle speech rhyme."

"It rhymed?"

Lorna rolled her eyes. "You're incorrigible."

Cate grinned, then felt it melt into a snarl. The dragon was on them.

She could see its face now, take stock of its head that mixed elements of lupine and serpentine features. There was a dry, malefic smell of crypts. A sickly sweet smell like uneaten cake at a funeral wake. Were the odors from its fur or its breath?

She found herself staring it directly in the eyes.

White but for red slits. The devil has eyes like that. A serpent's eyes.

In the instant before it seemed the dragon must strike the fortress walls, a convulsion of muscles in its back and shoulders brought the wings fantastically wide. Displaced air rushed over the company. The dragon opened its mouth wide enough to swallow a car, revealing those bumpy, serrated, too-full toolbox teeth.

No scintilla of orange at the back of its throat. No heat. No plume of exhaled fire.

Cate had time to think

(*Not a toolbox*)

(*a surgery kit*)

before the beast sucked in.

Inhaled, rather than *exhaled*.

And what it inhaled from their bodies, like soda through a straw, was blood.

Veins and arteries stood out with sudden, grotesque starkness. It turned the company's faces, their hands, any exposed skin, into roadmaps. There was no incision, no piercing, no laying open of their flesh. The dragon sucked and the blood responded to the sucking, winding out of them in dark red threads.

The sensation was unlike anything Cate had ever felt. Energized to crippling fatigue in a little less than ten seconds. A feeling of being explored, as if by the cold, blue-gloved fingers of a physician she was not allowed to see.

She was aware that at the front of the company, Kpelle and Steffan were bringing their fire and water to bear. Against what? Against nothing.

Aware, as well, that she was giving orders. Marcus, Eugenie, and Niccolo flung out their lashes at her command, the bluescarf and the thorny whip and the beatific chains circling the dragon's muzzle in an effort to close it. No good. If anything the dragon's jaws opened wider.

Eilandri Titansgrave going back. Not a retreat, a backpedal before a leap and then a lunge. She was going to jump off the battlements. That seemed an idea worth getting in on. Cate took a few steps and groaned as a wave of dizziness gushed up her, lodging between her temples and making porridge of her faculties. It was because she'd tried to move too fast. Slow, her body counseled. Slow, I can't handle speed right now. I'm lethargic you see. A dragon is drinking me.

The thought was an asylum level item, a frothing straight-jacket thought from the mines where the ore of madness was dug up by unwary brains.

But it was there and it carried the weight of truth.

A dragon is drinking me.

Her hand fumbled at her satchel. Something useful there. What?

An image arrived in her head—a reflection as displayed in something important, something that could save her, and yet indistinct, fogged and crooked. Meaningless.

Her gaze slalomed in blurred, uneven swoops. Baaack-and-fooorth. Baaaaack-and-forth. Back-aaaaaand-foooooooooorth. Nausea now, and that vulnerable sensation of being probed by questing, invisible fingers. Needles nuzzling each popped-out vein. She saw Steffan Cerulean looking at his gnarled-root fingers in mingled disbelief and horror. Rebecca Lupine thrown out of orbit, a tiny, parched moon becoming a pale, gasping woman, her expression haggard and so very, very bewildered. *What the fuck is going on?* That was the message such an expression conveyed. Cate saw it mirrored everywhere, a lake of stricken faces.

Mirror! That was the word!

And as though the word were a talisman, her fingers closed around a vial. Inside was a mirror, her means of fighting this wicked lethargy and the source of it, more wicked still.

God damn it if the bastard wasn't grinning at her.

She was sure it was, clueless as to how she could be, but sure nonetheless.

Flapping above them, strands of blood like DNA helixes passing down its throat, the dragon was peering down at her. Its slits were slightly wider, the pupil dilation an addict achieves when the time has come—finally come thank God—to shoot up again. And yes—below those eyes and the wrinkled snout, the lipless mouth was indeed peeled back in something very much like a grin. Its teeth were stained with their blood.

Not toolbox teeth. That description no longer seemed accurate. *This monster has a mouth like a quack doctor's surgery kit.* Scalpels. Long-handled saws. Tools for cauterization. Lobotomy drills.

Not a toolbox. A surgery kit.

And not the boogeyman of dragons, she decided. *A vampire.*

Chapter Thirty-Three

"Nice of your ex-girlfriend to give us a car," said Thud.

Behind the wheel Hughes made a noncommittal sound.

"Very obliging of her people to meet us with it, I thought. Handed over the keys like we were mugging them, and they were ay-okay with it. What was her name, that old flame of yours?"

"Creusa King."

"I must send her a Tinfrost card."

Another sound from their dark-eyed driver, this one even curter than the last.

Thud craned past the headrest. "You enough legroom behind me, Mr. Glint?"

"Lots."

Thud nodded and settled into his seat once more. It creaked pleasingly. "Quality seats," he said. "Leather?"

"Ikahaguan," said Hughes darkly.

After patting his pockets, Thud produced a chunky cigar. "Mind if I smoke?"

"Please don't," came Estelle's voice.

Thud peered over his shoulder at her, pulled an "if you say so" face, and popped the cigar back into his pocket. He listened as the blizzard battened uselessly at the car, watched the snows slam white puerile fists into the windshield. The wipers—glossy and sleek—cleared the mess without apparent effort. "Anyone else feel toasty?" he said. "Down there, I mean. In the nethers."

"The seats are heated," mumbled Hughes.

"That so? Leather and heated? I'll be damned." He took out the cigar, put it in his mouth, then remembered he wasn't able to smoke it. "Quality seatmanship, this vehicle. Tyres to beat the band too. Like tank tyres. Bogies, those were called during the war. And what's that thing you keep doing?" he asked Hughes. "Clicking those two buttons on the dash. We jounce right or left every time you press them."

Hughes cut his eyes to the buttons and back to the road. "It's a rapid lane-changing function. The storm's draped a white caul over the city's face. Obstructions all over the place. Tapping the buttons is faster than ahm..." He sped up, switched gears, lay both palms to the wheel again. "Than turning the ah..."

"The wheel."

"Yeah."

Thud nodded understanding. Heated leather seats, eh? Industrial-strength girding and exoskeleton. Thrice-toughened glass (you could tell from the sheen). Wheels that were the bloody business—not a single wobble when they hit an ice slick.

"What model is this car?" he wondered aloud.

Hughes fetched a breath and let it go. Exasperated. "An *Escateline Eschezmont.*"

An *Eschezmont.* Thud knew of only one of those in the city. There had been two, but Mr. Shine's had been impounded by the streetbeaters who had sold it to pay for leaky roof upkeep and general renovations to headquarters. That was after Shine's criminal organization had been dissolved. Raided and ruined, more like. The other *Eschezmont* was owned by Miss Shine, the crimelord's replacement. A clean-nosed sort, by all accounts, though that either meant she was very innocent or very careful. Thud suspected the latter.

"Can't help but notice you're a bit worked up," Thud said.

Hughes looked at him from the side of his face. "Worked up?"

I would be, thought Thud. *If my ex-girlfriend was Miss Shine, I'd be worked down, side-to-side, and diagonal too.*

"Don't mind me," he reassured the lad. "There's the *Duchess and Squirm.* Wonder if we'll cross into Leonidas."

Fifteen minutes later they did.

"Where are we headed?" Hughes murmured. "Where are you taking us, Jane?"

"To the house where leaves are crushed but no prophecies are foretold," said Desdemona, her voice distant. "To the shop where the walls are made of stories."

Thud had been toying with his cigar. He almost shredded it when Hughes slammed on the accelerator. They were thrown back in their seats.

"Hughes!" That was Estelle. Shrill-pitched. "We were already going too fast! What's wrong?"

"The Emporium, Estelle."

They all stared at him, all except Desdemona Cauldronpot, who was staring into a world of symbols and visions too occult for an ordinary person to fathom.

"The Emporium where I grew up." Hughes veered calamitously close to a trundling truck coming the other direction. Its horn blasted, dopplering to nothing as they sped by. The lad's mien was calm, but Thud knew better. Urgency moved just under the surface, a pulse-bubbling undertow. "Leaves are crushed there," Hughes continued. "The fixtures and furnishings are made of theater manuscripts and books. In other terms—"

"Walls made of stories," finished Estelle. "Oh God."

Hughes compressed one of the lane switchers. The car jounced left, narrowly avoiding a trio of garbage compartments left out to gather snow, white hulks hurtling by, the rotten smell seeping in through the air filtration, then gone a moment later as the pine forest and mint leaf perfume in the car hustled it out like a trespasser.

Hughes didn't have to vocalize what they all knew.

All of them, even Mr. Glint, for the gaunt man had, in the company of his former partner, threatened to visit the very *Emporium* they were now headed for. Glint's purposes had been evil indeed. Strange how the roles were reversed and he was headed there as a protector rather than a force for devastation. Funny old world. The other thing too. Terrible.

His dad, Thud thought. *Blimey. Jane's going to scrag his dad unless we stop her.*

Over his fingers, tobacco shavings spilled...

... and over the fingers of Gormon Hughes Senior, hot tea spilled.

One of his three bodyguards had just been thrown at him. Curiously the thrower was one of his other bodyguards.

During the last city crisis I had better luck with Boochums, he thought. He missed the stinky Saint Bernard. He missed Ernie Wilks, come to think of it. The old codger could handle himself in a fight, and it seemed that one was shaping up right here in the *Scriptorium and Flavored Tea Emporium.*

Gormon had brewed up a pot of his Special Winter Blend, poured three mugs—one for each bodyguard, who were okay, as thugs go—and put the mugs on the tray. Now he was on his back, hands smarting and scalded, and all three mugs shattered heaps with handles sticking up miserably.

Well, that was gratitude nowadays.

Sounds of fighting. Thumps, bumps, and hurley-burley. None of his business, really. He got up, pottered to the sink, elbowed on the cold tap, and held his hands under the chilly stream. Ahh. That was the stuff. Three mugs, written off. Gone up to that great kitchen cabinet in the sky. It was a bugger. Thank goodness the pot hadn't been on the tray. Hit a snag, dodge disaster, that was his motto.

Well, it would be, if he were a man for mottos.

Truth be told he was not a man of many words at all. Speeches, yes, when called for. A father can only do so much to avoid monologues. Sometimes they just happened to him. His mouth gave voice to something well-founded, almost mystical, without his head having so much as a contribution. Being a dad, you could keep it. At seventy he looked much the same as he had at sixty, only scrawnier, and yet broader too, as if life had pared away his body and added extra helpings to his personality. He liked getting old. Loathed it too. That was gratitude nowadays.

Nearby the bodyguards were getting on with it. Internal disputes. You could keep them too.

All at once there was even more commotion, so much so that Gormon deigned to glance toward it.

"Junior!" he cried.

"Hey Dad."

His son was there. Lot of other folks too. There was a young lady who looked completely washclothed, really dog-tired, and a middle-aged woman wearing a coat, blouse, a headdress of some kidney, and a noise complaint's worth of jewelry. There was a mustachioed man, and a very respectable bit of facial hair it was. Then there was a tall, rakish man in a sterling suit. The man himself was not so sterling. Gormon had never seen a fellow he disliked the look of more. Unearthed bones would be more appealing to the eye. That man is bad news, he thought.

In a mayhem of tumbling books and torn pages, Gormon Hughes Junior tackled one of the bodyguards, the other held his hands up and shouted something about not being involved. The last guard, the thrower as Gormon Hughes Senior knew him, the instigator of this ruckus, was accosted by the tall, rakish man.

"Peek-a-boo," he said in a voice that reminded Gormon of the spooky ear-rag horrors he'd listened to over the radio as a boy, the ones your parents warned you about, and that kept you up at night scanning the long shadows in your room in case something white-faced and smiling lurched out, lurched out and did unspeakable things to you. The bodyguard heard it, turned, and the gaunt man's hands closed around his neck.

"I see you."

"Mr. Hughes?" said the bodyguard Junior had tackled.

Hughes Junior studied him. "Not the one. You've got her, Mr. Glint."

The suited horror named Glint shook his head.

"Gone," he said in his awful voice. "Saw her pounce right out of his pupils." He set the bodyguard down. The guy rubbed at his neck, imprints of long fingers welting there. He seemed stunned but otherwise okay.

"Gone."

Gormon Hughes Senior heard his son mutter a curse not worth repeating.

"Watch it, boy."

"Sorry Dad. Are you hurt?"

"Burned hands. Nothing new there."

"Okay. Give me a sec."

Hughes Junior held court a while, clearing up the strange ordeal for the bodyguards. They seemed unconcerned. Evidently they were being paid well enough to withstand even a large dose of freaky-deaky.

Meanwhile the mustachioed man approached Hughes Senior.

"You're the owner of this establishment?"

"I am."

"Then you're Hughes' gaffer?"

Gormon grinned. "A gaffer, am I? That's a bit of slang I've not heard in a while. You a Leonidas man?"

"Yes sir."

"What line of work you in?"

"I'm a policeman, for my sins."

"My boy in trouble?"

"Yup. And me in it with him."

Hughes Senior nodded as if this were par for the course. "In that case I'll make you a cup of tea. I've got cardamon and fennel. Sweet plum and caramel. Apple, sesame, Jaenqui-jasmine."

"No, thank you," said the streetbeater. "I try not to drink the really hard stuff when I'm on duty."

"Desdemona's gone loopy again," said the young woman.

Indeed the bejeweled lady—Gormon assumed this was Desdemona—had a ghostly quality about her. Her lips were moving without sound, as if she were communing with something none of them could hear or see.

His son hurried over. "Dad, we've got to go."

"How's Cate?"

"Hm? Oh good. Away."

"Holiday?"

"Working."

"Give my love to her."

"Will do, Dad."

As the peculiar group rushed out of the Emporium, Gormon Hughes Senior rolled up his sleeves. "You there, big fellas. Two of you start to tidy in the main room, the other grab a dustpan and brush for the broken mugs."

In fairness to them, they were quick to task, gathering up the fallen books, righting them and making all as it had been, and the tinkling of the mugs in the dustpan was almost consolation enough to mend the trouble of them breaking in the first place.

The father of one of the most mysterious and powerful men in the city sighed, and made a note to order three new mugs, and sent his son whatever strength a parent could send across the divide all children inevitably build between them and the home-place, the home-people. It was winter, true enough, but that old chestnut the Autumn Waltz trotted on.

Sons. You could keep them.

He certainly kept his, or the idea of him, right there in a Hughes-shaped corner in his heart.

He sighed.

Then he went to put on the kettle.

***

The man with the tongue piercing rolled up outside the teashop on a motorcycle. Of the owner of the motorcycle, there was no sign.

Except for a whiff of cologne, and a little clot of blood and human hair on the back wheel.

He hadn't been keen to part with his ride.

Pig. These western people were all truffle pigs. Where are my truffles? Once I find them they'll be my property, and my property is me and I am it. Even the dragon woman was a pig.

The man with the tongue piercing looked up at the teashop.

A wrinkled old pig was looking down at him through a window. He had the look of the pig the man was after. The man with the tongue piercing would be satisfied when he caught up with the swine gang. Of course he did not view himself as a butcher, rather as a mildly evolved descendent of the boar. For he was also a pig, in his way.

All men were.

To think otherwise was grounds for being brought outside the barn and sodomized by the farmer whose name was Pride.

He watched the figure in the teashop for a moment or so.

The wrinkled old pig did a curious thing then. He could not have known about the man's eyes on him (he wore sunglasses to cover what the masters had done to his eyes), yet somehow he must have, because he lifted a mug as if sharing a toast with him, and drank deep. Then he left the window.

The man with the tongue piercing did not know what this meant.

Time enough to ponder its significance when the work was finished.

He revved the motorcycle into growling life and drove off, the pork hunt resuming.

***

No sooner had Cate thought that insane yet oh-so-appropriate word

(*vampire*)

than the antidote to such a creature made her move. Not a ring of garlic cloves or a sharpened bit of wood, or even sacred symbols of the old church, but a big woman and a bigger hammer.

With a running start, Eilandri sprang the distance, clearing the battlements, covering twenty feet, thirty, *forty-five feet* in a single jump. Sublimely quick, the dragon curled its bulk to one side. Instead of landing on its back, Eilandri was forced to grab a fistful of fur next to its left wing. Precarious, but apparently she was not the sort of woman to whom precarious much mattered. As the beast began to gain altitude—perhaps hoping to shake its unwelcome passenger off, making her plummet to a rather messy demise—Eilandri made a pendulum of her not inconsiderable weight, found the momentum, and drove the hammer's wicked head into the base of the dragon's neck, right where the clavicle broadened out into the body. The results were spectacular.

As a girl Cate had seen gross-out vids where Daethumbrish kids stuck gum-leeches to their legs, let them drink their fill of blood, and proceeded to squish them in the fingers. More gruesome than the mixture of pulpy brown slime and still-warm blood was the almost but not quite cartoonish *pop* these squishy interludes produced. Bursting too-full foot blisters would not emit such a sound. Hell, pressing a needle to a balloon would not emit such a sound. Something about the consistency of blood, or the leech, was vital.

Cate watched in breathtaking slo-mo as the hammer curved, and curved, and kissed the dragon's fur. *Pop*, went the sky-leech. The wound was craterous. Blood fountained out, pulse-pumping, drenching the fur, raining stickily, cloudily, torrentially. There was pinkish mist. The rusty-rail reek of blood. The guttural sound of hurt leaping up the dragon's hemoglobin-coated throat, like steam venting itself through the pipes of a nightmarish locomotive.

The dragon spun, trying to shake Eilandri loose, but the hammer was embedded. All it did was take her along for a thrilling, sickening whirl, blood sprinkling out of it in hot squirts and jets.

Out of range of its sucking breath, Cate felt the lethargy abate. *Thank you God*, she thought, although perhaps, Thank you whatever providence brought Ella and her together might have been a better starter. She took stock of herself. A frequent donor and no stranger to dizzy spells after doing so, Cate reckoned the vampiric dragon had siphoned perhaps three-quarters of a pint from each member of the company. If blood were biomass diesel, that would be a full tank of juice. The dragon had drained that out of them in less time than it takes to pick up a fuel pump, undo your car's nozzle, slide the pump in, and compress the handle. It was too much blood taken too fast, a reality that showed itself in the faces of her comrades. The agents of the Citadel were off-balance, sapped, confused. They spoke to one another in hushed tones, wide-eyed and languid, as if Eilandri—one of their own—weren't in trouble.

Her assessment concluded, Cate made a decision.

"Nyoni," she barked. "Hand me something cruel."

Blinking dazedly, Nyoni Snickerdrake gave her three fireworks, twizzled in curlicues and plasma-green in color.

"What are you going to do?" Lorna asked her.

Cate ignored this. There simply wasn't time.

"Liddicoat," she said. "When Kpelle lights the fuses, give all three of these fireworks a smooch with your axe."

Liddicoat-Smite-The-Naughty-With-Large-Implements wiped his pouchy, sweating face with his hand and said, "Couldn't do that. Not with you holding them."

"There's a delay to the explosion."

"Yeah, right, a delay—"

"*Right, now do as you're fucking told.*"

He cringed. But the force behind her words broke the spell for not only him but the rest of the company too, and the next instant they were galvanized into action.

"Kpelle," she ordered as the ranks prepared their defenses against a second breath, should it come. "Come here and snap those fingers, double time."

In a moment the fuses were fizzling, and Cate was lining up her shot. Overhead the dragon leveled out, dive-bombing the fortress, intent on splattering Eilandri against the mossy stones.

Almost.

Liddicoat swept the edge of his axe along the fireworks. The axe's magic set the air to whizzing and crackling and concentrating, a fabulous combustion sandwiching itself into the points of impact—gathering to go!

Almost.

Wings clapped the air.

Geometric shapes unfolding behind her eyes—Cate was clever as an outdoor cat when she needed to be and just as resourceful. No Pythagorean theorem here, no sir, a blooming basis for motion instead, no letters or numbers, but Point A and Point She and how to make the two align so, just so, just—

Someone screaming her name.

The heat, rippling, rolling over her in sweat-slick sheets, chrome-colored adrenaline dumped into her system, the explosion nigh, death by blast-radius—

Almost.

She saw the dragon. The dragon saw her.

Cate grinned.

Now.

At a squeeze of her fingers, two vials' insides arrowed out. Two mirrors crystallized, one below her, the other on the dragon's wing. She been waiting to see the top. She had.

Still grinning that grin—which by the way, was very similar in nature to the one the dragon had worn before it slurped its greedy fill from her company—she stepped onto the glass, vanished into the mirror, and reappeared atop the dragon's wing, her legs submerged into the glassy, fractal in-between so she would not be blown to her doom. Wind riffled her hair and whip-corded her cheeks.

With a bellow that carried far and wide, she crammed the still-pouring wound on the dragon's neck full of fireworks. As the beast's head turned, its teeth snapping at her, Cate saw Eilandri seize the moment. With the fortress blurring by, she kicked off the dragon. There was a shatter-crash of window glass broken and furniture taking the brunt of the Pale Giant's landing.

The dragon pinwheeled from its descent, cresting up once more and taking Cate with it. The dizziness oiling her senses multiplied tenfold. Meanwhile some synapse in the dragon's head must have given it a signal because its attention slid from the woman emerging from its wing to the tubes embedded in its pitted flesh.

Liddicoat's magic rippled the air—the heat of a desert mirage glimpsed through a lens of absolute thirst. Fizzzzzle, went the fuses, more and more frantic and sparking wildly.

As the dragon looked back at her, slitted eyes filled with some unreadable emotion, Cate slipped into the mirror. But not before tipping it a wink.

The patented Jubilee special.

When she came out on the other side, the explosion was already in progress.

Blood of such outrageous quantities as she had never seen splashed the walls, the battlements, the fortress itself. Great globs of it splatted against the stone. It soaked the moss and dappled the windows and began to... *Sweet God*, Cate thought. *It's filling the courtyard.* So it was. Decant an object with enough liquid, it'll slop to the sides and begin to fill. As the dragon writhed, they saw its whole shoulder was simply gone. A good portion of the neck had been vaporized. The wing on that side clung onto its body by a few wiry strands of muscle. The blow Eilandri had dealt it was bad—this was surely fatal.

But in spite of the agony it must have been experiencing, the dragon did not feel like sharing it. Not aloud, anyway. The only thing deathly about its struggles to remain airborne was the silence.

The company watched together, unable to look away.

They watched until its one strong wing and its other —barely hanging on—took it far from Betty's streaked and dripping crenellations.

They watched it land, rest, and take off once more into the mountain pass, which they would reach very soon.

They watched it vanish among the tree-speckled cliffs.

And then, at last, they exhaled as one.

"Sorry for mincing words," Cate told Liddicoat.

"To accept your apologies, it's an honor. To take your orders," he replied, offering his arm, "is a damned privilege."

She embraced him, arm clasping arm, her grin shading girlish now with delight rather than the impishness battle demanded.

She cast about. She saw elation in her comrades' eyes and no small amount of worry. She didn't blame them. That had been a close thing.

"Out of the slaughterhouse," she told them. "And the blood quagmire. Soon into the frying pan, then the fire."

"That one was on purpose," grumbled Lorna.

"Jubilee!" someone cheered.

They took it up, a merry chorus.

"Joo-bill-ee! Joo-bill-ee!"

Cate could not help but laugh. "Enough of that. I appreciate it, but you can applaud when we're home safe. For now, get something to eat and drink. Replace your sugar levels, especially." She stared past them. The mountains scooped up, blotting the horizon. A blue moon awaited them there, if memory served. Somewhere in those shaggy-haired pines, a dragon lurked. Frying pans and fire, indeed. Well, it had felt good to laugh. Headache nettled her, but that was good too. Laughter and blood-starved headaches meant your guts and skull were, if not in mint condition, then at the very least in coriander.

"Is the large one okay?" wondered Clothilda. "Tittens-something. I'm ghastly with names."

"Titansgrave," said Cate. "I'll check on her. Judging from her landing sounds, she probably broke something important."

Eilandri had indeed broken something important.

Their gas oven.

When Cate arrived the giant was picking her way out of the remains.

"Oh dear. That was unlucky," she said. "I thought that was the kitchen window you'd gone through."

Wincing, Eilandri took out a pen and a yellow card.

Cate read it.

At least this time there are no scorch marks.

Oh yes. Apart from funerals, there was nothing like laughter to remind you that you were still alive.

***

"There's a man in black and white, and red all over. Ten years ago he was a penguin for a day. Flies congregate, their fecal-stink and vibrating wings heading directly for him."

Hughes gave a curt nod; he read her loud and clear. He accelerated, pointing the *Eschezmont* like a tungsten trebuchet bolt at the boundary between Districts.

"You solved that one quick," Thud said.

"It's Falstaff. He's a butler. Black and white outfit."

"Red all over?"

"Redspire. He works in the tower."

"Thought I recognized the name. Why would Jane go for him?"

"He and I are close."

A letter arrived in his head, words penned and signed by the past.

You're amazing, Falstaff.

True. Try not to hop so much as you put on your trousers, sir. This is sharp.

What had been sharp? He couldn't place it for thirty seconds. Then he had it.

A razor! Falstaff was giving his stubbly face a shave before his first date with Cate. *The Pear and Princess* on the 31st of July. Boy, that took him back.

He had been fabulously nervous and so excited he could have swallowed a handful of coal and string and shit diamond necklaces. The butler had not exactly helped things. What was the line he'd dropped into the conversation?

Hughes had been putting on his trousers, jittering with the prospect of spending the evening in the company of the prettiest woman he'd ever seen, and Falstaff had asked him to keep still. Hughes had said, *Sorry.*

And Falstaff replied, in the same neat and tidy tone he always employed, *Hurt her feelings and you will be.*

The middle of a chase to catch a killer seemed an indecent time to smile, but Hughes felt that memory melt from sepia-tinted paper into whiskey, warming him up, sweet and good and fortifying.

The butler wasn't just Hughes' confidante.

He was his friend.

He spurred the *Eschezmont* to new speeds and it responded at once. Speaking of shaves, there were many close ones on that ferocious-fast zip from Leonidas to Ptolema District. But Hughes pulled it off fine, his reactions excellent, almost supernatural. He ran roadblocks, clipped other vehicles parked and puttering along and zooming, and generally made a public nuisance of himself. But then what are friends for?

Hang on Falstaff.

I'm on my way.

"What penguin?"

That had come from the backseat, an ominous quiet thunder.

Mr. Glint.

"Sorry?" said Hughes.

"Said 'ten years ago he was a penguin for a day.'"

It was Estelle who replied. "Oh, Desdemona meant the Hairy Autumn, Mr. Glint. Were you here in the city when everyone was turning into animals?"

"Nope."

"Oh, well you see—"

"Was in a dream."

Estelle frowned. "A dream?"

"Ate my way through the crust of conscious, me."

"Is that so?" said Estelle, doing her best to keep up. "During the Hairy Autumn?"

"Yeah," said Glint. "There were these witches, right, and—"

"Oh yes! The three witches of the Nightjar Coven! And um... they were in this dream with you and Frank Gallant and Hughes and Cate?"

"S'right."

"That's fun. You know, maybe it's exhaustion talking, but I can't honestly recall how the Hairy Autumn ended. The bits and bobs, you know. The details. What actually happened to the Coven in the end?"

There was a dreadful silence.

And into it Mr. Glint said, "Me."

There was another, rather longer silence, this one owned chiefly by Estelle, who was extremely embarrassed.

Eventually she pointed out the window. "That pharmacy has put up nice Tinfrost decorations. Wouldn't you agree, Mr. Glint?"

"The height of charm and splendor, Miss Corlum," said Mr. Glint graciously.

"Oh, that reminds me. Hughes. You were going to tell me about my malady."

No reply.

"Hughes?"

"Hmph. Sorry, Estelle. Mind on the road."

"No problem. Have you a moment?"

"For you? Always."

"Well ah... about my sickness, Hughes," she broached timidly, "you said you knew something that might shed light on it."

Hughes wondered if the soupiness in his bowels arose from complicated feelings on the chase at hand or simple apprehension. How did you tell a friend that an important figure in their life had poisoned them for almost ten years? It seemed gratuitously unfair that the responsibility for unmasking such a betrayal should fall on him.

Quit mousing about, he chided himself. *Drive like a maniac for Falstaff and pay Estelle the courtesy of the truth.* Maybe she'd call him a liar. *Okay, maybe she will. Cross that bridge if we come to it. One problem at a time.* That stupid, oddly gladdening mantra recurred to him: What are friends for?

In the rearview Estelle's eyes were bright expectant lamps.

Hughes could feel Thud's gaze on him also. The copper had a way of summing you up moment by moment. Annoying, but Hughes supposed his own pre-Performance observations touched on that same intrusiveness.

So he was resolved to do it. The million credit question was *how* to do it?

If it were done when tis done, then 'twere well it were done quickly.

A line from his second favorite play.

Quickly, then. He'd tell her quickly. No farting around.

Kindly too, some part of him counseled. Remember how Doctor Lanmoor spoke to you in his office that night in November? Remember how you were scared out of your mind—truly gaga and ready to come apart at the seams—and he took those fears and concretized them and laid them on you. Not a romance house of jelly but a heavy, burdensome duplex of solid grief.

Quickly was fine. Better than fine—essential! But if it were done well, 'twere best it were done softly and kindly.

"Estelle, hasn't it struck you as odd that your agoraphobia seems to have diminished in merely a handful of hours? Almost as though it were an immovable block that finally decided to budge? You've ran through buildings and braved a blizzard without grumble or complaint. You might be shrieking inside, in which case you're a finer actor than I could dream of becoming. By all accounts a full recovery."

"I had a breakthrough," she said. "A moment of strength."

"I don't doubt it. But why now?"

To that she had no answer. Luckily for her, Hughes had one ready.

He told her about rhylocaine—its effects when administered over a long period of time, as advised to him by the lackadaisical forensic Doctor Leborski. He explained that even a short gap in regular doses would in all likelihood result in the body ejecting the

(foreign matter)

toxins in a manner consummate with narcotic withdrawal. *Get your fix or take your kicks* was a bit of street parlance from Hughes' own childhood, one he elected not to relate at this time.

He told her about the envelope on Wendy's desk, that this discovery had for whatever reason—in combination with the chef's information about Wendy's daily visits to the eighty-ninth floor—set his alarm bells clanging.

He gave it all to her, withholding only the conclusion—that Wendy had built trust and a good, protective relationship with Estelle, and that she'd abused that trust to poison Estelle for almost half of her life.

He let her come to it in her own way.

Quickly. Kindly.

Even so it hit her hard.

Puzzlement crumbled from her face, replaced with a potion of suspicion and horror, one the rest of her body drank all-too-eagerly.

"That can't be true," she said at last. "There's been some mistake."

"No mistake," said Thud. "I vouch for Leborski. She's top of her trade. Takes precautions against false analysis."

Hughes couldn't see those bright eyes anymore. Her head was lowered. "I'm sorry, Estelle."

"She would never."

There they were, rising so he could once again see them in the rearview. Eyes bright not with curiosity, but with anger. *Which comes, or so the experts say, right after denial*, thought Hughes glumly. *Brick by concrete brick, the grief house is built.*

The atmosphere in the car rivaled the storm battering by. Colder than cold.

In the backseat, Estelle folded her matchstick arms across her matchbox chest.

"Wendy would *never...*"

Chapter Thirty-Four

ughes and the others were spared a tense, uncomfortable journey all the way to Redspire. This was not due to an accident—although Hughes' erratic driving might have caused a dozen or more—but because of an unexpected piece of communication.

It came as the car glided off the motorway and under a bridge with a banner on it. The bridge looked hammered out of a single block of ice—a troll bridge from a fairy tale. The banner was a poster advertising Leopoldo Fernassi facial creams and hand soaps: *Leopoldo Fernassi*, read the slogan. *Every man is a tiger to another man.* There was the Cleomenes District bank (closed), some sad, dark-windowed restaurants (closed), a pop-up frozen dessert shop (closed as closed could be), men's suit tailors, dressmakers, daycare centers, dance halls, and the huge marble pillars of the Wailing Lady Opera House. All gerrymandered by the cold political campaign of the storm party, cloud pundits lobbying loudly, snowflake volunteers making house calls and staging chilly riots and frosting up the ballot box of every street and corner.

Didn't Avery run for election once?

Desdemona thought he had done. Run and lost. In defeat he was not to join the ranks of the government, instead continuing to manage one of the city's three national banks. Not a bad consolation prize, getting to keep your cozy job with its pension and healthcare plan—still she bet he'd been fiercely peeved. Avery Mullinger was not a man who liked to lose the upper hand in anything.

Seeing the bank all rime-white and draped in icicles had called his face to her mind. His face led down a rabbit hole of memories.

From her seat next to Estelle Corlum and mercifully distanced from the heinous Mr. Glowy (or whatever the wretched man's name was), Desdemona Cauldronpot was busy thinking about her boyfriend, Avery, their early flirtations, and how she rather missed those since they'd apparently gone on holiday after she'd moved in with him, replaced by rather frequent requests to do housework, make home-cooked suppers, and give up all the things she thought she'd liked.

She was also occupied with how lovely this automobile was.

She couldn't believe Humphreys (or was it Hinkleman?) had been allowed to drive it.

But mostly, she gave herself to her occult visions while her subconscious mind dwelled on Avery, and his insistence that she was happy, and her reluctance to disagree because the man was just so... so *practical...* and...

And...

(*Desdemona.*)

She sat up straighter.

Who is that?

Frank, is that you?

(*Yeah, it's me.*)

Oh you poor lamb. You sound like you're in pain.

(*No time to plumb the sweet grains, sugarplum. Jane's leading you one way and going another.*)

How could she?

(*Don't know. But she's pulled tricks like this before. A little tiny bit of her is still going toward Redspire. The rest is going to Saint Wilhemina's Maternity Hospital.*)

The Maternity... Frank, she's not going to...

(*She is. You bet she is.*)

But they're only babies! Why would she be so cruel?

(*You know I heard once that male cicada bugs—when they get a special kind of fungus inside them—perform the dance the females do to get the males interested. Males come, and BOOM, now they're the bugs with the bug too. That way the fungus spreads because the original bug was just so damn smart. Sometimes nature is weird. Sometimes it's evil or so close as makes no difference. Tell Hughes to remember what I told him.)*

Frank?

(Yeah.)

I think... I think I might do away with Avery Mullinger. My boyfriend, you know. His nature isn't evil, but it's callous and... controlling. I'm all for manipulation of the mind by otherworldly powers, but by a man? Certainly not.

(So what are you gonna do about it?)

Well... Avery never likes to lose the upper hand. I've a mind to give him the middle finger.

(That's the spirit.)

A rush of giddiness swept her, the kind you got watching cute film stars with your girlfriends at thirteen or fourteen, the kind you lost somewhere along the way.

Honestly, Frank. You give a gal thrills galore.

Frank?

He was gone, a radio broadcast no longer transmitting.

Desdemona cleared her throat. "Hinkleman?"

No response from their driver.

It must be Humphreys, then. Hadn't Frank just told her it was Humphreys?

Drat.

"We must divert our course," she announced primly. "Jane has split herself, one tiny bit continuing to Redspire, the rest headed for Saint Wilhelmina's Maternity Hospital. We've got to go there at once and save the babies."

"Babies?" The policeman seemed outraged. "She's going to inhabit a nurse or another orderly and—"

"Yes," growled the driver who Desdemona was ninety-six percent sure was called Humphreys. She hadn't thought he could possibly drive faster in this weather, yet somehow he managed. The wonderful car was now a wonderful payload fired from the cannon of Absolute Urgency.

"Humphreys."

"His name is Hughes," said Estelle. Then she seemed to recall that she was angry with Hughes and retreated back into herself.

"Hughes," snipped Desdemona. "That's what I said. Frank imparted a message for you."

Hughes looked at her in the rearview.

"He said you must remember what he told you."

"Yeah."

"You've got that?"

"*Yes.*"

She ruffled like a proud owl at his tone. But she relented. The silly man was quite stressed, and he could be forgiven for that. It was a stressful moment they were in.

She would devise a suitably occult punishment for him later.

A pollution of his aura, perhaps.

A ghostly bird shit on his shoulder.

Unpleasant dreams.

First there was this Jane business to conclude. Afterward, a little chat with Avery Mullinger. Then the universal cosmic energies would be her guide. How chuffed she was at the thought!

Desdemona Cauldronpot smiled a brief, private smile, and then allowed stress to have its way with her again. Her nature was her own to decide. Right now it was hell-bent on whoever had hurt Frank Gallant. The woman who had shot him had been possessed.

So Jane, then.

Let Desdemona play her part in the apprehension and punishment of Jane.

Her fingers rambled over the bangles on her wrists and forearms, fluttering up to the earrings, and at last the diadem on her brow she'd marked with ink to signify the mystical opening of the third eye. *Gosh*, wasn't this exciting!

***

Pulling up outside the hospital, Hughes was overcome by a bitter, lemony mixture of enmity and nostalgia. Not the nostalgia that takes you back to good times. This was a shadow of that feeling, brooding and acrimonious, tracing his brain to his bowel and back again. Saint Wilhelmina's was where he and Cate had intended to welcome their little girl into the world. Saint Wilhelmina's was the best maternity hospital in the city. The best care. The brightest possible start to that grand adventure called Starting A Family.

Saint Wilhelmina's was also where Doctor Artemi Lanmoor had called Hughes into his office and proceeded to tear his still-beating heart out. Bad news, chief. Baaaad bad news. Your daughter's gone. Almost took your girlfriend with her.

It was where that sneering head nurse plied her petty power. What had her name been? Sarah, maybe. His usually flawless memory came up short.

Hughes' eyes drifted up to the hospital as he swerved the car into a vacant parking spot. This place was where he'd found out there would never be an adventure called Starting A Family. Not as intended, anyhow. Instead there would be an event called Picking Up The Pieces.

Quite literally in his daughter's case.

God, but that was too macabre to think about. About as grim as the Citadel saying, *assholes to apples, men to mulch.* Actually it was worse.

Jane's words, buzzing through their battleground in The Foundry, seemed to verify that.

I bet she tinkled, Hughes. I bet your baby girl tinkled like fucking sleigh bells.

Yeah. A whole lot worse.

He killed the *Eschezmont*'s motor, got out of the car, and the others with him.

Hughes cast an appraising eye over that motley crew—a criminal, a copper, a jailer, an occultist—and cramming his cold hands into his coat pockets, he turned toward the hospital...

... and turned back at the loud burring sound of an engine.

It was only a cursory glance, a dip of the head and a snatched peek before turning back. What that glance showed him was a huge yellow cone of light cutting through the pale haze. Then the motorcycle turned, and its front-mounted lamp bathed all of them in golden light. A little lovely. A little ghoulish.

The motorcycle rolled to a halt about five yards away from the Eschezmont's rear bumper—not parked, merely stopped right there in the middle of the parking lot laneway.

Dismounting from the saddle was a man. He made no move to turn the bike's engine off. It puttered as if in protest, tipped, and crunched into the snow, that cone of gold slashing across the man's frame and making him stark for an instant. Hughes gathered the impression of a tanned, glossy-haired figure. A tattoo crept from his collarbone along his throat, ending like an ellipse at his jaw. Excellent suit. Ruby cufflinks shaped like grinning yokai—the Mysicordelian word for demon. Hughes would have guessed (correctly) that the man was from Kirendei, the capital of Mysicordelia.

None of these details were altogether extraordinary. What was pretty weird—outright strange in fact—were the sunglasses. Evidently the man agreed because as he approached their group he reached up and took them off.

Take a stemless white lotus, fill a bowl with water, and set the flower to float. That was what the man's eyeballs looked like—closed lotus flowers, all white and wet and bulging from their sockets. To Hughes' rising fright they bloomed open, fat petals of eye jelly peeling back layer by layer. At the center of those horrific petals: a black bulb. It began to glow, black turning red like iron in a hot fire.

All of a sudden Hughes no longer felt chilly.

The base of his foot felt as though it were being dipped into scalding bathwater. His toes. His—

"My feet!" Desdemona yanking the words right from his head. Hughes heard her vent a helpless little gasp. "God that burns!"

"Magic," hissed Thud, his voice thick with pain. "Bloody bastard magic again." The truncheon was in his hand. Mr. Glint loped forward with that uncanny speediness Hughes had so completely feared during the dark days of the Hairy Autumn. Estelle and Desdemona were burying their feet ankle-deep in the snow, bending to the sparkling curb frost, their thin-lipped faces wearing panic like white exfoliant masks.

Hughes' own lips moved, the quiet invitation vaporized by the cold wind but carrying, carrying into this new enemy. For the second time since that afternoon, and to his abject dismay, the Performance failed him. But his attempt gave him crucial information.

"It's not her," he shouted, wrenching Chimera from its scabbard. "Estelle, Denise, run! Don't gawp at me—*RUN I SAID! IT'S NOT JANE!*"

He charged the lotus-eyed man, the heat climbing his calves into the muscle and meat of his thighs.

Mr. Glint sailed past him. He heard the gaunt man hit the bumper and sink to the snow. Hughes felt too hot for surprise. Every step felt like putting his feet into bags of broken glass. Kerosene-fueled fire pumped along kindled sinew. His muscles were surely wasting, skin boiling, bones cracking and gassing up dry clouds of vulcanized marrow, blackened husk bones you could crack with your thumbs like shaved coconut shell. Sweating now, shirt sticking to him with the barbecue heat. Packed sauna room moisture. An oven cranked too high and opened, that vaporous bilge boiling out, rashing skin out in red and jetting your eyes with prickly, implacable tears. Rising, rising up his legs—burningburningburning, his ears deaf to the crunch of his shoes in the parking lot carpet frost, his brain athrob with pain words, the language of hurt, a lump of solid scream spreading out to cover his whole self, and the burning rising some more, soon to lick and lap at his balls with a hot-pepper-swollen tongue wrapped in barbed wire—burrrrrrrrnnnnniiiiiinggggggGAAAAAAAAAAAAHHHHH—

And then Hoshrum Thud whapped the flower-eyed man with his truncheon. He had found a better vector of approach as the man dealt with Mr. Glint. Now the heavy length of hickory came back, Thud's fabled one-two, the same treatment he'd given Jane in The Foundry. It worked as well now as it had then, the man stumbling back.

In a thunderclap of relief Hughes felt the fire leave him. It slid down his thighs, his calves, his ankles, and poured through his feet as if attracted to the bitter cold harbor of the tarmac beneath the snow. Only his toes and the soles of his feet had a bit of aching residue, singed but not too badly damaged.

Hughes could have wept. He grinned instead. His head blazed with detectiveliness, not pain but the sheer deductive pleasure of observation. *Let your eyes answer the very questions they themselves ask.*

"It's those flowering eyes," he called to Thud over the blizzard's bugling. "He looks at you and you cook from the feet up. Takes a while but prolonged staring could be deadly."

"What a treat it is, meeting new people," said Thud, whacking his opponent about the head and shoulders, giving the man no quarter. "Now get out of here, lad."

Hughes slashed and was deflected by the man's fingernails. Enchanted sword steel deflected by a few centimeters of keratin.

That baffled him almost as much as Thud's words:

"I'm not going anywhere."

"Yes you are. Our Spring-Heeled friend won't wait for us to finish with this bugger."

Hughes' face hardened.

"I can't leave you alone."

"Hello, hello, hello," said a voice like loose paving stones in the last garden in hell. "What's all this then?"

The man fixed those peeled lotus-eyes on Mr. Glint and got a kick in the belly for his trouble.

"Might I assist you, officer?" said Glint.

Thud's mustache twitched. "Why if it isn't a concerned citizen. Yes, I think your assistance would be most welcome." He shooed Hughes with a jerk of his chin. "Go on. This has been your bailiwick for a while now. Jane. The whole case. Close it."

What was there to say to that?

"Careful," he warned them. "My sword banged right off him."

Thud nodded. He and Mr. Glint went for the man together. The man stuck out his tongue, a bizarrely juvenile gesture given the circumstances.

His tongue, Hughes thought, running at breakneck speed toward the huge indistinct building that was Saint Wilhelmina's. *Pierced with a red stone.*

Around him the storm wailed and crowed, its hands of gust slamming him into an ambulance shoed and puddled in snow, its teeth snapping at his coat, his sleeves, his naked skin, cold incisors burning in their own wicked way, the dentures and gleaming gums of December, that old bold month.

The hospital doors were automatic.

They slid open.

Hughes ran inside, hoping only that he was not too late.

Chapter Thirty-Five

They swarmed Betty the moment the fortress reached the mountain pass. Scores of them. Hundreds. Thousands. They mobbed out of the shaggy-haired trees and the carcasses of trees killed by the Troll's regional cold. They streamed from the mountain caves. They rose from shallow pits, fingers trussed in strings of soil mixed with deep wormy weeds. Their flesh was purplish-blue with lividity, attached or hanging off their scalps and rib bones. The older the body, the more spoiled the skin. Hair drifted from their skulls—greasy, lank wigs. Larvae, maggots, and fully formed flies—not the flies of Cate's home world, but massive crooked-backed bugs with wings made of caustic green membranes and long dripping feelers—made whatever rotted holes they could find their home. Their hosts did not mind. They came for Betty and all the people Betty carried, chanting a song that clawed up into the air, and this was what they sang:

Not so fast you poxy swains,

Why flee before the getting's good?

That leggy fortress we shall lame,

Then race atop and have your blood,

Your bones, and your most scrumptious brains.

We are the living dead, you see,

Necromancers died and waked.

Our Lord Burrows set us free,

Our hunger conquered, thirst slaked,

Your last breath, our supper intake'd.

And with that they flung themselves by the hundreds under Betty's legs. The most awful gut-gurgling *crunches* and *snaps* rose up to the Scarlet Citadel folk—the noises of corpses obliterated by moss-encrusted stone—made worse by the fact that with the sheer glut of bodies bunching up, the fortress was forced to wade like a dog through a fitful current. Betty's gallop slowed... and slowed... and then, incredibly, the first of the undead began to climb the fortifications.

There, however, they ran into significant difficulties.

After their initial bout of astonishment and worry, Cate Jubilee rallied her troops and gave them each tasks to which they were well-suited. The aim of these tasks was simple: secure the battlements against the forthcoming siege. Lay waste to the enemy. Withstand. Outlast. Reach the portal drop within the next scant few hours. This last part was important—according to the portal schedule detailed in her Citadel journal, should they miss that drop, John Isherwood's team of portal technician's wouldn't open the door of fire for another ninety minutes. Disastrous, in other words. The company would be overrun in forty-five. So they had to hold out, and they had to make the drop, all while saving their skins.

All this goes a long way toward saying that when the undead scaled the walls, their fleshless hands groping into the grooves between the stones, they had their heads shorn off by the sword and spear of Margherita Stranger and Kevlin Paladin. They were bashed to bits as the chains of Marcus Angel wound at terrible speed about the huge tent pegs set into the rock by Elowen Trammel. Kpelle Cinder and Nyoni Snickerdrake formed an explosive range, the latter slinging fireworks over her shoulders, the former lighting the fuses with her concentration, black smoke rolling from her eyes as she did so. The ice from the Troll's dominion had melted into runoff, and Steffan Cerulean was making ample use of it, whirlpooling the zombified remains and presenting their flailing bodies to Gilbert Wildsmith, Morvran Oats, Clothilda Toffington, Liddicoat Smite-The-Naughty-With-Large-Implements, Eugenie o'Nine Tails, Rosemund Valkyrie, and Xacorca Demon for the most violent bedlam of amputations, decapitations, buboes and boilings, severings, slices, cuts and cleavings, chokings, thunderous sneezings, and animal bebotherings you can imagine. In her bolstering lunar form, Rebecca Lupine took turns orbiting Eilandri Titansgrave and Cate Jubilee. That duo were the fulcrum around which that first part of the siege turned. Eilandri hewed and hammered, Cate stamped and kicked and clubbed, and they were both of them soaked in gore before long, and the gore crowning Eilandri's bald head in shards of sticky bone and tangled in Cate's disheveled mane like mausoleum decor. The company heard the hammer blows crash and bash and batter and bust, and they heard Cate's laughter over the growls and howls of the decayed horde, and their flagging energy shored up and gained fresh fuel—logs of courage for the burning.

The living dead were not so pleased.

Laugh will you, Cate Jubilee?
You midden maiden, sly hellcat.
We know of you, and your deeds,
How you slew Maelen, squashed him flat.
A marrow king you brought to knee.

He and his Bonemeal Boys were friends
Of ours, and our Lord Burrows;
King of kings, of beginnings and ends.
So we will slit you guts to elbows,
And with your entrails, make amends.

"Hellcat?" cried Cate. "I'm only a kitten." And in strictest evidence to the contrary she swung her boot at an undead head and sent it sailing like a prime shot in a game of football. The horde glared their sunken socketed hate at her. But she had their attention. Channeling Hughes, she enriched her voice with command and volume, with reason and humility and an undercurrent of threat. "Listen to me. I played some part in Maelen's death, I admit. But he was a witless tyrant. Don't be like him. If you've sense in your skulls you'll think like William o' The Wisps. My company and the wisps fought bitterly. Aye, and parted amicably. Give diplomacy its fair shake..." Her blood-and-sweat streaked face darkened. "Or I warn you, you won't name us Agents of the Red Death. You won't name anyone ever again."

At that moment, when the morale of the enemy might have developed a fatal splinter, a howl went up. Another rose to meet it.

Cate's gaze snapped to their source.

The fortress was still moving sllllllowly through the morass of the dead, so the effect was like a camera's fluid pan, a prolonged shot. The cinematic quality of the moment was not lost on Cate, who even more so than the rest of the company had reason to fear what she saw.

Up there on the mountainside, at the mouth of the largest cave, was a figure. Undead foamed out of the cave, scrambling along the walls, the ceiling, lurching forward into the fray. Motionless, as though the very act of moving was beneath him, the figure at the cave mouth was unnervingly tall and thin, sylphlike, with hair like silvery spindles of cobweb and gray, pinched lips. He wore a damask cloak of nighttime colors, patterned with gold, and a crown forged from the fangs of monsters, blunted and blackened with rot. The crown was draped with a veil like the one the Bride of the Fog had worn, though it covered only the figure's eyes and nose, not that pale, pitiless mouth. He rode a wolf with two heads.

That wolf was one of the worst things Cate had ever laid eyes on. There was something chemical about it, a pervasive wrongness like the lingering smell of mustard gas in an old war trench. One head looked solemn, the other snapping and crazy.

I've heard about you, she thought. *Hughes watched you massacre an entire unit in Iphigenia. A whole unit of Scarlet Citadel... including my friend Laurana.* But it couldn't be the same creature.

Hughes had killed it—him or whatever owned the long, feminine arms that had burst from the wolf's chest and placed its heart on his Krys knife. How then was the likeness so uncanny? Was this wolf a brother to that other? A sister? *A dark cousin?*

The howl went on and on, two-throated as the dual voice of the creature Skuggs. That sound rolled up from deep in the wolf's chest. A wild howl. A tempered howl. A howl to wake the dead and beckon them out of their graves. The horde threw back their heads and howled along with it.

"That must be Lord Burrows," Lorna Blacktower said.

"I think you're right." Though he was wearing that dark veil, the figure seemed to be looking right at Cate. She could almost feel it. There was something supremely arrogant about him. Disaffected. Disinterested. Bored. *Lord Burrows.*

Cate said, "Outlast him today. Kill him tomorrow. Ella, show him how we howl."

Eilandri Titansgrave brought her hammer down, splitting an undead's head with a sound like a rhubarb tart splatting on a tile floor.

More came, and more, a stinking, moaning, puling plague of them. Noseless, dry-gummed, gnawing, biting, festersome bastards.

Cate fought hard.

The company followed her example.

All the while the fortress called Betty slogged on.

They had but to last, and it would all turn out all right.

In the long blue shadows lining the mountain pass, a pair of furred wings rustled past the pines...

***

Thanks to the blizzard, Saint Wilhemina's was choc-a-bloc with due mothers and tense, flustered fathers; nobody wanted to be the one set of parents too cautious or indolent to get to the hospital ahead of the storm—such a fuck-up would mean a home birth and all the domestic hardship that entailed. The result was noisesome and palpably fraught. And crowded too, just as Jane would like it.

Over the tinny *pings* of elevator doors, yacking pre-parents, terse businesslike nurses, riffling papers, *ka-chunk*ing soda machines, pagers beeping, dry coughs, chesty coughs, and crying (happy or sad, it was hard to tell) Hughes heard Estelle call his name. She was signaling frantically from a stairwell leading away from the busy ground floor. He dashed to her.

"Desdemona?"

"She went up here. I think she's—"

"On Jane's tail, let's go."

They rushed up, creamy-sheened steps flashing below, three-at-a-time, Hughes' fit body setting the pace and Estelle keeping up. He thought the madcap quality of the case was taking its toll on her, judging from her expression, but he was wrong.

"Why?" It was as if the words had escaped her rather than consciously being formed.

Hughes grunted, "Why what?"

No response.

His friend bent her mousy head and ran, reaching the steel-handled door before him, hauling it open and holding it so he could plunge through. Hughes did just that. When he did, he thought he saw diamond strings glitter on Estelle's cheeks.

Diamond strings—my elevated senses approaching overdrive. They're only tears. And when she said "why," Estelle meant, "Why would Wendy Dragontail ruin my life?"

Hughes could sympathize—the question had needled him since last night—but right now he needed her at a hundred percent. He caught her hand and squeezed it hard enough to get her focused, then soft enough to let her know they'd find answers together, only later.

He saw her take that in, a little memo delivered through touch. She smiled, mouthed, *Thank you*, and they were hunters once more.

The first floor mirrored the one below—cramped and loud. There, ahead, the nurse's station as he remembered it. If he looked left Hughes knew he'd see the corridor leading to the calming yellow room where he'd relived his relationship with Cate, unable to help her as Artemi Lanmoor and his team fought a terrible fight against foreign matter, a baby become glass while it was still in the womb. His little girl—

No.

A command to himself, as close to a self-directed Performance as he could manage. Instead of looking left his eyes roamed right. They lighted on the shawled shoulders of Desdemona Cauldronpot. She was headed down a corridor lit by bright, clinical-white fluorescents. The corridor was labeled: *Postnatal Ward.*

Hughes' instincts had been right. Jane was going after the hospital's most recent litter of newborn babies.

He ran with Estelle, drawing irate frowns from the nursing staff and on-duty orderlies. One tried getting their attention—presumably to ask if they were visitors, and if not what the hell they thought they were doing here. She was stoutly ignored.

Details blurred for the pair. Hygiene signs, stainless steel water fountains, rogue wheelchairs in case one of the new mommas needed a place to park and get her wind back, bathrooms, men and women looking harried, tired, deliriously happy. Hughes took in everything and nothing. Was it his imagination up to its mean aunt tricks, or were the fluorescents *buzzing?*

There was something sinister in that noise.

Something accusatory.

They had caught up with Desdemona by the time the corridor broke apart in a T-junction. Left was a series of rooms where, ignorant of the danger their children were in, the new mothers sipped apple juice, watched vids, and caught up on sleep.

Right was a wide hall with snow-flecked windows. Blanching the overhead lights, their wan, cold glow touched a series of numbered doors. Beyond these were the babies.

A woman was in the hall. She was standing outside one of the doors. In one hand she held a plastic bottle full of drain cleaner. In the other, a syringe.

She gave Hughes a dreamy smile.

That smile seemed unwelcome on that seamed, serious face. When he'd last seen it in November, it had been glowering at him with thinly veiled contempt.

"You," he said tonelessly.

The door handle turned in her grip. She opened it and went in quickly, Hughes' hand closing on air rather than her blue hospital scrubs.

****

Head Nurse Sadie (known to her fellow employees at Saint Wilhelmina's Maternity Hospital as "Sadie the Sadist") was so radiantly happy.

She had, only a tad earlier that day, received the most wonderful letter.

Not a physical letter, mind. The weather was much too brutal for one of those to reach her. An electronic letter. Sadie had opened her computer that afternoon—grumbling that internal grumble all luddites espouse when forced to encounter a screen, keyboard, and mouse in that order—when she'd seen something unexpected. In her email folder, there was a message from L. Ansuble. Ansuble was Sadie's own last name. L. was for Lily.

Of all the things she'd hoped for that day—happy doctors, happy mommies, happy daddies, maybe even a few wearing wedding rings if God was good (the imprudence of the younger generation when it came to jumping into bed together never failed to grate on Sadie's nerves)—a piece of correspondence from her only daughter was nowhere near that list. As soon as it appeared though, it shot right to the top.

Dragging the cursor via her mouse with a trembling hand, she'd hovered over the letter and double-clicked. Words popped up. Two words preambling the others (*Dear Mom*) followed by neat paragraphs. As she read them, Sadie felt her whole body relax from a tension she hadn't even known was knotting it. When she was finished, she read the message again, as though to verify that (*yes!*) it was real. Really Lily. Several lines underlined and highlighted themselves in her head.

I regret what I said to you that night. I'm sure you do too.

And a little later in that same paragraph:

All I can say is that I'm sorry.

Regret. Sorry.

Sadie did regret the things she'd said that night. She had five long years of wishing and aching to show for it. And she was sorry. Sorrier than she had ever been about anything. When a wife and a husband fall out, that is unfortunate. When a mother and a daughter fall out, that is a full-blown disaster.

Here was another line that struck her:

That's enough about how things have been. I'd like to look to the future. Our future.

And even better than that were these:

I've seen on the news that there's a storm in the city. Maybe if it dies down I could get a train to you. We could spend Tinfrost together. It'd be nice for you to meet Gordon. He's heard a lot about you (don't worry, not all bad).

This last bit tickled Sadie mightily—partly for its tongue-in-cheek sensibility and partly for its honestly. There had been good times before their fight. What had the fight been about? Dumb mother/daughter stuff. What did it matter? Were some embers left in that particular fire? Perhaps. Who was she kidding?

There were embers, and they were hot and obscene and nasty.

She did her best to smother them, and what's more, she mostly succeeded.

Her flowering Lily had met a nice, conservative man with a promising career and provided the storm quelled she would come home for Tinfrost.

One of the orderlies (a big stupid lout whose name Sadie could never remember) had cleared his throat nearby and asked if she had a moment to lend a hand. Sadie registered the shock and mildly puzzled cheer on his face when she'd beamed at him, sunny and young-seeming as a woman half her age, and said yes, she would be delighted to lend a hand wherever she was needed.

She was scrubbing her hands with disinfectant and compiling a mental list of groceries she would need for Tinfrost dinner, just as happy as a tuba in an orchestra, when she'd begun to hear the flies.

***

Hughes' shoulder bounced off the door. He slipped, scrambled up without getting his bearings. Blue movement meant blue scrubs. There!

He lunged, arms flung wide.

He tackled Head Nurse Sadie just as the tip of the syringe needle brushed the chubby pink arm of Daniel Weiber (born two weeks late, healthy and with all his bits and bobs at half three yesterday morning). Where it touched little Daniel's skin, that needle's tip was wet, the syringe full of extra strength UNCLOG-O drain cleaning fluid. One of its main ingredients was sodium hydroxide, otherwise known as caustic soda or lye.

Hughes pushed his Performance, felt it roll in a wave, roll but not quite break, not yet, and grabbed at Sadie's hand. That hand was going wild, stabbing and weaving in herky-jerk spasms, the syringe dripping and sketching loony shapes in the air. Hughes seized it, fumbled, his palm clammy with sweat, and had it again. His gaze was fixed on that needle tip, like a spear of sharpened rain.

Sadie's dreamy bliss had faded. Her expression was hurt, petulant, with a fission of anger slamming through. He had no idea what Jane was making this woman see as she ate her joy, but

Hughes bet that it cast him as a villain to be trumped at any cost. That suspicion was confirmed, and fast.

Her free hand rose to rake at his face, clawlike. They missed his eyeballs, found purchase in his cheek, and gouged right into the soft flesh there. Hughes uttered a flat, barbarian sound of pain and drove his knee into her stomach. Breath burst through her lips, a harsh gush, then a wheeze.

From his spot amongst the rest of the newborns, Daniel Weiber blinked at the sounds of struggling. Thinking in his fluffy rose-pink province of a mind that this sounded interesting (although he had no word for "interesting," not yet anyway), he opened his tiny gumless mouth as though trying to say hello.

Estelle was coming, her face flintish with purpose.

Hughes gave a grunt. "Not yet. The Performance is close."

"Hughes, I've got to do this while—"

"*Stay there,*" he snapped. Sadie's hand whipped free. He strained, snared it, held it tight as she wriggled and cried out that he had to let her go, had to, had to, had tooooooooo.

Estelle was moving anyway. She understood that Jane and the woman she was infesting would be imprisoned together if she used her magic now. He could read that on her face, easy as the large letter row in an eye exam. What she didn't grasp was his absolute belief that Jane had done enough. She had done enough with her first killing. And if they didn't care about this mean-minded, supercilious, pompous head nurse, and said, "Okay, well, at least it wasn't a kind person who got screwed," then they *were* Jane. *He* was her. As evil as a criminal and a monster himself.

Estelle was closer now, inching her way toward the thrashing pair. One of the babies along the row of cots making uncertain sounds. Another sounding almost gleeful. Closer. The needle point weaving, patterning the snug baby-scented air with mischief and silvery evil. The corridor fluorescents *buzzing, buzzing.*

You must work, he begged his Performance. *Wherever you come from, whatever your grand design or insane plotlessness might be—you must work.*

I failed before in this hospital.

I failed the woman I love.

Not again.

Not

(he pushed)

again!

(and felt the waves of power roll and crash over his target)

Let's finish it. One shadow challenges another.

He saw Sadie's louring face go slack.

Come out into the light Jane. The dark will be fine without you for a while, and we shadows are defined by the light.

So come out.

One last time.

Chapter Thirty-Six

We, thought Hoshrum Thud, *are in deep didgeridoo.*

He brought his truncheon down, tendons like ropes in his neck, muscles he hadn't known he possessed straining savagely along the column of his back.

The man with the tongue-piercing and the white lotus eyes didn't even bother to stand aside. He took the blow on his temple, staggered, then like a coiled spring yanked straight, he lanced toward Thud, fist outstretched.

Now it was Thud's turn to stagger, hands clutching his belly, his air stolen, lungs deflated sacks, throat gasping. Pain's subtle irrigation poured liquid fury into his gut, tears of agony to his eyes, desperation into his limbs. Worse, the man was looking at him, which meant from his feet to his legs, creeping up and up, Thud was beginning to bake. Such heat didn't belong in December, in the clot of a windblasted blizzard, snowflakes spiraling and sticking in his eyelashes, his mustache, and lining his nostrils and his raw, hitching throat. Such heat didn't belong in the hottest heart of August. It belonged in the lowest, meanest pit of the deserts of Ikahagua where nothing human was suffered to live.

Then, just as quickly as it started, the feeling abated. All heat sapped. Thud looked up in time to see what had happened. None other than Mr. Glint had curled his hand around the man's head and was punching him squarely in the chest. It sounded like a butcher *thwapping* fat cutlets of rich red meat against a slab. That long-fingered hand ought to have crushed the man's head—Glint's strikes ought to have staved in his chest, just as Thud's blow to the man's temple should have done... well, something for God's sake.

But the man's head was not crushed.

His chest was whole.

His temple was in perfect condition.

We, thought Thud, *are so deep in absolute caca.*

The man broke Glint's hold, picked him up, and threw him into the side of an ambulance. *At least the bloody ambulance has the decency to cave in a bit.*

Thud could feel his grip on his truncheon sliding. He could have done with a lie down and a chocolate biscuit or one of those biscuits with the fluffy pink coconut shavings and jam. Matter of fact, he could have done with a holiday. He and Hettie could go somewhere with a beach. Or a pool. Smell of suntan lotion. Alcoholic drinks with little umbrellas in them, perspiration on the glass. No city. No street to beat with his feet. Nothing too cold to fathom or too hot to bear. Somewhere sensible.

The truncheon slipped from his hand...

... and his hand snapped out and grabbed tight.

A holiday?

Piss on that.

The city was his and he was its.

He advanced toward the man with the tongue piercing, a dog advancing on a bear, which is all the more intimidating because it really doesn't make a lick of sense for the dog to be snarling and baring its teeth, but it is.

Impervious as the man seemed to physical abrasion, he clearly had stamina that they were chewing into. He was bent over, his gruesome flower eyes averted, breath misting from him in white clouds.

"Got a confession," said a frightening voice by Thud. At least, it would have been frightening on any other occasion. It was oddly comforting now.

He glanced at his unlikely ally. "A confession, Mr. Glint?"

"Yeah."

"Go on, then."

"You know the way you were looking for Mr. Glint for a long time? You had a cell put aside for him and all that."

"Cell 13. What about it?"

"I am Mr. Glint," said Mr. Glint.

There was a tactful pause.

"R-right," said Thud. He rallied fabulously. An idea had just occurred to him—a brilliant idea that might get them out of the crap and into the clear. "In that case—since I've been relieved of duty—I am hereby making a citizen's arrest."

Mr. Glint nodded. "I enter a guilty plea. I'm an execrable so-and-so. Real menace to public order. Throw the book at me, copper."

"I'll do you one better—I'll pass sentence." Thud jabbed a finger at the man with the tongue piercing. "Keep that bastard busy. Call it community service."

"Right you are, Mr. Thud."

Thud took to his heels, heading for the hospital. Now if he could only find a nurse to point him toward the staff canteen...

Behind the sprinting figure of Thud, the hospital car park seemed like one enormous salt sieve, paleness shifting inexorably from here to there in a diffusion as sharp as vinegar, or hate. The wind whooped and cheered and hissed, a crowd of spectators to the violence that was sure to ensue.

They faced one another, the Incarnadine and Mr. Glint.

Mr. Glint paid no attention to the blistering heat rising up his body. He clicked his knuckles. It sounded like a bag of moldy walnuts being hit with a brick.

The man opened his mouth and extended his tongue, its gem sparkling in its damp pink cushion.

"Very fetching," Mr. Glint complimented. "And if you ever meet a nice girl, you've got the engagement stone sorted."

The man pulled his tongue back. Apparently the last thing he'd expected was a pleasantry before battle.

"What's your name?"

The man made no reply.

Mr. Glint shrugged his cadaverous shoulders. "That's all right. I shall call you Mr. Wall of Graffiti. I'm on community service, see."

The man was staring at him, his features screwed up in concentration.

The heat intensified.

"That tingles, that does," said Glint. He began to walk toward the man. "C'mere, Mr. Wall of Graffiti. Got to repay my debt to society." The wind hollered and screamed around them. Mr. Glint's sour-mouth stretched, so that the man could see his teeth, which were terrifying. The man took a small step back. Mr. Glint came on and on, death in a speckle-buttoned suit. "Got to clean you up."

***

"Dra*GON!*" thundered a voice, though it was impossible to tell who in the furor.

Balletic in the throes of murder, Cate sketched a plier, a pirouette, and a tourner, her whole frame curved with strength and motion—and just in time she saw the dragon's parted jaws. Before it could suck the blood from her veins she launched herself at it directly. Cunningly done, as it turned out, for the dragon hadn't expected her to go on the offensive, a lesson her boot taught it most bluntly.

But it did not retreat. Its slender, serpentine body flickered over the battlements, the red-and-white flecked fur on its body rasping eerily over the stone.

"Stop it!" Cate sent mirrors condensing in the courtyard. She was through them in a moment, her body pinwheeling, boots kicking so fiercely they punctured the dragon's hide in bursts of bright blood. *"Kill it–DOWN, BRING IT DOWN!"*

But the company were in dire straits. It was worse than the fight with the wisps, more taxing and atrocious by far. The enemy were without end, a supply of sordid flesh and bent bone and tenacity sent by Lord Burrows—a swarm of living dead rather than bugs. They turned Betty into a beehive and they an invasion of filthy autumn hornets. The smell creeping into the company's noses was rank, head-swimmingly foul perfumes of rot and putrefaction. The Citadel's weapons seemed heavier, their movements as sluggish as the fortress beneath them. Even Eilandri could do little to help Cate in that moment, her hands full keeping the others alive.

So when the dragon's rear claws swiped at Cate, it was all she could do to roll and tumble to a skidding stop, the courtyard stone hard against her back.

She watched the dragon worm its way through the keep doors, tail lashing, wings tucked tight to its body. In a flash she was on her feet and rushing after it. A hand closed on her arm. Cate snapped about, rage seizing her face in a rictus.

"Let it go, Cate," urged the owner of the hand: Rosemund Valkyrie. "If it goes for the dungeon, Igor and the others will give that dragon a nasty welcome. We need you here."

Cate searched Rosemund's face. There was something different about it.

An ear. She's lost an ear. Probably being gnawed by a bedraggled girl or boy out there in the undead throng.

Cate nodded. They did need her here.

As she and Rosemund rejoined the fray, she cast a look back toward the keep.

She had placed Igor, Brecht, Varjo, and Jennifer in the dungeon for a reason.

Still, it felt wrong leaving them on their own. That dragon was no dimwitted brute.

She wished the Murky Lurking Lads luck and waded back into battle.

***

After widening the entrance with its claws as sharp as the dreams of knives, the dragon slinked down into the deep dungeon murk, unaware of those who lurked there. Even Paris of Troy, who was an amazing mover before his run in with a certain sparkling duo in the days of the Hairy Autumn, would have been astonished at the dragon's capacity for grace. There was a sinuousness to it, a slippery, furry malignance. There went its muzzle, wrinkled as it inhaled the various smells of the dungeon. Various and interesting smells, yes. And here were its eyes, so colorless except for those narrow scarlet slits.

Down the steps it came, more like a snake with its belly whispering over the flagstones than a beast of the air. Before it were five cells and otherwise a deserted space. Shadowy, true, but surely deserted.

Gently, almost imperceptibly, the dragon's nostrils flared as it sniffed again.

Then faster than the naked eye could account for, it swung its head toward the thickest bit of shadow, opened its mouth, and *sucked.*

Pulled from that patch of dense shadow were wet ropes—wet and red. Into its mouth they streamed. The dragon gulped greedily. As it drank the shadow shrank. Revealed from its blackness were Igor Wight, Brecht Bedlam, Varjo Cutthroat, and Jennifer Goblingrin (not grinning now, far from it, glowering, groaning, simpering). The four fell to their knees. The threads of their blood grew thinner... thinner... gone. They collapsed.

At that a shape in one of the cells stirred. There was a grunting, snorting sound as of something sleeping coming awake. A pink-quartz eye blinked in the dark.

"Ruthven?"

"Good evening, Skuggs," said the dragon, moving forth and carving the bars of the cage with a claw.

"Ruthven! You got my flitter!"

"Indeed."

Skuggs offered up his manacles. The dragon called Ruthven pinched them between foreclaw and thumb, crumpling the sturdy metal effortlessly.

"What propoundable luck! I don't suppose you beat Burrows to me?" Skuggs said, sauntering out of his cell with a hopeful grin.

The dragon watched that grin curdle as he replied, "Burrows is here. He's laying siege to this perambulatory pebble of a fortress. Did you talk?"

"Did I buggery."

"They didn't torture you?"

A look of extreme discomfort passed over Skuggs' small, pumpkinlike face. It was swift enough in passing, but Ruthven caught it just the same.

"Nah. That Jubilee wagon doesn't have the axles. Quit ogling, Ruthven. They nabbed the compass, but nextly to that they didn't have a puking pissing phrase from me. Swear it by the Lady."

The little fellow met Ruthven's slitted gaze, his expression defiant, daring the dragon to call him a liar.

Eventually Ruthven made a guttural noise and turned away.

"On my back."

Skuggs' irritation changed. "I'll go below. Underground, since I've missed it so."

"Oh no. I insist. You invoked the Lady, after all, and by coincidence she wants to speak with you. It would be my pleasure to convey you to her."

If Skuggs' lips had curdled before, they were positively acidic now.

"Can't we linger and throttlest Cate Jubilee?"

"And risk our Lady's most invaluable communicator?" said Ruthven silkily. "Don't be absurd."

Skuggs gave up. He climbed atop Ruthven's back, grumbling to himself.

"Speak? With me? Yes. Yes, I suppose she does."

Poor Skuggs, pitied Ruthven privately, and with only a hint of amusement. *Poor, precious Skuggs. He really does have the most guzzlible luck.*

***

"Bastard."

The only ones who heard her say it were the living dead she was fighting. A hard word. A venomous word. A word that spoke to that most keen of frustrations—the one that shades to anger quicker than we care to admit.

It passed like an ugly spell through Cate Jubilee's teeth.

The dragon had taken wing once more, clearing the battlements and soaring toward the peak of the nearest mountain. On its back clung a small figure. Cate had recognized her prisoner at once, and in an instant she knew her people were dead and Skuggs was about to get away. She couldn't catch him. Couldn't mount a hunt. Couldn't conscript Rosemund or Morvran or any of the other fliers to follow.

A jailbreak, then, to free her prize. Her assumptions had been verified. Skuggs was a key part of Eurydice's invasion plans. The vampire dragon, Lord Burrows on his two-headed wolf, and Skuggs.

She could almost hear that tittering laugh of his—giddy in his freedom no doubt.

Ahehn-hen-hen.

We'll meet again, bastard.

Her eyes flicked to the dragon.

And you too, you bloated sky leech. I'll find out how deep the blood reservoir runs before it drains dry. I promise you that.

One of the undead lumbered into her field of view, grasping at her injured arm, trying to make her scream. Cate took the legs from under it and fed her boot to its hinge of a jaw. There was a *crunch*, and a puff of tomb-smelling powder.

Dear almighty God, but this was a bitter business.

Exhaustion and disappointment joined her blood in a second vital stream coursing right through her.

Leading as best (as Responsibly) as she could, her voice came softer, and this time not even Cate herself heard the words:

"Hughes, the letter. Read it and come to me, lover. Come quick."

Chapter Thirty-Seven

"–zzzzzzzzzhhhhhhhhhuuuuuuuughessssszzzzzzz–"

Where they lay in their cordoned-off units those newborn babies who were awake goggled, delicate butterfly eyelashes blinking, at the tumult of bugs. The bugs surged out of Head Nurse Sadie, out of her eyes and her nose and ears, her tongue a launchpad for locusts and beetles and spiders and flies. Hughes caught the nurse as she fell, his gaze fixed on the feminine shape forming out of the insect swarm.

"–Hughes, Hughes, Hughes. You keep barging in on my dinner plans," Jane told him. Her head was canted to one side, her dark hair frissoned with emotion, spilling over her face in wild writhing strands, and that long face so similar to Hughes' own. Curling her lips was a smile like a lepidopterarium—hard and glassy and full of moths. "People will say we're becoming involved."

Hughes watched her dark eyes swivel from him to Estelle.

"I know your face. I ate a slut who saw your photograph every day for a year. I see the mantelpiece of a brothel mistress, a woman with the look of you, a mother. She was a source of happy memories for my supper. You were younger in the picture. Who are you?"

"Jane," said Hughes softly. He rested Sadie's insensate body against the wall and stood. Steel whispered—Chimera sliding from its sheath. He held it out to her like a suitor at a dancehall. "I know you won't explain the things you've said to me. I'm sure some of it's been true, some not. I could ask you about it, but I guess you'd only dream up a new way to torture me."

"Don't hold me in suspense. Who is she?"

"No one."

"No one is no one." Jane was smiling from Estelle to Hughes and back again. A sword was in her hand now too, the insectile mirror of his own. She held it out, teasing the edge across Chimera's, the sound of steel's kiss strange and ringing, a finger-circled wine-glass chime. Around them babies cooed, made pillowy nocturnal noises, wept quietly, squalled. Estelle was stock-still, fascinated and scared all at once. Jane's gaze fastened on the object wrapping her arm.

"Funny looking glove. Lose the other one?"

The girl gave a tiny nod.

"Sad when a perfect pair is separated," said Jane with a sympathy that sounded almost genuine. Almost, but not quite.

Quite without warning she seemed to lose interest in Estelle.

"Even your baby was someone, Hughes. Not sentient, of course. But I bet before Cate's glass switched off the lights there were neurons glowing in your daughter's head. Pretty prisms of pre-thought. Couldn't you have convinced your woman to hang up the boots? Did it never occur to you?" Jane snickered. The room seemed to darken. "There once was a baby who turned into glass, her daddy's an ass. How's Frank?"

"Alive."

"Damn. Thought I got him." She shrugged, as if it were no great shakes. "I suppose if you can survive ritual parental abuse, you can survive a crossbow bolt. There's always next time. What about us?" she asked Hughes, still working her blade over his own, her tone a trifle sensual, and utterly vile. "What have you planned for you and I? This time, I mean. Want to fight? Want to fuck? That might be interesting. Iphigenia's a fertile place, and you are its shadow, as I have told you—truthfully. Maybe..." Oh her smile grew then, a larval egg splitting into a full grown fly of a grin. "Maybe we could make a baby."

As if to endorse the idea, the baby she'd been about to inject with drain cleaner brought its hands together. Like it was applauding.

Outside the room, Desdemona Cauldronpot cowered, her knuckles white as she held her accessories to keep them from jangling.

Inside, what little color there was in Estelle's face poured away.

Jane leered, searching Hughes' face for conflicted memories—oh what could have been, oh the hopes and dreams, oh the bitter mourning. He was her tasty joy-drenched bon bon, soaked in sorrow too. Sweet food sweet meat Gormon Hughes let's eat! That was what her expression said.

But when he looked at her, she saw the one thing she did not expect.

Hard to describe, but if pressed to confine it to a word, she would have been forced to admit Hughes looked *done.*

Not dismayed.

Not regretful.

Not sore or smarting or all busted up inside, as she had so hoped he would be.

She stared into his face, and the resignation there unsettled her. Freaked her the fuck *out.* Hadn't she taunted him? Pricked him deeply (glassily!) with that line about the two of them bumping uglies and making a shadow child?

Jane wasn't sure why, but the idea of Hughes ceding... no... *relinquishing* all that hot, feverish emotion she had once riddled him with so easily... the idea of him looking done with this whole scene

(*with me*)

... it galled her. Actually, that undersold it.

It infuriated her.

Okay, she thought. *Okay my poison honeycomb boy. You ointment fucking with my flies. Let's see how finished you look when I fill your little friend's eardrums with wasps.*

She feinted with her blade. Hughes took the bait. Slow, too dog-gone slow he riposted, missing her as she flowed in a buzzing cloud at the girl he'd brought with him. No surprise there. He had always been one step behind her. Maybe this time he'd take that to heart. Failing that, she could always stab him through his, just like he'd pierced hers.

Jane apparated before the tired, sickly little bitch. The girl's complexion was the color of cottage cheese. *I bet she's as soft as cottage cheese. She'll scream. How* done *will you be then, Hughes?* The girl's face smiling out from that brothel's photograph niggled Jane. But what did that matter?

The answer was that it didn't.

Jane listened to the babies, to Hughes' approaching footsteps (not fast enough), and her own beautiful *buzz*, savoring the bad sounds as much as the good. And as she listened, she folded the girl in her arms, and bent her like a lover getting ready to plant a kiss on her lips.

"I grew up in that brothel," the girl whispered.

Jane opened her bug-stuffed mouth, dismissing the words for what they were—inane bullshit.

The girl spoke again, louder. "My name is Estelle Corlum."

Corlum. In spite of the situation's urgency, the name gave Jane pause.

Corlum.

Where had she heard that name before?

It came to her like a lightning bolt out of a clear sky.

It's not a glove. It's a vambrace.

"No," said Spring-Heeled Jane. She wanted to run, to fling herself away from the girl, dissolve into flies, then the cusp of a sound, then a shadow, then nothing at all. But she couldn't move. She could only stare, her voice a beautiful buzz no longer but soft as a slice of fresh cottage cheese. Her murderous face was white as snow. "No. It can't be."

"It can," said Estelle. "This is for you."

For me? As if the anemic little bitch was giving Jane a gift for the holidays. *For Tinfrost.* Hughes was there, Jane could see him—*feel* him—watching.

She had to move. Had to escape.

She couldn't.

A fly caught in a trap.

The girl hugged Jane's helpless body close.

She was not sure how, but before the Perfect Prison finished the work it had begun the moment Jane had first touched Estelle, she somehow found the strength to look at Hughes.

He had been a worthy opponent after all. She ceded that. Relinquished it. Fat lot of good it did her now. On the floor, a drop of liquid beaded the tip of the syringe. It fell soundlessly, the way lazy bobbing bees drip from their stingers.

In the end I wasn't as busy a bee as I could have been. I got lazy. And stupid.

Or maybe she had simply indulged her hunger one time too many.

She met Hughes' gaze and had to physically restrain herself from bursting into tears. She wanted to beg for her life. She could use it better. She'd swearswearswear.

It wouldn't matter to him. He was done.

Jane supposed she was done too, now it came to it.

Full at last, only with defeat instead of victory.

What's that I see?

There was a flicker deep in those shadow-dark eyes of his. Her own eyes did that, she knew. A flicker of feeling. Hers went blue-ish white, as cold as winter. But his...

Green, she thought. *When he gets that flicker of feeling, his eyes go warm and green as springtime.*

"Goodbye," Hughes said.

She was too far gone to understand. Goodbye? What did such a thing mean?

BUZZ Buzz buzz—

Going, then losing all sense of going, then losing sense altogether.

In the last loaded cartridge of conscious thought, there buzzed a few final scraps of the shadow woman, the Spring-Heeled menace, the lady of the flies named Jane.

An epitaph. Last words of a kind, though not even Hughes heard them.

With silver bells and cockle shells and pretty maids all in a

***

The parking lot was in shambles. Mounds of snow lay churned as though a team of plough horses had been corralled through them. The Hospital Main Entrance sign had been knocked off its struts. Bumpers and bonnets were dented. Car alarms *honked* and *wheep-wheeped* forlornly, engulfed along with every other sound in the blizzard. Head-and-tail lights flashed. They turned the lot into a shaken snow globe strobed with mischievous fairy lights.

Next to an overturned ambulance, wrestling in the spilled medic equipment and crunchy frost and sugary lumps of crystallized rain, were Mr. Glint and the man with the tongue piercing and the eyes like white lotus flowers.

Glint had the man in a chokehold that, despite Glint's efforts, wasn't choking him. The man seemed as invincible to harm as the legendary Wendy Dragontail.

A figure labored up to them. Glint recognized Thud, who seemed to be shielding something from the storm with his body. There was a suggestion of a glossy surface and... colored teapots?

"Mr. Glint," said Thud, cutting off further speculation. "I would be very much obliged if you'd keep this nasty bugger's eyes open. Even one of his eyes would do."

Crrrrrack went Glint's jaw as it opened unspeakably wide.

His lower teeth wedged in at the nape of the man's neck. His upper row came around the man's scalp, passed the brow, and latched onto his right eyelid. They could not puncture the man's unbreakable skin, but they could tug that eyelid so the lotus eye bulged in an even bigger bloom.

Thud grinned a cruel, approving grin. "That'll do very nicely."

He strode up and pressed the object he'd fetched from the hospital to the man's face. The man's struggles renewed. More than that, they increased, as though spurred by sudden panic. His hands clutched at Thud; Mr. Glint caught them and held them fast. His legs backpedaled uselessly; Mr. Glint set his back to the overturned ambulance and refused to be moved further.

From under the object Thud was holding over the man's face came a harsh, croupy noise. It sounded like the Corinthian word "hack," only not quite so clear.

There was a smell like roasting pork.

Then the man with the tongue piercing went limp in Glint's grasp.

Thud removed the object and stood back, his expression wary.

Though warranted, that caution proved unnecessary—the man was unconscious. Those white flower eyes drooped like wilting tulips across his cheeks.

"What does 'aku' mean?"

Thud looked sharply at Mr. Glint, who was disentangling himself from the man.

"Sorry?"

"Aku," Glint repeated. "He said it over and over while you covered his face."

"Aku? Was that what it was?"

Not "hack." Aku.

"It's a Hortesian word," said Thud.

"What's it mean?"

"Stop."

They stood in the restless snow globe of the lot, those head-and-tail fairy lights playing their bright, strobing tricks, painting the pair standing up and the man lying crumpled in the snow like Tinfrost decorations, car alarms screaming, screaming.

"Come on," said Thud. "Let's get him inside."

It was no trouble to Mr. Glint, who set the man upon his shoulder as easily as a farmer ferrying a sack of apples. They lumbered toward the hospital against the wind. As they walked, Glint took Thud's object from the policeman's unresisting fingers. He examined it thoughtfully. It was an empty box, all mirrors on the inside and designs on the outside. The designs were indeed colorful teapots.

He said, "You're a wit, Mr. Thud. We couldn't hurt the man, so you made him look at his own reflection. That way the burning got inside him. That way he hurt himself."

"I have my moments," said Thud rather smugly.

"Could have used a mirror."

Thud's smugness congealed slightly. "Yeah, well. Had to improvise, didn't I? Besides," he said, taking the object back, "you must never underestimate the presence of a biscuit tin."

Glint nodded his horrible head as if this were a chunk of the most precious wisdom. Who knows? It may well have been.

The wind worked the snow and the dense wintry smells into their clothes, a chilly laundromat. They could make out the automatic doors of the hospital now.

Thud was wishing Hughes and Estelle luck with Jane and mulling over how he would explain the events of the day to Hettie when he got home, when quite out of nowhere Glint asked, "Why did you?"

"Why did I what?"

"Stop. You didn't know he was asking you to. So why did you stop?"

Thud regarded his unlikely companion. Glint seemed perfectly sincere.

Why had he stopped? Thud knew why, of course, but what was the point in chatting about it? He seriously considered leaving the matter lie, but then again, what the hell. After all that Glint had done for him and his city in the past week alone, Thud felt an explanation for a bit of mercy was the least he deserved.

"I didn't need to know he was asking me to because some part of me knew he was. Who wouldn't want someone to stop in such a situation? To be honest, Mr. Glint, I stopped because I know what happens to people when they don't stop."

"They keep going?"

"That's the difference between a criminal and a copper. If you want to carry the law inside you—a badge in your heart as well as your hand—you've got to let yourself be carried inside of it. And that means stopping before you become the thing you were trying to stop in the first place.

Stopping is the whole thing. The kit and kaboodle. As you say, if I hadn't stopped, *I'd have kept going.* Is it a city of murderers who murder other murderers we want? Or is it something measured, cautious, *better?* Yeah okay, be tough where tough is due. Whole place would be in terrible nick if there weren't rules and people carried by the law to enforce them. But I know where my bread is buttered on stopping and not stopping, thank you very much. Did you know the word policeman comes from 'polis' which means city?"

"So you are a man of the city?"

"Right you are, Mr. Glint. And damn well glad of it."

"Polis. Policeman. And what about 'Thud'?"

"It's short," said Thud. "For '*Thud*-Right-Now-Be-A-Sport-And-Fall-Over-There's-A-Good-Chap.'"

"Good joke," said Mr. Glint in his voice like a crooked coffin lid closing forever. "Four years ago, when Mr. Gallant and I were conducting a bit of business in Daethumberland, I found out where my name comes from."

"What, Glint?"

Glint nodded.

"Go on then."

"It comes from the word *glenten*," said Mr. Glint. "Means 'glass.'"

Thud made a polite noise of interest. But he was too occupied with thoughts of his wife and his work to think about etymology and glass.

Before them the automatic doors whispered open. Thud felt warm, conditioned air on his cheeks.

It felt good.

Chapter Thirty-Eight

With eyes that—in spite of everything—could not quite believe what they were seeing, Hughes watched as Jane's Spring-Heeled reign of terror came to an end. Estelle held her close, an embrace redolent of friendship rather than prisoner and jailer. They had spoken to one another, only a few terse words that Hughes had not quite caught. Now Jane was disintegrating. Not into dust. Not into ribbons of golden light, like the villain in a fairy tale.

Fluttering, and with more colors than the brain could keep up with, Jane melted into a kaleidoscope of butterflies. Their wings, so fine and so delicate, paddled the air. All around the room the babies were fascinated. Even the wailer had stopped to admire this development.

None of them would remember it tomorrow.

Only maybe that wasn't true.

To Hughes, memory seemed like an absent mother. Sometimes she took care of you, showed you what you wanted to see. Sometimes, though, she withheld. Perhaps because she knew, in the tired, beautiful way mothers seem to know everything, that you weren't quite prepared for those images, those sounds, those recollections of touch, or even more complicated feelings from your past. Perhaps she was trying to tell you that sometimes, not remembering is better.

The analogy was good, and it rang true for Hughes, whose mother had been so absent as to become tantamount to a dream.

Why should he think of his mother, a woman he had never really known, at this moment? It mystified him. Then, with a thunderbolt of thought, he did remember.

That day when she took me to Symbarr Square, the day I first saw Krys and The Mum present their Rotbloom Carnival of Bright Oddments and Dark Delights... there were butterflies.

He was not sure if they'd come with the carnival, or if they were as much a spectator to those bright oddments and dark delights as he was.

But they *had* come, and one had landed in his mother's hair. It had been so red his mind had enshrined it as a few seconds worth saving, the way a computer can be convinced to store crucial things that might come in handy along the digital road. Those wings had looked to his six-year-old self like envoys of the color red itself. The primary matriarch color from which all versions of red were born. Impossible to think of, but against his mother's hair it had managed to look redder still.

As Spring-Heeled Jane came apart, a butterfly just like the one from his memory passed before his gaze. Its flight seemed slow, almost drugged. It looked like it needed to rest. Unaware he was doing so, Hughes put up his hand, making his fingers a rest stop. But before the butterfly could alight, it faded, and faded some more. Then it was gone.

He raised his head. They were all gone.

It was over.

"What's happening?"

A panicky voice.

Hughes turned and saw that Head Nurse Sadie had returned from wherever Jane's possession had sent her.

"What's going on?"

For a moment Hughes stared at her, this woman who in November had separated him from Cate. It was clear that Cate had been in distress, that she needed him, but this morose busybody had separated them anyway. He had thought about her from time to time. His memories hadn't withheld the superior looks she'd given him. Nor had they withheld the disdain she'd shown him when she found out he and Cate had conceived out of wedlock. He had called her many names in the privacy of his head. He could feel them now, alighting on his tongue like poisonous moths.

"Nothing," he heard himself tell her. His tone was mellow. Kind. "You're in one of the infant care rooms at work. You had a fall, but you're safe, and so are the babies in your charge."

"Am I hurt?"

"No. Take my hand."

She did. He helped her up.

He was not sure she recognized him right away. The woman seemed too addled to recognize her own name.

"Desdemona," he said. And though he said it softly, his talented voice carried, and in a moment the occultist was there in the doorway, glancing about the room nervously in case it contained even a single trace of Jane and her bugs.

"Do you sense Jane out there? Any... manifestation of her at all?"

"No," replied Desdemona, visibly relaxing. "The shadow has passed."

Hughes felt gooseflesh prickle the back of his neck. *One of us has, Denise. One of us has.*

"Take this woman to the nurses' station," Hughes bid her.

For once Desdemona had no clipped words for him. She nodded, took Sadie's arm, and led her away. It was only when Sadie looked over her shoulder at him that Hughes knew. He was familiar to her, and soon she would make the connection.

He wondered if she'd feel guilty, then decided it didn't matter if she did or not.

He approached his friend.

"Estelle. I don't want to doubt your ability to use your father's magic, but I don't understand."

"Neither do I. Where is she?" Estelle was hugging herself, her triumph at having succeeded tamped down by uncertainty. "When Daddy imprisoned Frank, he put him at the top of Redspire behind a locked door. I tried to do the same thing with Jane, *but she's not there.*"

"You're sure?"

"Trust me. I would know."

"Okay." He walked out of the room so as not to further disturb the babies. He closed the door after Estelle followed him. "Show me the vambrace."

She brightened. "Right! Of course!"

They looked at it together. Where only a few minutes ago there had been two leather bands wrapping it, now there was only one.

"So it worked," said Hughes.

"That's good," Estelle said meekly. "Isn't it?"

He smiled at her. Anything to preserve the bravery he'd seen her demonstrate in that room. Anything to keep the anxiety from creeping back in and stealing her away again.

"It's good," he reassured. "A little perplexing. But good."

"Don't tell me we missed it?"

Hughes spun and saw Hoshrum Thud racing toward them, Mr. Glint right behind.

He grinned. "You missed it."

"Damn." Thud grinned back. "We've got her then? Your Perfect Prison worked a treat?"

"It worked. We're just not sure how it worked."

Hughes gave them the breakdown.

"Well it's a chin-scratcher, I suppose. But I won't scratch too hard." Thud shrugged. "If the lady with the dream visions says things are back to normal, then they must be normal."

His willingness to leave this particular mystery unsolved both rankled and pleased Hughes. He wanted to cross it out too, scribble it with thick marker and have done.

The word scribble keyed some rusted lock in his head. It opened on—not a memory—but a feeling of intense love and obligation.

Cate. She would want to know immediately.

He excused himself, went up the hall a ways, and took from his coat pocket the folded sheet of enchanted paper.

Thirty seconds later he was running as though his life depended on it.

Faster.

As though *Cate's* life depended on it.

Which was true.

***

For a sliver of a moment it seemed Estelle Corlum would run after Hughes.

Mr. Glint and Mr. Thud certainly did.

She actually felt her knee begin to rise... and then she thought of Wendy Dragontail's hand on that knee of hers. She thought of Wendy's hand on her shoulder. On her back. On her cheek.

Pat, pat, comforted that hand.

There, there.

As in *there, there. It will all turn out all right in the end. Like a story.*

And so Estelle chose not to pursue her friend. He had helped her, unquestionably. But she had helped him also, and now it was time to take stock of what he had told her. Take stock and process. Even if it injected her with the most awful, violated feelings.

She looked down the hall—empty now—and thought, *At least I'm in a hospital. What better place for a jab.* What might she be inoculated against?

Against that comforting hand, of course.

Pat, pat.

There, there.

"But why?" Now that Jane was dealt with (if she was dealt with, the missing vambrace strap said she was, but her absence was keenly felt in Estelle's perception), and Hughes had flown off on pressing business, she finally had a moment to think about that question. "Why would Wendy do that? What did I do to her?"

It went back and forth inside her, palindromic.

Back and forth—why, why.

Pat, pat.

There, there.

Painfully, predictably, no matter which way she examined it, the idea made no sense at all. She made a small, mousy noise, and at once regretted it because that was a noise that the girl in the tower would make. And she was there no longer.

She was—

As if in answer to the noise, a kind of echo floated up to her. A reply.

Estelle frowned at the floor.

A rat was there. Bizarre seeing so furry and twitchy and... *woodlandish* a thing on such a sterile floor. In fact it was so peculiar, Estelle forgot to be spooked. Another day she might have been. Or maybe she'd left the part of her that was scared of critters back in the tower as well.

"Hello," she said.

The rat gave a squeak. A decidedly friendly one to her confused ear.

An explanation presented itself.

"Are you one of Knickerbocker's spies?"

The rat brought up its pink tail and gave it a wag, just as a dog might do when it hears the name, or the voice, of its master.

Even with some of her puzzlement clearing, Estelle felt far from even footing. Holy moly, was she tired. Was this what it felt like to have adrenaline coarse out of you along the same pipes it entered by?

The rat seemed expectant.

Estelle couldn't imagine why. But then she knew why. It was the one "why" she could clutch firmly in that moment.

"Do I know you?" she said with a big smile because they did know each other. "Are you the rat who I used to catch roaming the eighty-ninth floor?"

Another squeak, this one somehow even friendlier.

"I thought so. Sheltering here until the blizzard dies down?"

An agreeable squeak.

"Well. You must take care not to be trod on."

A serious squeak.

In the wounded, but still sharp depths of her conflicted head, Estelle reached a decision. She wanted time to think. More than wanted. She craved it.

And just like that she knew what she was going to do next.

She got down on her haunches, so she and the rat could chat as equals.

"In some of the stories I've read, the princesses who escape from their towers have the power to converse with animals. Occasionally this involved singing. I used to think it was soppy, wooly-headed tripe. Now I think maybe there's something to it. Would you please help me with something? It means bending the truth to your master..."

The rat bristled.

"... but only for a little while. And it won't affect him in the slightest. I promise."

The rat seemed a trifle mollified by this.

Estelle sensed she must sweeten the pot.

"And I'm sure I can track down a slice of cheese in this hospital."

A disinterested squeak.

"Not a dairy person. I see. I suppose it *is* Tinfrost. There might be some candied pudding, but—"

Suddenly peace had been declared. The rat stood to attention.

Estelle's smile returned, fatigued in the cold fluorescent light, but happy all the same.

"Pudding it is." She giggled. "Okay. Listen closely..."

With a belly giddy at the prospect of rum-chocolate, frosting, and nutmeg spice, Whiskers 319 listened close as close could be.

***

Take a woman who has lost a child. Who has begun to reconcile the personal apocalypse of that within herself. Who has cleared a little of the mist fogging the glass inside, even if the stuff on the outside continues to grow and grow—

Not that she would wish it to stop—

Not that she would ever wish that—

Since the boots and the glass and the woman are inextricably tied—

Like laces that cannot come undone—

Take that woman and pare away all of the grief and reconciliation and every other traceable emotion (other than rage, of course), with a paring knife called Survival Instinct—

Carve her heart into the shape of a candle and take a flamethrower to the wick—

Sand her Responsible Leadership until its smooth and flat and unrecognizable—

Invoke and then provoke the Hurricane of who she is—

Then put something in front of her that wants to kill her.

See what happens.

See what the fuck happens.

By the time reinforcements arrived, pouring through the portal and sending Lord Burrows' undead horde scarpering for its life (or its un-life), Cate Jubilee had none of the wherewithal to recognize friend from foe. She had no sense of who had lived and who had died. If you'd told her *she* had died and this was hell, she would not have understood the language you were speaking, much less the implications the words inspired.

They found her where she'd landed, collapsed where the fighting had been thickest, surrounded by a veritable forest of bodies.

No one knew how she'd gotten there. No one except Eilandri Titansgrave, who gave Wendy Dragontail a little yellow card explaining things. According to the card, the undead had made a concerted push to take the fortress. Their numbers were very great, and in the bedlam they had overwhelmed Inez Symphony, breaking her violin and pulling her down into the throng and opening her chest like a cabinet door full of food. Cate had leapt off the battlements in pursuit. Inez had died, naturally, but so had her killers. And all of the undead nearby. And all of the undead in a radius the size of a football pitch.

Eilandri wrote they had all been far gone, and Cate was not to be scrutinized unfairly for her spate in a zone of animal violence. Quite the contrary. The Pale Giant was grateful. She wrote that more might have died if not for Cate. That went for today and the entire mission to Eurydice.

This was on the other side of the portal, back home, where Betty the fortress and those who had survived its final charge were recovering from the battle's aftermath.

Everything was in chaos. Medical attention. Shouts. Screams. Lunatic laughter. Inconsolable crying.

Through it all, Hughes shouldered his way. Cate's letter had done more than successfully raise the alarm, spurring Hughes to gather reinforcements. It had frightened him to the marrow in his bones. *Dragon attack. Come quick. Love you.*

Too many people. Too many.

He got through them anyway.

Come quick. Love you.

The words she'd written drummed crazily against his ribs like a second heartbeat.

First Head Nurse Sadie and now another world's trouble.

He and Cate had been parted forcefully. Love had brought them together after November. Now it seemed December wanted in on the action. It would test that love, and its terms, and its power to keep a man on the cusp of going mad with worry while keeping him sane with a devotion you could chart stars by.

Come quick.

He had done everything he could, as fast as he could.

What if I wasn't fast enough?

What if by the time I read her message...

No! No, I won't let myself conjecture about that. I'm already a wreck for God's sake, I can't—

He caught sight of hair, white as snow. "Wendy!"

The Estelle situation could wait. Evidently her Ladyship felt the same. The look she fixed him with was the farthest thing from accusation. It was bright, almost lambent with concern.

"Hughes," she said. "Cate's with the surgeon."

The surgeon.

Not again.

"Is it bad?" A damn fool question, given the circumstances. Right then, it was the only one he could think to ask. He looked from Wendy to the giant with sad, lavender eyes standing next to her, and back again. "Is she okay?"

To her credit, Wendy didn't shy from his gaze. She did him the courtesy of looking him in the eye when she delivered the words like a letter laced with arsenic.

"We don't know."

Epilogue
Something Ends, Something Begins

He really had to invest in a diary.

When Hughes opened the door of his apartment and saw Thud standing there, his first thought was that the Perfect Prison had only been a temporary solution to the Spring-Heeled Jane problem—that she was out there in the city eating herself fat and laughing at him.

Then he saw the bundle of ribboned boxes in Thud's arms and remembered the streetbeater had called him yesterday asking if he could swing by in the morning.

"Hello, Thud."

"Morning lad," said Thud, stepping inside. He was dressed warmly in blues and reds. As soon as he set the boxes on the living room table he teethed off his gloves and tucked them in his pocket. His eyes happened on Hughes' copy of *The Times*.

"So you've heard, then?" he said.

"Hm? Oh yes. Nasty, eh?"

"Nasty is one word for it."

The newspaper's chief headline read:

Streetbeater Commissioner Pleads Guilty To Hit-And-Run Slaying
Of City's Leading Journalist

Underneath were two pictures: the first was of the dead journalist, Tracer Gogen, smiling. The second showed Commissioner Vincent Winkles, his face crumpled in a moue of guilt and self-pity.

"Did he come forward of his own accord?" Hughes wondered.

"What? Vinny Winky obeying his conscience?" Thud snorted. "Next you'll ask if the restaurants in hell serve frozen yogurt. No, a neighbor spotted the commissioner parking his car round the back of his house—something she'd never seen him do before."

"Nosy woman."

"True, but thank goodness for nosy, suspicious, curtain-twitching women. One time out of ten their hand wringing turns up information more valuable than gold. Anyway she said the commissioner hurried into his house, came back a moment later with a bucket and sponge, and began scrubbing something from the license plate, the bonnet, and the windshield of his car. It was only when he squeezed the sponge over the bucket that she realized what he was cleaning."

Hughes, who had gone into the kitchen to put the kettle on, but who was listening keenly, called, "Tracer Gogen's blood."

"Exactly," came Thud's reply. "The cracked windshield, well, he might have explained that. Driving in the blizzard, and the wind blew one of the streetlamps right over. Bad luck. But the blood clinches it. Of course he disposed of the sponge and bucket, but after the neighbor contacted the Cleomenes Precinct, forensics got involved. Quickly too. Vinny made his fair share of enemies over the years."

"So the car is impounded and forensics find traces of poor Mr. Gogen's blood on it."

"Not just blood, lad. Bits of fabric and suchlike. A scrap of Tracer's fingernail lodged in the gap between the wipers and the broken glass."

Completely at odds with this grisly tidbit from the crime scene, there was a jolly *rumble-rattle* noise—the kettle.

Hughes' head came round the kitchen door frame. "Milk and sugar?"

With eyebrows raised, Thud looked up from his study of Vincent Winkles' despondent photograph. "Please."

Hughes vanished. He called into the dining room, "Forensics is mad."

"Mad as a spoon," agreed Thud. "The village loon kind of spoon. But useful as the cutlery kind as well, mind you. *Revolutionizing the field*, etcetera. Now the commissioner is the commissioner no longer. Resigned and pleading guilty to involuntary manslaughter. Can't say I'm overly miffed. The man was a cock with ears, if you'll excuse my Champleurs."

"You're excused." Hughes came in bearing the good stuff: two mugs of tea, and wedged under his arm, the biscuit tin Cate had bought him on a weekend trip abroad. There were pond-shaped ducks and duck-shaped ponds on it. Cate had found this almost hernia-inducingly hilarious.

Thud eyed this domestic horror with vast approval.

"Thanks," he said, accepting his mug. "Whatever about Vinny Winky though. I think you said it best. Poor Mr. Gogen. Apparently he was out rescuing people from the blizzard."

"Who?"

"Tracer."

Hughes hadn't read enough of the article—the knowledge that Tracer Gogen was risking his life at the time his own was snatched away was news to him. "Sort of a daredevilish hero, was he?"

"Not at all. Can't imagine what got into him. Same stuff that gets into a mother when she lifts a car off her toddler, I suppose."

Thud sipped his tea. His features pinched. He looked at the mug as though it had just performed some sort of extremely un-mugly trick.

"Ginger extract, chai, and a mix of Mysicordelian spice," Hughes explained.

Thud eyed him warily. With the air of a scientist who has seen something completely bizarre happen and is now going in for another go with calipers prepared, he took another cautious sip.

There was silence for a moment. Thud smacked his lips. His frown deepened considerably.

"Bloody hell," he murmured.

Hughes drank, smiling to himself. It was the exact same smile his father wore when people tasted his tea for the first time, a private smile that seemed to evoke a teatime nursery rhyme: *Toss the rest/oh leave the rest/no different will do/since my tea is best.*

See the two of them in tableau: both of the Leonidas dogs, the Bloodhound and the Labrador, enjoying the spoils of a tousle hard fought and harder won. Hughes' apartment was in a cozy-doze kind of disarray with shirts and trousers thrown over the backs of chairs, the wooden surfaces spiraled with those rings you get when you place hot drinks there for too long, and there was a slightly bachelor-like odor in the air. There were two large windows in the living room. Ushering through these were other guests who had invited themselves in that morning, namely bars of sunshine, in their way more valuable than gold (though perhaps only equally valuable as the germane insights of nosy neighbors). And with the gold of that light, December made its bargain with springtime, bribing it and coaxing it closer every day. The city was still cold—bitter cold and prone to plunges in temperature come dusk—but of big snow-burdened clouds there was no hint or premonition, and the sky was a devastatingly soft blue, and the gold notes minted by the wintry sun in that perfect blue bank purchased good humor everywhere in spite of what yesterday and yesterday held, as gifts are purchased with claims upon the mood and temperament of people we hold in contempt or in dear acquaintance, or hold close and dear, or simply hold.

It was Sunday, the 25th of December. Tinfrost Day.

"How's your Cate?" said Thud.

"Improving," said Hughes, grinning, and the day enriched its list of gifts by one. "She's going to miss the feast tonight, or so her doctor tells me. But yes, improving. How's Hettie? I assume this haul," Hughes gestured with his mug to the boxes, "is her way of thanking me?"

Thud was about to take a greedy slurp of tea. He paused. "Thanking you? What for?"

"Solving her husband's case."

"*Sorry?*"

"In time for Tinfrost," said Hughes, rewarding himself with a little triumphant sip. "First rule of police work. Do it with style."

"The cheek!"

"Okay, okay." Hughes raised a mollifying little finger. "I suppose you handled some of the extraneous details."

"The extra—Well, it's all coming out now!"

"Alas," said Hughes, "I'm too wrapped up in my life with the Citadel to take up the mantle of a streetbeater. I'm afraid you'll have to be Commissioner of Leonidas Precinct in my stead, Thud."

"In your..." The balloon of Thud's outrage deflated. "Commissioner?" he said, radiating puzzlement.

But Hughes had set his mug on the tabletop and was unwrapping the gifts. "Hope you don't mind if I open them now." Untied ribbons made their velvety noise. Wrapping paper crinkled. A box lid thumped open. "Oh." Hughes' head tilted slightly. "What is it?"

"It's an art piece," said Thud. "They all are. Hughes... lad... you think I..."

"I understand it's an art piece," said Hughes. "But what *is* it?"

Thud moved to stand next to him. They looked into the box together.

Eventually the policeman gave his mustache a meditative twist.

"Looks a bit like a pelican," he hazarded. "Maybe several pelicans in a bag."

"What's it made of?"

"The bag? Not sure. More pelicans, possibly."

"No, the actual material."

"How should I know? Listen now, you think I should—"

"Be commissioner? Course I do." Hughes tore at the next box's wrapping. "With Vincent Winkles off to the court and then the clink, and your suspension coming to an end in the new year, you should have his job. I'm sure there's others going for it, but they don't have friends in the Citadel."

"Hang on. That'd be—"

"Rigging a rigged system so it's rigged against the riggers?" Hughes made a fiendish face. "Heaven forbid."

"But—"

"Hettie could say, 'My husband is commissioner of an entire District, you know.' And I'm sure Leonidas could benefit from a commissioner who loves it as much as it needs to be protected."

He watched that slip past Thud's underdoggish principles.

In the span of a minute Hughes had the copper chock-full of the unfamiliar idea like a tin with strange biscuits. *Now to affix the lid and see how it fits.*

"It's like we talked about in the café the other day," he said. "Revolution's quick but too hot-blooded and too bloody-blooded for that matter. Reformation is a surer thing, but slow. Still, it has to start somewhere. Why not with you?"

The telephone rang.

Hughes gave the reeling streetbeater an apologetic smile.

He picked it up.

"Hughes speaking."

A pause.

"Falstaff! Merry Tinfrost. I—"

A pause.

"Okay."

A pause.

"Tell me."

A pause.

And the pause lengthened.

"Just now?" Hughes said eventually. His cheer was raisinlike—dried up, unrecognizable. He listened to the butler. "I see. And did—Sorry. Go on."

A pause.

"Yeah. Me too. And... Yes, I'll be at the feast. Okay. Thanks, Falstaff."

He returned to Thud much subdued. Thud was not so embroiled in mulling over his potential career prospects that he failed to notice.

"Cate still well?" he asked, fearing the worst.

An alarmed noise escaped Hughes. "Cate? Fine, she's... No, that was Falstaff. Priam King died this morning."

The significance of the bereavement came to Thud at once. "And your friend Hector?"

Hughes made no reply. He picked up his mug and went over to the window and leaned beside it, gazing out at the cars of people going blithely to breakfast, the closed shops, and the otherwise deserted streets rife with mirages of splendor, but only sunshine, only sunshine.

Thud left him alone for a while before he said, "Sorry, lad."

If Hughes heard him, he gave no sign of it. The brightness of the day sketched what little Thud could see of his face in an angelic glow. The lad's beard was clipped neat. The morning shone from the bristles. Hughes' hold on the mug seemed both graceful and perilously loose. Thud opened his mouth to say more, then closed it. As if he could wag his tongue a bit, balm the strife, make it better.

So he let his gaze drift to the newspaper. He took his case note pen from his pocket, flipped the paper to the back, scanned quickly, quirked a skewed smile, and finally bent to the crossword.

When he was done, he replaced the pen and said, "I'll be off."

"Um?" Hughes spun, looking for all the world as if he'd forgotten he was not alone. "Oh yeah. Your tea?"

"Finished."

Hughes walked him out.

"Thank you for coming, Thud."

"Thanks for the tea. Best mug of my life. Didn't even look at the biscuits. Give my regards to Miss Jubilee."

"I will." A touch of Hughes' charm slipped back into his face. Only a little, and it came ruefully, but it was there. "Send mine to Hettie, plus thanks for the gifts. Commissions from a commissioner's wife. Oh, I almost forgot." He offered the copper a square container. Thud took it.

The container showed a tiger's growling face. A strong fragrance emanated from it despite it being sealed. The label said: *Leopoldo Fernassi's Tiger-Tache Pomade: For The Dapper Dandy's Whiskers—Maximum Volume & Bounce.*

Thud held out his free hand. As he shook it, Hughes wasn't exactly sure, but he thought he saw a glimmer of amusement in the grizzled man's eye. Then Thud was heading down the apartment block hall, tugging his gloves back on, feet beating the carpet *thudda-thud-thud-goodbye.*

As he headed back into the apartment, Hughes checked the time.

Ten to ten. Damn. He was supposed to be at the carousel cottage for roasted chestnuts and figgy pudding at half-past nine. Krys would understand. The Mum less so. That carbuncular old gammidge viewed lateness to appointments the way crocodiles view overconfident fishermen. Oh well. Nothing to be done.

It was only as he was slinging his arms into his coat that he noticed the newspaper.

Instead of showing the front page headlines, it had been turned to that day's crossword. Festive hawthorn and tinsel draped the blank boxes, and little gnomes clustered around the prompts.

One of the crossword answers had been filled in.

Nineteen down.

Prompt: boon companion or comrade. No clues. Six letters.

Friend.

***

It was almost eleven by the time he made it to the carousel cottage.

The Mum was going to go absolute ballistic. When he raced in, laying out all manner of excuses and brandishing the gift he'd bought them (rare, speckled roses imported at fabulous cost from Yi-Shi) The Mum was going to turn her nose up at him, and he was going to feel an absolute pillock. He was going to feel like twenty pounds of sewage in a two pound hat. He was...

On the pavement—sparkly with the remnants of dawn's first frost but entirely cleared of snow—his pounding steps slowed... slowed... and came to a stop.

Hughes looked at the carousel cottage.

Or rather, he looked at the spot where the carousel cottage ought to be.

There's a particular feeling that overwhelms the brain when it notices that something is not where it ought to be. The gap is filled in by the willingness for the thing to reappear. This is usually applied to car keys or pots of jam left by one's toast, yet which has against all reason evaporated, or more likely left in the cabinet and not set next to the toast at all. When it comes to cottages, the mind has quite a gap to fill. The facial muscles have to put in some effort.

So Hughes gawped his astonishment. Meanwhile the place he had visited countless times failed to apparate before him.

Nearby, the datalog library with its obscene graffiti was just where it should be. The roads all seemed fine. Even the garden that had been installed outside the cottage was there, lush as ever.

But the cottage itself was, quite simply, gone.

Moving at their own discretion, his legs took him toward the plot of vacant land.

Tattooed there—much as Krys the Painted Girl's skin had been tattooed—were animals. He recognized them as the ones that had populated the cottage, formed the walls and doors and fixtures with their fiberglass. Golden-headed lion tamarins. Hornbills. Alligators. Goats. Geckos. Camels. Porcupines. Bears. Elephants. Dozens of them—hundreds!

They were all of them imprinted in the earth as though it were flesh. Insane, but undeniably true. He could smell the ink. The air was heady and rich with it, a million broken fountain pen's worth of black and blue and red.

The animals seemed to look at him from the ground. For his part, Hughes clutched the Yi-Shi roses (more for something solid to grasp rather than devotion to the blooms) and looked at the claws, the talons, the flippers, fins, paws, hooves, and even a couple of tails. Every countable "hand" was raised at the onlooker—raised at *him*.

As though they were saying, "Keep apprised of the satyr and the alligator, darling Hughes. We'll see-you-later.'

Make something of this, his mind insisted. *Investigate and deduce. Maybe they were taken away somewhere or maybe they went willingly. Either way track them based on circumstantial findings, otherwise known as clues. Four days ago you were in that cottage. It cannot just be gone.*

He took a deep breath, held it, let it go.

Okay.

If you assumed these rather amiable beasts had been left by Krys (a fair assumption, the uncanny way the things were waving at him was just so quintessentially her), then God knew what circumstances she had left them under. Indeed, the question of how she had done so and how the cottage had vanished in the first place, were compressed by the far more fascinating question of *why* these things had happened.

Summing up, he had no fucking idea. Flummoxed was the word.

How and why? Hughes didn't know. His observation could pose and subsequently frame the matter, but resolve it? No shot. Even rooted in magic as he was, it was a little too science-fiction for him to grapple with.

Feeling helpless and scared for his friends and optimistic that they could handle themselves, and yes, flummoxed beyond belief, he looked once more at the animals. All their "hands" (if you could think of them as hands) raised in salute. See-you-later.

Wishful thinking, probably.

They could have just as easily been left to say farewell.

***

"What?" said Jo, her great shelf of brow wrinkling. "A whole cottage?"

Hughes nodded. "With about as much ceremony as a fart."

"Upset?"

"Course. I don't have many close friends. Three of the big support pillars in the chamber of my heart have been removed today. First Hector. Now Krys and The Mum." He sighed. "Double feature."

Jo took a bite of her sandwich and washed it down with piping-hot cocoa. "That was very pretty, Hughes. Support pillars. Chamber of your heart. Lovely. Want advice?"

"Always."

"There are no prettier words in all the world than 'hello' and 'goodbye.' I'm as thick as clotted cream, and even I know that."

He looked at her. It was almost one o'clock in the afternoon, they were in The Foundry, and the workbench between them was cleared and spread anew with a splendid Tinfrost lunch.

"I think," Hughes said stiltedly, "that saying goodbye in the same sentence as the names of my friends will cause me to burst into tears."

Jo greeted this with a slope-shouldered shrug. "In that case say them inside. That way you'll hear them true, and our lunch won't get soggy."

Caught off guard by that, he grinned and agreed that a damp meal was a lamentable tragedy best avoided when possible.

They ate. He said that she seemed none the worse for wear after her possession at Jane's hands. Their party had reached her quickly, but Jane was a fast eater. Jo conceded that by times she had felt more glum and "emptysome," as she put it, than usual, but she pointed out it would take a lot more than a head-hopping madwoman to dissuade her from that which made her who she was. She took herself seriously and seriously is what she took herself.

"Still hear them now and then though," she said between bites.

"Hear what?"

"The flies. Will they go away, do you think?"

"Yes." His tone was confident. "Before he approached the Citadel with the case, Captain Hoshrum Thud of the streetbeaters traced Jane's activity to thirty-four years ago. It takes time, but even those worst affected by Jane's influence will make a recovery."

The same can't be said of their victims, but it'd be cruel to remind Jo of that. The loss of her own friend—Elderly Jolene—is still very fresh.

Out loud he said, "The flies won't be buzzing forever."

He felt a surge of fondness for the woman as her misshapen features shone with relief. "That's good tidings that is!"

"Well absolutely. Ah. Speaking of..."

From the hidden country of his deepest coat pocket, he plucked a comb of densest golden fibers. In the flickering light of the ever-burning furnace, that gold transmuted and seemed to make the comb a set of tiny dragon's dentures.

He stood and handed the comb to Jo, who took it curiously. "Happy Tinfrost."

"And to you, I'm sure." Those immense fingers of hers moved with unerring finesse over the comb, the pad of her thumb brushing the teeth of the comb. The reason for the abstract quality he heard in her voice became clear when she glanced at him, both of her mismatched eyes intent. "What's this made of?"

"That I cannot honestly tell you. I asked Frank Gallant if he could design something that would grant a person sweet dreams. He asked if the person had hair." Hughes grinned and nodded at the few thin locks wisping down from Jo's scalp. "I said you did." He spread his arms dramatically and bowed deeply, respectfully, charmingly. "Jo, your friendship has been an utter dream for me. Allow me to return the favor."

When he rose, he discovered Jo had moved. He was faced with her pectoral muscles, which could only be described as continental. All at once he was being enfolded in a spine-popping hug.

"Know what you are in my heart chamber?" Jo asked.

He made a muffled noise of inquiry. It was all he was currently capable of.

She let go but still held onto him. Three inches off the floor no less.

"Am I a supportive pillar?" he guessed.

In reply she set him down, shambled into the recesses of her workstation, and returned a moment later with what could only be described as a sheet of dull, unimpressive metal. Granted, there were some grooves resembling a plackart—the kind you might see in a breastplate. But other than that his diagnosis seemed correct. An unexciting slab with some lines on it.

Yet Jo seemed engrossed by the thing, fawning over it and muttering chippily to herself as she strapped it over the chest of a target dummy. She led Hughes to where she kept her homemade ballista (thank God that hadn't seen use in the Jane fight, else someone would have lost a limb for sure). She aimed the monstrously sharp point of the ballista's bolt at the sheet of metal, then stood back and nudged Hughes encouragingly.

"In your own time, maestro."

Hughes was at a loss. The bolt would puncture the flimsy metal easily. Jane was gone, but what now possessed his friend, he could not begin to guess at. Bugger it anyway. Indulging her seemed the best course of action.

He struck the release. There was a rush of sound, a tinny clang and a mighty splintering, and at last a rolling sound as of a large bolt that has not punctured a flimsy sheet of metal, and which is instead now rolling rather embarrassedly on the floor.

Hughes' mouth went dry. He approached. Jo came with him.

There was the bolt, bent out of shape, flinders of wood flecking all about. There was the metal sheet suspended above it. It was completely whole. Not a skewer, not a dent, not a nick troubled it.

He turned to Jo, his face the very portrait of the spirit of amazement.

She tapped the side of her nose with a finger. "I'll thank that rotten lady Jane for one thing—it made me look at the problem in a different way. Adaptive metallurgy and I have what you might calls a *truce*. We understand one another, see? And this," she knocked a knuckle on the metal sheet, "is only the beginning."

"Is it steel?" said Hughes.

Jo chuckled. "Steel*ish*."

That cleared up absolutely nothing.

Before he could ask her what she meant to do with such a creation, she grew shy. In her hand, her comb of sweet dreams shivered pleasantly with the firelight.

"For you, Clever Hughes, Kind Hughes... Handsome Hughes, who makes a misfit lumpen girl feel... just as welcome and comely as you are... For you, I will make a suit of armor as strong as my feelings for you. You've got the makings of a man on a dangerous road. I swear... *Swear* to you... You will not walk it unprotected."

She took three quick, lumbery strides up to him, darted down, pressing her lips to his cheek. Then she drew back just as hurriedly, her head bent, her face downcast. Hughes blinked, his ears reddening. It was, without a doubt, the most bashful peck he'd ever received.

He wanted to thank her, to lavish her with gratitude, but in that instant his instincts told him silence was most becoming. She had something else to say to him.

In the furnace, the low coals crumbled. Prisms of comforting red light worked in that dark, red as Hughes' ears, or nearabouts.

Jo clutched the comb to her chest like a precious bird, recently rescued.

Hughes listened and waited.

"You are the chamber itself," she told him quietly.

***

Sometimes, life presents you with a panoply of gifts.

Other times it takes them away.

As he hailed a cab to take him from Nikandros District toward Ptolema and thence to the Citadel, where he would be late for the opening ceremony of the Tinfrost feast, Hughes clung to two lines from the same poem. The first was this: *I felt a funeral in my brain.* And the second was this: *Then space—began to toll, as all the Heavens were a Bell, and Being, but an Ear.*

He was not sure if Krys and The Mum were alive or dead, happy or low, lost or found, but about Hector there could be nothing less than total certainty. Hector was dead. Second time's a charm.

And Hughes was sure about this as well: goodbye was—in its own bittersweet fashion—on a par with hello for prettiness.

No such thing as badbye or bleakbye or I'llmissyouforeverbye.

Only goodbye.

So he said it under his breath, and he pronounced his friend's name, and those of Cassandra and Paris who he also thought of with rose-colored care, and Priam King who he hadn't known, but whose decision had meant that he and Hector had a chance to know one another in the first place. He said goodbye to Krys and The Mum wherever they were: goodbye goodbye goodnight good morning good luck with the turn in your road, may it be longwidebright! Goodbye!

And through the cab window he watched the streets trussed up in Tinfrost go by. Afternoon sunshine etched the terraces and flowed in yellow-gold, stitching the spaces between buildings. A renovated church turned homeless shelter teemed with activity. Not many homeless in this District, but it was worth the trudge from Leonidas for hot bread and hotter soup, char-grilled sausages, bacon-chicken-and cranberry-sauce sandwiches, all handed out by glad-hearted volunteers, and the potluck presents waiting in the wings to make the down and out days slum-drifting in Corinth City seem forgotten nuisances, at least for a while. Meanwhile three guys had finished gluing up a billboard showing Father Tinfrost with a prosthetic arm bearing the tagline: *Who needs a staff of wood when you've got Spritlgood? Spritlgood Augmentation—Buy Now!* The sweaty workmen were sharing a thermos and a smoke. Hughes found himself hoping the thermos had mulled wine inside, and that the smoke tasted good.

A few kids thumbed the controls of mechanical trains and train-crushing behemoths, and they saw through the trains' dynamic camera lenses through their vid screens, giggling, eyes screwed up with baleful competitiveness, noses as rosy-pink as nostalgia with the cold, and their parents in cardigans and sweaters exchanging eye rolls and tired gum-tickling grins that would last until the day they grew old enough for their children to develop enchantment and cynicism of their own and have kids and set the presents under the tree, and all elegiac and all sublimated by time and as pretty as hello, as goodbye.

"I know your face, fella."

Shaken from his ruminations, Hughes looked at the rearview. The taxi driver was peering at him.

"I'm Gormon Hughes," he said.

"Wendy's Bloodhound? No bull crappy?"

"No bull crappy. That's me."

But for how much longer? Now there was a question.

He and Wendy had not spoken since his frenzied appearance at the Citadel, preluding the rush through the portal to whisk Cate and the rest out of harm's way.

"Wendy's Bloodhound in my car." The man blew out his cheeks. He craned around suddenly, taking a liberal attitude to safety, as well as the elasticity of his seatbelt. "Here. Weren't you the one who caught Spring-Heeled Jack?"

Hughes didn't bother to correct the false name.

"Close," he said. "I worked with the fellow who did. Hoshrum Thud."

"Never heard of him."

"Keep an ear out. He's going to make commissioner."

"Is that a fact? Well no wonder. Thud, eh? I'll give him this, it's a memorable name. No wonder."

No wonder indeed. There, Thud. Taxi drivers are a particularly gabby breed of gossip. I'll wager you'll be the talk of the city by next week at the outset. Won't you enjoy that?

Hughes could just see those pomaded whiskers twitching now.

He allowed himself a rather wicked, rather delicious smile... and that was when he saw Sheila Kofatch from the corner of his eye.

Persuading his driver to stop and to accept a sizable tip despite the truncated journey, Hughes took to his heels in the direction he thought she'd gone. He spotted her again past the Tyrant's Square, lost track of her near *The Coconut* club, and found her again on a road that, initially, Hughes didn't remember. The road was quiet, all the residents relaxing in their homes, probably watching the Tinfrost reruns or speaking with emigrated relatives over the telephone. At some distance trimmed hedges nuzzled the red brick of the train station. The clock set over the station's entrance was impossible to make out, but it was the sight of its glass face that jogged Hughes' memory. Years ago, he had left *The Coconut* and come here to catch an early morning rail. He and Cate had been starting out, and that night she'd told him how her father had killed her mother, a woman of infinite elegance who looked like the film star Ginger Dujour before the hammer staved in her head. Full of Cate's stories and his growing affection for her, he'd... yes he'd come to this road and he'd admired the roses that had once been in... there! That pot there which was now full of musky hibiscus, and speaking of musky, he had sneezed and Mr. Glint had said, "Gesundheit." It made Hughes shudder a bit. What a world that Glint and he should now be on the same side. It boggled the mind.

Another veritable boggler was the Sheila Kofatch lookalike. A lookalike she must have been. Hughes' old neighbor had died ten years ago, during the Hairy Autumn, not long after his sojourn down this very street.

The mystery cleared itself up when he saw her coming out of one of the road's houses. Not Sheila, but her daughter, Brenda. She was fiddling with her purse, trying to cram something inside—a package of some kind—when Hughes stepped into her path.

"Miss Kofatch? Whoa now. Sorry, I'm—I'm sorry."

"You startled me," she snapped. "Who are you?"

Hughes would not call what had just happened a moment of startlement.

If it was, her reaction would have been the small jump of surprise he'd expected. Instead her face had gone ashy-pale, her eyes had bulged with some fantastic emotion (dismay or fright, he was not sure which), and from her mouth he'd heard the beginnings of a shriek, violently cut off, the sound a fox might make when confronted with a mean dog off the leash in a wood full of hunters.

Letting his talents take over, he assumed the guise of someone to whom this information had not occurred. His posture relaxed. Both hands, raised to quell a storm, slipped easily into his pockets. His smile was the essence of lackadaisy.

"Gormon Hughes is my name." *I played a role in taking down the vileness that touched and took away your girlfriend.* He considered saying something tantamount to this, then ultimately decided he ought to work his way up to it. "I used to be your mother's neighbor."

It was obvious she had not been expecting that. She gaped at him, as if he'd told her he moonlighted as a semi-professional squid every other Tuesday. Then his words sank in and she recovered.

"Funny way to say you lived next to us," she said. She threw an anxious look over one shoulder at the house she'd emerged from, realized she was still holding the parcel half-in and half-out of her bag, zipped the bag as closed as it would go with trembling fingers, and began to walk away in a hurry. "I don't remember you," she said.

Casual as you like, Hughes fell into step beside her. "You've misunderstood me. I was her neighbor *before* she moved in with your father."

"In Leonidas?" More suspicion. Caution replaced by confusion. "I don't understand."

"Two things. Number one, you look just like her. The spitting image, really."

"You have some memory, Mr. Hughes."

"I don't know. We lived within high-fiving distance for years. Your mum had a distinctive face, one of the friendliest ever. When the rest of your neighbors are gnarled codgers and saturnine factory folk, that sort of face stands out like a rose in a field of thorns."

"Wait..." she said, slowing, then stopping so she could get a proper look at him. "You aren't... the bath guy, are you?"

The bath guy. Well, right now it was better than Wendy's Bloodhound. Hughes inclined his head. "That's me. I'm not sure what she told you about me. Nothing ever happened between myself and Sheila. It was purely platonic bath borrowing."

"Bath guy!" She vented a weird little hiccup of a laugh, one that didn't quite reach her eyes. "She said you used to blush so hard you looked like a kid's cartoon. Red ears with steam whistling out."

"Oh really?" It was Hughes' turn to laugh. His was more heartfelt. "Well the ears I can vouch for, if not the steam." Funny, he'd always thought Sheila was the embarrassed party in their admittedly pretty unusual dynamic. Yet she had told her kids stories about the shy blushing boy she'd let use her bath. He thought of that old chestnut: *when it comes to the past, we all write fiction.* "I hope you'll forgive me being so up front and bald about all this, Brenda. I always thought she did that bright, amicable face of hers justice, your mum. She dropped some kindness in my life when kindness was not so much wanted as needed."

"Yeah," said Brenda, her gaze misting. "Yeah, I can imagine." In her sadness and rapturous nostalgia, she was much less furtive than before. No anxious glances up the road. No great hurry to be gone. After a momentary trip down memory lane, she looked at Hughes with new appraisal. "So I have the look of my mum. That's number one. What's number two?"

Here goes.

"Your picture was in a file given to me by Captain Thud. I'm with the Scarlet Citadel."

She stared. There was no discernible shift in those eyes, but nevertheless when she spoke next her voice was tighter. As was—Hughes could not help but notice—her grip on the package sticking out of her bag. "You're *that* Hughes?"

"I'm sorry for what happened to your girlfriend. Before I say anything else though, I think I'd be remiss in not telling you something that hasn't yet been disclosed to the public. As her next of kin, you'll probably get a call from the police or the hospital to this effect, but I want to tell you now. Rummy Lou is going to recover. I know because the previous victims of the... the monster behind these crimes have recovered before, without exception. It may take time, months, maybe years. But that fugue she's in right now will break. She *will* get better, that I promise."

Stunned silence. It stretched as the afternoon shadows were beginning to, since winter evenings are eager, domineering things that demand their unequal share, and he worried he had said something wrong, had misjudged the situation somehow, and instead of providing solace he'd actually wounded this young woman, thrown a spanner into the works, further soured an already bitter business.

And then Hughes found himself staring into a face all weepy and luminous with hope. Brenda Kofatch's tremoring hand grasped his forearm like the corner of a life raft. "She's... going to be okay?"

He nodded.

"Oh God." She let him go, wiped the damp mascara from her cheek. "Oh my God. When?"

"As I say, it could be a long time."

"But it's a certainty?"

"I promised, didn't I?"

"Yes," she said, and this time her laugh was very fragile but oh-so-genuine. "Yes, I suppose you did."

"Miss Kofatch?"

"Brenda, please."

"Okay Brenda. What's in the package?"

"Oh um." Suddenly she was a child caught in an indescribable act, the depths of which she was only now contending with. She unzipped her bag and took it out, her smile curdling into a wretched grimace. "It's about three credits worth of Yellow Raven. Apparently I got a good deal on it. I can't tell. I've never done it before."

Hughes pulled a sympathetic face and nodded, as if admitting she had just spent a not insignificant amount of money on hard drugs was the most natural and ordinary thing in the world.

"I was only going to try it," she hastened to add. "I thought... maybe it would... Only with Rummy being sent to Taggart House, that made me think of my dad. He had to go there, you know. After he killed Mum and my sister Carrie-Anne. He didn't mean to. They were um..." She pushed a lock of hair over one ear self-consciously. "They were beetles at the time."

Hughes nodded. After the Hairy Autumn, stories like that really were the most natural and ordinary thing in the world.

"He got better. I can't tell you how happy I am that Rummy..." Brenda's fingers moved restlessly over the package. "Last night I got really drunk. I met this... guy and poured my heart out to him. He was really sweet and... ahm... philosophical, I guess, about the whole thing. He said whenever he's feeling overwhelmed, he does Yellow Raven. I was like, 'Isn't it dangerous?' He looked at me like I was crazy. 'No,' he said. 'No, absolutely not.' Then he did a spiel. And I was happy to listen as he described this thing that the drug dealers—he called them aviary boys, so silly—talk about. They say taking the edge off a sword makes it useless. But taking the edge off life, which is sharper than a sword, much sharper, is the opposite. It's amazing. Then the guy said something about joining the great rakery..."

"The great *rookery*," Hughes amended gently. "A house for ravens. Yeah, I've heard aviary boys say that too. Shoot it. Snort it. Swallow it. Do some Yellow Raven. Join the great rookery in the sky."

"And so I've come from his house. Nice one for a drug dealer. Anyway, I got this." She hefted the package. "After I paid, of course. Did I mention it was three credits? Very good deal, evidently."

"Uh huh. Brenda, you think you might give that package to me?"

"What?" She pulled it closer to her. Maybe she knew she was doing it and maybe she didn't. Either way, the message was loud and clear.

"Don't get me wrong," said Hughes, emanating reason and relaxation. "I'm not against letting the bird fly. We all have our vices. But Brenda, you're a schoolteacher. What if it got out? You'd lose your job."

"No one would know."

"They might. People are observant. Take my word for it."

"How could they? I'm not going to use it more than once."

"I know that's your intention. And the whole 'addicted after one hit' crap isn't what I'm worried about."

"Then what?" She was glaring at him now. No more reminiscing over borrowed bathtubs. "What are you worried about?"

He let a hint (any more would surely draw her further from him) of his concern suffuse his tone. "Months, years, it's a long time. You're going to think about her a lot. Your girlfriend, like. I'm worried that instead of sitting with that feeling—coming to terms with it—you'll reach for that rookery in the sky."

"It's not your problem."

"No. But it'll be yours if you indulge for refuge instead of recreation. Come on." He held out his hand. "Take a second and think about yourself and about Rummy Lou. Would she be happy with you doing this? You think she'd be glad you couldn't stomach the wait?"

That was callous of him. Hughes regretted it immediately and more so when he saw her features harden rather than soften as he'd expected them to.

"Thank you very much, Mr. Hughes. For the nice memories of my mum, if nothing else. As to that other subject, I'm a big girl, and as you so correctly point out, a teacher. I know more about discipline than you and about parsing what's best for me, in case you had inklings to the contrary. Happy Tinfrost."

"Wait—"

"Excuse me."

She brushed past him, her gait increasing in speed with every step.

Her name clambered up his throat, dripping with entreaty. Hughes bit it back.

I could call her name.

I could call and tell her not to take them.

And then I could call that an intervention.

The idea held an allure so strong it was almost scary. He knew what Cate would say. You can't interfere with someone's life unless they want you to. Tommy Fahrenheit was different. He wanted it, and Hector lent his voice in asking you. The Performance is an amazing thing, but it could be horrifying if you let it.

But what was truly horrifying was the notion that a young woman could throw her life away simply because life's edges weren't blunt or rounded. They could be sharp as blades. They could cut.

He wondered if he would say yes to someone erasing his emotions, or changing them, or inspiring them. Would he want that?

Would he have turned his nose up at such a thing when he was at his lowest?

He decided that he might have. Likely would have.

Only on some level he would have wished that the change would happen anyway.

Around him the day's shadows were lengthening. An invisible knife drew itself along the horizon, a red knife mixing with the daytime blue for that purple. Meanwhile coming nightfall bought up its share of the sky with coins made out of stars.

He thought about that knife, that scarlet blade, and about himself.

He thought it could indeed be amazing, and horrifying.

And sometimes, life presents you with a panoply of gifts.

Other times it takes them away.

And other times still, it makes *you* the gift.

"Brenda," he breathed, and his voice was fine and straight and sharp. He watched her stop about twenty feet away. "Happy Tinfrost."

The word insinuated itself between them

(CHIMERA)

and then it was only a matter of waiting...

Waiting...

Wai—

Brenda's back straightened. She turned around, smiling so bright she seemed to match the sunshine. On spring-stepped feet she sauntered back to him and thrust out the package of Yellow Raven with both hands.

"You know, I've thought better of it. I think I'm going to visit Rummy, then curl up on the couch with a movie and possibly too much ice cream."

"You sure?"

"Ab-so-lutely."

He took the package, unable to dismiss the idea that the Performance hadn't worked (even though it had), and this sprightliness she exhibited was completely genuine (which it wasn't).

"Okay," he said, returning her smile. "If you're sure."

***

"Hughes, you scallawagger heeldragger!" cried Elena Longfellow at his sheepish arrival. "You're late, you're late!"

Hard not to be goofy the moment the music and merriment swept you up. Hughes grinned. "Late you say?"

"Late as a pumpkin to the summer patch. Sit ye down, sirrah!"

"Are you drunk, Elena?"

"Getttiiiing theeeeeere! *Getttttiiiiiing theeeeere!*"

Eruptions of laughter along the table, so loud they almost shook the chandelier overhead, festooned in twinkling Tinfrost lights. Hughes sat and let the celebration take him. The Grand Hall of Redspire was full of tables like this one, resplendent with gleaming fruits from the countryside and across the sea, and there were pitchers of mulled wine fragrant with all manner of exciting spices, hot buttered bread, gravy tubs, smooth, creamy mashed potato, mouth-watering cuts of meat lathered in a lacquer of herbal coatings, adrip with fat, gristly here, bloody there, and there were shellfish and crab and lobster for the Daethumbrish crowd, balls of aromatic jasmine rice filled with marinated pork and raw fish tarts to please the Hortesians, chicken dusted in powdered spice from Ikahagua, so hot it would take your head clean off your shoulders and served with tasty jollof fries, and pies, dear sweet God, what a wealth of crusts and fillings, pecan and peach and apricot and warm, velvety dark chocolate with a walnut twist, beef pies and banoffee pies and lean melt-on-the-tongue veal pies, and on and on, each culture and tradition catered for in delicious abundance!

A feast! The music seemed to champion it, so lively and merry swerved its tune—a feast! A feast for Tinfrost day!

Hughes could see the surviving members of Cate's Company sprinkled throughout the Hall. Naturally they were the beneficiaries of many a toast and a cheer, as were the fallen, as was Cate who everyone agreed had done incredible things on the other side of the Door of Fire. Tales of trolls and giant manta rays and will o' the wisps fairly sparkled upon the lips of every other person, growing in the telling as stories tend to do. A toast was made to Cate's quick recovery. Hughes drank deeply for that one.

All of this was very quick, mind you. He was dizzy with the swiftness of it all. The *blub-blub-blub* of the wine pitchers pouring seemed a constant harmony for the band's melody. It seemed he'd only come a flash of seconds ago, and already he was three glasses of wine toward a pleasant boozy buzz, and his belly accepting what he gave it and craving more.

So it was only a few scant minutes before a hand clapped him a hearty welcome on the back.

Hughes turned with a polite smile—

—and almost choked on a rice-pork ball.

"*Hector?*"

"My apt pupil."

"Hector! Oh my God!"

He was up and throwing his arms around his friend before he knew it. Further, before he could think about it, he planted a huge smacker on Hector's lips for good measure. A thunderous cheer rose around them.

Hector was laughing. It was the most cinnamony carrot cake, autumnal, and utterly joyous of sounds. "Falstaff tried to reach you by telephone," he explained.

"This is incredible. How is this happening? Is this happening?"

"It's happening," affirmed a voice he recognized. He looked past Hector and saw Cassandra, her hard face softer than he'd ever seen it, and Paris, grinning crooked as a naughty bedtime dream of a lover, and both as alive (in a ghostly fashion, of course) as Hector. "Also cellulite will happen," Cassandra observed. "You must watch what you eat assiduously if you are to maintain your paltry excuse for a physique. Oh get off." She groaned as Hughes hugged her with fierce joy. But she did not push him away, not even when Paris chuckled sardonically and made the hug a thruple.

Hughes was deaf to the clapping and the thumping tankards and steins and smatters of laughter and catcalls.

"How?" he said, pulling away so he could see the three spectral siblings. Tears of pure exultant happiness slid down his cheeks. He hardly noticed. "How?"

"Our sister Creusa now wears the crystal crown," said Hector. "Its magic is hers, as is its burden. She made her choice. This morning the three of us died. This afternoon we were born again." He looked almost as jubilant as Hughes felt, but mingled in there was a deep melancholy Hughes understood at once.

His father is dead, and his sister has sacrificed her good health to keep her siblings alive as living ghosts. A difficult choice. In fact "difficult" doesn't sum it up.

"Is Kim here?" Hughes asked, calling their sister by the name he'd first known her by.

"In bed," Paris replied. "We'll visit her later. Come, if you like. She'll be glad to see you."

"I will."

"For the moment, I intend to drink with you, Gormy," said Paris. "Fuck your paltry excuse for a physique."

"Indeed," said Hector. "Fuck it."

Cassandra was so gobsmacked by her brother swearing that she consented to joining them before her stiff spirit could protest.

So it was that Hughes spent that first leg of the feast in the company of three ghosts—ghosts of Tinfrost past, present, and apparently Tinfrost future also.

He could not have been more pleased.

Or so he thought.

***

It was ten past six in the evening, a full moon shone in a blue-black sky, and from the Grand Hall they could all see that moon and feel just as full and aglow themselves. The Tinfrost lights strung here and there and everywhere from the decorated trees to the wall sconces to the mighty chandeliers seemed in direct competition with the stars. Not only that, they were winning.

It seemed a time for winning, for good results rather than bad. Alcohol played a role there, but the facts bore it up. Hughes' ears and heart were energized and topped up to the brim with ecstatic feeling. Jane's era of emptiness was at an end. He wished Estelle were here so he could talk about it with her. But she had vanished after their final fight with Jane in the maternity hospital. He raised a quiet lonely toast to her, sent his affection and gratitude out into the world for how things had turned out with her, and then drank and went back to feeling damned wonderful. Hector and Paris were testing for the umpteenth time their ability to get tipsy despite their not-quite-alive constitution. Cassandra disapproved enormously, mostly because she was better at sobriety than the other two. She bemoaned her lack of talent in getting sloshed. She espoused that it was her superior body that allowed this travesty to occur. Whereupon Paris called her a silly wench, stood back from the table, fell over, gurgled a bit, and declared himself the silliest wench of all.

"Hughes," said Hector muggily. "Wassat cake you dessribe me ass?"

"Carrot cake, Hector."

"Thassit. Used to love a slice o' cake when I was Prince of Troy."

"Have some then."

Hector blinked slowly. "There's cake?"

"There's several cakes by your elbow."

Hector looked at these for some time, frowning. "Dear God," he said eventually.

"He's drunk assa skunk," said Paris, still lying on the floor.

"It says forty-five percent," Cassandra growled, throttling a bottle of festive gin. "Where does it all go, I ask you? I have not pissed once since we got here. *Where does it go if not into my liver? Why am I sober as a carton of milk?*"

"Try quaffing," Paris suggested, waving vaguely. "Works for me."

"How do you quaff?"

"Iz like drinking," Hector said, his frown fixed on the cake in case they should disappear. "Only most of it ends up... *hic*... most of it ends up in your beard."

Cassandra reeled. "I do not have a beard!"

"Shame," sighed Paris. "You'd look lovely with a beard."

It was around that time that Frank Gallant and Mr. Glint arrived, drawing no small amount of attention from the celebrants as the arrival of those two so often did.

Hughes said he would see the living ghosts later and went to greet the newcomers.

"Happy Tinfrost," Hughes said, embracing Frank and not embracing Mr. Glint because he valued his bodily integrity.

"Deck the halls with tin and hawthorne," said Frank.

"Fa-la-la-la-laaa, fa-la-la-la," said Mr. Glint in the tones of an undertaker asking whether the family wanted an open or closed casket funeral.

"What shall we drink?" Frank asked Hughes.

Hughes considered the various options, scanning past the banquet-laden tables to the large round tables at the fringes of the Hall. These were dense with bowls of glass, boasting the yummiest punch and eggnog and cocktails, and every other drink that you in your secret, singing heart, might associate with the best of parties.

"Frank, let's you and I have a go at the champagne and crème de cassis."

"Delectable, my man."

"Mr. Glint..." Hughes pondered. "I'm sure we can dig out some weedkiller."

Glint bowed his head. "Yum yum, Mr. Hughes."

With drinks in their sights, the trio found themselves waylaid by Penelope Auspice.

"Hiiiii! Penelope, Penelope."

She gave her hand to Mr. Glint and Frank, introducing herself both times. "Soooo nice to have you at our, like, humble gathering? Um. Hughes, could we have a chat?"

"Sure. Frank and I are having champagne and crème de cassis. Come have champagne and crème de cassis with us."

"Actually that's..." She shifted close to him, lowering her voice to a classic Penelope whisper, which could only be heard, say, from a distance of forty yards or so. "I'm not sure it's the best idea, inviting Frank Gallant here, Hughes. You know, with her Ladyship? The whole 'you basically killed my dad by putting him into a sleep he never woke up from' thing? It's like *aaaaaaaagh*!"

"I don't see her Ladyship here," said Hughes. His tone was rougher than he'd intended, but he had no intention of letting Wendy Dragontail's name hinder his fun. But it was true. The whole Citadel thrummed and sang and swept the breadth of the Grand Hall, the whole Citadel, that is, save for its leader.

Penelope gave him a withering look. "Not the actual point? It's like, decorum, or whatever?" She looked at Frank, who was opening his mouth. "And you can save the charm." She pronounced this last word *chorm*. "I'm actually immune, unless there's another woman doing the charming."

Frank shrugged. "Penelope, I would never—not in a million years—dream of charming so astute and munificent a woman. Guy's gotta know the extent of his reach."

"Munifiwhat?"

"Means generous. When someone is as pretty as you are, every look is a wintertime gift warming up the cold core of a simple soul such as I. I'm not here to be winsome or to make a pass at anyone. All I can say is, whosoever does charm you, Penny... well..." Frank allowed his suit to shift, the fibers changing color until they matched Penelope's cream-white gown. In that white suit with a tie and cufflinks and shoelaces of indigo, he looked simply spectacular. "She is lucky indeed."

Penelope's furrowed brow cleared. "That... was actually really sweet."

Frank stuck out his arm. "Romance isn't everything. Wanna come have champagne and crème de cassis?"

Reluctantly, then with more confidence, she took it. "You know, I focking *do* want champagne and crème de cassis."

Hughes followed after them, shaking his head.

Only Frank.

At length it was half past six and the four of them were enjoying the bubbly fizz and blackcurrant tang of their drinks. Mr. Glint was entertaining Penelope, who had never met someone who had a past life of criminality. She was, by all accounts, thoroughly entertained.

Meanwhile Hughes and Frank lounged together on a convenient *chaise longue*.

Frank wanted to know, "Any chance we can call on Catherine later?"

"She hates when you call her that."

"I know."

"Hates it. No. No, Falstaff said she was sleeping when he poked his head in to check on her."

"You seen her since you got back?"

"Not awake."

"Her dreams have been troubled."

Hughes shot him a look. "You can tell?"

Frank nodded. "Her dreams are huge apparatuses made of dark materials. Not all doom and gloom though. Now and then there's bright spots." He said no more about it.

There was a comfortable pause while Hughes sent his heart to his lover.

The band was playing a new Tinfrost song, written in that new style that was emerging.

Jingle bell, jingle bell
Jingle bell rock
Jingle bells swing
And jingle bells ring

Hughes waved a dismissive hand. "This new stuff."

"I like it," said Frank. "I'm tremendously fond of it."

In his periphery Hughes saw the aurora in Frank's hair spinning and diffusing in time with the music.

"Please yourself," he said.

"Can I ask you something?"

"Go ahead. It'll drown out this racket."

"What do you make of the two-headed wolf?"

Frank was talking about the beast Lord Burrows had ridden at the back of the undead army in Eurydice. Hughes had learned about it from Rosemund Valkyrie, who had telephoned him on Thursday. They'd spoken for four hours. Afterward, he felt he had a single perspective on a complicated subject, though it was a rich one. Rosemund had a flair for clear recollection.

A two-headed wolf...

(put your heart on my knife)

(mine's broken, give me yours)

(hooyou)

Laurana... That thing bit her leg clean off and broke all her bones...

"Hughes?"

Frank's brows were up, his expression bemused. The way the *chaise longue* was built, his friend's face was close enough to mark out every detail.

"Lost you there for a minute."

"Sorry. This memory of mine sometimes seems more like a curse than blessing."

"I'll bet."

Frank's languid calm settled him a bit. Hughes reframed the question.

"What do I think of it? I think the creature I fought ten years ago was this other wolf's twin. A sibling, or a... relative of some kind. Maybe even a mate. The appearance of one a decade before the other implies that Eurydice—the Lady and the world—has been trying to push into Iphigenia for a long time."

"Any guesses why?"

Hughes shook his head, gave Frank a hopeful smile. "You? You used to call Eurydice home, after all."

"One little part. A squirrel can get a sense of a tree, but the whole forest? Nuh-uh."

"Yeah. Especially a forest that changes so dramatically from moment to moment. Worlds that think. Reckon this world thinks?"

"This one? Sure."

"Well it must be asleep. Leaving all the interesting stuff to the people living on it."

"To sleep, perchance to dream."

"Shut up."

"Want to get out of here later?" Frank asked suddenly.

"Lucky me."

"Lucky you."

They were laughing. Their glasses were almost dry and Hughes' head felt full of mirth and syrup.

"I meant to Dreaming Jija," Frank clarified, humor melting to excitement. "Let's go find out where your power comes from. What do you say?"

"I..." Hughes was aghast, delighted, skittish. "I'd love that Frank. I say we go."

"*Once more with feeling!*"

"Go, go, I say we go!"

"Tonight?"

"Tonight?"

"Want to?"

"Well..." Hughes thought about it. "Maybe I'm a little too jarred to meet Death. Better to be sober as a religious person selling car insurance. Could you pencil me in tomorrow?"

"Pencil, crayon, quill and ink! Come on, let's rescue Glint."

"So, sorry, let me get this straight," Penelope Auspice was saying. "You've been shot in *both* eyeballs?"

Glint grunted and sipped his glass of weedkiller.

"And you regained your eyesight?"

Another grunt.

"I cannot imagine. That must have been like *aaaaaaah*! Did you ever think of doing a television show? You could be—oh MY God—the amazing regrowing man!"

"Couldn't do that, miss."

The wind rushed from Penelope's sails. "Why not?"

"Need one of them 'charismas' for television, miss," said Glint. "Whereas what I have got is a 'charisntma.'"

Frank and Hughes shared amused glances.

"Hold that thought," said Penelope, who had stopped paying attention some moments before. She waved at her partner, Colin, at the far end of the Hall. "Okay, I'll be right back." She pranced away with the aplomb of a dancer and the social grace of a pickle sandwich.

"She's something," fluted Frank.

Hughes was smiling at Penelope and Colin and the whole Hall besides. "They all are. Oh hello!" He waved at a passing figure. The figure had the pasty complexion native to northern

Daethumberland, and they were bald and lavender-eyed and immensely, almost geographically tall and muscular. They were also wearing a shirt cut and frilled at the shoulders with a festive hawthorn branch design netting the fabric—green and red and black on white.

"I understand I have you to thank for Cate's life, and many of my friends too," Hughes told her. At her little bow of acknowledgment, Hughes allowed a tiny stream of his melodramatic side to trickle through. With a flourish, he announced the unfamiliars to one another. "Frank Gallant, Dream Warrior, Mr. Glint, his esteemed companion; meet Eilandri Titansgrave, legend of the Citadel. Tales abound about her. None do her the slightest bit of justice."

Eilandri jotted a message on one of her yellow cards and handed it to Frank, who read it, laughed a sweet, ceiling-climbing laugh, and handed the card to Mr. Glint.

There was a flurry of introductions and niceties, with Eilandri doing the majority of the listening and Hughes and Frank doing much of the speaking and reading. It became conspicuous, however, that there was something not quite right, something amiss. Hughes wondered at it, occasionally peeking outside their group in case some incredible thing was going on, but there was nothing. Whereupon Frank nudged him, caught his eye, and guided it toward Mr. Glint.

Mr. Glint was still holding Eilandri's yellow card.

Mr. Glint was staring with his mouth open, not at the card or its message, you see, but at the woman who had written it.

He was staring at her in what Hughes thought was a distinctly un-Glintish way. In his experience, when Mr. Glint looked at something for any length of time, he was either paying close attention to that thing, or he was about to eat it. Possibly both.

Hughes didn't know what to make of this stare, not until Frank made a spluttery sound into his glass of bubbly.

Mr. Glint, thought Hughes, *is looking at Eilandri the way a spotty teenager might look at the replacement schoolteacher who dresses like she's going out to a nightclub, and who chews gum, and who is passionate about teaching, art, and small niche wine-smelling bodegas, and poets who are very good or very dead or both concurrently, and buildings with folklore attached, and lots of other cool, cultural things.*

And Eilandri is looking at Mr. Glint as though they are both students at the same school, and they both belong to different friend groups. She is looking at him as if this distant and unsocial arrangement is perfect for her.

Now Mr. Glint is closing his sour, death-casket-lid of a mouth, and he's realizing he's staring, and that he has been staring for some time, and now Mr. Glint is frowning down at his shark-bone buckled shoes, and he is...

Oh my good Lord...

Mr. Glint's cheeks are...

"Well I'll be." Frank laughed. "Beautiful!"

Hughes was about to scold Frank for adding salt to an already soul-shrinkingly awkward moment.

But Frank wasn't talking about Eilandri.

There before the north-western door of the Hall, coming out from under the shadow of the balcony and into the gorgeous Tinfrost tree glow, was Cate.

She wore a cast on her arm where the creature Skuggs had gouged her with his knife and where the surgeon had done his best to repair the tissue damage. The cast was braced across her chest, but her other arm hung bare and unblemished by her side. Bruises mottled her skin like wine drops on cream sofa cushions. Stitches worked up her right calf and thigh like zips. Her hair had been shorn to the quick at both temples, one so they could sew up a nasty cut, the other for symmetry. Her heels were as big as her concession to the spirit of the event—not one for clicking and clacking when she walked was Cate Jubilee. They were not her hobnail boots, but their incongruence made them devastatingly sleek. Her dress was lime-green, off-the-shoulder, snug, and sexy.

Before Hughes knew himself—from his primary shock to his secondary awe—he was with her in the middle of things, not caring a jot for the hubbub waving and washing around them. Her arms slipped round his waist and pulled him close. He held her cheeks in both hands.

For the second time that evening Hughes kissed someone whose appearance sent him over the moon and back again.

For the second time that evening, the kiss was met with huge whoops, good-natured wolf-whistles, and cheers galore.

They came apart, breathless, grinning, and wordless like kids muted with love—to speak would be to dilute it somehow.

"Oh kiss again, for fuck's sake!" someone cackled through the raised voices.

Never ones to disappoint a crowd, they did just that. Victory over Jane was good. Champagne with crème de cassis was better. But the taste of Cate Jubilee was best of all. No debate. No question. Her tongue touched his, a little lizard flicker. He could feel her curling lips on his own, could sense her tensing body trying not to crack the romantic composure. How to laugh and kiss at the same time? *Gladly*, he thought. *Endlessly, if time were kind.*

Who felt the first brush of a wing against their face, it was never clear. The cheering had stopped. Cottony silence filled the Hall.

When the lovers paused to look around, they saw the butterflies.

Thousands—tens of thousands of fluttering shapes surrounded them. It was as if a great machine had appeared from nowhere, a fabulous gyre spinning and spinning. The butterflies made no undue sound, unless you counted the almost-noise their wings made, a papery thing that suggested itself to the ear like a sound flown out of the racing jungles and ruined forests of the past. They landed on Cate and Hughes, delicate and trembling, then took off again to join the cyclone of swishing wings. *Red*, Hughes' staggered brain supplied. *Red as red could ever be.* He realized that he recognized them. He had last seen them at Saint Wilhemina's hospital, when Jane, his fellow shadow, had breathed her last.

Now they were back.

The only question was why?

You might think there would be a big deal made of such a weird occurrence, but there wasn't. It was like a spell had been cast on the Grand Hall and everyone in it. A few feet away Frank Gallant's face was a mask of rapture. Eilandri took a step forward, paused as one of the butterflies lighted on her knuckles, as though to reassure her that all was well, and she need not trouble herself, and then stood frozen as all the rest when it soared off again to join the rest. Mr. Glint took advantage of the commotion and went back to staring at Eilandri.

Up above, where the columns failed to grow and meet the ceiling, for the Hall was open-topped and led to another floor of the tower, a woman with white hair laid a hand against the rail of the balustrade and peered at the swarm with interest.

Hughes instinctually drew closer to Cate. He was not sure if his heart compelled him to do that, or if it was the butterflies exerting some power over him. Maybe it was the latter because as they held one another something began to fill the space between them.

Overlapping, circling inevitably upward, the butterflies were a tower all their own. Gentle rustles, as of folded blanket pages, stories to slumber beneath. Wingbeats concatenated.

There was a tinkling, redolent of sleigh bells, but not quite.

It sounds like glass, he thought. *It sounds like...*

But the almost-sounds were gone. The butterflies too. The Hall was exactly as it had been before. With one small addition.

Cradled in Hughes' and Cate's arms was a baby.

It was tiny, smelling of softness, and quite asleep. As they watched it in utter incredulity, it opened its mouth in a big toothless yawn. Then it opened its eyes and looked at them.

It looked at Hughes.

It looked at Cate.

It looked at Hughes again.

His heart felt as though it had stopped a long time ago. Expectation wrapped him from head to toe. Not knowing if this was real, or if he had strayed into a place beyond dreams and the waking world, he followed the baby's movements, which seemed to play out in slow motion.

It put out its fist. Pudgy, and so small. The fingers spread wide.

Without knowing he was doing it, Hughes offered his own finger. The pinky. A small offering for a small goddess. Even then, some part of him knew it was a baby girl. Through a backward-facing window in his head, he could see the ultrasound technician's doodad gliding over Cate's goop-smeared belly. *Sliiiiide.* There was the monitor, and the fuzzy blob of life suspended in the nourishing dark, and the hand. Pudgy, and so small.

He came back to himself the instant the fingers closed around his pinky.

"Hughes." Cate's voice, barely more than a whisper. "Is this happening?"

The baby worked its free hand over its eyes, which had seemed so dark as to be virtually colorless but now appeared to be hazel-green. *You will meet her at the feast,* Krys had told him. *She and she and she. Two will have your eyes, shadow man, and one will have your heart.*

"Hughes?"

He croaked unintelligibly. His throat was too dry for words. He swallowed, tried again. "I think it is, honey."

"What do we do?"

Hughes hadn't the slightest idea. Best to improvise.

"This," he said.

He leaned down and nuzzled the baby's nose with his own.

She squeaked and gurgled happily.

Her grip on his pinky was very tight.

***

Nine-oh-nine in the night by the clocks' count, and the evening was full as the moon. Hours had passed, and everyone was talking about the baby. Some talked *to* the baby. Speculation and fussing, gossip, the rumor mill churning out its loaves like fresh bread. Where did it come from? What magic had conjured it? Was it sinister? Benevolent? A charm or chicanery?

The only thing everyone seemed agreed upon was the fact that the child had a knack for entrances.

After their initial bit of bonding, the baby evidently had enough of Gormon Hughes. She wanted Cate, a desire she made abundantly clear. Anyone had but to whisk her out of Cate's good arm, and as soon as she registered what had happened she would howl her lungs out until things were set right—more precisely herself set back into Cate's strong nestling embrace. This stoked a healthy amount of jealousy amongst the feastgoers and a healthy amount of amusement and delight in Cate herself, who quickly took to experimenting with what would make the baby do the squeak and gurgle routine. Nuzzling was not sufficient. Always one for doing things as right as they could be done was Cate Jubilee.

While he was apart from the deluge of admirers, Hughes spied a glimpse of stark white above him. When he looked, it was no longer there. But he knew who he'd seen, and he headed for the southern corridor and the stairs that climbed to the upper floor.

Murals commissioned by the Citadel showing the first generation of scarlet men and women. Themes of fellowship and strength and respectability were wrought in tiny fragments of colored stone, carefully assembled by the artists of yesteryear into astounding images that nevertheless lay dark before Hughes, the Tinfrost lights from the chandeliers and the trees below them straining to illuminate, but not quite, not quite. And they were macabre in the dark, those murals. There was something covert about them, as though their majesty was hiding something deeply frightening. There was a rectangle of railing that you could lean over and see the Grand Hall below you, and the acoustics were very fine so even without peering down you could hear its sounds all muddled in a mix. Here and there doorways were inlaid with gleaming panels of oak and elm. But once again these were ensconced in thick shadow. Through glass doors about fifty feet from where he crested the last step, Hughes could see a moonlit balcony. He made for it and stopped abruptly, not sure he believed what he thought he was seeing.

Bizarre, considering the events of tonight. Surely it would have inured him to anything. But one can never underestimate the determination of the mean aunt imagination and the dark—they still teamed up; still fucked with him when they could.

Patched in black shadow, one of the doors lay open a crack. A rat was squeaking at it. To a seasoned veteran of Corinth City, there was something conversational to its pitch. Or maybe it was just a case of the moon whispers. The night doing magician tricks to thrill the uncautious mind. Maybe. But Hughes didn't think so. He approached, quiet as he could. Not subtle enough. The rat's ears gave a twitch. One beady eye rolled to see him standing there. It let out a sound—shrill and alert—and scampered through the door. Baffled, Hughes strode up and tugged open the door.

For a moment he was convinced something would touch his hand in that implacable blackness

(something crawling)

(finger made of flies)

, but there was only the handle, cool and smooth against his palm.

Behind the door there was a corridor. He glanced along it both ways, keeping his ears peeled. No rat. Nobody at all. He scanned the floors, taking extra care. Nothing.

Pick out every spooky corner the light can't quite touch, his skepticism berated him. *Pick them and jump at them. Go ahead. See where it gets you.*

He gave that empty (or so it seemed) corridor a remote, stony smile, retreated, and closed the door.

When he got to the balcony it presented a scene carved from a fairytale. Ivy climbed the trellis. Potted cyclamen, hellebore, and snowdrops lined the curve of the eastern wall. Together they were sales assistants in a perfume shop, lacing their mellow fragrances in the dark doily of the December eve. The silver of the moon found its echo in the silver veins of the balustrade marble—in that stone the metal seemed alive, responsive in an organic way to the cratered lunar lugger up there riding the sparkling highway of stars. And there, the completing factor: backlit by the diamond-glitter city and the pale dusting moon was the Last Dragon herself. Her hair was in a bun, pinned there with a stick of toffee-colored corundum. No comfy sweater tonight. Tonight Wendy wore a long, trailing gown of blizzard-white. The breeze had blown the train of the gown so it clung to the bars of the balcony edge, making Hughes think of a dragon's tail.

She was facing away from him, gazing out over the city. He tried to imagine the expression on her face. Try as he might, the only one he could picture was a draconic leer—one that spoke to a ruling emotion, and one a dragon knows all too well: territorialism.

What to say, now that they were alone together for the first time since his betrayal, and his discovery of hers?

What would sum up his feelings? Could he entreat her? Shame her? Threaten her?

Hughes reached desperately for the right words and found his usually garrulous tongue limp and useless.

I can't be her Bloodhound. A simpering animal skulking close to question its master. I've got to be as Cate would be. I've got to be my best—better!

Her name is Winnifred. Talk to the woman, not the dragon.

Start simply with that. Address her by name so she knows you're meeting on even terms.

"My Lady..." he began.

Damn.

"Wendy, Hughes." Delivered airily, casually, like they were on the gentlest, friendliest terms and the idea of conflict between them was patently ridiculous. She made no move to turn around. "Always Wendy."

"Are you cold?"

"You know, usually the cold and I are jaundiced opponents. Tonight I find the chill bracing. Perhaps we've struck a truce."

"Good for you," he said, trying to sound brusque and failing miserably.

"I understand congratulations are in order. A Tinfrost miracle. Fate, it seems, has decreed you are to be a father after all."

"She... the baby... must be Jane."

"Must she?"

"The Perfect Prison," Hughes insisted. "There's no other explanation."

"This feels like the parlor scene in the detective novel," said Wendy. "The bit where the investigator reveals how it all happened." She turned. No draconic leer. Just that patrician face with its too-wise eyes, prone to twinkling, though not now. "Go on then. Explain. If the Perfect Prison was used on Jane, how then has it resulted in the birth of this child?"

Hughes took his time in answering. "I suppose the perfect prison for an evil person is to be reborn as a good one."

"And will she be?" said Wendy sharply. "Will she be good?"

There was a pause. Then Hughes walked right up to her, holding her stare, then taking up a spot next to her, elbows resting on the marble. He looked out over the city, his face bathed in moonlight, his hair dark and his beard dark and his eyes darker and his whole soul darker still. He smiled then, brief but true, and it was so wonderfully bright.

"I hope so," he said.

Wendy's elbows sank to join his on the rail, bony arms and wrinkled skin. Her veins and the veins in the marble seemed like one continuous stream, silver to blue.

"Elegant suit."

"Cate says red looks well on me."

"She's right. A man of the Citadel ought to wear red. He ought to remember his roots." Before he could frame a reply, she said, "My origins are in rebellion. You remember I told you about my days in Leonidas District?"

"During the Hairy Autumn, yeah. You said it was a different place."

"Quite so. Of course in other ways it was entirely the same. But that is the nature of places and the people in them, is it not? To change changelessly? To remain exactly the same while breaking down and being remade at every opportunity?"

"I don't understand."

"I'm trying to tell you that I know what it's like. I pushed back against my father. Distanced myself from previous entanglements. Got involved in others. Embraced the wild. I took on an exciting new role, if you like. All part of being young. And the thing about being old, Hughes, is that the young person you used to be never entirely goes away. It merely prunes in the bathtub of experience. It really is a fetching suit."

"Wendy..."

"I must say, I find the sword brings it all together."

Hughes felt his brows draw together of their own accord. "Sorry?"

"Your sword, Chimera. Completes your ensemble rather well."

Hughes frowned at his hip. The sword was there, sheathed in its scabbard. What on earth was it doing there? Searching his memory, he vaguely recalled fastening it to his belt. He must have decided to bring it when he left the apartment. But why? Why had he bothered? No one else had their magic items tonight. It was a celebration, after all.

The truth hit him, and it hit hard.

He looked at Wendy, his expression controlled but for his eyes, marginally wider.

I brought it because on a subconscious level I knew she'd be here, awaiting me. I knew that we would be alone, and that all of the tension between us would climax and be resolved, one way or the other.

Heed your instincts. First rule of police work. Shit.

Wendy smiled and shrugged her shoulders, as though reading his mind and dismissing the revelations there. "Does it perturb you, Hughes? The fact that we are so adept at observing others and so inept at observing ourselves?"

"What perturbs me is your smarm," he heard himself say. "What perturbs me is your ruthless side. What perturbs me is that I thought I knew who was holding everyone's leads and giving out the dog treats. Oddly enough the part about the leads and the reward system were ay-okay by me, but the *knowing*. That's what rankles. I do not know you, Wendy Dragontail. And I'm not sure I'd like to, now it comes to it. But I do want to know why you poisoned Estelle. There's no rationale that would justify it, of course. All the same, I want to hear it from you. What the hell were you thinking?"

"I tell you, and then what? Will you draw steel, the proud knight avenging the wronged maiden?"

"We'll see."

Her lips thinned, to show him what she thought of avenging knights and their less than ideal life expectancy. "When Idris Corlum sired a child in secret, he endangered his life. He could not have known that I had taken certain steps to ensure that the Perfect Prison would be passed on to a new caretaker."

"What sort of steps?"

"I had gas pumped into the room where he and his wife slept. They were rendered totally unconscious. A nurse entered the room and obtained a semen sample from Idris. That sample would have, upon Idris' death, been donated to a carefully selected woman, who would bear the child to term. That child would then inherit the Perfect Prison. Oh, don't gawp at me, Hughes, as if some fundamental line had been crossed. *Close it, boy.*"

"Wendy, you violated—"

"*Shut. Your mouth.*" He had recoiled from her. Now he stood, paralyzed by the force of that voice. She might as well have cracked him across the face: he was that stunned. The ferocity quenched behind her eyes. She sighed. "Forgive me. I'm observant too. Stubborn old me. I know

now that I went too far. At the time it seemed... practical. The Perfect Prison is a priceless resource. Its condemnation to obscurity would damn the Citadel and the city beyond to the claims of threats you and I cannot conjugate or pronounce because they have not made themselves known. Things more dangerous than Frank Gallant, whose existence I condone—just," she added bitterly. She searched his countenance, not liking what she found there. She looked askance, her lips peeled back over her gums in a pettish snarl. "I would prefer, Gormon Hughes, if you would wipe that look off your face."

Hughes supposed he must be glaring at her as though she had shaken off her skin to reveal scales and molten fire underneath. For all intents and purposes, she had.

She continued drily. "In some ways Idris' actions resolved the unpredictability of the matter. But he put himself at risk. *That* was the part that worried me."

That was quite enough. He couldn't hold his tongue if he'd tried. All of his worst suspicions had been confirmed. Worse, they had been accentuated. His outrage was a hissing, spiteful animal. It reared up his throat and vented itself on her. "You drugged Estelle every day for almost ten years... because you were paranoid? Not for her, but on account of an object tied to her blood?"

"She's your friend. You can't stand back and see how she fits into the grand scheme of things."

"How she *fits?*" The word shredded through his teeth, flecking spittle. "What the *fuck* are you talking about? She's a human being. You can't take what you like from people, do what you like to them because of their position in some plan. How would you like it if someone put their hands on you, and you didn't want it?"

She smiled at him, a lenient smile that forgave his petty world its petty values.

"My dear boy, what is sovereignty but dirtying your hands in the hope your efforts keep things clean?"

"You're mad. A mad brooding monster."

His fingers crept past Chimera's lion-headed pommel toward the sword's hilt. There were precious few yards between them. She was fast, blindingly fast. He had seen her demonstrate it before. In the hollow of her throat, he could see Faethe, Amulet of Dragons gleaming goldly.

"Hughes. I sent the Incarnadine to retrieve Estelle because I was ashamed. I wanted to put off you... looking at me this way. I admit that. I see how angry you are. I think you're right to be. My intentions were good, but when it came to seeing them realized I was cruel. I'm sorry for what happened with Idris, and I'm sorry for how I treated Estelle. I'm sorry that I lied to you, and for being a vindictive, stupid, stubborn old woman."

That last part I actually believe, he decided. *You want my forgiveness. But you don't regret what you did to the Corlum family. In that, at least, you're a fucking liar. I should know. I used to be good at telling those, Wendy. Like recognizes like. One shadow and another.*

"Estelle is gone," said Wendy. "I have it from Knickerbocker that she boarded a train. There's no undoing what's been done. Let's go inside." She took a step toward him. Hughes took a commensurate step back. "Why do you seem scared? Hughes. Look at me: I see your fingers inching over your sword hilt. Listen to me: I don't care. Draw it if it makes you feel safe. But I would never hurt you. Never. We will get through this together. We are going to talk as we did last week in my office. We'll um... We'll bicker and say things we regret later. And maybe that'll happen a few times. And then, one day, before you know it, we'll be all right. You'll meet me somewhere lovely and we'll have tea. It'll get better. I know that sounds crazy right now. I know it does. But I promise you that it will."

Outside Hughes was very still. Inside his heart was pounding.

Wendy took another step toward him. He made to retreat and found there was nowhere to go. Marble met his lower back. Past that was a drop to the city, far, far below. Wendy came on, her silk shoes whispering over the flagstone, the breeze working in her gown. Looking at it, Hughes felt as though the blizzard had come back. It wanted him after all.

"Let's go inside," Wendy said. "I'd like to meet your daughter."

"You monster!"

They spun in near flawless synchronicity.

The glass door to the Grand Hall's upper floor was open. Estelle Corlum was there. How long had she been there? How much had she heard? She was filthy, reeking, more tired than ever. She looked as though she had been sleeping rough since Wednesday, which was indeed the case. Chiefly, most importantly, she looked as livid as anyone Hughes had ever seen.

Afterward, when it was over, he had to piece together what happened. There seemed a lot of pieces to pick up. The last was the hardest.

What happened first was Estelle's charge.

She hurtled toward Wendy, her vambraced arm outstretched.

Quicker than a young person had any right to move, let alone an older woman, Wendy broke off a chunk of solid marble in her fingers and threw it with the force of a catapult. Hughes slid Chimera from its sheath, his other hand flung out to knock the stone aside. But he was only human. It struck Estelle, smashing her cheek to gory pulp and flipping her head-over-heels. She landed heavily, the breath crushed out of her, half her face staved in and pouring blood.

Hughes whirled, bringing Chimera about in a lethal arc.

Wendy caught the blade. She caught it in her hand and she *squeezed*.

There was a moment of terrible silence. Then a shattering.

Hughes stumbled back, holding half a sword. The other half lay scattered across the flagstones. His foot sent a shard skimming through the balcony's teeth and off, plummeting down toward the base of the tower.

Chimera. The word was a numb comet rocketing across his brain, its tail iced in a horror too keen to comprehend. *No.* He might have said it aloud.

At the same time he heard someone call his name.

With great effort he managed to tear himself from the ruin of his sword...

... just in time for Wendy's hands to lock around his throat.

Estelle was up—how, he had no idea. What little of her expression left ungrimed by blood was contorted into a rictus of hate.

Hughes tried to breathe, couldn't. Panic blotted out reason. The need for air, the impossibility of even one lungful, the terror that induced. Black spots tinged in fur pervaded everything. His Performance swelled up within him but could find no outlet. It was stuck, clogging him, and then it too was smothered in that baleful panic. His eyes rolled, cutting skyward. The stars were dim pinpricks in a lake of darkness. The moon no longer seemed full. It seemed a strange and barren jewel up there, cold as a friend's betrayal.

Wendy.

The name of his killer stirred something unspeakable in him. He forced his gaze down, and down, and down some more.

There she was.

Her eyes dark and hard. Her hair shaken out of its bun in a silvery nimbus.

Movement close by. Herky-jerky, spasmodic. Estelle. Hurt but advancing.

When she was done with him, Wendy would turn on her, he had no doubt.

He was not sure what brought his hand up. The one with the sword in it would have been advisable. But who knows what would have happened if he'd stabbed at her in that moment, when Tinfrost Day seemed to have shed its flesh for nightmare clothes, and all the lights shone without mercy? Who can say? No one.

Instead of the hand clutching Chimera, Hughes raised his other one.

He closed it around Wendy's, much as the baby girl had closed her fingers around Hughes' pinky earlier that night.

The Last Dragon's face changed. Or maybe it stayed the same, and the change was in his head. Hughes never found out.

All at once the pressure closing his windpipe let up. He fell in a heap, gasping, hitching as much air as he could, his throat a stinging raw tube. Wendy stood over him. She didn't look around as Estelle made a lunge for her. Not even as the arm with the vambrace closed tight.

When the Perfect Prison was used on Frank Gallant, it placed him behind a sealed door at the top of Redspire.

When it was used on Spring-Heeled Jane, it transmogrified her from a vessel of vileness to one of innocence—a woman becoming a baby in a shower of red butterflies.

And when it was used on Wendy, it killed The Last Dragon dead. Hughes and Estelle saw the pulsing vein in her neck go still. They saw a stillness come over her, like she'd been at sea forever, only now washing up on a windless shore. They watched her legs go out from under her. They heard her last breath leave her body.

Of course it killed her. Only one prison could hold Winnifred Dragontail. Only one could keep her from outwitting its jailer in the short term, or breaking its bars, or plotting her way free over months and years. The only prison sure to work was death.

So she died.

Estelle collapsed into unconsciousness, her pain too much to bear.

Hughes felt himself fading. Somehow he managed to stay awake. Leaving Chimera among its shards, he crawled to Wendy's body. Her skin was warm, but he couldn't feel a pulse in her wrist. He tried her neck. Nothing. Some part of him refused to accept it though. So he made himself look into her eyes.

That gave it to him straight enough.

A glow insinuated itself to him. Gold, it was, and growing brighter by the moment. He looked down at his hand. His fingers were tangled in Faethe's chain. It was not the chain shining but the amulet itself. Without thinking, Hughes slid his palm underneath it, cupping it like a wounded winter thrush. The gold leeched into him, diminishing. He felt it pass into his body, mixing with everything he was and had been and ever would be. He felt it join Chimera, snapped but still alive inside him. The power of the amulet and the sword seemed to weigh one another, then reach an unlikely truce. He felt their fusion like a moment of bliss after a period of hardship—every part of him exhaled, and that all-over breath tasted gold and green as spring.

Then he was back on the balcony. Through the open glass door leading inside, he could hear singing. And something else too. A baby. She was crying.

He looked at Wendy, her features somehow both slack and stiff in death.

He had just attuned to her magic item.

Which was impossible. Magic items were hereditary. They could only be passed through blood inheritance.

And suddenly Hughes thought about the first time he and Wendy had met. It was in her office. She had asked him how his dad was. *Still an old fuddy-duddy about his teapots?* She had been to Leonidas during... what had she called them? Her rebellious origins. She had been younger.

Then Frank Gallant had put her father into a sleep he had never awoken from, and she had returned to rule the Citadel. She had instigated sweeping changes by all accounts, including renovations to Redspire itself.

Hughes recalled Falstaff telling him that those renovations had been made about eighteen years before Hughes had arrived. Hughes had been nineteen, and he and his dad had been alone since he was one.

Except for his mother's occasional visits. The memories of her were murky and unclear. But on Wednesday, when they'd beaten Jane, Hughes had seen the butterflies with their incredible red wings, and he'd had the clearest picture of a butterfly landing in his mother's hair. She had taken him to see the carnival, which had just come to town. He was on her shoulders. The reason the butterfly looked so red in his memory was that his mother's hair provided a stark background.

Because it was *white.*

No, he thought. *That can't be right. Cannot be right.*

But it was. The proof was right there in her eyes. Dark, sure, but in certain lights they twinkled, which was when their color let itself be known. Hazel green. *Just like mine.* Hadn't he thought about that the first time they'd met? He had. And she had asked after his dad. She asked if he was still a fuddy-duddy about his teapots. Numbness giving way to a push of emotion so strong he couldn't stop it if he'd wanted to, Hughes looked into those vacant eyes, and he thought about Krys, who had told him that he would meet this woman—and two others—while they admired jelly biscuits in her carousel cottage. *She will meet you at the feast. She and she and she. Two will have your eyes, shadow man, and one will have your heart.*

Cate had his heart, that was plain as the moon glowing down on this impossible scene.

The baby girl had his eyes because Jane had his eyes.

And Wendy had his eyes.

No. I have hers.

He curled in on himself, a noise coming out of him that he wouldn't have dreamed of making had he been sensible to it. Pure anguish. Not a man's pain. A boy's, when that boy has made a discovery worse than bad, one that convinces him that happiness, no matter how great, can always come to an end.

He picked Wendy up. She was limp in his arms.

He held her anyway.

"Mother," he sobbed, his voice thick with grief. "Mother..."

END OF BOOK 2

ARISE ALPHA

By Jez Cajiao

When you steal a hundred grand from some very bad people, the best way to survive is to stay small and quiet...

Possibly its not to save a pair of drowning girls, not go 'viral' on social media and certainly not to let the local police take your passport, trapping you on a small 'party' island in the middle of the Mediterranean Sea.

But Steve isn't the average guy, he's ex-military, ex-enforcer and ex-human. He's a one-man nanite fueled nightmare for those that cross the line, and he's decided that it's time to clean up his act. He's going to make up for the things he's done, and save 'the little guys'.

It's a nice fantasy, but even he has to admit, it's really just a justification, because he's a very bad man, with horrifying abilities, and he's only just learning what he's capable of. He needs a reason to not go to the dark, and if that's hunting down the creatures of the night and beating them to death with their own femurs?

Well, he's just the man for the job.

Stolen money. Greek Islands. Werewolves and Enforcers...
What could possibly go wrong?

https://www.amazon.com/Arise-Alpha-Dark-LitRPG-Adventure-ebook

<u>THEFT OF DECKS BOOK ONE</u>

By Lars Machmüller
When the deck is stacked against you? Change the game!

In the frontier town of Isarn, Chase will never be more than the lowly Darkborn thief he is. Banned from training, banned from acquiring better cards, if the Lightborn had their way, he'd be banned from life itself.

He's not alone though, and the one thing he and his friends have is determination. Losing a hand to a brutal punishment only fueled his obsession to get access to his own amazing, reality-bending cards.

That is the path to power and a future for them all. Nobody cares where you came from when you're rich enough. For now, though, they're facing both established powers, churches and age-old prejudices. It's time to get to work, and if the Lightborn won't share and play nice?

Sometimes the only way to get dealt a better hand is to steal the whole damn deck!

D&D meets Magic the Gathering in this epic fantasy deckbuilding LitRPG

https://mybook.to/TheftofDecksbook1

QUEST ACADEMY

By Brian J. Nordon

A world infested by demons.
An Academy designed to train Heroes to save humanity from annihilation.
A new student's power could make all the difference.

Humans have been pushed to the brink of extinction by an ever-evolving demonic threat. Portals are opening faster than ever, Towers bursting into the skies and Dungeons being mined below the last safe havens of society. The demons are winning.

Quest Academy stands defiantly against them, as a place to train the next generation of Heroes. The Guild Association is holding the line, but are in dire need of new blood and the powerful abilities they could bring to the battlefront. To be the saviors that humanity needs, they need to surpass the limits of those that came before them.

In a war with everything on the line, every power matters. With an adaptive enemy, comes the need for a constant shift in tactics. A new age of strategy is emerging, with even the unlikeliest of Heroes making an impact.

Salvatore Argento has never seen a demon.
He has never aspired to become a Hero.
Yet his power might be the one to tip the odds in humanity's favor.

Buy on Amazon

WANDERING WARRIOR

By Michael Head

A divine quest to deliver justice.
One year to accomplish his mission.
After nineteen planets, there's something different about this one.

James Holden has reached the maximum level there is for a human. That's perfect, since he's the only one of his kind. A wandering warrior, without control of his destination, tossed between universes by gods who've failed to tell him why. James is the lone Judge on a new world in need of someone to balance the scales. He isn't afraid to do so with extreme prejudice. As the Chief Justice, he has to right the wrongs the innocent can't fix themselves.

As James quickly discovers, the roots of corruption run deep. Guilds choose to protect themselves rather than the people. Monsters roam the wilderness unchecked. Judgment is usually a decision between right and wrong, but nothing is ever that simple. This time, being the strongest human won't be enough to punish the guilty. James might have to recruit some new blood, even if he prefers to work alone.

On his twentieth world, he is going to win, no matter the cost. James will have to find a way to break past the limits of the system if he's going to have a chance at making a difference.

Buy on Amazon

KNIGHTS OF ETERNITY

By Rachel Ní Chuirc

When Zara awoke in chains she thought she'd gone mad.

She was Zara the Fury - mistress of flame and fear. Her name was whispered across the land, from ramshackle taverns to the royal court. Even the heroic Gilded Knights thought twice before crossing her path.
She was feared—*respected.*
Now she was curled up on a dirt floor on her fiancé's orders. Valerius, leader of the Gilded, mocks her cries for help. And the kingdom is on the brink of war over the missing Lady Eternity...
But that wasn't why Zara thought she had gone mad.
The reason why is that the last thing she remembered was blood, an arcade screen, and the gun that changed everything.

But no chains can hold the Fury, and when she gets out?
The world is going to *burn.*

Buy on Amazon

SOCIAL MEDIA

Jack Fields Author Page
https://www.facebook.com/JackFieldsAuthor

LitRPG Legion Page
https://www.facebook.com/groups/litrpglegion

LITRPG!

To learn more about LitRPG, talk to authors, and have an awesome time, please join the LitRPG Group.

https://www.facebook.com/groups/LitRPGGroup

FACEBOOK

Here's a few wonderfully active Facebook groups I'd recommend, as you'll get to hear about great new books and new releases.

https://www.facebook.com/groups/LitRPGlegion/

https://www.facebook.com/groups/GamelitSociety

https://www.facebook.com/groups

https://www.facebook.com/groups/LitRPGforum/

RECOMMENDATIONS

If you liked this novel, you might also like...

Creation's Bane by Kevin Sinclair

Knights of Eternity by Rachel Ní Chuirc

Quest Academy by Brian J. Nordon

Somnia Online by K.T. Hanna

The Good Guys by Eric Ugland

The Ten Realms by Michael Chatfield

UnderVerse by Jez Cajiao

Wandering Warrior by Michael Head

World of Chains by Lars Machmüller